Bluefeather Fellini

BLUEFEATHER FELLINI

Max Evans

UNIVERSITY OF NEW MEXICO PRESS
Albuquerque

2007 University of New Mexico Press edition
published by arrangement with the author.
All rights reserved.
Printed in the United States of America

13 12 11 10 09 08 07   1 2 3 4 5 6 7

Library of Congress Cataloging-in-Publication Data

Evans, Max, 1924–
  Bluefeather Fellini / Max Evans.
      p. cm.
  Bluefeather Fellini — Bluefeather Fellini in the sacred realm.
  ISBN 978-0-8263-4260-7 (pbk. : alk. paper)
  1. Indians of North America—Mixed descent—Fiction.
2. Pueblo Indians—Fiction. I. Evans, Max, 1924– Bluefeather Fellini
in the sacred realm. II. Title. III. Title: Bluefeather Fellini in the
sacred realm.
  PS35553V23B58 2007
  813'.54—dc22

                        2007001079

Book design and composition by Damien Shay
Body type is Minion 10.5/14
Display is Panjandrum and Minion

ONE FROM THE HEART

■ For ■

My wife, Pat, my number one critic, who also suffered safely
through all those long decades of my taking notes, thinking and
figuring on *Bluefeather Fellini,* and then the five and a half years
of actually writing it down. My profound and everlasting thanks
for surviving with me the roller coaster from poor to plenty over
and over and—on occasion—actual degradation, as well as sharing
the few glorious times of a treasured sense of accomplishment
in our other stories. Also, much appreciation for the colorful
painting you created for the cover.

■ For ■

Federico Fellini, the great director who taught me to feel the color,
see the sound, and hear the unsaid in such great films as
La Strada, La Dolce Vita, and *8 1/2.*

■ For ■

Burt Kennedy and Ed Honeck, who always kept the faith
long past its due.

■ For ■

Those deeply loved and influential amigos and amigas who have
gone on the "Long Adios," including my mother, Hazel, who taught
me to read, and love it, before I started school. Wiley (Big Boy)
Hittson, whose brief life of daring, courage, total loyalty and sudden
shocking death by gunfire inspired my novel *The Hi Lo Country.*
Luz Martinez, the "Santero" who followed me to Taos and carved
cedarwood into permanent beauty and dignity. Woody Crumbo,
the great pioneer Pottawatomie Indian artist, who became my
artistic and spiritual mentor and whose spirit is in every chapter
of this book. And finally to our little dog Foxy, who came to us as
a stricken stray and stayed to love and be loved through the last,
forever-long months while we sought the proper publishers
of the words and feelings inside these covers.

MAX EVANS
Albuquerque, New Mexico

Contents

BLUEFEATHER FELLINI

BLUEFEATHER FELLINI IN THE SACRED REALM

BLUEFEATHER FELLINI

■ Part One ■

SENSUAL YOUTH—FIRST REAL LOVE
The Scent of Gold

One

It was the time of youthful jubilation, and Bluefeather Fellini—the chosen one—knew that never, never, never before had anyone his age been so blessed. In just a few days, they would be rich—rich as bankers, rich as doctors, rich as movie stars, rich as kings. Grinder the Gringo was giving him this wondrous opportunity, and if he lived a thousand years, he could never show his ample appreciation for the golden opportunity afforded him by this generous genius sitting with him in the woods at this moment.

He sat across the campfire in Twinning Canyon north of Taos, New Mexico, watching the toothless old prospector, Sam Grinder, with respect. He could hear the voices of the night birds in the forest as clearly as violins, and feel the very earth vibrate with other more muted sounds of walking and flying life. The campfire flickered on the rump of the burro feeding contentedly from a feedbag and swatting, from habit, an imaginary fly with his tail.

Now that they had eaten, Grinder took off his hat, pushed at his gray, stringy hair and took a large chew of tobacco from a paper container. He chewed with long-suffering gums until the tobacco was soft and ready for spitting. He turned his head and exuded a stream into an empty coffee can.

Bluefeather thought, "What a gentleman." All the prospectors and hunters he had known before spat into the fire to test their accuracy and enjoy the little explosions from the moisture. Grinder looked up at him, somehow knowing the young man's thoughts were too complimentary.

For decades the old prospector had walked the sizzling southwestern deserts, climbed the jagged mountains, chewed the dust, dodged the blizzards without complaint or defeat. He had joyously spent his occasional discoveries on women, beer, and chewing tobacco. He was always grinding on forward just as his name implied.

Grinder studied his new partner with respect, friendship, and a learned cunning. He observed Bluefeather through slit, knowing eyes. The quality he looked for was definitely there. It flickered from the young man's large, black eyes and was obvious in the alert, almost regal, manner he carried his head and the way he climbed the Taos mountains with a long-stepped, but smooth, attacking stride.

Yes. Yes, Bluefeather Fellini was from the people of yearning. Whenever one walks or rides with yearners, the world becomes generous with great gifts of almost ceaseless adventure—and makes one pay terrible prices for the ultimate joys. Grinder knew this to be a fact, for he was a yearner himself. Now, right now, he must start his time of testing. The time of teaching. It must come from him naturally, without plan or precedence. Bluefeather was worth the effort—or worth nothing.

"You know, kiddo...?" he said.

Bluefeather, his large, dark eyes absorbing the flames and projecting them back even stronger, waited as Grinder thought over his next statement.

Then he got it in order and went on, "God is supposed to have made us in His image, but He didn't engineer us too good. When I was about fifty-five all my teeth fell out. Now I ask you, why didn't He take my balls instead? I really need my teeth." He spat again, kerpluk, kersplash, into the can and slapped a hand on one overall-covered knee, saying, "Get the idee?" A great boom of laughter exploded from him.

Bluefeather laughed as hard as he could to show his appreciation. The noise made the owls quit hooting, a mountain lion quit stalking a deer, a bear quit digging under a rotten log, and the burro stop chewing oats and turn his head to stare at Grinder and Bluefeather with curiosity and a tinge of superiority.

"You know, son, I never hired anybody I couldn't whup." He gave a quick pause and a knowing glance at the well-muscled, half Taos Indian, half Italian young man who watched and listened, then added, "When I was younger, that is."

The aspen wood fire, slow-burning and almost smokeless, reflected its orange light on Bluefeather's olive-reddish skin and chiseled features as he listened intently to every word the old man said.

"Well, except maybe once 'er twice." Grinder continued, "I remember this one particular time. This feller just begged me for a job. Said he'd do just about anything in the world for a chance to go prospecting with me. Well, I was so dang broke he wound up having to pay me for the privilege of getting to work for me. I worked him so hard he fell down flat on his face from exhaustion. And guess what!" Grinder paused for effect. "He found us a nice little placer deposit before he could recover and get back up. Get the idee?"

"Yeah. Yeah, I get it."

"Well, sir, that ain't all there is to this story." He spat into the can before continuing. "It was a profitable little find. With his percentage he bought a hardware store, and I been paying him money for supplies ever since." Grinder slapped both bent knees—and almost fell over laughing.

Bluefeather joined the mirth mostly out of respect and the old man's contagious sense of the ridiculous.

"Well, Blue, this feller has put two kids through college. The boy's a dentist, the girl's a schoolteacher. Now, all that was good for him, for his kids, for the community—even the country. Hell, he's a deacon of the church, a member of the town board, a pillar of the community."

He stared at the campfire a moment before continuing. "Me? I just went on prospecting, having fun, living outdoors with the rabbits and skunks most of the time. You see, son, those things is what's good for me, but if him and Old Grinder hadn't taken a gamble on one another, way back there, he might not be so deeply admired, so damn respected—even feared, . . ." he grinned grandly, "and the miserable son of a bitch he truly is. Get the idee, kiddo? You either got gold running through your veins or you ain't."

Grinder paused and stared off into the darkness. "Ah, robin piss, nobody ever hears these stories, 'specially young boys like you—and 'specially from an old man like me. You gotta make up your own mind where you're goin' in this world, then get after it and stay with it like a badger after a prairie dog."

Bluefeather smiled, but his dark eyes showed concern as he tried to interpret all the old man's messages. There was no way he could know that it was part of his initiation fee into Grinder's final trust. Now, Bluefeather made a mistake but had no way of knowing so in advance.

He said, "Well my Indian blood tells me one thing, and my Italian blood tells me another."

"Now, there you go—I've noticed it before. Ever chance you get it's, 'I did this 'cause I'm part Indian; I didn't do that 'cause I'm part Italian; that's my Indian blood talkin'; that's my Italian blood talkin'.' That's very tiresome. What do you give a shit whether anybody knows about your bloodline or not? There ain't a damn one of us ever lived who can do a single thing about our bloodline. Not one ever born. Not one in all history. You think you're the only one who's dark, light, short, tall, goofy, smart, crippled, or was ever cut down by your blood mixture? Haw. I say shit again and then again once more. Think. Go back millions of years, a minute at a time. Don't never be one of them self-bleedin' excuse inventors."

Bluefeather was stunned, paralyzed. For a moment he thought about knocking Grinder in the head with an ore sample, but control was definitely one of his strong points—one his Indian mother had deeply instilled in him. But he wasn't supposed to think about that, according to Grinder.

Grinder went on, "Now, listen up with very big ears. You want to talk bloodlines. Me? I'm a bunch of things: part Scotch-Irish, part Black-Dutch, Welsh, Choctaw, Polack, and no doubt some Mexican, Jewish, and colored blood has probably crept into the brew, and I know damn well, for sure, I'm part burro and a tad of coyote. We're all Americans, goddamnit, and we all got to grit and groan to earn our place here. Make it ours alone for just a little while. That's the only freedom, by God—getting your little spot on earth to work for you and you working like hell for it. There ain't no more than that, and I don't never aim for you to bring it up to me again, kiddo. Now go to sleep. Tomorrow's gonna be a long and great day for us Americans. Especially the very first ones like you."

Grinder chuckled himself to sleep, as young Bluefeather gritted his perfectly rowed, white teeth to keep his tongue silent and his muscles frozen. Soon he decided not to kill Grinder until morning, and his breathing slowed to normal.

He slipped into his bedroll and rubbed his hand across his forehead. His fingers automatically followed the thin, almost undetectable, scar that coursed at an angle on his forehead across the upper bridge of his nose between his eyebrows. At the touch and memory, he smiled. Then an even bigger, sparkling smile came. By the Great Spirit's worship, he would never bring that "breed" subject up to Grinder again. He had not been conscious of his using his bloodline as an excuse. He determined that perhaps Grinder the Gringo mongrel had just done him another "great" favor.

As the fire flickered down and he rubbed at the suddenly itchy sliver of a scar, he thought of how he had received it and about his childhood at Raton, New Mexico, where he was born.

The town hovered up against the mountains, which contained the coal seams of its livelihood. The famed Raton Pass north into Trinidad, Colorado, brought a few overnight travelers; the grama grass–rich ranchlands to the south and east fed thousands of cattle; but the coal mines were the black fossil lifeblood of the town.

Bluefeather's Italian father, Valerio Fellini, had married a Taos Pueblo Indian girl named Morning Star Martinez. He had met her while joining in the Friendship Dance at an open ceremonial at Taos Pueblo. She was delicately, darkly beautiful, and Valerio had fallen hopelessly in love with her.

It created a time of chaos, this marriage, for the family clans of the Taos Indians were just as strong as those of the Raton Italians. But enough authority can settle even the most entrenched disputes—even those of blood. Morning Star's father was a powerful shaman, and it was his position that determined the final acceptance of the marriage and mating from the Indian side. There also had been no argument when he gave his newborn grandson the spiritually strong Indian name of Bluefeather.

It had taken a little longer for the Italian family to come around, but after the birth of baby Bluefeather, both families were reconciled.

Valerio was a mine superintendent. He had earned this position by working underground since he was seventeen. His status in the community was greater than the mayor's. Besides that, he had the reputation as a fair man among the underground miners and one to respect in a barroom brawl. Around Raton he was considered in the league of Jack Dempsey and Jack Johnson.

Bluefeather grew up as an only child. The thought did cross his mind that this may have been chosen because of the mixed blood. He would never know. All his aunts and uncles had birthed multiple cousins for him to grow up with—to play with, fight, and love.

Morning Star was a caring, gentle mother who wanted her son to have the kind of education that she reasoned would keep him occupied and interested in life aboveground and out of the coal mines. She didn't want him "down in the hole." Her deep beliefs came from people who respected all that the Great Spirit had created—the whole earth, its animals, birds, insects, its all. She felt it was unnatural to scar the earth's beauty for wealth—wealth that always vanished in the end. She respected her husband and his family's heritage, but she pursued this goal for her son with a strong will.

She taught Bluefeather early on how to read and whetted his curiosity for varied, fine things. Valerio reinforced her when it came to Bluefeather's school studies. There was no shirking. Later Bluefeather would thank his family and his gods for this most priceless of gifts.

With all these blessings, Bluefeather's doting aunts, female cousins, and grandmothers almost convinced him he had one too many—he was almost too pretty to be a boy, and he hated it. From the time he could remember, all he had heard from them was: "Isn't that the most beautiful child you ever saw?" "Look at that hair, thick and shiny as a girl's." "What a girl wouldn't give for those eyelashes." "He's just too pretty to play baseball. What if he got hit in the face?"

By the time he was sixteen, his six-foot height, his wide, lean shoulders and his expertise at sports made him even more attractive. His father had taught him, along with the studying, how to hide his chin behind his shoulder, jab a left fist, fake another, and follow up with an overhand right that simply dropped whoever took the blow, like a sack of low-grade coal.

He overheard girls talking about his good looks and took advantage of it in a callous way, for a while. How was he to know if the young ladies cared for him for himself or because he was handsome? This became very important to him. He began to think that a few nicks and scrapes might change his image enough for him to discern the difference.

At first, he started friendly fights outside his family clan, over mostly nothing. Things such as someone not moving aside on the sidewalk fast enough, or someone looking at him the "wrong" way. He had a physical altercation with Eloy Gomez because he stepped on his shadow twice in one day. Unforgivable. Although he received many blows, bruises, and contusions, they all healed, and he was as handsome as before.

His second cousin, Guiseppe "Hog Head" Fontano, who was twenty-five years old, weighed 248 pounds and worked as a "collector" in Chicago, came to town to visit his kin. He loved card games of all kinds—mostly because he was a cheat and won a great percentage of the time.

Bluefeather was in a jokers-wild poker game with Hog Head and three other cousins. He noticed that his Chicago kin always won when he dealt. Always. Bluefeather knew no one could do that without rigging the cards. The odds were just too high against it.

He stood up and called Hog Head a liar, a cheat, an overgrown ape, and a disgrace to the family. His tactics worked. Hog Head hardly looked up, and he certainly didn't argue, as that would have been wasting time. In one motion he arose, reaching over the card table, and slapped Bluefeather across the side of his cheek and head with a huge open hand. He hadn't formed a fist out of respect for youth.

Bluefeather was knocked backward, whirling and falling face-first into the beveled edge of a dresser top. It split his forehead at an angle between his eyebrows. The flesh was peeled back and blood flowed wondrously into his eye and down his cheeks. He checked all this out after struggling a while to get his rubber-soft legs under his body so he could look in the dresser mirror. At first he was very sobered by the sight. It's true, he had wanted his features altered, but not quite that much. But it was too late; it was done. He might as well think of it as a difficult chore easily taken care of by his cousin Hog Head Fontano. He was suddenly very pleased.

Hog Head was dealing the cards again, uttering softly, "Don't nobody say I'm a disgrace to the family."

The betting went on as before. Bluefeather rejoined the game, wiping at his face with a red-stained handkerchief, saying, "Hey, Hog Head, would you teach me to deal someday?"

"Sure, kid. Anytime."

The old mine doctor had sewed him up so skillfully that only when Bluefeather got angry or highly emotional did the scar show. He resented the good doctor's skill for a while but soon found that when he sat almost directly under a light the thin scar invariably showed up. He had tried it from every angle with his mother's hand mirror. It would be there for as long as he was. Young Bluefeather was satisfied that now he could get on with his life in a normal fashion.

Soon after Hog Head's addition, he was disappointed to overhear his grandmother Fellini tell her closest friend, "Poor Bluefeather is so handsome, he'll be handed much without any effort on his part. Those Olympian eyes will bring him many delights and probably doom, for he is so naturally generous, he'll give all his earnings away."

"But they're such kindly eyes," answered her friend. "How could he not be a sharing soul?"

The cousin who overheard this with him later told a friend, "Yeah, he'll kindly knock you on your ass and kindly pick you up and generously do it to you again if you kind of don't like it."

As soon as he graduated from high school—to his father's delight and his mother's worry—he went over Raton Pass to Trinidad to work as an oremucker (shoveler) in the mines. His father's heritage was readily visible in his work, and rapid job promotions were forthcoming. He made shift foreman faster than anyone in the area ever had. His future seemed to be as vast as a cloudless sea. At first this success distressed his mother. She wanted him to go to college and pursue some other endeavor. His mother's expectations for him were yet to come.

Then, oh yes, then, he met the old gringo prospector who told enchanting tales of lost mines in Twinning Canyon north of Taos. The old man seduced his young mind with a simple trick of yellow sorcery. Grinder the Gringo had revealed a glass vial full of nuggets from the size of sand grains to the scope of a pencil eraser. He showed old geological reports and drew maps with authority and expertise. Bluefeather was properly entrapped.

It was natural that Bluefeather's immediate family and other kin tried to dissuade him from this foolishness; but toothless Sam Grinder could chew tobacco and drink beer at the same time and continue through many hours of dedicated conversation without any apparent injury. This amazed and convinced young Bluefeather that a man of such unique accomplishments should be followed listened to and learned from. All this and more would inevitably occur.

At first the Fellini family was more than a little upset with young Bluefeather for what they considered a very rash decision. Aside from his leaving the safety and security of home and friends, his joining up with a gold prospector was, in their minds, sillier and more risky than the venture undertaken by another ancient relation, Christopher Columbus. Bluefeather's leaving also threatened the future marriage plans of the Bertinoli family to their beautiful daughter, Margaret.

Bluefeather finally reasoned with everyone by pointing out that, in truth, he was simply going over to the other side of the Rocky Mountains. The Fellini family took some consolation from his being near the maternal side of his family at Taos Pueblo. They reluctantly gave their blessings, but not without many messages to relatives throughout the multistory adobe structure advising them on the manner in which the promising young company man must be guided back to his true and practical future. It was a wasted effort. The genes of gleaming dreams had been unleashed from his head. Many things might slow them down, but nothing could stop them now.

Bluefeather loaded up his gear in the back of the old prospector's battered Ford truck, and they headed toward what Grinder referred to as his "great hacienda."

The Gringo's great hacienda in Taos, just a mile from the plaza, turned out to be a four-room, slab (slabs being waste-wood strips from a sawmill) shack, the cracks filled with mud, with no electricity and no indoor plumbing. There was a well with a bucket on a pulley in the front yard and an outhouse in back. The hacienda did, however, sit on three acres of subirrigated pasture.

The old man explained as they emptied the last of Bluefeather's gear from the vehicle, "You see, son, a gold huntin' man has always got to own him a little headquarters somewhere. Then between strikes he'll have a place to plan and think about his next go. Cain't nobody shame and starve him plumb out. Get the idee?"

The first thing he did with Bluefeather—after introducing him to the house—was to take him out in the pasture and make him acquainted with his burro, Tony.

"Now another thing . . . always keep a burro or mule—mules, if you can afford 'em—and some feed. That way, no matter what, you'll never be afoot and at the mercy of functional folks—the vault stuffers. It's those functional folks that do in men like you'n me. We make 'em uncomfortable."

Bluefeather learned a great lesson standing there in a Taos, New Mexico, pasture. By necessity he found that he really could shake his head "yes" and "no" at the same time without breaking his neck. This ability would come in handy throughout his life. He also learned to be a good listener, mainly because he had no choice.

Grinder the Gringo ground on. "Now let's get on back to headquarters. We got things to discuss."

They walked the seventy feet back to the house with purpose in their footsteps. Grinder opened them each a beer and began to show Bluefeather ore samples from the entire Rio Hondo mining district—chunks of rainbow metallic copper; bornite from Frazier Mountain, shining with an iridescent patina as it was turned in the light; oxidized malachite and azurite, the grass-green and ocean-blue coppers, from Bull of the Woods Mountain—until Bluefeather's eyes and sense of color would be forever linked to chunks of rich ore samples.

Then came the clincher. The yellow metal would forever be imprinted on, and in, his entirety when Grinder showed him a fist-sized piece of white quartz with visible gold, some pieces as big as his thumbnail, splattered through it. Grinder placed the glass vial right next to the quartz rock and handed Bluefeather a magnifying glass.

"Now look carefully. The placer gold is the same as that in the quartz. It's the same color and grain. That rock is from the mother lode. No question about it. And that ain't no float rock neither. You can tell by the sharpness of its edges and the white shininess of the rock that it was just recently broke out of the mother lode vein."

Bluefeather asked, "Do you know the location of this?"

Grinder chose to ignore the question. He continued, "All great discoveries have come from finding jist one rock. Jist one and this'n here is it." He was chewing and swallowing the tobacco and beer with much enthusiasm as he pushed the white, shredded hair out of his little pea-sized, milky-blue eyes and walked around the room two or three times muttering to himself as if he were nearing the answer to all creation.

Finally he stopped, standing close, but just to the side, so he could look at an old, faded print of Christ on the cross where it hung crookedly on the wall. "I swear to the Almighty, I dug this here gold with my very own hands."

"Then we're ready to start our mining operation right off, huh?"

"Well now, son, I don't know how to tell you this, but after I found the placer and the vein—there they are right there on the table—I musta' fell off a bluff and knocked something loose in my head, 'cause all I remember is waking up here at headquarters with a big knot and a three-inch cut in my scalp and a whole case of empty beer bottles layin' about."

Bluefeather's strong young stomach did a little hula dance inside his ribs. He had not yet learned to handle the enormous changing of directions and gears that occurred so suddenly in the world of gold seekers.

"You mean . . . you actually mean to tell me you can't remember anything about it?"

"Well, it ain't 'cause I haven't tried. I've spent nearly a year now straining so hard my head sometimes felt like it spun off and rolled all the way to the Rio Grande. It sure ain't 'cause…" Then Grinder showed what makes a good mineral mountain man. "We'll find 'er, kiddo. And we'll be rich far beyond the greediest of dreams. Don'tcha worry 'bout that. Look here." He pulled a cigar box from a shelf and took out two neatly folded, official-looking documents. One was a geological report by a prominent, consulting geologist dated Albuquerque, New Mexico, November 2, 1900. He had written it for the now defunct Rio Hondo Mining Company. The other made for Messieurs Frank C. Smith and Son, Denver, Colorado, by Colonel L. S. Judd, mining engineer of Vicksburg, Arizona, dated December 14, 1907.

"Read 'em and you'll see what I'm talking about."

Bluefeather read about dikes, transverse veins, andesite porphyry, mica schists, incline shafts, crosscuts, estimates of ore bodies and values, and quotes from assay reports.

Grinder had waited patiently. "Well, kiddo?"

Bluefeather just sat and stared at the reports.

The old man said, "See, there's plenty of clues in those reports about enriched zones. All we gotta do is check ever' one out till we find our lode. Get the idee? Oh, yes siree, you are one lucky young man to be afforded this lifetime opportunity of adventure and riches. Riches, I say. Riches aplenty to buy all of Taos County, were you a mind to."

Bluefeather suddenly felt the need for "just one more" beer. He had five just one mores before he slept from several kinds of Taos exhaustion all occurring in his first night in the little mud village. It was a good thing he didn't know that this would seem like a placid night later on as he and the gringo explored the mountains, the saloons, and the artists' society gathered here from all over the world, and he would meet his greatest temptation so far—Lorraine Friedman from New York City.

Two

It was the time of harvesting early summer hay in the fields and money on Taos plaza. Bluefeather sensed that it was going to be a good, solid summer in the little mud village.

The winter snows had been heavy in the mountains, assuring an abundance of water for the irrigation ditches and the fishing streams that moved toward the Rio Grande a few miles west of town. Daily afternoon showers now kept the air crystal clear, and the dust settled on the unpaved streets of the plaza.

Heavy history had visited the village of Taos and stayed to mesh with the new that was always forming. The savage Pueblo uprising—which had forced the Spaniards all the way back to Mexico, and their ensuing bloody, permanent return—echoed through the adobe walls. From those of fame and power, who had once lived and loved here, there remained many historical, "spirit" presences. Kit Carson was one of the prominent trappers buried here. Hundreds of other mountain men chose Taos as their rendezvous place after trapping for furs in the Rocky Mountains. It was a town accustomed to fame. Names such as the late Governor Charles Bent and the deceased Padre Martinez were as familiar in the village as the name of the current mayor.

To Bluefeather and other casual observers, Taos seemed like a normal, unhurried world, but deceivingly so, for underneath and mostly hidden was a creative force, like artillery explosions taking place in selected spots in the mountains, in unseen art studios and occasionally along the curving side streets of the adobe town.

The tiny mud settlement was like a magnet. The artists and their colony attracted visitors and buyers from around the world. People came and rented homes for a month or the summer to paint, to take photographs, to try to absorb a mystique that mostly defied their attempts at description.

People of worldly import like Georgia O'Keeffe, Leopold Stokowski, and many, many more would visit the matriarch of Taos (and possibly matriarch of American art and artists), Mable Dodge Luhan, and her Taos Indian husband, Tony. The Taos masters, Oscar Berninghaus, Bert Phillips, Ernest Blumenschein and others, were all painting, enjoying growing sales and recognition around the world.

The Pueblo Indians tolerated the visitors, posed as artists' models and allowed photographs in designated areas, both at the multistory adobe dwelling and in town. Their images, including many of Bluefeather's kin, were being hung in homes, buildings and museums across the United States and in other countries. Unimpressed by their fame and attractiveness, they went about their farming, horse and cattle trading, fishing, and mostly private ceremonies just as they had for hundreds of years. They accepted the invasions of varied peoples with astounding grace and dignity, as long as the visitors didn't interfere in their ancient religious ceremonies without invitation.

Almost the entire east side of the plaza was a large, vacant lot surrounded with hitching rails for saddle horses and wagons and teams. Bluefeather loved and belonged in this place of unhurried activity. The Indians, blanketed like bedouins, would come and go and gather in colorful groups to wait, talk, trade, and drink or just enjoy the warm sun as did the old men—*los viejos*—of the Hispanic world.

The sparkling atmosphere gave the great bluffs and forested canyons of the sacred Taos Mountain—north of the village and the pueblo—such a clarity that it dominated Taos, its people, and all the wild creatures as if it were the first and largest cathedral built by the gods.

It was on the other side of this massive prominence, up Twinning Canyon, that Bluefeather and Grinder started their search. To form their main camp, they pitched their tent by the creek at the foot of Frazier Mountain.

They could see the green malachite, oxidized stains of copper, painting the bluff above them. It was real, but still an illusion, because the fifty-yard-wide stain was just that. Many a prospector had been lured up those bluffs thinking the stain was a massive deposit of solid ore.

As they started their search for Grinder's lost mine, he told his new protégé, "Remember son, everybody in the whole world is a treasure hunter. Most of 'em never find much 'cause they haven't got the guts to take the extra steps. Anyway, you gotta have the smell for gold. I can smell it like it was a skunk. I can sniff it out no matter where it hides. I ain't no rock hound. I'm a pure and sure gold-dog."

Bluefeather would have followed him unhesitatingly off a thousand-foot bluff if he had said the vein was at the bottom. He wasn't sure, yet, but he felt he was gonna be a hell of a gold-smeller himself.

Three

Bull of the Woods Mountain is just above timberline, over twelve thousand feet high, in the Sangre de Cristo Range just north of Wheeler Peak, the highest point in New Mexico. They moved their camp up there with the help of the burro, Tony, right by the headwaters of Twinning Creek.

As they packed to climb, Grinder said, "Don't worry. It's just three whistles and a fart to the top of this mountain."

After eight hours, on a trail suited only to the agility of mountain goats, they finally reached their intended campsite just at dusk. Bluefeather was a tired young man marveling at the old man's stamina but questioning his mathematical calculations.

They soon found the porphyry outcrop mentioned in the geological report, just forty or fifty yards east of the highest point on the mountain. There were flowerlike crystals of malachite and azurite copper in it. They found other rich-looking samples of ore in many old tunnels scattered over the sides of the mountain, but no visible gold.

They cut samples of the best prospects, and Grinder showed his young protégé how to thoroughly mix up the rock cuttings in a sack, quarter them on a tarpaulin, and then quarter them again. They reduced the weight of their load enormously by following Grinder's advice: "One of the great failings in prospecting is high-grading yourself when you know the values are not there. You ain't cheatin' nobody but yourself."

Bluefeather and his Raton relatives were miners, but black coal was always easily identifiable. Over and over he had felt the bloodswell of discoveries that turned out to be yellow, shiny iron pyrites (truly fool's gold) or chalcopyrite copper that was an even duller yellow and closer to the hue of real gold.

After he had excitedly shown these discoveries to Grinder twenty or thirty times, the old miner sat him down and said, "Look," handing

Bluefeather the ore glass and a nugget from the vial. "Now look at the pyrite. See. It's shinier. It's like glass. It's fake gold. Raw gold is more loosely grained, and that takes the luster off it. You getting the idee, kiddo?"

"I'm beginning to, I think...just a few more days and I'll..."

"Well now, I'll tell you the secret of this wondrously malleable metal. See this here nugget? A jeweler can hammer that so thin it would reach halfway to the bottom of the mountain without it separating. Now ain't that a wonderful thing?"

"Yeah. Yeah, it sure is, but what's the secret you were gonna tell me?"

"Oh, that. Okay. If there's any doubt at all about it being gold... it ain't."

Bluefeather soon learned the truth of this and thereby saved much time throughout his life for better, more productive activities.

They worked downward now to the many caved-in tunnels on Frazier Mountain, sampling the outcroppings above them, digging, chipping, looking for the twenty-foot-wide brown dikes where they intersected with much narrower quartz veins, hoping every second to finally look upon the spot of Grinder's rich lode.

Bluefeather slithered into tunnels that were still open, sometimes almost getting trapped. In case there was a hang-up or a cave-in, the rule was that one man always waited outside any tunnel entered by the other.

The insides of the tunnels were hauntingly beautiful with the damp copper glowing in all its varied blues and yellows. Most of the tunnels on Frazier Mountain slowly leaked water from the heavy winter snows through their minute cracks and perforations.

Bluefeather finally learned that one could become entranced by the silent beauty, the sound broken only by his own chipping or the occasional dripping of water.

Grinder had to tell him again. "Hey, you're gettin' carried away with the purty and wastin' valuable samplin' time. I know. I did the same thing when I was your age."

Bluefeather heeded the advice. They had covered every visible prospect on Frazier Mountain that they felt had any merit, when they suddenly discovered a streak of ruby silver on the edge of a tiny hole. Bluefeather bent down and shined a flashlight down into the darkness. There was a huge hole under them, and their weight was on very thin rock. They retreated quickly, walking ever so softly.

"That's a stope. Miners drop ore from above when they find a rich pocket. Those guys came upon an enrichment of ruby silver and just let it drop."

Lower down they saw where the tunnel had been blasted under the vein. Bluefeather began digging furiously at the portal. Grinder sat down to cut a big chew of tobacco. He stuffed it into his cheek and worked his gums in amusement at Bluefeather's wasted efforts.

"Well, he has to learn it all," Grinder thought to himself. "Might as well let him chance a look."

It turned out to be a hell of a risk. The minute space he had dug suddenly opened so big that the light barely reached the top, revealing the tiny opening they had almost stepped into earlier. Bluefeather had some difficulty enticing Grinder to join him for a look. With their carbide lamps and the flashlight, the massive stope was revealed. They could see scatterings of silver still hanging above, absolutely unrecoverable.

"Somebody took a wad outa this stope. I'll bet there was high gold values along with the silver, but they ruined the mine forever," Grinder said with a sad hurt in his voice.

Bluefeather didn't need this explained. He could see it would be impossible to timber the hole where tons of rock hung loose, ready to fall. The mine had been raped and plundered so drastically—for a quick gain—that it could no longer be worked. The previous miners had ruined it for anyone who followed.

Bluefeather had already been in several tunnels on Bull of the Woods that were in the same condition. These were the first undeniable physical signs of the waste of human greed that he had witnessed. As he thought of the long-ago miners, he was stunned and enraged. Then he wondered if he would do the same when he and Grinder found their place to stope. He swore he wouldn't, no matter what Grinder did. But of course, he was young, and his elders had told him that ideals were either thrown away in youth or kept and expanded in old age. There was no in-between. Hell, he didn't know for sure what he might do.

He was relieved to hear Grinder's voice say, "Let's get out of here. A strong thought could send this mountain crashin' down on us, kiddo."

"Kiddo's got the message," Bluefeather answered as they started for the opening, the nervous sweat curling his dark hair and running down his face so the salt filmed his large eyes with tears.

The assays came back and told a story that verified the validity of the old geological reports. So far the veins revealed in the tunnels and the surface cuts showed an average of one and a half percent copper and a little gold and silver by-products—too low-grade to mine without a huge, expensive mill. The intersection of the veins and formations showed an enrichment, but nothing to compare with the placer and rock Grinder had found; most of these had already been usurped by tunnels and stopes underneath them.

Grinder put a confident voice to it, explaining, "Lookee, son, we've narrowed it down now. There's a lot less to prospect, so that means we'll be finding her soon."

Grinder walked stiffly but recklessly about the mountains, weaving, wobbling, moving on as carefree as a blue jay. Bluefeather knew that the crazy gringo's equilibrium had been knocked askew ever since his fall at the discovery point, and he worried every second they were climbing, even though the old man rarely fell hard enough to break the skin.

Then early one evening Grinder got up from the campfire to empty his tobacco juice can, stumbled, and fell in a little rocky wash not two feet deep and broke his left leg below the knee.

"Now don't that scald the hog. We're gettin' close to the find, kiddo, or the devil would never have tripped me like that."

By the time Bluefeather hauled Grinder into town, got his leg set, delivered him two cases of beer and a carton of Beechnut chewing tobacco, made a trip back to the camp to get Tony and all their gear, he was ready for a small vacation. He could afford to take one, since a widow who lived three houses away from Grinder, Maude Cisneros, would visit, comfort, cook, and drink with him. Bluefeather decided to go visit his relatives at the pueblo.

Maude assured him, "Now, boy, you take all the time you might need for a good visit with your grandpapa. I sure enough take care of the gringo here. We been amigos for seventy million years."

A friendship that old could mean nothing but good company for them both. Bluefeather was totally relaxed with her now.

He motioned for Maude to follow him outside where he handed her nine dollars, saying, "Maude, we want that leg to heal properly, so you be sure he gets some meat and eggs and try to get him to drink some fresh milk along with all that beer."

"No worries." She waved a heavy arm in the air. "No bother. I take care of him like leetle baby boy." She smiled so big her cheeks rose up and almost hid her dark, happy eyes.

"I'm sure you will, Ma'am. I'll drop by in a week or so."

"Now you stay right over there at the pueblo long as you like, and don't worry yourself none. Get the idee, kiddo?" And they both laughed at her mimicry. She had obviously done a lot of careful listening to the gringo in the past.

He left feeling free of responsibility. His natural-born, coyote ears heard the two old friends talking inside the house as he readied to leave.

"Hey, you beautiful old Spanish woman, get us a new beer."

Maude answered, laughing with him, "Only the rich are Spanish in Taos. I'm a Mexican because I'm poor. Better you call me Mexican. Don't you savvy nothin', you toothless old gringo? Huh?"

Bluefeather moved away smiling for them. He felt good because his friends did. That's the way he was.

Four

It was the time of things that moved about the earth at Taos Pueblo. Bluefeather eagerly pitched in and helped his grandfather and uncle make the first cutting of grass hay in their allotted pasture. It was a good crop from plentiful summer showers this year.

Two horses pulled his grandfather on a mower that cut the long grass close to the ground. Bluefeather drove another team pulling a rake and piled up the long windrows to dry. When it was cured enough they would stack it next to his grandfather's barn to feed to the livestock throughout the long, harsh winter.

They worked in the fields all day, skipping the noon meal. By evening they were ravenous, but the long day seemed a little shorter for the field hands because of the feast they anticipated at the end of the day. They knew Bluefeather's grandmother would have beef and corn, or sometimes a stew made from soaked venison jerky with several kinds of vegetables and chiles. And always, she would have many loaves of fresh bread she baked in the *horno* (outdoor oven). Bluefeather had missed her bread with its thick crust and tender insides. Just the thought or smell of it made him dizzy and caused saliva to accumulate in his mouth. Then his absolute favorite thing was the dessert she would serve made from fresh fruit, when it was in season; if not, she used dried apples or apricots.

The little time that was left after the cutting and the stacking was spent repairing barns and equipment and looking after the livestock. Lots of visiting went on with his kin in the Bear Clan. However, his grandfather, the shaman, was always on call to those in need of spiritual or physical healing. They were a team, his grandparents, because during the time he spent in the cedar-burning ceremony to rid the body of bad spirits, she would prepare whatever combination of herbs it took to benefit any fleshly illness. Bluefeather was constantly amazed that they made no discernible signs to each other or conversation as they worked so perfectly as a team.

He remembered when he was about seven years old and his family had been visiting here while his father hunted deer with his uncle Stump Jumper. After the hunt Bluefeather recalled watching them dress the deer out when a signal, unseen to him, came from atop the highest level of the mud building from a kiva chieftain denoting "the time for staying still." (For forty days, beginning December 12 and ending January 20, the pueblo occupants do not chop wood or dig in the earth. They can, if needed, ride horseback only at a normal walk, to care for the livestock, but they cannot drive a wagon and team. For this period of time, they try to become as close to dormant and as in rhythm with the earth entering deep winter as possible.)

When the quiet time would come upon the pueblo, Valerio always loaded his family in the car and eased off the reservation and back to Raton to hold down his job in the mine. Bluefeather could never forget the sudden switch in tempo of his two worlds. There was no concern this summer, though, for he soon adapted to the pueblo ways as his mother once did.

Although visitors are allowed to attend the Turtle Dance, Corn Dance, their very special Deer Dance, and a couple of other ceremonies, the core of Taos religious events is rigidly protected from anyone outside the pueblo. The kiva and Bluelake rites are the most carefully guarded.

Just the year before, Bluefeather had been honored with participation in both. So it was no surprise to him when his grandfather advised him one evening that they would be going to the sacred cave on the northwest side of Taos Mountain. He was allowed no supper that night and no food the next day.

They were all elders of the Bear Clan who rode through the foothills to the Mother Mountain. They wore varied colored blankets of fine weaves, used only in ceremonies. While doing ordinary work the elders wore Arab-style blankets made of plain cotton from the local J. C. Penney department store and folded them to cover their heads and the sides of their faces as well as their bodies.

Bluefeather was riding in the center of the group and knew that he was the focus of this trip. He was not afraid, nor did he question the hunger of his empty stomach but instead looked forward to whatever would occur with confidence and a feeling of warm and total trust.

They rode across a canyon and up a trail on its side and tied their horses. It was just sundown. His grandfather took his medicine bundle. The others carried skin drums and a large blanket. They walked the final distance to the cave. There was a neat stack of twigs and larger sticks piled near its entrance waiting for them. They would replace them when they left.

The youngest member present of the Bear Clan was his uncle Stump Jumper. He was allowed because he was a shaman-apprentice to his father. He was in direct line after uncounted centuries to carry on the sacred traditions. He built the fire as the night swallowed the last sunlight.

Bluefeather's grandfather, Moon Looker, motioned him to sit in the middle of the blanket and watch the fire. He performed the cedar-smoke cleansing, spreading the smoke in all directions with an eagle feather. The drums beat softly. The shaman walked into the cave alone for a few silent moments then returned to the circle. Chants were sung. The fire flickered and danced to the beat. Drum. Drum. Drum. Chant. Chant. Drum. All was one.

Bluefeather saw a rabbit jump out of the fire. It leaped playfully on the far end of the blanket, then another and another rabbit played there until there were six. They were cottontails, fat with full, soft fur. They paid him no attention as they moved about touching noses. Then four of them ran swiftly in different directions toward the four winds. One dug swiftly down into the rock, and the last leapt straight into the sky. They all vanished.

Now a stranger stood between the blanket and fire smiling at Bluefeather and speaking, "Well, hello there, dear brudder Bluefeather. I come to meet you, for sure."

"Who are you? Where did you come from? What are you doing here?" Bluefeather asked.

"Just like other white feller, asking three questions at same time to be answered. Okay, all right then. One. I'm Dancing Bear," and he did a little dance that did indeed imitate an upright bear. "Two. I come from other side. Three. I been called up on assignment to be your guiding spirit."

"I don't think I need any spirit guide. I'm doing just fine."

Dancing Bear did a fast step that might have been part Deer Dance, Turtle Dance, and the Texas Two-Step, saying, "You don't need me this time right now, but things change from one sun to the other. Maybe so, you could use a little professional help someday. Maybe."

Bluefeather jumped to his feet, and Dancing Bear flew up on a rock to avoid possible attack and great danger. He squatted there on the precarious perch smiling at Bluefeather with flickers of firelight washing back and forth across his face and looking like a big sitting bird.

"What kind of Indian are you anyway?" asked Bluefeather, studying the beaded moccasins, the soft buckskin suit, the featherless band around his head that held his loose, iron-gray, shoulder-length hair mostly in place.

"That is one good question. One. I'm proud of you for being brief already."

"You still haven't answered my one question."

"Well, now lookee here, then," Dancing Bear said and leapt from the rock, whirling in the air all the way down next to the fire. He did dances so fast that Bluefeather thought his legs must break off—Cherokee Stomp Dance, Apache War Dance, Ute Rain Dance, Creek Eagle Dance, Taos Deer Dance, and on and on—until Bluefeather's eyes were dizzy and his hearing impaired.

He shouted, "All right. That's enough. Stop it, you hear? Stop it."

Dancing Bear stopped with both feet several feet off the ground, arms outstretched, motionless as if he were carved from the magic mountain itself.

Bluefeather took a deep breath, staring wide-eyed at his guide. "It may come to pass that I need a spirit guide someday, but I don't need a cockeyed whirling dervish telling me what to do."

"Oh, oh, oh, hi, yi, yi. I never, for sure, advise my dear brudders. I let 'em build their own trails."

"Well then, what good could it possibly be if a guiding spirit doesn't guide?"

"One good question. Thank you. Maybe we are titled wrong. Maybe we should be addressed as pointers, like bird dogs. Huh? What you think of that, dear brudder? Maybe you can call me Dancing Bear the pointing spirit. That please you more?" He proceeded to dance around bent halfway over, pointing first with one finger at parts of the mountain, then doing the same with the other, and then into the star-speckled heavens. Then he whirled like a scared cat, pointing both index fingers at Bluefeather's heart, and laughed until he could no longer hold his arms out. Anyway, he needed his hands to wipe the tears of mirth from his eyes, shiny as little black diamonds.

"I got to go now. Authority is calling me. Remember, dear brudder, you don't own no earth here. It on loan, see? See?" Bluefeather tried to speak, but Dancing Bear paid no mind and spoke on. "Same thing 'bout you. Nobody around here on this earth own you either. Fair? Fair? Huh?" And he was gone.

Bluefeather's yell traveled across the western foothills and miles of sagebrush-covered desert all the way to the Rio Grande Gorge. "Hey, come back here...you deserter, and tell me what I'm supposed to do. You can't just start me out with dances and talk that wouldn't make sense to a corncob and then leave me. Hey! Hey, you!" But Dancing Bear was gone. In his spirit mind, he had done all that was necessary.

The fire was low. The elders encircled Bluefeather again. He lay on the blanket and slept deeply like a played-out puppy.

Five

Bluefeather rode in the wagon beside his cousin Smiling Dog, who drove the gray team past the Manby house on North Pueblo Road and on down to Taos plaza. Smiling Dog tied the team to a hitching post near three saddle horses. Several of Smiling Dog's friends were standing about in twos and threes waiting to visit. Bluefeather knew if Smiling Dog got the chance, he'd get drunk today. Even though it was against the law for Indians to buy whiskey, those who wanted it did so surreptitiously out back doors of saloons and from bootleggers. Since the Indians were constantly afraid of being caught, fined, and jailed, the pints were emptied as fast as possible. This sudden jolt of alcohol to the brain could have made even an elephant stagger.

Bluefeather wasn't interested in drinking today. In fact, he drank only occasionally, and only when the situation seemed to demand it. He loved to explore Taos plaza—the center of the village, a permanent local stage. It often held a sampling of the entire world. Bluefeather loved to watch the kaleidoscope of colors—the blankets, clothing, jewelry, hair, and skin. He was fascinated by it all. The shops held beautiful paintings, Indian pottery, religious *bultos* (upright crucifixes) and *retablos* (paintings on flat wood to hang on a wall), Navajo blankets, and every other southwestern art and craft.

There was always a generous mixture of colorfully blanketed Indians from various pueblos present on the plaza. Then there were the Spanish Americans or Mexicans (as some preferred to be called). Most of the town's public officials, city and state, plus the police force were of this nationality. Then there were the mongrelized gringos, some with bloodlines beyond research.

A few tourists were taking photos of the adobe architecture, but their main interest seemed to be the Indians. Boom! It struck

Bluefeather that he had adapted so well to the pueblo life, he'd forgotten that he, too, was wearing a faded pink blanket and had allowed his hair to grow into two respectably long braids. What would he do if a tourist approached him for a photograph? Would he be a fakery if he posed as a full-blooded Indian? If not, how could he explain? The problem lasted only a moment, for the passing of scattered conversations made him forget. He relished just walking along overhearing bits and pieces of all the varied conversations. He rarely looked at the speakers. It took strong will not to, but this was part of the game. He wanted his mind to picture the person, not his eyes.

"That lady in the curio store said the governor is coming tomorrow to give a speech here on the plaza. Shall we stay over?" one male voice said.

"I can't imagine why you would think we'd like to hear a political speech while we're here. This plaza says all the things I'm interested in," another male voice replied.

Then Bluefeather heard a female voice join the two male ones so strongly he almost broke his neck to keep from turning his head.

She said, "The tourists don't come to New Mexico to see politicians. They come to see the Indians, the cowboys, and the artists that inhabit these adobe buildings."

Then, on a few more steps, he heard, "Did you folks come through Amarillo, Clayton, and Raton?"

"No, we came down from Denver."

"That's also a beautiful drive. We came that way two years ago."

More walkers and talkers moved perpetually along the rectangular boundaries of the plaza.

"I know that the greatest thoughts are never told or written, but let me try and explain this dream I had last night..."

Bluefeather really would have appreciated hearing the rest of this and was tempted to follow them—even if it was against his eavesdropping rules—but the voice moved on, diminishing, as another floated into hearing range.

"He always picks the dumbest women."

"Yeah, but boy are they lookers. Give him some credit."

Bluefeather moved on, stopped in front of La Fonda de Santa Fe Hotel, and turned to look across the center of the plaza.

He heard a hurried voice that didn't seem to fit Taos but was of the village just the same. "Terrasita read the cards for me yesterday. I've just got to tell you all about it."

"I have something to tell you, too. Mabel has insisted we come for cocktails before dinner tonight. She has this artistic genius she wants us to meet."

"Introducing genius is Mabel's business. We should go. Let's go into La Fonda and have a drink and catch up on our visiting."

Bluefeather saw a young couple crossing the corner of the plaza in front of him. This time he watched them as he heard the Anglo man say, "Taos is as mysterious and indecipherable as knowledge itself. The more you feel the mountains and mysticism, the wider the cavern of the unknown becomes."

The pretty girl, holding her mate's arm, leaned her head into his shoulder and said, "Oh, I know, and I don't want to leave here. I wish we could just stay here forever."

He watched them while their voices trailed off into silence as if caught in a vortex of crosswinds. Bluefeather thought they were strangers, but somehow they were also his kin. Maybe the young man's thoughts were felt deeply enough and spoken honestly enough that they would always be part of Taos plaza.

The next voice he heard was as melodious as a great song, youthful as the first sunflower bloom, and vital as water.

"Excuse me, but may I please take your picture?" He didn't move while he waited for another voice to answer her. None came. Before he realized she was speaking to him, there she stood, camera in hand, directly in front of him.

He turned his blanketed head slightly to stare at a golden young woman. How could it be? Had Grinder the Gringo mesmerized him with visions of the precious metal to the point that everything he saw was impregnated with it? Her blond hair was streaked with golden strands. Even her wide, hazel eyes contained little, sparkling gold nuggets. The sun had caressed her skin and carefully brushed it in even strokes with the color of its rays.

She moved directly in front of him, looking up intensively as if she was trying to read his mind—his very soul.

"Will it be all right?" she asked, suddenly relaxing, exuding vitality and eagerness.

"You're speaking to me? I...I...uh, well okay."

"Oh, gladness," she said.

Gladness? Bluefeather thought, "What kind of woman is this who uses the word 'gladness'?" Well, whatever, she doesn't hesitate once she gets your attention.

"Hi, I'm Lorraine Friedman."

"Good to meet you. I'm Bluefeather Fellini."

"What an unusual name."

She looked at him through the camera lens and snapped a couple of shots. Then she stopped and studied him as if he were a new dress she might consider buying. She backed off, her eyes never leaving his face, and stood by a shiny, new 1935 Buick roadster. She said to him around the windshield, "Everyone takes pictures on the plaza. Do you mind if we go somewhere different?" She didn't wait for him to answer. "Okay. Get in."

Bluefeather couldn't believe what was happening. He removed the blanket from his head and wrapped it around his waist. He walked slowly, half hypnotized, to the other side and got into her car without saying another word.

She drove expertly around the plaza and headed east to Taos Canyon. It was a short drive of five or six miles. She parked by the creek and directed Bluefeather in many poses in the sunlight and shadow, totally absorbed, instructing him with many "pleases," "move here," "move there," "tilt your head up," "look at the mountain," "look at the creek."

"Good. Good. Perfect. Ah yes, delightful. Beautiful. Beautiful. Now look straight at me. Hold it." Click. Click.

All the time she was posing him, she was intermittently explaining that she and her divorced mother had rented a summer home here; that they were from New York City; that her mother owned and operated both a modeling and advertising firm, but she was not one of her mother's photographers; that hers was a different calling with the camera, although she wasn't sure what it was yet; that she was filled with gladness that he was so kind to pose for her; and would he please call her "Lorrie," and she would like to call him "Blue."

"It seems everyone—professionals and amateurs—wants to take pictures of the older Indians whose lives are written on their faces and in their eyes. You see, Blue, I want to try something different. I want to capture that fragility of youth looking forward to a life not yet formed...like watching the pyramids going up."

Bluefeather thought that was sure a fine ambition, but his head was overloaded with all this sudden posing and bountiful information. He'd asked for none of it. How had this happened?

He had been on the verge of getting testy when she said, "That's enough for today. I've imposed on you far too long. Could I express my thanks? We'll go back to town and have drinks and dinner on me."

Now he faced something else he had never before experienced. His long hair and his Indian attire posed a new problem. He did look like a full-blood now. Earlier, Lorrie had thought he was joking when he told her his father was a full-blooded Italian.

He blurted it out. "Don't you know it's against the law for Indians to buy whiskey?"

Lorrie suddenly became still where she was sitting on a log putting her gear in a camera bag. Then she lifted her face up to his with a mixed-up emotion emitting from her eyes and said, "Oh, I'm sorry."

Bluefeather knew she meant it. He said, "It's all right. I really don't care that much about drinking, but if we want it, it's easy enough to get. There are bootleggers all over town."

"Well, I'll feed you then. There's no law against that." They laughed.

They laughed for the next few hours. Bluefeather would never be able to remember at what. He was rapidly being enclosed in the sweet-scented cocoon of young love.

It happened on the mesa west of town where they parked and watched the sun go down across the Taos desert. So many people had tried to paint this happening, and most had failed. It was just too much. The sky was on fire, with streaks of purple clouds fracturing the sun's rays so far into the clear sky that it seemed as if it would take the whole universe to dissipate them. The suddenly brassy oranges and violets glowed momentarily like a gift. Then there were the last rays that flared up as a good-bye before the day and night blended in a profound stillness and quietness.

They talked and caressed there in the desert, walking about in the twilight smelling the sage that pungently perfumed hundreds of square miles. They kissed and closed their eyes so that all this was integrated into their nonthinking, purely feeling moment of magic. They understood the coyote that howled in a draw near them, because on this evening they were as much a part of their surroundings as the animal. Youth. In fluorescence.

She drove him back to the plaza to see if Smiling Dog's wagon was still there; if it wasn't, she would drive Bluefeather to the pueblo. It was a good thing the team was still tied there. It was difficult for them to go their separate ways. They kept holding on to one another as if they would be parted forever. Finally, after agreeing to meet the next day, Bluefeather gathered the will to part.

She reluctantly backed the roadster onto the plaza street as he untied the team's lines and crawled up on the wagon seat. There was Smiling Dog, lying dead or passed out, in the back of the wagon. As Bluefeather backed up the wagon and reined the horses around toward the pueblo, Smiling Dog sat up, pushing at his eyes with the backs of his hands as if to be sure they would still open.

"I got too much fun goin' over there at Taos town. I think maybe it's a good thing to own some of this fun stuff."

Bluefeather agreed, guiding the horses toward a moon-burned Taos Mountain, breathing wine, feeling heaven, moving on a road of rapture. It was the time of no thinking.

Six

Yesterday Bluefeather had intended to spend a couple of hours exploring Taos plaza and visiting his partner, Grinder. Instead, he had spent from just past noon until almost midnight with Lorrie Friedman, Taos summer resident and photographer from back East. Of course, Taos being the absolute and only center of the universe, everything else was "back there," "over there," "down there," "up there," and especially "out there." Golden lady Lorrie Friedman was the center of the center.

Bluefeather drove Grinder's old Ford truck slowly away from the pueblo, for his mind was dangerously elsewhere. He was pleased that Lorrie liked to drive, because in truth, he didn't. While riding a mule or walking, he could think. A mule would not deceive him and run off the road or into any oncoming traffic. Walking was such an ancient instinct that he could descend a mile-deep shaft, climb a two-mile mountain, or make love along the way in his picture-mind, without falling or crashing into objects. Driving a car was an entirely different matter, and it was particularly dangerous in his present state of mind. He woke up this morning to find himself so in love with Lorrie that he would certainly die if he didn't hold her again soon.

It felt just like first love, but it wasn't. No, Lorrie was actually his third love.

First love had struck Bluefeather's heart at age eleven, as suddenly as lightning bolting a tall tree. She was Leesa Curry, a petite, soft-spoken blond in her early twenties. Miss Curry was his fifth-grade schoolteacher.

It was the third day of the fall school term. Billy Martinez had brought a garter snake to school in a cigar box, and it was causing a considerable amount of girlish squealing in the back of the classroom. Miss Curry, unable to get the class to come to order, straightened herself to her full five-foot-one-inch height and marched to the scene of the excitement.

She calmly reached over, took the snake in hand, held it up for the rest of the class to see, explained that this harmless little creature did a considerable amount of good in its natural habitat, and asked Billy to please set it free during the lunch break so it could get on with its business of ridding the world of unwanted pests.

When she gently returned the snake to its captor's care and returned to her desk, Bluefeather was almost blinded by the dizzying surge that passed through his being—it stayed with him all year.

It was, in the end, a very productive happening. He did all kinds of extra schoolwork, and his homework was always handed in on time and done as neatly as possible. He read many more books than were required of him and found that reading was just as exciting and rewarding as Miss Curry had said it was. Zane Grey and Jack London showed him vistas of deserts and snow, action and adventure, even beauty that he had looked at without seeing before. He became more open now to everything. Aware. His major goal in life was to gain her smiling approval and a gentle hand on his shoulder, and he received them both.

His second love had come at the age of sixteen when one day, in one second, he had noticed that Margaret Bertinoli had the longest black eyelashes, the biggest dark-brown eyes that danced with mischief and mirth, and the shapeliest long legs of anyone in high school. He spent over half his time thinking about rubbing his hands over them. Then he found himself finally thinking about the rest of her, most of the time, and would have gone uneducated and frothing-mouth mad if he hadn't decided that the only answer for him was to eventually marry her.

Once he declared this to be his lifetime commitment, both families were pleased. After he graduated and went to work in Trinidad, Colorado (only eleven miles away), his anticipated progress in the mines and ability to start a family were proven.

The day he received his second promotion at the mine, he decided to start the formal proceedings of asking Margaret's father for a meeting that would determine how he would spend the rest of his life. Before this could come about, though, Grinder the Gringo and his golden rocks had come crashing into Bluefeather's world.

His decision to follow a golden dream to Taos, thus leaving his intended bride and his glowing future in the mines, sent waves of despair and anguish, mixed with anger, among the planners and plotters of his entire future. He did not blame them, and he felt much agony and shame before they were finished with their admonishments. He could not stop this terrible move any more than he could block the blood flowing through his veins.

He thought of the long-legged Margaret often with aching and deep regrets, but such thoughts slowly receded into the mists of Twinning Canyon. There was no doubt in Bluefeather's soul that Miss Bertinoli would marry a mine owner's son and become part of those two families, bearing lovely and talented children for all to love and admire.

Bluefeather had broken all family tradition and was becoming excitedly mired in this new world that he himself was inventing as he raced along—second by minute, by hour, by day here in Taos.

Now, this third love, Lorrie, walked out before the imagination of his misty eyes. Her perfect legs moving so gracefully, he expected her to break into ballet steps at any moment. When she pushed the long, thick ponytail of sunshine hair from her face and smiled at him, bells clanged, the lame became well all over the world, and dogs had pretty puppies. It was indisputable to Bluefeather that never had there been anyone as intelligent, humorous, and beautiful as Lorraine Friedman. She was a genius at photography, and her kisses would have caused Cleopatra to expire from jealousy. Besides that she had 20/20 eyesight and perfect hearing and smelled like a pasture full of spring flowers. Bluefeather was to be complimented no less, especially since he had acquired all this knowledge of his love in less than one day.

Bluefeather was just as surprised on his second date as he was on his first. Lorrie took him home to meet her mother.

The Friedmans' summer house was located at Ranchitos just above Taos Creek on the mesa. The meandering dwelling seemed to have sprouted out of the ground from an adobe seed. All the mountains to the north and east as well as the entire valley were visible from this high point. On the west side, the patio offered a full panorama of the sunsets.

"Mother, this is Blue. Well, I should be more proper; Bluefeather Fellini."

Lorrie's mother moved forward and extended a slender, soft hand with two large, turquoise rings and said, "Hello, Blue. I'm Candi Friedman."

The young prospector was suddenly glued to the floor, and his eyes were surely lying to his brain, for what he saw was a woman so striking she would have turned heads at the Resurrection. Candi Friedman was almost six feet tall and moved like a walking python. Her dark green eyes were even larger than Lorrie's, and her almost blond hair was pulled back in a bun so smooth it made her creamy cheekbones as prominent as an Indian's. Her neck was long, slightly curved, and elegant under a small but firm chin. Her face was delicately and softly colored except for the brilliant vermilion she wore on her full lips. Her nose accentuated all these attributes, precisely placed and shaped, to finish off a truly classical beauty.

Bluefeather did not remember any more of their introduction. He found himself sitting in the patio with a drink of Scotch in his hand, astounded that there existed two such females in all the world much less a mother and daughter in the same house.

Candi, who sat in the chair across from him, wore a long, gathered, red-print "squaw" dress with a Navajo concho belt around her waist and a heavy, squash-blossom necklace hung about her neck. Two long, thin slivers of silver dangled lightly from her earlobes. She smoked from a silver cigarette holder, waving it and punctuating sentences with it like the director of a symphony orchestra. She had, in fact, directed the conversation so smoothly, without obvious interrogation, that Bluefeather never realized he had been played like a zither.

Candi had found out his reading preferences, his current ambition as a potential mine owner, his bloodline, and his immediate madness for her daughter, and had made him feel comfortably at home while doing it.

"Now then, darlings, shall we have another drink? You know, Lorrie dear, your friend Blue could make a top model with the proper grooming."

Lorrie went to bring another round of drinks, saying, "Oh Mother, please. Can you just forget the agency for now? All right?"

Candi spoke to Bluefeather so confidently in a voice so strong and smooth that he felt they had been coconspirators for life.

"Of course, dear Blue, you can see what a fine model Lorrie could be, but she'd rather tinker with a camera instead. She won't even use her little hobby in the agency. A pity, don't you think?"

"I don't know anything about that kind of business, Ma'am," Bluefeather said with much sincerity.

"Of course, how silly of me. I forget that people have other interests. It's just so lucrative to loll about for a few hours a week with the photographer doing all the work. There are many fringe benefits to be had for the asking as well."

Before Bluefeather could be made aware of all those fringes, Lorrie returned with the drinks. He had lost count of the number consumed. Bluefeather was floating in the ancient Taos mist of vast mountain green, desert sage, adobe walls, paintings, books, and an old, old mystical air that both exhilarated and calmed, with all the edges knocked smooth from booze, beauty, and conversation. There was a feeling he had never dreamed existed. This mellowness would surely continue through eternity, since a million years had been enjoyed already, this second day with Lorrie.

They watched the sun go down and the glorious colors rise, catching on the clouds and filling the sky with quickly changing beauty, and then they had dinner. Bluefeather was amazed that Candi and Lorrie had prepared the meal so casually while visiting, mixing drinks, and absorbing the stunning sunset.

They had roast leg of lamb, green beans, potatoes, a green salad, and for dessert, a spiced bread pudding. The red wine was dry and smooth.

Bluefeather Fellini enjoyed the food, the company, and all the world that evening. After giving them each a kiss on the cheek, Candi Friedman bid them good-night.

"It was so good to finally meet you, Blue. You will come back often, won't you?" she said with a powerful, smiling gaze that seemed to push his eyeballs into the back of his skull.

"Well...thank you very much...I sure hope I get to see you again sometime." Bluefeather suddenly realized that Candi had said she was so glad to "finally" meet him. It had seemed like many generations since he had met Lorrie, but the word "finally" made Bluefeather aware, for an instant at least, that he and Lorrie had been acquainted for something a little less than two days.

Lorrie walked him out to his car and gave him a good-night kiss, pushing him away as he felt his hormones and adrenaline mix with the booze in a truly lustful manner.

"No, no. Tomorrow. We have tomorrow."

With the strength and will of a war elephant, Bluefeather drove away. He was so extremely charged up that there was no way he could quit now. He wanted to go to a saloon but couldn't until he got his long hair cut.

He drove to Grinder's house and was thrilled to see the glow of the kerosene lamp that meant Grinder was still up. He went to the open back door and found Grinder and Maude sitting at the kitchen table drinking beer.

They listened to him go on and on about the Friedmans. In his elevated state, the young man thought they were having a normal conversation; however, Grinder the Gringo and Maude Cisneros could easily discern otherwise. Bluefeather never stopped talking except to go to the outhouse occasionally.

During one of Bluefeather's outdoor trips, Grinder spat tobacco juice into a tin can, took another swallow of beer, and said to Maude, "There's only one thing that'll take a prospector's mind off gold even for a little while, and that's brand-new love."

Maude agreed. "Seems like he's got both kinds of fever real bad."

Bluefeather came back inside, speaking as he closed the door. "Say, did I mention that Lorrie's a hell of a good cook? I never had a better meal in my life."

A few hours and many empty beer bottles later they all slept. Bluefeather enjoyed his dreams on the kitchen floor, where Maude had tossed a Navajo rug over him.

Seven

Bluefeather got a short, neat haircut and bought some new clothes. He shaved every day and took a bath in the number-four washtub so often that Grinder remarked, "Son, if your hide springs a leak you're gonna drown."

Bluefeather and Lorrie were together most of each day and night now. They had picnic lunches in the mountains up Twinning and Taos canyons. They walked in the desert and studied the lizards and insects. Lorrie was taking pictures all the time in such a casual, unhurried way that Bluefeather was mostly unaware of it. He took her often to see Grinder and Maude and Tony, the burro. They all liked one another right off.

Lorrie and Bluefeather drove over Palo Flechado Pass to explore the now-vacant gold workings at Elizabeth Town near Eagle Nest. It was only a short drive from there through the canyon to Cimarron then northeast to his hometown of Raton. He ached to show her off to his folks, but somehow never brought it up. He did not want to face the scorn and possible retaliation of having deserted Margaret Bertinoli. He had given no promises about his future intentions toward Margaret, but somehow his thoughts had escaped, giving the relatives of two good Italian families a different idea.

Bluefeather admitted to himself that he just did not have the courage to make such a bold and tradition-insulting move as taking a beautiful New York lady into the family lair. Not yet.

He took her to Twinning often, where they would sit and listen to the emerald water sing and chant and whisper old stories. Once they climbed up Frazier Mountain. He showed her mineral outcroppings and broke off richly colored specimens for her.

Then she wanted to go into the main tunnel and was momentarily shocked when he said, "Oh, nooo. A woman can't go inside a mine. It'll cause a cave-in."

She looked at him with many questions on her face, but she did not ask him why. Bluefeather was so relieved at her silence, and felt so guilty at his abruptness, that he broke all rules and told her about Grinder's lost quartz vein. He was very pleased when her attitude was one of shared excitement. He had feared that she would ridicule their search.

They went out for meals and drinks a couple of times, and no one even questioned serving him liquor. The short haircut and the new clothes had made him someone else. Just a few weeks back he was a pueblo Indian, and now he was a young Latin squiring about a classy lady from Manhattan. People stared and whispered to one another, "What a handsome couple those two make."

With this freedom, Bluefeather could wait no longer to take Grinder, Maude, and Lorrie to the Don Fernando for a party. Not all the plans worked out. Maude's youngest son had an upset stomach. She felt he shouldn't be left alone, so she missed the revelry.

After a fine Mexican dinner, Grinder said, "Let's take a table near the bar so we can get down to some basic lying and drinking and have some serious fun. Get the idee, kiddos?"

Once they got Grinder off his crutches and his busted leg propped up, he began to stuff his lip with chewing tobacco. Bluefeather felt a twinge of apprehension about how Lorrie might react to seeing Grinder gum tobacco on one side of his toothless mouth while drinking beer with the other. His concern was unfounded. If it bothered her, which he was sure it must, she did not allow it to show.

They had already consumed several beers. Bluefeather and Lorrie danced many dances to the jukebox music and were feeling uninhibited and full of play. When they went back to their table, Lorrie gave him a smile that would have candied acid. Her eyes poured almost visible emotions into his chest, of such warming and primal opiate that he truly thought he would explode. So he decided to express the special joy he was feeling by leaping upon their table, with the agility that a leading ballet dancer would have envied, and performing some of the dances that his guiding spirit had created and initiated. He was certain his rendition would meet with Dancing Bear's approval.

Grinder shouted and pounded his crutches on the floor, trying to help his exuberant protégé any way he could. The bartender watched tolerantly. As long as they were spending money, and there was no great damage or overwhelming disapproval from the other patrons, he would allow the extra exertion of fun. Some of the other customers actually smiled and yelled encouragement. Only a few seemed to resent joy being carried to this extreme.

Lorrie marveled at his dexterity, although it took a few beats to acquire such a sanguine attitude as Grinder had accepted as perfectly natural. The beer glasses shook, but none were touched, and not a drop was spilled. Bluefeather made what appeared to be a misstep and Lorrie was quick to chime in, "No teetering on the table, Blue. 'Tain't allowed."

"Don't worry, precious one. I've already drunk myself completely weightless and I'm almost floating."

Grinder understood this perfectly and said, "Hell, that's nothing, kiddo. I can drink myself invisible. Like right now. I bet nobody in here can see me—maybe the crutches, but not Old Grinder."

Bluefeather sailed gracefully to the floor then sat down and suddenly became profoundly serious, looking all around with great concern. "Where's Grinder? When did he leave? I hope he didn't miss all of my dance."

Lorrie pitched right in, "I don't know. I didn't see him go."

"Well, he'll be back in a minute or he wouldn't have left his crutches dancing all by themselves."

"Of course," Lorrie said, slapping her hands on the tabletop, "I hadn't thought about that." Then she said, "Oh look, Blue. He's come back," and she pointed in exaggeration at Grinder.

They all laughed as freely as three-year-old children, raised their drinks in a wordless toast, and then had a moment of quiet seriousness.

Grinder seized this opportunity to launch into one of his adventures about hunting Maximilian's treasure on the Yaqui Reservation in northwestern Mexico. He was on the part where some of his crew had—against his strict orders—tried to mess around with some Yaqui women. The resultant little war had left seventeen bodies for the buzzards. He was not quite to the juicy part of his story when he was interrupted.

A very large young man loomed over their table, cleared his throat, and with the tiniest crooked grin said, "The old man's messy mouth is making my wife sick," and pointed to the table where a very pretty black-headed woman sat glaring at them with dark eyes of disgust.

Grinder was so busy setting up the geography of his private Yaqui war that he did not even notice the man. He talked on with a little stream of tobacco juice making a muddy creek from the corner of his mouth and on under his chin.

One thing Bluefeather's father had told him was always to try joking his way out of trouble before taking extreme actions. Bluefeather said, "Tell your wife not to worry. He'll swallow the cud any minute now."

The man put two hands, big as a fence-builder's gloves, on the table and hovered over Bluefeather like a lightning-burned thundercloud.

"Get that filthy old man out of here right now or I will do it myself."

"He's got a broken leg and he's a little deaf. It might take till about closing time."

Lorrie was watching the mean interloper and trying to hear Grinder's tale at the same time. The fun was beginning to be drained out of the evening.

"You gettin' smart with me, feller?" the mean one roared.

People at other tables stopped visiting, their mouths open from partially finished sentences, and were quiet. Some froze with drinks tilted to their lips while other drinks remained in midair.

"Please, sir, we don't..." Bluefeather started to say.

The man put his hand on the back of Grinder's neck and started to speak. "Say, you old..."

Bluefeather had slipped his left foot behind one of the man's legs. He smashed his right foot into the knee with all he had. The trip and the kick were supposed to flip the mean man backward so hard his head would bounce off the floor, and his knee should be so damaged that upon regaining consciousness he would be in no condition to leap up and create harm to innocent people.

He did go backward and crash into his own table, knocking his wife upside down so that her full skirt flipped up, giving the bar patrons a brief floor show. He scrambled up growling and sounding beastlike.

Bluefeather was a little late. He threw a punch that had all his 170 pounds behind it, but it didn't land solidly on the moving face. The blow that grazed along the side of the jaw and connected somewhat with the cheekbone did turn the 220 pounds around and halfway over another table, where three occupants fell crawling on hands and knees, swift as lizards, trying to escape the turmoil.

The agitator did a surprising thing for an overgrown adult; with mighty arms spread to grab and crush Bluefeather into syrup, he ducked his head and charged like a Mexican fighting bull. One hand did manage to close on Bluefeather's shirt as the youngster swiftly and wisely leapt out of the way. The man's head hit the adobe wall after passing through the glass covering a watercolor of the Ranchos de Taos Church. As he staggered back with a four-inch, bleeding gash, along with many small slivers of crushed glass in his skull, he dropped the remains of Bluefeather's shirt on the floor. This irritated the young prospector since it was the first time he had worn the garment, having saved it for this special evening with his special friends. It was his turn to roar, although the actual sound was more like a piglet shrieking. There was no denying the sincerity of the highly creative words that went along with it, however.

Bluefeather frothed out, "You dirty no good, second-rate chicken plucker," then he took a heavy swing and connected. "You...overgrown, fuzzy-brained descendant of an inbred tax collector," and he struck again.

Everything had been a blur before. Now it was all a red haze, and the two men rolled over and over knocking things out of the way, smearing blood like paint. Bluefeather was kneeing, hitting, and occasionally biting. Nonetheless, he wound up with his back on the floor, and the man of many names was sitting on his stomach pounding on his neck, shoulders, and chin. His inaccuracies were preventing total destruction, so he decided to choke Bluefeather to death.

The long darkness was descending on the valiant but outmatched young warrior when relief suddenly came. He gasped wonderful smoke-filled air into his desperate lungs as the massive hands slowly released his throat.

Lorrie, seeing her lover beginning to lose the fight and maybe his life, had jumped on the man's back and was reaching over and ripping at his face and then his eyes with her sharp fingernails while screaming sensible things like, "You vile beast. Take your filthy hands off my man."

At the risk of permanent blindness, he released his grip. He fell over on the floor, rubbing blood from the top of his head and other spots into the furrows of fingernail tracks across his eyes, crying, "Oh, my God. I'm blind. Oh, my God, I can't see. Oh, my God."

Bluefeather stumbled up, not caring about his several cuts and purplish lumps, just thankful to have his breathing intact. Now the pretty black-headed, black-orbed, pale-faced wife with the weak stomach who had started the entire thing was bent over her husband, wiping at his face with the remains of Bluefeather's new shirt, saying, "Oh, my poor, poor darling. Oh, my precious, what did...what did these terrible people do to you?"

Grinder precariously crutched his way forward looking at Bluefeather's abrasions as he stood there with no shirt and one blood-smeared arm around a now-shaking Lorrie. Grinder's gaze dropped to the messy people on the floor.

"Well, looks like you folks been having a whole pile of fun," he said, taking out the paper Beechnut container. Leaning expertly on his crutches, despite the many beers he had consumed, he took out a fresh wad of tobacco. He now swallowed the last chew just as Bluefeather had promised he would. Timing is everything. The fight had all been for nothing.

■ ■ ■

Eight

Grinder indirectly complimented Bluefeather the next day. "I admire your courage, son, but question your judgment. That bastard you fought was as big and dangerous as a runaway train." He spat a wad of tobacco juice out of his unmarked face into a coffee can and continued, laughing, "I've found that honor is often extremely expensive... but sometimes dishonor is more so. Huh, kiddo?" He was, of course, proud as a dominant stallion of his young and very active protégé.

Bluefeather had many points on his body that were a mixture of greenish blue to varied hues of purple. There were places and tissues, stiff and throbbing, that he had never felt before. They nursed along a couple of bottles of beer easy and slow, afraid to make any rash or sudden moves that might cause an imbalance of mind, or flesh and bone.

"You gotta admit, Grinder, that Lorrie is one hell of a woman."

"I admit. I admit," Grinder said throwing his hands up. "And by jingos, I'll never know how she talked those cops outa taking the whole bunch of us to jail."

"Kind and smart cops, I'd say, Grinder." Bluefeather laughed softly. "You did get a good look at what she did to that bastard's face, didn't you?"

Grinder was feeling no hangover. He was charged up because he would be able to take the cast off his leg in another week, and he could not control his eagerness to get back on the trail of the lost vein that had birthed the one rich offspring of white quartz and yellow gold.

Grinder was entering the ancient gold-fever zone now. He took out his vial of little yellow nuggets and set it on the kitchen table. He intermittently tapped its bottom on the wood and turned the precious rock to view its multifaceted fractures and light reflections.

Bluefeather opened them each another beer and slowly sipped. He watched Grinder's battered, big-boned hands moving the gold as delicately as a mother touching her new firstborn infant.

Grinder was talking, but the beat-up young man was not his usual, attentive self. Somehow the gold and his thoughts of Lorrie had become mixed together like a pattern of sun shining on wispy clouds—vaporous more than real. He felt a warmness that came from far away. It washed and numbed the pain of his bruised flesh, and he was totally enveloped in a veiled cocoon of fuzzy rainbows. There was no hurt here, no danger, no turmoil; only a soft, even cozy peacefulness, a blessed euphoria. He never wanted to leave it. If he did not move or think, the glorious transparent shroud might stay with him, protecting and consoling him with a delicate nothingness.

Then Grinder's voice penetrated the enveloping shield. "You know what a gold prospector is, son? He's a bullshitter of truth. Never forget this, my boy. Never. Gold is the aphrodisiac of power and greed."

Grinder looked at him sideways across the neck of his beer bottle, which just missed the tobacco in his mouth. His eyes were bright and glowing with laughing sparkles as they studied his young protégé for reactions. He was pleased to see that his words had penetrated for a brief moment, but then the longing look of young love transposed the knowledge he had so freely imparted. Grinder had seen that look many times and had felt it a few himself. He was sure it was the one power capable of overcoming that of gold, but of course only temporarily, at most.

Grinder was not consciously dredging up these words and thoughts. They just came forth from the special caring he had for the young man. If the old man had bothered to analyze his feelings, he would have admitted seeing much of himself in the lad across the table from him who was so engrossed in his feelings for Lorrie.

He pushed a few strands of the lank, gray hair out of his eyes and got up saying, "I feel like cooking. What do you want? Bacon and eggs or eggs and bacon?"

"I'd really like some plain bacon and eggs if you don't mind."

"That's exactly what I was thinking, too."

Nine

Bluefeather had not yet learned how to get out of unwanted social obligations. So he went to the Friedmans' cocktail party.

It started in midafternoon and lasted until after midnight for him and Lorrie's mother. He was amazed at Candi Friedman's casual easiness as she entertained. The only help she had was the eighteen-year-old-daughter of her neighbors, the Archuletas, and a bartender borrowed from La Fonda de Taos.

Guests wandered in and out of the patio and settled in varied-sized clusters. Unlike at most cocktail parties, there were more sitting than standing. People drifted around, ate hors d'oeuvres, refilled their glasses, and then sat down somewhere to have conversations.

The adobe hacienda was regal without arrogance. Magic enfolded. Replete. Paintings by many local artists decorated the walls. They ranged from the realism of E. Irving Couse to the abstracts of Emil Bisttram. Primitive cedarwood carvings of Patricino Barela and colorful pottery from the Zuni and Santo Domingo pueblos were placed in shelves and on tables with deliberate balance in mind. Old wooden church crucifixes and retablos joined company on the walls. Well-worn Navajo rugs softened the floors, while the midafternoon magical sunlight of the high desert cascaded in slanting patterns of tender yet strong designs across the patio and through the large window and open doors.

The serene beauty of this atmosphere, the softening effects of the booze, and the rush of adrenaline began to give Bluefeather a feeling of sublimity and confidence. He had not felt comfortable at first—perhaps even out of place. But why should he feel that? No one could be out of place in Taos unless he or she was far beyond ordinary offensiveness. The gathering here was proof of that. The guests ranged from the world famous, to those wanting to be, to those not caring about either but enjoying the repasts and the greatly varied companionships. There was no escape from the dominant outdoors with its almost arrogant skies, the reserved, sometimes awesome mountains, the sagebrushed desert—more changeable in color and mood than any ocean—that penetrated the thickest adobe walls and permeated the living beings like ectoplasm, or hot syrup on pancakes. There was no escape. Either the ambience was absorbed and enjoyed or a person was shrunk to a body of walking dust.

Whether it was the drinks, Lorrie's beloved presence, or the fact that half his blood had been here around a thousand years, Bluefeather felt robustly at home. All doubts of his personal bearing vanished in the warm haze of the time of Taos. It was his now. Forever his.

The attending age groups ranged from the nineteen-year-old Lorrie all the way up to the next-door neighbor, eighty-five plus Doña Archuleta. Eclectic.

There was the accountant, Rodriguez, and his wife, Mary; a famed writer and painter he had yet to visit; a designer of squaw dresses for a shop on the plaza; a banker; a restaurateur whose establishment specialized in chile rellenos; a remittance man from Saint Louis and a remittance lady from Syracuse; an ex-cowboy now in the automobile business; and others just as varied in their occupations and preoccupations.

Everyone was dressed in elegant, casual comfort with an emphasis on bright colors. The black, formal look was not popular in Taos. Long pleated squaw dresses dominated the scene, with their wearers usually weighted down with turquoise and silver jewelry. Cotton slacks or even faded Levi's were enhanced with the richness of handmade and embroidered Mexican shirts.

The mingling and murmuring grew to a certain pitch and then slowly subsided as some guests left. There were no loud protestations about either leaving or staying. Restful excitement. Some overloaded on hors d'oeuvres while some preferred to drink. Intellectual conversation, if desired; fortuitous meetings, if one wanted. Even solitude amongst the multitudes, if desired. It was a typically successful Taos social. A pleasurable gathering of old and new bloodlines in a mystical unawareness of time.

To young Fellini, however, it was a wondrous occurrence, even though he had resisted yelling like a pack of coyotes several times, and his legs had felt betrayed when he'd done only a couple of little jigs instead of a wild original dance of great invention. Although he was totally unaware of it, he had been watched the entire evening by Candi Friedman. Her daughter had appeared, and reappeared, by his side, touching him on the back, grasping his hand for just a moment, sometimes joining in his conversation with someone else, and yet never in an intrusive way. She just let him know she was with him—there.

Spud Johnson chose a spot at the end of a couch and stayed. People came and went, visiting and serving him the little food and drink he desired. If there was anyone who represented the sociability of a Taos party, it was Spud Johnson. He was special, even in a village that specialized in a concentration of special people. Formerly a writer for the *New Yorker*, he had wound up in Taos by way of visiting his friend, the poet and writer Witter Byner of Santa Fe. The indefatigable Mabel Dodge Luhan had convinced Spud to move to Taos. He did. Forever.

Spud wrote a little journal called *The Horsefly*. It was a newspaper insert of Taos's main weekly paper, *El Crepusculo*, or as the locals called it, *El Creeps*. He was a bitingly humorous writer, and no one who did anything escaped his penetrating attention. This, of course, included his many world-famous friends, such as Frieda and D. H. Lawrence, Georgia O'Keeffe, and many other notable personalities. He could, on rare occasions, be generous in his praise of a book, a poem, a painting, or a worthy incident of any kind. In person, Spud had a kindly acceptance of people's foibles and was good humored as a bonus. Nevertheless, most people were afraid of him because of the little journal he wrote.

Spud had a cadaverous face, even in his youth. This made his brownish black eyes prominent indeed. At first glance Spud's eyes said they had seen too much and done too little about it. They could be interested, amused, and in agreement, with moods changing so fast that the projections could be lost on the viewer. Today he sat in the corner of Candi Friedman's couch and held casual court, sponging in almost everything, as he occasionally sucked on his curve-stemmed, usually unlighted, pipe. Few knew that in addition to his journal and his poetry, he was the editor and typist for all of Mabel Luhan's writings. His indirect contributions to Taos were as great as those of Kit Carson or Padre Martinez.

Candi took Bluefeather by the arm saying, "Darling boy, you must meet our Spud." Bluefeather's olive-brown face was enhanced with burning crimson and she said, "Spud, this is Bluefeather Fellini. I'm sure you've heard of him. He and my daughter, Lorrie, are the barroom brawling champions of Taos, New Mexico."

Spud smiled out at Candi's lilting, easy laughter and said, "That is quite an honor to hold in a place known worldwide for its savage little wars."

Bluefeather was guided to a seat next to Spud and joined in the best his amateur cocktail party talk would grant.

"I hope we're not so overrated that someone else issues an immediate challenge," Bluefeather said.

"Not to worry, my boy. In Taos the gossip is altered daily by swiftly changing sins."

Bluefeather was surprised how comfortable he was with the small legend of Spud Johnson. They visited easily on many subjects. He was pleased even more when Spud discussed the mining history of Twinning Canyon and Frazier Mountain with far more knowledge than he had heard from anyone who had been there before—even Grinder the Gringo.

They were interrupted often by someone paying their respects to Spud's little power structure. He invariably introduced Bluefeather as a friend of the Friedmans' and a mining entrepreneur. Sitting by Spud this length of time, and being a Friedman friend, gave Bluefeather an immediate respect that most people could spend a lifetime desperately seeking but never achieving. Candi Friedman was aware of this even with her back turned all the way across the room. She was very pleased.

Finally, Lorrie came and excused herself to Spud as she led Bluefeather away saying, "Blue, I want you to meet one of my favorite Taos people ever. She never stays very long, so we have to go see her now."

Now, Bluefeather had a remote knowledge of the Honorable Lady Brett's importance in the history of Taos and beyond. She was born of royalty and had chosen art, as well as D. H. Lawrence, as her calling. Her following Lawrence and his continuously growing entourage to Taos had appeared puppylike to many, but she didn't care what people thought about it. Brett's art studies at the exclusive Slade School in England would have little use in the way she wanted to portray Pueblo Indians. No matter. She was beginning to be noted for her combination of primitive and classical interpretations of the Indians.

When Bluefeather was introduced to Lady Brett, he felt awkward, not only because of her world-famous associates, but also because of the curved metal horn she was using as a hearing aid. But when the large woman with frizzy, whitish hair and a long, wonderful nose that came to a little, almost beadlike, point gleamed forth a natural heart-grabbing smile, Bluefeather's uneasiness disappeared.

Lawrence was once asked why he liked Brett and he replied, "Because she lights things up." This she did like halos turned into holograms.

Bluefeather didn't remember their conversation, except that she knew his grandfather, Moon Looker, and had hired him to model for one of her paintings. He was puzzled at how easily Brett and Lorrie were discoursing. He felt that this particular meeting had been a failure, but of course, it hadn't.

He excused himself to go get another drink, leaving his love—his destiny—communicating freely and with exuberance. He took a longer look at two of Brett's paintings on Candi Friedman's wall and felt a trueness to one half of his ancestry in spite of his current, amateur knowledge of painting. He felt something emanate beyond the frame. He would forevermore judge any work of art by this sudden discovery and unsolicited gift from Lady Brett.

Between the two paintings hung a framed short poem. He stepped closer to read it.

Autobiography
One of my dreams is very old
And never has been or will be told
But three of them have long been sold
And ten have caught their death of cold.
—Spud Johnson

He was strangely touched by the little thoughts of the kindly man he'd just visited. He had another drink and became more gregarious.

Candi managed to join Lorrie in her bedroom where she was combing her hair, each stroke reminding her of Bluefeather's loving caresses.

"Darling, I must ask a favor of you. It's for your own welfare, of course."

Lorrie dropped the comb in front of her, holding it in both hands as she turned wordlessly to face her waiting mother. She was long familiar with the sincere but authoritative tone of her mother's voice when her mind was glued to a certain thought.

Candi continued, "As you know, our little gatherings are over when I say they are, and I addressed everyone to the fact it would be from six till eleven. They'll all soon be gone—even the drunks. They know my rules."

Lorrie waited, then said, "Well, Mother, what is it?"

"I want to keep Blue for just a twinkling. One brandy perhaps."

"Please, Mother, don't interfere. He's too intelligent not to know what you're doing. Please don't."

"He is, of course, well-read and smart, but he doesn't have the experience, you see, the background—certain advantages must be pointed out. Now don't you worry a second, darling. Have I ever let us down?"

Lorrie could easily have begun a debate that might possibly have risen in volume and extended time. She gave in, trusting that Bluefeather would reach his own decision with her in mind.

"I suppose you just want me to disappear?" Lorrie asked.

"Just for convenience' sake, dear. We must not clutter his head in advance. Now that's a good—and wise—girl." Candi kissed her daughter on the cheek and reentered the little, temporary Taos world she had created. Lorrie followed a discreet forty seconds later.

Spud motioned for Brett to bend closer to him, and cupping his hand around her best ear he said, "Candi is going to acquire young Fellini for Lorrie—and her advertising firm."

Brett whispered back, "'Tis a pity to remove such a handsome and charming young man from this valley—from his roots actually."

"Not to worry, Brett. He will return. You and I always have, you know."

"But, we, dear Spud, were not born here. We came here at Mabel's bidding."

"Nevertheless, our roots sank here in spite of all our travels."

They chatted on in private about memories and experiences that only those who are wealthy and famous, or those who associate with them, can conceive.

Bluefeather emptied his drink and gathered Lorrie into his arms and danced her around and around the kitchen. Her warm blood flushing her skin and the smell of her, the glorious smell of love and excitement and the physical totality of holding her against him moving, moving as the whiskey did in his brain, disturbed a center of his being he could no longer control. He tilted his head back and yelled all the way through all the walls and ceilings of the adobe house. It was coyote. It was lion. It was eagle and owl. It was Bluefeather. It was of such loud and exuberant suddenness that an almost unseen shock washed over and through everyone present, but they controlled it and acted as if it had never happened. One could not show resentment toward someone who had been anointed by Spud, Brett, and the hostess, Candi Friedman.

Bluefeather danced on wildly with Lorrie, who laughed as she said, "Blue, you crazy idiot. I love you."

A couple more twirls and Bluefeather suddenly stopped, saying, "What in hell has happened? I've drunk myself sober."

Then Lorrie quietly poured him another. The crowd started leaving, offering both real and obligated compliments. Then, without anyone actually realizing it, Candi and Bluefeather were alone. Just as Candi had planned.

Lorrie, now sitting rigidly in her nightgown facing her bedroom mirror but not noticing her reflected image, combed furiously at her hair.

The sun had long ago gone to light other worlds; the moon came up, replacing the yellow glow with soft blue across the green sagebrush and painting the sides of the adobe houses in the same settled softness. The valley had a scattering of tiny artificial suns peeking from the windows of the homes in the village. Somewhere in the valley a dog barked, and the distant hum of a pickup motor diminished, and it was quiet in the night.

Bluefeather hadn't remembered much of his limited conversation with Lady Brett, and he couldn't figure put how he had ended up here sitting across the kitchen table from Candi Friedman. But here they were.

Lorrie's mother had just served them an exquisite, supposedly "good-night" brandy. She smoked as elegantly as ever from a long, slender, inlaid-turquoise holder. He would never forget the beauteous force of her strong, green eyes looking through him as easily as through steam from a teakettle. He might someday forget their color, but he would always remember their intelligent strength.

"You get along well in mixed crowds, young man. I'm sure Lorrie is proud of you. Of course, she's prejudiced, being so damnably in love with you."

"Where is she, anyway? She's been gone quite a while. Has she gone to bed?"

"Oh, to tell the truth, Blue, it was at my insistence. We must talk, you know? You and I."

They looked at one another, the olive and the cream. The powerful, green eyes of experience stared into his misty, ebony ones that were almost as large. Although younger, they drew on other abilities, such as instinct and long-past experiences buried deep within his genes.

Bluefeather became extremely calm now and sipped his brandy slowly as it was made to be enjoyed.

"She's a child-woman of great potential as both a wife and a photographer...or whatever else she might take a fancy at becoming. I don't want her hurt any more than necessary in this world of uncalled-for pain. Do you understand?"

"I think so. I'm pretty sure I do."

"Well, let me put it to you, dear Blue, as clearly as words can express. She loves you passionately and with reasonably good sense. You have the looks and a proven social ability to fit in beautifully as a top model for my company. The benefits for you would be numerous. To name a few—the pay...the position...yes, even the surface glamour...plus, my lovely daughter."

Bluefeather tried to say something, but she continued on with such determination that he politely held back.

"You two could have a wonderful life...free from financial wants...a creative life, if you please, and you'd have sufficient time to figure out what other pursuits might call you...all the while living in and with beauty and abundance." Then she struck with her well-planned clincher. "Manhattan is full of gold that's already been mined."

It was then that Bluefeather realized he could never explain to her that piles of yellow bars in a bank vault were not his goal. Never in a million aeons could he get through to her that it was people like Grinder who made it possible for bank vaults to fill up at all, or that what Bluefeather and Grinder shared in the mountains could never be calculated by a genius a thousand times more intelligent than Einstein. It was so precious and private that words, maybe even thoughts, were inadequate. Feeling, absorbing it silently was the best anyone could do.

So, silence now.

She poured them each another but smaller brandy, looked him directly into the eyes, and said, "Well?"

Bluefeather could not comprehend how the next words could come out of his mouth, but they did.

"I never would have believed in ten zillion years that a little half-breed like me would be made so grand a gesture." In his imagination, he genuflected an apology to Grinder for his last statement and smiled so enchantingly at Candi Friedman that it turned her experienced soul—calloused and formidably shielded to the core—to warm-stirred Jell-O. She smiled formidably back, taking his words as total acceptance of her just-verbalized wishes. Those two mighty smiles met and resounded silently in beauty, and in both, but in different ways, love for Lorrie. It was not yet known which one had diffused first.

Grinder and Maude Cisneros had partied all night, celebrating the removal of his leg cast. Bluefeather joined them for a while. He just wasn't up to their enthusiasm, so he soon excused himself and went to bed. Candi Friedman and her daughter had him feeling indecisive. This was against his nature. He was a young man who, after asking himself two or three questions, made his choice and acted on it.

Maude, after entertaining her boyfriend until three in the morning, had gone home to take care of her chores. Grinder was sleeping in. It would be his last party before returning to the mountains and resuming his search.

The next morning, Bluefeather walked out into the pasture to think things over and visit Tony. The subirrigated grass was as thick as beaver fur and about a foot tall. It was a grand day with the air so clear it seemed to squeak. The mountains stood out against the northern and eastern skies so clearly that they appeared to be only a mile away. He did not notice these goodly enchantments as he rubbed Tony's neck. Candi Friedman had offered him a piece of the world that nearly all people would lie, rob, and cheat their brothers to attain. Some would certainly commit murder for the position he had been offered last night, all because his unique bloodline had so profoundly affected his physical appearance.

Then there was the main reason for all this—Lorrie. She, too, could not help the physical and material benefits bequeathed to her by her father and mother's joining of flesh. The fact that she was pursuing one of her many gifts through photography and had overcome all her birth advantages to be a loving, caring, and celebration-of-life lady made her very special indeed.

He cared for her so much his very eyeballs ached. His chest was about to explode, and his toes were frozen almost for certain. So what the hell was the quandary about? He could almost grasp the reason, but then it melted and dissolved into an unreachable mist. "God uh mighty," he thought, "is love always such terrible, sweet agony?" How could he know that this was one of the prices of youth? The main one, in fact.

The burro dropped his head back down to the luxury of the earth and casually grazed at the bounty of the grass. Then Bluefeather was startled to see Dancing Bear sitting a few yards in front of him chewing on a grass stem. Dancing Bear stood up smiling. His hair was braided in the double Taos style. That first night on the mountain his hair had hung loose under his headband.

"What kind of spirit are you anyway?"

"Same as always, dear brudder. The helping kind. I fit the needs of my clients the best I know how. 'Course, I'm limited by the knowledge of the subject."

"What kind of talk is this anyway? You sound like a combination preacher, lawyer, and cop."

"Now you catching on. Dear brudder, I see you are in turmoil. Allow me to dance for you. Your choice. Greek? Yugoslavian? Scottish? Irish? Swiss? Maybe German or French?"

"Stop. Stop all that." Then, seeing the rejected look on Dancing Bear's face, he changed his mind. "Greek...Greek will be okay."

Dancing Bear certainly danced. His beaded Cheyenne moccasins whirled in the grass. His hands were above his head, fingers snapping as loudly as castanets, then he slowed down and sang something that sounded Greek, yet moved on and on, with the fringes of his buckskin suit slapping in time with his stylized movements.

Bluefeather glanced around quickly, embarrassed that someone might be witnessing such a crazy Indian of undetermined origin doing Greek dances in an open pasture with a young man and a burro as his audience. When he saw that Tony grazed unconcerned and unaware of the activity, he was enormously relieved.

Bluefeather clapped politely, hoping no one would notice, and whispered as loud as he could, "Thank you. Thank you. That is enough for now...I feel better already."

Dancing Bear smilingly stopped, obviously pleased, his dark brown face happy with achievement and his body poised for more consoling. "Maybe Russian dance?"

"No. Later, please. Thank you."

"Ah well, I suppose we have to talk now."

"If you wouldn't mind."

"Why, dear brudder, that is a good portion of the business I'm in...this talking stuff."

"Well, these people, these women, I don't know how to say it, they're just fine people, both of them, and they want me to go to New York and become rich and famous and all those kinds of things. They're pretty and nice and..."

"You say that already before."

"I'm sorry, but you see...it's the mountains. I think Lorrie might stay here with me in the desert and the mountains, but I'd be gone most of the time on my business. It wouldn't be fair. My business seems so unpredictable; of course, if Grinder and I find the mother lode...well that would be..."

"Whoa. Whoa," said Dancing Bear. "Whoa, too much talk at one time shrinks the space for thoughts. Now, let's see here once more. Maybe you go to mountains and somebody done robbed 'em. Huh? Huh?"

"Goddamnit, talk so I can understand. I thought a guiding spirit was supposed to give guidance."

"That is too true. Guidance. Not doing. Guiding spirits ain't mamas. Men cain't nurse babies. Great Spirit put teats on 'em by mistake. What you think anyway? Experience is still a stranger to you. You haven't even had the clap or ever been in jail yet or fought in a big war and here you are thinkin' I'm gonna do everything for you. You gotta pay for the trip, dear brudder, whether you enjoy it or not."

"Jesus, you're gettin' worse. I wish Great Spirit would send me another, smarter guide. You talk like you been eating peyote buttons and locoweed soup for a hundred years." He fervently wished that Dancing Bear didn't cause him to say such rude things. He vowed to control himself better.

"Not near that long, dear brudder, and now we say to you the truth. A feller told me once—when I'm still on your side of the river—'Hey, Dancing Bear,' he says, 'step lightly on the strongest mountains and harshest deserts, for they have delicate skins.'"

Now Bluefeather ran this last statement through his addled head several times. It made sense for everybody else, but what in holy hell could it possibly mean to him right now?

"I tell you true, dear brudder, you shouldn't do it, but the mountains will stay 'round a while even if you treat 'em badly. Say, before I go, you want a nice Norwegian dance?" And he whirled and dipped and dallied right out over some cottonwood trees along an irrigation ditch and went somewhere else.

Bluefeather, being as yet unadjusted to the company of spirits, was startled, then angry. "Hey, please come back. Dear guiding spirit, come back here and tell me things I can understand. Hey, please, I say. You didn't tell me a single thing worth hearing. I'm gonna report you... you hear?" He didn't, however, have the slightest notion of where to turn in his complaint.

Bluefeather suddenly turned and strode with purpose back to the house. Grinder had arisen and was haltingly cleaning up beer bottles, ashtrays, and stale dishes. Neither one uttered more than two or three grunts.

"I have to go make a phone call. Do you want me to get gasoline while I'm at the filling station?"

"Yeah, fill 'er up."

Bluefeather went to the telephone, which felt like acid-coated steel produced by the devil, and managed to call his love. "Lorrie, I love you. I've got to go to the mountains and help Grinder set up camp. I don't want to go, but..."

"You have to go now? Right now?" she asked.

"Yes. I've got to, honey. His leg is still stiff and sore. Believe me, darling, I don't wanna go. God, I want to be with you, but I'll be back at noon in three days."

"Well, I love you, too. And Blue,... I'm really glad you're coming back on Saturday because we're leaving Monday for New York. We're already doing some packing."

This last comment brought misty, sticky, pointed pains back to certain parts of his body.

They said, "Good-bye," "I love you," and "I'll miss you," three more times. It was with bone-aching difficulty that Bluefeather hung up the instrument of bad news into silence. He stared, tempted to pick up the appurtenance from its hanger and call again. He shoved his hands in his pockets and turned away.

■ ■ ■

Ten

The two prospectors were anxious to set up camp and get about the business of finding the vast wealth assigned to them by the Great Spirit. They were convinced it was ordained. They had to leave the pickup with Grinder's friend Pacheco in Arroyo Hondo, and pack in using their strong backs and Tony's much superior one. They were close to the last place near Twinning Canyon that might gift them with rocks that matched the single precious one that drove them on and on.

They pitched tent near an old tunnel about a mile and a half northeast of the village. The tunnel had collapsed about forty feet in, but with a half-day's digging they managed to scramble over the top of the fill and get to the ore face. They were disappointed that it had little quartz—and no gold.

Somebody had found enough values to drive a 180-foot tunnel here, so Bluefeather agreed that they must work the area carefully before moving on.

On the second day, Grinder found a piece of quartz float rock that slightly resembled the precious one. Its edges were worn smooth and its luster was dulled, indicating its movement atop the earth for aeons. Grinder excitedly broke it open with a prospector's pick, and the fresh edges did resemble the gold-laden one. However, there was no gold visible to the naked eye, and the glass revealed only quartz; but not all rock, even in the richest of veins, carried visible gold. Their excitement rose.

The next day they carefully worked up the rough little canyon toward an outcropped bluff where there was scant overburden.

That night after supper Grinder pulled out a piece of parchment with a crudely drawn map on it.

"I been meaning to show you this for a couple of weeks. Ol' Paul Burch came by the house the other day, and knowing what prospectors he and his brother, Elmer, are, I showed him our sample rock. He liked to of fell over. He told me he'd seen the same kind of gold-bearing rocks several years ago. Sheepherder had sold them to him. Paul's crippled from that car running over him, you know? So he drew me this map describing where the sheepherder said he'd found them."

The map showed a line that traveled off Twinning Road across Twinning Creek on a logging bridge, up the South Fork Creek to a small lake where several springs converged to form the headwaters of the stream, and up a steep game trail to the west, perhaps half a mile. Thirty or forty feet along the trail, where it curved back south, the sheepherder had slipped and fallen down a steep eastern slope and had accidentally found the small pieces of gold-filled quartz.

"Now, Blue, this copy is for you in case anything should happen to me." Bluefeather tried to protest, but Grinder would have none of it. "We gotta play as close to a cinch as we can, you know? I done bumped the point of discovery out of my brain before I met you, and I've broken my leg since. We gotta split up this information. Hellfire, I might break my goddamned ol' stiff neck next time."

"It might be me who falls. Who knows?" said Bluefeather, staring into the red, orange, and yellow patterns of the piñon campfire.

"Naw, hard-peckered boys like you don't get hurt so's it lasts. Especially you, Blue. You got too much livin' of life to get in yet. I can tell these things. You're gonna do wonderful things 'fore you're through, son."

They sat on their bedrolls, sipping coffee, staring off into the purple night. The fire crackled loudly and a night bird chirped as if to say "the prize is here"—the same as the mountains way down below seemed to whisper it.

They could see the dim lights of two small houses on the rim of Arroyo Hondo Canyon, struggling to be seen in the seemingly limitless space of night around them. Bluefeather stared at the lights trying to imagine the occupants inside one of the houses. The mother would be putting three kids to bed while the father smoked his pipe at the kitchen table listening to a song on an old battery radio. The woman was still young, and she bathed in an iron tub by the cookstove. She dried her smooth, olive body, rubbing it even after the wetness was gone. Now she became Lorrie in Bluefeather's scenario, and he was the man who turned off the radio and led her to the fresh covers turned back on the ancient, carved bed. Lorrie stretched out under the low, flickering light of a kerosene lamp. Fresh as clothesline-dried sheets, fresh as springwater, fresh as virgin life. He was nude himself now and was lying beside her. After caressing her breasts, he was moving his hands up her smooth spreading thighs when three things happened: Grinder reached for his coffee can, missed, and spat a saved-up mouthful of tobacco juice into the fire that caused a minor explosion of sparks and spittle; a single coyote howled as loudly as a dozen in the canyon just below them; and the staked burro decided to bray into the moonless night.

When these sounds broke the nocturnal silence, Bluefeather's inner being was turned all around and moved on past the great Taos Mountain south to the village and on to the Friedman hacienda. It would not stop. He didn't sleep that night until almost daybreak.

Lorrie had been all over and through Bluefeather no matter how he twisted in his bedroll, and her mother's great green eyes were turned on them like circus lights, following their every move and thought, pulling them both along with her, all the way to New York. They screamed, kicked, and cried, but she dragged them on without ever touching either one.

Grinder also had a restless night. He dreamed of Bluefeather leaving by train, on foot, or mule and even flying off without wings.

When daylight awakened Bluefeather, Grinder had the fire going, his face washed, and his hair combed. He threw some sourdough into one Dutch oven and some bacon and the last of their fresh eggs into another.

Grinder's fine, later-than-usual breakfast helped Bluefeather only a few moments. The hot coffee was swallowed but not tasted. Yesterday by this time, Grinder would have had at least two hours of earnest labor done, but today he busied himself feeding oats to Tony, studying maps and geological reports, and cleaning up around the campsite.

Bluefeather just sat on his open bedroll and stared into clumps of trees, searching their shadows for an answer. None came. None.

"You know, Blue, I hate to admit it, but I just can't call up the location of that damned vein no matter what I do. I've tried conjuring it drinking whiskey, beer, wine, and water. I've tested out starvin' myself into a trance and eatin' until I could barely breathe. I've rolled over a thousand times a night and spent another thousand hours staring at the universe. I've prayed to God and cursed Him. I've tried to sell my soul to the devil and even threatened to castrate the horned bastard if I didn't get a fix on the gold's location. So far nothing has worked, and if I had any teeth I'd uh ground 'em to chalk by now."

"We'll find it, Grinder, don't worry anymore. We're getting close. I can feel it."

Grinder was both amazed and pleased to see and hear Bluefeather escape his reverie, even for a moment. Grinder had stayed in camp that morning to make his last speech, knowing that something about Bluefeather's new love was tearing at his guts like a ravenous hyena.

"Well, I'm sure glad you got that feeling, Blue. Makes me feel better already. Say, it's none of my business, but when is that Lorrie and her mama going back to New York?"

"Monday."

"Monday?"

"Yeah... I gotta bring it up one time or another, Grinder. I promised I'd meet her tomorrow at noon. Is it all right if I leave early tomorrow? I'll be back Sunday to see you, even if I'm..."

Grinder's tough, old guts twisted up like a den full of freezing rattlesnakes, but he said casually, "Sure, son. No problem at all. I think we'll just hang around camp today so we'll both be in good shape to tend our chores tomorrow. I can't wait to get that country prospected up to that bluff. I'll bet that's what you're feeling... the vein is right there in that bluff. I'm close to smelling gold, son. Real close."

"There's something else I gotta... well... no use waiting on this either. Grinder, I... that is, they've offered me all kinds of rich folk's stuff to go back to New York with 'em."

"Well, son, you're free to go, far as I'm concerned, if you think it's best for you... for your whole life. Even though I'd sure hate to lose you, you got Ol' Grinder's blessings." He remained dry eyed, but the tears inside almost caused them to explode.

Bluefeather went on. "I sure appreciate that, but I just can't make up my mind. I can't sleep or nothing. I think I'm going to go flat-ass crazy if I don't decide soon. I never could take much indecision, anyway. I love that damned woman as much as I can, but I love that mountain there, too." And he pointed at the north slope of the magic Taos Mountain where the sun was waking it up with caresses of warming orange light.

"Hey, son, we all seek the truth that pleases us."

Bluefeather really thought this one over before he spoke. "You're just as correct as you can be, but I've been trying to figure what's really right for me instead of what pleases me."

"Yeah, sometimes it's sure enough damn near impossible to figure out what we're supposed to do—which could be what we really want to do...if everything is in balance and our luck's runnin'."

There was silence for a couple of minutes as they both watched the sun changing and enlarging the light and shadows on the sacred mountain.

The old man hid, with practiced care, his fear of having lost Bluefeather. He had just now reached a point of total trust after having risked both their lives in old tunnels of rotten rock. They had laughed and played together, cementing the other side of a total friendship— one for which a man should be willing to die. He hid the ache that numbed his heart at the vast loss of a companion—the one he had chosen to share his upcoming fortune. A true partner was rarer than all the gold he had pursued his entire lifetime.

Bluefeather was suffering the same emotional struggle. His young mind jumped back and forth from Grinder to Lorrie until the confusion caused him to eradicate, on the surface at least, the deep hurt he was going to feel either way he decided. He thought of trout fishing, timber, bears, and his grandmother's horno-baked bread.

Then Grinder sort of mumbled to himself, "A feller's got to make up his mind about problems and then kick one and piss on the other with all he's got. Right or wrong, kiddo?" He spoke louder now and with much certainty, still staring at the mountain. "It's true that the sun comes up every single day, but it comes up one time less for me and thee each morning." He hesitated a moment and broke wind so loudly that the burro raised his head and turned to check out the disturbance. Bluefeather was so shocked that he fell back on his unmade bedroll and laughed his indecision right out into the mountain air.

Grinder jerked the floppy, greasy, old hat from his head and fanned his fanny, laughing so hard he could hardly boast out, "Knocked a hole plumb to bedrock with that'n. Right, kiddo?"

Tony went back to grazing.

Eleven

He met her on the plaza in front of Skeezix Rodriguez's drugstore. He disliked unnecessary driving, but today he asked Lorrie if he could take over the wheel of her car. She seemed pleased at this sudden change in him. He drove south to Ranchos de Taos and turned left on Talpa Road. They passed the house of modern artist Andrew Dasburg. Both commented on the young cottonwood tree next to Dasburg's adobe studio that seemed to have grown with perfectly balanced limbs and leaves just to please the artistic sensitivity of its owner.

Bluefeather drove on in silence with no conscious plan. Finally he turned southeast up the winding gravel road into the heavily timbered forestland toward Little Pot Creek.

Lorrie slumped down in the car seat watching the twisting stream as it caught light and shadows, sparkling, yet dull, like an old Navajo silver necklace. But her mind wasn't there with her eyes; it didn't even seem to be in the car. She was not with the wilderness either. She was in some blank, unseen, unfelt place she had never been before. Today a decision would be made and her natural courage was failing her. It would be up to Bluefeather to bring up that which she had anticipated, longed for, and yet feared the entire summer. Words. Yes, words must be spoken from his tongue now. The time of young passion and heartwarming love must be put aside for a brief spell.

Although Bluefeather, too, was distracted and introspect, he tightly gripped the steering wheel and kept the roadster on the proper side of the road. He was only slightly aware of the wooded scenery, like a man knows a chimney is on the roof of an old house. Well, he could drive on and on for over a thousand miles to Brownsville on the southern tip of Texas on the Mexican border and it wasn't going to change a thing. He had to face it.

He glanced at Lorrie—his Lorrie—where she had scooted down even farther, so her eyes were now barely level with the dashboard. Lord, oh Lord, how tender and helpless she looked. Of course, she had proven in many varied ways, including her saving him a terrible beating in a barroom brawl, that she could be as tough as large razors when the chips dropped from the ax blade. But at this moment, he wanted to hold her against his chest and tell her everything was all right—now, later, and maybe forever.

He choked a little, swallowing frequently, pushing back the moisture that was trying to ooze beneath his eyelids. They arrived at the top of a pass overlooking the vast new world to the east. He stepped on the brakes awkwardly. The stop jolted Lorrie up and returned her to the now of things. Yes, now. Here.

"Lorrie..." He could not go on for a moment. Then he put his hand out and touched her on the shoulder. He started again, "Lorrie, you want me to go to New York, don't you? You want us to marry, don't you? Well?"

She looked at him with the eyes of a doe who had just given successful birth to her first fawn and caught the scent of a lion on the cooling breeze. "Yes. More than anything."

Bluefeather was tempted to question the "anything" bit. Anything, after all, could mean her staying here in the great Southwest, waiting month after lonely month, year following longer and longer year, while he pursued his own peculiar and particular madness with the earth-blessed rocks. It wasn't right to terrorize her into agreeing to suffer this fate just out of his desperate need for them to be joined. It would not be fair to either of them. There was no sense now in being altruistic. Charging straight on with the lance, hoping it would glance off some piece of invisible armor was the only way. Rough.

"Oh, Jesus, how it hurts to say it, Lorrie, but I can't do it right now. I can't go to New York with you. Not now."

"Don't you love me?"

"Yes, oh God, of course I do. But I've got this sudden feeling—I don't know where it came from—that the love we speak of is not enough."

"It would be for me. I'll do anything you want. Anything."

"I know that's what you think. I know you even mean what you're saying, but I know better, because I keep getting the same feeling. Then..."

"What are you telling me? That I wouldn't be able to give up New York and all the things my mother has in mind for us? Blue? Please tell me the truth. What are you feeling? I can't take it any longer. Just say it and get it over with."

"Well, I don't know exactly how to say it. I don't know if you'll understand. I don't want to hurt you. That's the last thing I would ever want to do, Lorrie."

Lorrie already knew he was saying "no" to her. Every word pained her more. Still she was hoping, grasping for the component that would make them cohesive. "Is it the modeling for mother's firm that bothers you?"

"No. It's not the modeling. Hell, some of my Pueblo kin have been modeling for Taos artists for years. No, it isn't that. Maybe it's because I had already made a decision, before I met you, about what I have to do next in my life. And I have to stay right here in Taos to get it done. That's the way I am once I've made up my mind. I hope you can understand. My parents sure didn't. But I am doing it anyway. It's just that everyone has to have his own work....It finally becomes more than...ah, hell, it's just the way I am."

Bluefeather was not thinking of these words in advance, and he didn't speak them as knowledge either, but they came on out anyway.

"Damnit, darling, I can't marry you and your wondrous mother. It would be bigamy. I'm already committed to Grinder and that mountain," he said as he waved back over his head in the general direction of the mighty, rocky bulk that dominated Taos Pueblo, the Spanish village, and the rest of the canyons and deserts for hundreds of square miles.

"Well, I guess it just comes down to the fact that you can't go there and I can't stay here," Lorrie said as she blotted her tears. He realized how she hurt, from the way her body jerked as she sobbed as quietly as her emotions would allow.

He was numb. His emotions were dry. He knew this had to be finished as quickly as possible.

There were few other words between them as he drove back down toward Taos. As he circled the plaza he felt none of Taos's sometimes glorious, sometimes infamous, history. The only history that mattered to him at this moment was the one that was ending with Lorrie.

He drove her to the front of the Friedmans' hacienda, got out, and walked around to open the door for her. He was hurting to touch her one last time, to feel her heart pounding against his chest and push his face into her soft, blond hair so he could smell it and her essence just once more, but he didn't. It was done.

Candi stood on the porch wearing a turquoise dress that emphasized her colorations and exquisite, rich form. The welcoming smile dissipated as her daughter numbly opened the front-yard gate and walked quickly toward her. She took Lorrie in her arms, pushing her face between her breasts, and stared after the strong, young figure walking away toward the edge of the mesa down the road to town. She stood and wordlessly held her daughter. Her chest was pierced with a sudden, but ancient, pain of knowing.

The figure of Bluefeather could only be seen from the waist up now, then the head, and then nothing. Gone.

Bluefeather drove north out of Taos toward the village of Arroyo Hondo. Breaking up was something like boiling one's soul in carbolic acid. There was this feeling of far, faraway loss combined with a short breath of relief. Yesterday his vision seemed hypnotized by the road, and he couldn't even look at the land. Today the blindness had cracked open to let in light, color, and form.

He glanced off to the right at Taos Mountain. The evergreen and sagebrush foothills sloped down like great stone roots. There was his part-time home, Taos Pueblo, at the bottom of the looming prominence. What an irony that its five-story main structure was the tallest building in northern New Mexico. Even so, it was barely visible, like a few grains of sand on the arm of a giant.

He pulled off the road and stared at the huge sacrosanct upthrust. Then he spoke aloud, alone, as if imagining a conversation with a close friend, "I salute you, oh precious, perverted, eminence, sister of powerful spirits and first daughter of the gods." As he crisply saluted, the shape of his face was slightly altered by a small smile.

He drove down into the tiny village of Arroyo Hondo, gateway to Twinning Canyon. The land hovered on both sides of the life-giving creek that traversed all the way from the top of Bull of the Woods Mountain and other nearby peaks. The controlled turmoil of a lost love was barely subdued within him. His youthful exuberance to get to the mountains and start the adventurous work of seeking lost gold with his partner was almost more than he could handle. No matter what his aches and desires might be, he had to visit with Grinder's old friends, the Pachecos.

He drank coffee. He talked politics—although he knew little of this pastime. That was the way of the blood of Spain mixed with that of the mighty Mayan civilization. He bounced little Juanita and Adelina on his knees. He honorably thanked the quiet and solid wife of Gilberto Pacheco for the libation, and he told Gilberto how much he and Grinder appreciated being allowed to leave their conveyances on the Pachecos' property.

Everyone had been properly honored and pleased. He left, walking with much strength and agility up the swiftly steepening slopes to their prospecting camp.

It was midday when Bluefeather arrived breathing deeply, sweating some, but with plenty of strength to spare. He spoke to the burro and told him he was going to seek his master.

In the soft bottom of a little draw perhaps fifty yards from the bluffs, he found his partner's tracks. They moved erratically back and forth searching thoroughly for evidence on the surface of the earth. After a while Bluefeather decided that the tracks were certain to lead to the bluff, so he just walked as straight as the treacherous terrain would allow to their private landmark.

He was excited now, for he would soon rejoin his partner in the hunt. Maybe he could share in the excitement of discovery. All other concerns vanished. There was a freedom of choice tingling through his surging blood. He was home. Home to the mountain. Joyous. Thrilled. Pure.

He stopped as he saw Grinder's tracks approach the bluff and looked up in search of his form high in the deceivingly rough and creviced rock face. He strained, but could not see, or hear, anything of his friend. His eyes moved on down.

Then he saw the upraised hand sticking out through a tall clump of bunchgrass. The handle of a prospector's pick lay across the open palm. Grinder had slipped somewhere up there, concentrating so hard on the hunt that he had missed a step. He had crashed swiftly to the ground to have the life broken and jarred out of his body by one of the mountains he had loved so very much—that had given him his reason for breathing.

Bluefeather hauled the old prospector's body down the mountain on Tony's back. He would retrieve their camp gear later.

He and Maude Cisneros buried Grinder at her family plot at El Prado on the northwest edge of Taos. Only Maude and her children; one bartender; the two prospecting Burch brothers; Patricino Barela,

Grinder's friend from Canon; and Bluefeather's uncle Stump Jumper and his cousin Smiling Dog were at the graveside. About a dozen in all.

Bluefeather spoke the eulogy: "Grinder the Gringo's earthly run is over, and I will always feel humble that he shared part of his life with me. He was full of wisdom and fun. He was loyal to his few friends and ignored his enemies. He was not an observer of life. Grinder was a partic-ipator in love and sorrow and the wondrous mixed adventures it gave him. He was a true walker of deserts and climber of mountains. We miss you already, ol' pardner. Good traveling to you, amigo. Amen." Bluefeather made the sign of the cross and briefly raised his arms in a burial chant.

He poured a knapsack of their mineralized rocks into the grave and turned and walked away with the others, leaving Maude alone with her last love. She stood there motionless in her black dress, veil, and shawl seeming to grow smaller and smaller as if part of her was already join-ing Grinder. Bluefeather was stunned by the loss of his two main loves within twenty-four hours. It would take a special gathering of will to lose no time grieving for those already gone. He didn't.

Bluefeather was surprised that Grinder had left a recent will. Maude got his house and land. Bluefeather got all his mining equip-ment, his old truck, Tony, his vial of gold, and his prized rock speci-mens, among which were five more large vials of nuggets.

Bluefeather smiled and mumbled, "The wonderful old digger had put away enough gold to provide for himself, Maude, and over a year's worth of prospecting. He had just practiced his survival con on me and then decided he enjoyed the company." Bluefeather laughed aloud with abandonment. He felt good, just as he knew his friend had arranged. Then Bluefeather remembered that just two days earlier Grinder had said he might break his neck. Revelation.

Bluefeather took care of all the legal details with a wise, old Spanish lawyer. He delivered the necessary papers to Maude and enfolded her in a crushing, silent hug. He gave Tony to his grandfather at the pueblo, then came back and began loading his things into the old Ford truck.

He wrapped the rock that had driven Grinder to make his last climb and the Burch brothers' treasure map in waxed paper and put them both in the cigar box in the bottom of a footlocker with the rest of his special rock specimens. He planned to sell the vials of raw gold to Candelario's Curio Shop in Santa Fe for a nice wad of cash. He drove around Taos Plaza and turned right toward other worlds yet to come.

Before the highway dropped down into a horseshoe curve, where the Taos country would vanish from sight behind him, he pulled over to the side of the road, got out, and swept his eyes back across the world's greatest panorama of big sky, big earth. He could see all the way west to Tres Ritos where the sagebrush fused into infinity. He moved his eyes back across the vast sagebrush desert to the curved malpais gash of the Rio Grande Gorge creating a volcanic scar seven hundred feet deep. Then his gaze moved on to the blur of the scattered mud rectangles of Taos and on up across the Sangre de Cristo Mountain Range.

It was already late enough in the day that the color of the blood of Christ was tinting the mountains' open spots. At last his eyesight was pulled to the limitless sky above it all. For the first time in his life he could not find a single cloud there. His orbs raced back and forth across the immense sky, but there were no clouds. None. There was something else. Something that he had never seen before in the limitless forming and reforming of the sky above the divine mountains.

He strained to discern its form, its dimension, by squinting his eyes and alternately opening them wide, like someone looking at the color and form of a painting. Something alive, pulsating, was there! It hovered above the vast upper spaces centered over Taos Mountain. It floated and poised like a giant transparent stingray of the sky. One instant it was billions, trillions, of gold specks, then it turned red and violet. During the tiny time of a single, swift glance, it became colorless to the point of near invisibility. It was there! Then streamers dropped down from the massive form like slowly writhing, silent tornadoes. Some of the tendrils from the sky were as light and delicate as a sleeping fawn's breath, and a few darkened and appeared to be shadows in the sky. Threatening and tender, raw and refined, all at the same instant. He knew that the thin, diaphanous feelers touched the earth of the Taos land and all its creatures in an energy that was filled with creation. The dominant thing was the ephemeral penetration of the light that shimmered as nowhere else in any other sky.

Then suddenly it was removed from his perception. He stared, straining. He could not make it return. Beyond being embraced in awe, he was humbled at the great privilege of the vision just gifted to him. He felt guilty he'd been given this omnipotent honor. Why him? Then it came to him, straight out of his heart, that the floating "Taos energy evolution" surely had been seen by others, but they, like he, would never be able to describe it. And if so, how, or why? For beneath the fabled mountain, massive plates of rocks rubbed against one another embracing, making a humming music that a few could hear. Bluefeather was one who could.

He drove on around the horseshoe and then soon alongside the rock-churned Rio Grande south to Albuquerque to reorganize his life. The Taos days of both earthly and inexplicable "other" experiences were behind him but would always be a splendiferous virus in his blood. Young Bluefeather Fellini would soon be ready to run, ears back and head down, toward many other wondrous and magic worlds.

Twelve

Bluefeather had wandered for a spell from the Big Bend country of Texas to the Superstition Mountains of Arizona, half-heartedly prospecting, wholeheartedly drinking, dancing, and accepting the attention of several women. The last was against his true nature. He was, in fact, a one-woman man.

Then, in Nevada he met Nancy, a fancy dancing girl who turned out to be much more. It seemed to him that every young man, at one time or another, had wanted a saloon dancing girl. This one, though, wanted him.

Nancy said to him, "Now, look, Blue, I've been everywhere and done everything. I know all men intimately. But I don't know you. You ask nothing of me but my love. Well, here it is, Blue. Take it, but don't throw it away. Come with me. I'll show you the tricks of the cards and we can tour the world. Just you and me. You'll never have to worry about a grubstake again. It will be better than it would be if you made a big strike. You will have all you ever need and more."

She made it sound so good, so easy, so sure. He enjoyed her talk and her love, and decided to give their relationship a mountain of a try. Unlike Lorrie Friedman of New York, Nancy was from this harsh land and worked it with skill and tenderness. He was influenced by this.

Many times Nancy would hold and tenderly, slowly, stroke Bluefeather's face, running a fingertip along the thin scar on the bridge of his nose. She was constantly amazed that he could be so perfectly sculpted and still have so little vanity and so much kindness to give, so much thoughtfulness to offer.

She taught him how to work the gambling cards and was patient while his hard-rock hands softened so he could finally manipulate the cards and deal to win. He cleaned their living quarters. He looked after her needs beyond anything her jaded life had known. She could not keep her hands off him, not knowing that this eventually would repel him.

He finally fell for the "easy way home" routine and began to thoroughly enjoy it. Nancy slowly had gathered together a talented burlesque company. Combining this with her notable singing voice and her lusty figure, the group was quite a draw. They traveled all over the West, with pleasure and profits growing all the time.

She was pale skinned with black hair and gray eyes, full figured for such a fine and light-footed dancer of exquisite invention and skill. Even so, there were women more beautiful than she in her dance group. There were women everywhere he went who were more handsome, but it was Nancy whom his young body was in heat for and his young mind fantasized after.

They had accrued enough savings to make a down payment on their own place. It all came together, and then apart, at Tonapah, Nevada. Tonapah was a mining town, and Bluefeather felt comfortable there among his own kind. Nancy's show was a yelling, stomping sellout twice every evening. Bluefeather kept all the gambling tables moving and paying.

How could he complain? She managed it so they could go to San Francisco together every two or three months. They drank the best whiskey, ate the finest foods in the most elite restaurants, and stayed in the luxurious suites of stately hotels. She dressed him like an Oxford dude or an imperial prince by tailors of her personal acquaintance. They attended every worthy show in the city that was boiling with lust and life and illusion. The opera, the cabaret performances, and the myriad of single and group entertainers who had come here to blend into the excitement of grand adventures and tragedies of the same scope were appreciated and rewarded with applause and generous tips by the two lovers from Tonapah.

These trips became a narcotic—a warm, sensual, ever-moving, eternally changing, other place. Then, after indulging several times in all that money and young bodies could desire, the first stale taste entered his mouth and the first slight sullying of overused nerves set in.

He told Nancy, at last, that he appreciated all the operatic indulgences, but the truth was that changing his outdoor nature was "like asking a piss-ant to play a trombone."

Nancy answered, "Lincoln was born in a leaky log cabin, but he learned to love living in the White House."

"But you see, Nancy, my darling one, Lincoln never watched the vision of a Dancing Bear nor did he climb mountains with a man who could chew tobacco and drink beer at the same time."

She ignored these retorts as simple jesting and said, "Your dried-up desert will still be there just like it is when you're old and made of sandpaper. Now, while your skin is smooth, we must enjoy our bounty."

But just as he would start to consider getting his two mules from the stable and scuttling into the night mountains and rocks, Nancy would trap him again with caring thoughtfulness and velvet deeds. A man could stay in this bejeweled cocoon and die of benign contentment.

Her bookkeeper and confidante, Rosalie, told Nancy, "Don't get your heart set on a 'forever deal' with this man. He's looking way off at something none of us can see—not even him."

"Since you're so clairvoyant, dear, explain why he can hardly wait to bed me; explain his thoughtfulness, his gentleness," she paused a second, "except when he has a rare spell of anger. Oh, Rosie, he'll stay because I'm giving him all any man needs."

"Believe me, honey, he ain't any man. He's . . . he's, oh, I don't know. I just know that I don't want you hurt again, that's all."

Sensing his growing lack of enthusiasm during their last trip to the West Coast, Nancy had a true and impressive surprise waiting for him upon their return home. In his private room, where he kept his unused prospecting equipment and his treasured mineralized rocks, she had had shelves built and carefully lined with black velvet and special lights to spot his displayed rocks. He appreciated her gesture of understanding where his true soul was hidden, and he felt humbled and obligated. That was part of the problem.

True, his gambling skills had been considerably refined under her expert guidance, since his earlier experience with his second cousin, Hog Head the collector, in Raton. He also had learned to dress and act the part of a gentleman gambler, again through her knowledge. He felt a combination of gratitude and resentment toward her. One good thing, though, all these things were forgotten in bed. In fact, after all this time of easily earned luxury, he was afraid their lovemaking was what had pulled him to her and held him, even now, instead of all the easy living. More and more often, he pondered this.

Slowly, like water rising in a large lake, he was becoming jaded with the "foreverness" of luxury and soft flesh. He would not deny that he enjoyed her touch, her careless laughter, her generous gifts. Damned right he did. But the chefs of this particular life had served up sweet delicate pastries far too often. He longed a little more each morning for the lonesome hunt, for the singular search, and for the thrill of possible discovery. He longed for the things hidden by the wary earth; little clues to search for; tiny pieces of float rock; looking with the glass at stones for the first time with one's heart aware of the possible beauty, a hint of riches that might magnify before his eyes; the company of the mules, the deer, the eagle, the bear... ah, and that was another thing—his guiding spirit, Dancing Bear, had never once visited him here in Tonapah. He must get up from their bed, scented with lovemaking, early the next morning and call him up. He had tried to evoke the dancing one many times since he had arrived in Tonapah. Nothing. But today?

In a half-vision he lay there and "mind-talked" to Dancing Bear. "Look at me, ol' pardner, I'm so loved out I'm limber as a rotten rubber band. I'm as thoughtless as a sick chicken, and I haven't got any more dreams left than a rusty bucket. My spine has turned to worn-out rope, and my mind is as dead and worthless as a used eggshell. Please, dear Dancing Bear, come and give your meek and desperate subject help. Please beautiful, attentive Bear. Assistance, please, now. What good is all this silver and gold that's already been found and is handed to me at the mere turn of a card? Where is the accomplishment? The fulfillment of successful struggle? You don't need to dream of lovely women when you're sleeping in a whorehouse. Huh? Huh? Answer me if you can. If not, show me a sign. Just one. Please... please... please."

As the half-vision cleared away to instant reality, he sat up in bed and turned to see the strong, delicious figure of Nancy spread wide open before his eyes, with her head turned over one arm, breathing steadily so that her breasts moved just enough for him to feel the same stirring that had become a mink-lined jail.

He almost went down to her. In her natural knowing, she would raise her legs around his hips and moan love sounds at the ceiling before she even opened her eyes. Temptation. Indecision. Decision.

He dressed, acquired one of his mules, and rode out through the mineralized blue and dull purplish hills of Tonapah. It was against his nature to ride and not search the ground for special rocks and colorations of the earth, but this time he ignored the earth. He looked out ahead, searching for the exact, right ridge.

The mule walked with brisk confidence, and Bluefeather could sense the feelings of escapement and discovery in the mule's muscles just as his own lungs relaxed and tasted the desert air scented like wafting caviar. After a while the town of mined metal from beneath the earth, with its silver dollars sliding across green-clothed tabletops, was gone. Now he could see folding and unfolding, obtruding and intruding, large bulks of rocks and earth bluing off into the distance. Oh, how he craved to go and explore their sides, canyons, crevices, and sandy wrinkles that Nancy had so casually dismissed. If he had properly supplied himself and brought his other mule, he knew he would have ridden on without looking back.

Then they stopped, the man and the mule. Here he could see in a complete circle. Bluefeather reined the mule around a little so he could scan the entire panorama. He could hear two birds talking way off somewhere and see a soundless pair of buzzards circling far to the southwest. Quiet. Ah, what beauty. What peace. He felt his soul settle perfectly into the form of his body from where it had been dislodged by all the cards, booze, overindulgence in rich foods and Nancy's lush body, as well as the adrenaline-pumped, stomping crowds who thronged the casinos searching for all of the above. Winning was the quick fix; losing the quick sad. Starting up again; the sudden surge of new hope. The old, old cycle.

All was forgotten the instant he saw Dancing Bear sitting on a cactus.

"I'm going to rename you Smiling Bear," Bluefeather said, spreading his own lips over his teeth in mirth like his spiritual mentor. "I thought you had deserted me forever when you didn't answer my half-vision."

"Dear brudder, I wonder why it is that apes and humans are the only creatures that pull their lips from their teeth when they are both happy and angry. What do you think of that, dear brudder? Tell me, please."

"There you go, Bear, asking questions when I'm so desperate for answers. Didn't you hear me talking to you, begging you like a man condemned to hanging, of my limited time? Huh? Huh?"

"But you haven't asked me a single question yet."

"I haven't had time."

"Take all of that time you wish, dear brudder, I got many minutes for listening. Maybe years, eternities even."

"Okay then. Listen, Bear. I'm gettin' mixed up about all that stuff over there at Tonapah."

"How's that? Isn't Tonapah a mining town? Aren't you a mining man?"

"Say, you really haven't been paying any attention to what's been going on with me, have you?" Bluefeather let out a deep breath and started to remind Dancing Bear that he had already broken his word and was proffering questions instead of answers just as before. He decided it was no use confusing the rare meeting even more, and he went on again. "That is true what you say, Bear, but it is all the other things—all that money and fun, and the women, well, a woman, and everything else a feller could possibly want. I just don't know how much longer I can take it. Nancy's a fine lady, and I don't want to hurt her feelings or anything like..."

Dancing Bear yelled, "Whoa, whoa, whoa," just like Bluefeather had at him once before. "Well now, we got a brand new one here. I got clients complaining all the day throughout the world about not enough money, not enough food, not enough women. To tell you a sure-enough truth, most of my clients are crying, screaming, and just plumb overrun with 'not enough.' This here is one damn brand-new one for this old Bear. Hold it right there. I got to go higher up for consultation and advice." Dancing Bear zoomed up out of sight faster than a fiery comet.

Bluefeather leaned back on the mule, looking up, wanting his guide to return with advice from above. Dancing Bear returned swifter than sight, for certainly Bluefeather heard him before he saw him. "Dear brudder Blue, the One on the high horizon says He's too busy right now over at Beijing to bother with problems at Tonapah. His associate tells to me this..."

Bluefeather interrupted, "I don't want to hear any of your lame-duck, weasel-whining, secondhand blather. I want first-cabin stuff or nothing. Right now. Right here is when I need to hear words of wisdom. You hear me, Bear? You hear me begging you like a kid wanting permission to go to the bathroom? I beg you like a street corner pencil peddler."

Dancing Bear was leaping as light as a fruit fly from one cactus to another. He was whirling around on one toe yelling gleefully, "Wheeee, whoopee, pisseroni."

Feeling helpless, Bluefeather jumped from his mule and vigorously started throwing rocks at the dancing spirit. But the rocks ran together, creating a figure of two stone apes, one chasing the other with a stick in its hand. The ape sculpture just grew larger with the heavier rocks that Bluefeather hurled at his untouched guide. Finally he had thrown all the rocks within reach and had not even touched the spirit who danced like a swift ghost. Not even a single glancing blow had dusted Dancing Bear.

Bluefeather shoved enough breath from his lungs to shout, "Quit playing those magic games on me. I want the pure truth. You hear me? The pure truth." He gasped the frustrated air back into his lungs for a few moments then continued, "You know I love and respect you like my grandfather, the pueblo shaman. So treat me good and kind and thoughtful and do it real quick like he would."

Dancing Bear quit dancing, squatted down, and started drawing pictures in the dirt with his trigger finger, saying softly but firmly, "A sunbeam penetrating a great forest mist in the canyons of Taos Mountain, an antelope giving birth to twins, lightning bouncing across a great lake. That is all magic. Magic, you hear? Even a mirror is magic, but real to the one making the image. What I do over on this side of the river is real. You hear, dear brudder? Real!"

Bluefeather was upset again, ornery upset. "There you go spouting all these highfalutin things at me like...like that. You're no good to me this way."

"Listen careful, dear brudder. You are lucky to have me around sometimes. Most people don't ever get to see their spirit guide. Only a few get to feel and a few get to hear, but most people have the insides of their heads squeezed so tight they never know we exist. Poor, poor people. Lucky, lucky Bluefeather. Huh? Huh?"

Then he cocked his head, listening far away, and said as he danced an Icelandic shuffle across the scorching desert out of sight, shouting, "Have a good Thanksgiving when you finish carving the big, wild turkey."

Bluefeather sighed. "Here it is only April and he speaks of Thanksgiving."

He stared for a time at the empty place from which Dancing Bear had vanished, then he looked at the statue of the two apes hovering in midair. He watched it slowly descend to the ground, then turn into a sculpture of a little man carrying two mules. By the time he had remounted his mule, the figures had become a pile of sand, and the next breeze, before he reined away, had started scattering the grains of the statue across the desert.

He went back to work as was his nature. Reluctantly.

Bluefeather had refused, even with Nancy's protestations, to take money from the underground miners in head-to-head games; however, the owners and the professional drifters were another story. He deliberately started the game that would bring about his turn at disaster. He didn't even know the man he was to finally beat.

The game of five-card stud went on all day, all night. The stakes rapidly had grown too big for all but the best. By three o'clock the next afternoon, only Bluefeather and the stranger, who called himself Grady, were left playing. There were a score or so of losers watching, taking sides. Many thousands of dollars were now on the table. This same situation was probably happening somewhere else in the West at this same instant, but one thing was turned around: Grady had caught Bluefeather dealing the second card, but he had said nothing until Bluefeather went for the third selected winning card under.

Nancy had warned Bluefeather that very few men in the gambling world could smoothly go that deep into the deck, so the other pros seldom looked for it. All Bluefeather's years of practice went to hell in a glance; Grady called him on it. He knew he was caught, but professional honor would not allow an admission of guilt, or rather, of making a blunder. At Grady's cursing, he felt his skin tighten where the back of his neck joined his skull, and a searing of swift heat prickled his nose scar. Then, Grady's words and knife came at him all in a blur of motion and diffused sound.

Bluefeather deflected the knife from his heart, and it sliced along his ribs cutting a sudden little red overflowing creek that bottomed out against bone. He shattered and tore Grady's elbow over the edge of the card table, but Grady used his other hand to put a lock on Bluefeather's neck bones. He kneed Grady in the groin, gouged at his eyes with both thumbs, and bit his right ear mostly off. Grady's fingers stayed locked as if they had been cast in solid bronze.

Bluefeather's vision was turning into a whirling gray mass as he fell. He was not aware that he had secured Grady's knife until after it was over. Later he remembered the feel of the blade slicing between Grady's cervical vertebrae. He choked and coughed away the violence, desperately seeking air until he could see again. Grady's throat was cut open all the way back through his cervical bones. Only a couple of tendons attached his head to his body. For just a last, heart-pumping moment, the blood spurted almost up to the high ceiling, then its spray dropped to a seep, like a suddenly dry courtyard fountain.

Nancy, her fellow entertainers, and almost everyone in the Tonapah area had tried consoling Bluefeather, assuring him that it was self-defense. Some came forward with true tales of great and evil deeds Grady had committed in other states to many helpless folks. None of the words worked on the heart of Bluefeather Fellini. The rightness or wrongness no longer mattered to him. If he had stayed in the mountains where he belonged, it simply would not have happened. That's the way he felt.

So he left the fine wines, big steaks, the feather bed where he and Nancy rubbed skins, and all the other delights. He went back to the mountains. Riding one mule and leading another, he left Tonapah that night just as Nancy and her girls started their show.

He rode across the moonlit desert until the sun came kissing him with kind warmth at first, then searing him with savagery by midday. He had a canvas bag full of water and a wide-brimmed hat. Nothing could stop him from reaching the coolness of timbered country somewhere toward New Mexico.

Thirteen

Bluefeather rode down out of the southern Colorado mountains toward the town of Breen. He brought his saddle mule to a stop in the foothills overlooking this place of humans. The pack mule pulled beside them and tried to graze at the long bunchgrass.

He surveyed the setting and saw that there was a good-sized waste dump to the west and some movement around an ore mill below it. He reasoned there would be some action in the town since at least one mine was working.

To the south of Breen, he could see where the sagebrush of the high desert mingled with the thinning timber of the high country. This had always been his favorite kind of land—timber to the north, sage to the south. The Rio Bello edged the town in a half circle, sparkling blue-green where it was banked with cottonwoods golden as egg yolks and oak brush red as fresh blood. Little gardens and orchards that tempted his taste buds were visible even from this distance. He could see the activity on the main street. Several saddle horses and a few wagons and teams were mixed in with a few automobiles. There were even some new mid-1930s models. This was a good sign of local prosperity.

The houses were mostly wood and rock with steep, sloped roofs to more easily shed the heavy winter snows. On the southern edge of town, a scattering of adobes hinted at the Spanish influence of New Mexico.

Yes, he felt good about this town. The terrain suited him—rolling foothills, high desert, timbered mountains, water that had to be good fishing, and even an operating mine. It was the right size for its surroundings, too; he figured Breen's population was about fifteen hundred.

But there was something else he felt. Something waiting for him that was good. He sensed this the way an old hunter knows there is a deer behind the oak brush before he sees it.

He smiled and spurred old Jackknife on down the trail. Nancy followed taking quick, short steps to keep the pack balanced. As the mules picked up their gait, there was a smile in the rhythm of their hooves as well.

Bluefeather's sense about Breen was correct. He tied his mules at a hitching post next to the little courthouse square and followed the allure of a sign across the street: *Mary's Place—Homemade Pies—The Best in the World.*

Although he always took dried apricots and apples whenever he went on long prospecting excursions, he never seemed to get enough sweets.

After a fine plate of roast beef with steaming brown gravy, Mary handed him an ambrosial quarter of an apple pie as thick as a two-by-four, with crust as delicate as a spring cloud and a flavor as delectable and lasting as first love.

Bluefeather said to himself, "Now that's a pie worth digging for."

Mary smiled at him from her naturally rosy face under her red-blond hair that could match the fall colors of the mountains. Her blue eyes sparkled like polished turquoise and with the same expression of pleasure that danced around her full, pink mouth.

She asked expectantly, "Could you eat another slice?"

Bluefeather looked at this face of womanhood knowing that the body underneath was both strong and elegant like her cooking. "Yes, Ma'am. I think I could. I surely do."

The patrons—miners, drifters, a few cowboys, and diverse others—were all a simple blur. He could not force his eyes to focus on anything but the little cardboard sign by the cash register that said, *House for Rent. 10 Acres. Inquire Here.*

Mary delivered Bluefeather's pie. He sat straight back in his chair rubbing his powerful, rock-digging hands tenderly back and forth on the red-and-white-checked oilcloth covering the table.

He looked back and forth from the pie to Mary's eyes. Back and forth.

She stood away from the table rubbing her hands lightly on the sides of her apron just below her hips. Neither one could think of anything to say that would break the spell of their transfixion.

"I'm Mary. Mary Schmidt O'Kelly."

"I'm Bluefeather Fellini."

Finally, Mary, feeling her face flare hot, turned hesitantly, looked at the kitchen, and uttered something about "biscuits burning." She went to her iron range and became very busy.

Bluefeather sliced off a bite of pie so large it nearly choked him. He was saved by swallowing what was left of his water and coffee. He needed to gasp for breath but somehow got his lungs working before he turned blue or made any embarrassing noises. After that he kept his head tilted down over the pie and took very small bites. He ate it all, even picking up his spoon and scraping the remaining crumbs of the crust into it with the fork until the plate appeared freshly washed. He faked taking another bite of invisible pie as Mary hurriedly filled his coffee cup. She knew he was staring after her as she walked back to the stove.

Suddenly, Bluefeather felt a presence behind him, oppressive, and projecting disturbing vibrations into his back. It came from a table of four men, but he didn't have to look to know exactly where this uncomfortable feeling was coming from. It had happened many times before during his lifetime and was always right in its invisible warnings.

One of the men—big, with wide shoulders and heavy hands, a nice-looking face, except his eyes were somewhat close together—came over and politely introduced himself.

"I'm Stan Berkowitz."

Bluefeather knew this was the man whose presence he had felt and he said, "I'm Fellini."

"Pleased to make your acquaintance. I see by your mules," and he motioned out to them, "that you're a mining man. I'm the mill foreman here. If I can do anything for you, all you have to do is ask."

"Well...thank you, Mr....?"

"Please, just call me Stan. The widow Mary and I have been dating for some time now. She makes some kind of pie, don't she?" He smiled like a braying mule.

Bluefeather somehow knew that the man was going to do something to him. He had met a few gracious losers in his time but never a joyous one. He must watch his back for a smiling dagger. If, of course, he decided to stay in Breen a spell.

Bluefeather wandered around the town for a couple of hours, then returned to Mary's Place to inquire about the house that was for rent. He had decided this was where he wanted to be. Maybe for the rest of his life.

Things moved so smoothly it caused a slight blur of memory. Somehow he had joined Mary in the kitchen to help clean up after closing. Then her elderly father, Ludwig Schmidt, had limped over to walk her home.

Bluefeather couldn't recall all the things they said that night of their first meeting in the cafe, but it left a sweet melancholia like a fine mist of honeyed air. He knew he would carry the scent of her, the feeling of her, through many dimensions of moving time.

At Ludwig's insistence, Bluefeather had joined them, after getting his mules and introducing them as Miss Nancy and Señor Jackknife as formally as if he were introducing royalty. Ludwig examined the mules and their packs in the moonlight with an experienced eye. He approved of both. Mary smiled fleetingly, knowing that her father had just accepted Bluefeather as the new tenant.

"Almost as fine a pair of mules as my last ones," Ludwig said.

Bluefeather was happy to unpack, brush down, feed the mules some oats, and turn them loose in the corral. There was a nice shed for a stable, and the ten acres of grass were ungrazed and seeding out.

As he stepped up on the porch he noticed a small sign above the front door: *Ludwig Schmidt—Assayer*. Great spirits alive! His new landlord was a mining man. Nancy would have said, "The cards are falling for you, darling. Push your luck."

Ludwig stayed in the main house while Mary showed Bluefeather his new home and helped him get set up. She lighted the lantern hanging on the back porch and two kerosene lamps inside. The house was spotless, even though Mary kept apologizing for not having it cleaner. Bluefeather wanted to laugh at this. If the place had been more polished, it would have been too smooth to stand or move about in without falling. He was really pleased with the three rooms. There was a kitchen, a bedroom, and a supposed sitting room.

He threw his bedroll on the floor by the bed and pulled it open.

Mary said, "Oh, no need for that. Here, I've kept clean sheets and covers ready." She pulled off an old spread that she used to keep the undercovers dustproof.

Bluefeather said, "Ahhh, well if you don't mind, I'd rather get a bath before I use such a special bed."

"Well, in that case, there's firewood and a washtub on the porch." She demonstrated the hand water pump over a galvanized sink and got a couple of pails and set them up on the stove. She looked around hesitantly, holding her hands together in front of her as if there just had to be something else she must do.

Bluefeather said, "Now don't fret. Everything is fine. I'll just heat some water, take a bath, and I'll see you both in the morning."

"Are you sure there's not something else you need?"

"No. No, you've already been too kind."

"Well, I'll be going then. Papa likes a bourbon and hot milk before he goes to bed." She started out the door and then hesitated. "Papa fixes his own breakfast about half past six or so, because I have to get to the cafe for the early birds. Good-night then."

"Good-night, Miss...Miss..."

"Actually it's Mrs. I'm a widow. But call me Mary," she said with almost an order in her voice.

"Mary it is."

And she was gone. He missed her before she had reached the back door.

Bluefeather slept later by far than he had intended and felt a little guilty. The sun was over the trees by the river when he arose. He fixed his breakfast from his prospecting supplies but vowed to get fresh eggs, potatoes, and much more for the next meal.

He fed the mules a coffee can of oats before he even thought of feeding himself. He looked again at the pasture of lush grass and knew he had not needed to worry. Even in deep snow the mules would enjoy digging down to the grass because they would know there was plenty of oats in the barn. It would just be exercise for sunny days. It suddenly hit him that he had been so pleased with the entire situation that he had forgotten to pay Ludwig. He blushed until his face felt singed.

"Jesus H. Christmas Christ," he muttered to himself, "what a rude, thoughtless bastard I am." Well, he had cash, but because of his unforgivable oversight he decided it would make a better impression if he paid in gold dust. He knocked on Ludwig's door and after a while he heard the old gentleman limp to it.

"Ahhh, good morning to you, Mr. Fellini. Come in. Come in. Did you sleep well, Mr. Fellini?"

Bluefeather said, before he realized he was imitating Mary, "Blue. Blue, it is."

"Ah, yes."

Bluefeather apologized for neglecting to pay the rent, and although he was offered coffee, he insisted on getting business over with first. Ludwig led the way into his assay room. There were great rock specimens everywhere as well as old and relatively new mining claim maps all over the walls.

Bluefeather was stunned and highly pleased. Ludwig was not just an analyzer of other men's labors; he had been a seeker himself.

Ludwig, seeing Bluefeather's expression, said, "Ah, yes, Bluefeather...Blue, I've been far more involved in prospecting than assaying. I've wondered many times if I've wasted my degree in chemical engineering. No. I suppose not. The money I've earned has allowed me to follow my...my dreams. Can I use that word with you, Blue?"

Bluefeather was thrilled even more than he could have hoped for. Here he had a landlord who was not afraid to be labeled a dreamer, and say so. After weighing out three months' rent in gold dust, Ludwig told him the history of many of the rocks. Bluefeather recognized some of them from mountain ranges he had visited himself. All green malachite copper might look the same to the casual observer, but to those who breathed it, every location had a slightly different cast—a differently hued host rock. Only true professionals had this capability.

It was midafternoon when they realized they had been lost in their worlds of hard earth and rainbowed minerals. To Bluefeather it had seemed like only a second ago since he had knocked on the back door; now he must leave. He suddenly felt that he had most certainly overstayed his welcome.

As Bluefeather apologized and opened the door to leave, Ludwig said with a strong voice that somehow gave confidence and comfort, "Oh, sir, never apologize for having true adventures and fun. That's what rocks are made for."

Bluefeather walked out into the late sun of the wondrous southern Colorado fall weather and talked to his mules.

"Say, kids, we've found us a home at last. Now don't you worry. There are hundreds of thousands of acres to prospect next spring right near here. We'll have a lifetime of that and a home too. Now, how do you like them pinto beans? Huh?"

They both listened, looking at him as they moved their ears to catch the special resonance, but then simultaneously they dropped their heads and started grazing again. This move was not done out of disrespect for their partner, but they knew that now was the short time of easy grass. They grazed accordingly.

In the next few days Bluefeather and Ludwig made many new discoveries about each other. For one thing, they were both avid readers. Bluefeather was pleased that they shared a love for Balzac and Dostoyevski. The Schmidt family room had been turned into a library, a music room, and a place for contemplation. A great bay window looked out over thousands of acres of high timber and desert combined.

Before Ludwig realized that Bluefeather was staring at the rows of books with joy, rather than insecurity, he half apologized, "Well, you know, Blue, many of the mountain men read Shakespeare as a religion."

Sometimes they would talk for hours; then there were times when silence was the rule as Ludwig played his beloved Wagner records and the works of other composers on the Victrola. Occasionally he would play a Strauss waltz and, limping slightly on one lame leg, dance to the music. A quick change of mood might call for Beethoven.

A surprising cultural bond was developing between these two men of mountains, but they didn't spend all their time together. Every day, Bluefeather had gone to lunch at Mary's Place, and every day, he had helped her clean up the tables and dishes. He soon learned that she had taken on the restaurant business so her father could afford to spend time with his music and books during the fall and winter months.

Mary was very pleased that her father had someone to share his rocking-chair adventures with, but a different, strong emotion tore at her now. She herself wanted more time to spend with the new tenant. Being a practical person, she trained additional help so that she and Bluefeather could be together a great part of Wednesday and all day Sunday.

They fished the cold, Prussian-blue waters of the Rio Bello, and Bluefeather was amazed at how dedicated and skilled she was. Unbeknownst to Bluefeather, she was just as pleasantly surprised with his abilities.

On their third outing together she wandered downstream from him about a hundred yards and cast out into a deep, dark hole of twisting water next to a fallen log. The sun came bouncing across the ripples of the current and created a vibrating halo around her red hair. The shimmering rays cast little dancing lights over all her body, delineating her femaleness so strongly that Bluefeather missed two good strikes in a row. He jerked so hard at the third fish, while his head was still turned enraptured with the highlighted vision of Mary, that he slipped and fell into the water. Fortunately he was mostly below a cut bank so that Mary could not see his embarrassment, as long as he stayed bent over almost double.

He hooked a six-pound brown deep in the throat. The fish showed much resentment at this, diving, jumping, and shaking with all its watery strength. Bluefeather finally landed it. He had fought the fish in his bent-over position so long that he couldn't straighten up to show it off with the proper shouting and bragging—the key element when fishing with a companion. When one is in the company of the most beautiful, intelligent, kindliest, and best baker of pies in the entire world, it is an absolute requisite. Shame. Instead he lay down on the grass in a curiously bent position with the water squishing in his shoes and his clothes sticking to his skin.

He extracted the hook from the fish's throat with some difficulty, saying, "Forgive me, you flopping bastard." He hid in a circle of bushes until the slanting sun had him mostly dry. Then he went looking for his Miss Mary.

Mary caught three ten- or twelve-inchers, providing them with enough fish for a feast, and indeed, they had one that night.

Bluefeather had a little more bourbon than usual before the repast, and later, after the great meal, he had an extra two or three glasses of wine. He finally gathered the courage to tell Mary and Ludwig the whole truth of his fish story. Mary laughed so hard her eyes watered, and Bluefeather swore he could hear her entire body tinkling like a thousand ceramic bells.

Ludwig roared and shook. His face, strong as a lion's and chiseled from granite, turned a little softer with his mirth. Even so, his broad-knuckled hands that appeared strong as a rock crusher shook the room as he alternately slapped his good leg and then the tabletop.

Good people. Good times. Simple.

Fourteen

In the memories of all, there had never been such a long-lasting fall season in the Breen, Colorado, area. Everyone said so. The yellow-gold of the aspens and cottonwoods and brown-red of the oak brush stayed in the leaves that clung and quaked on the trees for extra weeks. Precious weeks.

Bluefeather and Mary rode the mules high into the mountains several times. They looked out over little streams at an occasional bear, deer, and even elk. Once they caught a glimpse of a reclusive mountain lion. It must have been old, because its back was swayed so that its belly appeared to almost drag the ground.

Bluefeather enjoyed spotting tracks of all the wild creatures and showing them to Mary. He pointed out the varied shapes of a wild turkey, a coyote, a bobcat, a raccoon, and a porcupine. He explained how the distances between tracks and the depths of indentations told stories of haste, slow walking, or even attack. She would ask questions and smile at his answers, as excited as a child at a frog pond.

Their last trip before winter was celebrated with a meal of fried chicken, potato salad, and sourdough bread with goat cheese, heightened by a bottle of red wine. They chose a little highland meadow for their picnic, where the thick, cured grass was surrounded by spruce trees and a few aspens. These kept the wind to a teasing breeze.

They could see for almost a hundred miles to the south into New Mexico, across colorations of timber thinning into the sage and cedar of the high desert. Richly colored mesas twisted across the vast area like waves on a mighty sea of dirt and stone. Then on and on, purples and blues as the land broke and reformed. Finally the horizon and the sky met, creating different shades of blue to every eye that had ever looked upon their joining.

The sun was low in the sky, even at two o'clock in the afternoon, but warmed the little park just enough to take the bite out of the sharp, thin air.

Bluefeather felt at home where he sat and the same as far as he could see. The two mules grazed contentedly. He reached over and touched Mary on her temple and twirled a flaming lock of her hair.

She turned her face to him, took his hands in hers, and held them to her lips. Then with a little glance of wide, blue eyes at his dark ones, she moved his hands between her breasts and squeezed them with some force. They loved. Later she slept.

After a short time, Bluefeather got up and stepped away, as quietly like the Indian he was, into the timber. He sniffed the sharp evergreen scent and felt the needles, leaves, and twigs crunch softly under his feet. This was his first choice for a home. At this thought he needed to touch Mary again.

He moved quietly out into the clearing and stood looking down at her where she lay. She was so lovely, so at rest and at peace, that he was totally entranced. Immobile. Even though her breasts lifted up and down in slow, deep breaths, the flush and touch of love still pinked her face.

He had no idea how many eternities he stood there absorbing her, but suddenly he realized her great, blue eyes were staring up at him, and he could read their message. He felt warmer than the sun that would bless them for only a few more minutes.

He was suddenly as drunk as a bottle of bourbon, as weak in the legs as a very old granddaddy spider. Then an instant surge of energy and exaltation possessed him. He bent and lifted her up, carrying her over the little meadow to a gap in the trees looking south.

She was awake when he let her feet down in the grass. They stood shoulder to shoulder staring at the southern panorama all the way across the invisible Colorado state line into New Mexico. She leaned her head over on his shoulder and he put his arm around her back. There was a stillness now. A silence to hear, and air so pure it breathed itself. Their outer vision joined their inner vision as Bluefeather raised one arm sweeping wide in front of him.

"We belong to that," he whispered.

"Yes. Yes, we do. Always."

In three days the leaves lost their yellow and red brightness and turned brown and gray. In two more they started drifting toward the earth's eternal gravity, delayed in their descent a fractional degree according to the cold gusts of wind.

Bluefeather felt some guilt. He'd been so absorbed in being with Mary, he had postponed crucial winter chores as he had never done before. At least he had put an old wagon in good shape earlier. Now he and the mules must get busy hauling wood for both houses—piñon for the fireplaces and cedar for the cookstoves. Cedar was better suited for the contained cookstove because it creates a quick, popping heat; piñon, which burns steadily, emitting a rich, earthy smell, would give much comfort and delight in the fireplaces the entire winter.

After hauling the wood down out of the mountains, he chopped it all into proper lengths and stacked it in neat rows. He worked furiously, sweating in the early winter winds, his strong, young body enjoying the extended exercise.

The snow held off even though the winds were icy from heavy, white moisture farther north. He caulked doors and windows and nailed down anything that was slightly loose. He saw to it that the grain bins were filled with sufficient oats and corn. He had already bought plentiful supplies of grass and alfalfa hay; he liked to mix up the grains and the roughage for his animals in the cold months. They would come out of the long winter in good shape, ready for the heavy work of spring. This thought brought others to Bluefeather's mind.

He had had only a few long visits with Ludwig when the old gentleman brought up what he called his "great secret." Bluefeather would never be so foolish as to take him lightly. If Ludwig chose to describe something in this manner, Bluefeather *knew* it was great. Even though the word seemed so overused almost everywhere, he did not doubt the quality of Ludwig's secret to any degree. Ludwig had promised to tell Bluefeather at the right time. Well, when would that be? When he was ninety?

It was very difficult for Bluefeather to admit to himself that he craved—yes, ached—to ask Ludwig what the hell it was all about, but he knew he must be patient and refrain from any questions until Ludwig chose to tell him. Even though Bluefeather was taught early in life—like most Indians, cowboys, and mining men were—not to ask personal questions, it was still going to be very hard not to break the rules. It was the code. Oh sure, it was fine to ask people questions about the welfare of their spouses, or their children, or even their parents.

Also, it was permissible to ask someone about his crops, the weather, or how his arthritis was getting along. But the great secret? Never.

He realized that when Ludwig felt like it, he would tell him, without any impolite questions being asked. If he didn't, then Bluefeather guessed it was just no one's business. Bluefeather was suffering great pain wanting to know. But damn the code—it held.

Again and then again he played over in his hearing-mind what Ludwig had promised: "I'll tell you, Blue...at the right time, of course, dear boy...I shall reveal to you a great secret. Your wildest fantasies are nothing at all. Nothing, I say. None of your dreams could touch my revelations, unless God made them for you personally at the right time."

As Bluefeather was saying, "Yes. Yes...?" Ludwig's voice faded and he fell asleep.

Bluefeather repeated, "Damn the code!"

His curiosity kept him awake for three days and nights. He made medicine, chewed peyote, and had natural hallucinations, but no answer came.

He finished storing the apple crop in the cellar, wrapping each apple tightly in newspaper or pages from the Montgomery Ward catalog. He saw the long shelves loaded with vegetables and fruits that Mary had canned all spring and summer. Now he rearranged the jars of apricots and peaches in bunches on the wooden shelves. To his joyful anticipation, there was a whole winter's worth of pies in those jars—enough for the restaurant and plenty for them personally.

There seemed to be only one thing left that he felt he could add to the winter food supply. They needed a buck deer to hang in the meat house.

If only he could get Ludwig's secret off his mind, everything would be just rosy. Why? Why did Ludwig have to use that word "great"? Why couldn't he have simply kept quiet until the right time, or at least have said something like, "I have something to tell you in a few days, or...in the spring or...in the summer or..."

He decided to force himself to quit thinking about it. Anyway, he knew it would have something to do with a mining secret. He was sure of that. What else could the two of them share that deserved such words?

Bluefeather saddled Nancy, took his .30–30, and rode into the mountains. He wore a sheepskin coat and chaps, and had his hat tied down with a bandanna. When they got to about eight thousand feet, it was blowing so cold that he tied another scarf around his face just under his eyes so he could breathe warmer air and still see. If the snows had come on schedule, the deer would have been in the foothills, and hunting would have been easier.

Today he had seen some old and some recent signs of both bucks and does. Tracks and droppings were plentiful, but so far he had spotted nothing fresh. His young eyes could see fine from the top of the mule, but even so, at every clear patch of earth he would stop Nancy and lean over to carefully examine the ground. He figured the deer would be on the east side of the slope out of the wind and in the sun if possible. He was right. He saw where the larger tracks of a single buck had followed a trail and then left it just ahead of him. He had a choice of getting down, tying the mule, following the tracks, and eventually coming at the deer from a downwind direction, or he could stay in the saddle and save a lot of walking and time.

He reined Nancy out after the deer. He watched her ears work. Soon they came to the easterly edge of an open meadow heavily circled by spruce and some pines. He pulled the mule back and rode all the way around to the east side as he had planned. In a spot where the trees thinned a bit, he pulled up and carefully looked across the opening to the other edge. No matter how hard he tried to conjure up a deer in the varied shapes of scattered dead timber, he just could not make one appear in the flesh. Well, he had figured wrong. The buck must have moved on farther than he had figured. He would just have to ride higher to the north in hope of cutting the sign again.

They moved out and up now. Bluefeather was in the netherworld of doubt. He was in that highly charged condition that comes after one finds evidence of the immediate presence of prey, and then the sense of loss, or of a vacuum, when the prey seems to have vanished. Bluefeather was determined to conquer the spell.

He slipped the .30–30 from the scabbard and decided to gamble entirely on Nancy. She stepped delicately but surely through the scattered trees as only mules can do. Her long ears worked back and forth, listening. Her head was up, she was alert, sensing with all her body.

On they moved, and now, even as quietly as Nancy walked, Bluefeather felt that the noise was as loud as a landslide and that all the deer between southern Colorado and northern Canada could hear them. But that was sometimes the wisdom of hunting from the saddle— the wild animals heard the rhythm of four legs walking instead of two.

Bluefeather felt the mule's muscles tighten under the saddle and her steps shorten as she turned her head to the side with both ears pitched forward. She came to a stop like a bird dog on stand. There. About eighty to a hundred yards away stood the four-point buck. Its head was up, and it was looking in their direction. There was an open space to aim the rifle, and he could shoot to the side so the noisy explosion of the cartridge would not hurt Nancy's sensitive ears.

He took a deep breath and held it as he lowered the barrel down so that the sights entered just behind the deer's shoulder. It was the best he could do at that angle. He squeezed off the shot, his spirit going out the barrel with the lead, through the trees and the heart of the deer. Then it zapped back into his body as the majestic creature seemed to float just above the ground for an unmeasured instant, then fall dead without time for pain.

He reined toward his prey, the ancient hunters' genes within him causing his blood to flow like a flash flood. He dismounted, put the palm of his left hand on the forehead of the deer, and said softly, "Forgive me, kind and generous brother."

He gutted the deer then swung it across the saddle. With leather thongs, he tied its feet to each stirrup. Then with another thong, he secured the stirrups under the mule's belly. It was done.

He mounted behind the saddle and headed home with the game, as men had done for uncountable time. There was no gloating here, and there would be no bragging later with Bluefeather Fellini, just a warm, pleased feeling at having done his job right. The cold mountain breeze went unnoticed now. He thought of a warm Miss Mary and hot peach pie.

Fifteen

All the town's roads were open again. The cold dropped down and surrounded everything but flame. Some days were the coldest ever recorded in the United States. Even so, the people adjusted and simply went on with their work the best they could. It was the time of acceptance.

Ludwig was delighted at the news of the engagement, asking Bluefeather, "When?"

"We've decided to do the deed when all the snow is gone from that long hill behind the house. The one Mary calls 'Clock Hill,'" and he made a northerly gesture.

"That is good, sir. That is splendid. It'll be some day in April or May then. We'll watch closely." Ludwig started making all kinds of plans. "Durango. We must go to Durango for the wedding. We'll stay in the Strater." The latter was a four-story, brick hotel built in 1887 and one of America's finest. After his pleasurable tirade, Ludwig added solemnly, "That is, of course, if it's the desire of you kids."

A few days after his initial elation, Ludwig became quieter and more withdrawn than Bluefeather had ever seen him. Bluefeather's first honest thought was a fear that Ludwig was ill. He had grown so fond of the old man that he would be greatly troubled if Ludwig missed the great day because of an indisposition. He talked over his concerns with Mary, and she said he was always like this before a moment of meaningful decision.

She was right.

Bluefeather fed the mules and walked on the path he had shoveled through the snow over to Ludwig's to have some coffee.

Ludwig fussed and limped about, insisting on fixing and pouring the steaming liquid himself. He drank only half a mug. Then he brought a bottle of Napoleon brandy from the whiskey cabinet and, without a word, poured them each a portion large enough to fill their coffee mugs.

Bluefeather was surprised that the old man would drink brandy so early in the day. They sat, staring into voids, these two men linked together by their love of the precious rock from the earth and a lovely lady called Mary. They sat in silence, each waiting for the other to speak.

Finally Bluefeather came out with a cliché as he set his mug back down on the table. "This really hits the spot."

"Yes. Yes, the spot. Certainly. Certainly does." Ludwig twisted in his chair and looked out a frosty window, turned his mug on the table, looked at Bluefeather, and grinned. He scratched in the white shock of hair on his large head as if he were cultivating it. He cleared his throat and glanced at Bluefeather, smiling so quickly an eagle would have missed it. He cleared his throat. Again. Then again.

He emptied the coffee and brandy in one mighty swig. Then he stood up on his bent and battered legs, straightening his spine, stuck his chin out, and headed for his workroom with hardly a limp.

Bluefeather half expected a drumroll or maybe the music of a military band to blast forth. Ludwig returned carrying a leather-covered box perhaps ten by twelve by fourteen inches and placed it on the table right in front of Bluefeather. Then he inserted a key in the small lock secreting the contents of the box. He placed a massively boned hand on each end of it, hesitating as his old lungs moved his chest bones under the skin, in and out. Faster and faster, his eyes widened and brightened, and then with a flourish that would have done credit to most highly acclaimed illusionists, he raised the lid on the box. There it was at last.

Yes, finally Bluefeather gazed upon the great secret. It was a rock of rose quartz that almost filled the box. It was filigreed with wire gold as if sewn in by a large, magic needle. The snakes of gold seemed to twist and writhe around one another in ancient shining splendor.

Ludwig said, "Well...there it is," in a voice that could just as well have said, "Answer the doorbell....God is standing on the front porch."

Bluefeather knew well that some of the greatest high-grade gold discoveries had been made in rose quartz, and he also sensed correctly that Ludwig would not be displaying this wondrous specimen unless he had found the mother vein that had given it birth. At a glance Bluefeather knew the rock had not been dug from the vein but rather that the elements had freed it. Then the float rock had moved a short distance downhill over many years. He knew this by its slightly smoothed edges. If it had moved a long distance, there would have been no sharp edges left at all.

At last he could give voice. "Thank you, Ludwig. Thank you for allowing me to gaze upon glory."

This pleased Ludwig immensely and he said, "Go ahead, go ahead and lift it out of the box. Examine it with your glass. Go ahead, sir."

Bluefeather did as he was bid. He could barely lift it free in his fear of dropping the rock and smashing the lovely gracious container. He thought the specimen was well over half gold. He placed his prospector's magnifying glass close, adjusting it as the entire visible world turned to precious gold before his eyes.

"Ahhhh. Ahhhh," was what he said.

After a time he raised up, breathless, stunned, but before he could think of another proper comment Ludwig broke in. "I found it. I found the big dream. But I had to know if the vein carried any distance before I mined it. Naturally I called the claim the King Tut. As you will soon see, that part of the forest is covered with heavy overburden. So I took the strike of the vein, and sighting along it, I could see where the penetration of some rock bluffs must occur, perhaps a quarter mile up the mountain. If it did, I knew I would have the bonanza that all mining men seek—nay, all men and some women. There would be enough gold to buy a city, build a large lake, or feed a million mouths. So, Blue—and I know you can understand my thinking—I climbed and slid, and climbed and fell, until I reached the edge of the jagged bluff. It sloped back slightly and had sufficient crevices and indentions to make an easy climb. It was not so. The gold had blinded me at about thirty or forty feet up. I'll never know. I slipped. I fell. I broke many bones, and my innards have ached now for these five terribly long years, but aside from my smashed and mangled leg, I am able to get along quite well, as you can see."

"Yes. Yes, of course," Bluefeather agreed. He did not know why, but he had thought that Ludwig had been crippled in the flash flood that had taken the lives of his wife and Mary's husband.

"Neither one of us knew it, but we have been waiting for one another, looking for each other. It was fated beyond recall that you'd ride your mules into this town and stop at Mary's Place exactly when you did, Blue, my son."

Bluefeather couldn't think of anything to say, but he believed, with all his being, Ludwig's every word. The old man spoke softly, always, but even so his voice was as powerful, smooth, and penetrating as rubbing alcohol. It moved out in the air and surrounded him like a tent.

"Now, now, at last, you are here to fulfill my dream," Ludwig said. "Your dream. Mary's dream. Your strong, young legs will carry you—more carefully—to climb the cliff and uncover the vein. It is you, dear Blue, who will finish the dream for us all."

In this mesmerizing moment, Bluefeather gave his hand, his word, his vow, to Ludwig Schmidt, currently of the village of Breen, in southern Colorado. He was further thrilled when Ludwig showed him the map he had sketched out while recuperating from his fall. The vein was only half a day's mule ride from the room in which they now stood.

Late that night, Bluefeather stared from his bed into the darkness of the ceiling and smiled at the Great Spirit, voicing softly his thanks. He could have great riches, a loving wife, a father-in-law friend, and his home, all right here. Here. Who had ever been so blessed? Who, indeed?

Bluefeather walked into Mary's Place in midafternoon. There were still two tables of coffee drinkers, cursing the government and talking hunting and fishing. Bluefeather spoke to them politely and they answered back only because of Mary. He did not, and had not, ever joined their tables for small talk. It just was not in his nature. When he had a friend, that person got his time, his attention, and his thoughts as long as they lived. Grinder the Gringo had been one of those. Nancy had almost been a friend, but Bluefeather's sudden departure had prevented it. Now his number-one friend was old Ludwig. The fact he was to be his mining partner and father-in-law was truly a meaningless matter as far as their friendship was concerned.

So he chose a corner table like a regular customer, which he intended to be before he shared with Mary the churning tidings he held inside with such difficulty. It took a tough man to control knowledge and feelings desirous of exploding like a full case of old dynamite.

Mary sent him a smile of love and a little wave that said she would be there in just a moment. Oh well, he could handle it. As soon as the meal was finished he would take her into the storeroom so he could share his elation with the love of his life. Mary looked at him again as she was finishing cooking something on the stove.

Ah, thought Bluefeather, how special that our warm thoughts can cross the restaurant, ignoring the customers. But suddenly her face seemed void. He could not see the talking smile or feel love projecting like sunbeams through a forest glen. What had happened? In one instant he felt alone in a deep canyon beyond the reach of light. There was a stream flowing and roaring there, but it had no fish in its currents and no animals came to drink. No birds or insects would ever bother to seek its repellent banks. What in hell was he suddenly doing there?

Then he saw Mary do a strange thing. She turned the OPEN sign around to CLOSED and began talking to the other customers. They were slowly standing, looking as confused as Bluefeather.

He heard her say, "No, no. It's all on the house. You'll forgive me this inconvenience, just this one time, I hope. Something has come up that must be settled. Now."

They shuffled out, glancing and mumbling lowly to one another. One of the most important daily rituals in their lives had just been disrupted. They were suddenly without a single thing to think or do before dinnertime.

Mary locked the door after them. She brought cups and a coffeepot to his table without looking at him or speaking. She poured the coffee and placed the large coffeepot in the middle of the table between them.

She took a sip, glancing across the rim of her cup at him as she did so. Then she set, or slightly slammed, the cup on the table just under the breaking point and said in a voice that would have charred fine oak beams and shattered knife blades, "He told you, didn't he? Well? Well, answer me."

"I . . . I . . . I . . . what do you mean? I don't under . . ."

"He told you about the King Tut. I could recognize that gold-mania stare all the way through the walls of a bank vault. I've seen that glazed look of greed since I was an infant."

"I thought you'd be thrilled that I'm to be partners with your father."

"Thrilled? Thrilled?" And now she stood up and walked to a wall before turning. "Thrilled at the chance to see someone else I love maimed or dead? My God, he's been crippled for years from trying to climb that bluff looking for more. More. Always more. He was an old man then. I'd just lost my mother and my husband, and he falls off that damned rock and nearly dies. Did you know he dragged himself for three days just to get down to the old truck? Three days. His hands and the rest of his body were a solid bleeding sore."

"It seems to me that Ludwig showed great courage and love for you to survive all that."

"Courage? Oh, he's got plenty of that. But consideration? None. When the gold takes over and becomes all...all, do you hear? Then thoughts of others are secondary." She hesitated a moment, pushing at her hair and wringing her hands as if she wanted to twist the blood out of them.

She finally started to talk again. "We had no one left but each other. Oh, maybe somewhere in Germany or Ireland, and then...then he goes and climbs in the rocks like a kid."

"It was just professionalism. You have to know if the vein is long enough to risk the expense of digging. That's the way it is."

"You sound just like him. There's always some excuse—some reason to perpetuate the obsession—the madness. I thought you were different. I thought you wanted to make a home here with me...with us."

"I do. I do. I love you, Mary, and I want to be with you all my life."

"Ha...haaa..." She stomped about, looking unnaturally awkward and repulsive for a moment. Then she was quiet and, still breathing heavily, cast her all-enveloping blue eyes on him, saying softly, "You'll let the mad dream go, won't you, Blue?"

"Well...I can't, Mary."

"What do you mean, you can't?" she screamed, her eyes suddenly turning green as malachite and hard as sculptor's marble. "Are you so weak that you simply can't say no? I thought you were a man. You're just a little, measly wimp. A joiner." This last hurt deeply, but Bluefeather made a desperate effort to understand.

"But I gave my word to your father. It's his last dream. I'd rather die than take that away from him. Don't you see?" He begged, "Mary, I'll be careful. I'm young. I'm strong. I'm experienced. We'll all be rich."

"'Rich, rich, rich'—that's the word that never leaves gold. They're glued together so strongly that families, friends, homes, and lovers are ripped apart and destroyed, but not 'gold' and 'rich.' Oh, no." She was shaking now and beginning to choke to hold back her sobs.

Bluefeather had to reach her somehow and make her believe him. "I have never let gold possess me, darling. Please believe me when I tell you it never could, never will."

"Listen to you. Just listen. Empires have fallen. Millions upon millions of people slaughtered, tortured, until madness sets in on both the robbed and the robber. It's never stopped. It never will."

"But I'm different. Me. Bluefeather Fellini. I'm not the same as the others. I swear to you, I'll dig only what gold we need. That's all. No more. Ever. I give my promise to you on that, the same as I did your father. Both promises can be accommodated and honored."

"So you're going ahead with it? My father hypnotized you with his dreams. You're crazy. You're both crazy—filled with yellow madness."

"You are not hearing me correctly." Now he was shouting. "I said that I could keep both promises. I give you this vow on my soul. I will never let the gold obsess or dominate me in any manner that would jeopardize our love, but you must know that I have to keep my word to your father, or nothing matters—not friendship, not love, not honor, not gold."

He was exhausted and drained from the shouting, but not Mary Schmidt O'Kelly. She trembled even more, broke into sobs and moans of anguish beyond his reach, and then grabbed the coffeepot and hurled it at him. It splashed its contents about the room, clanging loudly in a strange tune with her own terrible angst.

"Get out. Go away. I hate you. I never want to see you again. Never, ever again."

With a pain so dull and deep it was not of his body but some other part of him, he tried to speak the right words to salvage something very special that was being lost—tossed away, like cold, winter ashes.

She scrambled for the kitchen, running into tables, and picked up a meat cleaver still screaming things he couldn't or wouldn't hear. He barely got the latch to the outside door open before she attacked him.

He walked away in the snow path, his shoulders humped up like a cow's back in a blizzard. His heart beat erratically in fear and unspeakable sadness. There was no measurement for such a loss.

Sixteen

He had wanted to stop in and talk to Ludwig about the disaster, but it would not be proper. Mary was his only child. He had to face that. Now was the time he could have used another friend in Breen, but he only had a few acquaintances.

He thought about going to one of the three saloons and getting drunk. He discounted that thought faster than he had discovered it. Bluefeather didn't drink except for pleasure...for fun. So he went to the shed and fed the mules two hours early. They only smelled the grain and picked at the hay. They knew something was mightily wrong with their partner and moved about nervously, observing with both their large eyes and ears.

"Oh, cherished ones, my heart is in torment and my soul dangles over the escarpment of hell. We...we have lost our new partner. She has cast me out and beyond her, for reasons that are wrong but understandable. She has taken her tragic losses of recent years with much bravery and good cheer, but underneath she must have suffered the distress of the damned. I see it clearer now. She finally reached the point where she couldn't even think of any more losses of loved ones. Is that it? Am I right, Jackknife? Is my thinking correct, Nancy? I see that you feel I'm on the right track."

Bluefeather whammed the bottoms of his clenched fists into the walls of the shed, shaking it and causing the mules acute concern.

"What does understanding Mary's hidden feelings matter when the entire world has been ripped into fragments? Huh? Huh?" He demanded a reasonable answer from the mules and himself, but none came.

Bluefeather went to his house and built up the fire until it roared and the iron stove seemed to bounce from the floor. He tried to eat but threw up. He opened a book and the words were all blurred and made him nauseous again.

He stretched out on the bed and tried to sleep. Nothing worked. He saw Miss Mary. Her eyes washed him in lustrous light, her voice soothed and excited him all at once. Her body moved in rhythms that gave him pleasure to the point of blankness, blindness—the nonknowing of the ultimate intent of love and creation. Hours passed before he moved.

He rebuilt the fire, but the room was still cold, so he walked about, back and forth, like a newly caged coyote. His stomach felt like he had been disemboweled and his temples pounded as if he had competed in a head-butting contest with a bull buffalo.

He was still up when the sun rose. By then he had another affliction. Someone had extracted all the blood and bone from his legs and filled them with water one degree below freezing. His thoughts rattled around in his head and made weird, uncontrollable sounds.

He craved to cry and sob aloud to relieve the rusty barbed wire that was rapidly tightening around his heart, killing him for sure. Had he known that Mary suffered even more, he would either have started feeling better or fallen dead. The pain from torn and lost love finally caused him to feel like he was floating around the room with a high fever.

At last, on the beginning of the third day, he fell belly-down on his bed and sobbed so long and hard he threw his back out of place. This bit of destruction hurt so badly, he only thought of losing Mary two out of every three minutes now.

Bluefeather had slept so hard from pure emotional exhaustion that he had forgotten about his dislocated back. He stood up and started to stretch. A pain that truly made him go blind struck his whole body, and he fell to the floor. He was afraid to move for a spell, but then, pushing himself slowly to a sitting position with the strength of his arms alone, he braced for the shock of expected misery from his lower back. It didn't come. Cautiously he eased to his feet. It was gone. The fall had knocked it back into place.

He was so relieved that he built a fire and cooked a big breakfast of coffee, sourdough biscuits, venison, eggs, and milk gravy. And ate it all. Of course, it was his first meal in several days. He tried to count them. Two? Three? Five? A million? Well, somewhere in there.

He heated some water in a large pan, shaved, and took a sponge bath. He put on clean clothes and actually combed at his tangled black hair. He raised one knee up and then the other. The back held. This gave him enough courage to actually make a decision. By damn it, he was not going to let the woman of his life get away.

He had just put on a heavy coat along with a muffler and was reaching for his hat when he heard the tentative knock. He hung the hat back on the hook and moved to the door. He could see the outline of a figure through the frosted glass as it tapped hesitantly again. Could it be...? Was it possible that...?

His breath was suddenly hard to find, even though it was strong enough to heave his chest up and down above his thrashing heart. He opened the door, close to fainting.

The air was turned to frost as her lips, red as her hair, moved and said, "May I come in before I freeze to death?"

"Oh...oh sure, come on in here." He stepped as far aside as he could when she entered, then swiftly but gently closed the door.

She untied the scarf over her head, unwound the muffler from her neck, then straightened up bravely like a Joan of Arc and said with much firmness, "I'll work the mines with you. Then we'll both know what is what. All right?"

Bluefeather could certainly be forgiven for stuttering and saying nothing clearly.

Mary continued in a businesslike manner that would have made the secretary of the treasury proud, "I know all about the worldwide superstition of impending doom if a female enters a mine. It all started in Wales when a lady member of the royal family inspected a mine and immediately afterward there was an explosion and a cave-in, killing many miners. Yes, I know about that, and I also know that she had inspected several other mines that week where nothing of obvious danger occurred. You're not superstitious, are you, Blue?"

"Oh no...no, of course not. There's not a superstition," he swallowed hugely, "in my whole body. In fact...this will be just wonderful, because you and I know it is all foolishness." His excitement was escalating. "But all the other foolish prospectors will be afraid to come near our mine. Oh yes, Miss Mary...why, it's just made to order for us." He was hastily removing his coat and saying, "Would you like some coffee?"

She hesitated a blink and said, "No. Not now."

Then, in a synchronized movement, their flesh moved together from the floor to the tops of their heads, and between kisses, Mary said with an infinite sound of relief, "Oh, Blue. Blue."

And he said, "Oh Mary. My Miss Mary."

Moving, still clinging together, they sought a more comfortable spot. They eventually found it and everything fit in its proper place.

The branches had been traumatically stripped from the pines, but the trunks had held strong. Now the branches grew back new and even stronger, in an amazing few minutes.

Seventeen

All the denizens of the Breen area suffered the long winter of deep snows and iron-bending cold with commendable fortitude, but now that the patches of brown earth and vegetation were widening daily, they became irritable and fussy, issuing complaints at the slightest cause. It was the in-between time.

Mary and Bluefeather rode the mules, nearing home. The sun still slanted low, but nonetheless gave some warmth and a touch of promise to the ever-nearing, full awakening of the earth and all its seed. They had gone south for their outing where the mules could bypass the snow with ease. The last mile home, they dismounted to walk. It was warmer that way.

They led the mules and held each other's free hand. Their youth, health, and love of loves awaited the green flush of spring with impatience. They felt like springtime, just as the weeks nearing would be.

Bluefeather chuckled to himself and said to Mary, "You know what? We'll have to name our first child America. Nothing else will do. He will be Indian, Italian, German, and Irish. If that isn't America I can't conjure it up."

"America Ludwig Fellini. America...Ludwig...Fellini. Yes, it does have the ring of the nation."

They chattered on about spring, the wedding and the mine. As they neared their houses, both sets of eyes looked at Clock Hill, checking the evaporating snowbanks by immeasurable inches.

Bluefeather unwrapped the beryl crystal he had chiseled several years earlier from a pegmatite dike south of Taos near Penasco. Now he was glad he had not given it to Nancy. The six-sided gemstone was the most beautiful he had ever found. He put his glass on it. Clear, blue light radiated out of it like the birth of a tiny planet. To him, it was lovelier than a solid gold bar, more precious than a large well-watered ranch or a royal castle. He was sure the jewel had been invented by the Creator especially for Miss Mary, whose eyes were often the same color—with the same dancing lights. So he sent it off to Denver to be mounted in silver for a necklace, and he ordered a diamond wedding ring from a Saint Louis catalog. They both miraculously arrived at the post office on the same day.

He immediately rushed home to get a full view of Clock Hill. There were only two snowbanks visible in the shady portion of a long draw. The time of union was near.

His gold dust was gone and his cash was getting short. They would need money for the trip to Durango and the lavish party they were planning. After the wedding there would be the expenses of powder, dynamite caps, drills, and just plain living to fulfill his promise to both his good amigo Ludwig and the other half of his bouncing, gleeful soul, Miss Mary of Breen.

He knew a way he could earn the money. It was his honor and his duty to do so. He would win it using the trade Nancy had so carefully taught him. Suddenly, he no longer resented the incidents at Tonapah so much. Maybe the experiences, both delightful and deadly, could be transposed and used on a grand adventure of love. Maybe.

His footsteps became livelier as the idea became more acceptable to him. The purpose was very strong in his soul, and he began to appreciate the thrill that was beginning to stir in him. It was almost the same feeling he got when hunting deer rabbits or other wild game for food.

The Breen Palace Hotel was small in room numbers, but it had a large bar with a dance floor. On Friday and Saturday nights a three-piece band consisting of a fiddle, banjo, and guitar played there. The First Thought Bar, as it was called, had a steady clientele of miners, businessmen, salesmen, and a few ranchers. On the weekends it howled with revelry. However, the most expensive action took place two doors behind the bar. Patrons had to pass through a large storeroom to get to the gaming room.

The bar was luxuriously appointed for this sparsely settled area. A fireplace with a five-foot open face had a large framed original oil painting of a reclining nude hanging above it. On one wall hung a print of Custer's Last Stand that was passed around the West by an alcohol manufacturer. It showed Custer standing, fighting gloriously,

amidst thousands of charging Indians whose bullets, spears, tomahawks, and arrows had somehow missed him.

There were several soft-cushioned leather couches and chairs. A
walnut, glassed-in liquor cabinet, with accompanying front bar, held all
the mixes of the time. Just beyond the huge fireplace was a green, felt-
covered poker table. It was well-lighted and covered with ashtrays. It
had been in almost constant use for twenty-five years now.

Skimpy Jones ran and banked the game. Although he played as an
outsider, he took ten percent of each pot for the house. Even if Skimpy
himself sometimes lost, the house always won. The players got new cards
whenever they asked, and free drinks as long as no one got rudely drunk.
If this happened, Skimpy, who weighed around three hundred pounds—
a hundred of that was belly- and face-swelling fat—would escort the violator out in whatever manner it took. Admittance to this back room was
gained only if one knew the bartender. Bluefeather knew him from his
many meals at Mary's Place, so he was immediately passed through.

The first night he played, Bluefeather lost a little money and quit about
midnight. He was studying the game and feeling his way. The next night,
Friday, he felt the high voltage as he walked in. There was a lot of money
in front of the five players. The game had started about two o'clock in the
afternoon, and seven or eight players had already gone broke by six o'clock
that evening.

Stan Berkowitz seemed to have the most chips, but Skimpy was a
very close second. Wally Ward, the railroad super, also played. There was
a mining promoter from Denver, who the players called Birmingham and
who had a noticeable southern accent. The last surviving player was the
owner of the light, telephone, and utilities company of Breen, Saul Kahn.

Bluefeather mixed himself a light bourbon and water and told
Skimpy he would wait for the next empty chair. In about thirty minutes
Kahn stood up saying he had guests coming for dinner, and since he
was nearly even he would cash in. Bluefeather took his seat. It was the
nearest one to the fireplace, and he was directly across the table from
his one-time rival for Mary's favors, Stan Berkowitz.

The game grew in intensity as the night deepened. They switched
games often here. Instead of playing draw or five-card stud all the time,
they played hi-lo-split a lot and seven-card stud poker. The house rules
were dealer's choice. So a player who was unable to almost instantly
adjust his mind to a new game could wind up a loser.

The players came and went except for Bluefeather, Skimpy, and Stan. In the fog of smoke and concentration of Bluefeather's personal mind-clock, time ceased to exist. He had no idea whether the other players had sat in for the jolting, high-adrenaline charge of a full house, or for four of a kind, or whether some of them just needed the money. The players changed like substitutes in a basketball game.

Bluefeather knew that he and Skimpy were playing for a grub-stake and a living, in that order. Bluefeather always sipped his drinks slowly, very slowly, so that the players who drank more heavily would not start watching him, feeling he was setting sober traps.

So far it had been an honest game, except for the salesman who had tried to deal the second card but had done it so awkwardly he never tried it again. Bluefeather deliberately had run a couple of bluffs on bad hands to get caught so that later, when he did have a locked hand and the pot was big enough, he would be able to suck the other players in.

Sometime after midnight, a player from Taos sat in next to Bluefeather. At two o'clock in the morning, Bluefeather was two thousand dollars ahead. That was surely enough to supply their needs for the trip to Durango and get the gold moving out of the King Tut.

Bluefeather played carefully now. Since he was the principal winner, he knew it only natural that everyone at the table was after his jugular. That's the way he liked it.

The last loser had said it was two o'clock in the morning when he gave up his chair, so Bluefeather guessed it was now about three o'clock. That, of course, is the "genius hour" when drinkers—real tough drinkers—think they know everything in the entire world. That's when Bluefeather planned to knock them off. The kill.

There was just one problem: the man from Taos had somehow wrangled it out of Bluefeather that he had once lived there. Between deals the Taos man made unusual small talk, asking if Bluefeather knew this merchant, this artist, that remittance person. Since Bluefeather knew none of these people, the man obviously thought he was a liar and a phony and was making small hints to that effect.

"You must have been just a baby when you left Taos if you don't remember the artist Joseph Sharp. Everyone knows him. Ol' Joe is a legend in Taos and so is Long John Dunn."

"I'm sorry to say, I have heard of them both, but I never knew either of them personally."

"How could you miss Long John? He ran the stagecoach lines into Taos in the early days, and even at his age he's still dealin' at Mike Cunico's place."

"Just my bad luck, I guess." Bluefeather tried to dismiss the subject.

Everyone was staring at the two men now. Stan Berkowitz, who had been extra polite all night, now had that genius-hour grin on his face from boozing. The rising and falling of adrenaline over and over had left him somewhat narcotized. Skimpy was not much better off.

That's when the hand Bluefeather had waited for for two nights fell. Stan had dealt the cards himself. Four kings and a deuce. Bluefeather threw away the deuce and drew a queen. He was hoping they would think he was going for a straight and had missed. He started his bluff just as he had done before. He acted just a little overanxious as he immediately raised the pot a hundred, then two, then three. It was close to perfection.

Three opponents, Stan, Skimpy, and Mr. Taos, must have drawn good cards, too, for they stayed. Mr. Taos was done and in for the pot on the second raise. Skimpy was in for another pot on the fourth. Then Bluefeather surprisingly checked. He figured there was six or seven thousand dollars in the pot. It was more than enough. He figured Stan would come at him with all his remaining chips, but Stan checked as well, sensing too late what had happened.

Stan turned over his three jacks and two tens. When he looked at Bluefeather's four kings, he got up and poured himself another drink and came back saying to Skimpy, "Deal 'em, Skimpy. If my check's good, this game just got started." He took a swallow of whiskey and said, "I can't let this newcomer beat me at everything."

Bluefeather felt the bristle hairs on his neck rise and speak to him in warning, but he knew he had to stay another hour or so. If he tried to leave, Stan would surely insult him. Even Skimpy, Taos, and the other player would all know they had been suckered for their greed. No. He would play another hour and even more carefully lose a thousand or so back.

It wasn't working. The remarks from Stan kept coming and then Mr. Taos finally drove it all home with a direct question just as Bluefeather was shuffling the cards to deal. "Exactly where did you live in Taos?"

Bluefeather had been so totally involved in handling the game properly for Mary, Ludwig, and their partnership that the question caught him at the wrong instant. "I didn't exactly live in town. I spent a lot of time at the Taos Pueblo visiting my grandfather."

"Oh, so he taught at the Indian school there, huh?"

Then Bluefeather really blew it. "No, my grandfather is a medicine man named Moon Looker. My mother is Morning Star."

"Then...then you're an Indian? A Taos Indian? You don't look like..."

"I'm half Italian."

"Say, it's agin the law to sell drinks to an Indian, and it's agin the law for you to buy one."

"I didn't buy any drinks. These were given to me."

Stan said, just as Bluefeather finished dealing and before he looked at his cards, "You bought into the game and the whiskey is part of it, huh, Skimpy?"

Skimpy looked around and added up the situation like any good professional. Mr. Taos was a very successful car dealer—not to be counted lightly. Stan Berkowitz was a regular player and steady customer with very strong local connections in the mines—where three-fourths of this establishment's business came from. The other player was the owner of a large cattle ranch with landholdings in both New Mexico and Colorado and was also a friend and strong supporter of the governors of both states. Skimpy was naturally respectful of such a powerful person.

He took a quick tally and said, "Stan's right. The Indian was deceiving us and breaking the law by buyin' in, because the whiskey sure as hell goes with the deal."

They all four, plus an onlooker friend standing behind Stan, stared at Bluefeather. The silence seemed extended through many changes of seasons and much eroding of rocks. He felt enclosed in a tight shroud made up of thoughts and eyesight so strong it could crush him into breathlessness.

A light somehow flickered in his brain. It was true, after all, there was always one son of a bitch to throw gravel in the gears. The man from Taos, who should have been his friend and compatriot, was that one.

Stan said as he looked around for support, "In a case like that, I reckon house rules would call for the Indian to return the money, huh, Skimpy?"

Skimpy nodded "yes" and clicked a stack of blue chips up and down in a hand so big and fat the chips were hardly visible. He puffed on the fat cigar between his thick lips, and the smoke clouded his face so that Bluefeather could not see his eyes already slit and almost closed by surplus flesh.

The coldness of fear, of danger, emanated from Bluefeather's being, and the bristles of his neck were about ready to scream and leap out of his skin. He saw a year's worth of looking in just a few seconds. Hours ago, he had, out of habit and training at Nancy's establishment, spotted a sawed-off ax handle just behind Skimpy and the fireplace iron that was almost within reach. Bluefeather rubbed at the sudden burning of the thin scar between his eyebrows.

Skimpy was huge, experienced, and mean but he would be slow. He figured to get Mr. Taos first. Stan was bigger than he was and, according to what he had heard, had a punch that would make a water buffalo cringe. Stan's friend's power was probably just under that or he would not be that close to the mine super. The rancher was totally unknown to Bluefeather. He was a year or so younger than Bluefeather, about five feet eleven inches, and built strong all the way, except his hands looked a little delicate. He might be carrying a gun. Well, Jim the rancher was just about his size except for the hands, but he was probably a gouger, kicker, and biter—anything to protect himself.

There were two out of the five, Stan and Skimpy, who had a chance to take Bluefeather if they got in an early blow. So he had it figured. He had to shock them so that their forces were scattered, and he, in truth, would be taking them on one at a time if—if he moved with enough speed. He knew without having to analyze that each man must go down wounded badly enough to stay down.

They waited for him to answer; all those staring eyes expecting explanations, a bartering suggestion, or possibly even a bit of begging.

Bluefeather grabbed the ashtray in front of Skimpy, threw it and its contents in his face and at the same time whacked his left elbow on the bridge of Mr. Taos's nose. Taos went down screaming with the blood, struggling all at once for a way out of his badly broken nose.

While Skimpy was trying to scratch the ashes out of his eyes with one hand and reach for Bluefeather with the other massive one, Bluefeather got to the shillelagh and brought it down across the sixth cervical of Skimpy's neck as hard as he had ever swung a miner's pick.

As Skimpy dropped to his knees bellowing, cursing, pawing at the air for something to crush, Bluefeather swung the ax handle so hard along Skimpy's jaw that he thought the piece of hardwood had snapped. He was wrong. It was the jaw that was broken.

Bluefeather saw a blur somewhere and punched his weapon at it like a sword. The blur moved back saying "Aggggh." There was another blur to his side. He ducked under it and swung the ax handle low with great force. It made a popping noise that felt good as it busted Stan's right kneecap in three parts, driving some splinters of bone between the joints.

Stan rolled, screaming and cursing right beside Skimpy, who now just frothed at the mouth, spitting out blood and teeth to keep from choking to death. Now Stan's friend, who had been knocked backward, came at Bluefeather with a chair. Bluefeather ducked the blow but it came down on one of his kidneys. His breath went as he dropped to one knee. As the man raised the chair for the coup de grace, Bluefeather drove the ax handle, with every last tiny fiber of strength he had, into the man's port of entry. The chair went sailing out over him right into the fireplace. While Stan's friend was bending over moaning and holding his pulverized privates, Bluefeather bounced the flat side of the weapon off the side of the man's face, fracturing his cheekbone, knocking six teeth loose, and turning his nose forever south.

Bluefeather whirled to the side, and there stood Jim pointing a .38 special at his belly, smiling as if he had just sold five thousand head of steer for the biggest money ever paid. Ordinarily Bluefeather would have taken time to consider maybe making some kind of careful statement or cautious negotiation with a man who pointed a gun at him and grinned like that, but he was still full of mad.

When the chair burst into flames in the fireplace it popped exactly like a gun. Even one as sharp and watchful as Jim was fooled. He whirled pointing the gun at the new enemy. That's when Bluefeather, aiming to sidewind him in the jaw, hit him full in the ear so that it knocked the rancher spinning, and he dropped the gun.

Bluefeather kicked the gun across the room where it scooted under the whiskey cabinet. Jim came out of his whirl and kicked one of his fancy boots at Bluefeather. His aim was awry, as he was yet off balance from the blow to his ear. Bluefeather grabbed Jim's leg and twisted the ankle out of place, while at the same time jerking his foot as high as he could. He pounded one of his heavy prospector's boots right where the rancher was spread into a wide Y. Jim joined the others on the floor, but he had difficulty concentrating his moans on any one spot—he was wrecked from top to bottom. When he could talk, Jim gurgled out, regretfully holding his hurting places as much for protection as pain, "By the Almighty, I'll never, ever forget this shame. I didn't get to play a single hand of poker and still got the shit kicked out of me."

Bluefeather slapped him upside the face again, and Jim became the quietest he would ever be for the rest of his life. Bluefeather turned and kicked the Taos man in the belly, saying, "You're the goon who started all this. You're gonna remember to keep your stupid mouth shut or I'm gonna empty it of teeth and fill it with a two-by-four."

The Taos man rolled over twice, stifling bad feelings and bad thoughts, and stared at the little stain of blood on the floor as if it had dropped from the palms of Jesus Christ.

Stan Berkowitz, the mining super, had never let up his bawling and bellowing, "My balls, my balls, my balls are mashed. What am I ever gonna do without my balls? I'll be helpless as a little baby. Oh, my God. My God."

Bluefeather gave him the most considerate, comforting answer he could think of, considering the activities that had led to his becoming indignant and resentful. "You got most of that correct, Stan. A great big, young, and healthy man like yourself can't get a hell of a lot going without his balls. Even so, you're about the luckiest man in all the Southwest."

Stan stopped moaning for a second and, although his tongue could not utter the question, his tortured eyes expressed, "How's that?"

Bluefeather graciously answered, "Why that's obvious...I didn't scalp you...you lucky son of a bitch."

Stan was trying to stand up. Bluefeather kicked him precisely on the tailbone; this time he stayed down hurting so badly that he could only gasp out dull, moaning sounds.

It should have been over, but Bluefeather grabbed a chair and braced it under the knob of the door to the storeroom. He need not have bothered. The place had cleared out at half past one, and the last worker had left at least thirty minutes before the disagreement had set in.

Bluefeather hurled the ax handle into the fireplace where the chair looked like the skeleton of a small monster as it was engulfed in flames. Then he got the fireplace poker and walked back and forth around the room punching people with its heavy, sharp end to be sure they would hear what he was about to say.

"Now, I've still got some mad left in me so don't any of you bastards interrupt. You hear?" When there was no answer, he jabbed Skimpy in the belly and tapped Stan on his good leg's shinbone. "I said, do you hear?"

There were nods and even some words that sounded like "yes."

"Well, that's better." Now and then he swung the iron in the air like a baseball bat. "I am a crusader against injustice—especially when I'm the victim. I want all of you to know, if either Miss Mary Schmidt O'Kelly or her father hears one word of this in the form of gossip, written words or any other way, I'm gonna look up your milk cows, your chickens, your kids, and maybe your wives, and I'm gonna spank 'em real good, you hear?"

There were quick nods of understanding now.

Bluefeather continued, "And if that ain't enough I'll waylay every one of you and split your bag and run your leg through it. Then I'll really get mean. Now, my Indian ancestors were here thousands of years before anyone else and then one of my other blood brothers—old Columbus—was hired by the Spanish, and he came over here and found the Indians. So you folks are all latecomers to this part of the world. You still hearing me? Huh? Huh?"

Much affirmation amid stifled groans could be ascertained.

He continued, "I repeat. If one sentence, or even a part of a sentence, gets back to my people, on top of everything else I'm going to do to you, I'll put a Tiwa Indian curse on you that will last through every member of every one of your families for a thousand years. And if that doesn't get it done, with the rest of my blood I'll put out a Sicilian hex that will hold good for ten generations of pestilence, plague, and penury."

He calmed down now and put the poker back in its holder with care. He walked slowly around the room kicking each man in the ribs with a light but solid tap to be sure the battlefield contained no dead. He counted his chips twice to be fair and told Skimpy he wanted $6,033. Skimpy pointed to the tin box on the shelf where the ax handle had been. Bluefeather counted the cash twice to be certain it was correct. He didn't want a cent—not one—that wasn't his.

He took the chair out from under the doorknob and returned it to its proper place by the gaming table, which amazingly only had one leg askew. He walked proudly through the storeroom, the whiskey and smoke funnel bar, lifted the bar door lock. As he stepped out into the cold, star-speckled night with a half moon sitting on top of the massive black mountains, he took a deep breath of air and walked toward home.

A coyote was yapping and howling just outside town trying to sound like a dozen. Bluefeather just could not help it. He raised his head and howled right back. He could feel the thick bulge in his pocket packed full with his honest day's work.

Eighteen

Mary, Ludwig, and Bluefeather were watching the snow on Clock Hill almost hourly now. The two remaining drifts were shrinking fast. They had to move swiftly to make the pledged date.

Bluefeather had heard it was against the rules—or maybe even the law—for either the groom or the bride to converse about their matrimonial garments. So he went it alone, although fearful of his choices and ability in this particular endeavor. He had no experience to guide him and hadn't attended a wedding since leaving the family home at Raton.

He had three handsome black suits left over from his gambling days in Tonapah, so he chose his favorite to have cleaned and pressed. He bought a new white shirt and a dress tie. He assumed that bow and string ties, common in houses of chance, might not be suitable for such a grand, if small, wedding party.

Mary, of course, had far more work to do than he because she had the responsibility of getting Ludwig ready and everything packed for the both of them. She also had to dispose of the restaurant. She leased it to the two ladies who had worked for her part time. The papers were drawn for one year with a two-year renewal and an option to buy after that. This gave Mary the freedom she needed to prepare for the wedding. She spent many anxious hours with the seamstress getting her wedding dress just right.

While Mary was away shopping, Ludwig called Bluefeather over to the house and presented him a bowler to try on for size. Unfortunately—at least in Bluefeather's mind—it fit perfectly. If Bluefeather had not loved and respected jackasses so much, he would have accused himself of looking like one in the silly little hat.

"Ah, yes, my dear Blue, it's an elegant fit to say the least. Yes...yes, Mary will be quite proud of you, sir."

Bluefeather said, "I sure do appreciate this, Ludwig. I would probably have had to travel all the way to Denver to find a hat like this."

"Oh, farther than that, my boy. Hats of this quality are only made in two or three places on the Eastern Seaboard."

Bluefeather had moved about town more in the last few days than he had in the ten previous months. People gave him great respect. There was even a fear, an awe. There was no question that something had leaked, no matter how distorted, of his devastation to the gamblers. But no one had breathed a word of it to Mary or Ludwig. That, he would have noticed. However, the intensity and worried concern of getting ready to bind with Miss Mary made him oblivious to this new respect—a respect that can come only in the conquering of very small towns or very large cities. Totally unbeknownst to him, a tiny legend had begun about Bluefeather Fellini.

Then it happened. Ludwig and Bluefeather were in the former's workroom going over the rough maps and other production ideas about the King Tut, when Mary charged into the house shouting with rapture.

"It's gone! It's gone!"

Before thinking the two men chorused, "What's gone?"

"The snow, you idiots. Now, my darlings, we leave on the 8:45 train in the morning." Mary's eyes were filled with the color of a clear, clean sky, and her naturally pink face was flushed to a shade near the color of a ripe watermelon heart. Her excitement radiated out, giving Bluefeather the tingling of a near lightning strike. He was certain the entire world shared their elation.

She said, "At last. At last. At last," throwing her head back and clasping her hands in front of her.

The train ride was quite an outing in itself. Scores of brand-new little streams cascaded in frothy good humor from the crevices in the canyons' sides, dropping finally into the wondrous Rio Bello just as Bluefeather and Mary would merge and begin to assail the world tomorrow. Wet wisps of mountain fog clung here and there. The fog was welcomed by the heavy growth of evergreens and made one's eyes strain to see wild creatures, both real and imaginary, in the primeval-appearing forest. The three were silent in their awe of the vitality of earth, water and trees.

After some two hours the canyon widened and little meadows of new grass were visible. The cows, horses, and sheep grazed in these open spaces relishing the tender, green treat. After a long winter of white cold and dry brown feed, the grass was like a before-dinner dessert to them, and they hardly ever raised their heads to look at the chugging train.

Birds were returning from the southern deserts. They flew about constantly chattering love messages and territorial threats before either sound-signal was ready to be consummated.

Mary and Bluefeather held hands, comfortable with each other's silence, absorbing the rebirth of their world all around. Ludwig had blossomed like the timbered canyons. His face glowed with a newness as well. The craggy features had softened and the corners of his mouth and the inner light of his eyes revealed the positive emotions besetting him. He could contain himself no longer. To hell with the lovebirds.

"Look. That's the tungsten mine I found in 1920. See it up the canyon there on the left? See the waste dump? And there, right there below those corrals, that's where my friend Eloy Irick was killed. You remember Eloy, don't you, Mary? Good man, Eloy, but foolish when on horseback. He was chasing a gut-shot lion and tried to jump that dead tree. It's still there." He strained to look back as a little spot from his past was left behind by the train disappearing in its smoke.

He talked on about the silver find at Leadville, Colorado; the copper prospect outside Billings, Montana; his long-dead dogs; his friends that were all gone now. He included Mary's mother, Ila, in most of his remembrances. He even mentioned, over and over, how hard the decision had been to leave the assaying business. "Hard on Ila and Mary, more than me, because I was out looking and digging up dreams. Little dreams. Broken dreams. Big dreams." Then his voice trailed off and both of the lovers had to strain to hear, "... the King Tut ... yes ... yes ..."

The canyon had dried and widened, and ranch houses and homesteads had become more prevalent. Then the ridges spread apart like the handles of a pair of steel pliers, and the wedding party looked at the top of Durango, Colorado.

Inside the historic Strater Hotel, Mary fussed about in the bedroom of their suite, dressing. Bluefeather was in Ludwig's room across the hall. Ludwig waited impatiently, roaming in and out of both rooms, stopping in front of first one mirror and then another to adjust his vest, straighten his tie, or tilt the fedora just a mite more. He liked the feel of the gold watch in his vest and the gold head on what he called his "exorbitant cane."

Finally he knocked on his daughter's door, and she asked him in for a final inspection before the main event. He drew his breath in with delight. "You are divine, my dear. You—especially in that dress and veil—would have made Cleopatra jealous and Josephine rant and rage. Now let me be off to check on our groom."

Bluefeather met him in the hall. He stood and posed. "Well, what do you think?"

Ludwig paused a moment, tilting his head from right to left, inspecting Bluefeather. "As for you, dear fellow, just tilt the bowler ever so slightly. As I see it, that's the only touch I might suggest."

Bluefeather obliged.

"That's right,...now back about a half inch...ah yes...we are ready, I'd say. Ready for the ball."

Mary stepped into the hallway. Bluefeather was speechless at the sight of his beautiful bride-to-be.

And so with an arm on each side of Ludwig, so he could hang the gold handle in the slight bend of one elbow, they marched down the stairs, out of the hotel and along the main street to the justice of the peace.

After the ceremony they were escorted by the maître d' to a private room off the main dining room in the hotel. There was already a magnum of fine champagne chilling and a tray of delicate appetizers awaiting their arrival. Bluefeather had arranged for a private waiter. He was a middle-aged Mexican man with an exquisite, thin mustache and a neatly trimmed beard below a head of iron-black hair.

Bluefeather also had arranged for the music. He imported Ramon Hernandez from the tiny immigrant coal-mining town of Dawson, thirty-five miles southwest of Raton, where he was as highly respected for his music as the Taos masters were for their paintings—even though he was barely grown. Ramon was smiling broadly as he placed the guitar strap around his neck. He not only loved his work but enjoyed every note like a new adventure or gift.

Bluefeather poured champagne for the three of them and yelled at Ramon, "Hey, *compadre*, would you care for a tilt before you play?"

Ramon was pleased by the offer but politely refused for the time being. He was a professional and would drink only when his duty was done. He started playing an old Spanish love song very softly. His music was soul-satisfying and made the fine food taste even better.

Bluefeather didn't really care much for champagne, but he kept this to himself. During the eleven months the three had been together, it had become a ritual game with them to make toasts to many things, but now, right here, was the top time of toasting.

Ludwig had the honor of offering the first one tonight. "To life, love, and music."

Bluefeather swallowed the French liquid saying, "To earlier, to later, to now. To my family of the 'forever' world." Of course they all knew there was no such thing as forever, but it sounded right at the moment.

Then Mary raised her glass high and uttered, "For the fine times, and the trying times, but always to our times."

Bluefeather yelled, Ludwig clapped, and Ramon grinned broadly and kept on playing. Their waiter waited. Their toasts continued.

"To the moon's mother."

"To the father of the universe."

"To all the ships on all the oceans."

"To all the sailors on all those ships."

"To the cactus and the coyote."

"To music of all tongues."

The waiter started serving the meal. Everything was elegantly presented from soup to dessert—the latter, of course, being a double-tiered wedding cake. Bluefeather and Mary cut the first slice together and fed each other big bites.

Now the mariachi band came in with sombreros, big as umbrellas, and played. The musicians circled the room and yelled as they tilted their heads. The music was wild. The laughter was happy.

Ramon had a drink with them, making his own toast to the newlyweds, "May your days be filled with work and laughter, your nights with love and rest, your life with dancing children of delight."

Everyone clapped and even the mariachi players joined in the applause. It was their cue to play their way out of the room, and it was also the cue for the violinist to join Ramon and play the first dance, but Bluefeather made them wait as he took the beryl necklace from his pocket and placed it around Mary's neck. Bluefeather had planned for this to be presented with some gracious, profound statement, but he couldn't remember the three or four hundred lines he had memorized then cast away, searching for a better one, so he said, "Darling, I dug it up myself."

Mary grabbed him and pulled his head down, saying, "That makes it so very, very special. I shall never take it off."

As the groom guided his bride around the table for the first dance, Ludwig stopped them, took out his prospecting glass, and examined the gleaming new stone hanging between his daughter's breasts.

He exclaimed, "I found a yellow one once in Colombia, but it was not as lovely as this."

Ramon and the violinist started right back at the beginning as Bluefeather and Mary began dancing slowly, slowly. They held each other and felt the moment with all of themselves. The room turned with the music under their feet, without effort on their part being necessary. It was their private heaven for this little time in eternity, all enclosed with their scent, their touch, their taste, and their flesh and souls becoming the same.

Then, as if coming slowly out of a perfumed anesthesia, they awakened and went to Ludwig. Bluefeather helped him to his feet. He took his only daughter, his only known kin, in his arms to dance, but Mary nodded at Bluefeather and he understood that the intoxication of the evening may have been too much for her father. So Bluefeather danced with them.

The trio worked perfectly. Ludwig was held up by them but also was separate and leading the dance. They went around slowly again and again. Ludwig's old heart pumped other songs from long, long ago into his eardrums. The slow little threesome moved across the floor as they patiently circled and finally arrived back at Ludwig's chair. He braced himself against it, and with some risk gave them a bow as gracious and meaningful as grand opera.

One last glass of special imported brandy and the ceremony was closed. The musicians were gone, but the essence of the day and night permeated the air and their hearts like the scent of a mile-high rose garden.

Ludwig was in his bed already sleeping and dreaming things that were special and known only to him. The La Plata Mountains were framed in the window like a calendar painting of the Swiss Alps, their white upper reaches way off behind foothills and the warmth of the room.

The light from a tiny lamp cast a soft, bronze-colored glow around the man and woman. Bluefeather took her hands, trying to look and put himself behind her wide, waiting eyes.

He spoke softly as a breeze from a butterfly's wings, "I shall love you past history."

And she whispered, "I shall love you longer than memory."

They held each other. They were silent and immobile for a spell. The man and the woman could hear an old, old song from before their births—from before fossils. The ancient melody accompanied them to bed.

Nineteen

Bluefeather insisted, and Mary agreed, that they get a camp set up before they started digging the crosscut marked on Ludwig's map. He had covered it back up so carefully that a quick look revealed no changes in the overburden.

They chose a small clearing for their campsite, disturbing the bushes and trees as little as possible. These gave added protection from wind, provided more shade, and left the clearing's beauty unchanged. A tent held their double bed, and a tarp tethered out in front on strong poles added to the protected space. A rock-encircled fire pit would take care of the cooking until Bluefeather could get the wood-burning cookstove set up. With a rope, they hung their food box from a large limb to protect it from bears and insects. Some crude wooden shelves in the tent held their utensils. A table, which could be moved easily in and out of the tent for dining according to the weather or their whims, completed the necessities.

He had already cut enough firewood to last a month. His next task was to install a temporary hand pump in a deep hole at the nearby creek, which also held some nice brown trout.

Mary was busy getting the entire place in her own kind of order so she could do her share of the chores as easily as possible under the outdoor conditions. They had gone back and forth to town in the old truck every other day since the wedding, finishing the trip to the camp with the pack mules.

Ludwig wasn't concerned about any of this activity, even though he had experienced these setups dozens of times by himself. He was waiting for the dig. Well, now he would get it.

Bluefeather waited patiently until the sun totally illuminated the opening. Bending down, he narrowed his eyes like an art critic would to check out the patterns of shadows in a painting. At first, he felt helpless. He could discern no difference in the topsoil. Ludwig would have made a top trapper because of the way he could disguise a disturbance in the earth.

At last he saw the very slight differences in the patterns of the tiny shadows made by millions of fallen leaves, twigs, limbs, bird droppings, and everything else that had fallen for millions of years in the scattered forest. He was able to see the line of Ludwig's dig, and before he lost its strike, he dug spades of dirt several feet apart. His excitement was growing with every breath, every thought.

Bluefeather dropped the shovel on line with the old cut and went to tell Mary. They had made a pretty good guess. The camp was only twenty or thirty yards from the cut.

"Hey, Mary. I found it. I found the sign."

"Wait for me...wait till I finish unpacking these pans. I want to dig with you."

"It's okay. I'll do it."

"No...no, I want to help. I want to be there."

Bluefeather knew by her voice she was determined. So he waited. Then they dug the crosscut trench together, scraping down to solid soil with the shovels, then pitching the overburden back to form a trench. They were both perspiring in the still-crisp spring air, without noticing.

Bluefeather constantly tested the earth with his prospector's pick. Finally he heard the unmistakable ring as his shovel blade dragged across rock. He scraped the spot with much diligence and soon had the slightly undulating vein uncovered. He squatted wordlessly, as Mary stared down, digging furiously trying to dislodge a piece of the eight- or ten-inch-wide vein.

A small chunk finally broke loose. The damp earth was stuck to it so that its quality and content could not be judged correctly even after he had rubbed it with his hands and against his pants.

"Come on, let's go to the creek and wash it."

They ran without being aware of the hundred yards to the creek. He stepped into the edge without even noticing its wetness. The swift water helped the scrubbing of his hands. Then he raised up, stepped back on the bank, and fumbled to get his mineral glass in focus and adjusted to the bright sunlight. He smilingly handed it to Mary.

She looked and looked. "I can't see anything but rose quartz."

He pointed to the outer edge near one end. "Here. Look right here."

"Oh, yes, there it is. I see it. A nugget. No, it's wire gold. I see the tiny tendrils emanating from it now. My God," she said, "we found it. It's exactly like Daddy's rock." And even though she was a little ashamed at the tremendous burst of elation that encased and penetrated all of her being, she still fell into Bluefeather's arms as he held them open to her. They danced across the forest laughing and giggling as they whirled.

Mary sang like a little girl, "We found it. We found it. We found the pot of gold."

They danced up the hill, around trees, between trees, through the overburden, and in and out of strong shadows and brilliant streaks of light. Where the sunbeams touched her hair, they glowed orange; his hair shone as blue-black as newly tempered steel.

Finally they fell onto the soft layer of leaves and grass of the topsoil and rolled over, giggling like children on their first school recess, until stopped by a young sapling. They kissed and loved for the best reasons—the celebration of discovery.

When their breaths were back and their minds had stopped dancing and making love, Bluefeather knew he must find the location of the tunnel or shaft before they confronted Ludwig with the news he had waited for for so long.

The vein seemed headed in the general direction of a suddenly steep, rising slope where a huge boulder hung fifteen or twenty feet above it. They dug there and found it. Bluefeather was afraid if they tunneled under the boulder, it would hold an imminent danger of falling on them or possibly sealing them inside the tunnel. If so, it would have to be blasted apart.

He climbed up and around to examine it with much care and was elated to find that it was lodged between two outcroppings of solid rock. So there was no danger that he could see.

They knew exactly where to dig now, so they carefully covered the crosscuts just as Ludwig had done years before. Bluefeather was extremely pleased that they could tunnel in horizontally instead of having to dig a vertical or incline shaft. There would be no need for a head-frame, hand windlass, and ore bucket. They could avoid the terrible and constant battle with gravity involved in lifting the rock straight up.

Of course, there was also much to do in horizontal mining: acquiring and hauling dynamite and powder, cutting timbers to secure the entrance or maybe the entire tunnel, and clearing away the dropped ore were among the major things. Right now they would use a couple of large wheelbarrows, but later they might want to lay track and run an ore car.

All this would come shortly, but now they must return the great secret to its first finder, Ludwig Schmidt of Breen, Colorado, who waited with understandable trepidation for their return.

Bluefeather had forcefully stiffened his neck to keep from looking up across the jumbled boulders to the fore of the bluff that had maimed Ludwig. It couldn't be ignored. There it was waiting for him, not quite, but almost, perpendicular. The bluffs had just enough slope to make their climbing seem possible. The protruding sheets of rock would not relinquish their unavowed information freely.

The long-expected good news seemed to make Ludwig grow several inches in height, and the measurement of his bony chest showed a like expansion. He insisted they go out for dinner to the Railroad Cafe where they specialized in huge T-bone steaks. Bluefeather felt a little guilty that they didn't go to Mary's Place, even though it was leased out, but he also felt that the event called for something different.

It was an odd dinner. At the beginning they strained to speak softly and in riddles so that no other long-eared patron would know what they were talking about. Soon though, the game became fun just as their toasting ritual had. The old man seemed about fifty now in his movements and conversation.

They were so caught up in their own private world that Bluefeather had not noticed Stan Berkowitz with three strangers in a booth across the room. He hadn't even felt Stan's presence as yet. A dark sign indeed.

Stan was talking animatedly to the men as if he had not seen them in a while. He acted as if the people at Ludwig's table did not exist; but once, as he leaned forward across the table, gesturing with his strong hands as he talked, Bluefeather saw Stan shoot them a glance so swift, it could have been the natural movement of his eyes. But Bluefeather's days at the green-topped tables of Tonapah had taught him the difference; Stan was thinking of them under the disguise of other voices and movements.

For just a moment Bluefeather felt a slight irritation. Then his joyous thoughts and feelings dominated any emanations from Berkowitz, and his attention rejoined Mary and Ludwig as the old gentleman raised his glass of brandy. He held it out to theirs. They waited for the game to continue. It didn't. This was a toast too precious for Ludwig to express in words. He held his glass against theirs a long moment, looking from one to the other with a smile that was working itself inward from the surface. His eyes reflected his joy back out to his compatriots. He was filled with total contentment. They would never see him that way again.

■ ■ ■

Twenty

They went back to the mountain together, yet apart. Mary drove the small truck as far as the terrain would allow and walked the short distance on into camp. Bluefeather rode Nancy and led Jackknife, packed with the powder and caps, hand drills, iron bars, saws, and just about everything they would need to open a small operation like they planned.

He dug a small cave around the edge of the mountain, facing away from their camp. He framed it and built a door with a lock on it. This was their powder box to keep the explosives dry and safe.

He started picking at the mountain's overburden until he could shovel it free to the hard rock and the rich vein. Now he would have to dig holes for his dynamite and blast out an even face of rock.

He drilled by holding the forged steel rod against the rock face and pounding it in rhythm with a broad-faced heavy hammer. Bing. Bing. Bang. Over and over for hours. Then he used a longer drill rod called a bull prick. Hammer. Twist. Remove. Hammer. Hammer. The tiny holes were placed just right so they would shatter and drop the boulder into pieces. With a smooth wooden spatula, he carved a space in the dynamite for the explosive cap. He inserted a short fuse inside the cartridge-like cap and crimped the edges around it; this was then delicately placed in the dynamite and bound there. He placed a stick in each of the holes. The fuses were cut at slightly different lengths, so when he lit them, each would explode a split second apart allowing him time to count and keep track of those that had fired. This was terribly important, because an uncounted round could later blow a man's head off. It took many years of practice to do this perfectly.

If he had planned to mine on a larger scale, he would have used a battery box and long wires to set them off all at once, but here the old ways would be fine.

He set the fuse. He and Mary crouched around the curve of the mountain as he yelled, "Fire in the hole." This was an old, old unwritten law to protect any strangers walking by or workers nearby. With the shock of the first multiple explosions over, the work on the tunnel proceeded rapidly. He soon had the portal braced neatly and solidly with hand-hewn and notched logs.

Now was the dangerous period. They feared someone might unexpectedly walk up while they sorted out the rich ore that had been so clearly visible from the outside. They felt fortunate that no visitors appeared until they were about ten feet inside, where they could separate and hide the rich ore, thus leaving nothing but dead rock for anyone to see.

This safety point had just been reached when a lone prospector came through the clearing and saw Mary, a woman—the unthinkable—push a wheelbarrow out of the mine entrance. His eyes as well as his cringing movements showed his superstitious fears. He spoke but made every excuse to get his burro watered at the creek and remove himself from this dreadful travesty.

Bluefeather and Mary were pleased that the old superstition—a woman in a mine causes cave-ins or explosions—was still in powerful effect. Bluefeather was certain, and relieved, that word of this madness would spread swiftly and they would be left alone.

They sorted out the richest of the wire-gold ore, put it in gunnysacks, and hauled it back to the house in Breen. They always covered it with firewood or some other disguise. They secured it in the cellar, covered with loose straw. That would have to do until they had time to think of something better. They scattered the rest of the rose quartz in front of the slowly growing waste pile, immediately covering it with dead, worthless rock. In effect, their waste dump concealed ore of a secondary, but still valuable, assay. Even though there was no gold visible to the naked eye, a torch or smelter furnace would melt lots of minute specks of the yellow metal from the rocks.

On their third trip home with the high grade, they were surprised to find Ludwig gone. Mary drove down to the restaurant and had coffee. He wasn't there. She didn't bring up his absence because her lessees would have mentioned it if he had been in that day.

Bluefeather saw Ludwig's odd, limping tracks imprinted on the trail to the Rio Bello. He followed them and discovered him sitting on a chair overlooking the river, staring motionless across the waters toward the mountains. Bluefeather wondered how he had gathered the strength and courage to carry the chair, use the cane, and arrive safely. He was wearing a topcoat. Bluefeather felt it would be an infringement on the man's privacy to approach nearer. So he sat down, some distance away, and waited.

When the sun tipped the mesas to the southwest, Ludwig stood up stiffly, adjusting his cane, and walked with his permanent limp toward Bluefeather and his home.

Bluefeather dodged behind some bushes and walked swiftly back to the house just as Mary arrived. He felt as guilty as a spy spying on his own country. He told Mary what he'd seen and she became more worried and puzzled.

Soon Ludwig arrived. They prepared dinner and tried to share the day's adventures at the King Tut. They received mostly grunts, headshakes, and very little other communication from Ludwig. Every day he returned to the chair and stared across the space between himself and the mountain. He sat almost straight up with both his hands on his walking stick held between his legs.

Mary became so concerned with this strange behavior that she and Bluefeather both agreed she should stay home a few days with Ludwig instead of going back to the mine. She decided her father was just too lonely. It did no good. Bluefeather missed his new bride enormously, and Mary could establish no understandable contact with her father.

The next time Bluefeather returned home, Mary brought him up to date, speaking with confusion and compassion in her voice. "Blue, he just sits out there staring. He doesn't even move. It causes his joints to stiffen up even more, and he can barely make it back to the house. I keep feeling that someday he won't make it at all. I'm afraid he'll fall or something."

"I know. I know. He's having his half-visions, Mary."

"What do you mean, 'half-visions'?"

"Just that. I don't know how to put it in exact words, but... but he's not ours anymore, you see."

Then he couldn't explain further; she would just have to feel it for herself. Bluefeather knew the old man was preparing to go away—away to the next stop, to the next beginning that comes to all, sometimes suddenly, sometimes slowly, but eventually to all for dead certain.

Bluefeather knew that Ludwig was one of those few fortunate enough to be so highly honored by the spirits. He was being gifted with a little more time to stare backward at his old trails. It was the order of all things that Ludwig daydream the important times of his life so he would know what knowledge to save and take to his next birth. How could Bluefeather explain to Mary this special tribute that Ludwig had received? This complimentary time meant he could advance to the next dimension without fear of having to return and do more work and penance in the one he currently occupied. Bluefeather was very happy for his friend's unseen prestige, but Mary was suffering, feeling inept and unforgivably helpless.

Bluefeather volunteered to stay home now as well. He tried to convince her that the high grade was all hidden, that there would be no danger to the mine and camp. Mary disagreed.

"Oh, no. You're the one that convinced me of the value of keeping your vows to my father. Now those vows are mine, too. We can't risk anything hurting him in that way. The mine had become his whole life until..."

They agreed that Bluefeather would go on back and work the diggings for a week before returning. Mary insisted that they give a week apart, each in his or her own way, to Ludwig. She to his home, he to their mine and mountains.

Early on the third morning of his return to the mountains, Bluefeather was awakened by the howling of three coyotes trying to sound like thirty. He listened raptly, but with no analyzing. He arose, fixed a sparse meal out of habit, saddled one mule and, leading the other, headed for Breen.

He was there by midmorning and found Mary and Ludwig sitting in the music room, drinking coffee and chatting merrily with each other.

Ludwig smiled with all his life's wrinkles and said, "Ah, good fellow, I was hoping you'd come back today. The air has never been purer. The sun will give us seventy degrees and the wind will only whisper good tidings. Have some coffee, my son."

"Thanks, I will."

"I can tell by your bearing that all goes well in the mountains."

"Yes. So far it has been better than one could hope for. We're not even going to timber the mine, only the portal. The rock is solid and safe."

"That is good. That is superb."

Bluefeather suddenly chilled and cringed, thinking for sure Ludwig would ask him if he had checked the continuation of the generous vein high on the outcropping of the waiting cliffs. He didn't.

"Well now, sir, shall we all sin and slip a little morning brandy in our coffee?"

"Sounds better than good to me," said Bluefeather.

"It is ordained then," smiled Mary, highly pleased at the instantaneous and stunning recovery of her father's health and attitude. She moved quickly and poured the brandy, sitting back down so as not to miss a second of this astounding resurrection.

Ludwig tasted it saying, "Ahh," with pleasure. The others did likewise. Then he held it out for a toast. "Here's to the world and all that's in it."

Mary said, "The same."

Bluefeather said, "The same."

Suddenly, with the quick movements of a child, Ludwig gathered his cane and topcoat and tilted his fedora exactly right.

Patting Bluefeather tenderly on the back as he bent to kiss Mary, he jauntily left the room saying, "I feel like a long walk," and departed through the front door.

A relaxed Mary said, "Can you believe it?" She watched him out the window take the path toward the river. "He's walking almost as if he'd never been injured. Come look."

Bluefeather indeed saw that the old man was only touching ground with the cane every other step or so. Then he vanished around Clock Hill.

Mary decided to cook Ludwig's favorite meal—peach pie, pork roast, and sourdough rolls. Bluefeather played Wagner and Mozart records, although he did not really care for that kind of music in midday. This was middle-of-the-night music, when a man could be alone or share listening time only with those very few choice people. He didn't ask himself why he was making this exception with Ludwig's favorite composers; he simply acted.

The sun dropped, and the latent breeze came to life moving limbs and leaves in little rhythms. Mary was working as if the end of the world could only be averted by her cooking this special meal. Bluefeather brought in wood, drove in a few barely loose nails around the house, and replaced some loose putty on a couple of windowpanes. They both seemed to be trying to elongate the day, but nothing stopped the sun from hiding behind the mesa, flaring mightily with shafts of gold fanning out like wagon spokes across the whole of the western sky.

Then Mary stopped working. She washed and dried her hands, took off her apron, and got her scarf and coat from the hanger on the wall. She looked with anxious questions in her eyes at Bluefeather, who had already donned his jacket. Neither one said a word as they left the house with Mary's hand clutching Bluefeather's arm. They didn't hurry and they didn't dawdle either.

At the clearing, they could see the figure of Ludwig, sitting upright in his chair in almost a military posture, facing the violet sky and the very last tip of orange on the snow-covered mountain. The beams were dragged out of the sky by the father sun and taken to the other side of the world. The orange tip on the mountain blazed stronger for only a second because of the darkness gathering swiftly all around the other half of the world. The two walked arm in arm up to the figure. They knew.

Bluefeather stopped behind the chair with a hand on Ludwig's shoulder. Mary moved to his front, looking at his face a moment before tenderly touching his eyes. Then she took his face in her hands and said, "Oh father, dear father, we will miss you so."

The cane dropped to the ground as the hands fell limply in his lap. The breeze across the Rio Bello was especially cold for this time in early summer.

■ ■ ■

Twenty-One

Bluefeather wondered why every small-town funeral he ever attended was wind-whipped. Ludwig's was no exception. There were close to a hundred people, he guessed, gathered on the edge of Clock Hill to pay their last respects to the music- and literature-loving mining engineer.

A few came because they admired his intelligence and thought he deserved some last regard. Some were there out of curiosity, wondering at their neighbor's attachment to the man who married his daughter. There were those who thought it good business to be seen among the citizens of Breen country. A very few loved him and were already missing him.

Bluefeather stood with Mary in silence as the monotonous words of the preacher created impatience in the crowd. Mary had already grieved. Now she was simply putting the funeral in its place as a last dignity for a truly fine and feeling man.

Bluefeather felt an invisible disturbance in a shaft of air before he glanced up from the coffin and over the crowd. Behind them, on the hill, he saw Stan Berkowitz standing, staring at him. He was accompanied by the same three men he had had coffee with in the Railroad Cafe.

It was over. Everyone sighed and pulled their coat collars up against the coldness of the late spring wind. Scattering into little groups, they walked to whatever mode of transportation they had.

A hawk dove from the sky, screeched and widened its wings to stop its descent, then whirled and flew south until it vanished somewhere in the corrugated horizon. Just like the wind, a bird always seemed to visit the funerals.

About forty of the crowd showed up at the surviving daughter's home. Several ladies had brought food. Lots of food. People ate, visited and felt free, even joyous, as they talked about what a fine man Ludwig had been. They shared incidents, the loss to the community, but none spoke the dominant truth; they were venting their relief that it was Ludwig underground instead of themselves.

Bluefeather was miserable. He was a man dedicated, almost totally, to a few people who were his friends—those he loved. A surplus of people scattered his emotions. He had been born and reared with close clans just across the mountains from one another. It was one too many for a single human being to handle properly. So he had taken the trail with a few, but very close, friends. The crowds and masses were for politicians, power worshipers, religious fanatics, and their foolish soul-shattering followers, not for a man who walked deserts and mountains alone, except for two mules. Not for a man who loved reading fine books and hearing masterful music and who, by the moment, had hundreds of landscapes available to his inner eyes that were painted in his picture-mind by the Great Spirit.

He slipped out the back door and proceeded to the shed to enjoy the company of his longest-lasting friends, Jackknife and Nancy. They were always glad to see him, even if he placed heavy burdens on their backs and led them to otherwise inaccessible places.

A few days after the funeral, they returned to the King Tut and their labors of love. The next morning Bluefeather began felling trees—all as nearly equal in size as possible—and started building a one-room cabin. He thought this might help take their minds, especially Mary's, off their grief. He had fenced in a bush-encircled meadow for the mules with a spring along one edge so they did not have to worry about them while he and Mary roamed the creek, worked the mine, or went into town.

Almost immediately upon their return to the King Tut, they had a surprise visitor. Tracy was a miner for the local company. Mary knew him quite well, but Bluefeather had only seen him about town a few times. Both were inwardly terrified that somehow the knowledge of the wealth-giving discovery had leaked, but their fears were unjustified.

He visited easily over coffee, laughing as he said, "I just couldn't resist a little spying on you,..." the two felt their breath vanish, "hoping I'd catch Miss Mary making one of her wonderful apricot pies. Kate and Ellie are pretty good cooks all right. You couldn't have leased the restaurant to better people, Mary, but nobody, and I do mean nobody, can bake a pie like you."

Although Bluefeather agreed with Tracy's compliment, it was hard for him to understand the full reasoning behind this overwhelming desire for a chunk of pie. He saw that Mary was both pleased and embarrassed, but just as puzzled as he was.

Bluefeather decided to test the man, saying, "Miss Mary doesn't have much time for fancy cooking right now. She's been too busy helping me in the mine."

Mary pitched right in laughing a little. "If you can call it a mine. So far we haven't found enough metal to make a wedding ring."

Bluefeather said, to cover and make Mary's statement seem like the gospel, "There are traces, though, and where traces go you just might find the mother that gave birth. Right, Tracy?"

He had directed the last at the miner, who unaccountably found his coffee cup more fascinating than the rest of the world.

Mary said casually, "Well, I've still got a barrow of rocks to remove." She walked to the mine and disappeared inside.

Tracy watched with total disbelief at what was happening—a woman was actually going into that mine right before his sure-to-be-blinded eyes. The tin coffee cup that had had the miner hypnotized only moments before was now shaking so that he had to put it on the table out of embarrassment. He got to his feet knocking over the heavy wooden bench and fell backward with it. He tried to regain his balance but tripped again over an ore pick, twisting and falling this time on the palms of his hands and on his knees. He was thoroughly mortified, blaming his clumsiness on the cruel spirits that were angry because a woman had broken an inviolate law by transgressing into the mine, thereby sentencing all participants to unspeakable horrors. He slithered off down the trail toward Breen sure that every eye in the world had seen him falling about.

Bluefeather stared delightedly at the receding figure as did Mary peeping around the edge of the portal. They shared a satisfied glance and grin with one another, certain that they would be free from any but the most accidental invader of their privacy from now on. Tracy would spread the threat of doom like a flu epidemic.

This part of early summer became the time of Eden. Bluefeather had made an art out of the blasting. He was using half loads of powder and drilling the shallow holes with a short drill only. He learned how to blast the tunnel face so that the waste rock shook loose and left the vein inwardly sloping on the side called the hang wall. Then, once it was slightly loose from the careful blasting, he could pry the quartz free with a large, steel crowbar. It cut their hand sorting by eighty percent with the same amount of rich recovery. This gave them free time on Harmony Creek.

They both came to care for, and delight in, the many gifts the creek had to give. Bluefeather dug out a seep near camp, rocked it in, and made a good well of cool water for all their drinking and cooking needs, but they saved a special hole in Harmony Creek for their bathing.

Bluefeather had never dreamed he would ever make the acquaintance of a person as infatuated with mountain trout fishing as he was— much less marry one. In truth, Mary was better at fishing than Bluefeather. She had as her domain a couple of favorite, deep fishing holes where the water backed up and circled slowly. She would fish an hour or so in one pool, then move to the other. Once she had worms and sometimes kernels of corn attached to her two small hooks, she would sit motionless, patiently, until she hooked one. Then Bluefeather could hear her excited screams no matter where he was on the creek.

He, on the other hand, would slip up quietly to a likely looking spot, hide behind a bush or boulder, and sometimes hook one as soon as the water engulfed his bait. If ten minutes passed without a nibble or strike from the elusive native trout, he would back off and seek another spot. Sometimes he would walk several miles in a day, climbing over boulders, pushing through heavy brush, slipping, sliding, totally exhausting himself. At day's end, Mary would usually have more fish and probably hadn't moved over forty or fifty yards the entire time.

Harmony Creek had many varied waters. In some areas it cascaded down steep inclines where the water frothed as thick as whipping cream. In places where the beavers had widened and blocked it with their expertly engineered dams, the water moved slowly. On sunny days the creek turned an emerald green of such beauty it made Bluefeather feel like he could float up like a balloon so high he could look down on the sky.

The first day they had fished, Mary became so excited at her initial strike that she slipped and fell into a large circular hole of water bluer than the deepest ocean. She went under briefly, then stood up gasping and pushing her red hair out of her eyes. The next thing Bluefeather saw, to his surprise and pleasure, was Mary tossing all her clothing upon a smooth boulder.

She said, still spitting out water, "Evidently this hole was made for bathing. We shall hereafter share it with the fish," and she swam about as happy, smooth, and free as the trout. Bluefeather joined her and it became a daily ritual.

Some afternoons, after they had sorted the ore, they would simply walk together looking for fish where the water was shallow and clear, reading the signs left by all the animals and birds that habituated, bathed, drank, and hunted its sides. Occasionally they would actually see a deer, head high, watching them for a frozen moment before bouncing out of sight into the forest.

There was a special glade with thick grass and no wind where they could lie back and study the sky, the clouds and the birds flying. It was home to lots of chattering squirrels and chipmunks. They scampered up tree trunks and leaped from limb to limb, hiding and peeking at the intruders like little woodland voyeurs.

They could hear the creek softly playing like violins and then increasing in tempo to include horns and wet drums. The creek had become their artery. They ate from it, bathed in it, indulged in many forms of mental and physical recreation with it. It gave life and death, pain and pleasure, like the whole world did. They were the fortunate ones, for it was a treasured liquid trail of near ecstasy for them. They did not own it nearly as much as it did them.

One day as they sat side by side near a gleaming, rippling stretch of the precious creek, Mary said softly, "You know what, Blue? We just have an unwritten lease here along with all the other creatures. Each time one of them becomes extinct the rest of us shrink a bit more, until finally we will shrivel to nothingness."

Bluefeather tossed a little twig in the water and watched it bob up and down, go underwater for an instant, then twist and turn, hang a moment on a rock, break loose, and move forward on through a stretch of churning water, and come up on the other side in a quieter pool where it circled and circled, finally finding its way peacefully downstream and out of sight.

"Yes," he said. "Yes. You are right."

She had already forgotten what she had said in her reverie.

Saturday afternoons brought different kinds of entertainment: they drove Mary's old truck into Breen to do their weekly shopping, to hide their high-grade ore in the cellar with the rest of their growing treasure, and to attend the matinee at the Lyric Theater. They liked watching the children who attended almost as much as watching the movie.

They ate popcorn and yelled for the cowboy heroes just as loudly as the youngsters.

After the shopping chores were done, they would go to the Railroad Cafe to eat and have cocktails or wine. If they didn't want drinks with their meal, they would go by Mary's Place and dine. Then they would spend the night in the big house playing Ludwig's records or reading. Sometimes both.

Sunday morning would start with an unhurried breakfast and then back to the King Tut in time to get ready for work the next day and hear the coyotes howl.

Their young bodies were hard from all the physical work and play. Health and love and lust and all of life was theirs when and where they chose. They lived a little paradise. The world was a golden smile.

Three days passed before Mary was absolutely sure of something. Then, while things were as near perfect as humans can have them, she decided it was time to tell Bluefeather another great secret. She waited until all their work was done that day and they had eaten an early dinner. The summer sun was still shafting a few soft beams through the tops of the trees. There would be a new moon that night as well.

"Darling, Blue, we're going to give birth. We're going to start a population boom."

He stared and smiled at her, holding in his enthusiasm for an heir and another partner.

"When?"

"I don't know for sure, but I think April or May."

"Just in time for the spring runoff. That's right keen. Now let's see, . . . I think we decided on America Ludwig Fellini, huh?"

"Well maybe, but you see, there is just as much chance at it being Americana Ludwina Fellini, don't you think? She'll be called Cina for short." It was settled. Bluefeather stepped around the table, stood Mary up, patted her belly, and then danced her tenderly in a circle singing some made-up madness.

"Roll out the barrel 'cause my baby Cina's gonna smile at me." Happiness flooded the King Tut mine and the Harmony Creek area like an August cloudburst on a field of green corn.

Then one night the coyotes failed to howl. The night birds waited for their signaling sounds, but they too remained silent. There was no perceptible reason for this. Anyway, Bluefeather and Miss Mary and little Cina inside her belly all slept so soundly, they missed the coming of the silence. They got up as eager as the sun, thinking it was the same wondrous world as yesterday. It was not.

The morning of the day the men came, Bluefeather looked up at the bluffs. The sun was washing them with colors so warm they were not only lovely, but enticing. They called to Bluefeather and he heard. They spoke to him of a waiting enchantment. He closed his mind's ears and did not look up at them again that day.

He was eager to get inside the solid walls of the tunnel to sort the ore he had blasted the afternoon before. The carbide lamp revealed the face of the tunnel as solid ore. They had hit a pocket—hit a wide pocket bounty of extraordinary dimensions. The entire tunnel face including the hang and foot walls were solid rose quartz, laced with wire gold in many visible areas.

Miss Mary was busy working on their expense book, so he mucked the tunnel out himself. There was no time to sort the ore from the waste. He had to see if the pocket widened and went down as well as up. He dug his blast holes with the eighteen-inch bull prick and placed the full loads of dynamite. This time he angled the holes so the explosions would break as much rock as possible.

Mary, sensing his excitement, crouched with him around the rise as he automatically repeated, "Fire in the hole."

The earth shook under them and the dust blasted out of the tunnel in a brown cloud. They waited impatiently for it to settle. They each took a carbide lamp and walked inside. The blood rushed through their veins like the waters of Harmony Creek. In the quiet of the tunnel, they could hear their hearts thumping like the drums of a war dance.

There it was under the revealing glare of the two lights. Their minds coursed and scattered around the universe with mighty surges of emotions, thoughts, and feelings.

Bluefeather shoveled three or four scoops of ore into the wheelbarrow, but instead of dumping it outside, he decided to do the sorting several feet inside the portal, safe from inquisitive eyes. He tippled the hand-separated richness into a little pile out on the waste dump so the sun could fully illuminate every tiny indentation and projection of the sunflower metal.

They both stared at the ore, bending down, feeling its heaviness, seeing its luxuriance. Thoughts of castles on mountains, privately owned hunting and fishing preserves, great gardens of flowers and shrubs, food and drink from every field and garden of the earth, walls adorned with masterpieces, scores of servants, opulent silks and perfumes were theirs on demand. Demand. Power to control their destinies and those of innumerable others. All.

Then...then came the next feeling, simultaneously, to both Bluefeather and Mary—fear. Fear there would not be enough gold to own all these things, not enough to last forever. Fear that others would plot and gather expert and terrible forces to take it all away from them. Fear of losing their pleasures, their powers. Fear of being murdered, mutilated and, even worse, relegated to shameful poverty with all the earthly demons staring at their ragged, starving dementia, pointing at them in ridicule, with shrieking laughter that caused such shivering that they would turn into little piles of dust out of irresistible fear. Fear beyond time.

All these things and more accelerated through their beings with such speed that they were unable to get any order to their emotions at all. They looked at one another, recognizing that each had succumbed to the ancient call of covetousness.

With a strange, stiff walk, Bluefeather dragged a bench from under the protective awning out into the sun and sat down on one end. Mary joined him on the other. They sat as far apart as the hand-fashioned bench would allow as if each was afraid of contaminating the other with their stricken and avaricious virus. They stared at each other in soul-searching silence.

Mary finally said, "We must not dig anymore. There's enough to last for several years already."

"Yeah...we can just live here from snowmelt to snowfall enjoying the creek, the woods...protecting the property. Of course, later when we have time to plan, we can decide how to help the poor, the crippled, the disenfranchised. We must do it in such a manner that no one will know."

"Anonymously, of course. There is always our baby to think of, Blue."

"Oh, I am. Believe me, I am. We'll see that he has sufficient funds put aside for any sort of education, in whatever field he desires."

"And we can have a modest but nice winter home in Denver or San Francisco in case she wishes to pursue music or the dance. There's no way she could do that here in Breen."

"No, I suppose you're right there." They were both silent a spell, then Bluefeather said, "We must remember my vows."

"They're mine, as well."

"No. They're mostly mine. I made them only for myself as a gesture to you and Ludwig."

"Just the same, they are my vows too. Now, with the baby coming and..." she motioned at the tunnel, pulling her head back as if a serpent would strike it, "and...that...in there."

"I suppose you're right. We must not let a single thought of the 'yellow madness' enter us. Right? Isn't that right, Miss Mary? Huh? Huh?"

"That is our vow. Our blood vow." Mary stood up with an entirely different demeanor suddenly suffusing her vital body. "It's all settled then?" She said cheerfully, "I'll race you to the pool."

Bluefeather looked at her, and the concentrated strain vanished from his face and eyes and was replaced by one of challenge—of fun. At this recognition, Mary turned her body, and her long graceful legs carried her swiftly down the trail with a good twenty-yard head start, her hair of fire stringing out behind not quite able to catch up with her momentum.

Soon their many partners of the forest turned ears and heads to listen to the squeals of joyous abandonment as Bluefeather and Mary splashed water over each other's naked bodies, firm and supple as steel cables, and washed the last vestiges of sunflower fever into the purifying waters of Harmony Creek. The mules brayed in such volume that insects crawled under rocks. The forest creatures didn't understand the shouted human words, but they felt their meaning and rejoiced with Bluefeather and Mary.

After their swim, they walked back to the camp slowly, completely relaxed from the cold bathing and warm lovemaking that followed. There was a look and feel of repletion about them.

Bluefeather was thinking how absolutely gifted they were—young, strong, healthy, and in love. He envisioned their beautiful baby running and laughing across this special glade. The baby would stop and turn at the dark edge of the forest, eyes wide with the elation of discovering the world, and wave at them with only the tilting up and down of his fingers as little children so often do. Mary was thinking similar thoughts.

As they returned to their soon-to-be-permanent summer home, Bluefeather felt the bristling of hair on the back of his neck, ever so slight, and an itch on his nose scar like a grass stem rubbing across it.

He tried to ignore it, but the tingling was persistent and stronger now. There was no sign of the camp being disturbed. Maybe a bear or a lion had passed nearby. That must be it. That would explain it . His ancient survivor's blood was still working, that was all it was.

Then his rock-trained eyes scanned the pile of ore they had dumped on the ground earlier. A chill jabbed at all the skin on his body. He instantly knew the pile was smaller. There were three or four chunks of ore missing. He checked the ground for signs. Whoever the violator was, he had been very careful. Bluefeather could see where he had brushed his tracks out with an obviously heavily leafed limb, but he had missed one tiny imprint of the edge of a rubber heel. Bluefeather didn't miss it, though.

He had to tell Mary about the intruder. He hesitated, looking over the huge boulder that crowned the King Tut's tunnel portal, on up through hundreds of tons of large rock that had fallen over the aeons from the mountain, concealing the possible strike of the vein, all the way up to the waiting bluffs. Waiting. Waiting. "Oh, Great Spirit, the greatest of us all, it is a terrible thing that may happen here," Bluefeather thought. "If the vein has length, as I'm sure it has depth, it is of such value that men will dig millions of tons out of the mountain's bowels, and the waste and chemicals will fill and destroy the canyons and crevices of Harmony Creek. They will wash and blow down for millenniums, polluting the town and the gorgeous, giving Rio Bello. The wealth will be taken elsewhere, to many cities and many lands, while Breen and its lush forests will only be decimated, until finally even the miners, who will live and prosper until the mountain is gutted, will be gone."

Mary said, "What's that, Blue? I didn't hear you clearly."

He didn't hear her speak as his mind-voice continued, "Oh, what do I do, majestic and wise one, and where is my guiding spirit now that I need him the most? Dancing Bear, you ol' darlin', where do you hide, huh? Huh? Have you gone and left me like an alcoholic husband deserts his wife and children for the saloons? Well, you ol' dancing lush, you better show up or I'll kick your ass until your nose bleeds like a razor-sliced artery and your butt flops in the air twenty feet above your head. Now, you wouldn't like that to happen, would you? I'm sorry, Bear. Of course, I'd never go that far...unless you..."

"What? Blue, what are you talking about? Have you gone ringy-dingy on me?" Mary's voice finally penetrated. He apologized and told her of the theft.

"My God," Blue answered. "I know that they know about the ore; they'll kill us for this kind of wealth. They'll kill us for sure, and then the real madness will begin. They'll kill the creek and destroy everything beautiful here."

"What are we going to do, Blue? How can we find them? We don't even know who took our rocks." Mary's anxiety increased.

Bluefeather quickly calmed down and tried to reassure her. "Do not worry your beautiful, little red head for a single second, dear Miss Mary. I'll take care of it for sure."

He momentarily ignored the rest of her questions while he put on his moccasins and tied a rolled bandanna around the long hair he had chosen not to cut that summer. He picked up his .30–30 and checked it for shells, dropping several more into his pocket. As he shoved a hunting knife in his belt, he turned to answer her growing protestations.

He said, "Defilers. Infiltrators of our property and our honor. Desecraters of Ludwig's dream and our work. Usurpers of others' souls, that's what they are. When the devil sinks his horns into your loved ones, his head must be severed."

Mary grabbed him and hugged him. Tears puddled her eyes, as she pleaded with him not to resort to violence. As her belly full of baby pressed against him, his rashness and his madness slowly diminished. He finally promised her that he would strike only to save their lives. He kissed her, held her closely and patted her back, comforting her until she believed him.

He left the camp making a small and then ever-widening circle to seek out the steps of the perpetrator. He regretted his promise, made under such stress in the arms of his love. One did not make those kinds of promises without some pain. He made another silent vow to keep his last verbal one to Mary. It would not be undemanding—this keeping of one's word. It never was.

He moved on, head down, all senses applied to the hunt now. There was no mine, no Breen, no memory. Only the enemy to be found and confronted with... with what?

■ ■ ■

Twenty-Two

It did not take Bluefeather long to locate the tracks. The man had evidently felt no need to cover them after a hundred or so feet. Bluefeather could tell he was a large man by testing the depth of the tracks against his own—of course, making allowance for the gold quartz the thief carried. He also limped on his left leg some, but the regularity of the tracks left by the injured leg showed that the injury was not a new one—the man had adjusted to it.

Now Bluefeather could see by the moisture still oozing from bruised grass and bushes that he was gaining on more than one man. He stopped, leaning his rifle up against a forked limb, cupped both hands behind his ears, and listened. It was fortunate he had stopped when he did because he could hear muffled voices coming and going with the gusts of the mountain breeze. He carefully worked his way downwind, at the same time moving nearer to the source of the sounds.

The voices were indistinguishable but becoming louder. He was in thick timber now, occasionally skirting a small meadow. He must move as slowly as a mother cougar after prey to feed her hungry young. With ultimate patience, foot by foot, then inch by inch, he eased closer. If they were on horseback, or worse yet, on mules, and were acute enough to watch their animals' ears, they would know someone was approaching. He would have to risk being discovered, but he felt that his patience and the favorable direction of the wind gave him a good chance of going undiscovered.

He was right. There they were in the meadow, sitting around a small fire with a large coffeepot hanging above it. Bluefeather could not hear any muzzling sounds of horses. They had most likely come in a truck, parked a mile or so below and packed their bedrolls, grub and guns in on their backs. The man he had followed was Stan Berkowitz. He was standing. The others sat on bedrolls.

Stan was saying, "I know you believe your eyes as far as those three rocks are concerned, but I keep tellin' you that they've opened up a solid face of ore as rich as what you're holdin' right there in your hands."

One of the three men whom Bluefeather recognized as having been in Stan's company at the Railroad Cafe and Ludwig's funeral said, "I never seen nothin' like it. Never."

Another said, "I heard about a strike like this over in California somewhere, but I bet it wasn't this rich."

Stan, who moved about agilely considering the stiff leg Bluefeather had given him, spoke now. "What do you think I had you boys come all the way down from Leadville for, anyway? There ain't ever gonna be a chance like this again. We gotta take it. That's all. Take it now before somebody else finds out about it."

"How you figger to do it? That goddamned Indian is a mean son of a bitch from what I heard he done over in Tonapah. Cut a man's head clean off with one swipe and stuck it up on a stick right on the main drag.

The other said, "Look what he done to you, Stan. That feller ain't anybody to..."

Stan yelled, raising a large hand for silence. "Yeah, well, he'll damn sure pay for that, my friend. I don't care how much man he is. The smallest .22-caliber bullet made, placed exactly between the eyes, will kill the biggest, meanest, toughest bastard that ever lived."

"Well, I reckon you got that right, but we're gonna have to kill that woman of his, too."

Stan interrupted again, "She's mine. That's another little debt I'm gonna collect. I'm gonna do her special."

"That's just fine, but we gotta get rid of the bodies so nobody can find 'em—not ever. You know there's gonna be a big search when that Mary woman comes up missing. People 'round here sure do think a lot of her. They don't know what to make of that blanket-ass Taos Indian 'ceptin' they're scared shitless of him. Some folks say he casts spells and things."

"Aw, bullshit," Stan protested. "Listen, I know where there's a mine shaft less than five miles from here that's seven hundred feet deep and too risky for anybody to ever reenter, unless they were dead. Couldn't find them bodies in a thousand years. We can pack 'em in on the mules and then turn 'em loose way over there," and he pointed northwest.

There were mutters of frightened approval.

Then Stan cinched his pitch. "Listen, we can mine it ourselves and split it all four ways. In one season we can buy up half of Denver and all that's in it, if we want. You want a stable of racehorses or women? You want big automobiles and the fanciest clothes in the world? You want to eat and drink any damn thing you like and all you like? Well, what do you want? You wanna buy the next Congress? The governor of the state? Well, what in hell? Let's vote on it right here and now."

Bluefeather had seen the rifles leaning on the bedrolls and the holstered pistols as well. Even so, he could down them all before they could get organized enough to fire back. He knew that he would only have to pump five shells into the chamber of the .30–30 and pull the trigger five times. He could do that in five seconds. They would never make it out of the glade alive. None of them. When they had mentioned Miss Mary's name he had sighted down on Stan's backbone just behind his heart and fingered the trigger, but he held off because something kept whispering to him. He wanted to hear it clearly, that whisper—to know what it said.

Bluefeather was also shocked by the things they had said about him. He had no idea that anybody around Breen ever gave him a tiny thought, outside of Stan Berkowitz and Skimpy Jones, and they did not want to talk in public much. How could Stan explain about having his balls mashed like pecan hulls? Bluefeather did not appreciate them bringing up his trouble at Tonapah, much less twisting and turning it into something it wasn't. It was bad enough to kill a man to save your own life without having some low-quality people spread it around all out of kilter. He felt the mad enter the back of his neck, trying to get in deep enough to enter his bloodstream. If the mad got that far it would be all over. He would kill the deserving bastards, and then his vow and prayers to Miss Mary would be ruptured and so would all the love they shared.

He fought, straining mightily against the mad, but he was slowly losing as he heard the men's voices vote to kill him, Miss Mary, the baby, Ludwig's dream, the world.

Then the whispers he had been struggling to clarify cleared some.

"No. No, dear brudder. Come. Come visit with me. Here behind you. Follow this voice, dear friend."

Bluefeather turned and rose to a crouching position to follow the blur in front of him, a blur that talked in magnetic tones, enticing him to follow. Finally he walked around the edge of some rocks opening into a small canyon and saw it. The "it" was Dancing Bear, smiling, shuffling about in his moccasins as if he was getting loosened up for a marathon.

"Here we are, dear brudder, all together again. You look strong as an elephant, fast as a deer, miserable as a wounded wolverine. What's a matter? You gettin' the angries cause you cain't kill them sorry folks?"

Bluefeather sighed and sat down, leaning his back and rifle against a big rock. "Where in hell have you been all this time? I been needing you for a long spell. Bad. Why didn't you show up earlier today when I was begging you?"

"I don't know why you white men always ask at the same time two questions, maybe more. Dadburn, it makes answers hard to get."

"There you go, just like always, avoiding the immediate issue, making excuses, making me wait, when I'm near disaster."

"Okeydokey, okay, then. I been over in Los Angeles, California, helpin' a friend get into the movies."

"Movies?"

"Yes sirree, that's what I do. He's gonna make people laugh and fall down doin' it. That is an important thing to do, making people fall down from havin' much, much fun instead of fallin' down bein' clumsy or drunk on whiskey."

"Bear, I don't give a damn about any comedian in Los Angeles. I want to know how to stop a big killing right over there on Harmony Creek. You don't want to feel responsible for that, do you? Did you hear what I said? Say, did you hear what I was gonna do to you back there at camp a while ago?"

"Of course, and for sure, dear brudder. Why you think I'm here? I ain't no dumb Indian spirit guide. I don' want my hind-end kicked way up there in the air where eagles and falcons might tear it in pieces. I say 'no' to any that stuff. I say 'yes' for helpin' my dear brudder Blue Fellini."

Bluefeather felt relieved that Dancing Bear hadn't taken too much offense at his recent threats, but still he had received no answer. His guide had guided him around in circles that got smaller instead of bigger. A few more turns on the trail would finally shrink it down to a dot. He'd seen ancient rock drawings do just that.

"Now listen and listen carefully, Dancing Bear. I can't wait around here visiting with you—as much as I enjoy it. I got to have answers now. There are four men right over this hill with two rifles and four pistols getting ready to kill me and mine. Now, how in all hell am I gonna stop this without shooting bullets of my own? Huh? Huh?"

Dancing Bear was sitting way up in a ponderosa pine on a dead limb looking down at Bluefeather like a great horned owl looks at a mouse. He stood up on his moccasined toes like a ballet dancer, dived off backward, and stopped about three feet from the ground upside down just in front of Bluefeather.

"Now, dear brudder, I tell you this. You hearin' me for sure?"

"Yeah, for sure."

"I tell you this again. Go invite them sorry white men to dinner."

As if it had not been difficult enough to listen to somebody floating, resting, or whatever it could be called, upside down in the pure mountain air, how could Bluefeather be expected to sit there and consider such an insane suggestion?

"Invite them to dinner?" Bluefeather couldn't believe what he was hearing. "At our camp? You are crazy, crazy, crazy. Insane, I say. I reckon they are going to come over and enjoy our hospitality so much they'll help with the dishes, apologize for ever having bad thoughts, and just walk away."

Bluefeather could have emptied the .30–30 into Dancing Bear's delirious brain, but then he remembered that it was pointless to attempt to murder spirit guides—that was how most of them had gotten their jobs in the first place.

Dancing Bear turned sideways in the air to make verbal visiting easier. "No, no, no, they don' walk away; they run like little rabbits with lions big as clouds and claws longer than pine trees chasin' 'em. Ah, dear brudder, the authorities done sent for poor, poor Dancing Bear. I go work on Saint Louis now. Then I gotta go to London and do the queen's maid," and he was gone.

Bluefeather was puzzled, but his killing mad had flown away. Dancing Bear had helped, but, as always, he couldn't figure how at the moment.

As Bluefeather walked toward the enemies' camp, he started whistling sweet love songs as loudly as he could prior to his advancing into the clearing. They were surprised.

He ignored their hands placed on guns and said in a kind and courteous voice, "Good day, gentlemen. I've been trying to pick up the tracks of a camp-robbing bear for hours. Have you boys seen any sign of one? Well, hello, Stan. I haven't seen you since Ludwig's funeral.

How're you doing?" Bear was right. He had asked two questions at once again, but he got more answers than that.

"I'm fine. Just fine, Fellini. Say, I'd like you to meet some of my friends from Denver." He quickly introduced them by their first names only—Bluefeather would never remember. "They're in the lumber business. Thinkin' on maybe puttin' in a sawmill hereabouts. I've been showin' 'em about looking at the stands of timber. Thought another payroll might do the folks of Breen considerable good. You never know when the mines will run out of ore, do you, Blue? They figger on maybe hirin' somewhere between forty and fifty people. Be good for everybody, I figger."

Bluefeather had gotten answers in the neighborhood of three to one on his questions. He felt like that was a good percentage in his favor. His luck seemed to be running. At any rate, he sure did crowd it about as far as a man could. He could hardly believe the purely bizarre words as they emanated from his mouth.

"Why don't you folks come on over to our camp for dinner. We're not far from here. We've got a bunch of fresh trout that are just begging to be cooked. Besides that, Mary's making up a Dutch oven full of peach cobbler. You know how expert she is at makin' those pies and cobblers, Stan."

They all looked around at one another feeling just as amateurish and imbecilic as Bluefeather. Finally Stan stuttered out, "Why... why... why, I reckon that's mighty hospitable of you, Blue. I reckon we'd be much obliged, huh, boys?"

"Yeah."

"Much obliged."

"Our pleasure."

Stan responded to this "our pleasure" part, getting a gleaming of proper conniving back, "Yeah, Blue,...tell Mary it'll be our pleasure."

"Then it's settled. See you about an hour to sundown. I'll have a big pot of coffee ready."

Bluefeather's moccasined feet moved swiftly away, craving desperately to get his broad back out of rifle range. Even so, he never glanced behind him.

Stan Berkowitz swung his lame leg expertly in a movement that kept his three companions straining to keep up. At each stride, the exultation grew in him at the almost laughable irony of Bluefeather inviting him to dine with them. Yes, these other men were just shadows that he needed temporarily. He realized that now. After they had served his swiftly forming designs, he would dispose of them just as he would the two fools awaiting them beside Harmony Creek. As soon as the mine's reserves were proven, he would be the only one around to watch the great mill be built. There would be no problem with financing—any bank in the world would be delighted to draw interest on such wealth. Instead of being a mill foreman, he would be the sole owner. After a time, he would accumulate so many cash reserves that he would expand around the country, maybe the world, certainly to Brazil where he had heard of great caches of gold to be taken from the Amazon wilderness—if one had the power and guts. He, Stan Berkowitz, would have plenty of both.

He had told his underlings to wait until after dinner to eradicate the male host. He had warned them not to harm the woman. He wanted to be sure her last thoughts were of him.

Now as they moved within a few minutes of the camp, the covert part of his surging blood shoved many thoughts into his brain. Bluefeather had taken the woman away from him so easily, he had not even known that he was permanently damaged by the loss. Bluefeather had beat him in the poker game and crippled him in the fight. And now, now he had casually invited him to dinner. My God, what a final insult. Well, he would be the one counting all the gold and seeing the world with all its creatures in attendance, but before that he would satisfy his prior defeats. He would have that woman in every way his fevered being could imagine, and then roll her over for his underlings to finish off, like the remains of a carcass after the hyenas and vultures had dined. Too bad Bluefeather would not be allowed to witness his retribution, but he was too dangerous and the sunflower metal was too near Stan's grasp to risk it.

Mary had been angry because they—foolishly in her eyes—had only one rifle at the camp. She could shoot as well as anyone. It had been natural. Ludwig had given her shooting lessons when she was twelve, and she had become more accurate than he was in just a few short practice sessions. She had never hunted much, only a few times when they needed the meat, and then only with her father.

Bluefeather consoled her by leaning the rifle next to the cook bench with a gunnysack draped over it. He had the .44 pistol stuck in the back of his belt under a light jacket. Mary wore a sweater. The evenings were cool enough at this altitude to justify them anyway.

Bluefeather was certain that their guests all would be wearing jackets in spite of the warming, mile-and-a-half walk through the woods. It made sense, because of the finality of the situation, that they would come with hidden guns. It would have made a lot more sense if they simply slipped up within rifle range, and with two or more shots blew them down. However, Bluefeather did not expect it to happen in this practical way. It was simple to him at this moment. There was not now, nor had there ever been, anything practical or even slightly understandable about humans dealing with the worshiped metal. The paradox was inconceivable because the metal itself was totally predictable. It was magnificently malleable into any shape of stamped or sculptured glory and would last in beauty as long as the world. Was there some undiscovered emanation from it that all of mankind's soaring science had been unable to detect? Had it been chosen by the great gods as a constant test material of almost inhuman, irresistible allure as a device to test and try men and women to the ultimate? If not, what then?

He could not answer these thoughts, but he did not have to think about his next actions. They just came with his ancestral nature. He crushed the peyote buds into powder in a rock mortar with a marble pestle. He added several dried seeds from the Southwest earth to the mixture as well. He dumped it into the simmering coffee and stirred it with the long wooden spoon. He set the table with a large tin coffee cup by each plate. He poured the cups for Mary and himself almost full of plain water while she busied herself getting the trout breaded with cornmeal. He took the remains of the cornmeal and cast them up in the four directions of the compass, up into the sky and down at the earth. He chanted softly to himself and the Great Spirit. He burned cedar in a prospector's pan and whiffed the smoke all about the campsite with a hawk's feather. An eagle feather was used on most of these occasions, but Bluefeather used that of the hawk, which wasn't as strong as the eagle but had more resilience and survival abilities. He gave special attention with the cedar smoke to the places soon to be occupied by the guests.

Mary had just put the heavy, iron Dutch oven on the woodstove filled with the ingredients that would make a luscious cobbler. The sourdough bread was baking, and the aroma had already begun to drift on the air. He had just put the stomped ashes from the gold pan behind the tent when he knew his enemies were nearing. He could feel it on the back of his neck and smell them, even above the cobbler.

Mary added a couple of sticks of cedar to the fire. As Stan and his men entered the camp area, they were hit with the subtle remains of the cedar smoke and the gland-stirring smell of the bread and the cobbler.

"Welcome. Welcome," smiled Bluefeather from his black diamond eyes with the olive-brown complexion surrounding them. "We're almost ready for you."

"I could smell Mary's cookin' a mile before we got here," said Stan.

Everybody exchanged greetings and introductions as the occasion demanded. The atmosphere was absolutely tense with such an abundance of cordiality.

"Here, here, here, Stan." Bluefeather seated them, giving Stan the head of the table, but next to his own elbow. He left his wife's seat open, saying, "The cook must be nearest to the fire." He graciously poured them coffee, chattering on furiously in competition with the birds of the forest. He faked pouring his own, using the same skill he had been taught to deal the cards with in Tonapah—by misdirecting the viewer's vision with an opposite action. It worked.

Mary was tending to pans and all sorts of cookware that needed no attention at all.

Bluefeather was watching all four of the invaders, but mainly Stan, as he knew the mill foreman was the general of this little campaign.

Stan volunteered a polite remark about the "delicious-tasting coffee," and the others nodded and commented just as favorably. Bluefeather was pouring refills by the time they finished their compliments.

Stan's eyes now darted from Bluefeather to Mary. The orbs of all the men were becoming erratic, looking inward a moment and then jerkily outward. Bluefeather knew they all had pistols hidden under their jackets. One guest thoughtlessly touched its bulk under his leather jacket and came within a fraction of a second of dying.

Bluefeather raised his under-filled tin cup with his left hand while he reached to secure his pistol with his right, as if he were scratching his back, which indeed he did as soon as he saw that the man's gesture was a thoughtless one.

Now Stan's eyes lingered on Mary. She felt them and gave swift, hopefully unnoticed, glances at the .30–30 under the gunnysack.

Bluefeather saw that these men were now possessed by the vision-buds as far as he could allow.

He slowly raised up and said, "Gentlemen, it's only a moment until you will be served. So, with your permission, I'll play the drums for you before the repast of your lifetime."

Every move had to be smooth. The slightest jerk and the six harmless guns would be put into an action from which there would be death, pain, and deadly disruption forevermore.

Bluefeather took the old, hide-covered, Indian drum and beater from where they hung on the corner log support of the lean-to. He squatted without looking at the armed and increasingly befuddled and ominous trespassers. The air was twanging and trembling as it became thinner and harder to breathe.

Mary moved and stood next to the rifle as Bluefeather pounded at the drum with swiftly increasing velocity. He sang now, songs of the Pueblos, the Anasazi before them, and the ancients even before them. The sounds vibrated into the air like the noise of a million geese rising in migratory flight.

The men stared at him, mouths slowly opening, eyes flickering as things began to flutter and move in their peripheral vision. Things they tried not to see, but could not hide, nor could they deafen the increasing racket. The trees of the forest were uprooting and flying through the air leaving a vast circle, and the ragged holes they had torn in the earth were filled and smoothed with tall grass. The trees that had moved aside now rocketed upward with whooshing sounds, and the air they displaced whammed against the earth in downbursts of such force that the impact sounded like explosions of dynamite as it shook the earth and rattled all the matter inside their skulls.

Lightning ripped jagged holes in the sky without letup, crossing, crisscrossing, and colliding with such force that great balls of whirling blue and orange lights were formed, whizzing so fast the best of eyes could not begin to follow, much less endure the brilliant kaleidoscope of plunging, bouncing lights that inundated everything. The skeletons under all things were visible, even the inner textures of wood and rocks.

Then the lightning stopped in an immeasurable instant, and thousands of tepees circled up and around the clearing and through the forests and fires. Dances and old, old songs were seen and heard separately and together. The lights and sounds filled every twig, every rock crevice, everything. And there on the edge of the circle was Alexander the Great and all his legions astride mighty stamping horses that snorted fire. Their eyes gleamed in blue lights of beauty.

The Roman Coliseum now appeared, alive with roaring lions. A lion, as big as three elephants, slung nude human bodies around like apple boxes in a tornado. A human body made only a single bite for the monstrous creature, and a solid river of blood drained from the terribly beautiful beast's jaws in a stream that flowed in a cresting flood toward the camp.

Thousands of blue-gray souls moved across the opening in silence. Endlessly they came from many directions, moving through one another and finally walking around the great round clearing in the circle of infinity.

All was quiet now except for a low moan never before heard. It penetrated out into the universe and down toward the molten, gut center of the earth. It was the sound of eternity—methodically, ceaselessly marching.

Suddenly the displaced trees all melded into one massive trunk, so high above, it seemed only a twig. Then with a roaring of ten thousand racing trains, it headed toward earth and the campsite. As it neared it became bigger than a town, as big as a city, bigger than anything. Its roots were like mile-long, clutching claws of a gigantic lion. It would, within seconds, be close enough to rip a hole in the earth a mile deep, creating scars like the Grand Canyon.

Stan became unparalyzed. He ran away from the camp, crashing over the table, screaming unheard-of utterances. The other three tried to follow, falling, then scrambling up so fiercely from the earth that they ripped the skin from their palms and the tips of their fingers.

One ran into a tree, crunching his nose flat and breaking his cheek open so that the sides and back of one eyeball were in open air. Another ran into his companion. They fell together, rolling over and over, kicking, biting, scratching at one another, sometimes with rocks and dead tree limbs in their hands until they were crippled and crawled away into hidden places of the forest to die alone like wild animals.

Stan got his good leg hung up in the crevice of some rocks at the edge of a ten-foot drop. Gravity and momentum carried his heavy body freefalling the ten feet to a slope where he rolled until he hit level bottom. All the bones of his good leg were twisted and shattered beyond repair.

After the guests' unannounced departures, Bluefeather and Mary finished off all they could hold of the delicately prepared trout and the hot, buttered sourdough buns. The cobbler bubbled up slightly around the edge of the just-right brown topping as Mary set the Dutch oven out to cool. Ordinarily it would have been hard to wait for such a sweet-smelling treat, but they had lots of time now. There was no doubt in their happy minds that their working and playing retreat would never be perforated again.

They decided to have a cup of the coffee themselves. It would not harm them. They had brewed it. They clanged the cups together for the toast.

Bluefeather said, "Here's to warm campfires and great visions."

Mary said, "To the gods, God bless them."

For reasons that needed no exact understanding, they laughed with the great joy of release, looking at one another's chortling faces as they did so to double their pleasure.

Stan was found three days later, dragging himself with his upper body and a slight assist from the leg Bluefeather had worked on earlier. He was discovered on the eastern road into town by two nine-year-old boys who had intended to spend the morning fishing on the enticing banks of the Rio Bello. Instead, they threw down their poles and ran down the street screaming that there was a crazy man crawling toward town. Indeed they were right. Neither Stan's legs nor his mind ever worked correctly again.

Two days later a man without a face, at least without a recognizable one, stumbled and fell into town, and the most sense he ever uttered the rest of his life was, "There's a long-toothed lion bigger than the state of Texas after all our asses."

Twenty-Three

Mary and Bluefeather did not bother to sort and haul the ore from the King Tut tunnel. With the outside threats to their personal province permanently removed, they simply relaxed for a few days. Anyway, whenever they decided to sort the ore there would be no need to mine more for two or three years. They could live abundantly now from their prior work, and a couple of heavy charges in the widened and enriched part of the vein would probably give them ample resources for a lifetime. They could take time to enjoy more music, reading, loving, and fishing, without anyone knowing or noticing the difference. Not that the citizens of the Breen area would dare to intrude. There was enough wild gossip and individual imaginings of unknown forces to deal with if one messed around with the half-breed or his lady.

Mary shared none of the blame, but people said things like, "How could she be so blind to this magician of the devil?" Other statements about her were made out of hidden but surely jealous emotions.

The couple now pleasantly planned their quiet but assured future, while enjoying the present warm days, fishing, swimming, and walking the banks of Harmony Creek. They also enjoyed riding the mules down the canyons and around the mountains. They even rode over to look at the Ruby Dove workings and tried to guess which shaft Stan and his boys had intended to toss them into.

A few headframes and some remnants of buildings that had collapsed into great, gray splinters were the only remains of a settlement. Even the ghosts seemed to have deserted the Ruby Dove. But people had lived and died here. There was a weed-covered cemetery to prove it. The wooden crosses had almost all gone to the bugs, and the iron ones had fallen and were mostly covered over.

Two of the old mine tunnels were still visibly identifiable by some odd-shaped rock markers that stood upright and in good order.

Mary pointed to one of them and said, "That's the one they had picked out for me. I can tell by the chamisa growing around it. I love the smell of chamisa."

Bluefeather said, "Okay. That's yours . . . I'll take the other one with the small piñon tree sprouting out of its edge. Piñon is my favorite tree in all the world."

"I think I've seen enough of the Ruby Dove for this lifetime," Mary said, and reined Nancy back onto the trail toward Harmony Creek.

Bluefeather said, "You're right. Those are old, dead dreams and not for people like us who own all the world worth having." He lightly nudged Jackknife in the sides and followed his love.

For a change, that afternoon they sat and had hot tea. Sipping quietly, they stared into the forest filled here and there with the light of the sun forming little temporary, natural cathedrals.

Bluefeather's eyes went up to the waiting bluff. He couldn't stop them. He couldn't grab his eyes with his powerful miner's hands and pull them back down to more peaceful sights. Nor would his will—which was stronger than a thousand such hands—control the orbs either. He could hear it whispering again, growing seductively louder and louder, "Come, dear brother, I'm waiting. Waiting for you to keep your vow. Do not worry. You will conquer my sides as if I were only an infant bluff three feet high. Come, come to me. I'm tired of waiting to show you your desire. Have no fear. You will return to your camp without harm. I am waiting. Waiting just for you. You. You."

At that moment he almost screamed at the bluff to hush before it upset Miss Mary, but she had come over to sit on his lap. She pushed his hair back from his forehead and held his face tenderly in her hands, looking straight into his eyes, saying, "Blue, dear Blue. I want to try to tell you how deeply I appreciate you keeping your word and not letting the . . . the blasted gold possess you. You were right. You were strong enough to whip the madness and you're the only man I've ever known or heard of who has. I have to confess, after all my lecturing, that at the sight of the new discovery—that fabulous face of ore—I had momentary flashes of grand castles and diamond necklaces. I am so ashamed."

"No. No, it's only natural. It's . . ."

"It was over as quickly as it possessed me, because of you. Anyway, I have to tell you now, and I'll try not to bring it up again, how much I admire and respect your willpower."

Bluefeather was pleased almost to tears and so embarrassed that he just gathered her breasts to his chest and laid his head in the comforting bend of her shoulder and encircling arm. Then she said, "Blue, my partner, I love you as much as ... as ..." Her voice faded into her thoughts.

They were still and silent in their embrace until the coyotes howled again. And again.

Bluefeather arose at daylight, built a fire, and put the coffee on to boil. Then he sat by the bed and watched the restful breathing of his Miss Mary. He reached out and touched her hair where it was in very bold relief against the pillow. She was so quietly beautiful at that moment, he almost dissolved. She sighed, smiled so slightly that he nearly missed it, and took his hand in hers, holding it to one cheek.

"I can't put it off any longer, my darling. I must climb the bluff today." She opened her own piece-of-the-sky eyes just long enough to look up at him and say, "Yes, I know."

He had glanced at the bluff surreptitiously hundreds of times and had studied it seriously through a score of sessions. He had glassed it until his eyes and head throbbed, hoping the vein would show up clearly under the magnification and he would not have to make the dreaded climb. There were just too many cracks and crevices to see it any other place, except there on the bluff in the flesh. His.

He worked his way through the tumbled mass of boulders carefully so as not to strain any muscles or ligaments. To get up to the conclusive evidence he would need all his physical powers to help parlay his mental capacities.

He had decided to come at the bluff from an angle he had picked out earlier. It appeared to his naked eye, now that he had neared the spot of resolution, that he could angle sideways and upward, and at the same time avoid the straight ascent that had broken Ludwig. One thing he had spotted with the glass was the flat-looking ledge two-thirds of the way to the top. He had located it earlier in the spring when he saw an eagle land there.

The first going was not so difficult. There were plenty of indentions for his hands and feet. The bluff angled back ten or fifteen degrees giving his body something to rest against between moves. Already, though, he realized he had misjudged the height; it was much greater when his eye was six inches from the bluff's hard, unforgiving face.

Slowly he moved one hand, one rubber-soled boot, at a time. He could feel the sweat just beginning all over his body, but it wasn't bad as yet for the early morning gusts of wind cooled and helped dry him.

Suddenly he was on the edge of a crevice only about a foot and a half deep and perhaps four feet across. Leaning as far as he dared with one hand out, he still could not quite reach the other side. It was just barely beyond his reach. He would have to retreat and attack again where the indention was narrower. On his attempt at the second step backward, his right foot could find no hold. He moved it about, seeking, touching, scraping it across the rock. How could that be? Where had that foothold gone? He was returning the exact way he had come.

He stretched down as far as possible, straining his fingers, precariously grasping the rock to the limit and pushing the knee of the solid leg hard against the unyielding stone. The sweat came now and he didn't feel the breeze anymore. He was trapped. He could not descend an inch. There was nothing to do but try to get back to the crevice.

He kept one wet cheek against the rock now as he inched back up. Twice a hand slipped from the sweat and his weight. He was suddenly much heavier than he had ever been in his life. He was pulling his muscles tight between all his joints. As he lifted his body, he felt they would rip and twist into the form of steel coils.

The gray nothingness had come upon him, because he was back at the crevice without consciousness of having groped the last few feet. He held a moment to gather what was left of his courage and strength before he leaned out again straining, reaching, until he touched the rock. There was a handhold—just one, but he could not force the extra fraction of the half-hand's distance it would take to reach it.

When he returned to his four-point position he realized that he was in about the most perilous position he could imagine. He could not go down without falling probably seventy feet onto jagged boulders, and the same fate awaited him if he tried to go up. Or there was the impossible choice of grabbing at the single handhold as he shoved himself across the thin mountain air between the edges of the crevice.

Finally, as sweat started trickling down into the corner of one eye, he made up his mind to try it. Once that was done he said in a whisper, "Well, Ludwig, in a moment I may be keeping you company on the hill outside Breen, but here I go." Again he extended his arm across the space with all his force. The far tips of his searching fingers were almost there, but it was the limit at last. He propelled with the other three members, grasping outward for his life. The hand locked into position on the rock and almost ripped apart as the weight of his body struck the bluff. He clawed with his hands and feet for any notch of any size. The fingers of his free hand shoved into a small crack so hard it peeled the hide on his middle finger to the bone. He found another little niche for the toe of his left boot and held. The one leg that hung heavy, loose, and unsecured in space, gave him the impetus to claw his way upward through the gray nothingness again.

At last he opened his eyes to the flinty vision he was spread laboriously against. It was strange to him that the granite did look like flint this close up and smelled like old gunpowder.

He discovered he didn't know where he was on this massive outcropping any more than he would if he had been hurled past Mars without a compass. Bluefeather reasoned that there are many ways to break rock: by repeatedly freezing and then toasting it under the harsh sun for several million years, by earthquakes of great magnitude, by encroaching glaciers, by swinging a sledgehammer enough times with powerful arms, and with explosives of devastating power. But one thing he knew for certain, no matter how many ways one could find to break rock, there was still no known way to stretch it. None. That was for sure.

Almost mindless, and certainly mostly blind from the sweat that drained off his forehead, around his eyebrows and into his eyes, he moved upward with a Herculean effort. His hands were becoming so slippery from the wetness, every grasp felt like his last. In contrast, his breath was gasped in and out of his hurting lungs as dry and terrible as desert warfare. Then nothing moved but the bluff. It heaved and moved in wobbly, shaking laughter as he clung to its face. Cold and hot. Weak and strong, but always scared.

Then he said to the bluff, "You deceiving bastard, I know that rock can't stretch. You're not moving except as the world turns. That's all. You're playing little dirty tricks on me. That's for sure. Hey, I'm coming to your ledge, you vain old fool. Your ego can't take it that I'm going to sit right astride your golden vein and take a big, healthy dump right on top of it. How do you like that? Huh? Huh? Why so silent now after all your laughing and taunting? Answer me that."

Bluefeather's rebuttal to the mountain worked as far as his valor was concerned, but his indomitable will could not find a tiny pit for his wet fingers to hold onto. He was stopped here as sure as one of the recent evil imposters in their camp who had run into a tree.

He tried to move one hand up and then the other, over and over, but they would not hold. He was forced to return again and again to the handholds that were deep enough. The increasing sweat made every second more slippery and precarious. He didn't dare drop even the weight of one leg in an attempt to move downward. That much weight would certainly jerk his slick hands loose and hurtle him to eternity.

He could not even see the rock face anymore. Everything was slipping away. Without a conscious precept, he had begun singing the death song taught him by his Indian grandfather, Moon Looker. As he chanted on, the fear began to leave him. He cried out silently for his guiding spirit, Dancing Bear, then several sweet visions of Miss Mary undulated back and forth in the stone—smiling, laughing, beckoning. At this he stilled and braced himself, looking up for the first time. There it was just out of reach. The ledge. There was no question, because he could see the sticks of the eagle's nest protruding out from it. But it was no matter, for he could not move in any direction.

"Well, I'll be a cockeyed, castrated, one-eyed goat. There it is right up there, but it might just as well be in Chicago for all the good it's gonna do me." He didn't actually speak aloud. It was more like guttural rumblings in his throat. His face was jammed against the stone so hard he was afraid even to move his jaws. Even his eyes could only cover about a one-yard circle without tilting him loose. Comparatively this was the smallest piece of real estate that had ever owned him—less than a foot above his uppermost hand to the edge of the rock shelf.

Right here, within a few inches, was the whole world: all the books he had read; all the songs he had heard; all the fine food and drink he had tasted; all the love he had felt for Mary, Ludwig, his mules; all the mountains and deserts he had borrowed from the Great Spirit; all the deer and bears he had tracked and respected; and all the coyotes he had heard as brothers and sisters. Here, too, were the moon and the sun he had followed and avowed, along with the immeasurable space of the white-freckled blackness beyond. Water, wind, breath, life of the whole earth—these things and more were right here this instant. All.

Now he put his thoughts down to his one leg, bent at the knee, and about even with his waist. He concentrated with all that was left of him on that one limb. With an exuberant, reckless, and joyous yell, he shoved

his body with that pivotal leg. As he did so, a slab about twelve by sixteen by ten inches broke loose and plunged downward, bouncing crazily
at odd angles because of its irregular shape, like the broken club head of
a giant warrior's battle-ax.

Bluefeather reached through space and hung just a fleeting, horrible
second on the edge of the rock above, with fingertips digging in so desperately the fleshy ends burst open. Then the elbow of his other arm and
one leg swung over the precipice. He was there. He had made it. He just
lay on the stone as if it were made of goose down. When he was able to
move again, he kissed it like a returning prisoner of war when he first
steps upon his homeland.

Bluefeather said, "Ahh, sweet bluff. You have given me back my life,
so I will cancel my threat to dump on you. I think my pants are dirtied
from the last lunge anyway."

Miss Mary had not looked up at the bluff that had crippled her father
and seductively beckoned her life's love. She ignored it and went
about separating the little bit of muck from chunks that made up
their treasure trove. She had put all the waste rock on the dump and
piled the high-grade ore next to their camp table so they could sit and
replenish themselves while admiring its colored, crystalline beauty in
the sunlight.

She was pushing the last barrow load out from the portal when she
finally stopped and turned her head to look up for her husband. That's
when the sharp edge of the plunging rock struck her. Only a half inch of
it touched her.

Bluefeather slowly crawled around the edge of the ledge until he could
peer over its back side. There was no vein here that he could find. Of
course, he knew it would be weathered and dull. Just the same, he had
far better-than-average eyesight and lots of experience for his age at
spotting rare rock. He noticed that the back side of the bluff would have
been impossible for him to climb; it angled in toward the bottom. No,
he had climbed up the only possible way. He must not allow his
thoughts to linger on what might have been.

He turned carefully, futilely scratching at the most likely places for
the vein with a sharp chip of rock. He failed to find the completion of
Ludwig's dream. He had a moment of sadness as he asked Ludwig's

forgiveness. He didn't bother to apologize for the fact that only boiling nature could make a rock vein.

He had placed the rope on the eagle's nest. As he reached for it, he realized that the nest was built on the edge of the crevice that had almost consumed him. It took a lot of strength to raise the edge of the large interwoven nest, but he did. There it was. He had found it. He swiftly gathered pieces of rocks and built a stone post to hold up the edge of the nest and crawled under to examine the vein. He chipped at it with his prospector's pick, and when that didn't work he took his pocketknife and cut at it, finally working loose a small piece of gold stuck to a gravel of rose quartz. That was all the proof he needed to show Miss Mary so she would know that all vows had been kept.

Then he noticed that the vein formed one side of the crevice. He peered over and saw that a narrow projecting part of the vein itself had been the singular handhold that had saved his life when he had taken the little leap across the narrow void.

He crawled out from under the nest and removed the rocks. The nest would be ready for the eagle's eggs and a new brood of eaglets next spring. Now that his eye was adjusted to the weathered colorations of the vein, he could see where it wove its way on up in the crevice and dis-appeared. It was there—solid in the belly of the mountain. Just between his spot on the bluff and the tunnel's face, there was enough ore to mine and supply ten lifetimes. That didn't matter. What counted was Ludwig's dream. They had fulfilled it, and in doing so they had created their own.

"Hey Ludwig, ol' partner. It's done. You can rest easy, ol' boy, on your travels through the other worlds. Bon voyage."

His thoughts left the ledge now. They sailed above the treacherous, tumbled rock pieces toward Miss Mary. He secured the loop over an outcropping, wrapping the rope around his hips and jerking back with all his weight. It would hold. He rappeled down the face of the bluff, having great difficulty taking the necessary care in his descent across the random roughness of the mountain.

Finally he reached grass and bushes with solid dirt underneath. He felt no tiredness from the ordeal. Only jubilation. He rounded the edge of the rise and reached in his pocket as he walked proudly toward the camp. He took out the little sample of truth and held it in his open palm for Mary's eyes.

He yelled, "Mary! Miss Mary! We did it, darling! We pulled it all off!"

He saw her sleeping there on the barrow of gold ore. He felt guilty for shouting. A quick glance around at the ore separated and piled told him that she had worked very hard. She was plainly exhausted from the night of emotion and the day of labor.

He tiptoed up to her, smiling with reverence. He put his arms under hers to lift her up. Her head flopped over, and through the hair the color of fire, he saw the narrow gash just barely cutting into her brain. He knew, but he could not accept, that the blood on his hands was from her body. The cold numbness held him a moment as he talked to her and told her of their victory. He tried to get her to look at the little specimen.

"See, my darling...see how lovely it is. Your father will be so pleased. I know he is raising a toast to us right now. He is saying, 'Here's to Miss Mary and Bluefeather, my children who loved me very much.' Can't you just hear him? Huh? Huh?"

It was no use. He got control then. On the way to get a blanket to wrap her in, he saw where the fallen stone had imbedded itself in his homemade cabinet. He vaguely, as if from a time before dinosaurs, remembered the rock cracking loose under him as he made his final leap at the bluff's edge.

He wrapped her tenderly. Then he had an almost overwhelming desire to tear the baby from her—to salvage that part of her breathing life. But he killed the beastly thought. It was too late for that. The baby was not old enough to live anyplace but its mother's belly. So it would have to crash through and travel on with her.

His body turned to pain. The dull but excruciating throb of sorrow in his breast finally broke loose in long, shuddering sobs as he cradled Miss Mary across his heaving chest.

Bluefeather drove to the morgue. He told the mortician to deliver the coffin containing his wife and baby to the main house. The man tried to get him to sign papers and kept saying things about arrangements. Bluefeather did not answer him. He handed him a large roll of bills and said, "Do what I tell you."

The mortician did.

That night with some difficulty Bluefeather managed to secure the coffin in the bed of the old truck. He drove out into the darkness toward Harmony Creek.

He unloaded the coffin after cutting log rollers, and slowly, with many stops and endless adjustments of the rope and rollers, he finally got Miss Mary to the portal of the mine and then back into the tunnel.

By lantern light, he dug, with inconceivable strength, a large hole in front of the portal. He took the lamp and, scooting through the hole, entered the tunnel. He hung the lantern on an iron spike, then opened the coffin lid, straightened the beryl necklace on her throat, and placed the small specimen from the bluff ledge in her hand. Bluefeather looked at his love for a moment. The last moment.

Then he kissed her on the forehead and said, "Someday. Somewhere, my love." He closed and nailed the coffin shut.

Bluefeather picked up an anvil and carried it over, placing it next to the pile of ore. He leaned his rifle against the table. No one—no one on this earth—would be allowed to interrupt his duties to Miss Mary.

He hammered and chipped, hour after hour, until all the nuggets, wires, and ropes of gold were mostly free from the rose quartz. It took him the rest of that day and most of the night by lamplight to complete the task. He did not eat, drink, or sleep. All the gold was piled on their table now, almost covering its top.

He carried his labors into the tunnel. It took many trips. He scattered the sunflower mineral across the top of the coffin until it was completely covered. Then he got the other lantern and filled it and its companion with fuel. He drove a spike in the other wall and hung one lantern across from the other one where they shined down on Miss Mary's coffin. The tiny pieces of rose quartz caught the minute flickerings of the two flames and sparkled as if handfuls of diamonds had been sprinkled amongst the gold.

Bluefeather was pleased at last. Mary's tomb would be no less than the greatest of Egyptian or Mayan royalty. Considering the clean face of solid ore revealed at the head of her coffin and the just-proven length of its richness, all other tombs in history were amateurish.

He didn't pause now but turned and walked toward the light of the world shining outside Miss Mary's place.

Now Bluefeather was all professionalism. He studied the two rocks that held the huge boulder in place above the tunnel. He hammered and drilled at specific angles and measured his powder charges to his own perceived expectation. He wired it with care and then without hesitation knelt beside the newly acquired charge box, pushed the plunger down, and blew the barrier out from the front of the obelisklike rock.

It was freed and dropped down into the hole, sealing the tunnel so perfectly it could not have been better planned and executed by an entire family of gods.

It took Bluefeather three days to tear down everything in camp and haul it away. But at last he had cleaned, shoveled, and swept with branches until the spot was returned as near to its natural setting as was humanly possible. Then with a hammer and drill he chipped new petroglyphs on the curving face of the fallen boulder.

First he made a cross three feet high; next a peyote messenger bird, sleek and streamlined, flying the message as swiftly as thought straight up to the proper spirits in the heavens; and last he put his own personal sign that he had just invented without conscious thought. It was a circle inside a circle, and then he chipped three little dots in the interior circle. This represented Miss Mary, Bluefeather, and their child. The family in the world and universe. He dug up and planted thorny bushes in front of the boulder. Then he watered them and smoothed everything again.

"Now no amount of greed or need will ever allow me to upset the sanctity of this tomb."

He packed his remaining gear on his mules and led them down to drink from Harmony Creek for the last time at Miss Mary's pool. Just for an instant he was sure he saw her body—shining wet, smooth, vibrant, swimming across the pool—and heard her exultant laughter filling the canyon and the woods. Then it was gone.

He mounted Jackknife's back and rode away from the talking waters of Harmony Creek, leading Nancy. Their lease had run out. He did not look back. He couldn't. Ever.

He and his mules wandered in the mountains for several days. Bluefeather was unaware of his actions as he packed and unpacked the animals, automatically making camp and preparing just enough food for bare sustenance. Numbness prevailed.

Then finally, they dropped down out of his beloved San Juan Mountains where he followed a game trail into the northern New Mexico hills. There was a mixture of grasses, sage, cedar, and other small evergreens scattered around them as they moved down the curling trail.

He was beginning to notice the tracks and other signs of wild animals again and walked ahead of the mules for a change. Suddenly he saw a movement in an opening perhaps a quarter mile below. Dancing Bear was shuffling about in circles as if preparing, but not quite ready yet, to perform a full-scale dance. As they neared him, Bluefeather raised an arm in greeting and opened his mouth to yell a hello to his spirit guide. In this brief instant Dancing Bear skipped through the air over three treetops, landing on his toes and up again in ever longer leaps, becoming small as an eagle in the growing distance, then he appeared no larger than a sparrow and vanished altogether. Before Bluefeather could shout his dismay at this shoddy treatment, the whole of the firmament before him turned into the face of Miss Mary. The top of her head appeared thousands of miles above him. Her lips smiled at him bigger than the Grand Canyon. He stopped. The mules stopped behind him. He stared, but his keen vision was far too limited to encompass the entirety of the wondrous projection of the loving expression on her face. Was she God now?

As he struggled to absorb the massive transparent vision before him, the various parts of her beautiful face started separating. The cream of her cheeks floated down and became part of the mesas stretching flat topped across the high desert before him. The crimson of her mouth became part of the iron-blushed streak through the center strata of the mesas. Her sun-flamed hair swept from the sky and joined the barren vermilion hills farther on. Her great blue eyes of such vital mirth and knowing energy fused, dancing and vibrating, to intermingle with the boundless sky. The whiteness of her teeth whirled in a burst of light and motion to blend with the crowning snows far to the south and east in the Sangre de Cristo Mountains. Miss Mary's soul impregnated all. All.

A mighty surge of ecstasy inhabited Bluefeather's being. He offered both hands high above him in a silent thanks to the Great Spirit. Then he leaped down the game trail, agile and strong as a deer, shouting to the mules first and to the rest of the world next, "She's in the mesas, the mountains, the sky. Our darling Miss Mary is everywhere. Everywhere we look. Everywhere we step. Every breath we take. Everything we feel. She is around us, beside us, below us, above us, and inside us for eternity. Oh, joyous thanks a billion, a trillion times!"

Then he sat down on a flat rock, and with a smile made of amalgamated happiness, he stared across the ever-changing, ever-moving landscape of the earth, the sky, and all its flora and fauna that in their totality were his very own Miss Mary. He would never be alone again.

■ ■ ■

■ Part Two ■

TRANSITION—MISTS OF GOLD
Mists of Blood

Twenty-Four

Bluefeather never knew for sure why he chose the small, personal, adobe village of Corrales, New Mexico, on the northwest edge of Albuquerque, for his headquarters. Maybe because it had the same reminiscent qualities as Taos—just as varied, but with a smaller collection of nationalities and artists. It even had the domination of the mighty Sandia Mountains to the east. All this was a plus along with the natural rural feeling. Its small orchards, vegetable farms, and pastures were irrigated by the nearby Rio Grande.

He found the exact acreage he needed to keep his two newly acquired young mules happy and a pleasant, well-built, five-room adobe house. But what clinched it all were his new neighbors, Tranquilino Lucero and his family.

He took an instant liking to Tranquilino, and the feeling only increased when he found out he, too, liked and understood mules. It was decided. (Bluefeather would never regret this purchase, through all the times of horror and wonderment that he would be plunged into like a wheat straw in a tornado, inexplicably driven into a telephone pole.)

He settled in, patching up the adobe-mud house with Tranquilino's expert help. Bluefeather paid him a few dollars that the Luceros were happy to get. Their orchard, garden, pigs, chickens, and milk cow kept them in food, but Tranquilino had to do outside repair work for any extra spending money they might have. It was nice for him to get employment right next door.

It was a pleasant time for Bluefeather. He had the best of neighbors, a place just the right size to go with the house, small barns, and outbuildings. Everything was in good repair now. The two huge cottonwoods framing his house were well-watered and healthy. There was an old grape arbor under which he built an eight-foot-long table with benches on each side. He and Tranquilino enjoyed sitting there sometimes in the late evening, sipping beer and talking about mining, ghosts, and Hitler's war that was cracking and scorching a large portion of the earth. Or they simply stared out over the lush ditch bank at the elms and cottonwoods across the bosque (the sixty-mile-long cottonwood forest), which hid the fast-growing city, and up at the Sandias turning just as pink as the San Juan Mountains above Breen that he had left almost a year ago now.

Bluefeather had patiently trained his mules for packing and riding, and now the time had come to get on with his life's work. Arrangements were made for Tranquilino to look after the land and see that all was well in the house. He headed into the San Pedro Mountains north and east of the Sandias near the little mining towns of Golden and Madrid where, in the 1600s, the Spanish had taken out many millions in gold.

It felt good to get back into the hills again. He enjoyed the quiet companionship of his mules, which he had named Nancy, after his Tonapah lady, and Mary, after his love in a hidden tomb, or temple, as he liked to think of it. He had made the uncomplicated decision to name all his future mules Nancy or Mary. It was a point of honor, both ways.

He walked and studied the earth and hundreds of chunks of float rock. He assayed samples from many cuts and some old tunnels, but the best he came away with was a little bed of dry placer. Prospecting and mining were his chosen way, but he did resent having to pursue gold right now. He hunted for other minerals but found none that would pay.

He rigged up a good, dry shaker and recovered some color. Since he still had a few funds left from Breen, he did not have to worry about starving or having to hunt a grubstake. He accumulated three small canvas bags of mixed dust and small nuggets, but he could see that the sand would be gone in a few months, and he had found no other pay.

Every couple of weeks, he would ride down from the hills to Golden. He would drink and eat in the combination bar-restaurant and listen to all the war news. That was all anyone talked about anymore. Friends and relatives of just about everyone were scattered around the world fighting or preparing to do so.

He got a letter from his mother in Raton saying that all seven of the Marchiondo boys had joined up. This was admirable, but after Mary Schmidt O'Kelly Fellini, even the war was having a hard time affecting him.

Finally, though, he felt the pull of all these bodies, moving and gathering for the greatest storm of steel the world had ever known. It was irresistible to him. Since Tranquilino had too many kids and was just over the age limit, he would not be going to war. Bluefeather made a deal with the Luceros to oversee the property until his return. His mules could be profitably used and cared for by Tranquilino.

The Luceros did not know what was in the letter Bluefeather left with them, for it was to be opened only in case of his death. It contained instructions that the adjoining Fellini land would become theirs, along with the mules and the contents of a locked, iron box they were to care for—the box held about $30,000 in nuggets at the current going rate.

Bluefeather, the Luceros, and some other close neighbors had a three-day party, a fiesta, a drunk, a feast of red chile in great pots, tamales and posole, and hollow pillow-bread called sopaipilla—made properly only in New Mexico. They drank tequila, beer, wine, and even a little brown whiskey. While Tranquilino played his violin like a master, others accompanied him with guitars and dances. Oh, it was fun enough to last the war, he thought the day before he sobered up. Then over many tears and embraces he left to join the army.

Naturally, having knowledge as great as most graduate engineers and a high degree of reading ability that would have made him an ideal candidate to write and prepare general orders, he was put in the walking infantry.

Well, by God, he had done that too. He could outwalk anyone at the Fort Walters, Texas, boot camp and shoot better than anyone he met, but he was too accustomed to being his own boss—answering only to the dictates of mountain lightning storms and three-hundred-pound black bears—to take orders very well. He could have stayed in the army until retirement age and still would have been a private, but he went to war believing it was what one did if one's country, and possibly the freedom of the whole world, was threatened. That's what everyone said, and wrote, and repeated on the radio over and over and over. He believed it with all his soul. Later he was amazed at its truth. Hitler would make five mistakes that would save the entire world from torture, slavery, and death.

■ ■ ■

Twenty-Five

They were on the waters of the Bristol Channel, June 6, 1944, moving in support of the First and the Twenty-ninth divisions already landing and dying on Omaha Beach. Bluefeather's regiment, the Ninth, was an old, old, warring number first organized in 1798. But today the regiment and the world were all brand new to the mining man, who was now a rifleman in Company G, Second Battalion.

The troop ships steamed on out around Lands End and into the English Channel. Selected parts of the division had already landed in engineering and assault units to help their brother and sister divisions claw their way out of the water and onto the land, just as at the very beginning and birth of man aeons ago. The transports of the launching ships for troops soon heard, saw, and became part of the biggest military buildup in the history of mankind.

Bluefeather felt smaller than the most minute grain of sand. By nightfall the First, the Twenty-ninth, and elements of his division had secured a foothold and moved on past most, but not all, of the initial, heavily armed cliffs.

The night of June 6 and the day of June 7, Bluefeather was so seasick, he truly did not care when they landed or if they sank. Surprisingly, the German air force that was supposed to have been knocked from the sky that day staged daring night raids. The roar and explosion of bombs, the antiaircraft guns, the flaming barrage balloons, and the clattering of flak falling like steel rain on the decks of the ships stretched out in a convoy farther than any eye could see, made the night a circus of power and death; a display so large and unimaginable in scope, it finally became indescribable.

On the beach were parts of men, and in the water were parts of men. A small percentage were whole, however, having drowned as their landing craft disgorged them in water too deep for solid footing. The beach was a caldron of chaos beyond the limbs and bones and scraps of torn flesh mingled with discarded gas masks, useless punctured canteens, broken and bent concrete and steel beach obstacles, erratic piles of smashed and destroyed equipment, and disabled and destroyed vehicles already being reclaimed by the sand and sea. Destruction incarnate.

Many of the seventy-two known elements of the earth, which were of such beauty and sparkle in their natural veined and disseminated forms, were here fused, amalgamated, and alloyed into terribly efficient instruments of death. The same elements whose seeking and finding was Bluefeather Fellini's life's work were now particles of booming savagery just before the stillness of death. His sought-after beauty was trying to kill him, but of this he was mercifully oblivious. Violence—violated violence. Piercing, screaming steel, twanging off hard objects and thudding, slicing, piercing softer things, and on impact, blood flying into the convulsed air and becoming a red mist before running in rivulets, sinking into the wet sand searching for the birthing sea. This was the ultimate exploitation of the human wholeness—its severance. The bodies floated facedown calmly now in the sea, moving only as the mother ocean did. On land, the living crawled through the motionless dead and paused over and over next to the nonmovement to gather a bit of sulfurous air into their heaving lungs, and another tad of courage. Then forward again. Again. Again.

Bluefeather saw a lot of this, and none of this, as they moved out of the water into all the above—up little canyons, in the cliffs with sniper fire and artillery harassing them almost every step. Every few yards this harassment also killed someone. But the stench of his own vomit and the excrement and urine in his olive-greens helped disguise that of exploded entrails and the vast nauseating blood-smell strong as a thousand slaughterhouses.

The war was a blur. Like a barroom brawl. There were no great organized plans and brilliant military tactics, no inflamed thoughts of glory and winning of great battles, no patriotic images of heroics and the flags of one's country waving in victory. There was simply a moving blur of frazzled images in a twenty-yard circle. The war, the world, everything, was all in this very small twenty-yard circle. That's all he knew. All he felt. All he realized of existence and nonexistence. All.

They fought their way off the beach through the swift signatory howl and crashing boom of the eighty-eights intermingled with the "BrrrrrpBrrp" of the automatic weapons. The maiming and dying continued.

They moved to the outskirts of the lovely French town Trevieres, with green fields and apple trees and solid old Norman stone houses. The Germans fought like bulldogs, house to house. They actually had to be dug from the cellars before they would surrender.

On to the villages of Saint Germain de Elle and Saint George de Elle. The Germans were desperately attached to the latter because of the good observation posts it afforded and its protection of a major highway. Attack after bleeding attack was launched by both sides. The village changed hands like a million steel Ping-Pong balls. No matter what side was on the attack, the stones of the old homes were blasted until they were mostly powdered, random heaps. Each house cost a gallon of blood and a hundred pounds of powder and steel to destroy—an ancient formula. It stretched out for hundreds of zigzagged miles. Civilians, made up mostly of elders and children, cattle, goats, chickens, pigs, and pissants, were smashed and pierced to death.

Bluefeather followed, and moved, and fired the M1 whenever he got a glimpse of the gray enemy and sometimes when he didn't. He saw only little movements of the opponent but felt the earth shake like a cow's hide trying to dislodge a bloodsucking fly. He was so far beyond ordinary fear, he became numbly unaware of it.

Now they let the Germans have the ruins of Saint George de Elle and consolidated their lines digging in, preparing for a large-scale attack at the heart of the interior of Normandy—the day and moment unknown.

Men on both sides still suffered and died from intermittent artillery and sniper bullets, but on a much smaller scale. The reduction from intense second-by-second violence to hourly caused Bluefeather to pause and consider the odds of his card-gambling days in Tonapah, Nevada. If a man listened for the cough of the enemies' mortars, the zapping song of the eighty-eights, hit the ground on time, and kept his head below the tops of the hedgerows, he had a reasonable chance to live until the next big charge came off.

The soldiers had a chance now to wash, shave and eat their first K rations since the invasion. Bluefeather looked up at the sky and said, "I'm alive."

Now they could look at their living friends and see their gaunt, sunken features, say their names, speak and then a little later make jokes. They also had time to add up the number of missing and really miss them. The generals, the colonels, and all the higher officers were meeting, studying maps, casualty reports, the supply situation, the projected remaining air power of the enemy, and the growing support of their own uncountable tons of ammunition and supplies moving up.

The thick, stone hedgerows made almost perfect fences for the farmers' fields. Over the centuries the many plants that had seeded there covered the hedgerows with lovely, picturesque foliage. Their roots also wove around the stones with such a strength of possession that each and every hedgerow made a natural fortress. Hundreds of thousands of them stood so strong that tanks had to take long and dangerous time to break through. This was the great advantage the Germans had. Outgunned on the ground and in the air, they still had a new fortress every hundred yards or so for mile upon mile that seemed forever. For thousands it already had been.

A sergeant of infantry, who had been a mechanic in civilian life, solved this greatest strategic problem facing the Allies. He designed and welded a huge, pointed iron ripper on the front of a tank. It worked. Every available engineer and expert in this field was put to work. The idea that a workingman soldier would save uncounted lives and wounds of the flesh was of grand proportions. He should have been as honored as the greatest general, but it was only the dog-faced foot soldiers who truly appreciated the vastness of the contribution, and only a handful of them even knew who had created the smashing design.

Guns were cleaned, oiled. Muscles had a chance to limber and gain strength. Minds and emotions were pulled back together. The second most important thing besides breathing was the mail delivery. They read of home and the special ones there, over and over again, like listening to a favorite song.

Bluefeather said to Pop, "Well, Pop, you think we'll be home by Christmas?" (Every soldier in a long war asks this question, whether it's January or July.)

"No," Pop said, "not even if we live." He had come up as one of the replacements for the dead and wounded a few days before. He was really too old for a front line infantryman. He was thirty-five. Ancient. He looked sixty after a few days on the line.

Bluefeather felt old at twenty-six. Most of the warriors were eighteen to twenty. It has been said that kids fight and old men make the plans. Of course, there was no practical way to reverse it. But here was Pop. Bluefeather wondered how in hell Pop had survived basic training and transport across the seas and on right here to the front. All he had to do was say he had a pain in his chest or his knees were locking, and he would have been instantly discharged. Why was he here? How? Not only that, he wrote poetry in a little book wrapped in heavy waxed paper—poetry, by god almighty, in battle. He was soon known as Pop the Poet.

The child-soldiers were in awe of him and many were afraid. He seemed to them a man far too old to carry the heavy burden of a rifle, shovel, ammo, hand grenades, and other gear, under fire, falling, crawling, running, digging into the hard earth they slept on through long days following longer nights. Men who could accept the embrace of violent death surrounding them—inescapable for thousands—were confused and fearful of this simple old man who wrote of tender flowers and steel flak, of happily singing souls and agonized doom—but not Bluefeather.

Bluefeather had known real poets at Taos, and he had felt the poetry of Twinning and Harmony creeks and a love for his Miss Mary that transcended even the magnified destruction of Normandy. Instead of awe he felt respect for Pop. Instead of fear he felt a closeness, a kinship. He was certain that Pop had been guided here by Dancing Bear, as his own personal companion and mentor. How else could Pop the Poet be explained?

Pop was small, perhaps 130 pounds of bent weight, five feet, seven inches, and had sunken eyes and a long, thin nose over a mouth curved to kindness. He had much trouble keeping up on the forced marches of battle, and he was usually too tired during the rabid fury of combat to scoop out more than a shallow indentation in the earth. Part of his body was revealed, more vulnerable than others. He didn't seem to care, but now during the time of only small storms of steel, he had a deep foxhole between Bluefeather and Daniel Wind, an Osage from Tulsa, Oklahoma.

They were sitting, smoking and visiting on the edges of their foxholes as Pop quit putting words down and carefully wrapped the notebook with the waxed paper.

Wind watched him with much curiosity, finally asking, "Hey, Pop, you ever sell any of that stuff?"

"Never have," Pop answered. "Nobody wants it."

"How come you write it then?"

"Don't know." He sighed with a tiny smile. "I just don't know."

Wind said, "Well, maybe you're like me. I got ten, twelve dogs all the time. People always asking me what I do with 'em. I say, 'Hunt.' They say, 'What?' I say, 'Rabbits.' They say, 'Ain't no rabbits in a mile of this farm.' I say, 'See? Now you got it.'"

Bluefeather wasn't sure he got it either, but he and Pop laughed as hard and loud as possible without giving their position away to the foe. Bluefeather had an enormous craving to read some of Pop's lines, thoughts, feelings, but his old-fashioned raising—no personal questions to your elders—prevailed. His family had carried this unwritten tradition through centuries in Sicily and northern Italy and three generations in America. Politeness prevailed.

So he said, "For years most folks thought Melville's *Moby Dick* was just the wasteful scribblings of a seasick sailor. It didn't sell over two thousand copies for a decade."

Pop grinned. "So you know Melville, huh?" He seemed pleased, but even so, he added, "Well, he has me beat by exactly two thousand copies, and I've been putting this stuff down on paper since I was seven years..."

The shout came down the line, "Air raid! Air raid!" The three friends, along with many others, fell into their foxholes.

Two German fighter planes dived at their line, ripping the earth with machine guns. Then they were gone, roaring up and back to somewhere in France.

"Medic! Medic!" came the now-familiar cry of the wounded and dying.

"Oh, mama, oh, mama, I'm hit. Oh God. Ohhh God."

Bluefeather and Pop were the first ones out of their holes. It was Corporal Nye who was wounded. He had been straddling a slit trench with his olives tucked under his knees. Pop bent over and dragged him out of the excrement. The blood from three holes in his stomach was already coursing out through the fingers futilely trying to hold his life's fluid inside a sieve of a body.

Bluefeather jerked his first-aid kit out and opened it. He started to apply a bandage. Pop raised his writing and shooting hand, saying, "Too late." It was.

They cleaned up the best they could by the time the medics arrived. They radioed back for a burial detail. In a little while they carried him away covered by his raincoat.

Bluefeather was numbed by the suddenness of Corporal Nye's destruction. The vileness, the waste, maddened him, but the planes were gone. He was helpless to avenge his buddy. He had known him for nearly two years now. They had trained, and strained, long and hard together. They had been drunk and chased women together and recently fought and suffered together. This made them deep friends. Close—close as humanly possible. Closer than the blood of any kin.

As much as Bluefeather was shaken, Pop seemed more so. He was pale beyond his norm. It was as if his blood had all drained out the pores of his skin along with the corporal's. He leaned against the hedgerow trying to light a cigarette. His hands were shaking terribly, and when he finally got it lit he could barely hold it in his mouth.

Then he said softly as if talking to a sleeping baby, his dark, hidden eyes glowing from within, "We'll never know. Only a few will ever know and then it'll be too late."

Bluefeather took his helmet off and pushed at his dark, sweating hair, staring hard at Pop, wanting to question him, but at the same time having no idea what he would ask. Later, perhaps, if they lived.

Wind said, "Got drunk with the corporal over there at Wales. Gonna miss him many days."

Daniel Wind had spoken for them all, but he was wrong about the days. So many more would immediately follow Corporal Nye's destruction that there would be too much remembering to handle. In combat there is no time for the luxury, and relief, of weeping.

Twenty-Six

For days now it had been rumored that they would make the big push. Their artillery had been firing Time-on-Target for a week. This TOT was set so that every hour the regiment artillery would concentrate on a given spot. The Germans absorbed a great deal of these messages from hell and were supposed to weaken therefrom. Instead they fired back, but of course, in much smaller volume. The last two days, they had picked Bluefeather's Company G Second Battalion of the Ninth Infantry upon which to concentrate their heavy mortar fire. Each time the "carrummmp...carrummmp" coughed from the German mortars, they all dropped in their holes like frightened prairie dogs—and suffered waiting, waiting. Then the soft death whisper of the dropping shell and the "ha—whoomp" of the explosions cringed them into the bottoms of the holes as they attempted to bury themselves completely from the ripping, uneven chunks of hot steel. Even so, casualties were always present somewhere on the line.

Pfc Shadow Requenez, a Mexican American from El Paso, Texas, absorbed a direct hit from a mortar shell. He was dug in just past Daniel Wind. He came screaming up out of the earth. One leg was gone at the knee, and part of the bone stuck out, whitish and barren of the red. As he thrashed about in the mudding dirt, he kept jabbing the bone into the ground as if he wished to dig his own grave with the protruding sliver.

Bluefeather and Pop held him while Wind and Sergeant Pack—the lean, almost frail lover of war—tied several first-aid pads over the end of the shattered leg. Bluefeather twisted a tourniquet over the thigh. As soon as the medic arrived he gave Shadow a shot of morphine, but he went on screaming and thrashing about. Finally he quieted, and they lifted him onto a stretcher.

"Carrrummmp!" They came searching again. Everyone dived for their foxholes. It was automatic now. The Germans had the range down perfect. The shells made the earth twitch and bounce. Gravel and spent pieces of shrapnel showered in on them. Quiet. Waiting.

When the numbness of trying to make their bodies amalgamate with the earth eased, and they could gather courage to breathe a little again, Bluefeather listened a moment. Then he raised up, peeking over the edge of the dirt mound. Other heads appeared and saw that the medics were upright now. One was limping badly, a spot of the red soaking through his olive-greens just above the knee. Shadow's stretcher was riddled with shrapnel. The motionless, soundless figure of the Latin-American lad dangled the remains of his other leg off the stretcher. The medics stopped, lowered the stretcher, replaced the leg and a dragging arm back on it. They walked away—one of them needing to be carried himself. Pfc Shadow Requenez would never need an artificial leg.

Everyone had returned to their separate earth wombs, except Shadow. He had been Daniel Wind's very best fun-loving, hell-raising, drinking buddy. Even though the mortars came again, Daniel foolishly sat on the edge of his foxhole sticking his trench knife, over and over, into the earth as the shells burst all around him. Not a single piece of shrapnel touched Daniel. When the shelling stopped and the perpetual motion of diving swiftly into holes and slowly easing back up, listening for the cries of, "Medics," "Mama," "God," then looking around with silent relief when none came, then, only then, did Daniel Wind speak, and only to himself. "Hey, Great Spirit, you keep good care of that Shadow man. We got lots of laughs we gotta share someday...some-where...maybe."

That night on guard duty, Bluefeather had a sore tooth that finally abscessed. By the next day his jaw was swelled to double its normal size. Every shell that whammed the earth anywhere near him seemed to hit his jaw point-blank. The following day the entire side of his head was swelled like that of a snake-bit cow.

Pop told him, "You better go back and get that infection taken care of."

Bluefeather mumbled and settled back down in his foxhole.

Soon Sergeant Pack leaned his thin face over the hole and said, "Fellini?"

"Yeah."

"Get your ass back to the medics."

"I'm okay, Sergeant."

"Yeah. Well it's sort of embarrassing to insist on this, what with men gettin' their legs and heads blown off, but we're gonna need every man we've got in a few days."

"Okay, I'll be right back."

Bluefeather walked down a lane, each step jarring him so the diseased tooth felt big as a anvil. It was a lonely lane for sure. He walked past a dead black and white cow whose belly was swelled to the bursting point, with all four legs sticking out like posts. There were a few more signs of death, such as a helmet with a shrapnel gash in it that had reached somebody's brain, a riddled cartridge belt, and a couple of empty first-aid kits. All these things only emphasized the absolute vacancy of life here. It was as if the lane was poison itself.

Then he knew why. "EEEEeeeeeooooowwww zip, boom!" The eighty-eight shells shrieked down the lane in bunches; an observant artillery spotter had mistaken Bluefeather for a troop movement. Well, it was a one-man movement. He ran sweating, his heart trying to thump his ribs apart, hitting the ground, running, falling, rolling, crouching. On and on for over half a mile. The shells had shaken and jarred the lane to pieces in places, and a pall of dust and smoke hung over it. Not a single fragment of steel had touched him. He had forgotten all about his tooth, but as his breath came back and no more shells pursued him, the throbbing pain returned.

He found the medics' tents in a field shielded by a lot of trees and camouflage netting. It took more courage to walk through the newly maimed and low-moaning causalities and ask to have a tooth pulled than an attempt to catch an eighty-eight shell in his bare hands would have. Only the horribly maimed, or the dying, moaned in this war. It was so strange to see these men hurting so terribly, be in pale pain and swallow their inclinations to scream. He wondered about it as he would many things to come.

The tooth must be pulled. It had to be done. His friend Sergeant Pack, the war lover, had ordered it so. Medics, if they survive, become the most heroic of men. They do, after some time, become weary of imposters with little "nothing" wounds.

It took Bluefeather a few moments to gather the presumption to say, "Please sir, I have a tooth,…well, I have a tooth that is giving me,…well, I say, sir, could I bother you just a moment? I can see you're busy. Pardon me, sir, but I need a tooth removed. I know it seems like nothing...but...but, you see..." Then he grabbed one medic by both ears, jerking his head so that he had to look at him and said, "Forgive me, but I have orders from a superior officer to have this friggin' tooth removed. There is still some fighting left to do."

A few moments later Bluefeather Fellini acquired some more useless knowledge. First, all available sedatives were for more serious war injuries than his; and second, the roots of an infantry private's teeth are very long indeed—they go all the way to the ankle bone. While two strong medics held him from the rear, another put his knee on Bluefeather's chest and removed the tooth. It was a tragic operation. He was positive that his head had been pulled off along with the tooth. By the time he could stand upright without weaving in circles, someone had stuck his head back on, but he was still a little bit blind and did not see where the medics had disposed of his tooth.

Bluefeather said, "What'd you do that for? I wanted to use that tooth for the head of a prospector's pick when I get back home."

The medics were in no mood for any misplaced jokes, and since that was the only one left in him, Bluefeather spit out a wad of blood, blinked his eyesight back into focus, put on his helmet, and took a different route back to the front line.

The rumors of the big bust, later to be known as the Saint Lo Breakthrough, came about. The Twenty-ninth Division was on the right, poised to hit the heavily defended town of Saint Lo face on. He could hardly wait for the order to attack the almost impregnable position.

Hill 192 had to be taken from the Germans as it afforded observation for the advancing Twenty-ninth Division to the orchards surrounding Saint Lo in front, all the way back to the ship-clogged beaches.

They were ready. The tanks were gassed, greased, and the guns were loaded. The dirt-loving fighters hung hand grenades and double bandoliers of ammo on their clothing. The black snouts of the artillery waited, zeroed in. Stacks of shells were laid by, waiting for their controllers to lift them and send them singing through the sky to fulfill the two reasons of their manufacture: money for the maker, death for the receiver.

The little 60-mm mortars were right next to the rifleman ready to be fired. Farther back the heavy mortars waited. The machine guns were loaded with extra belts ready to be fed into the steel jaws that would spit them out in clustered groups that seemed to make the air itself become pieces of flying lead, inescapable in the numbers that spewed forth so fast it sometimes sounded like one continuous solid sound.

The Big It. This day, they were all poised to ride the wire-thin edge between life and death to its ultimate destination. Wherever the hell it might be.

The roar from above came lightly at first, then stronger and louder. The sky was sundered with hundreds of bombers. Their bombers. Horizon to horizon across the sky in such force they seemed to have come from a faraway place where no one on the ground had ever been or would ever know about.

Slowly. Oh, so slowly they moved forward, these mighty dragon birds of war. The smoke bombs had been set all along the front lines, all the way to the left and the right. However, several high gusts of unpredicted wind had blown the smoke back over the waiting soldiers in spots, making it impossible for the planes to drop their bombs with complete accuracy. Nature had always altered even the greatest of battle plans.

The men of this "day of true destiny," feeling smaller than microbes, looked up from the foxholes as the bombers droned, in a solid sound and perfect formation, above and toward them. The wisps of smoke slightly obscured their vision in places. The planes vomited their bombs—tons and tons and tons of them.

The skin of the earth crawled and shook in mighty agitation at this infringement. The earth did not just tremble, it was possessed of a vibration that must have reached to its molten core. It shook. Shook. Shook. The tops of the foxholes actually narrowed, spread and closed and then opened, while much of the abused earth floated in the air. But all the genius of science had failed to a degree. Many of the bombs fell on friendly forces. When they arose to attack, many were as numbed and shocked as the enemy. But rise they did. Those who still breathed.

The artillery, hundreds of pieces, hurled a massive mess of poisonous steel in the sky above them. It crept fifty yards ahead of the tanks. The engineers dropped shoulder charges that exploded both sides of the hedgerows so the tanks could burst through with their newly welded heavy metal spikes. The infantry followed, firing all their weapons. It was synchronized, from the planes in the sky to the creeping artillery, the heavy weapons and then, as always, the man on his belly, the man running, crouching, falling to fire or to die. The footmen had to wrap it up, always. The chatter of the machine guns and the crack of the rifles were lost in the density of sounds—endless, punishing, excruciating sounds. The mind-warping, wanton noise pierced all fibers of being. Every atom of the earth and air above was quivering with it.

As in all great battles, the front lines became staggered. Sometimes the men of the Ninth were out ahead of the main lines among the Germans. Then it became a very personal thing. The war narrowed to each man and the eternal twenty-yard circle.

Private Price of North Dakota died with a rifle bullet in his left eye as he tried to set up his light machine gun. A burp gun pinned the squad behind a hedgerow. Sergeant Mitchell of New Hampshire caught a burst from the burper across the neck. He died trying to give orders, but all that came out was a burbling sound as he choked to death on his private blood.

The Germans had dug tanks into the earth with portholes at the bottom of the hedgerows so that they could rake an entire field with cannon fire. Machine guns were dug in at corners so they would have sweeping cross fire. They were great improvisers, these outmanned, outgunned soldiers, and they almost made the battle even, with their tenacity and skill. Almost.

Now Bluefeather and the men around him were becoming aware of another sound in the deadly din. The enemy artillery was coming in return, searching through the sky looking for living flesh on the ground.

Lieutenant Noble ran through his men shouting, "What in hell's the matter? One man's holding up a whole company! Come on, we're going to take this nest."

He jerked a pin from a grenade and rounded the corner of the hedgerow at an open gate, hurling it at the enemy dug into a round hole in the hedgerow corner. As the grenade left his hand he caught a full burst of Smeisser shells in the chest.

"Come on," yelled Sergeant Pack. "Come on with me."

Daniel Wind rounded the abutment just ahead of Bluefeather. The lieutenant's grenade had knocked two German parachute troops out of the hole. One was trying to reload. Wind shot him in the head with the Browning automatic rifle. The other raised a rifle and Bluefeather shot without aiming. The M1 bullet hit a rock in the hedgerow and ricocheted into the bridge of a German's nose. The middle of his face exploded.

Sergeant Pack was fighting hand to hand with one of the enemy. He stuck his trench knife in a German's side with such desperation he lost his grip on it. It hung, gradually shaking loose, as they bounced on the hedgerow, each man's hands at the other's throat.

Bluefeather started for them just as Pop the Poet struck the German in the back with the butt of his M1.

"Kill the bastard," Pack screamed.

Pop pointed the gun at him and just stood there. The stunned and wounded German somehow jerked the pin from a concussion grenade. Daniel Wind shot him in the chest and stomach as Pack picked up the grenade and hurled it over toward the other side of the hedgerow. It exploded in air. The blast knocked Pop down and staggered the others, but it was too far away to do critical damage.

A hell of a soldier, Sergeant Pack, from Clovis, New Mexico, where he had been a state golden-gloves champion and a runner-up as a six-foot welterweight in the nationals. It was an amazing accomplishment for one who now seemed so fragile. Bluefeather, observing Pack, began to realize the gods of war do not necessarily choose weight lifters or shot-putters as great infantrymen.

It was all clamorous chaos now. Everyone here in the bloody little circle was so confused and lost, they had no idea whether they were winning or losing this battle. Bluefeather's remaining squad members were separated from the rest of the company. Men from other detachments lay all around.

The spotter for the German artillery evidently saw that the soldiers from many scattered and varied elements of the division had overrun their positions. First the eighty-eights started firing for range. Now they had it, and the high, whining impacts fell among them.

"Medic! Medic!"

"I'm hit! Oh, God, I'm hit!"

"Help me, please, help me."

"Hurry. Hurry. Help. Please help."

"Mama, mama, I'm dying. Oh, God help me."

And those who were mildly hurt said nothing, trying to patch the wounds themselves.

Somehow the medics always came.

It was possibly redundant, but bad wounds, whether on altar boys or atheists, brought out screams for their mamas and their God.

Sergeant Pack yelled, "Come on, we're dead here," and his men, so thin in numbers now, followed.

They came to another hedgerow. Machine-gun fire tore the brush along its top, and the eighty-eights were firing almost flat trajectory over their heads. They moved crouching, hitting the ground as shells burst some forty yards out in the open field behind them. Then Captain Marson showed up with scattered portions of other squads and the rest of what was left of Company G.

Bluefeather squatted and leaned back against the hedgerow exhausted, awaiting further orders. Three or four yards in front of him, two men slept still and peaceful. He couldn't imagine such casual courage in the midst of the devastation. A shell burst only a few yards out and to his right. A piece of shrapnel banged off his helmet. Others zapped into the hedgerow around him.

He crawled over and grabbed at both the men, one in each hand, attempting to shake them.

"Get over here next to the hedgerow," he shouted, trying to penetrate their ears through the crescendo.

There was no reaction. No movement. There was no blood. No broken skin. The men had died of concussions. Strangely, after all he had seen of shattering savagery, this was the most repugnant. He was chilled ill. To die without even the honor of a wound was somehow unholy. But then, what wasn't in this maelstrom of purposeful insanity?

A tank clanked past. A squad of engineers fired a large charge of high explosives, ripping a wide path for the tank in the hedgerow. The iron Goliath lumbered around and rumbled into the new opening, with cannon and automatic weapons firing bursts across the open wheat field.

Sergeant Pack yelled, "Up now, all of you! Up and fire!"

Those who could slowly, even reluctantly, rose. Although the enemy was unseen across the field, he was certainly there.

Bluefeather fired on every shadow among the brush-topped hedgerow a couple of hundred yards away. A stranger fired next to him, methodically, as fast as he could empty and reload the M1.

Then as Bluefeather reached for another clip, the man wheeled toward him staring with his mouth open, his lips moving as if to speak. He fell. A bullet had penetrated his helmet. Bluefeather knelt by him and saw that the bullet had struck high in the forehead and come out the back of his skull. His last thought would never be verbalized. Incongruously, he realized that the greatest thoughts of humankind were never written or spoken.

It was very close to impossible for Bluefeather to rise once more, but he did. He peeked as low as he could over the hedgerow, like a squirrel watching a hunter from over a fallen log. Just at that moment a shell struck the tank and fire leaped out from it. A soldier raised the hatch to escape the oven, but the enemies' automatic weapons drilled at him. He fell, hanging half out, half in the tank. He had not felt the fire.

Suddenly, for just a moment, things were very still, like the unexpected brief quiet that comes occasionally between the crashing waves on a long seashore.

Then Captain Marson shouted again, "Move out!"

He had a radioman with him and was receiving orders to continue the attack. The cost had not been discussed. There was no option here. As he led the way through the open gate across the clearing, the same machine gun that had caught the driver of the tank perforated both him and his radio operator. They fell face-down. The captain moved his left leg only once. A private, a new replacement whom Bluefeather had never seen, ran to help the fallen men and died alongside them.

Sergeant Pack held up his hand, signaling a halt at the edge of the gate opening—perhaps fifteen feet across. It was a tiny opening in such a large field, but far bigger than any shell. It was pure, naked space. About every thirty seconds a machine gun fired a short burst into it.

"Get ready," Pack yelled. He raised a hand, looking at his men, waiting.

"Rrrrrrapp . . . rrrrrrrrrrapp."

"Now."

Feeling as nude as the space they ran across, they made it. That is, Pack, Wind, Pop, and Bluefeather made it. The next two men were caught. Others succeeded, too. Finally, there were nine fallen men pouring blood in little dirty red rivers across the opening. One had his neck artery shot in half, and a stream of blood spurted in the air at each pump of his heart like a tiny West Texas oil gusher, only it was red liquid instead of black. Strangely soft moans filled the air that was defiled with acrid smoke, the fumes of burning gasoline, oil, and the essence of arteries. The mist and scent of blood was prevalent above all. It dominated even the smell of tons of exploded powder and singed metal.

Bluefeather watched in agony as Corporal Bulto, a heavyset, American machine gunner, tried to outrace the German machine gunner's finger. He almost made it but slipped in the blood and fell face-down in it, his weapon hurled safely on ahead of his exposed flesh.

"Rrrrrrapp."

He took an entire burst in the side. Bluefeather reached out and grabbed him by both hands and dragged him across the slippery earth up next to the hedgerow. There was no use crying "medic" for Bulto. Following, with the wrong timing, was another radioman. He was shot in the ankle as the machine gun spit out its last bullet before reloading. Pack, alertly and bravely, slid out, jerked him to his hands and knees and dragged him falling, slipping, rising, falling again, in the blood-mud, across the terrible place. He had saved his life, at least temporarily, in the uneasy safety of the hedgerow.

The radio would not work. The German gunner was back at his deadly pastime now. The bullets were striking the dead bodies, moving them a fraction. They didn't care.

"Mortars," Pack yelled. "We've got to have mortars." He raced right back across the opening, almost sliding down, but the German gunner was a fraction too late to get him. A fraction. Now, all up and down the endless rectangles of hedgerows, men were lying, hurt, afraid, dying. And when it seemed they could not possibly bear anymore, the eighty-eights sniffed them out again. The unmaimed dug in.

Bluefeather ripped a hole in the earth with a small GI shovel faster than a dozen badgers. When the eighty-eights were once more quiet, he sat on the back edge of the foxhole looking across the field at a tree with an empty, two-wheeled cart under it. He thought that just a short time back a Norman farmer had rested his team of horses there and had taken his noonday meal. The alterations of war are as varied as fingerprints. Now and then a shell cracked into the tree. It was broken and torn and stark against the sky. The clouds were not real at all. They must surely have been drawn with a huge sky-pencil. No one looked up but Bluefeather. He felt silly and sad.

A soldier came stumbling along. He was blood all the way from the soles of his feet up. One eye socket was empty and left a little cavern in his head. It was obvious an antipersonnel mine had exploded right in front of him. He just stumbled on by, moaning like a long-lost child. An eyeball dangled from a string of flesh down onto his cheek like a rotten plum. One hand flopped loosely, the tendons revealed like white wires. The numbed soldiers tried to stop him, but he walked right across the opening, moaning. The machine gun spat at him and missed. A medic helped him across the last of the opening, kneeling beside him. The man was silent now. The medic took a raincoat and covered him.

Another soldier, without a shirt, casually walked along. He had a hole in his chest from which a thin trickle of blood oozed. Bluefeather stopped him before he hit the opening. The soldier hesitated only a moment.

He gasped. "Look, I'm bleedin' like hell inside. I can feel it. I got to get myself to a doctor. I ain't goin' to last long, friend." Amazingly he gathered the will to cross the opening and made it.

Bluefeather could see where the bullet had peeled the meat away from his back like it would the bark of a small tree.

Then a shell came whipping in from the side. Bluefeather flinched down into the small space he had initially scooped from the earth. He knew that part of his body was revealed. The shell hit in the field with a dead thud. Bluefeather bunched all his being against the impact. It didn't come. It was a dud. He looked to the side where the shell lay. He could feel the powder wanting to burst apart the steel and, subsequently, his body. He stared at it like a field mouse hypnotized by a rattlesnake. It was a long, long time, in battle time, before he could pull his gaze away from the unspeaking shell.

A jeep stopped across the way. It was a medical conveyance rigged to haul the stretchers of the badly wounded and those beyond that. The experienced driver waited for the machine-gun fire, then gave it all the gas he could across the opening. Everyone watched the successful maneuver and gave tiny applause somewhere in their minds. The jeep was on a farm trail perhaps twenty yards out from the hedgerow. As it neared a tree, it just raised up off the earth and blew to pieces along with all the well, the wounded, and the dead bodies on it. A mine. Up there in the tree hung what had a moment ago been a man. Strings of shredded flesh dangled, along with pieces of his insides.

Bluefeather stared and stared. He glanced at Pop. He was vomiting. Bluefeather tried to heave but only dried air came up. He looked at the tree once more and then back at the dud eighty-eight. There was Dancing Bear squatted down sitting on the shell. Bluefeather started to scream a warning at him before the dawning of who it was stilled the cry.

"That's perty fair fightin' goin' on around here, dear brudder."

After what Bluefeather had seen and survived in this single day, he was qualified to make a year-long speech if he so desired, but because he felt too weary to work his vocal cords so heavily, he simply said,

"Hey, I learned something, Bear. Ground war made me realize that one can breathe blood...and nothing is unbearable." He was silent for a while, then he finally overcame his weariness enough to try to be angry. "Where the hell have you been?" He motioned at the carnage around him. "Can't you see this is the worst day of my life? What good are you if you aren't around when the going is tough? Answer me, Bear."

Dancing Bear did a friendship dance around the shell and followed that with one of his famous toe dances right on top of the murderous object. Bluefeather's anger dissipated like an alcoholic's memory. Dancing Bear had presented his message clearly enough in his delicate association with the unexploded shell. Not even Dancing Bear would have blamed him for his flashing thought of suicide. It was just too damn much. However, better judgment did prevail. If he wanted that, all he had to do was raise his head above the hedgerow. The Germans would be delighted to accommodate him.

Instead, he croaked out like a sick chicken, "Answers, Bear. That's all I'd like." He glanced around him guiltily at the motionless forms now slicker-covered. Then he remembered that his voice could be heard by the dancing, maniacal Indian spirit guide.

Dancing Bear slowed down to a shuffle dance now. "You are right. Going is tough all over around here."

"You been around here today?"

"Oh, for sure, dear brudder. I been working my ass off for my clients on both sides."

"You been consorting and consulting with the enemy?" Bluefeather was mortified. "I shoulda known that's why they had us zeroed in all day. That's treason, Bear. You oughta be hanged."

"Whoa. Whoa, to you I say, for sure. They are your enemies for now. Not mine. I don't have any of those. That's not the way it works when you crash through to this side of the river. Why, just last week I was down in the South Pacific comforting some of my Japanese clients."

"My god, the Japanese, too?" Bluefeather was aghast. "Oh, dear Great Number-One Spirit, banish this bastard straight back to this dimension right here and give me three seconds with...three seconds, that's not much to ask for."

Dancing Bear decided he didn't want to hear this kind of talk, so he didn't. "Also I been over in China and Russia doing work. And I been to Brazil and Lebanon and the Philippines and..."

"Stop. Stop it. That's enough. I got the idee, kiddo," he said from his mentor, Grinder, without even knowing it. "Don't run it plumb into the ground."

"Oh, no, dear brudder, ground too bloody."

"Look, Bear, I'm sorry. I've just had a touchy day."

"That's all right, young Blue. I get shouts from people having troubles all the time. Everywhere I go. Don't matter. Folks all over think they're the only ones with troubles. They don't think I got troubles over here. Now let me tell you what happened to me in Detroit last April. This woman, she…"

"Bear, Bear, Bear, you're forgetting what your position is. What your appointed duty is. You are supposed to listen to my troubles. Give advice, not ask for it."

"Oh. Oh. You're so right there, brudder dear. I haven't slipped up like that since the San Francisco earthquake. Whew. I hope my supervisor was too busy and didn't hear that. I might get sent to Antarctic—barefoot—on that one. I sure hope this tiny, teeny, little-bitty, minute mistake don't get back to the Authority. He would have no mercy, at all. He might even send me to Bakersfield again."

"My god and little dandy daisies, where did you get that idea about Bakersfield? That's good farming country, and now they're gonna drill for oil there. We need oil for these tanks and guns and unruly hair and stuff."

Then Bluefeather realized that he was getting silly and out of line with his spirit guide. They both were overreacting from a hard day on the job. He decided to be nice and polite and make amends for them both. "Please, dear Bear, I wish you would get me outa here before the Germans do. I've been at this steady, by the minute, for a lot of days now. I'm wearing out. It's getting close to unbearable. What's the answer, old amigo? It's your turn now."

"I say to you the truth, ain't no way for right now to change jobs. You know what the feller said about horses in midstreams, and another one talked something about leaving sinking ships, and then there was the lady in Paris who wrote down about being loyal to your friends. What was her name? You remember her, don't you, dear brudder? That wolf- and deer-hunting president one time who talked about those good men who get down in the arena. What was his name? What all was it he said? Boy, something is happening to my memory."

"I knew it. I just knew it. All I'm gonna get outa you is questions. Millions of goddamned shit-eatin' questions. I tell you what I'm gonna do, dodging Bear, if you don't help me on past right now. I'm gonna make prayers to the Number-One Spirit, until that entity lets me skip across the river and leap up two or three dimensions until I'm in yours. Then I'm gonna jerk both your ears off because you don't use them anyway. Then I'm gonna jerk your shoulder sockets loose and break your arms in so many pieces I can tie them behind your back in a bowknot. Then...then, hurting Bear, I'm gonna fill all the way up with mad. I think you can tell I'm almost full of mad right now. Huh? Huh?" Bluefeather giggled his position away. He rubbed at the scar on his nose for the first time in an hour and started growling in mock anger. He had so many thoughts he could hardly keep them in his mouth. "Hey, Bear, you know I'm just joking. This day's work was as much fun as a free trip to Hawaii...and I'm gettin' paid almost forty dollars a month for it. Think, and be jealous of all these benefits."

"Say there. I heard that one real good in both ears. Give me a few seconds and I'll think of something sweet and soothing for my dear brudder Blue."

One of the most stupid things Bluefeather had ever witnessed was before him now, especially since Dancing Bear had just promised him sweets.

Bear was doing a war dance around the shell. Bluefeather started to scream about the idiocy of this act, considering how many guns had been fired all over the world within the last horrible hour, but no sound issued because he was witnessing some odd and unusual movement, even for Dancing Bear. He had quit dancing, picked up the shell, and it turned into three.

Bluefeather suddenly wanted to clap and yell, "Bravo."

Dancing Bear juggled the shells over his back, catching them on one moccasined heel and then the other, and pitched them right back over his head into his masterly hands. He juggled them through and around his legs. He slowly rose in the air, pirouetting and rolling sideways a spell. Even upside down, still moving his head this way, a leg that way, he was still in complete artistic control of the shells. Such dexterity was truly the show of all shows, except, of course, the one taking place down below in the hedgerows.

Then he was so high above the shattered tree, so randomly decorated by the power of gunpowder, that he appeared small indeed.
Dancing Bear grasped all three shells in both hands and flung them
straight up. They changed into three masses of golden mist that floated
slowly toward the earth. The sun, lowering in the west, beamed through
the three clouds of mist, turning them such a golden brilliance that the
beauty almost blinded Bluefeather momentarily. The three clouds then
settled around the tree of life, the tree of death, and dropped into the
Norman earth. Six hundred fourteen sunflowers instantly grew nine
feet and four inches tall and bloomed, turning their faces toward
Bluefeather, shining through the decimating smoke of battle in a red
haze. The flowers swayed to some unheard music in lovely peaceful
rhythms. For a moment, the floral aroma wafted and washed away the
awful, forever-imprinted smell of death.

Bluefeather waved one friendly hand as he looked back in the sky
where his Indian spirit guide had been. He was gone. Everywhere
Bluefeather looked it was peaceful as a baby's smile, until six British
fighter spitfires zoomed across the space. They, too, were gone in just
a glance.

Sergeant Pack came back with a 60-mm mortar crew. They set up
the guns across from the opening, and the instruments coughed out
three rounds for range. The gunners dropped the shells into barrels. Out
they belched, arcing high into the sky then down, down, faster, and "carrummmp," right on target. Pack was exultant. He danced around gleefully, reminding Bluefeather of his other-world-across-the-river friend.

It was unbelievable, but Bluefeather took the trouble to ask himself
a couple of hard questions. Are we all war lovers like Pack? Or was Pack
simply more honest?

The firing ceased, except for long-range 150 artillery from the
Allied side. The day's battle was done. There was no strength left on
either side for night-fighting foolishness.

The surviving Germans would magically recover most of their
dead, retreat under cover of darkness, and take up new fortifications by
dawn—waiting, waiting for the metal and men to come again.

Twenty-Seven

Only intermittent artillery fire could be heard now. The bestial symphony of war had taken intermission.

After cold rations, Bluefeather and Pop were getting in a last cigarette before dark. They talked in lowered voices, seeking anything living to communicate with. There had been so much of death that day.

Pop was writing in his eternal notebook. Bluefeather loved books, even poetry on occasion, but he had a hard time believing that Pop was writing a poem now—not now. And then he handed Bluefeather the book. He strained to read the words in the rapidly failing light, but they blurred together.

"I can't make it out. What did you write, Pop?"

"I don't remember now," he answered, his anemic, bony face standing out around his sunken but powerful eyes. There was a tiredness about him that had nothing to do with the terrible struggle of the past day. It was as if he had finally given up. Not on himself, but on everything else. He looked more than twice his age and a frail weakness possessed his being. He looked so old his nose was wrinkled.

Bluefeather realized, too late, he had taken the wrong tack in trying to cheer up his blood brother. "You know, Pop, as horrible a defamation as war is to the human species, it's still the greatest adventure we've discovered to date."

Pop looked at him from inside his head. He didn't speak. The cigarette hung unlit from his mouth.

"Pop, why don't you quit?"

"Quit? Quit what? Quit smoking?"

"Quit the war. Just tell Pack you can't go on. Hellfire, pardner, at your age, nobody expects you to go on with all of this."

"It's like the poems," Pop said softly, "I don't know why I write them, and I don't know why I stay here."

"Look," Bluefeather argued, "the odds are out on you. There are only seven or eight of the original men left in the platoon now. It's going to get us all. All. But you can just walk off from here in five minutes. Listen, I'll go talk to Pack myself while you get your gear ready. Okay?"

Pop acted as though he had not heard the last of the plea. "I know the odds are getting short. Don't you think I know that, Blue?"

"Well, then?"

He didn't answer, but said, "You know, I was just thinking about my kids a while ago. Thinking about 'em while I was writing. I was telling myself that maybe they would never have to go through what their daddy did, and that's what I wanted the most. But now I wonder."

"Wonder what?"

"I wonder if it's right they don't know. Somehow they have to know. If I really believed they could understand just a little about it, maybe that would be enough. It's not true, though. You have to be here a long time to understand the tiniest bit."

"Pop, nobody understands. I mean, nobody I've ever known anyway. We just flat-ass haven't learned to love enough, I suppose. But shit, that's nothing new. Well, I take back a little bit. I did love...uh...never mind. Hey, you know something that just came to my mind?" Pop slowly turned his gaunt face, leaning forward to listen as Bluefeather continued, "Well, we've been up here fighting and killing for nearly two months now, and I haven't heard one man—not a single goddamn one—ask why we keep doing this over and over and over again. What in the hell are we doing here and all over the crazy world destroying one another with all the strength of our beings? It can't just be over land and religion and boundaries and doctrines, can it? We aren't that stupid, are we?"

"I'm afraid we are, Blue."

"What is it then?" Bluefeather asked, realizing he had asked a question of Pop no man or woman had ever satisfactorily answered. He was suddenly ashamed and embarrassed to have spoken of such things. He certainly didn't feel like talking about them, but somehow it had brought Pop back—this terrible pondering.

Pop wrote almost furtively now, glancing up as if he didn't want anyone to catch him at such an embarrassing activity. Not here in a dirt hole—not this instant.

Bluefeather was silent, trying to act like nothingness. Then Pop handed him the page. "It isn't a poem. It isn't what I know. It'll just have to do until I can bring myself to say it."

Bluefeather could tell that Pop intended for him to read this no matter what. He pulled a blanket over them and it took two matches to read the few words.

Bluefeather read. "Hate is equally amorphous with love, every bit as ghostly, as unexplainable, just as mysteriously enticing and alluring. Jealousy can force feed love and activate hate. Both love and hate can be powder-triggered into single or mass murder by the stupidly shameful inferiority of new or ancient defeats, both actual and imagined." Bluefeather sat looking into a cloud of his own creation then handed the paper back to Pop.

"That, Pop, is a whole bunch of something. A hell of a start, but I still don't get it clear."

"I know. I told you. I told you I'd tell you...when..." Then Pop said resignedly, "I know. I can't put it into words right now. It's more than words. I been trying with these poems and this page." He wadded it up and threw it out over the edge of the foxhole. "I'm just not good enough at it."

"Please, Pop, you should never have owned up to it. Please, I gotta know what you know."

"I tell you, Blue, I can't right now. It's nearly time for me to go on guard."

Pop and the newly arrived replacements, Privates White and Burton, had the first guard. Before they left, Burton came by.

He said to Pop, "I hear you're a poet."

Pop looked up at him, through him, and beyond. "No. No, I'm writing imaginary notes for an imaginary audience."

Burton said, "Oh."

Bluefeather was to relieve Burton in four hours. He fell asleep almost instantly in the bottom of the hole.

It seemed like four minutes instead of four hours when Burton shook him gently. He woke up reaching for his rifle.

"It's me, Blue. Burton," he said in his soft, North Carolina voice.

"Anything out?" Bluefeather asked, referring to German patrols.

"Nothing. We've got 'em whupped. They're headed the other way."

Bluefeather got up and walked numbly to his post, on past the motionless, stiff figures, lying under slickers or blankets with only their feet sticking out to make known they once had been living humans.

It was a long night in Normandy, but a bird sang just at dawn in the shattered tree above the place of the giant sunflowers.

Twenty-Eight

They attacked early the next morning. Burton was wrong about one thing—the Germans had not pulled back very far. Before nine o'clock they were under heavy artillery bombardment. They worked their way along, cringing against the repeated shock of the shells. Most of them hit short or went over their heads some distance, but they were there all the time.

It was difficult to segment the enemy's shells from the Americans' with the guns firing so close behind. They fell into the ground and rose to run forward and then back to the earth until it was all of existence: father, mother, home, life.

Miraculously, Bluefeather's squad escaped any casualties until midmorning. They had not created any either. It was a duel of the heavy guns for now.

Then it started. The shells came howling in there and smelled them out. Bluefeather felt the earth toss under him and his helmet was blown tight against his skull. He grabbed the helmet as it was nearly torn away and pushed himself into a slight indention in the earth.

It seemed endless. Then the cry came—a frail, little cry. It didn't have words to it, only a message. He tried to ignore it, but it came again, weaker. It took all Bluefeather's will to raise his head.

Then suddenly he was up and running through the artillery bursts toward the cry. He was too late. Sergeant Pack was already in the shell hole along with Pop. They were working on Private White. His buddy Burton was already gone. A great chunk was torn from White's side, and the shattered ends of his ribs showed where Pack had tried to stop the bleeding.

"I don't wanna die," he gasped. "I don't want to die now. Oh please, please don't let me die now. There's something I have to...."

They were done. White and Burton were numbers now. The placid stillness of them made the movement and sound of the living artillery shells sound louder, viciously intruding on the sacred moment of passing.

As always Pack said, "Come on. Let's move out."

And move forward they did—all who were physically able. There were two moving lines on the Americans' side that day. One attacking and another heading back with their perforated skins leaking blood.

The Germans fought tenaciously for every fortressed hedgerow. They crisscrossed their machine-gun fire with the guns dug in under the hedgerows. Even under constant moving barrages of Allied guns, they zeroed their mortars and artillery at every troop crossing. When the Ninth Regiment artillery raised to let the infantry move up, the Germans rose from their foxholes and fought with rifles, grenades, and bayonets. Whether a compliment was in order, Bluefeather would never know, but he felt there was no honest way he could visualize a better all-around fighter than the German soldier. The Germans were natural warriors, sensing every weakness, every strength, and moving on them with deadly resolution. The numbers of shells they had to absorb were so great they would finally be forced to retreat so they could fight again. They even fought with tragic effect while in retreat.

Bluefeather and his few old and mostly new comrades paid a very high price for every yard of earth they gained that day in Normandy. Pieces of men, machinery, insects, dogs, cows, horses, birds, wings, bumpers, feathers, chunks of skulls, and the insides of all these things were scattered forcibly but randomly about.

That night was very quiet for a while, as it often is in war. The replacements—the new, green men—came up from the rear to take the place of those who had died or had been maimed. They tried to appear brave, but fear came like an ugly perfume with them. Suddenly everything they had been trained for seemed different than they had expected. They were needed intruders in a disoriented landscape.

The unforgettable smell got to them the most because they only made hasty, denying glances at the slicker-covered bodies and the stained, broken pieces of people and their discarded equipment. If they could last seven or eight days, the incoming and outgoing fire sounds would become more familiar than their own breath. They might survive a long spell after that. Few made it through the learning stage. The turnover was great.

"You'll be sorry," was the singsong refrain from the ten-day-or-more veterans.

Most of the new men were sorry to begin with and missed the humor of the statement entirely. Pack always had a line for them—only one— that was different and unexpected by the longtime survivors each time.

From his pallid face—which would make most dead appear vibrant but alive, because of the minute, inscrutable but permanent smile— Pack announced, "You know, men, life would have been miserable for me without hand grenades." Then he surprised everyone by allowing himself an actual outburst of laughter as he scuttled along a hedgerow under fire. He hurled a grenade that silenced a machine gun and calmly strolled back to take two more of the explosive devices from a body under a slicker. It would never be known if this random act of courage gave confidence or shivers to the new arrivals—probably both.

Pop said, "You know, Blue, it's a funny thing. I talked to White and Burton a little bit last night when we were going off guard. They both were absolutely certain they were gonna live through this thing. I swear it. They believed they had some kind of protection. They could feel it."

"They were wrong, huh?" Bluefeather said, feeling rather stupid at stating such an obvious fact. "Look, Pop, the Germans might break. A man might hold out till then...if...if it's not too long."

"Yeah, he might."

Then Pop talked about his wife and children, fishing trips to Oregon, his little newsstand business. He asked Bluefeather for the first time if he had a wife.

"I did. She died."

Miss Mary had come visiting in his random foxhole dreams, but mostly he tried not to think of her—not even the wondrous times they had shared. Looking back sometimes made a man look forward, and all he could handle was the day, was now, for now. Pop didn't pursue the conversation any further. Bluefeather was relieved and said, "You know, we should be talking more about fishing and girls and whiskey and dancing and yelling, huh, Pop?"

Pop gave him a little grin that knew too much and started writing in his notebook. Bluefeather dozed off, partly asleep—in the state of half-visions, and he saw the aspens on the Sangre de Cristos back in New Mexico. He saw the trembling of their new, green leaves. They shook from the joy of existence unlike the fearful, quivering leaves of Normandy.

A wispy parade of people with misty smiling faces, some waving their hands and speaking in unheard voices, passed through his vision: his parents; his Raton, New Mexico, friends and kin; Old Grinder; Lorrie; Stump Jumper; and there in the parade was a mariachi band. He saw Nancy and his darling, Miss Mary, and his mules. In spite of Grinder's advice—he had a clan. Here in the bloody air.

Now all his friends were marching across the Nevada desert then on to the red-rock areas of Arizona and New Mexico, all smiling and waving at him.

Then there was the spirit of Dancing Bear, and he heard him alone and would never forget what he said. "Ah ha, young man, there awaits you a greater adventure than war. Yes, dear brudder, even greater than that." Bluefeather was protesting and asking when and where at the same time. Dancing Bear continued, "In land beneath the trees where the water burns." Then Bluefeather's half-sleep and his half-vision vanished.

Pop was gently shaking his shoulder saying, "I've never given you anything, Blue, except worry, and this probably won't change that at all, but..." and he tore some pages from his precious notebook. "They're not much. I know that, but I had to put it down somehow. It's for you and...and all the rest."

GUARD

It was White
It was Burton
It was me
Standing guard by the light of the half-moon.

Eyes dead tired
Bodies numb, aching
Listening hard ahead
88s fiery above
Boom Boom Boom
105s way behind
White he whispered
Burton did too.
That's for sure
They would live.
Long, long night

Staring, blinking, staring
Rifles held taut
On through darkness
To surprising day
Ahead, ahead attack
Into the steel
Burp guns chatter
Cannons belch red
Mines rip earth
Bellies to the ground
Dead flesh smell
One cow here
One horse there
Closing in, closer now
Burton yelled stay
White yelled go
We'd like to live
But we don't know how
The bursting shells
Blow life away
But it's not mine
I'm almost sure
Sweat wet here
Blood wet there
Against the ground
Praying for night
Knowing your buddies
Are too dead to cure

White is gone
And Burton too
It's just me
Standing guard by the light of the half-moon.

It was signed, "For Bluefeather Fellini, my friend in France, forever. Pop Marsten."

My God, he had even forgotten his friend's last name. Bluefeather wanted to cry. He tried, but the best he could manage was a tiny sniffle in his left nostril. A great loneliness came over Bluefeather. He could not imagine, ever, how Pop had gathered the strength to write about fate throwing a detour in the path White and Burton had been so sure of following. It had wiped Pop out, all right, for he was sitting up asleep in his foxhole.

Bluefeather wanted to say something, but couldn't bring himself to disturb the exhausted old figure. Pop looked older than any attempt at measuring time. He was as still and lifeless as a dead car battery.

Bluefeather crawled over to Daniel and said softly, "Hey, Wind, do you know what an old, worn-out cowboy from Taos once told me when I asked him what thirty years of that kind of work was like?"

Wind said, "No."

"He said it was just shit, hair, blood, and corruption."

Wind thought a moment and said seriously, "He left out canvas and leather."

Bluefeather took a little time now, then speaking to himself he put their words together, "Shit, hair, blood, leather, canvas, and corruption." He whispered it several times before he reached in the foxhole and patted Wind on his perpetually tilted helmet. "Hey, Wind, you're a bloody genius. That ain't only a fine description of cowboying, but that's a damn near perfect description of this little old war we're in here right now."

About then, a light machine gun started firing bursts a short distance down the hedgerow. They all grabbed weapons and leaped up, except Pop, who slept on. The rest stared out across the uncut wheat field, expecting a night attack.

The gun fired an entire belt and then a noise came; a crying noise, but not human. It was a minute or more before Bluefeather realized it was the dying bleat of a flock of goats. The Germans had herded them out into the field, and the new man on the machine gun had become trigger happy.

Some of them bleated all night. It upset the men far more than would be expected. The goat incident cost them some casualties the next day because of loss of sleep. Bluefeather heard several soldiers mention the fact that they couldn't get the sound of the dying creatures from their minds. This was odd, since the cries of dying men were all around.

About noon they were held up by heavy automatic fire. Their artillery seemed unable to dislodge the Germans from a strong gun emplacement.

Sergeant Pack's tall, emaciated figure ran by, hunkered down just below the top of the hedgerow at least part of the time.

"Dig in," he ordered. "We're launching a tank attack in about five minutes." Bluefeather was astounded to see the rapture glowing from Pack's sallow, war-loving face. They welcomed this chance to burrow into the mother earth.

Pop had only enough strength to scoop out a shallow hole, that might, or might not, cover his entire body.

As Bluefeather dug he thought, "The damned old fool, he's going to get it today. There's not a chance. He's done. Why'n hell doesn't he go back?" It was driving him crazy, all this unnecessary worrying about the old man. Everyone wanted him to take his goddamned notebook and go home to his wife and kids. Everyone, of course, except Sergeant Pack. If a man could raise one arm and open one eye, he figured he should be able to shoot a gun. Damn the crazy old man. He could be out of artillery range in fifteen minutes. Safe. Everyone would silently applaud.

Pop was throwing Bluefeather's survival rhythm off, and he was talking serious crap to him when he should have been concentrating on nothing but escapist fare. All who had survived more than ten days in heavy combat knew that heroics and cowardice were from the same mold. Survival is the only bravery after the odds have thinned far enough against you.

Angry from his love for the old man, Bluefeather dug furiously up against the brush and rocks of the hedgerow. He dug deep. Some insects were bothering him, but because of the clanking roar of the tanks coming across the field, he ignored them.

The enemy had held up their artillery for a couple of hours. The six U.S. tanks ground out onto the field firing ahead at German emplacements. Then from higher ground the eighty-eights came. There was no firing for location now. It was a perfectly executed trap. The shells whammed all around and into the tanks, in one grand explosion. At least ten or twelve cannons must have been concentrated on the field.

Bluefeather hit the hole with shrapnel zipping across the edge into the hedgerow—very close, for the thousandth time. Then the insects covered him. He had dug into a wild beehive. In a moving mass, they covered his hands, his face, even his closed eyes, ears, mouth, and buzzed under his helmet. Bluefeather almost panicked and raised up out of the foxhole, but there was no choice. Nothing could bare itself to the hail of steel up there and live.

He made prayers in Pueblo Indian, Sicilian, and English. He lay perfectly still and made more prayers and promises of bribery. He told all the great spirits, no matter what their religious preference, "If you'll let me survive these bees, I'll go and accomplish that great adventure under the trees by the burning river. I swear it on the souls of all my grandparents as far back as the Sicilians and the Tiwas go. Even further, if needed, Dear One."

Not a single bee stung him. Not one. And after a while they all left at once. It was a very difficult thing for the young soldier to believe. He had seen much in life already, that was for sure, but this deliverance made him humble, profoundly so. He surely would attempt to fulfill Dancing Bear's prophecy and his own wild promises. But he didn't have much time to repeat his vows; the shells came on all that day. My God, how the Germans fought for land that wasn't even theirs. Vire, France, only a few miles away where the Twenty-ninth fought, had been conquered by the Germans, and now the GIs of the Second Division had to go on dying until they took it away from them for good. The town wasn't theirs, either. For a moment Bluefeather lost sight of the rules. Who in hell was refereeing here, anyway?

Finally, in between bursts of the eighty-eights' coordinated fire, he could stand it no longer in the bottom of the visionless hole. He raised up and took a quick look. All six tanks were knocked out, their hulks torn and rent and burning. The smell of cooking flesh was almost unbearable. Bluefeather felt guilty thinking that the smell was probably as mouth watering to the gods of war as to the early-rising inhabitants of a hunting camp.

Bluefeather wished he were someplace else. Say, right on top of Taos Mountain with a gallon of wine and Ramon of Dawson playing his old Spanish love songs for him. He would feel so good to be there that he would do one of Bear's toe dances all the way to the Rio Grande, where he would go fishing. These were nice, little, foolish daydreams, but one wish of all his buddies was granted an hour before sundown. The P-38s came.

They dived on the heavily fortified hill and dropped bombs and fired rockets. Ah, what a sight of splendor. For the first time since the beaches, they all stood up in their foxholes and cheered at the beautiful life-taking, lifesaving sight. Bluefeather wondered if the German infantrymen had done the same when their artillery had demolished the American tanks a few hours earlier.

Bluefeather told Pop about the bees. Pop grinned weakly and said, "I promise you I'll laugh out loud, later."

The next morning they moved on to the crushed, but still heavily fired upon, city of Vire, seeking to cut off and entrap the entire German army there. Sergeant Pack, Daniel Wind, and Bluefeather were the only ones left of the original squad. They walked on, and fought and dug, and were thirsty and seared, and sick and cowardly, and brave and lonely.

The battered Twenty-ninth Division held Vire. The Second relieved them late one afternoon and moved toward a high spot in the powdered town. The Germans shelled the living hell out of them as they took over the bunkers. They were good ones. In spite of the shelling, the protection they offered gave the gift of light casualties through most of the following day.

Pack sent Pop and Bluefeather to get two cans of water from the supply depot to the rear, and if they felt they could carry them, some dry rations.

They moved down the main road—clear, but pulverized now. It had once been blood and stones, but the red stains were not visible; the shell-shocked earth had settled over it as dust. The street was a deserted Sahara, made of even finer grains.

They got the water and half a pack each of C rations and struggled nakedly back up the street. Now, several more GIs from different platoons were on water and food details. As the war gods would have it, they all met next to a bombed-out building with a cellar still partially revealed.

Pop put his water can on the edge of the cellar, moved down some concrete steps, and sat down, saying, "I finally have to admit it, I gotta rest a minute. Blue, come on down in the shade and let's have a smoke and talk about fishing in Oregon."

Bluefeather had heard, since the first hour he entered the army, that you never hear the shell that gets you. Well, they must have been talking about small-arms fire, because he heard the "boom" and then the heavy, rustling "swoosh" of the shell from a railroad gun displacing air like a runaway train. He, of course, didn't hear it hit about ten or twenty yards away.

Bluefeather woke up blind. He flailed his arms out to his sides in the rubble in the bottom of the cellar, desperately seeking to feel what world he was in. Then with great trepidation he put both hands gingerly to his eyes. Maybe he was dead. Maybe that would be better. If he was dead, why wasn't Dancing Bear there to quiet him with the glowing white light? No . . . no, there was wet flesh around his eyes—probably his brains—but how could he have these thoughts if his brains were blown out of his skull?

"You okay, Blue? Speak to me, Blue."

Well, at least he wasn't deaf, because he heard Pop's voice as he pulled the entrails that once belonged in some other GI's body from around Bluefeather's face and eyes.

Bluefeather sat up. Then he stood and then stumbled to his knees. His head hurt beyond anything he had ever imagined, and the world whirled so fast the dizziness made him throw up. The world slowed. He could finally stand. He was bleeding from the nose, the mouth, and one ear. Only one tiny piece of shrapnel had hit his forehead. He rubbed it, pulled it out, and stuck it in his pocket for a souvenir, like a child keeps a pretty rock.

Pop washed his face with a little of the precious water from his canteen, saying, "You'd better head back to an aid station."

Bluefeather knew that he probably should, but he had spent so much time trying to get the old man to go home that now a stupid, stubborn streak possessed him.

The other GIs would need no medics. Bluefeather had been blown about twenty feet out into the basement, and he couldn't see a whole part of any of the others—anywhere.

It had been two days of miracles. Pop had been below the main force of concussion and steel. His water and food were intact. Bluefeather sent him on saying he was going to get a checkup at an aid station and would catch up later. What he did was go down and trade in his shredded can—that looked like a cheese grater—for a new one full of water.

He delivered the water and rations to Pack and a new corporal. Pack said, "What took you so long? You been takin' in the sights?"

Pop pointed at Bluefeather and said, "Sergeant, you oughta send him back. He got a concussion that blew him almost across the basement of a big building. Look, he's bleeding from the nose and ear again."

"Hey, Pack, don't listen to that worn-out old bastard. I'm all right or I wouldn't be back already."

Pack's entire life was spent running yellow lights. It was the way he had been made by two relatives copulating his final genes together in some dark jungle ancient times ago. So that's all Pack had to hear. Anyway, men with Bluefeather's experience were scarce around Vire, France, that day.

The next morning, August 9, the Ninth Regiment and the rest of the Second Division attacked out of Vire, toward Linchebary. They did not know it then, but the main line of German defense had been broken. They only knew the twenty-yard circle, but the immediate result of their foray across Normandy was the crumbling of German resistance in the sector, and ultimately led to the crushing out of the Normandy Peninsula and the end of their first great war campaign in France. They did not know what they had done at the moment, and the few of them left did not much care.

They attacked. It was the usual battle of attack, the enemy retreating, fighting back, on and on. By August 13 they had taken Linchebary. Immediately thereafter the division was notified to pull out of the line and prepare to head for Brest, France, and the Brittany Peninsula. There a hardened group of German paratroopers had received orders from Hitler to fight to the death. Some of his select SS soldiers were also dug in to help enforce and inspire his wish. It was a crucial submarine base, and a little piece of the Führer's pride still left intact, on the French coast.

On the day Linchebary fell, the Third Army moved north from Le Mans around the southern flank of the German positions in the direction of Argentan. At the same time the British, the Canadians, and a Polish brigade swept in from the opposite direction from Caen toward Falaise. These pincers created a pocket out of which over one hundred thousand German troops were captured—on top of the multitudes of dead and wounded—and millions of tons of enemy armor and trucks were smashed along scores of miles of fields and roads. To the generals, the politicians, and the composers of news headlines, this was a great victory. To those walking men with rifles, it was the same little bloody, twenty-yard circle. That's all.

■ ■ ■

Twenty-Nine

They were moved by truck across Normandy toward Brest. Riding was new to them. They had run, walked, fallen, and crawled every step from Omaha Beach to Linchebary.

As they crossed Normandy, the signs of war were everywhere. The shell-blasted fields, the artillery- and bomb-shattered towns, and the absence of people on the roads all gave evidence of the struggle just past. The loss to the inhabitants as well as the invaders was stifling. However, as they moved into Brittany the feeling changed. Except for a few bombed railroad stations, the countryside was green and peaceful under the late summer sky, so peacefully blue. The people had been liberated from the Germans by the rapid dash of General Patton's army. They came out en masse along the roadways, waving almost hysterically in their relief.

The Brittany faces showed only a portion of the strain the Normans' had. The people still laughed. It was good for the soldiers to see. The fresh beauty of the young women was almost too much to bear, but the trucks rolled on. And then they began to notice there were no young men; only old men and children were scattered among the French flesh. Yes, war was here just the same.

On to Brest they rolled in a great snaking line of wheeled vehicles, moving in a constant grinding roar—moving men to fight and die sooner.

Pop was weak and listless. Bluefeather could not get him to talk, and he was worried about his health. But there was nothing to do but wait and hope. This thought seemed somehow foolish to Bluefeather, no matter how true. He would not ask any more stupid questions of Pop about "the answer" now. He felt that he was the only soldier in the world so dumb he could even have dreamed of a partial answer to this madness. Then he became dizzy for a spell. Since the railroad shell explosion, he had been having these sudden attacks. He hid them well from the others, but now, as he withdrew into himself, he had these imaginary debates and questions. Damnit.

He could stop the talk with Pop, but he couldn't stop his own thoughts. The parade of friends started by. It was the time of half-visions again. They all formed a partial circle around him, smiling and muttering things he still couldn't hear. He spoke anyway. "There is only one General Eisenhower who is the leader of the Allied Forces. Not a hundred. Not three. There can only be one Number One. Why can't all these religions, which have never, ever stopped hating and killing one another, realize that just because their prayers are said differently, they nevertheless all pray to the same commander in chief?"

Bluefeather waited for his father to answer, his grandfather, Moon Looker, Lorrie Friedman, old Ludwig, Miss Mary, and all the others. He looked from one to the other, but they just smiled and chattered on all at the same time.

He tried again. "How, oh, God, oh, Muhammad, oh, Buddha, oh, Jesus, oh, greatest of Great Spirits, can they be so bleeding dumb and ignorantly blind?" He pleaded to Old Grinder now, "Are we really that goddamned infantile? Is vengeance a disease in the genes of entire nations? Huh? Huh?" Then they all moved, skipping, whirling lightly in single file over the top of Sandia Mountain and out of his vision.

The trucks stopped. They had moved as near to the new front as they were going to. The men unloaded stiff bodies, packs, rifles, and all the weighted things it would take to make a new little war.

They expected the battle of Brest to be over in a week. A rumor spread and grew that they would soon be relieved for garrison duty, guarding prisoners of war. How foolish. Generals did not pull strong, proven divisions from the line for lesser duty. The better they fought, the tougher the front line they would be thrown at, and the more they would suffer. Nevertheless it was a silly little hope they wished to survive on.

In spite of Hitler admonishing the Brest garrison to battle to the death, General Herman B. Von Ramcke had set his holding mission there at ninety days. He had at his disposal troops ranging from the highly trained Second Parachute Battalion and select storm troopers to civil service workers and naval personnel. He had ample weapons and deep concrete defenses. The antiaircraft guns were skillfully set so they could fire both air defense and flat trajectory against ground troops. The German forces controlled the high ground and were dug into some of the strongest concrete bunkers ever built. They had been told that every shot fired at them by the enemy was one less fired at the Reich. The defenders believed these words and fought accordingly.

In every major battle ever fought, somebody occupies the main hilt looking down on their attackers—throwing rocks, sticks, and spears; shooting with bows and arrows then with caps and balls; and finally, up there on hill 154, semiautomatic rifles, fully automatic burp guns, mortars, machine guns, and cannons. It had taken only a short while to graduate from the bow and arrow to the machine gun, and it was not done to put meat on the dinner table either. Methods of killing humans were escalating with vast speed.

Hill 154 had eight concrete bunkers and many and varied guns. Besides those, circular trenches were dug all around its base. The hill had to be taken before any progress could be made on the approaches to Brest.

The Third Battalion attacked that day near the end of August, moving in single fashion, Indian style, taking cover anywhere they could: in slight indentations, in clumps of grass, behind rocks, behind fallen bodies—wherever.

Finally two men from L Company, equipped with a bazooka (a hand-held rocket launcher), crawled forward and knocked out a self-propelled gun that had held the entire battalion to almost a standstill; but because of at least twenty-five heavy machine guns, many high-velocity flat trajectory weapons, as well as mortars and small arms, the hill remained in enemy hands throughout the first day and night. Casualties were heavy on both sides.

The battalion was finally completely pinned down, and in spite of heavy fire from the U.S. tank destroyers it was up to one man to break the battle open.

Infantry Sergeant Carey crawled forward. He shot down a German rifleman at forty yards with his own rifle and crawled on until he was able to finally lob a grenade into the mouths of the main pillbox. Although severely wounded, he continued to do so till he died. This was one of the few, true heroes of war. A very dead one.

Bluefeather's company was moving around the edge of the hill while others took the top. But in his twenty-yard circle nobody knew the others had succeeded. The fire of cannon and many sorts of weapons seemed to come from all four directions and the sky itself.

Bluefeather had to lift and half drag Pop along several times. After the two days of heavy battle, the gun and pack he wore were just too much for his weary little legs to hold up.

Over and over, Bluefeather picked him up and said each time, "Enough, you old goat, haven't you had enough?"

Pop just created a thin smile of thanks and weakly staggered on. It was rapidly becoming one additional burden that Bluefeather, and their little circle, could not handle. They were pinned down.

Men were scattered all over. Some would never move themselves again. Others shoved themselves into the lowest spots they could find on earth. At staggered moments, one, two, or three soldiers would rise up and charge forward only to fall, never to stand again.

Sergeant Pack was rolling, crawling, gathering hand grenades from the dead. As he neared Bluefeather and Pop, he handed Bluefeather several.

Then the eternal cry of battle came from nearby just ahead of them. "Medic! Medic!"

Pack and Bluefeather moved up, their bellies dragging heavily from the weight of the extra hand grenades. A medic was somehow there, and then another. It was a waste of precious time and risk. The man they had crawled over to help had his entire lower jaw blown off, revealing only a burbling hole down into his body. There was just enough lower jaw left to hold two dangling teeth on one side. Bluefeather had an irresistible and futile impulse to pull them free before the dying man could swallow them and choke. He pulled them loose just as one last gasping spurt of warm red liquid gushed over his hand. The final bubble broke. All that remained was a hole with the lungs underneath bubbling up little red froths and a rattling sound. Then nothing.

Bluefeather stared numbly, turning to look at Pack, who also stared. Then it happened. Bluefeather felt the scar on his nose burn as if it had been painted there with acid. If the hairs on his neck had been long enough, they would have been standing up like the quills on the back of an agitated porcupine.

Pack whirled toward Bluefeather, his usually calm blue eyes filled with rage. This rage was so great that some of it lopped over and penetrated Bluefeather's already lambasted being.

Pack yelled for the thousandth time, "Let's get the bastards, Fellini!"

Bluefeather followed like a simple, unthinking servant infected with some of Pack's own frenzy. They charged through shells and bullets, crawling, firing at the enemy's emplacements, grinding into the trembling earth, spurting ahead like track stars only to fall, jolting the joints of their bodies loose but feeling none of the pain.

Others rose at Pack's cries of relentless inspiration and fired and fought blindly in the new little circle. The fire from the emplacements cracked at them, and Pack's usable troops were bloodied and thinning rapidly.

Pack yelled, "Stay, Fellini!" He dragged two wounded men through the storm of steel to a swale and stanched their blood, tying it off so they could remain alive. He did the same three more times on his way back to Bluefeather, who had been happy to obey orders and lie with face and body as thin against the earth as fear could force them. The little bit of fury that Pack, and the blown-open throat, had imparted to him was gone and he felt like he had been in this losing, pounded position for years; whether he lived or died, he never wanted to move again. But Pack did. When his rifle ammunition was all gone, he crawled and screamed Bluefeather along with him. Now he hurled the grenades at the bunker openings. They were so close that the enemy couldn't lower the line of fire of the machine guns enough to touch them.

One bunker became silent. Pack had demolished the living there, and one of his beloved grenades had exploded on the edge of a dirt emplacement and trench. He was fixing his bayonet to charge when a shot came from somewhere and Pack fell.

This brought life back in Bluefeather, and he threw a grenade at the emplacement himself. Before he could reach Pack, the maniac was up and charging, blood streaming from his forehead into one eye. Bluefeather followed, so afraid that his legs buckled several times. Pack shoved his bayonet through the chest of the last enemy soldier on this Nazi machine gun. Stabbing with lethal precision, he killed two other riflemen.

He wiped the bayonet on the side of the trench, saying softly under his silently heaving chest to Bluefeather, "Well, Fellini, ol' partner, we sent several of them to the kingdom of all wishes." Then from a curve in the trench a concussion grenade was thrown at Pack. It dropped into the trench in such a way that part of the exploding force was absorbed by the earth, but enough was left to knock the sergeant down and into blackness.

Bluefeather crawled over the edge of the emplacement just in time to catch a small part of the blast. He ignored the light concussion and threw his last two grenades down into the curving trenches. One German soldier was blown up on the edge of the trench with the side of his neck gone—two vertebrae dangling loose. The fire from this particular bunker, in this particular little circle, was silent.

Bluefeather knelt by Pack. The bullet appeared to have grazed his head just enough to take away a tiny furrow of bone and leave the lining of his brain untouched, but he had no idea what the concussion grenade had done to Pack's insides.

Bluefeather was the one to yell now, "Medic!"

The soldiers rose from below and moved on up and took over the conquered trenches. Then Pop just rolled over the edge and lay there prone, looking into the pale, pale face of another hero, Sergeant Pack of the Ninth Infantry. Bluefeather could not decide who looked worse, Pop or Pack.

They came and took Pack away on a stretcher and Bluefeather felt empty, lost, and lonely. He just patted Pop on the shoulder softly and sat there speechless, too tired to be thankful he was alive and unmaimed—on the surface at least.

He thought, for the moment, that most heroes of war are created by the acts of men gone mad, but of course, he too, now qualified. Many of the great fabrications of man had been instituted by people thought to be crazy at the time, and often thereafter, most were.

After the Third Battalion had topped out on the "killing hill," the three attacking divisions, the Twenty-ninth, the Second, and the Eighth, straightened up their lines and began preparing for the major assault on the port city.

Bluefeather's depleted company moved up into their part of the line. There was a small, delaying party of Germans along the other side of the next hedgerow. They held the company pinned down temporarily, but the 60-mm mortars silenced their fire. There was no return fire now. The riflemen loved the 60-mms when they needed them desperately, but at the same time feared their sound because they almost inevitably drew return artillery and mortar rounds. The 60s were the bastards of infantry, but they had allowed Bluefeather's company to advance one more hedgerow.

Bluefeather cautiously raised up, and to his surprise, a German soldier jumped out of a hole and started racing erratically across the field right in front of him. Bluefeather figured the mortar rounds had knocked the German's senses loose. The high moan of the German eighty-eights and the flatter tone of the American 105s drowned out the report of Bluefeather's M1. The German's knees buckled. He fell forward, then rose again.

Bluefeather eased off another shot, surprised at the sudden deep pain of guilt he felt toward killing a man who a moment earlier had been trying to kill him. The German whacked against the earth facedown. One foot twitched and that was all.

Then, at last, they settled down for a few days of hot food and some rest. The Germans only fired at large troop concentrations or patrols now as their lines were being straightened again. They were conserving their ammunition for more numerous game soon to come. The men were beginning to spit bathe, shave, laugh a little, write letters home, and start dreaming of all those July 4 celebrations, white Christmases, their wives and girlfriends, or those envisioned to become so. Pretty little songs were being played all around the world saying for sure these dreams would come true.

Bluefeather kept thinking of the dead German lying out there in the wheat field. He could see the dirty, gray uniform above the stubble between the shocks of wheat, like a big, dead rat.

Finally on the fourth day he could stand it no longer. He passed the word that he was going out to the soldier. He slid over the hedgerow and moved toward the stiff figure, even though his body cringed at the thought of enemy fire concentrated on him alone. No bullets came his way. None.

The instantly identifiable stench was already there, aided by the summer heat. The flies had done their dirty work, and the body was turning the usual gun-barrel black. He could see the round holes in the German's back about three inches apart. Bluefeather was only briefly revulsed at his good marksmanship. He grabbed a shoulder of the uniform and pulled the German corporal over on his back. The entire front of the dead man's uniform was blood-covered—some dry, some sticky wet where it had been between the clothing and the ground.

He extracted the wallet carefully, for half of it was blood-soaked. He was later amazed at his disappointment because the man had no valuable ring or wristwatch or gold teeth. My God, had he become more vulture than human? Was he so jaded and empty that the man he had killed was meaningless? Was humankind a joke the Great Spirit had pulled on the universe? Was mankind just a big, bloody laugh for deities, war lovers, warmongers, and eternity as well? If so, even memory itself never had been.

These thoughts came later. As for now he was more troubled by the little photos he found of the man as a civilian having a joyous-appearing picnic in a park with his wife and two small kids. They were all smiling, and one little two- or three-year-old girl was waving at the camera. The poor unlucky son of a bitch had loved and lived the same things as everyone else. Ah well, he should have had the sense to surrender instead of trying to escape across an open field.

Bluefeather felt better when he saw how many thousand franc notes were in the wallet, and he was glad the soldier hadn't carried Reich marks, for they were worthless to the GI.

Bluefeather walked purposefully back to the foxhole he had covered over with bundles of wheat. He carefully extracted the notes from the wallet. They were all stuck together at one end with blood. The other half was perfectly clean. He poured a canteen of water into his helmet and cautiously dipped the bloody ends of the bills into it. Then even more delicately he laid each out to dry. The bills had the odor of the dead, but he was sure that the combination of water and sun would take it away. He lay back against the hedgerow and took one of his rare smokes, waiting for nature to do its work.

He dozed a while. When he awoke, he inspected his newly acquired wealth. The first bill he picked up looked almost clean. He decided the others would pass. He could hardly control his anticipation as he walked swiftly down the hedgerow to a poker game going on there.

"Hi, fellers. Got room for another sucker?"

"Come on in," said Private Jenkins from Texas.

"Money's money," said Sergeant Gallagher from upstate New York.

Corporal Kreuger from Wisconsin said, "Feeling lucky, eh?"

"I am lucky. Whose deal?"

Bluefeather stacked the money in front of his folded legs. It was wrinkled from the fast drying of the hot sun and would not stack neatly. Bluefeather pitched one note in the pot. It was the equivalent of a twenty-dollar bill in 1944.

He played carefully because he didn't know the cards yet, and he would have to play it straight as long as the others did. He had just robbed the dead, but he would never be able to bring the skills of his cousin "The Bookkeeper" from Chicago, or his Tonapah, Nevada, tricks to use here against his own men.

Every time someone took a pot, he would ante the soiled French note. It was repeatedly pitched back into play until Bluefeather wondered what in hell was bothering these guys. The game got quieter. At dark it broke up.

Early the next day the game continued. Bluefeather lost all the change from the first note and managed to get a second in the pot. The players tossed it back in over and over just as the day before. The dampness of all their hands seemed to make the odor exude from the bills even stronger. Now it was Bluefeather's turn to ante up, and he, too, pitched the stained bill back in the pot.

The three remaining players stared hard at the note. Bluefeather tried not to acknowledge it, but even he couldn't help noticing the pinkish stain across one end. His eyes kept moving from the dirty end to the clean one. Back and forth. He shuddered suddenly and felt like the pink stain was spreading over all his body. The other players got up and walked away. He sat alone. Jesus H. Christmas Christ! He was becoming immune even to the blood of the dead—by his own hand, no less. He had to stop this numbing of his soul before it was too late. Too late?

Bluefeather got up slowly and crawled over the hedgerow. He looked out where the burial detail had just that morning removed the corpse. He walked slowly toward the dark stain and smashed wheat stubble where death had overtaken a son of the führer. A little to one side he dug with his bayonet and buried all the money. Then he walked slowly back and picked up a V-mail letter and wrote his parents way, way off in Raton, New Mexico. He told his father to go down on First Street and give a twenty-dollar bill to the worst-looking bum he could find. He would pay him back and explain later. He never did either one, but somehow felt better for now. He also felt a little cleaner than he had for many hours.

Pop finally decided to shave. His whiskers had been out about half an inch in thin patches that made him appear older and more worn than ever. One could hardly see his eyes now unless directly in front of him, but this morning he had received letters from his entire family and it had pepped him up. His hands were still shaking, and he had cut his face in several places with the razor.

Bluefeather said, "We attack in the morning, you know?"

"Yeah, that's what I hear."

"It ain't too late, Pop."

Silence.

Bluefeather went on with his seemingly lost and grinding purpose. "Well?"

Pop said, "The only way out is to plunge right in."

Bluefeather almost held his breath as he tried hard yet again. "There are just so many times an old tire can roll over on a rutted road. We're travelers with thin-soled shoes."

Pop thought a moment, rubbing at his clean face. "A few days back I didn't have enough air left in me to blow up a balloon, much less a concrete fortification, but today I'm ready to wipe up the town," and he made a casual wave in the direction of Brest.

If Bluefeather had known Pop in peacetime he could easily have strangled him. Well, there was just no use trying to help him anymore. They both felt pretty good this day. Might as well try to enjoy it. Pop was also exuberant because he had somehow bribed a mailman to send all his notepads of poems to his sons. He, like Bluefeather, had seen many causes for disillusionment in the last few weeks, but he still believed they had to go on fighting this war for their country and the children of the world. Naive, of course, but true as well.

Pop said, "When this is over, I'm gonna take you fishin' up in Oregon. I know a..."

Bluefeather didn't hear the last; he had become obsessed watching a bird that had landed in a bush on top of a rear hedgerow. He could see the bird raise its head to sing, but he wondered why he couldn't hear it and what the bird was doing this close to the front.

Then they heard a German machine gun rattle three times in the distance, the flat crack of an antiaircraft weapon and then the returning song of American 105s searching for the sounds to bring them to permanent silence.

Pop the Poet said, as he made himself consciously listen, "You know, Blue,..."

Bluefeather waited.

"...all things make music if you listen. Water, wind, even war."

"Yeah, yeah. The cottonwoods of Corrales and the Rio Grande make music—music together from the wind. It is like having your own private chimes big as mountains, big as forests. You are right, Pop, all you gotta do is listen. Really listen."

"What kind of town is Corrales?"

"Oh, it's what might be called a little Mexican town in the Southwest. If you're poor, you're Mexican American. If you're rich, you're Spanish. 'Course, all that'll be changing, I suppose, after the war. Some people think they'll even let Indians drink in bars someday. Corrales looks a little bit like a spread-out Indian pueblo, too. The gringos are mostly involved in the arts some way. I like it there, Pop. My old mining mentor, Grinder, said a man had to have a headquarters so he could dream about returning to it. You gotta have a place to keep your mules. I like mules, and I like little towns to live in, and big ones to go to."

"Having good neighbors sure counts a lot," Pop agreed.

"I got the best . . . the Luceros." Bluefeather proceeded to describe every detail of the Luceros. He left no praise unspoken. They were the most loyal people on earth. They had the most beautiful and brightest kids ever to eat chile. Tranquilino's violin could accompany the music of angels. Their garden produced the sweetest tomatoes in the whole valley. That's the way Bluefeather felt about the few people he loved.

Pop said, "We've got this old bachelor, Dave Boston, right next door. Gripes all the time. The bastard's personality is so sour he'd give a buzzard ulcers. Turn right around, and there's hardly a week goes by he doesn't bring the kids some kind of unique present. Car breaks down, he's right there to give you a pull or a lift into town, griping all the time. We wouldn't trade him for a dozen do-gooders and four church deacons thrown in.

"Our mailman is prejudiced against everybody that didn't come over on the Mayflower. As if that bunch of thieves were his kin, Blue. He was cussing some nationality or other and said, of course, that didn't apply to a white man like Mr. Boston. Mr. Boston yelled back at the letter carrier, 'You prejudiced son of a bitch, I'm not a white man, I'm half Irish.'"

These two friends went on like this for a couple of hours, sharing, laughing, living for a moment with the folks back home.

Then Pop inadvertently broke the spell. "We got a new lieutenant named Cohen."

"Yeah. Well, he won't last till noon tomorrow without Pack around to show him the game."

"Probably not, but he survived three days before the lull."

"It seems to me it takes about a week to get your sea legs of battle. How many lieutenants have we already gone through, Pop?"

"I lost count, and you've been here longer than I have."

It was true. An infantry lieutenant was the most exposed of creatures. Few ever had a chance to learn the different voices of the shells before one of them blew his breath away.

"Pop, we don't have to worry about that. We'll never make lieutenant. You and I will be privates till the day the war ends."

"Yeah, you're right there, Blue, unless we're the only two left. Then we could promote one another. Say, I overheard Lieutenant Cohen and Sergeant Gallagher talking, and you're up for a Distinguished Service Cross."

"I'm what? What in hell for? I haven't done anything but survive."

"That's not the way they figure it. The sergeant said the report quoted some soldiers saying you saved a bunch of wounded, blew away a machine gun and antiaircraft cannon, and bayoneted several German soldiers. Hell, I don't know what all. Cohen was feeling bad because they hadn't put you in for the medal of honor."

"Oh dear...dear Number One Above, forgive us all. God uh mighty, Pop, I didn't do nothing. I just followed Pack out of pure-ass insanity. He did it all. All of it."

"Shhh, Blue, quiet down. You'll wake up the enemy."

"I don't give a shit if I wake up the whole damn SS Corps. This is crap. That medal should go to Pack. I didn't do anything but throw one grenade after it was all over."

"They've even got a recommendation from Pack, soon as he comes to."

"Well, it's a hell of an embarrassment to put on a man who's half coward and half...well, half something..."

That put them back in a good mood again, and Bluefeather scouted around in bombed-out cellars until he found a half bottle of Calvados.

When he returned, smiling big at his scavenging victory, Pop said, "I was getting worried. Thought maybe you'd gone back to the reservation."

They had just enough Calvados to get a little drunk and laugh at all the nothing things they said to one another. In fact, for a couple of hours they were not only already on their way home, but were two of the world's greatest humorists.

Then Bluefeather looked into the sky and said, "I haven't caught on to all I know about this world."

They started laughing again.

Pop gasped out, "One good laugh will cure a thousand tears."

Bluefeather replied with great difficulty between spasms of mirth, "Our souls are scattered about like glass from a wrecked auto, but we have...we have...what? What in hell do we have, Pop?"

Pop said, looking at the almost-empty bottle, holding it right in front of his eyes, "I'm sorry you forgot the little jewel of wisdom, but I'm glad we've got one big drink left each."

"Hallelujah, amen, and forty fast Hail Marys."

They drained the bottle, crawled into their foxholes, and slept.

Thirty

They didn't get to talk about anything but blood and ammunition for several days. The enemy occupied their time quite well. The Ninth Regiment moved relentlessly on toward Brest, just the same. Every field was costly, but that's the way with wars.

Finally, the enemy was contained within the fortified city itself. Few buildings were totally intact. The artillery of three divisions had made it a ghost town, and even the ghosts seemed to have left. But the German soldiers, with their uncanny, even unholy, ability to improvise on any spot, made the Americans pay with many limbs lost for every yard gained. The Germans were particularly adept at inventing diabolical devices of death; booby traps and mines filled with charges of powder up to three hundred pounds infected everything. Some were made from 75-mm artillery shells with pressure igniters dug into the roads. They also had pulled torpedo heads forward from the naval yards and rigged them with trip wires and pressure devices, along with antisubmarine mines. Several road junctions had been mined with over a ton of explosives. It was said, by a division historian, that here the infantry and their engineer units found the most horrendous concentration of explosives on the European continent. The infantry engineers and mine platoons suffered and paid their dues uncounted, terrorizing times during the next three days.

Bluefeather knew some of these things in a foggy way, like struggling to get out of a bad dream and back to a reality that's even worse.

The Americans breached the fortress of concrete and buried powder, and were ready for the final assault. The units consolidated their positions once more. So did the Germans. There could only be one assault left. It only took one to die.

Already, up and down the line, men were talking about a long leave and the war's end for their outfits. This invention of wishes came about because they had been under fire for almost three and a half months now—those who had been there since the beginning. A small arms bullet killed a man just as dead as a thousand-pound bomb, but it was the hundreds and hundreds of shock waves, over mile after mile of hedgerows, that shook more than a soldier's body loose. It was the never-ceasing artillery barrages that finally made him grasp blindly at the earth in a silent pleading for succor.

They injudiciously believed they had done their fair share, somehow forgetting the old, old, knowledge that war was the very last place to seek fairness. Justice belonged to the lucky. To compensate for this mistake the troops figured the least they should get was a long-deserved rest before being transferred to the new front in Germany itself. They were looking forward to a real shower bath, some play, and a short time without shell burst. At least this. A man might even find a woman if he had some loot, or was lucky—or both.

These thoughts were what made it so hard on them the morning of the Big Do—and this was one reason why the commanders didn't like their solders thinking too much. They knew it would be, at most, only two or three more days of deadly conflict before a reprieve.

Bluefeather was especially nervous this morning as they advanced into the heart of the city whose soul was out to the nearby sea. The windows and doors were the vacant eyes of the dead, until a sniper fired from one and brought life back to the building by sending death into the street. Sometimes the hollow buildings, with walls standing so precariously, belched forth such resistance that the Americans had to hurl phosphorous grenades into the streets to disguise their sprint from one side to the other.

Bluefeather moved with the others on past the body of Lieutenant Cohen, a child officer, who had not lived long enough to gain the necessary experience to go on living. Bluefeather fired at movements in the building, and he hit some, but he had no adrenaline left for the lust of battle. He just wanted to live. One sniper's bullet struck the corner of the doorway he was peeking around, less than three inches above his helmet. Three inches. It was the same sniper who had shot Lieutenant Cohen in the chest, puncturing his heart. No inches there.

Then G Company's firing on the city almost ceased. Intermittent only. The tank destroyers that had moved in ahead of them had done a fine job of explosive ferreting. It was said that General Ramcke was negotiating a surrender. Bluefeather—recklessly now because of possible booby traps—rummaged around several ruins hoping to find a bottle of wine or Calavados for a little victory celebration with Pop and Daniel Wind. He thought about Sergeant Pack, too, and then remembered he was hospitalized. Pop followed along as he tried to plunder futilely. There was nothing left but tiny remains of papers and pipes, empty or broken cans and bottles. It was mostly pulverized. Waste.

Then, as they exited a corner building, on the opposite side, Bluefeather saw the German private's body. A tank destroyer shell had struck him right at the belt buckle. He was blown completely in half except for a few strings of flesh on his right side. His severed ribs stuck out, and the inside of his chest cavity was almost empty. His arms were flung back as if he had reached out for something compelling with all his strength the instant of his death.

Bluefeather stood, staring and staring, somehow never getting used to it. The suddenness. This one had moved his arms up and out in a desperate grab, in a minute, immeasurable, split part of infinity.

Pop walked around the edge of a caved-in wall saying, "What's the matter?" before he saw the hollow body.

Bluefeather pointed.

Pop stared too.

They had seen many hundreds of fractured bodies, but now, here at the end of this battle, far apart from the main ones, on a French peninsula in the month of September, on a clear and lively day away from the city, they were both hypnotized by the fragmented form that had once been like themselves.

Pop began to shake from something other than exhaustion and fear. He quivered like an old Model-T Ford that had been started for the first time in months. His paled face turned pink and his breath came short and hard.

"Look," he said, moving with the sudden agility of youth. "Look at that! You see now, don't you?"

Once it seemed, long ago in a land made of trances, Bluefeather had wanted Pop's answer. Now this day, right here, he plain didn't give a shit. It was as unstoppable as it was meaningless, he thought.

Pop made sort of a dance in front of the body, agile, but pitiful, too. Then he bent down to look inside the corpse. He suddenly, shockingly, straightened up and leaped into the air with grasping hands. Then he ran about grabbing at air with his flexing fingers.

"Where is it?" he shouted. "Where, oh where has it gone?" He made a motion as if he had caught something out of the air, and he ran back to the hollow part of the body and pantomimed shoving the "something" inside it. "It won't stay," he shouted. "It won't return. Ohhh, ohhh, where has it gone?"

Then he ran around in a circle looking under stones, bricks, slivers of wood and peering into the crumbled corners of the building. "Is it here? No. Maybe it's over there. No? It is gone. Gone. Gone. It is gone and no one knows where."

Bluefeather was possessed by an impulse to grab Pop around the neck and hold him until he shut up. Instead, he stood still, silent.

Pop raved on, "What was it? Where did it come from? Where did it vanish to? Ah, my dear friend, Blue, we don't know, do we?" Now softly, almost whispering, he went on, "We don't know what it is." His voice rose again. He shouted so that Bluefeather thought Pop's mind was altogether gone as well. "It is so simple. We don't know what we are. Remember the goats? Remember, just remember, how upset we all were. Well, that's because we know what goats are. Don't you see?" He pleaded desperately, standing crouched forward with his arms waving, begging in the air.

Then the hands stopped and he slowly spun around and settled to his knees and his face fell forward on his chest as if he were praying. His arms hung limp as he rolled slackly over on his side.

For a moment Bluefeather was paralyzed, then he ran to his buddy. There was a black hole under each temple. A tiny bit of red began oozing from one, but it was from gravity that he bled, because the blood Bluefeather saw had no life pumping it. It had none of the element he had but a moment ago grasped so frantically for.

Bluefeather heard a rattle of friendly small-arms fire a short distance away. The sniper was now on the same trip as Pop.

Bluefeather straightened him out, took the raincoat from his friend's pack, and found in it a lost, unmailed letter to his family back home. He covered as much of him as he could with the raincoat. Tenderly. Then he walked back toward the rear. He had to mail the letter as quickly as possible. He had to find Sergeant Pack and Daniel Wind and tell them about Pop. Then he remembered that Pack was gone. The first ghosts were already returning to Brest. The port was never used by the Allies.

■   ■   ■

Thirty-One

The city fell and they took a lot of prisoners. Bluefeather was amazed at the arrogance of the defeated SS officers. Most other armies would have executed them without hesitating. Hitler had done such a masterful job of brainwashing his SS children that, for centuries, psychologists would be entertained, and other dictators educated, by his feat.

The portable shower baths were enjoyed, relished. The first hot food in weeks was gulped as if it were gourmet. As he stood in line for his first meal, dangling his mess kit, Bluefeather remembered his late grandmother Fellini's cooking. She had been from the Calagari family of Lombardy in northern Italy. She always kept Franchia cheese, with its brown line over the top, for snacks and dessert. He could see her hands now, as she made crespelle cheese pancakes, mixing the three cheeses. He could taste the sharp tanginess of the provolone cheese that she used in everything possible. She mixed the flour, eggs, and nutmeg for the pancakes, then, with expert, loving hands, she poured the cheese batter inside them. His heart was full of the nostalgic smells and tastes of his grandmother's house—but then he wasn't there any longer. He was here—near Brest—waiting, waiting, as soldiers had forever done.

The laughter, the sleep, the letters to and from home were exulted in.

Bluefeather won a pocketful of money in a poker game and invited his one remaining close war buddy, Daniel Wind, to a nearby village for relaxation. It was the time of fun.

The place was loaded with GIs who had had the same thought before them. It took quite a spell for the two friends to get drunk on the cheap wine. The villagers kept what good stuff they had hidden. Wisely so, for they knew its rare and precious vintage would grow in value almost hourly. They would need all the resources they could muster to rebuild their steel-shattered land.

Finally, Bluefeather put up enough money, a lot, for a bottle of the good stuff. It was the time for remembering.

"Dan'l, ol' pardner of the storm," Bluefeather said, "here's to those who died and to those who lived. Here's to the worlds that have come and vanished and to those adventurous ones yet to be. And here, Dan'l, ol' foot soldier, here is a brimful glass to the poets. God rest their scarce hearts."

Daniel wiped the wine from the corners of his mouth and said, "Yeah," and poured the balance of the bottle into his empty glass and drained it just as fast.

It took all the rest of Bluefeather's poker money to find them a woman. The few women available for this sort of social contact were outnumbered by the partying GIs by at least fifteen hundred to one.

Bluefeather had more money left than most, so he cut a line short. They got this very important relief and pleasure over with, even though they had to share the same lady.

"Buddies to the end," Bluefeather told Daniel right after.

Daniel replied, "For sure."

Way into the night, they started stumbling, drunkenly, back toward the company bivouac. Somehow, they went astray off the road and wound up staggering across a railroad bridge high above some body of water—a stream, or pond.

Bluefeather never considered the ocean to be in the reckoning. He had never heard of anyone building a bridge over an ocean. He wondered how it had escaped bombing and was about to ask Daniel Wind what he thought about it when he heard a splash down below.

He muttered something to himself about that crazy Indian going swimming at this time of night and went on doing an imaginary stomp dance in his picture-mind.

About noon the next day, Sergeant Gallagher woke Bluefeather and told him that Daniel Wind had evidently fallen off a bridge and drowned. Some E Company boys had seen him floating on top of the water about a mile from camp.

"Well, I'll be damned," Bluefeather said, wiping at his dehydrated eyes. "Say, Sergeant, have you got a drink of water on you? My canteen's empty."

All around Brest, back in Normandy, out on the South Pacific Islands, down in Italy and over in Russia, the worms, the ants, the dung beetles, the roaches, the flies and millions, billions, and trillions of insects

waited in the earth, the grass, and the bushes for the juicy parts of det-
onated flesh to come to them. They could handle the meat of any size
mammal, from the elephantine to the microscopic, as long as it was dead
or dying. They grew gluttonous and fat. These were days and years of
surplus riches for the under-earth.

As soon as the troops had healed their exhausted bodies and minds
enough to start getting into trouble, the commanders knew they would
fight again. This sort of knowledge is what had gained them their
power to begin with—and end with. The ability to get men to fight and
die for you took a special talent. Custer had understood this long before
he attacked the twenty thousand Indians with two hundred fifty men.
He was already a minor hero, after dashing and driving hundreds of
soldiers to their deaths in the Civil War, and as the fate of fractions
would have it, survived unscathed. He, in the end, outdid them all. He
accomplished his goal of world recognition. What did he care if he was
infamous as well, and they all died to the last man?

It was the time to return to battle. The commanders passed down
the orders. Part of the Second Division made the trip to the Ardennes
Forest and the Siegfred line in old boxcars, stopping at every railway
station along the way. Others were moved through France and the edge
of Paris by motor convoy along the Red Ball Highway, made famous by
motor drivers of the Red Ball Express. They were mostly black troops
and made both the highway and the convoys famous. The rest walked
the seven hundred miles.

Before the new choices of travel had been made for them, a fresh
replacement asked Bluefeather, "Which method of transportation will
we have?"

Bluefeather smiled and said, "Guess."

The walk into the foothills of the Ardennes was through mud as
thick and sticky as half-set concrete. The rain came on down, good for
the trees and brush. They slept in the water until it turned to snow and
then slept in that. They took up positions along a thin, thirty-mile front.
Here Bluefeather had just passed completely across the land of his
admired Balzac and had not seen a single volume of his work, nor would
he have had the time to read an opening chapter if he had seen one.
Now, here he was in the country of Bach and Wagner. At this time in history it seemed impossible that the beauty of their music had made it

around the entire world and the conquering dreams of Hitler had not. He had to listen to the chants of the erratic music of the screaming meemies (German short-range rocket launchers) and to Hitler's vaunted V-2 weapons. Eight hundred twenty-nine bombs and twenty-six rockets were recorded—most of them on the way to rear areas. The total damage from this great expenditure of energy was two minor wounds and two trailers crippled. Then the buzz bombs came, looking like small planes as they flew over, adding to the symphony with ear-shattering noise on their way to England. At night the music continued, seen and heard as streaks of roaring fire in the sky. Some flew in circles and dropped on the Ninth Regiment, while others returned to their sender. The music makers played on.

Bluefeather told the new lieutenant from Beverly Hills that he was going to have to assign him some help. "I'm wearing out running through this forest, pushing trees apart, making a path for German rockets."

To amuse himself even more and keep his mind in tune, he did some mathematics. Bluefeather figured that in Normandy and Brest he had dived to the earth a minimum of thirty times a day. Figuring at the low end of three months and ten days, he had whammed into the earth three thousand times, at least. This, loaded with a full pack, as well as ammunition, grenades, rifle, canteen of water, a bayonet, and a GI shovel. He had dug at least three foxholes every day. So he had moved enough dirt to have created a massive meteor crater. The molecules of his body had absorbed the continuing shock of enough exploding bombs, artillery shells, mortar rounds, and concussion grenades to turn granite boulders into prisoners-of-war soup. Yet he felt pretty well and anticipated fulfilling the prophecies of his spirit guide having these great adventures to look forward to "after the war."

There was still much pain for many here, beyond the explosives. The snow melted and froze over and over. The infantrymen had to put a layer of sticks in the bottom of their foxholes every two or three days to stay ahead of the water buildup caused by the living warmth of their bodies. Some had frozen feet and toes. Some lost them to trench rot or black foot.

He had survived long before, and long after, Burton and White. He believed now. Dancing Bear had given him notice of the great adventure to come "below the trees where the water burns." The division patrolled, and occasionally fought, in three countries—Belgium,

Germany, and Luxembourg. Sergeant Pack came back. His presence assured Bluefeather of a close friend and war mentor all the way to victory and home. No doubt. Pop was gone. Daniel was gone. Burton and White were gone, and...and...and...but Pack was back.

The division went through the Battle of the Bulge, the Rhineland, and on to Pilsen, Czechoslovakia, to greet the Russians. Bluefeather went methodically on, but since the deepest snow of December in the Ardennes, his spirit had returned to roam the red mesas of the great Southwest in the company of two amiable mules, and he heard the voice of his Tiwa grandfather saying, "Oh, wah, ha, water, wind, breath, life of whole earth." The sonorous song of comfort drifted across the fields and foothills of Taos Pueblo, vanishing in the struggle to reach the top of the sacred mountain.

Then he heard someone else singing that old-time favorite, "Wake Up and Dream, You Sleepy-Headed Bastards."

He was home before he got there.

■ Part Three ■

NEW FRIENDS—NEW FOES
And the Return to Taos

Thirty-Two

It was the time for family, friends, and fun. The prophesied adventures of Dancing Bear would just have to wait for their space on the turning wheel.

The Luceros had taken great care of his place in Corrales. In fact, the garden was like a small farm now with spaces for tomatoes, chiles, squash, and corn. Bluefeather could not believe the size of the children. Had it really been that long? They were all big enough to chop wood, and Tranquilino was joyous, heavier, and even more lovable.

Bluefeather brought each child a souvenir: an SS belt buckle, a small Nazi flag with bullet holes in it, and a German paratrooper's knife that had multiple uses and a blade that would spring out of the handle by pressing a small lever. He also brought a ten-pound bag filled with every kind of candy he could find for sale. He gave Tina a shawl, a silver comb, and a mantilla to wear during special Mexican-American ceremonies.

Tranquilino stared, puzzled at his gifts. The goodies were in a large box divided into two sections. The top half held dishrags, dishtowels, dishscrubbers, and a cuckoo clock. Tranquilino received his gifts, with Tina's great black eyes pouring tears of laughter as she slapped her left leg over and over with both hands. The kids even forgot about their own presents and joined their mother, Bluefeather and, finally, their father in the laughter over the surprising idiocy of Tranquilino's presents. He had never washed dishes in his entire life. The second section of the box was a little more to Tranq's liking. There was a bottle of very scarce brandy, a fancy and complete shaving set, an eighteen-karat gold pocket watch, and a paid-up certificate for a new John Deere tractor as soon as it was available. Now appreciation gleamed from Tranquilino's eyes, and he drank about a fourth of his liquid present to show it.

Later, after a great meal of Tina's enchiladas—made from Verlarde chile—Tranquilino and Bluefeather went out to see the mules.

Tranquilino had them both brushed and in the pen. The sun caused bands of light to glisten across their sleek bodies. They were too well cared for—too fat.

Bluefeather exulted in the smell of the corral, the hay, the oats, as well as the animals. He would have to get them out in the San Pedro Mountains and walk them lean and tough again. He rubbed their necks and their foreheads. He felt certain they knew him. Mules never forget a kind friend or an abusing enemy. Never. Then he put his arm around one lowered neck, and silent tears flowed from his body and out his eyes. Then his chest heaved in mighty silent sobbing. He was home.

Tranquilino walked out of the corral and examined the garden with great care, keeping his head down. All of Bluefeather's grief for lost loves and dead buddies had been necessarily repressed for years now. The mules' scent, their living warmth, their environment, and their loyalty finally released the pressure and it was eased.

He bought a secondhand truck and loaded it down with gifts for his parents, uncles, nephews, and nieces at Raton. He wanted to give everyone he loved the world and would have done it, too, if the Great Spirit would have sold or traded it to him. He hugged and kissed so many people that he had to get drunk to keep going. His mother and father and sisters all tried to love and feed and drink him to death. He told his cousin Mario that surviving the war had been easy, but an Italian homecoming was damn near impossible.

His Italian blood pulled at and nearly, but not quite, magnetized him into falling into the comfortable womb of protective family love and expectations. It was hard to leave the constant rolling talk, hugs, laughter, and the promises and suggestions for a great future in the mines awaiting a war hero. There also was the ready-made wedding, planned all the way through his honeymoon, kids, grandchildren and beyond, to where he would meet the Heavenly Father and a family of waiting Fellinis and their kin for thousands of years on into eternity. It was terribly tempting.

He was amazed that all seven of the Marchiondo boys had returned home safely. His mother had saved him a copy of the *Life* magazine they had been written up in. Finally, he could stand it no longer. He would have to go back to Corrales to see his mules and rest. He would also have to cash in some of his gold nuggets to maintain all this loving, eating, and drinking.

Then his mother had to take him to Taos to visit his grandparents, his uncles, and cousins. He was required to get drunk at least once with Stump Jumper and Smiling Dog. The venison from the mountains and the hot loaves of bread from his grandmother's horno were as enchantingly delicious as all the finest nectars.

All this multiplied love only led him to remember the words that he had promised his mentor, Grinder, never to forget. How was it exactly? "You are not half-Indian. You are not half-Italian. You are a whole Bluefeather. Bluefeather is Bluefeather. Blue is Blue, and you are you." He was almost certain that was it. The words. It didn't matter. It was the essence of the meaning, and he would travel his own trails just as he had given his word to the old prospector of gold and truth. He would make new trails. He would invent them, if necessary. Here too, the Bear Clan was strong—very strong. Again, he had this easy temptation to stay under their protection in the shadow of the blessed mountain.

Soon he returned to Raton and took a room at the El Portal Hotel. The family condoned the time of change that was here. They left him alone unless he wanted to see them. He loved the old hotel with territorial furniture in the rooms and dining area.

His friends Charlie Musso and Charlie's sister, Rose, would occasionally neglect their business and join the sporting activities. Mugs Moss and Pal England from the village of Hi Lo, about halfway between Raton and Clayton in a southeasterly direction, moved into the hotel. Both had been shot down on the same bomber just after crossing over the English Channel and had parachuted into the waiting clutches of the German troops. They had spent over two years as prisoners of war and had, what seemed to them, a small fortune in back pay. They were obliged to try and spend it all. They finally got it done, but before they did—with much help from Bluefeather—the party, the laughter, the wildness of freedom possessed them. No one seemed to mind.

Mugs fell in love with Rose, and for a while it was beautiful, but Rose finally left for Denver. It was too much for her. Her family had already planned her future, and it was apparent that the only thing this bunch wanted was endless fun.

It was fun, too, until it ended. When Mugs and Pal had used up their back pay and then their credit, the imaginary bullets and crashes of their dreams slowly dissipated along with the cushioning haze of total abandonment and alcohol. The old, old reality of new obligations to themselves, their families, and the new world slipped into their beings and took over. Ambition itself helped crowd the war into second place, then third...then way back, for the great majority of them anyway. For a few, of course, their real lives ended with the signing of the peace treaties—they stayed at war as they grew older and weaker. They could imagine no other adventure that could ever touch it, and consequently bored people to death till their own demise talking about it. These were truly the exceptions, though.

Something finally ended for Bluefeather as well. He realized he could play Ping-Pong the rest of his life between the Indian and the Italian clans and have a lot of fun doing it, but he had promises to keep and dreams to fulfill. He decided to go study mining engineering at New Mexico Institute of Mining and Technology in the Spanish-gringo, high, dry mountain town of Socorro, eighty miles south of Albuquerque. He was a student of great perception when on field trips, but the chemistry of the classroom did not suit him. Even so, his grades were good, and he held himself in place there, mainly because it was an easy drive back to Corrales for the weekends.

He dated some women, as nature demanded. Occasionally he would go on a weekend ripper of a party, dancing, yelling and, once in a while, having a little fistfight if someone insulted a friend. It was purely for fun and did no harm at that time in his life, at that time in history, at that time in New Mexico. Times change. It also just wasn't quite exciting enough. He became involved in a minor mercury smuggling operation out of Old Mexico. Nothing too important, and not illegal, in his eyes. Bluefeather was not clearly aware of it, but he was moving about hoping the spear of Dancing Bear's prediction for the rest of his life would pierce him and activate the greatest of all adventures.

About three months before he was to graduate, he packed up his mules and headed for his placer spot in the San Pedros, but someone had cleaned out all the remaining gold while he had recently been otherwise busy. Somehow he resented this, but at the same time, he was relieved that the mine was emptied. He put it immediately from his mind.

After World War II, most of the prospectors used jeeps and all kinds of four-wheel-drive vehicles for prospecting. They only searched for massive deposits of ore and overlooked small rich ones. Bluefeather was aware of this, and he sampled the little, tiny, overlooked veins of silver hoping for a modest discovery to keep him and the mules busy and alive. He, like Grinder, could smell gold, but he did not want any more of its scent of constant disaster. He didn't find the silver either, because he had unknowingly limited his avenue of searching. The prophecies were still in his mind. He knew they would start being fulfilled, but he didn't know when.

Half of the gold he had stashed was cashed in and spent on indifferent prospecting, assays, food, drink, and fun when he was back in town. There were three bags left from all the riches he had found at Breen and at his other small strikes. He also still had the three specimen rocks: two from Breen and the one from Old Grinder. He would starve before he would let them go. It didn't make good financial sense, but he borrowed money from the bank to survive rather than cash in the last of his stash.

He had paid his own way through school, but he could have applied for help from the GI educational program and gotten his degree. Somehow this seemed redundant to him and a step backward, whether it was true or not. He could go back, way back, to the mines at Trinidad, Colorado, or for that matter, almost anywhere in the world. Among the many things Grinder the Gringo had told him for sure, was that a man had to have his own headquarters to fulfill himself. By God he believed it when he had first heard it, and he believed it now, but he was just about to put his at risk.

He would make up his mind to do something about this situation in a couple of days, but he didn't know what in hell it would be. Of course, there was no way he could visualize, without the unpredictable help of Dancing Bear, that the new world he had so lightheartedly thrown away was going to abruptly change.

Thirty-Three

Bluefeather sat on an Ortiz Mountain peak resting and contemplating while his mules grazed nearby. His eyes wandered way up north past Santa Fe and the Sangre de Cristos, down to the Jemez Mountains to the west and to the San Pedros and Sandias to the south just outside his current hometown of Albuquerque. It was a magnificent view encompassing over a million acres and four different mountain ranges. However, he didn't give the awesome sight its proper concentration. He only saw it with his outer eyes; his inner eye was practically blind to the spread of beauty. He had just discovered that someone had trespassed and dug out his placer mine during the three years he was in the armed services. It created a multitude of emotions.

At first there was a sense of loss and betrayal. How dare anyone— anyone on earth—take advantage of his patriotic absence to loot his claim. For a few moments his nose scar seared, and he wished to feel the perpetrator's neck encircled by his hands.

These feelings began to vanish as he sat staring across the land. He mused hopefully that someone with a large family to feed had worked the dry placer, or maybe it was an old veteran from the last great war. Anyway, it was only a nice little survival claim. No one had gotten wealthy from it. That was for sure. He decided he was lucky. He still had three bags of ninety percent nuggets and gold dust stashed back at Corrales.

The last of his ill feelings had disappeared and full acceptance of the situation had set in, when he first heard the distant "whack whack" of a helicopter. Before he could pinpoint its location and direction, the whirling blades almost blew his old leather hat off. It circled in the opening between two peaks less than forty yards from him, almost level with his gaze. His surprise kept him from getting a good look at the two occupants. The machine clattered on around the peak again and slowed, hovering about thirty yards out.

A young woman looked straight at him, smiled, and waved. Suddenly his heart filled the entire cavity of his chest and seemed to be struggling to burst out of his body. It restricted his breathing so that he had to gasp the high-altitude air into his lungs. It was Miss Mary! How could she have reincarnated so soon? No, it couldn't be. He waved feebly back at her and realized that it was the auburn hair and the red, full lips that had fooled and stunned him. No, it wasn't Miss Mary. This woman had higher cheekbones and a leaner jaw than his last love, but the totality of her coloration was shockingly similar.

He stood up, having trouble keeping solid footing in the wind wash from the chopper propellers. Smiling, he removed his hat and graciously bowed toward them. At that, the male pilot and the lady clacked off through the air toward Santa Fe.

He sat back down and watched them move out of sight over the hills. What were they doing out here? What could they possibly want from him? Why did they go to the trouble to take an extra look at this lone prospector, Bluefeather Fellini? Maybe it was a simple joyride. Maybe they were uranium prospectors. Maybe. Maybe. Maybe. Whatever, he would always remember that face, that woman.

He tried to cajole Dancing Bear up for one of his confusing, puzzling answers, but the emotions of finding his mine had been robbed, and the initial shock of having seen a Miss Mary facsimile had left him without the energy.

By the time he got back to Corrales, he had decided to leave his relatively new team of mules at home for a time. He had named them the same as his other mules: Nancy, after his first notable love at Tonapah, Nevada; Miss Mary, for the love of his life from Breen, Colorado, and Harmony Creek.

He told them, "Do not worry your beautiful heads, inestimable ones. In my absence, Tranquilino will treat you like the queens you are. I will make the trip as brief as possible. Please, bear with me and grant me patience. The excitement of making it back home from the war to my loved ones has caused my mind to vacate. The pleasure of celebration, and haphazardly—mainly in fun—prospecting with you, my dears, has created a meagerness in our funds. Forgive me for this oversight. The only excuse is our enjoying the wandering too much. We only halfheartedly sought those earthly treasures we so expertly know how to sniff out. I have erred against the advice of my mentor, Old Grinder, and put our property here—our homestead—in slight jeopardy. But do not allow my meandering voice to dismay you, sweetest ones. I shall increase our stash soon and all will be well. Do you hear and get my offerings clearly?"

They looked at him with shining eyes of velvety softness, large as a doe's, and understood.

"Good," he said. "Good."

Then he proceeded to the house, picked up the heaviest of the three bags of gold, and got into his already-loaded jeep with a canvas top. Previously, he had visited, dined, had drinks, and jamboreed with the Lucero family, so now he was free to make another run at the world and continue what began when he had met Old Grinder in Trinidad, Colorado, and fortunately had fallen for his yarns of gold and glory that were as true in his mentor's mind as a church steeple.

He started the jeep and drove toward the main city on the south side of Sandia Mountain. He had to cross the Rio Grande and finesse his way through the city traffic of Albuquerque.

He stopped at the office of a dentist who had always paid him cash for his gold. As he left, he wondered if Dr. Dingel illegally melted it down to make crowns for his patients' teeth.

He circled around the east side of the mountain past Golden, on to the old coal-mining town of Madrid, and then to the tiny outpost of Cerrillos. Nearby, before there was any other nationality on this part of the earth, the Indians had mined turquoise and many before him had sought and found some gold. Even Bluefeather had accumulated enough gold near here to allow this trip. Cerrillos had been bad to some, good to others. It had always been comfortable and lightly rewarding to him. Why not start his next and continuing quest here? Why not, indeed?

The hills moved by as fast as fence posts as he elatedly spurred the jeep toward his destiny.

The Cerrillos Bar had the usual smoky mirror, western prints, and beer advertisements scattered about on the walls, a jukebox, three or four customers, and that same old smell. It was unmistakably an icon of the great Southwest. It was also a sort of restaurant. Customers could eat at the bar—if they weren't slobbering drunk—or they could choose one of the seven tables scattered all the way across the forty-foot room.

Blessedly, the kitchen was next to the bar. The restrooms were in the far northwest corner. For utility purposes, the jukebox was halfway between these two rooms of the absolute. The tables circled around a small dance floor. All in all it was an establishment to succor the body and replenish wounded souls, with a touch of ancient history in its often stale air as a bonus.

The owners, George and Mattie Gull, handled the entire operation. He tended bar and waited tables part of the time. She cooked and waited tables part of the time. He was big and hairy, with a laugh that would have startled a charging rhino. She was also big, but deft and skillful in her work. Her laugh was not big. It was a light, almost continuous, titter for convenience's sake. The Gulls knew how to please without condescension or arrogance. They were the power in the village of perhaps a hundred living bodies. This power element was simple: they had control of the necessities of life for this sort of land—namely booze, bread, and music.

"One could do worse," Bluefeather thought as he sat drinking a cola and looking out the only window into Cerrillos's mostly empty main street. He had casually observed the uranium prospectors at the bar telling Big George about their claims. They were holding "hot" rocks next to their Geiger counters, thrilling at their buzzing the signal of radioactivity in the specimens. They carried and handled these instruments with the same pride a Texas Ranger had in his badge. These "hunters"—for most of them had so little experience one could not justifiably call them prospectors—were scattered by the hundreds of thousands throughout the valleys, mountains, and bars of Colorado, Arizona, Utah, and New Mexico. They were from every state in the Union and several foreign countries, searching for the bonanza of "yellow cake" that could be turned into power enough to blow up the world. None of them thought of this. Druggists, accountants, farmers, grocery store owners, gas station attendants, all kinds were obsessed with the glorious riches to be found and the glorious worship they would receive from their neighbors back home when they found them. It was only an idle curiosity to Bluefeather. The uranium fever had escaped him. He was aware that countless little restaurants, bars, and motels across his part of the world had found a lucky bonanza of business.

While Bluefeather mused about going back to the New Mexico Institute of Mining and Technology to earn his degree in mine engineering—it would only take him about six months—he saw a man walk past the window. There was something that emanated from the figure right through the glass to Bluefeather. He rearranged his chair so its back touched the wall. He sipped his cola, watching the bar entrance.

The door opened. A combination of light and shadow filled it. After tipping his tweed cap to the bartender, saying, "A good day to you, George Gull," he walked straight across the room toward Bluefeather.

"Why, why, hello there, Dr. Godchuck. How're you doin' today?"

The man ignored this as he moved on. He was dressed all the way in perfectly fitting tweed. A tan silk ascot encircled his neck. The thick showing of white hair underneath his cap had a sheen to it even in the soft light of the Cerrillos Bar. He wore a perfectly trimmed white mustache exactly one-eighth inch in width and two inches in length. His brisk walk was accentuated by a cane that was somehow part of his being, but obviously not needed for any type of physical impairment. His left hand carried a briefcase, or a leather valise, at least. The bottom was flat, ten inches wide, and the single piece of leather on each of its widest sides sloped up and came together with a hole in both forming a perfect handle. It had gold-buckled pockets on all sides. It was different and elegant, just as the man.

He sat right down at the table in the corner next to Bluefeather, placed the odd-looking walking stick on the table, and removed his cap, placing it very correctly atop the handle of the cane. The briefcase was pushed up against his right leg. He had hardly finished these movements before Big George placed a glass of ginger ale in front of him and poured the liquid into a glass as if it were rare French wine.

"Thank you, George Gull."

"My pleasure, Doctor."

The man raised the glass now, his piercing dark eyes looking directly at Bluefeather, and said, "And a good day to you, sir."

Bluefeather stuttered, "Why sure... sure enough, and an even better one to you."

They drank the toast. A swallow each. The man stuck out a hand smooth and spotless as the butt of a fresh-powdered baby, saying, "I'm Dr. Merphyn Godchuck."

Bluefeather took the soft-looking hand and almost winced at its crushing strength as he replied, "I'm Bluefeather Fellini. Pleased to meet you."

"Ah, ah, ah, let me guess. Bluefeather Fellini. Yes, that would be Indian-Italian ancestry, I believe," he said with just a trace of the Old South in his voice.

"Yes, sir."

"Fine, fine people. Are you here prospecting for uranium, Bluefeather Fellini?"

"To tell you the truth, I was just thinking about going back to school for a few months and getting my M.E."

"Good, good. I'm glad you're not a follower of the uranium tide. These poor creatures will have to sell their claims at a price the big companies choose. You see, these corporations have the only permits to mill and process the ore, and most of them are merciless. Of course, only one in a million or so of these hill climbers would know a worthy deposit if they found it."

"Well, it's good for local business," Bluefeather said, motioning to the bar.

"Indeed, it is that. Also good for the sellers of penny stocks."

Bluefeather agreed and added, "There are always more sellers than buyers in the mining business."

Dr. Godchuck seemed highly pleased at this statement and said so. "You display considerable wisdom of how the great metal scam works, Bluefeather Fellini."

Another blur moved past the window.

Dr. Godchuck cleared his throat and motioned to George Gull, who leaped around the bar and politely opened the front door. A young lady of perhaps thirty or maybe thirty-five years entered with a silver tray balanced on the bent palm of one hand. It held an elegant, old silver teapot and four teacups with saucers. She pranced delicately across the room toward the doctor and placed the tea ensemble on the corner table just as caringly as he had placed his accoutrements. Dr. Godchuck rose and stood until she was seated.

She was something, all right, but Bluefeather could not figure exactly what, except of course, woman. She had a short pageboy cut to her light brown hair and a 1920s hat—one of those soft-looking kind with one side curving down over her left ear. She wore a fine silk dress the color of her hair. It fit tightly over her lower breasts, revealing the upper portions of the smooth, creamy flesh as she bent over to pour the tea. Her mouth was almost painted in a cupid's bow, and her dark brown, gleaming eyes seemed to exude liquid sparkles of joyousness. She expertly poured a cup of tea for Dr. Godchuck and herself.

Bluefeather stared back and forth from one face to the other. His hunter/prospector eyes could not discern a single wrinkle on either face, although the doctor had to be sixty or older in spite of his agility and smooth hands. There should have been at least the first sign of smile wrinkles around the lady's face, but he could see none. Both of these people moved with such expert quickness that the two cups were correctly filled and properly placed before she glanced at Bluefeather.

The doctor caught her swiftly moving eyes and thoughts, saying, "Ah, ah, ah, this is Mr. Bluefeather Fellini, dear. Bluefeather Fellini, please meet my aunt, Tulip Everhaven."

Bluefeather stood up, bowing and kissing the tender rosewater-scented hand of Tulip Everhaven. He was certain the doctor had meant to say "niece" instead of "aunt." It had to be. He was almost stunned at his sudden courtliness when he said like a practiced Kentucky colonel, "It is a great pleasure to meet one of such delicate beauty."

She put one hand to her cheek, blushing—or feigning one better than a great actor—smiling with red and white profusion. "Oh my, you are such a gentlemen. Tea?" The southernism of her speech was undeniable. There was no exact location to it.

"Thank you, I will."

"Good, good," she said as she poured the hot liquid and smoothly moved the saucer and cup to the space on his table an inch from his hand.

"Mr. Bluefeather Fellini is a mining engineer, Tulip."

"Oh deah, how exciting. My third husband, Franklin Debonshire, was an engineer of some kind...or was it my fourth, Wilby Strick, Merphyn?" She set her cup down and tried to make wrinkles of thought on her forehead. The puzzle was so great that Dr. Godchuck deigned to solve his aunt's quandary.

"No, Tulip, it was your seventh, Farmley Casino. He wasn't an engineer exactly, more of a...a caretaker of floors."

"Oh, that's right, Merphyn deah. He was the one who electrocuted himself by...by..."

"Lightning struck him while he was emptying a pail of mop water in his client's hedge."

"Of course. I sometimes get them mixed up and especially how the deahs departed. Eight of them, you know." She smiled in confidence at

Bluefeather. "Whistle-Stop Everhaven was the last, of course. He was a fighter for prizes, but alas, one too many blows to that precious head and it exploded inside. He was blessed, though. Never knew what hit him. He had been out on his feet for three rounds. God does have his ways, you know."

Thirty-Four

Bluefeather had been soberly considering his next move at the perpetually challenging world when these two—these two individuals—had simply, elegantly barged right into his thoughts—his being. Just a few moments ago he was seriously considering finishing his education, when an older man with the skin of a healthy baby and a weirdly gorgeous young woman finely attired in flapper fashion that had ended twenty-odd years ago had suddenly become part of his space. He felt as if his previous world had suddenly been moved over, like a chair, but a thousand or so miles away.

For a young man, Bluefeather felt that a sufficient number of adventurous experiences had befallen him to make him at least somewhat worldly. He had grown up in two strong but separate cultures. He had been fortunate to have a great, a trusting, a loving mentor in Old Grinder. He had placed his life in jeopardy countless times on steep mountainsides and in carelessly dug tunnels. He had gambled at cards and dice against the best. He had fought for his life in bars, at gambling tables, and in a mighty bloody war. He had loved, by varying degrees and ways, a few fine women. He had experienced assorted spiritual initiations and involvements with a dancing spirit guide who gave erratic advice.

Yes, he had been places and done some things. Now he felt inexperienced, even amateurish, at life. These two people—within less than five minutes, but what seemed like several eternities—had invaded his person, his place on the planet, and somehow taken it over. The "deah this" and "deah that" of Tulip Everhaven, and Dr. Merphyn Godchuck consistently calling everyone by his or her full name, had temporarily thrown him off balance. Everything seemed to be reversed, and yet somehow promptly and properly normal. Even the doctor's clothes, which were more suited to a lord of a Scottish castle than a little worn-out mining village in New Mexico, seemed as natural as onion breath, as did this aunt of his, who dressed like a playgirl flapper and seemed to be about thirty or more years younger than her nephew.

Dr. Merphyn Godchuck had been talking a while now, and he continued in his smooth gentlemanly way. "I can see by your demeanor, Bluefeather Fellini, that you are a strong-willed man and indecision is against your nature. I sensed before I entered George Gull's place that I was about to have one of those rare, gifted, and fated meetings."

Strangely, Bluefeather now felt the same way. He had told them he was deliberating about renting a room in Cerrillos or possibly going on up to Santa Fe. They both offered and insisted, with such diligence, that they had a special, unused room for him. Not only that, their home was only two blocks from where they presently sat. He could not bring himself to refuse.

Ordinarily, he would never have accepted such an unheard-of offer but did so now without hesitation, feeling at home with these people and their house before he had ever entered it. Rare, indeed.

Now they had an easy, comfortable visit and talked of many things. Bluefeather told them of his relatives at Taos Pueblo and his Raton family and some of their ways. They each in turn related scattered incidents from their past lives and how they had lost their plantation to robber barons, rapists of good people, and purveyors of tax bills so huge they would have been unpayable by the Rothschilds. The proud Godchuck family had been shamed beyond repair. All, except the good doctor and his flexible aunt, had found ways to depart the accursed land, hangings, alcohol, train wrecks, and murderous constipation from eating too much red-eye gravy and shortening bread.

Tulip let out a soulful sigh, reaching out to pat one of Merphyn's hands with tender remembrances, uttering with pity, "Deah, deah, it seems like only this morning that we moved the bed to the center of the room for Merphyn's birth."

Dr. Godchuck explained to Bluefeather that the left side of his body was born in Louisiana and his right side in East Texas. He made a motion with one hand down his middle. Tulip picked up the descriptions where she had left them. "You see, deah Bluefeather, the Louisiana and Texas state lines ran exactly through the center of my deah sister's bedroom. You understand of course, why everything, and I dare say, my deahs, I do mean everything, had to be centered. It did pose a slight difficulty since Merphyn's mother was in full labor, but with the help of several hired hands and a tape measure we managed to deliver deah Merphyn in one piece but in the two states of Texas and Louisiana." Tulip smiled and looked wide eyed—very wide eyed—at Bluefeather for approval.

He gave it. "An extraordinary achievement indeed, dear Tulip. Few men have had the great fortune to be related to an aunt who realized the importance of being born in two states at one time. Why, it enlarges one's homeland by several million acres and gives a special stature to the recipient of such a majestic privilege."

While she was shyly thanking him for his appreciation of the special event, he realized he was already beginning to sound like his brand-new friends. He would have to be careful and stop this unintended imitating right now.

He had little time to worry because the man from two states was talking, using his smooth unmarked hands to emphasize. "Everything, everyone, takes many jagged, seemingly random detours in this life, but you can draw a straight line right down the middle of your final existence, from your mother's womb to your last breath, and that will be your life. By the way," the doctor continued, "I believe that a normal life span should be between 135 or even 150 years." He paused a beat, then said, "All a reasonable-thinking person has to do is take a glance at sweet Tulip," and he smiled affectionately at her as she coyly accepted the compliment as her due, then clasped her hands together in front of her upper cleavage and beamed her pleasure at her nephew's words at Bluefeather. She had evidently agreed with her nephew somewhere near one hundred percent.

After about third or fourth thoughts, Bluefeather backed up to what the doctor had said about the "seemingly random detours" and saw much truth in the simple declarative statement. Hadn't his cousin Hog Head changed Bluefeather's direction drastically by slapping the arrogance, vanity, and other things out of him with one fateful blow? Hadn't his meeting Old Grinder, by pure accident—or was that fated, too—led to his searching for his own dreams of gold instead of digging those of others? If Grinder had not fallen, killing himself, would he, Bluefeather, have left Taos, or would he have wound up with Nancy, the grand lady of gambling? Would he? If he hadn't killed the man in Tonapah—even though it was in self-defense—would he have gone to Breen where he met Miss Mary, the love of anyone's life? Would he have moved to

Corrales and eventually on up to work the placer mines south of Cerrillos? If he hadn't heard about all seven of the Marchiondo sons going into the armed services would he himself have joined up, fought, bled, puked, and felt horrors and loves beyond description? Would he?

It must have been the influence of the powerful spiritual number seven. Certainly it had worked for the Marchiondos. New Mexico governor Mabry had invited the parents, Anna and Troy, to spend a day and a night in the governor's mansion. Both the state and American flags had been flown in their honor. The next day Governor Mabry presented the proud parents and entire family the American flag, saying, "In a small attempt to repay and show appreciation for an Italian immigrant family who offered the lives of their seven sons in World War II, I hereby give this symbol of freedom." A true miracle.

Yes, like he, they had all returned, battered but alive and free. The *Life* magazine cover story as well as a pictorial feature in *American Legion* magazine about the immigrant family had made Bluefeather feel good and offer up many prayers of thanks.

But now he continued his cogitation of his own fate and destiny. And without Old Grinder's early company, love, and advice, he never would have had the patience to enjoy his present delightful, eccentric companions. Without all the previous events having happened, including the robbery of his last mine, he would not be sitting here with these two wonderfully preposterous people right now. The old-young Dr. Godchuck spoke eternal truths. His life, any life, of seeking and purpose was linked to another, like a tapeworm tied in a bowknot at its ends. And now the voracious worm had fed itself into a growing new link for Bluefeather—the doctor and his aunt. It was all tied together just as the doctor said. Simple.

Tulip poured them each another cup of tea, since the cola and the ginger ale were all gone, saying, "I hope Mr. Barkitch and his son are on time for dinner. My tummy tells me I'm neglecting it woefully."

"Patience, my Tulip," said Merphyn as he took a heavy gold watch from his tweed vest, "it's only an hour yet."

"Oh, that's wonderful, deah. I do hope they come in faith."

Bluefeather's head was clear in spite of the odd company and thoughts surrounding him, but he felt it a miracle on its own that Aunt Tulip could speak with such a southern accent and still not drop many of her *g*'s and *r*'s.

Merphyn pushed, just once, at his vast array of crowning white hair, stroked his perfect moustache, just once, and said, just once, "I'm frightfully delighted, Bluefeather Fellini, that you're going to be there to lend your strong emotional support when I make my sacred presentation of ideas of actuality to John D. Barkitch and his attorney son, Joseph S. Barkitch."

Bluefeather swallowed in embarrassment at this show of faith. "I won't know what to say since I don't know what you're going to present."

"Do not be concerned. I don't need words from you. I have millions of words of my own. All I need is the support of your mind, the force of your will, and the presence of your special spirit."

"Well, if that's all, you've got it."

It was the time of silent giving now. All three seemed to hold a quiet moment of support for whatever the upcoming struggle might bring.

Then Bluefeather saw her. He was almost certain the woman in the helicopter had just driven by in a Cadillac convertible. He leapt up and ran around the table, leaning into the recessed window, anxiously staring down the street. There she was at the gas station getting out of the car. With her was a huge man with a scar completely angling across his face—a deep scar, for he could discern it from where he stood. The scar-faced man exited the other side and stood leaning against the door looking up and down the street without stopping, as if both Chief Joseph and Geronimo had singled him out for attack.

Bluefeather said, "Excuse me, please. I'll be right back."

Before his new companions could answer, Bluefeather dashed the door and outside, fully intending to accost the woman. However, the fullness of the scene made him stop and look around for the great Indian warriors himself. The attendant, Rocky Ames, pumped the gas, wiped the windshield, and then checked under the hood of the sleek blue car.

The woman walked several steps down the street, where she had a dead-on view of the high-desert sunset. The warm, pink-orange afterglow caught her features as she stood raptly absorbing the solemn event, hands on Levi's-clad hips. For just that moment, the sinking sun found one last opening between the spearlike clouds, giving her a burst of illumination that made Bluefeather feel he was intruding on a sacred moment of a goddess. He walked back toward the bar, reached to open the door, then took one last glance at the divine vision. She was looking straight at him with a smile that beggared quick description. He swiftly reentered the Cerrillos Bar feeling as if he had spied upon the birth of Christ.

As he sat back down, Dr. Godchuck spoke in a voice so smooth it would make silkworms go into jealous tantrums. "Bluefeather Fellini, you have just gazed upon Korbell's only daughter. The man with her is head of his security."

"Korbell? The one we read about doing all this business around the world? That Korbell?"

"That Korbell."

Bluefeather suddenly felt helpless. There had been some unknown bond in the air between them. The link was there between them, even when she was hanging high above him in the helicopter in the Ortiz Mountains, and now again as she enjoyed the late-day explosion of color in tiny Cerrillos. Korbell. Just the name had damaged the invisible binding that stretched between them.

"What is a woman like that doing in Cerrillos?"

Dr. Godchuck answered, "Something, for certain. The Korbells never do nothing."

That made as much sense to Bluefeather as he felt he was going to get.

With the tips of her exquisite fingers, Tulip touched the edges of her brown hair and unconsciously covered her cleavage with the other hand, volunteering, "I visited with Marsha, Marsha Korbell, for a few exhilarating moments. She is a lady of charm, grace, and decisiveness. She is also beautiful in a...a fresh-air way."

Merphyn reached over and patted her hand, saying softly, "That is generous of you, Aunt Tulip Everhaven, but she is not nearly as alluring as you, my dear."

She gave him a beatific smile, replying, "Oh, deah Merphyn, you do use such honeyed praise. Of course, that's why you have always been my favorite."

Then the Barkitches came. There were only two of them, but the floor seemed to shake and the walls to quiver at their arrival. They both had fattish faces with slit eyes and widespread nostrils that somehow reminded Bluefeather of a pig's snout—although he would never mean to insult that noble creature. They both wore the same dark gray suits, ties slightly askew. In fact, nothing exactly synchronized here. Their hips were too wide for their shoulders and their hands too small for such large-boned wrists. But they forced smiles with ease as the introductions were completed and they were seated. They were in the heavy construction business—highways, bridges, and such. Surprisingly, few people questioned how they seemed to always bid their jobs just a very few dollars under second place.

"Well now," said Barkitch the elder, "how about some drinks? What's this tea service doing in Cerrillos anyway?"

Mattie Gull had come tippy-toeing and twittering up, appearing to float her substantial weight in between her dainty steps. She passed a menu to each and then said, "Care for drinks first?"

The junior Barkitch motioned to Tulip. "Lovely young ladies first." His eyes stayed on her, roaming back and forth from her cupid lips to her milky, soft cleavage. She felt this, and after careful thought ordered a dry red wine. Both contractors desired bourbon on the rocks, and to make it simple, Bluefeather chose a bar Scotch with water and ice. It was understood with the establishment that Dr. Godchuck would order Irish whiskey aloud, but would be served ginger ale and ice.

The drinking was on. Mattie would not let their glasses stay empty long. She would wait just the right amount of time to take their dinner orders.

After silly small talk through two drinks, Dr. Godchuck said, "Gentlemen, I assume you've perused our documents and are ready to talk business."

The elder Barkitch said, "I leave most of that to Joseph. I've got to get something back from all that money I spent on his law school." He laughed at himself, alone.

Joseph became so serious, one would have thought he had just been notified of the death of the world. He said, "Well . . . well now, the patent on the sage oil is only good for a few more months. We feel there's too little time left . . ."

Dr. Godchuck had spent a lot of the "time" Joseph spoke of with him and his father already. Precious time. "I believe that I explained this clearly at our last meeting, Joseph S. Barkitch. If we set up our processing plant ahead of any competitors we will be so far ahead that . . . certainly you can't deny the gingivitis cures?"

"We must be cautious, Dr. Godchuck. Our finances have come about the hard way. We've had to outperform and outbid all competition. We can't just gamble on any project, no matter how promising."

Tulip gracefully chimed in, "My nephew's invention is not just 'any project,' sir. It can lead to great benefit for all humankind, including yourselves."

"Well yes, we're taking all that into consideration, Miss Everhaven. May I call you Tulip?" Joseph's eyes gleamed rapaciously at the overall softness, smoothness and classiness of Tulip Everhaven. His father, observing his son's obvious weakness for Tulip's delicacy, reentered the fray.

"I tell you what, Dr. Godchuck. Why don't you just run the deal down step by step, and then we'll make our decision after we eat. How's that, huh?" He beamed around at everyone, feeling in control now. He was gratified.

Dr. Merphyn Godchuck did not hesitate a second. "I first heard of the wondrous curative powers at your old home, the pueblo just north of the town of Taos, Bluefeather Fellini. During the terrible flu epidemic of 1918 and 1919, people were dying like the black plague was upon them—over three hundred in the small village of Taos itself. However, a shaman of some grandeur ordered the Taos Pueblo tribe to boil the leaves of the sagebrush and drink it several times daily and inhale its wondrous curative vapors. The death rate was nothing in comparison to the rest of the land. I was already practicing medicine then. It was only a couple of decades back that I could force myself to start my experiments. It's very expensive to have a chemist distill small amounts. That's why, John D. Barkitch, we need the pilot plant now."

"Yes, yes, I understand the urgency of that all right, Doctor."

"Now you've had in your possession records of over four hundred cures of gingivitis, and when taken orally with two other herbal compounds the sage oil relieves ulcers almost instantly. The common cold, if caught early, goes in remission in less than twenty-four hours. I have already quoted you an endless succession of enormously promising cures and other remissions such as . . ."

In spite of Bluefeather's dedicated interest in Dr. Godchuck's elixir, he felt an unknown but powerful force toward the bar. He could not stop himself. He turned his head and eyes and there sat the huge, scarred man and Marsha Korbell. He could swear she was staring at him and had lowered her eyes just as his lined up with hers. But it was so swift, he could not be sure it actually happened. He was pushing his chair back, preparing to go introduce himself, in spite of her gorilla companion. Then they arose and walked out, nodding and speaking unclear words to Big George as they exited into the darkness. In a moment he heard the convertible start and saw the headlights flash on the bar's lone window as they made a U-turn and drove toward Santa Fe.

Bluefeather felt a strange loss at his unnatural inaction. He forced his attention back to the business at the table. Joseph had just said something to Tulip as an excuse to place his hand on her warm, soft arm. He was conjuring how those silken arms could enfold him and crush his back in ecstasy.

"Ten thousand seems a little high for just five percent of such a risky deal," said Barkitch the elder.

"Well, I can't see how we can build the pilot plant for any less, John D. Barkitch. We have to gather the sage leaves first as well. That takes wages for the pickers and, again, time. Time, you see, is all we own. Everything else is on lease or borrowed. Everything. We must not waste the one single thing that the great mystery has deigned to grant us to use as we please. We may waste it joyfully on occasion so we can better use it wisely the rest of our lives. Now is the time for wisdom, for vision, Mr. John D. Barkitch. Now, if ever."

"Well, I dunno. What does that legal mind of yours tell you, Joseph?"

The lawyer removed his arm from patting Tulip on the back and said, "Oh well, I think we need more time...a few more meetings." Bluefeather saw Junior's telling glance at Tulip as he said this last and continued, "Why don't we dine now? Is everyone as starved as I am?"

The doctor would have no more waste of his precious gift of time. He said in a voice that eradicated any thought of interference, "Very well, then, John D. Barkitch and Joseph S. Barkitch, I will give you a demonstration of another of the oil's wonders. If this won't convince you, then I withdraw my own offer."

He bent over and took a small bottle of sage oil and a box of kitchen matches out of his unique valise and set them on the table in front of him. Then, methodically, he opened both the matchbox and the bottle of sage oil. He held his smooth, unblemished left hand out flat in front of everyone. With his right, he struck one of the kitchen matches and held the flame under his left middle finger. All were transfixed.

Bluefeather forced his eyes from the burning sacrifice and watched the impassive face of the doctor. However, when he saw the jaw muscles knot up in pain he turned his eyes back to the match. Dr. Godchuck held it until it extinguished itself against the forefinger and thumb of his right hand. Then he turned his left palm up and there on the obviously burned finger was a spot almost swelled to a blister.

He took the bottle and, with the dropper suction cap, applied a tiny drop to the burned spot. Then with the two fingers he had singed while holding the match, he rubbed it into his burnt skin. The oil vanished almost instantly.

"It takes so little because of its unheard-of penetrating power," he said.

Throats were cleared. Glasses of alcohol were emptied and unbelieving eyes stayed on the finger now. The swelling diminished and disappeared. There was only a slight pinkness left to show where the flame had burned.

"Think. Just think of the ramifications for saved suffering, scarring, and death all over the world from this one use alone."

The elder contractor laughed dryly, saying, "You are a magician. A real good'un, Doctor. That's some trick you pulled there. You really had me goin' there for a minute."

Tulip sat straight up with the palms of both her hands on the table and said, "Any faker of small skills can be a magician, but only the chosen can make real magic." She stared at them with a look so proud, and hovering anger so dangerous, that the contractors both swallowed three times almost simultaneously. But they could not allow their control to be lost.

However, before they could think of a put-down, Dr. Merphyn Godchuck sat as straight as his aunt. His white, glossy hair seemed to capture power from a source above his head relaying it down through its roots and into all the elements that went to make up the body of the doctor.

"Sirs," he said, "I shall point out one last series of verification for you. The last one. Look at the skin of my hands—smooth, full fleshed, no brown spots. See if you can." As he leaned forward toward them, he said, "Examine my face with care. Can you spot any lines, wrinkles, or blotches natural to a man seventy-four years of age?"

They leaned forward to examine him like a jeweler does a diamond. Then they reared back trying to think of the thing to say. Their minds were not that quick.

"I speak to you in truth and faith, Joseph S. Barkitch. Since you are next to Tulip Everhaven, look at the full handsome breasts."

Barkitch did so willingly for the fiftieth time.

"Examine with your own hands the firm skin under her arms."

He did so eagerly as the rest watched enraptured.

"Now, Tulip, turn your face full at Joseph S. Barkitch and let him try to find a wrinkle around those wondrous eyes or the corners of those luscious lips."

Joseph S. looked hard, all right. He looked willingly.

"Ah, ah, ah," said the doctor, "before her startling beauty blinds you, did you find a single fault when you examined her as I instructed?"

"Well...well, no, Mr....Doctor. She's a beauty all right, but we've all known that since our first meeting. What does that have to do with our deal?"

"Have to do? Have to do? Why, everything. Have you ever seen a seventy-four-year-old man and a ninety-six-year-old woman, like me and my dear aunt, with such skin? Well, it came from the smallest application of the sage oil mixed in a lanolin base applied lightly twice daily."

"You folks look pretty good all right, but you cannot be a day over sixty, and you, Mrs. Everhaven, must be an expert with heavy makeup to make it look that smooth. I've seen 'em do it in the movies," said the elder Barkitch.

The younger Barkitch spoke decisively now. "You must be crazy, Godchuck. Plumb raving, wall-butting nuts. This pretty little thing here you call your aunt couldn't be a week past thirty, if that. Now isn't that about right, honey?" he said, grabbing one of her dainty hands.

She spoke softly with a coy glance as she moved her hand so that his missed hers. "Well, I do color my hair a wee bit."

The lawyer said, "Are you people putting us on? The only reason I'd advise Dad to invest in this phony deal is if you went with it, Tulip. What kind of suckers do you take us for, anyhow?"

Bluefeather's nose scar was hotter than the demonstration match the doctor had burned up. He was clenching his jaw so hard he felt the tops of his teeth had been mashed down even with the edge of his gums. The only thing that stopped damage from occurring was Tulip, dear Tulip, opening her purse, casually taking out a little vanity mirror and redoing her lipstick with expertise. She touched the hair that bobbed out so evenly under her 1920s hat, turned a smile on the two enemies that would have charmed a snake that had just swallowed a baby porcupine. She spoke in a syrupy voice, barely above a whisper, "Snakeshit, you bloodsucking soul snatchers. Remove instantly your fat, stinking asses from the exalted presence of my deah nephew and our most esteemed associate Mr. Fellini. You and your kind only meet with 'givers' such as ourselves to steal time and take advantage of those you know to be your mental and moral superiors. It makes you feel almost equal for a moment to toy with the grand thoughts of grand people." And then louder now, yet smooth as catfish skin, as deadly sharp as a cottonmouth's fangs, she finished, "Away assholes! Away!"

They had scooted their chairs back from the table and had risen, no doubt, to say crude and insulting things, but on observing Bluefeather standing, feet spread to leap, his finger to his lips motioning, "shhh, shhh," and the honorable doctor poised with his pointed cane like a swordsman, they were caused to knock both their chairs over, and three others as well, as they hurried from the premises talking to themselves in unknown tongues.

In a voice without rancor, but of solid certainty, Dr. Merphyn Godchuck said, "Taking into consideration our few geniuses and near geniuses along with our uncountable idiots, I cannot visualize the collective intellect of the entire human race being sufficient or deserving of its permanent survival."

Bluefeather and Tulip Everhaven thought and nodded in agreement.

As they sat back down, in order to hasten the forgetting of the Barkitches, Bluefeather said, "I've been meaning to ask you about that distinctive cane, Doctor."

The doctor handed it to him saying, "It is a bull's prick cane. Here, take it and examine it carefully. You'll see where my friend, Luz Martinez, the great wood-carver of Taos, made the handle from walnut."

Bluefeather was amazed at how it had been carved, waxed, and fitted so one could hardly tell where the bull started and the tree parted. "Excellent work here, Doctor. A prize cane for sure. I've never seen one before. I'm honored."

"I'm pleased you like it. If we can manage the time maybe I could get you one made. After the penis is removed from the bull—at a slaughterhouse, of course—it must be dried properly in the sun. It takes quite a spell for proper curing. Then, of course, Mr. Martinez is a perfectionist, and he uses up several days and nights for his part of the construction."

"Well, I won't mind waiting."

"Let us, as gentlemen, consider the deal done then."

"Agreed."

Tulip said, with near happiness, "I'm so terribly delighted that we made some kind of deal tonight. Would it be unreasonable to suggest we order our dinner now before it's too late? And if you would join me, Blue...may I call you Blue?"

"You already have. Please continue to do so, Ma'am."

"Thank you. I was going to suggest that you and I share a carafe of dry red wine. It's too early for my deah, deah, nephew to have his allowable two bedtime bourbons."

Dr. Godchuck said, "Please, let us proceed."

They did with unabashed joy.

Thirty-Five

It had not taken them long to retire from the Cerrillos Bar to the Godchuck home as Bluefeather drove his jeep up and moved in. It was a comfortable six-room adobe house decorated with a strange combination of Navajo and Persian rugs. There were prints and paintings of, and by, southwestern artists as well as English fox-hunting prints.

While the doctor poured one of his two bedtime bourbons and settled among the colorful pillows on a colorless old couch to enjoy it, Tulip swiftly poured Bluefeather and herself a glass of dry red wine—make unknown, since there was no label on the half-gallon jug.

Bluefeather followed Tulip, paying the usual respects to each room. She saved the doctor's office for last. His degree from Columbia and a few photographs were displayed. In one of the doctor's graduation photos, Tulip pointed out so many attending family members that Bluefeather lost track, but he did discover Tulip looking almost exactly the same age as she did now. He was again startled, although only a moment ago he was still accepting her as the world's youngest ninety-six-year-old.

At his voiceless consternation, she, without looking directly at him, said, "It was only a few years after this photograph that I became Merphyn's guinea pig. He's made oh so many experiments on me. I've enjoyed and survived them all quite well, don't you think, Blue?"

"Oh my, yes, you most certainly have."

They glanced at one another with mutual respect and, of course, Tulip added to her wide-eyed glance of innocent expectation one more little dash of spice—flirtation. There was an old examining table and other medical artifacts that Tulip proudly pointed out, adding, "Of course, deah, you can appreciate the lack of patients in such a small and healthy place as Cerrillos, but deah Merphyn has a respectful clientele who occasionally drive down from Santa Fe or up from Albuquerque. You see, it's enough to care for our necessities, but not sufficient to progress onward to the pilot plant. It takes so very long for an individual to obtain a medical patent. I'm sure you, being an engineer and all, understand this better than I do."

"Well...I..."

"That's why Merphyn chose the gingivitis patent first. It was the easiest to prove and therefore the fastest to get registered, but there are so many far more important cures we've proven to ourselves that must have patent proceedings finished and others begun. That is, in order to benefit the world. Don't you see, Blue? You do realize the urgency is to get a sufficient supply of sage oil on hand from the pilot plant in order for Merphyn to prove his findings once and for all?"

He was trying to think how to properly answer her when she said with a powerful longing that was also somehow a pleading, "Don't you see, deah Blue?"

"Yes, Tulip, I believe I do better than most."

He realized she had been pitching a perfect con at him, but he felt it was sincerely unintentional. The few belongings he had with him certainly made him look like he was unemployed, and there was no way she could know about the seventy-eight hundred dollars in new hundred-dollar bills in his billfold. No, it was simply her love and belief in her nephew's work and vision that gave such a passionate chime to her velvety voice.

They rejoined the doctor. She was her demure self again. It seemed she either chattered in long discourses, made short pungent observations, or remained smilingly, enigmatically silent, seeming to absorb every sound and sight around her with acute awareness. Bluefeather thought this Tulip woman was so full of life there was enough to slosh over and spill on those in need of the elixir.

The doctor had put on a soft smoking jacket and was comfortably enjoying his allowable second Kentucky bourbon.

"I see Tulip has bored you with our humble abode, Bluefeather Fellini."

"No, Doctor, quite the opposite. I thoroughly enjoyed the all-too-brief tour," Bluefeather said as he sat on a couch opposite the doctor.

Tulip refilled their glasses and joined him on the couch making a slight gesture of pulling the short dress over her knees. It was only a movement of habit, but the little movement served to draw the eye to the graceful, even sensuous, legs protruding thereunder.

Bluefeather made the first toast, looking past the burgundy-colored liquid at Tulip's oversized brown eyes, then to Merphyn's dark ones. In the soft lighting of the room his eyes appeared as black as the center of a cannonball and just as penetrating.

"Here's to a night of new friendships. May it be one to remember as warmly as its actuality."

"Well done, Bluefeather Fellini. May those precious thoughts increase a thousandfold for you as they are certain to do so for us."

Tulip simply whispered, "Agreed."

And they all took a sip in perfect unison as if they had trained a hundred years to do so. The three were attuned in soul and possibly deed. Bluefeather suddenly felt that he had done enough talking in the presence of such exemplary company. He would speak a few more words and then go into action, rightly or wrongly. It was his true nature.

"I beg your forgiveness in advance," he said, "but could I have a match and the bottle of oil for a moment?"

The doctor surprised him by saying almost eagerly, "Of course you may."

Tulip volunteered her services and obtained them for Bluefeather. She placed both on a hand-carved coffee table in front of him. He carefully took the lid from the little bottle of light golden-colored liquid, opened the matchbox, and removed one. Then he held his left hand out, palm down, just as Dr. Godchuck had done. He struck the kitchen match on the box and placed the resultant flame under his middle finger. The first second he didn't sense the burning, but then the pain came. He could feel his eyelids wanting to close in agony, and his lips screamed silently to curl away from his teeth and pull tight to the sides. He controlled this somehow, although the effort made his breath feel like it would explode his chest into the four eyes of the anxious observers. His only flinching was the uncontrollable clenching of his jaw muscles, just as Dr. Godchuck had done before. It was beyond the comprehension of a snail how long the match burned. Again, just as Dr. Godchuck had, when the flame neared the end of his fingers, he tipped it so the flare would continue until it singed itself out on the tips of his right thumb and forefinger. All three were holding their breaths, eyes transfixed on the tiny diminishing blaze as if watching a tornado disappear in the distance. Then it flickered out. All breathed in unison again.

Bluefeather tipped only a tiny bit of oil onto the fingers that had held the match and began to rub the swelled spot on his testing finger before it could break into a blister. For the hundredth time this night, he was pleasantly surprised. The pain was reduced with almost the same speed as the swiftly penetrating oil disappeared through the skin pores to begin its soothing healing. In a few minutes the main swelling was gone, and there remained only a pinkish residue of injury and a slight combination of both warm and cool feeling.

Now at last, he raised his eyes to the expectant ones staring at him, awaiting his decision with both confidence and a slight, understandable uncertainty.

Bluefeather said, "Dr. Godchuck, you and your aunt are among the rare chosen. Your formula works beyond words. Congratulations."

They were all so suddenly overjoyed at the wonder of mutual understanding and respect that they silently drained their respective glasses.

Dr. Godchuck arose with a new agility and went to pour a third forbidden drink, saying, "One must become a fool occasionally to appreciate rare moments such as this."

As soon as the doctor was seated, Bluefeather took out his thick wallet and swiftly counted out six thousand dollars on the coffee table. "Please honor me by accepting my minor partnership for this pitiful amount. I shall do better as we move forward."

"Ah, ah, ah," said the doctor. "Blessings be tendered to us all. Tomorrow we shall move into La Fonda de Santa Fe. That's where the funding for our pilot plant shall be acquired."

Tulip clasped her hands over her cleavage and beamed. "I deahly love that hotel lobby."

■ ■ ■

Thirty-Six

Bluefeather sat at a familiar table in the La Fonda dining room awaiting the arrival of his two compatriots for brunch. It had been over three weeks since they had loaded his jeep and the Roadmaster Buick belonging to the Godchucks and settled into the hotel. The load, in volume, had consisted mainly of the doctor's many variations of tweed and her mostly flapper-era wardrobe. Besides the necessities, Tulip had insisted on taking Merphyn's framed diplomas, awards, and her favorite picture of their family, whose members were now scattered somewhere amidst demons or angels. Bluefeather's wardrobe was easy to handle, consisting of one blue-gray suit, several pairs of Levi's, a dozen or so white shirts as well as some plaid Pendleton ones. He had two pairs of prospecting boots, two pairs of shoes, and one pair of rubber galoshes that could be worn over either. Today he wore pressed Levi's and a white shirt.

The doctor had acquired a two-bedroom suite for him and Tulip. Bluefeather's room was directly across the hallway from Tulip's door. The suite's living room area was furnished with heavy, territorial-style furniture, a mirror with a hand-worked tin frame, a short bar, and it had a view across adobe house rooftops to the Sangre de Cristo foothills. Tulip kept the multiple-use area dotted with a few green plants, chocolates, snack chips, and nuts of various kinds. These items were not only for their pleasure, but for the occasional interviewee who would be subjected to the mildest of suggestions that it would be wise to invest in the development of the oil of sage and its vast restorative qualities.

The doctor acted as adviser and Bluefeather as front man for their presentations. Bluefeather soon learned that other medical men were skeptical and often ridiculing. This was confusing to the young entrepreneur, because Old Grinder had told him that doctors and dentists were the most inclined to take gambles. This group actually seemed afraid of Dr. Godchuck. It was a while before he realized most of them were possibly jealous of Merphyn's courage and felt insufficient around a man of medicine who was, and always had been, more than willing to give up the private clubs, the golf, the tennis, the many comforts of mercilessly combining the gods of medicine and money. It was a fear of an unknown territory that they would never dare to tread upon.

He had raised five hundred dollars from a truck driver, a thousand from an insurance salesman, and fifteen hundred from a sheep rancher. The profit was not as much as he would have liked because it had taken many steaks, cocktails, and wearing conversations to arrive at these small contributions.

Dr. Godchuck had told Bluefeather to avoid the elderly, or the second-generation rich and the wealthy from inheritance, as they would mostly just take up his time and use up his soul for their own entertainment, then pass, saying, "My accountants have turned the deal down," or "I have an enormous tax burden coming due." One woman of this kind had surprised him by speaking straight and saying she understood real estate but had no knowledge of the sagebrush that sometimes covers it.

At his admitted failure with this play-it-safe-at-all-costs group, the good and great doctor said, "If you insist on wasting time in the effort of acquiring inherited money, get a group of them together. They don't mind gambling a little if they all do it together. That way if the deal turns sour, they can all laugh in chorus. No one person is singled out as the fool. You do understand what I'm telling you, don't you, Bluefeather Fellini?"

As yet, Bluefeather had been unable to get more than two of these types of people together at one time. However, today he had meetings with several prospects: a Ford car dealer, the manager of a grocery store, and an admitted cow thief. There was one order that Dr. Godchuck had handed to him with much sincerity. He was told that the lovely woman of the helicopter and the Cerrillos Bar was also staying at La Fonda. The woman of shocking beauty and forceful feline movement, the adopted daughter of a real, self-made, world-class power, Marsha Korbell must be approached for bigger things.

"Now, listen carefully, Bluefeather Fellini," the doctor said, "Korbell is the kind of man we want to join us after we have properly used our pilot plant. We must not waste a man of his caliber on small stuff. He would not be interested. We must tap into his funding through his daughter for all the hay in the fields—for the factory, the worldwide distribution, and the advertising."

Bluefeather replied, "Then I should wait to approach her until we have succeeded with the pilot plant?"

"Ah, ah, ah. No, oh, no. Make the run when it feels right. We must get started with Korbell, for he will check us out right down to the exact count of the pores in the skin of our big toes."

Bluefeather said, "That will take some time."

Now as he sat in almost, but not quite, half-vision, the woman of his thoughts was standing, talking to a couple of men in the dining room entrance. She shook hands with each as they turned to leave. She was then guided by the Spanish hostess to the table next to Bluefeather. He looked around instantly for her entourage of guards, or whatever they were, but could recognize none. It was the right place, at the right time, as the song went. He waited impatiently, surprisingly nervous, for her to get her order in. He did not know how, but knew he had to make a move.

"Excuse my rudeness, please, but aren't you Marsha Korbell?"

She placed the coffee cup back on the table, turned her head full at him, and smiled inquisitively, nodding "yes."

"My name is Bluefeather Fellini. Would it be too much of an imposition if I joined you for just a moment? There's a question I'd like to ask you."

She hesitated, then making up her mind motioned toward a chair opposite her and said, "Please do," in a tone that removed his doubt, calmed his nerves, and caused him to trip over his own chair in eagerness as he followed the route of her casually directed hand to the seat at "the table" with "the woman."

"Thank you. Thank you very much," he said.

"Have you ordered yet?" she asked.

"No. Actually I'm waiting for Dr. Godchuck and his aunt to join me."

"You mean Tulip Everhaven? I've visited with her casually, of course. She is a charmer."

"That she is. Please don't think me impertinent, but recently I think I saw you fly right by me on a hill in the Ortiz Mountains."

"Fly? How do you mean?"

He could not help but choke back a laugh. "Oh, you were in a helicopter, and the pilot held position while you looked right at me."

She calmly took another sip of coffee as the waitress waited to fill her cup, saying, "Oh, it's possible. I fly all over the state checking out state land for oil or other mineral possibilities."

He was a little let down at her appearing not to remember him. He sure as hell remembered her and how he had felt the invisible rope that tied them together. She obviously had not recognized him or the connection.

He was uplifted some, however, when she unexpectedly shared her current work with him. "As I'm sure you're aware ... you are in minerals, aren't you?"

"Yes. I have been."

"Well, as I started to explain, I'm sure you know that New Mexico holds monthly auctions of mineral rights on state land."

"Yeah. Sure."

"Well, that's what I do. That's why I'm here. We're looking to bid on oil possibilities only."

At that moment Bluefeather regretted deeply that he had not majored in oil geology instead of mining at the Institute of Mining in Socorro, and oh, how he wished he had finished. Here was the opening everyone would dream of charging. Well, he had not majored in oil geology and he had not earned his degree. He would just have to get his mind back to Dr. Godchuck's project where he was obligated, and forget stupid, wasteful regrets with a vital vengeance.

"Folks say you're Mr. Korbell's troubleshooter."

"They do? Well, what a compliment. I've never felt qualified for such a title, but will accept it as great flattery."

"Oh, I'm sure you measure up, all right."

For some reason they both laughed as she said without any vanity showing, "My measurements have sometimes led to embarrassing situations, mostly to the measurer."

Bluefeather reserved any more comment. She had somehow made him just as comfortable as he had been hesitant earlier. He no longer doubted that he could bring up the oil of sage without being ridiculed or insulted, so he decided to be just as open as she was and see what happened.

"I was curious about seeing your lovely eyes out in space in front of me and my mules on the little peak, and I also noticed you looking at the sunset in the streets of Cerrillos and later in the Cerrillos Bar having a drink. I have also pleasantly observed your movements in and out of La Fonda and a couple of times here in Santa Fe while you were shopping, but right now I have a serious business venture I would like for you to take a look at. It, too, is oil. But a different kind."

Well, there it was, he had made a speech. A goddamn speech. However, it was all truly felt. He waited.

She looked at him straight on and said, "Shoot."

He did not remember the words as they poured out, because of the intensity of his feelings about Dr. Godchuck and his work. She interrupted now and then with sensible questions about the quantity needed, overall plans, and other things so rational that she made the pitch easy for him.

Just as he asked her if she would present the larger view to her father, if he could prove to her beyond any doubt at least one of the oil's possibilities, they were approached by the doctor and Tulip.

Bluefeather and Marsha both stood up as Marsha said, "It's so nice to see you again, Tulip. You look wonderful."

Since the citizens of Santa Fe had always dressed in any manner they chose without undue alarm, Tulip's short red dress and wide-brimmed red hat could legitimately be called charming, Bluefeather supposed. That was the word almost everyone seemed to feel suited the ninety-six-year-old flapper.

"Why, thank you, deah. And this is my nephew Dr. Godchuck."

"So good to meet you at last, Doctor. Tulip and Mr. Fellini have both spoken so highly of you."

"I am as pleased to meet you, Marsha Korbell, as I am to hear about the kind words of my associates."

Marsha insisted they join them at the table. Through bits of conversation, all managed to order again. Surprisingly, eggs Benedict was the mutual choice. Dr. Godchuck insisted that their Saturday brunch be accompanied by a bottle of chilled champagne. It was agreed.

The food was better than usual, the champagne was better than ever, and the conversation was somehow lost in the enjoyment of it all.

Bluefeather's keen hunter's eyes were now in their proper mode of observation. There was nothing false he could find in the warm welcome Marsha was attending them. Her charm and beauty matched those of Tulip. He felt that invisible cord pulling at his chest and other portions of his anatomy in a sultry touch that infused his entire body, his heart, and his highly pleased mind in a glow of beginning fondness.

After the successful meal, Marsha surprised them all by ordering another bottle of champagne.

Tulip said, with the usual hiding of her cleavage with her clasped hands, "Oh, deah Marsha, what a delightful suggestion."

They had fun. Tulip hesitated to take the last glass, saying as she did so anyway, "Oh my, my, I'm afraid I'll be dancing on tables."

The doctor smiled, touched his flowing white hair as if to assure himself it was still there and said, "Please do, my dear. Remember the last time you enjoyed that particular procedure?"

"Why yes. Yes, I do, Merphyn. It was right after Schoozie Felts's funeral, wasn't it?" She looked apologetically at Marsha, continuing, "Please forgive Merphyn and myself, deah, for talking about an event neither you nor Blue attended. You see..." then she turned with great seriousness to the doctor, "Schoozie Felts was my third husband, wasn't he, Merphyn, or was he number five?"

"Felts was sixth."

"Oh, oh," she was thinking, counting mentally, "but of course, he was. My precious, redheaded number six. Oh, that Schoozie was a dandy dancer, I can tell you. Smooth as glass he was for certain. That's how he died—just started on a dancing drunk in Baton Rogue, danced right on through Mardi Gras at New Orleans like that's all there was or ever would be. Schoozie died shuffling both feet, holding one hand around my waist, and snapping his fingers with the other." Tulip raised a hand, snapping her own smooth fingers, and then pointed at the floor. "Poof. Just like that. He was on the floor dead as a seventy-year-old dream. Now, deah Marsha, isn't a beautiful death like that something to dance on the table about?"

"I can think of many reasons and excuses for such celebratory activity, Tulip, but none better than you've just described."

Now they all laughed in joyous vision.

In spite of the easy fun they were having, Bluefeather caught the doctor's signal as he changed positions with his cane and gave Bluefeather a look so swift a barnyard cat would have missed it. However, before he could start his deal-closing remarks Marsha said, "That's a remarkable-looking cane, Dr. Godchuck. What kind of...what is it made of?"

Tulip saved the doctor from having to explain his favorite accoutrement. She was good at it. She spoke now very softly, as she often did.

"The cane is made from a bull's prick. A Jersey bull. They have the biggest ones, you see. They're also the most dangerous."

Even in the jaded, ancient city, nearby heads turned, chairs grated, and half-suppressed giggles ensued. Tulip was oblivious to these onlookers and Marsha didn't seem to care either.

Without hesitation or frustration Marsha replied, "Perhaps the danger and the size go together," and she looked at Bluefeather with one of those "almost" smiles of hers. He felt naked as a porcupine with no quills.

Tulip belatedly said, "Why, of course, my deah, they do both go together."

Bluefeather and the doctor realized they were about to lose possible great gains to a happy time of camaraderie. Bluefeather took the situation over, saying, "Marsha, while we're feeling good, I'd like to demonstrate something of vast importance." He asked the doctor for the objects from his always present wide-bottomed case. The doctor was surprised and pleased that Bluefeather would suffer this act himself for their cause.

As he moved painfully through the match, burned skin, and oil trick, Marsha watched with unblinking, unmoving eyes. When the flame was out, she took his hand, examined it with extreme care, then closed the fingers, holding on a moment more in silence before saying, "Draw up a proposal and I'll present it to Korbell." Suddenly she was all business. She got up saying, "It has been a pleasure dining and visiting with you. I have a meeting in fifteen minutes. Enjoy."

They all muttered nice things to the delicious, decorative force moving so enticingly away from them. Bluefeather held his hand, not feeling the burn, but still feeling the touch of her hand.

Twice now in just three weeks, Dr. Merphyn Godchuck had broken his rule of drinking alcohol even though he had only had two glasses of champagne. Nonetheless, he was in high spirits.

"I'm not one for complimenting in advance, but you gave our project a big boost today, Bluefeather Fellini. Your presentation to the extremely intelligent Marsha Korbell was first-rate."

"Thank you, Doctor, but it was simply spontaneous. I won't be doing the finger-burning part again.

"I understand. One can only crowd luck so far. An overburn would take two or three days to heal and the observer wouldn't be around to see it."

"Precisely."

"Then I have my notes to work on while you two celebrate the victory, minor though it might appear." The doctor took his cane and custom case and prepared to exit the dining room.

"Why, thank you mightily, my deah," Tulip said, "I'll share a carafe of wine with Blue . . . if he'd be so generous with his time."

"Granted," said Bluefeather. "As long as you wish." Then added, "Tulip, why don't we remove our bodies and place them in the bar for convenience's sake."

She happily agreed. So they did just that. They ordered the wine and looked at one another in satisfaction for a chore well tended.

"You are quite taken with her, aren't you, Blue?"

He was surprised at her unfamiliar familiarity. He stuttered, "Well . . . I . . . she . . . seems like a very intelligent woman . . . and she . . ."

"She is lovely, too, huh, all the way up and down?"

"Sure, but . . ."

"I'll not meddle anymore, Blue. Merphyn doesn't like me doing this, but Marsha is a thoroughbred, a strikingly beautiful thoroughbred, and she's rich, just terribly rich, my deah Blue. Don't ever sell that rarest of combinations short." At his growing discomfiture from her so very true observations, she changed the subject and continued, "We must forgive Merphyn's single-mindedness for now. He's so terribly, terribly torn about which curative source of the oil to pursue next. You know, several skin cancers he treated disappeared in less than ten days. Of course, he's been experimenting with different mixtures of herbs and other chemicals with the sage oil for years now. He feels it is equal—with proper development—to the perfecting of penicillin. Possibly greater."

"You don't have to sell me, Tulip. I'm one of the team, remember?"

"Oh, deah me, I'm rattling on like an idiot. Forgive me, will you, Blue? It's just that we've given ourselves to the concept for so many decades."

"It's okay. Hellfire, I've had obsessions too, and I made them work . . . but then . . ."

A small Mexican band was set up now. They could play, and did with expertise, popular music as well as Latino. Bluefeather and Tulip listened without speaking for several minutes. Tulip was inwardly glancing back at moving people and objects from her long past. Bluefeather was thinking some of his two new associates, but mostly of Marsha Korbell. He still imagined he felt the touch of her hand on his. He knew he was being childish at the tingling that rippled through his body at the thought of her, but he didn't care. Yes, he was afflicted with an almost embarrassing puppy love, and it showed. Tulip had not put it in exact words, but they both were aware that she knew. Of course, he'd had considerable experience in this area, but nothing to compare with her eight husbands, and even the great mystery in the sky might have difficulty keeping track of her flirtations.

They were both surprised when the group started playing "Begin the Beguine." Bluefeather moved, taking Tulip's soft hand, then her soft body in his arms. They danced—or rather they flowed. They were in such unison that they moved as smoothly as water over glass. She felt he was Bluefeather at the beginning, then Herman Slats, her first husband, during the rest of the dance. Bluefeather would have been amazed at her suppleness if she had been only nineteen, but for ninety-six, she was one of the world's great wonders. Someday, when he needed it, he must remember to ask her for the exact formula of the sage oil she had been taking for over forty years.

He soon forgot about all that, and he too imagined she was Nancy of Tonapah and Miss Mary of Breen. Then she metamorphosed into Marsha Korbell and seemed to stay that way through a dozen dances and another carafe of wine. Their intermittent but almost continuous dancing caused them both to perspire slightly, thereby creating a reason the two bodies were sticking closer and closer together as they danced. Her breasts against his chest, her thighs pressuring against his, and all the movement in between caused their breaths to increase in volume.

Just when Bluefeather felt he was dancing alone outside a tropical cabin under a damp tropical moon with Marsha Korbell, Tulip said softly in his ear, "Come with me now. Let us have one flirtation. Just one, deah, to do me the rest of my life."

As she led him to the elevator, Bluefeather's half-vision was still in the tropics with Marsha, and they were going hand in hand to the cabin covered with bush-green jungle growth. The adrenaline-jumping acceptance of their project by Marsha, the champagne, the wine, the whirling dances, holding the sensuous transcendental body of Tulip Everhaven against his own and his orgiastic imagining of Marsha Korbell had left him weak and susceptible.

He followed her to her room. They entered from the hallway door. He followed her to her bed where they both disrobed and eased into one another's arms and he into her in a warm soft glow of hard and tender flesh. They were both easily and subconsciously in earthly heaven for this moment.

Then the action from the ageless Tulip "Began the Beguine." During these blissful moments, the strongly built territorial-style bed held together in spite of a ninety-six-year-old who would have severely tested the talents of a world champion bareback bronc rider. Bluefeather was to be commended for his skill, strength, and courage. But all the lastly named attributes began to shatter as Tulip Everhaven screamed like a badly wounded elephant or several chimpanzees fighting over a banana. She made other rug-curling cries that were so loud they could be compared to nothing less than a pen full of male dogs with an equal number of females in heat at the same time. His ecstasy was stentorian. Bluefeather was simply hanging on now in great fear as her cries became verbal, and he was certain she was awakening everyone in the hotel and maybe even other nearby hotels.

"Skin! Skin! I haven't felt skin for sixteen years," she shouted to the world. "Oh, Herman, sweet Herman, I love you, Herman! Herman! Ohhh, Herm..."

And then she was so still and silent, Bluefeather was sure her uncontrollable desire had killed her heart dead. He hurriedly jerked on his pants, clutched at his unbuttoned shirt, grabbed his untied shoes, and was in the process of fearfully taking Tulip's pulse when he heard the knocking on the door and concerned voice of Dr. Godchuck.

"Aunt Tulip? Are you all right, dear? Answer me, Please. Tulip, do you hear me, dear? Now, listen here, no more of this..." There was a frantic twisting of the locked doorknob.

Bluefeather was startled as the lovely sweating body bolted to a sitting position in the bed, pushing at her hair trying impossibly to pat it into neatness, saying, "Everything is fine, deah Merphyn. I was just having a dream. A beautiful dream of Herman Slats, my first husband. We were in the first throes of our honeymoon night. Ah, Merphyn, what a beautiful dream it was, deah. It seemed as real as roast beef. Do you hear me, Merphyn?"

Bluefeather exited swiftly, guiltily, into the hallway before he could hear the doctor's answer. The closing of the heavy door sounded like the clanging of a prison door on a man condemned to death row. He leapt across the hall to his own room, but before he could enter, the house detective and the night manager descended upon him. Three other doors were now open with people who had been shocked awake, staring down the hail wondering if a vile and bloody murder had taken place.

Bluefeather kept one hand on the doorknob and raised the other outstretched palm to stop the two unsettled men. He took the initiative, which was his nature to do.

"Whoa, there. Stop right there. The lady has had a bad dream about the demise of one...of her late husband. As you know, her nephew is an imminent physician. He's giving her proper care at this very moment."

"But..." said the house detective.

"What? How do you know?" asked the night manager.

"Listen. Let me warn you that any uncalled-for or unnecessary disturbance at this critical time could open this establishment—and you as individuals—up to a very large lawsuit."

"Well..."

"I don't know..."

"You can hear the silence now. Don't jeopardize it and yourselves. Get back to work while all is quiet and you're still safe."

They stood, mouths slightly open, in massive puzzlement. Bluefeather turned loose the doorknob momentarily and took a step toward them, pointing a decisive arm back down the hallway, silently saying, "Go."

That was the decision maker. They both halfheartedly slunk away, mumbling under their breaths to one another but prudently in very low voices.

Tulip stayed in bed for three days. She was not ill, rather she was festive. She simply liked her bed more than anything else.

Thirty-Seven

While Tulip was in bed reliving her extreme ecstasy or letting her vocal cords heal, or both, and while the doctor worked on his formula notes, Bluefeather staked out the lobby for Marsha. She didn't show. So after reading the *Santa Fe New Mexican*, the *Taos News* and both the *Albuquerque Journal* and *Tribune*, he wrote her a note: "Marsha Korbell. Stop your march to glory in time for dinner at El Nido. Seven o'clock tonight. Good time guaranteed. Blue."

El Nido was a fine restaurant a few miles north of Santa Fe. It was owned by a French couple who, oddly enough, specialized in popular American food such as steaks. Of course, they also had a few French specialties disguised as purely American.

Bluefeather walked out of the hotel and started around the plaza. He stopped as he passed under the old portal of the first governor's place, to study the jewelry, rugs, and pottery that the various Indian tribes had displayed on blankets on the brick sidewalk. He went down Palace Street to the New Mexico Museum of Art. He found a special exhibit of the Taos masters there. He got a feeling of great nostalgia when he looked at a painting done high in the aspens of Twinning Canyon, featuring two of his uncles and their horses. He felt he was talking to them as if they were still alive. Well, they were on this canvas by Joseph Sharp for immeasurable time. He was proud.

He moved on through the painted landscapes, adobe houses, and mystical mountains painted by the sun, the moon, and the clouds of an invisible brush wide as a county. He had walked on these mountains. There was a Blumenschein mountain that climbed up in cubist tiers that was his favorite at this show. He wondered why the Taos artists were always stuck with the title of "realists" when so many of their works were so highly impressionistic. These "tags" must have been invented by people who had seen only a few of their paintings. He decided that en masse they would fit any designation and average out with the greatest of schools. The Joseph Sharp painting of Twinning Canyon brought back a tearing image of Old Grinder as well as a warm missing of his elderly kin. But the Berninghaus with one rider high up Taos Canyon imaged his mind's eye with young Lorrie Friedman for a moment. He didn't know why he was momentarily sad. They had enjoyed only the finest times of flesh and photography up this particular canyon. He brought himself out of the nostalgic musing by reminding himself that not all was from the past. He presently knew and liked many Berninghaus descendants, the Brandenburgs, and on and on.

He ended his tour feeling fortunate to have been a tiny part of that area and era hanging there on the museum walls, and went across the street to the Palace Restaurant and Bar. He was relieved that nobody approached him while he finished off his green chile omelette. He was thinking deeply about the doctor's vision and the great possibilities to help lessen the many perpetual pains of the human race, but no matter how he struggled to keep his mind there, it kept disjointing and flashing on the woman of the auburn crest and the cerulean eyes—Marsha Korbell.

He finished his meal long after most of the businessmen had returned to their offices and the politicians had retired to other negotiations. He had three coffee refills then decided to go back to the museum.

He passed by the Taos paintings and wandered slowly through the other rooms, absorbing the land he worshiped from the palettes of others—many who were not born upon it as he was, but who had parts of their souls imbedded in that same earth and repeated in oils, watercolors, ink, and many other mediums for everyone to see and enjoy in the head and heart. How lucky he was to be able to sponge up these wonders both in the vast lands and on these canvases that were just as widespreading—if one knew how to look. Here in the whispering silence of the museum, he was both sad and happy to know that these works of art would show how it once had been in spite of the scarring of the land that was sure to come.

It was closing time at the museum. He was pleasantly shocked at how long and involved his visit had taken. When he got back to La Fonda, he went straight to the desk. Marsha had taken his note and left one for him. His heart beat like first love as he unfolded it. Her note said: "Well, Bluefeather, I must fly to Lea County for consultations with geologists. The bids come up next week. Our timing is off today, but some mañana? Dinner at El Nido soon. Marsha."

He felt like he was walking on the breath of friendly dinosaurs as he skipped the elevator and bounded up the two flights of stairs and knocked on Dr. Godchuck's suite. The doctor was glad to see him but was preoccupied at the same time, ordering room service for just the two of them, saying, "Tulip has been eating in bed all day."

Then they turned to business, took a few moments to add up their finances, and realized there was just not enough to gather the large amount of sagebrush leaves, build the pilot plant, and at the same time keep their fund-raising going. They had been selling a quarter-percent share per thousand-dollar investment, but they had not raised enough to realize a surplus. They were not acquiring the needed extra funds, but were giving up parts of the whole rapidly.

Bluefeather volunteered to approach Marsha with the problem upon her return, but Dr. Godchuck nixed that instantly. "No, my dear Bluefeather Fellini, we must risk it all. Even if Marsha Korbell could persuade her father to invest the funds for the pilot plant we would have used up our one source for the big 'run.' We must not risk him while we are risking everything else. He just won't be interested at this stage. I have known these big club-wielding types all my life."

"He might do it as a favor to his daughter."

"No, she would know better than to pressure him at this time, unless I've vastly underestimated her."

Bluefeather put up no more argument. The dinner was served and, shortly thereafter, the two men were friendly and comfortable enough to sit in silence. Bluefeather suddenly made his mind up. He would go to Corrales and get his next to last bag of gold. According to the figures they had just perused that should be enough, with what they had on hand, to gather the sage, build the pilot plant (really a large whiskeylike still), and process enough of the oil to continue proving up the patents pending. He'd do it!

"Dr. Godchuck, why do you insist the sagebrush be gathered at Taos?"

"Ah, ah, ah, well, your own ancestors proved it worked on respiratory ailments long ago. We must not risk lower-altitude sagebrush until I've got all my formulas and my herbal mixture correct for the Taos sage. Then...then we can start experimenting with the sage at other altitudes."

There was no way Bluefeather understood the exact differences these altitudes would make, but Taos it would be.

The next day he drove his jeep to Corrales, visited briefly with the Luceros and his mules, then moved on with decisiveness. He pulled up the floor in a crowded closet and looked at his stash. The three gold rocks he would "never let go of"—or so he thought—and the two leather bags of small nuggets and dust were all that were left. He took out the largest one, leaving a single small one behind, and headed for his dentist friend to cash it in. He was on fire with true purpose now and puckered up tight to win.

Thirty-Eight

Bluefeather was not ready to return to Taos under the present conditions. It was possible to be laughed out of the state by the majority of Spanish Americans for picking sagebrush. Once, they had probably known of some of its medicinal qualities, but for now he would have to somehow come up with another reason for its procurement. Long, long ago, the old Spanish dons, who were mostly sheep barons, had overgrazed the grasslands so that the sagebrush took over. The result was a lot fewer sheep and a lot more artists around Taos. Just the same, it was not like harvesting corn or picking cotton around here. The gringos would join in the laughter as well, maybe with even more hilarity than anyone else because they would understand it less. Even though some great medicine man had used it so effectively back during the massively murderous flu epidemic, Bluefeather was somehow afraid to tell his true duty here to even his closest kin. Of course, his uncle Stump Jumper was the exception.

After a short visit at the pueblo, he and Stump Jumper moved into the Sagebrush Inn a little over two miles south of Taos. A favorite cousin, Smiling Dog, wanted to join them. It was difficult for Bluefeather to refuse, but they could not risk his fondness for alcohol and his actions thereafter.

The inn was a large adobe establishment inspired by the real pueblo. It was a fine place recently bought by a short, fat, bespectacled fellow, Myron Vallier, and his wife. The lobby was one to remember as long as one had any sight at all—and maybe after that. The north wall was at least half picture window, and what a landscape it framed.

The blue-green sagebrush mostly hid the highway into town so that one could see the plants for a considerable distance, enhancing the sight of cottonwood trees and glimpses of adobe walls before the great Taos Mountain seemed to boom up and take over. The picture was different by the minute as the clouds and light changed dramatically. The window alone brought visitors from around the world to headquarter their exploration of the Taos area from here. Those fortunate enough to have lived or visited there at a time before that inevitable scarring would occur were blessed indeed.

The lobby was filled with Mexican carved furniture around a massive fireplace. On the walls hung paintings by some of Taos's finest while the floors were decorated with Navajo rugs. It didn't matter, summer or winter, the warm feeling of the lobby and the bountiful views for the eyes and souls bequeathed by the window were truly beyond compare.

Just off the lobby was a large dining room of pure southwestern decor and delectable food. A small, intimate bar joined it. One could hardly drink there without somehow striking up a conversation with a stranger and often making a lifelong friend. The patrons ranged from local day workers, artists, and writers, to Texas oilmen, or often international celebrities, from politicians to symphony composers. It was extremely eclectic in its clientele.

At the time Bluefeather and his uncle moved in, Jay, the only black bartender in Taos County, ran the small corner of delight. The setting was one of the finest on earth, and their duty was one of possible wondrous contribution to all who lived on that same earth. The pressure of finances made it a requisite that they keep this endeavor to themselves. Any interruption could doom the project. That part would be a struggle, for Stump Jumper's natural reticence around strangers would—after half a bottle of alcohol—turn to unlimited information about the world and all that was in it.

They got settled in their double bedroom, then got back into the jeep and drove immediately west about two-thirds of a mile to a little farm surrounded by a three- to five-foot-high carpet of the material they sought. Emilio Cruz owned the place and clawed out a living with a medium-sized flatbed truck, hauling anything from furniture to garbage. The Cruz family kept a milk cow, pigs, chickens, goats, and a garden to supplement his small earnings. His wife, Elena, had borne six children—three were still at home. Bluefeather had known the couple as long as he could remember.

They sat down at the kitchen table of the extremely clean, four-room adobe house. The only modern appliance was an electric refrigerator. It was given a place of honor in the modest room. In the living room was a small area of worship on top of an old, carved chest covered with a hand-crocheted scarf. Candles in small, red glass holders burned at the base of a statue of the Virgin Mary and two *santos* (carvings of the saints). There were some pictures of Christ on the cross hanging in a group with a couple of retablos.

"Hey, Emilio, I got a good job for you."

"Need some ore hauled?"

The question didn't surprise Bluefeather because once Emilio had worked the mines north of Taos at Moly Corporation.

"No, no. Don't need any ore hauled." How in all hell could he say it? It was a scary statement that had never been made outside the Taos Pueblo in the history of the West. "I want to rent your sagebrush and hire you and some of your compadres to pick the leaves."

Emilio stared at him like he was a dog puking on the kitchen table. Elena dropped a spoon that rattled on the floor like tiny machine-gun fire.

"You want to lease the sagebrush, not the ground?" Emilio finally asked, wide-eyed with a silly half-smile on his face.

"That's right. Just the brush itself...and for only a few weeks."

"I never heard nothing like this before. What do you want it for? You gonna make something and sell it to the tourists, huh?"

Bluefeather had to give some kind of answer to Emilio's question without telling the truth. He twinged because he was afraid that the true use of the plant was buried deep in Emilio's mind and he might dig it up.

"No, Emilio, we just want the leaves. We'll pay good wages. You can hire your brothers to help harvest. Stump Jumper here will oversee the operation."

"Well, I don't know how to do a deal like that. I just haul stuff, you know that. Like cows, horses, manure, anything I can load and get paid for, but I don't know nothing about dealing like this here. I never heard..."

"Look." Bluefeather counted out five twenty-dollar bills. "Here's a down payment. We'll work out the details later. Gather a lot of gunny-sacks full of the younger leaves. We want the leaves hand picked. Then when we get a truckload of full sacks, I'll pay you again for hauling them all to Cerrillos."

"Whew," Emilio said looking at his wife, hoping for some kind of silent advice from the expression on her face. He got no help. She was moving about wiping at things that were already spotless. Her kind heart pounded out strange rhythms in her chest at this one possible bounty of their entire life.

Emilio said, "Whew," three more times then went on. "Well, it'll take me the rest of the day to get my brothers and maybe two *primos*, huh? Yeah, that's okay. We can get started first thing in the morning, say seven o'clock."

"Now, you got five brothers and you're gonna use two cousins, so with Stump Jumper that makes a crew of eight. Elena, you think you can handle the noon meal for that many? We'll pay two dollars a person."

For that kind of money she would have taken on a hundred diners. "Yes, ah yes. I feed 'em good—beans, bacon, tortillas, chile . . ." and she went on counting long after Bluefeather had agreed to the deal.

Emilio followed them smilingly out to the jeep, having great difficulty keeping from laughing out loud. It was the hot feel of the hundred dollars in his pocket that kept him under momentary control, but as they climbed in the vehicle he just had to ask, "I know it's none of my business, Bluefeather, but what you gonna do with them sagebrush leaves, huh? They're not good for nothing."

"I know you're not gonna believe this, Emilio, but my clients are going to distill this stuff." There now, he had told the truth and had not given anything away.

Emilio nodded his head in agreement and understanding. "You mean distill them like run them through a whiskey still, huh?"

"Yeah, only bigger."

"Well, I'll be a . . ."

"See you early in the morning. Be sure you get the sacks and the hands gathered. We don't have any time to fool around."

"Okay. Okay, old compadre. We'll be ready," and strangely he started trotting to the house holding one hand over his mouth. Before Bluefeather and his cousin could get turned around they heard screams of laughter coming out the open front door, windows, and cracks.

Emilio said to his wife, "The goddamned fools are goin' to make wheesky! Sagebrush wheesky! Ain't nothing but a crazy artist would ever drink that stuff. Goats won't even eat it 'less they're starvin' to death. Goats won't even . . ." and then he and Elena could not utter words for a moment for their hilarity. The last thing Bluefeather and Stump Jumper heard as they sped over the corrugated dirt road was, "We are gonna get rich on sagebrush wheesky. God is good."

"God is getting better."

Before they were out of hearing range Stump Jumper, who had shown exemplary control, suddenly burst apart with long wails, cackles, and guffaws too pent up to control any longer. He was trying to say something, but couldn't squeeze it out.

Bluefeather drew back one hand to hit him in the mouth and then remembered he had sworn off violence in 1945. In spite of a valiant struggle he soon joined his uncle in howling humor so drastic he had to brake the jeep to a halt. He could not see the road for the tears.

Thirty-Nine

Bluefeather decided he would work along with the pickers until he was certain the operation was moving smoothly, even though Dr. Godchuck had insisted his time would be more valuable promoting the project than in the field.

The workers had all lined up a few yards apart. Holding their gunny-sacks in one hand, they started picking at the pungent sagebrush leaves with the other. In varying degrees and minutes, they all learned things about sagebrush they had never even thought about, even though all had been born and raised near hundreds of thousands of acres of it. First, the leaves grow gracefully on the ends of the stalks in an umbrellalike formation, giving the appearance of ten times the actual amount of leaves. Second, the leaves do not pull clean like corn, cotton, or green beans; it took more time and more care. Then they found that it took far longer to cover even the bottom of the sack than they had thought.

Emilio was the only one who thought to bring gloves. By noon everyone but him had sore, bleeding hands, so Bluefeather sent Stump Jumper into town for leather work gloves for all. It took another two hours of work before Bluefeather realized that the leather gloves were too tight and stiff—the pickers were dropping half of their production on the ground. Now he sent Stump Jumper to town again for gloves made from cotton that were much better. They could feel the leaves and handle them much more cleanly, but they found that they wore out a pair every other day. So they bought out the entire town's supply of canvas gloves.

All these delays and learning processes had slowed the gatherers greatly. By the fifth day they only had ten fully packed bags. Bluefeather had long ago forgotten about promoting. He labored, cheering on his workers.

"Do not worry, amigos," Bluefeather encouraged, "we'll get it done if it takes a month."

The sun beat down in the supposedly cool seven-thousand-foot altitude of the Taos area like a symbol from hell. The dust from the sage got into their eyes, ears, pores, and noses, causing alternating sneezing and watery-eyed spells among the men in the fields.

Two brothers and one cousin decided to quit at the end of the first week. Bluefeather heard one of them say, "I'd rather starve for five years than spend one more day at this work for fools."

Brother answered brother with, "I agree. This is work meant only for prisoners or someone being punished for some terrible deed."

Bluefeather wisely called it a payday and said, "From now on you will be paid in cash, plus two ice-cold beers at the end of each workday."

It was a delicate balance between the daily pay and cold beer, against the itching, sneezing, back-tearing, sweat-soaking, sore-handed work. However, Taos had long been a hard place to make the barest of a living. So the longed-for treats at day's end kept them going—for now.

At night, Bluefeather and Stump Jumper showered, put on clean clothes, had a couple of drinks with their meal in the inn's restaurant, then fell into bed half dead and asleep. Bluefeather was so exhausted he didn't even dream—none that he could remember, anyway—and he was a man of many dreams, mostly memorable and all in full color.

Bluefeather was proud of the way Stump Jumper was performing. He worked harder than anyone and took most of his money home to his wife and two sons. And he hadn't even looked at the bar. Of course, there was great wisdom in that action for him. Temptation. Stump Jumper was sometimes misunderstood. He had attended Bacone College in Oklahoma—the college that had graduated many Indian notables—intending to make his clan happy by becoming a grade school teacher. He had done well in his studies, but the confinements of a schoolroom were not for this Indian. What he liked was fishing, hunting, alfalfa-hay farming, and occasional drinking. The last would create small problems on rare occasions. Contrary to popular attitudes he was by no means an alcoholic or even a so-called periodic drunk. He might go six months without a drop or he might get zapped two weekends in a row. What made his drinking seem like a continuing event was his total enjoyment of it from the time he made up his mind to do it until he slept it off. The impression of his having fun was so strong that often people would see him acting in the same happy, crazy manner and would assume he was always like that. A mistake.

However, things—little things at first—began to occur in the harvesting fields that could cause even a man of total control to take to strong drink. At first, there was just one carload of people driving slowly down the road next to the slaving sagebrush harvest hands. Then two. Then three. They drove so slowly, staring hard in amazement, that the drivers often ran off the narrow dirt road. At first they were just onlookers making little gestures of diversion to one another. Then finally a pickup from Arroyo Seco drove by with three passengers in front and three in back.

One melodious voice boomed out across the field. "I wanna go back to them old cotton fields of home. Away, Dixieland, away."

They all chorused, paraphrasing the old song.

"I wanna go back. I wanna go back to them dear old sagebrush fields of mine, away Dixieland, away Taos land, away."

Then a carload of beer drinkers joined in the musical competition and switched songs. They drove back and forth singing in reasonable harmony, "Bringing in the leaves, bringing in the leaves, we shall come rejoicing, bringing in the leaves."

As if the stupid singing wasn't enough, they began shouting things like, "Hey, amigos, why don't you get a hay baler and save all the work?" or, "I got a million acres for you to clean up soon as you finish this little job."

Mostly, though, they just pointed and said unheard things, gigging one another in the ribs with their elbows as they broke out in insulting mirth.

The constant travel churned up the hard ground of the narrow dirt road so that there was a permanent fog of choking dust in the air, which settled on the sage to further discomfort Bluefeather and his men. The difficulties of the hand-tearing labor were enough without being joked to death about them. The men made quick shameful glances toward their kibitzers at first, but as nerves, bodies, and fractured souls were kibitzed almost ceaselessly, the glances and mumbling became angry.

Bluefeather realized mutiny was at hand. So, after paying the pouting men that late afternoon and waiting for their two-beer allotment to take effect, he suggested they dig a ditch across the road. All cheered up and pitched right in.

The sage was so thick on each side of the road, all were certain the ditch would stop the traffic dead. They scattered the dirt out on the open land so that a driver would be upended in the trench before he knew what had jolted him unconscious.

For the first time they could hardly wait to get to work the next morning. It was a day of little progress. Everyone kept raising their head from their task to look and listen for an automobile engine. Bluefeather was biting big enough slices of flesh from the inside of his cheeks to enrage a sloth. They were losing precious time and money. Dr. Godchuck's money. Well, it had once been Bluefeather's, but now it belonged to the maker of great medicine. The waste of effort and energy in anxious anger galled him meanly, which was against his postwar vows. The scar on his nose burned in such controlled fury that he could not keep from rubbing it. That action filled his eyes and nostrils with sage dust so he could hardly see, and he had fits of sneezing that would have done justice to a blacksmith's bellows.

Reprieve. There was the engine just around the hill. The workers stopped now, looking, their expressions changing from extreme anxiety to hopeful anticipation. It was a big old rusty gravel truck with only two passengers in front. As they crept forward, the driver started honking a tune of mockery. They ground slowly along now, closer and closer to the ditch.

Bluefeather took command. The driver's eyes must not spot the ditch in advance. He shouted at his troops, "Smile, wave, dance, do anything to divert the driver's attention."

Oh, what a performance the sweating, long-taunted, long-suffering men put on. One sang "El Rancho Grande." Another danced an artificial flamenco. Others whirled about clapping their hands above their heads like Greek celebrants. Bluefeather and Stump Jumper simultaneously started a war dance, chanting and yelling and making motions of stabbing with spears. Not only was this action courageous, but it was also somewhat hurtful, as their movements were greatly, painfully hindered by the now-hated sagebrush. They persevered, gaining momentum as the truck neared the ditch. All eyes were wide and eager. Mouths were ready to fly open in hee-haws, and hands itched to slap knees and their companions' backs with vengeful glee.

The truck was within inches now. All breathing of the workers stopped, so did all motion. Their eyes riveted on the coming crash. The truck stopped just on the very brink of the hand-dug trench.

The driver waited while his companion got out and looked at the ditch with such lingering care, one would think it was his first visit to a bordello. Then ever so slowly, he unbuttoned the fly of his pants and relieved himself in the ditch as he watched a couple of ravens fly across the soft blueness of the summer sky. Then he shook his apparatus several unnecessary times and buttoned his pants while still showing the intense interest of an ornithologist in the flight of the birds. He then walked slowly back to the truck looking into the distance at different mesas, mountain ranges, and various species of smaller birds, as well as a couple of cumulus clouds forming over Taos Mountain. If the word "forever" had any meaning at all, this was a time and place where it applied. When he took out a cigarette and lighted it, using six matches to do so, Bluefeather could see with his eyes closed and feel with his back turned, the blood baking in the arteries of his hired hands, who now had become friends through their shared responsibilities.

He raised one silent hand that held them back momentarily. As the casual one climbed back into the truck and took three slams to get the door closed, Bluefeather could sense the danger of his compatriots bursting forth and dragging the men from the truck and tearing them into such small bits that only the hardy desert ants would be able to find the pieces.

The driver backed the truck up. Its reverse gears resounded across the land as if metal were eating metal. He stopped, put it in a low forward gear, and plowed a new deviant road around the ditch through the sage and back on the other side to the old road. He drove on toward the highway next to the Sagebrush Inn, honking clever little ditties as they rolled past.

Even though it was only eleven o'clock, Bluefeather swiftly declared it was time for lunch. He led the way back toward Elena's kitchen, walking through stripped sagebrush that looked like dying plants on a dying planet. It did nothing to ease the terrible joke the "saints" had played on them by making a latrine of their ditch.

In spite of what the moguls, the greedy, the evil politicians, and the first-rate accumulators of the world might collectively believe, there exist a few things that money cannot buy. One was right here and now at the home and in the fields of Emilio and Elena Cruz. These men were not going to go back to work for any amount of money that Bluefeather could afford. The humiliation of having their ditch pissed in, and their certitude of the tables of mirth being tilted away from them, were simply too much to endure. No reasonable human being should expect more from them without some sort of uplifting compensation.

Bluefeather had long ago proven he was a fast thinker in desperate situations, so now he said, with all the conviction he could draw out of his limping genes, "Men, I have to go to the inn and make an important phone call. Wait here at the house for me after you've enjoyed Elena's delicious repast."

Grumbling.

"No matter what," he continued, "stay here in the shade of the porch and enjoy in advance your after-work beers. No more work until I return, you hear?" Grumbling. "Now promise me again not to leave this site until I return."

With a swift glance and nod to Stump Jumper indicating he was to stay and take control, Bluefeather swiftly moved to the jeep and took off before his workers could ask questions that might expose the possible vacancy of good news. It burned his ass some more to be forced to follow the bumpy trail of the gravel truck around the ditch, thereby helping make a permanent detour in the road, further defiling and insulting this patch of desert.

The first thing he did upon entering his room was call Dr. Godchuck at La Fonda.

The answer came over the phone purring like a madam's cat, "Dr. Merphyn Godchuck's laboratory."

"Tulip?"

"Blue?"

"It's me, darling. Are you having fun?"

"Why, of course, deah boy. That has been a custom of the Godchuck descendants for centuries."

"Good. Good. Keep it up for my sake. Is the doctor present?"

"Oh, no, he isn't. He's in Cerrillos composing his plant. He insisted I stay here and take phone calls until he's all done down there. Why don't you just call the bar, deah. The Gulls are such nice accommodating people, I'm sure they'd be more than pleased to conduct Merphyn to the phone."

"Aww, it's okay. I just wanted to pass the word on that we should have the hay...I mean sage picking and sacking done in ten or twelve days. You can pass the words on to the doctor if you wish, and I'll just get on back to work. Oh yeah, before I go, have you seen Marsha?"

"Yes, we had tea day before yesterday. She was asking about you. In fact, she seems curious beyond the ordinary. That's good news, deah. I know you've forgotten my telling you not to resent that such a fine specimen of femaleness is going to be terribly, terribly rich. That's a rare combination, deah. In fact, it's just as hard to find an all-'round woman among the poor as the rich. You do understand me, don't you, deah Blue?"

"Right down to the rabbit's hole. I must go now...and give Marsha my...my...best."

"That will do quite well then."

"Bye, Tulip."

So she had asked about him, huh? That made Bluefeather ready for his next move to save the sage. He went to the lobby and had a visit with the owner, Myron Valuer. If he could have dug up the courage he could have mustered at least a small smile at the irony of the Sagebrush Inn's name. Everything had suddenly turned to sage or thereabouts.

Now the square and roly-poly Myron imagined himself as a helpful and trusted nonmember of the CIA, the FBI, or any other semisecret organization that was supposed to protect the sanctity of the good old U.S.A. and its protectorates. This attitude probably came partly from his having served with the OSS in the war. He was as sincere about this as a guard dog, and even more ready to freely serve any cause for his country. That was the feeling Bluefeather drew upon, and in fact, took no little advantage of. He assured Myron that the gathering of sagebrush leaves was heavily related to experimentation that had a lot to do with the welfare of America's citizenry. It must be kept hush-hush for now, but later he would explain in detail, for he knew Myron was one of "us." That did it.

Myron immediately discerned that Bluefeather was in the secret service of his country and said, conspiratorially, "I understand. Is there any way, any manner at all that I may help?"

"Well, now that you've broached the subject, maybe, just maybe, there is a way you could be of service. We would be most grateful," he whispered, taking a quick glance around to be sure no one could hear the vital secrets. "I've let it drop, Myron, that we are going to make sage whiskey from these leaves. Can you believe the workers fell for it? Can you believe? What am I saying? Of course, you can. You've had the training."

Whatever all this meant, if anything, Myron took it seriously. His entire fat-laden body became tense, strong, and ready to assist in the cause.

Bluefeather continued, "Just to keep their minds from wandering and possibly endangering our cause, I thought it would be prudent on our part to throw a little diversion. Say, food, drinks, and music for just one evening out here in the patio," and he made a motion out toward the large space enclosed on three sides. "Diversionary tactics worked quite well in fooling Hitler at the Normandy invasion. As I'm sure you well know, having been in on the planning personally."

"Well the OSS did have a role. Yes, they played their part." Myron seemed to be stretching upward, now taller and much thinner. He was ready to do duty. "I'll talk to my wife and the staff immediately. When do we begin the . . . the diversion?"

"Oh, if it's all right with you, say an hour before sunset tomorrow."

"Done."

Myron clasped the deal-closing handshake with such surprising strength that Bluefeather's sage-picking hand was numb for a bit. That was a good sign that patriotic and sacrificial adrenaline was flowing freely in Myron's previously Jell-O–type body. Bluefeather was certain that handshake was the most physical act Myron had extended in a decade or more. Bluefeather was highly pleased, at least for the moment, with his unthinking, inspired actions. Instead of the coldness of dread, he now anticipated facing his men with the happy news, face on, full force.

He drove now toward the Cruzes' with a heart that sang with violins, guitars, and the warbling of meadowlarks and canaries. The air had suddenly turned to a fine champagne mist, and the corrugated road caressed the wheels of the jeep like velvet-palmed hands. Oh, glorious day of days.

In his relief, he felt all and nothing. He saw much and little. That's the way of sudden deliverance from almost certain disaster.

It was a quarter of a mile before he realized that sometimes there was a transparent figure poised on the toes of one foot on the hood of the jeep. Then the figure leapt from the vehicle to the ground landing a few yards in front of him. He jammed his foot on the brake pedal so desperately and with such force that not only did the jeep come to a jarring, skidding halt, but also the motor died. There, thirteen inches from the radiator, stood a smiling Dancing Bear.

"Lookee here, dear brudder, at this." He did a side shuffle and a couple of whirls with an imaginary partner. "Fred Astaire and Ginger Rogers," he said.

Then he did a single dance of great action, whirling back facing Bluefeather and shoving his arms back and forth to the sides dancing in place. "Gene Kelly for sure, dear brudder." Then he did a tap dance with so many accurate steps and tricks that Bluefeather forgot to be agitated. Even though his spirit guide had been absent lately when he was so sorely needed, Bluefeather's mood was so elevated that he welcomed Dancing Bear's presence.

"Who is that?" Bluefeather asked.

"Roosevelt Martin Luther Jones."

"I'm not aware of him, Bear. Does he do movies?"

"No, dear brudder, not yet. He ain't been born yet. Forty maybe fifty years to go. Watch for coming attractions. Watch this. He's gonna be the best for . . . I betcha a hunnert years."

Bluefeather thought he was about to be bored with another toe dance representing the upcoming reincarnation—not so. Dancing Bear whirled so fast at times, he nearly became invisible. At other moments he took circular steps on the heel of one foot and the toes of the other at the same time, and that was hard to do. Then he zipped back and forth, changing the position of his feet from front to back in the process, and finished with a whirling leap and six knee bends with each leg. He then bounced up and stood stiff as a flagpole with one arm angled straight up and out to his side while the other made wild circles at the exact same angle, only downward. Then he got his crazy dancing self together. Smiling, he bowed as if a half billion people were applauding. One was.

Bluefeather jumped out of the Jeep, clapping to beat of the half billion and said sincerely, though unthinkingly, mocking his guide, "Bravo, dear brother. Wonderful, terrific, and downright done good."

"Ah ha. Thank you, Blue. Thank you very much. I have to practice the Go, Ho, Hey dance all the time. The authorities will not tell me where on earth Mudball Eclair is going to reincarnate."

"Mudball Eclair? How did he . . . I mean, how is he going to get a name like that?"

"Well, when he first comes around this dimension here that you're hung up in, he is gonna be first born in Florida swamps. He's gonna learn to dance in the mud 'cause there ain't no other place to do 'er. Understand? Huh? Huh, Huh?"

"Makes all the sense in the system to me, Bear. Say, ol' missing-when-I-need-you pard, how have you been? Where have you been? Have you traveled a lot lately?"

"Just like always, you ask more fast questions than my slow ears can hear. I'll just finish up, maybe, that Korea war is going on, you know? There's lots of folks staring at one another across the invisible line. Guns all cocked and eyes peeled like fancy grapes. Both sides been gettin' the nervous jerking disease. I been plenty busy. Say, how come you am t over there? The Second Infantry Division is right on the front line right now this beautiful day."

"I've done been, Bear. More than I can bear. Forgive that awful pun, okay?"

"Okay. Ain't much to forgive."

"Right. Well you must know I've sworn off all violence."

Dancing Bear began to laugh and tramp his knee-high Apache moccasin boots into the dust over and over. Bluefeather could not see for the life of him and all of Taos County what was so funny.

"What's so funny?" Bluefeather asked with annoyance.

"You done said it just like everybody else. Since I been working for the high-upper folks—kings, dictators, generals, politicians, ax murderers, serial killers, wife beaters, husband beaters, and retired combat marines—" Dancing Bear laughed heartily, "they all say," still laughing, "the same thing. Ever' time, I tell to you. It's so sad it makes it funny to me. All these no-gonna-do-no-more-violence-anymore kind of folks, all these I-been-born-again-to-be-a-pussycat folks. All these..."

"Whoa! Whoa! I got it. I got your feelings clear. But it doesn't make any difference to me. I've got proof. If you'd been around the last few days you would know that I had many justifiable reasons to commit dismemberment."

"Chure. Chure. There's always excuses aplenty."

"You're not getting it, Bear. I didn't do it. You hear me? I did not do it when it would have been allowable."

"I hear now perty good, but if you had not talked to the fat FBI man over at lodge, maybe you don't keep away from dismemberment violence. See what I mean? Huh? Huh? Huh, dear brudder?"

"All right, I concede a little there. Say, what are you doing listening in on secret service conversations without letting me know you're around, anyway?"

"Sometimes it much better when folks don't know too much. Savvy the burro, kid?" he kidded.

"Bear, I like to have fun as much as you do…well almost, but you know this oil of sage business is serious. A lot of pain, and maybe even lives, could be saved with Dr. Merphyn Godchuck's inventions and formulas. Why don't you take a little time off from your other chores and help us when we need it?"

"Well, there's too many lives scattered 'round places as it is. No way I can take care of just my little share. No way, brudder. Believe it, dumb ass."

"You don't need to be calling me names just because I'm seriously concerned about the success of our project."

"Sometimes people don't listen to politeness. Sometimes the world is full of gaps. Sometimes fences have water gaps. Teeth have gaps. Sometimes dreams have gaps, and sometimes, great inventions have gaps."

Before Bluefeather could ask him to decipher those "sometimes," Dancing Bear changed the subject, chuckling almost evilly, saying, "Dear brudder, I hear from my fellow guide amigos that you been lookin' hard at almost redheaded lady. I hear she is tough and tender like steaks from two different cuts. I hear she got so many smarts between her ears that her eyes are wide apart like a good quarter horse. I hear she got a daddy with enough money to buy…to buy…well, to buy maybe Hong Kong. I hear…"

"For once, Bear, I want to thank you for overhearing these things from your spirit guide friends, and I want to thank you for telling me what you did. I'm gonna level with you, Bear. I think I like her a whole bunch. Now, after all the trouble you've gone to, straining your slow ears to hear all these things for me, why don't you just haul off and tell me what to do about her. I'm adding a little-used and very special word to my request. Please, Bear, please, please, please, advise me about the almost red-haired woman. She is red when she's in sun or bright indoor light. Red as fire. Red as a ripe tomato, red as…"

"Hey, hey, you beginning to sound like me," Dancing Bear said. "Hokay, hokay. I see you don't quite understand about gaps. So, I say enjoy yourselves together between the gaps."

"If you think I don't understand, why do you keep using the word over and over? Why don't you explain it to me in clearer terms?"

"Beat a frog with the same stick long enough and he'll finally piss. Hey, dear brudder Blue, I just got a commission to save a senatorial candidate from gettin' the clap. That's a real emergency. Bye-bye, Bluebird."

Then with a little one-toed whirl he became less and less visible until he was gone. Bluefeather walked over and looked where he had last stood. There was a perfectly round hole in the hard roadbed. He did not try to guess how deep it was. He crawled back into the jeep with the not-quite-understood but well-taken suggestion that he and the almost-red-headed woman, Marsha, should "enjoy together" each other in spite of gaps. Whether he had decoded his spirit guide's message properly or not was of no matter. He intended to fulfill that "enjoy together" part with all the power of pleasure he had.

He drove to Emilio Cruz's place as the bearer of multitudes of joyous tidings. The workers were given the rest of this day and the next off to prepare for the little entertainment.

■ ■ ■

Forty

It was the time of waiting. Mrs. Vallier supervised the tables and bar being set up in the patio. Except for a few clouds guarding the highest points of the Sangre de Cristos, the sky was a blue of great purity. The sun gave warm blessings on all the area, and the breeze across the desert was just enough to make breathing effortless.

About three o'clock in the afternoon, Stump Jumper, who had showered twice trying to rid himself of what was to many the enticing aroma of sage, finished wrapping the two plaits of black hair down the back of his head, put on a heavy silver and turquoise bracelet, a black shirt and clean trousers, wrapped the folded white bedsheet around his waist Taos Indian style and headed, without a word, toward the bar.

The hired hands, with wives, girlfriends, and a few extra "cousins," started arriving about an hour or so before sunset. Jay, the bartender with a gleaming white smile of great anticipation on his black face, started serving drinks assisted by Jack "Rattlesnake" Sowers, who had volunteered to help out.

The women wore every kind of apparel from Levi's to squaw dresses. The men were mostly in Levi's and plaid western-style shirts, but some had on their best suits and neckties. Many wore silver Indian jewelry and bolo ties. This was not a diamond and ruby crowd. But there was sparkle—and color. Lots of color. A spirit looking down would have sworn the crowd was a large moving flower garden.

The buffet was laden with a variety of sumptuous delights: cheeses, fruits, sliced meats, and Mexican dishes. Many took their food and drinks to tables, while others stood around in handshaking, hugging, kissing, and happily chattering groups. Neighbors who lived only a small farm or house away acted as if they had not seen one another for years.

It was supposed to be a festive, relaxing event, and it was. Of course, Mr. Vallier had used his connections with the forces of law and had Sergeant Leach and Officer Gallegos on hand. All knew them. In fact, the policemen had several kin here themselves. They joined in, visiting as casually and comfortably as if they were at a family picnic; however, as Myron had so keenly foreseen, it gave the crowd the freedom of fun without the worry of violence.

Bluefeather held back as long as possible, then headed for the bar figuring to have a quick drink before joining the main party. As he entered the bar he was greeted by Stump Jumper in a manner to create thirst.

"Hey there, Bluefeather. Here's my nephew Bluefeather I was telling you about. Remember? The mining engineer and manufacturer? Hey, Blue, get over here and have a drink with these fine folks from Texas."

These "fine folks from Texas" consisted of a group of seven from Dallas and Fort Worth. Bluefeather never did understand who they were, what they did, or exactly why they were here, because too many people were talking at once. Happy. Happy. Happy. Rattlesnake, the substitute bartender, was frustratingly trying to keep the swiftly emptied glasses refilled and had already given up on keeping tabs and correct change. He just served.

"Hey, Blue, these Texas people are coming to the party with us. Hey, bartender, give 'em another toddy all round to get 'em in the mood."

Bluefeather downed two drinks, and in the midst of the babble headed, at a speed just under a trot, for the great outdoor patio. He was fondly greeted from so many different directions, he was momentarily confused as to how he should respond. Then he remembered that when Tulip Everhaven did not feel like making small talk, she just smiled and nodded lightly. It worked. Of course, he felt glad that his vow of nonviolence was sanctified as he shook hands and visited a while with a quietly beaming Myron and his two brothers of the law.

Then Bluefeather was shocked to find here the guitarist Ramon Hernandez of the Dawson mining camp from over near his birthplace of Raton. He had not seen him since Ramon had played so sensitively for his marriage to Miss Mary at the Statler Hotel in Durango. Their mutual embraces were deeply felt. What better frosting for the cake of fun than to have a man of such giving music in attendance.

Ramon then introduced Bluefeather to the other guitarist who had been hired for the evening. He was stocky, curly-headed Antonio Mendoza, who had recently arrived from Old Mexico. Antonio exuded a love of music and life that was a privilege to absorb. Here were two true givers. Oh, how they played. Oh, how the listeners danced. Oh, how they all ate, laughed, yelled, clapped, and loved, and later on some—like Dancing Bear—did their own private dances.

Myron Vallier's importance and connections were mostly under-rated by everyone but Bluefeather. Myron was that rare human being—he delivered—and he and his wife had delivered in high style here.

A photographer and reporter moved about, mixing in the crowd. Myron quieted Bluefeather's concern with, "Don't worry. It's all taken care of. You'll be proud when you read the paper."

Bluefeather had danced with every woman there. At this moment, at this time, in this patio with these friends, it was all first cabin. Bluefeather felt inspired. As the awestricken quietness of a short-lived, blazing sky turned the night a soft blue-green, with a three-quarter coyote moon, Bluefeather let out a triumphant howl of fulfillment. He was certain it could not get any better than this.

Oh, but it could, for instantly following his jubilant yell his eyes were whipped in the direction of the lobby door as if directed by a powerful beam of energized light. Through that door stepped Marsha Korbell.

She stopped, looking widely about until her blue eyes sighted down the invisible beam straight into the coal-dark ones of Bluefeather Fellini. Her smile of radiance dimmed his of stunned delight. They moved to each other. He took her in his arms and they danced. She smelled of incense from the Orient, rosewater from the Deep South, frankincense from the Mideast, flowers that grew someplace far away in the sky. She smelled of the female Marsha—blood stirring and distinct from all others in the world.

She whispered in his ear, "I heard you asked after me."

"Yes."

That's all they needed to say.

As they moved smoothly past Ramon, his guitar strings seemed to turn to fresh clover honey, and he nodded at Antonio with knowledge. Antonio also expressed his utmost feelings and stirrings of love on the guitar strings.

Bluefeather did not dance. No, he simply moved with Marsha in warm air a foot above the patio. His face had already melted and joined with her cheek and shoulder. His slow but heavy breathing was filled with musk and mystery. It was the divination.

Then she spoke softly. He felt his feet on solid material once again and pulled his head free to look into her eyes. She put two fingers from her lips to his, and he somehow heard her words, "I must go now. It's a long drive this time of morning back to Santa Fe. It was a wonderful time."

She walked toward the lobby door, paused, turned her head back, giving him a smile that could have projected through a mile of darkness. He started to raise a hand to wave good-bye but decided that would have been superfluous. She was already gone.

He slowly made his way through the swiftly thinning crowd to the bar. Rattlesnake was sitting in a chair unconscious from serving and participating at the same time. Jay could handle the crowd alone now, anyway.

"What'll it be? A nightcap?"

"Yes, Jay, thank you. A brandy, perhaps."

Jay reached under the bar and lifted a bottle of Courvoisier. Then he brought up a snifter and poured three fingers of the golden liquid.

Bluefeather leaned on an elbow on the bar saying, "It was a great one, wasn't it, Jay? A truly great party."

"Yeaahh, that it was. That it was."

Surprisingly, Myron came up and asked for a nightcap himself. His last drink of the night was also his first. He and Bluefeather raised their glasses in a silent toast to Jay and then clicked them together for themselves.

Myron said, so pleased at his efforts he actually smiled a bit, "To the cause."

Bluefeather replied, "To the cause, forever, sir." He finished his brandy, set his glass down with a fifty-dollar bill showing from under it, turned, and walked with deliberate steps to his room. Ramon and Antonio were putting away their guitars as they saw him retreat.

Myron said, "A fine American."

Jay appreciatively pocketed the fifty and said to his boss, "He is that," and began to close his bar.

The sagebrush gatherers, at least those fully conscious, had gone home happy and honored.

∎ ∎ ∎

Forty-One

After the party a day off was certainly needed, but that afternoon the clouds spread away from the mountain and inundated the valley with rain, making it impossible to work in the desert clay, anyway. However, the weekly *Taos News* could be delivered. There was a big headline: "Secret Government Sagebrush Project May Bring Prosperity to Valley." There were captioned photos of the festivities and a shot that included Bluefeather and Stump Jumper, who were named as heading up the work. Myron Vallier had taken all this to his officious heart and almost overdone his job.

It turned out quite well, though. The American Legion, along with a few local police, volunteered to protect the workers from the dust-raising traffic and eyes of possible foreign agents. The workers now felt honored. They really went about their leaf picking with diligence. Emilio's small barn was almost filled to capacity with the full gunnysacks. He had informed Bluefeather that in a couple more days his truck would be loaded to the limit.

Bluefeather, now satisfied that this end of the venture was a success, left Stump Jumper in charge and went to the inn to catch up on his phone calls. Besides, the successful ruse of secret government work had certainly nullified any chance he might have had in selling shares. He was looking up the number of the Cerrillos Bar when his phone rang.

He picked it up with anticipation, saying, "Hello."

The sweet voice came back at him. "Bluefeather," Marsha said, "I might as well get straight to it. Korbell turned down the proposal. I know you want to know why."

"Well, yes, I suppose I do."

"His turndown has nothing to do with the potential of the various formulas using the oil as a base. He thinks there are great possibilities eventually." Bluefeather was silent. "Are you there?"

"Oh, yeah. Yeah, I was just waiting for you to finish."

"Oh. Well, he simply thinks it will take too long to do the research to prove up all the patents. He's only interested in projects he can move on right now. He's always been that way. I am sorry."

"Don't worry about it. I figured—and so did Dr. Godchuck and Tulip. We all knew it was a long shot."

"I must say I am relieved at your attitude."

"No worry."

"Good. How is the leaf gathering proceeding?"

"Fine. We'll have our truckload day after tomorrow."

"You'll be coming back south then?"

"Be back in Santa Fe and Cerrillos in four or five days. You gonna be around?"

"I don't know from one minute to the next right now. We've been checking out a large parcel of state land to see if we want to bid on it. Please, call anyway, and we'll get together the first time we're both free. Promise?"

"Promise."

They said good-bye and for the moment the turndown by Korbell was secondary to her insistence on his calling. He was truly thrilled in a childlike manner just thinking of being with her again. Then it slowly seeped into his being that he must call the doctor and break the bad news to him. He wanted to run to the mountain behind the pueblo and hide like a rabbit. He craved going on across the mountain to his kin in Raton and absorbing their healing love. He could go into the bar only a few seconds away and forget the unpleasant duty for a while at least. He decided against that. He would just face it and get it over with.

He picked up the phone and called Cerrillos, asking Big George Gull to please seek out the doctor. He did.

Dr. Godchuck's voice was almost instantly on the other end of the line, "Ah, ah, ah, Bluefeather Fellini, what a pleasant surprise. We must be near a truckload."

"Day after tomorrow. I . . ."

"Fine. Delightful. We've just an hour ago finished testing the plant with some local sage and it's working perfectly, I'm happy to report.

"Well, that is great news, doctor," he swallowed, turning a little numb, and continued, "but I'm afraid I have some not quite so good news for you. Korbell turned us down. However," he crowded in, "he did say he thought we had great potential." Bluefeather waited for the doctor to have a heart attack, a cursing fit, or a show of terrible disappointment, but instead he seemed somewhat jovial at the information.

"That's good, Bluefeather Fellini, very good. I never expected him to come in now. No, no, his kind waits until all the gamble is taken out of it ... then ... then they move in like stabbing rapiers. It's all just as I expected, dear boy. Congratulations on your fine work."

Instead of complaints or reprimands, he was being complimented for what he considered a failure. It was a feeling of relief, but he could not believe he and Marsha had delivered. He decided to make a quick trip to Raton, leaving a note of explanation for Stump Jumper.

The drive through Taos Canyon was one of sweet nostalgia as he remembered Lorrie Friedman and their many visits there. But now Marsha dominated his mind almost equally to his thoughts of the healing elements of the oil of sage. Banished was the massive effort it would require to make his thoughts go on over the mountain to Eagle Nest, Cimarron, and then home to Raton.

There was a big family dinner that night as he was loved half to death. His mother remembered well the life-saving uses of sagebrush. Surprisingly, she was seriously concerned whether it was the thing to do.

"But Mama, it will ease burns, arrest colds, cure ulcers, slow the aging process, and that is just the beginning of what can come to mankind with the oil used as a base with other herbs and lotions."

"Well, of course, son, that is probably all true, but will it work without the blessings of the tribal council?"

"They would never give it. You know that. It would just get lost."

"Well, I do not know whether it's right or not."

"But Mama, millions of ailments and lives could be helped."

"Not if the Great Spirit hasn't approved."

Bluefeather was so knocked back that his mother was, as yet, even after all her years away from the pueblo, still set in concrete when it came to the old ways. He simply changed the subject to Hog Head's adventures in Chicago and how mine production was going in York Canyon. He had wanted to tell his mother that anything so good for the Pueblo Indians should be shared with everyone but was glad he had dropped the subject because when he did the family camaraderie returned immediately.

His father got him out on the back porch—alone, except for a bottle of good red wine—and wanted to know all about the venture. It was all quietly discussed, but when Bluefeather casually mentioned he had been associating with Marsha Korbell, his father slapped him on the back so hard he felt like his spine had joined his chest bone.

"Korbell's daughter, you say? Well, now...now there's some real handy work you've done there. Congratulations, my son. Who would ever think a coal miner's son would be hitching up with the likes of the Korbells? Wait till I tell your Uncle Alberto. He'll celebrate for a year, huh?"

Bluefeather tried to tell his father he had only been with her three or four times, but he was so overjoyed he would not listen and insisted they empty the bottle as a toast to his great accomplishment. They did.

His father said, "I think I have a feeling she is part Italian. In fact, I know it. I know it in here," he said quietly and pounded his chest. Then he jerked Bluefeather to his feet with surprising strength. With his arm around his son's neck, he led him back into the house, proudly and loudly announcing the upcoming joining of the Fellini family to the Korbell name.

Bluefeather was embarrassed and did his best to deny it. He might as well have tried to swim the Pacific Ocean with lead weights tied around his neck and feet for all the good his protesting did. It was a done—very well done—deal to his family that night in Raton, New Mexico.

The morning arrived in a few minutes.

It was completed. The gathering was finished until later, when much bigger acreage and many more workers would be needed. The field looked like a half-plucked chicken, but it would swiftly grow to normalcy.

After the truck was loaded and tied securely with ropes, Bluefeather paid everyone off with a little bonus he couldn't afford. They all thanked him sincerely, shook hands, happily volunteering to be first in line at anything he might need them to do.

Years before, Emilio had hauled ore from a mine in Cerrillos, so he knew exactly where and how to go. He drove away with the load. Bluefeather went over to the porch where Elena stood waving after her husband. He gave her a hug of thanks, reminding her, as he had many times, how vital her cooking had been in keeping the strength and mood of the workers up. He also slipped an extra twenty-dollar bill into her palm, in spite of her protests. He walked away with Stump Jumper, refusing to take it back.

The last words he heard from her were, "May the saints bless and keep you."

He drove Stump Jumper to within a half mile of the pueblo. He let him out, explaining to his puzzled look, "I don't have time right now for any more family celebrations. We've got to get this thing on the way, savvy, Stump?"

Stump Jumper did not savvy at all. He had forgotten they had already celebrated at the Sagebrush Inn all night long. That event no longer existed. He was ready for fun now. Everybody was supposed to celebrate the finish of any harvest or hunt. It had always been so.

"Hokay, you go on and work like a white man. I'll celebrate enough for everybody."

As Bluefeather drove toward the hotel to pick up his clothes, he had a moment of remorse knowing he was going to dearly miss some wild, crazy fun with his uncle. Ah well, such is the life of inventors and men of medicine.

Forty-Two

He stopped in a shop on Kit Carson Road and bought a vase in a shape that pleased him. Then he took the twigs of spruce he had cut at Palo Flechado Pass, between Raton and Taos, and the few select sagebrush twigs he had left in the jeep from Emilio's field. He drove to the little graveyard near El Prado, got out, and knelt at Old Grinder's gravesite. He tenderly placed the bottle with its spruce and sage next to the headstone. The sage and spruce represented what Grinder had loved most, besides silly fun—the mountains and the high desert. So did Bluefeather.

"Hey old pardner, I've been mining sagebrush for gold. Bet you don't believe that one, huh? It turned into quite a bit of fun, but I'm sure you were poking around somewhere and know all this anyway. Now I got to go see about milling the blue-green ore. Miss you old buddy, but you're always with me anyhow. Bye for now."

He got up, took a quick look at Taos Mountain and the pueblo, got into the jeep, and headed into his other worlds looking forward to every change of weather or turn in the road.

He checked in with Tulip, whose old-young skin and wonderful round brown eyes radiated good cheer and excitement at the pilot plant actually having been assembled and distilling the potent Taos sage.

"Oh, just think, deah Blue, at last Merphyn will have enough of the oil to finish the research to secure his patents. Isn't that the most stunning feeling?"

"It is indeed, Tulip."

"I always had faith it would happen, but these last few years I'd begun to have some concern for poor deah Merphyn. He's spent most of his life, you know? There's not much left in the purse."

"Yeah, well, now no matter what, he'll have the necessary material to finish his experiments. What's more, I'm going to see to it that he has enough money to go along with those materials," he said with an urgency in his voice.

Bluefeather hurriedly finished lunch with Tulip and excused himself from the table. He called Marsha and left a message. He started scouting the town for prospects to whom he could sell small interests in the one patent that existed. He felt the pressure of time, but he just was not clicking yet. He had been too long in the rhythm of the fields to just instantly switch over to the rhythm of sales. This did not slow his trying, though, for he believed the more effort extended now, the sooner he would reach his best form. He was a long way from that ideal now. All he was getting from his prospects were strange and doubtful looks and the proverbial promise of "I'll think about it" or "I'll talk it over with my associates" or "We'll talk it over with our accountants" or "Just got to talk it over with my wife."

He counted the cash he had left. It added up to $482.68. He checked at the front desk and was pleased, at least, to find they were paid up for another week there. He was disappointed when he found Marsha had not answered his message. He felt guilty at this feeling because he knew she tended to business before she played. Just the same, he missed her more by the hour. It was a longing.

He forced his mind back to Dr. Godchuck. There was no way to know without asking—which he would soon do—what the doctor's financial predicament was. There could not be much left after hiring help, renting the garage, buying parts and constructing the plant.

He decided to drive on down to Corrales and check on the Luceros, his mules, and the gold in his last precious bag. He would cash it in immediately. He planned to hand most of the money over to Dr. Godchuck. The last bag was the smallest of all and weighed out only forty-five hundred dollars, but maybe, just maybe, it would be enough to distill an ample supply to finish all the experiments. If so, he would somehow work, promote, or rob, as a last shot, to see that the dedication of this rare man would be fulfilled.

Tulip was thrilled that Bluefeather was taking her with him to Cerrillos. She said appreciatively, "Deah Blue, how thoughtful for you to ask me on a little outing. I'm dying to see Merphyn and his machine. Just nearly dying."

Bluefeather drove the Roadmaster. Tulip chatted the entire way about everything from mint juleps to a Basin Street jazz joint where the music was so grand that "one is simply transported."

Then, in the casual manner he had learned to expect under the most trying situation from the two remaining members of the Godchuck clan, she suddenly tossed him a lap full of live hand grenades. "It is so wonderful that deah Merphyn will have a chance to go right on with his other patent applications since the one on gingivitis runs out the third day of next month. What fortunate timing for us all."

He did not run off the road as she so lightly tossed all his efforts for them away. He did not grind his teeth or turn pale with fear. He did not even glow with anger. He was simply numb and cold somewhere deep inside the stomach area.

She went blithely on, "I do hope he pushes forward with the age-slowing process. We know that works. Just look at the two of us. Of course, Merphyn only applies it externally, while I've taken it both inside and out for decades now. I've never noticed any side effects, except in the beginning; I felt slightly queasy when I danced all night, but aside from that, ..." and she talked on and on with total sincerity.

They pulled into Cerrillos. Bluefeather slammed on the brakes right in the middle of the street and leapt out. Bluefeather's lower-mind showed his eyes a disjointed, distressing sight.

Tulip said, "Deah, deah me, it looks as if we've suffered an incident."

There in front of them stood almost the entire population of the village, surrounding a capless Dr. Godchuck, his necktie uneven and his mane of white hair turned anywhere from lamp black to dull silver, blown awry as if he had just walked through a tornado bareheaded. Smoke and soot smears covered his face, his moustache, and his tweeds, as well. Several other persons were in the same condition.

A man stepped back from the doorway with considerable strain and hacking. "The fire's under control, but we gotta get them smoldering bags of sagebrush outa there."

Bluefeather rushed up to the straight-standing, perfectly controlled doctor, breathlessly asking, "Are you all right?"

"Of course, Bluefeather Fellini, of course," and with his bull's prick cane he pointed, smiling, at the two safely packed drums at his feet, saying, "We have two pure quarts here."

"What on earth happened?"

"We'll never know for sure. Something stopped up the distillate machine and the pressure built to an explosion."

Bluefeather ran and looked in the building. It was a mess. The large still was distended, distorted, and destroyed. The coiled tubes looked like a den of dynamited snakes. It reminded him of a direct hit by an eighty-eight-millimeter artillery shell. Men were dragging the remaining sacks of sage out a back door. Some of the sacks were giving off an acrid smoke.

He went back to the doctor. Tulip stood calmly holding one hand on his arm as if they were about to enter a Broadway theater presenting a Shakespearean play.

"Was anyone hurt?"

"No, no. We were lucky. Only a few little burns and bruises. Nothing to cause concern. The building is mostly intact and we have two quarts of pure liquid gold." He glanced endearingly, still smiling, at Tulip. He patted her hand and then stood even straighter-appearing than a healthy pine tree, his walking cane by his side as a decoration only, and continued, "We shall proceed forward." He then asked Bluefeather, "Would you be so kind as to take Tulip back to the hotel? I will get this slight delay straightened out and join you both shortly."

Bluefeather hesitantly agreed to obey.

He drove—neither one spoke. They stopped a moment to check for traffic at the main highway to Santa Fe. Tulip sat still, and her eyes were motionless but looking inward.

She said, finally, "Merphyn is a brave and totally dedicated man."

He answered, "None more so." He glanced at her and instantly saw through the smooth ivory skin and body, like a living ghost. He could visualize the ninety-six-year-old woman underneath. A silent tear followed the lovely contours of her face as she whispered in a cracked voice he had to strain to hear, "So very, very brave."

Forty-Three

It was the time of uncertainty. The first day he found out that Marsha was still in the southern part of the state in Lea County. The second day Bluefeather called Merphyn at Cerrillos because he wanted to return to help him. The doctor said everything was going well and that Bluefeather should remain in Santa Fe and keep Tulip company.

This became very hard to do after she told him, "Merphyn is selling our property in Cerrillos, deah Blue. We're especially pleased that our deah friends George and Mattie Gull are the purchasers. Such a peachy couple, don't you think?"

The third day, Bluefeather called Merphyn again to talk about the money.

"Look, doctor, I forgot to tell you, I've got several thousand to get us started again. Should I bring it down?" He acted as if he didn't know the doctor was selling his property.

"No, my dear Bluefeather Fellini, the gods have suggested other approaches. I'll be done here in a day or so and apprise you of the situation. My heartfelt thanks, however. Love to Tulip, as well." He was gone from the line.

Bluefeather took Tulip to dinner at Claude's up on Canyon Road. The food and wine must have been excellent, as always, but he really didn't notice. He did not notice enough to remember much of their conversation either; just a few lines of hers and none of his own.

"My deah Blue, how loyal you've been to us. But you must not let our endless endeavors come between you and Marsha. I've had much experience along those paths of roses and thorns, you know? One can conquer armored dragons with one who fits. That's the secret of life and love, my deah. Two who fit. So simple, isn't it?"

He halfheartedly looked for investors in and around the many and colorful watering holes of old Santa Fe. Excuses. Promises. Then that did not matter so much. He waited for Marsha's return. He was ecstatic to find a message at the desk saying she would be back sometime the next day.

He got up at dawn, had breakfast, and drove around the hills north of town looking down on it, feeling the centuries of oxen, mules, horses, Indians, Spaniards, gringos, traders, artists, gamblers, business people, politicians, soldiers, madams, and princesses who had fought, frittered, and loved away centuries here, just as he himself was doing today. The costumes and transportation were the only differences.

After a while, he drove back down to take Tulip to a late lunch. He decided to go to his room and take a shower first, for he was certain that later he would be with Marsha. There was a little framed photo and an open letter on his desk. The picture was of a woman looking almost exactly as Tulip did now, holding proudly, with a smile, the baby Merphyn. His usual steady hand quivered some as he picked up the letter on La Fonda stationery, and read:

Dear Bluefeather Fellini,

If during a lifetime one can truly help twenty people change their lives or work for the better, then that person is truly a fine and fortunate individual. You have two on that small list in Tulip and me. You have given of your most precious possession—your time— and you have given it unselfishly and with faith and dedication, as well. You have delivered.

Remember always, my son, that you have participated in a grand medical movement first proven by your own ancestors during the terrible flu epidemic of the First World War. The three of us together have given it a momentous kick into the stratosphere and it will forever move until someday it will enter someone else's brain and soul. Then it will be carried on, and then perhaps on again, to its fruitful, life-enhancing destiny, with our labors being improved upon over and over. Radio came to first attention, and then invention, from the amazing mind of Lee Marconi to be passed on to Edwin de Forrest and thence on for more key improvements to Howard Armstrong until eventually the wireless could send voices and music—some of great importance and renown—around the world. Entrepreneur David Sarnoff made the relay of inventors' dreams and work "his" and spread the use and sale of radio around the world through a company called RCA and finally NBC, as well.

We were able to communicate from shop to shop, from ship to shore, from land to plane and nation to nation. Then in 1939 we moved on into television, and I'm sure someone is continuing the perpetual motion right now, moving on to molecular transport and perhaps finally to complete the earthly circle, with teleportation, so that the supernatural will once again become the natural.

So, you see, Bluefeather Fellini, that our part of the medical movement is no less significant than the parts played by any of the above named. You have helped move a little goodness forward for others. That alone makes you blessed.

We are off to Brazil to study combining Amazonian forest herbs with the sage oil. I shall concentrate my next patent process, for expedience' sake, on skin revitalization. Most people feel that looks are more important than health.

In faith forever,
Dr. Merphyn Godchuck and your Auntie Tulip Everhaven

For a moment the letter caused him to blanch like an atheist at the sight of the archangel and to feel as uncomfortable as a dog plagued with diarrhea. Then he perused the letter again and yet again. With each reading he felt more merited, more complete, and finally filled with a warm truth of major accomplishment. He had done his part. His molecules all returned to their proper position, relaxed, joyous even.

With a confident and purposeful stride he went down, crossed the lobby and, as he knew he would, found a message from Marsha saying she was back. He rang her room from the lobby. No answer. No matter.

He strode out, walking around the portals of the plaza. Then he saw her inside a curio shop examining some heavy silver and turquoise jewelry. She was so enraptured, he slipped in and stood back making as if he was interested in a rack of knickknacks, but he was looking at her, and his heartbeat and breathing changed pace almost instantly.

Then he saw the dealer reach under the counter to a hidden shelf and pull out an old squash-blossom necklace. Bluefeather could tell it had been created with exquisite hands and much love. It was a very special piece, just as Marsha was.

He walked up and whispered in her ear, "Buy it."

He moved with smooth but swift steps on outside where he faked studying the window display as he watched her try on the necklace.

Then she turned to him for his approval through the glass. She waited for his decision as the saleslady looked back and forth in puzzlement. He nodded "yes."

In a few moments she walked out the door, wearing the piece, and said, "You have very good taste, Mr. Bluefeather Fellini."

"Yes. Yes, I believe I do."

"If you're free, we can finally make our long-awaited dinner at El Nido," she said, tilting her head slightly to the side and giving him a flirtatious smile.

"I'm free for a lifetime."

"Meet me in the lobby at six o'clock then."

She walked away. He moved away from the window to appreciate her elegance more clearly. Both males and females stared at her as she came toward them and then looked back as she passed. Maybe the average man and woman on the street were smarter than he gave them credit for. At least they saw, smelled, or somehow felt when they were in the presence of a true princess, no matter how brief the encounter. He wanted to rear back and crow like a fighting rooster.

She stopped just before entering the portal and looked through the moving crowd to find him staring at her as she hoped he would be. She smiled with an overwhelming expression that spoke to him, radiated along the invisible connector between them, vibrating into his wide-open soul. She tossed her hair back with a movement of her head and vanished from his sight into the hotel.

It was around four now, by clock time. The next two hours would seem an eternity. It was one he was happy to spend. Bluefeather Fellini of Taos and Raton, New Mexico, danced a little jig forward, sideways, then forward again, as his whole body smiled.

Two Navajo jewelry makers passing him noticed his happiness, and one said without rancor, "That crazy man there looks like some kind of Indian I never seen before."

"Cannot figger it. He dances like the original white man."

"Maybe he eats locoweed."

"Maybe he is in love."

"Same thing."

It was the time of anticipated ecstasy. Bluefeather Fellini danced on to many kinds of music. He laughed out loud—twice.

BLUEFEATHER FELLINI IN THE SACRED REALM

■ Part One ■

ON THE TRAIL OF
THE GREAT SURPRISES

One

Bluefeather pulled the envelopes out of the mailbox as if they were a handful of glowing lava. Without daring to look at them, he unlocked the front door, entered the house, and dropped them on the kitchen table as fast as he could remove his fingers from the repellent paper. He knew he would have to look at them later, but he needed time to gather up his waning courage. Bluefeather had used up a lot of his reserve bravery in recent infantry combat across Europe during World War II.

He started to open the refrigerator for a cold beer and then remembered that the electricity had been cut off a week ago. Bluefeather lifted a bottle of room-temperature beer out of a six-pack container, found the beer opener, jerked the cap off, took a swallow and walked out into the living room to cogitate.

He had just sat down and taken another swallow of his refreshment when he saw his guiding spirit, Dancing Bear, up on the ceiling, looking down, grinning like a hog cracking peach seeds.

Dancing Bear spoke first. "Hey, dear brudder, I'm glad to see your Indian blood overtaking your Italian half so you can see me again."

Bluefeather yelled, "Get down off that ceiling, you crazy Indian, and lay some more of your cryptic advice on me."

"I ain't on the ceiling. I'm sittin' on a tree limb."

"Your ass, you are."

"That's right. My ass it are."

Bluefeather took another big swallow of Schlitz, tightly closed his dark brown eyes, and rubbed his hand through his black hair as if to get a new perspective on this whole situation. He was in this mess because nearly all the gold reserves he had mined before going to war had been spent on good living, attending college, and halfhearted prospecting. Then he had willingly followed the legitimate dreams of Dr. Godchuck and his Aunt Tulip through their failed attempt to develop the medicinal values of the oil of sage.

He did not regret these activities, but wondered where he had lost sight of the strong advice his old mentor Grinder had drummed into his head about always keeping a home place secure and safe. After Dr. Godchuck and Tulip left for the Amazon, Bluefeather had borrowed from banks, mortgaging different things at different times for different purposes, until now all was gone. The only things left clear were his two beloved mules, and they would probably be going next. How had it happened? There had been plenty of caution signs, but he had simply ignored them, and right now he was feeling some bitterness and wanted to shift the blame somewhere else.

Maybe he had gone blind with his infatuation of redheaded Marsha Korbell. The woman had begun to possess his brain when she left him dangling, waiting for their long-planned "proper" date in the lobby of La Fonda Hotel in Santa Fe. She had checked out without leaving a note, and all his attempts to contact her at the eminently powerful, wealthy Korbell estate had been rebuffed.

Maybe it was Dancing Bear's fault. Why hadn't his guiding spirit guided him through all this properly? Why had Dancing Bear taken the job of guiding if he didn't guide? Bluefeather felt a moment of resentment and a possible need for chastisement, but he remained speechless as he watched Dancing Bear climb off the invisible tree limb and float down, twisting slowly around until he landed on the floor in a sitting position with his legs tucked under him, saying, "Now, dear brudder, I ready to guide and help."

"Listen," Bluefeather said, "ever since you first showed up at Taos, I've been in trouble."

"That's true for sure. I probably wouldn't drop by at all if you were gettin' along good."

Bluefeather was getting increasingly puzzled. "What kind of a guiding spirit are you, anyway? All the others I've heard about were Indian chiefs or, at the lowest, a prince or princess of Tibet or ancient Egypt. Look at you in those ragged old buckskins. I bet the highest position you ever held was dog feeder. I have a powerful need for a Geronimo, a Crazy Horse, or a Sitting Bull to help me out of this mess."

"Do not worry your head. Authority send me to other peoples lately. Mebbe fifteen or ten. Me, Dancing Bear, guides 'em all to happy hour. Now I catch up on my business. Got plenty time for you now a days."

"Now cut out that Indian dialect. You're talking like you had never left the 'rez. You mean to sit there and tell me that during the most difficult period of my life you've been guiding ten or fifteen other people?"

"That's just last week. Yessum, I do what Authority tell."

"Authority. Authority. Why doesn't he talk to me about this in person?"

"You not listening with ears open. I told you before, dear brudder, Authority busy, busy, busy person. People all over got plenty troubles. Plenty. This Indian see it around town and in the trees."

"Well, maybe I was asking too much, Bear. Sounds like you might have troubles of your own. I'm real sorry."

Bluefeather felt a little foolish. He hadn't been trying to call on Dancing Bear for a simple, friendly visit. No, he waited until he was about to lose everything he had. His own selfishness was also something to ponder on.

"Okay, Bear, you got any suggestions for right now?"

"Maybe you oughta think about white man's metals that cause you big problems."

"Yeah? Go on."

"Maybe you read little letters and do business with glass."

"Glass?"

"Glass. Yessum." Then Dancing Bear pointed to glass objects in the room—a glass ashtray, a bottle, a drinking glass, a windowpane. "Glass, uh huh, glass."

Dancing Bear leapt up from the floor and started dancing in a circle around the room chanting, "Hay, yi yi, hay yi yi."

Bluefeather yelled, "Jesus H. Christmas Christ, can't you do anything but that buffalo dance?"

"How about Greek?"

"I've seen it before. I've..."

Dancing Bear did a "Zorba the Greek" right around the room and out through an unseen crack in the wall. Bluefeather could hear the zithers zinging all the way from Athens.

He shouted at the vanishing point, "You're no spirit guide. You're a cockeyed entertainment director."

He sat staring at the spot of Dancing Bear's disappearance. There were no thoughts of the dancing one right now, however. He was remembering something his father had told him long ago when he was growing up in the northeastern coal-mining town of Raton, New Mexico: "You know, son, when I get the feeling I'm goofing up and can't find the reason in my mind, I start back aways and write things down. It slows the head, and the problem will usually jump out at you."

The thought of his father, Valerio Fellini's, confident voice warmed him. Because Valerio was a "super" in the York Canyon coal mines, his words carried authority with everyone in the area, especially his young son, Bluefeather. So Bluefeather found a pencil, a sheet of paper, and geared himself to write. He did not know exactly how far back to go so he started at the beginning.

> *Born Raton, New Mexico, to Valerio Fellini, son of a Sicilian*
> *immigrant, and Morning Star Martinez, daughter of a powerful*
> *Taos Pueblo shaman. Played with lots of Fellini cousins in*
> *Raton and in summer played with lots of Indian cousins at Taos*
> *Pueblo. Then went to school. Did good at studies because my*
> *parents read to me a lot and made me do my homework. Liked*
> *baseball. Also a pretty good fighter. Fell in love with my fifth-*
> *grade teacher. What was her name? Leesa Curry, that was it . . .*

He stopped his note-taking and took another sip of the beer. It was not nearly as easy writing down his thoughts as his father had made it sound. His mind kept jumping back and forth like minds do. Well, he would have to concentrate all the harder.

Okay, he thought, and wrote:

> *I was embarrassed a lot of the time because almost everyone*
> *thought I was pretty. The cure: insult my cousin Guiseppe*
> *"Hog's Head" Fontano (who was employed in Chicago as a "col-*
> *lector") when he came back to Raton for a visit. It worked. He*
> *changed my features all right. He gave me this scar on my nose*
> *and it did stop the "pretty" talk for a while.*

Bluefeather stopped and thought about the incident. Hog's Head had obligingly whapped him in the face so hard he had ricocheted around the room with blood spurting from a beautiful split from one eyebrow all the way down across his nose. Bluefeather thought it was perfect except that the family doctor had performed too fine a job sewing it up. It had, however, accomplished its purpose, because it was permanent. Bluefeather rubbed lightly at the scar. It gave him all kinds of signals, this thin mark. When he was angry the scar burned. The greater the anger, the hotter the burn. It gave other signs of his emotions, when he could remember to feel. Even when he was in love, it tingled like little electric needle stings.

He stopped daydreaming and starting writing again:

Graduated high school. Worked as a "mucker" in Trinidad, Colorado, coal mines. Mother was sad because I didn't go to college right then. But I was promoted real quick. Family expected me to marry Margaret Bertinoli. Might have, but met Grinder the Gringo, the gold prospector. Told me great stories of mines near Taos. He was a great man. Could chew tobacco and drink beer at the same time with no teeth. Great man. Followed him to Taos. Prospected. Learned from Old Grinder. He taught me much. Taught me respect and love for mules. Taught me much. Great man he was. Fell in love with Lorrie Friedman.

He paused and let thoughts of Lorrie race through his mind. It all ended because of her mother. He liked and respected her mother, Candi. She was a beautiful woman. Talented. Rich. Strong-willed. But she made a mistake with him—she tried to buy him. She did not need to. He was sincerely in love with her daughter. Candi had offered him whatever kind of business he wanted if he would marry Lorrie and return to New York with them after the summer season in Taos was over. He was tempted but just couldn't do it.

He stopped the scenario, and began writing:

Left Lorrie. It hurt like hell to do it. Grandfather—shaman, elder of Bear Clan—and other elders took me to the sacred cave in Taos Mountain. Had the ceremony. My spirit guide, Dancing Bear, appeared. Got him for life, I guess. Left Taos. Went to Tonopah, Nevada, with beautiful dancing girl, Nancy. Learned to deal cards. Good woman. Fun in San Francisco. Had to leave. Killed man over poker game. Sorry for that. Me or him though. Left again with mules. Drifted back to Breen, Colorado.

Now he stopped, leaned back, and reminisced. How could he think his current predicament was important after remembering Miss Mary and her elegant old mining engineer, Mozart-loving father Ludwig? They were both buried in Breen. Ludwig on a hill near town and Miss Mary hidden for eternity in the tunnel she and Bluefeather had dug together with so much love. After her death, the great vein of gold they had found had become meaningless to him. He had left her there in the mine after covering her with pieces of their treasure. He had caved-in the tunnel, hiding it so well that even a shaman of the highest order, much less ordinary gold seekers, could never find it. Ludwig had died because he was ready to do so. His beloved blue-eyed, sunset-haired daughter, Miss Mary, had died from a falling rock accidentally dislodged off a bluff by Bluefeather's own foot.

He could not bring himself to pencil on past the lingering scent of Miss Mary and then the great war he had just returned from fighting. Nor did he need to write down anything about Dr. Merphyn Godchuck and Tulip Everhaven. The mind imprint of the medical visionary was indelible. How could the vision dim of a man obsessed with the curative powers of the oil of sagebrush, who could dress in Scottish tweeds and carry a cane made from a bull's prick and always appear elegant? What manner of man could show the proof of his beliefs with his own seventy-four-years' skin looking like that of a healthy thirty-year-old? A rare man indeed, but they had failed to promote his patented formula somehow, even though Bluefeather had given the project quite a boost with a considerable amount of funding from his gold reserves. If only the wealthy and powerful Korbell had just come through with the needed financing. But then it was his own adopted daughter, Marsha, who had made the presentation. The same Marsha who had left Bluefeather in the paddocks. The why of her unexplained desertion and disappearance jarred Bluefeather back to the present. He was surprised he had grown to care that much for her in their few brief meetings.

Bluefeather shook away his thoughts long enough to read back through his notes. Nothing happened to hint at how he could solve his current difficulties. Even so, he did not feel it had been wasted time. He chugged down the rest of the beer and went in the kitchen to get another.

In spite of his natural fear of the pile of mail, he sat back down at the table, put aside his recent writings, and picked up the letters, shuffling them like a large deck of cards. He dealt them out in a row into an oversized poker hand. He opened them in the sequence they had fallen. There would be no favorites today. He had already lost his Chevy Deluxe, and in just ten days he would lose his two-seat canvas-top jeep. The second envelope graciously explained that the bank had made every effort to help him save his adobe house and irrigated acreage. Since he had failed to respond to their repeated notices they had no choice but to file foreclosure papers in two weeks and one day. Nothing surprising so far.

The third missive was something else. Bluefeather mused on the number three. Why was it that the third of anything seemed to move the cogs of the modern world most of the time? Was it ordained? Well, he might as well find out now. He opened the heavy, gold-embossed envelope.

The typewritten note was vibrating in his shaking hands like a mini-earthquake. It was an invitation from Mr. Ricardo Korbell. Korbell! A car was coming to pick him up this afternoon at three. What had happened? Would Marsha be there? The questions came so fast that any possible answers were immediately lost.

Bluefeather looked at the envelope again. There was no stamp. No postmark. It had been hand delivered. Bluefeather looked at the clock on the table across the room. It said five after four—that, of course, being the exact instant the electricity had been cut off a week before. He grabbed the phone to dial for time. He listened to a dead nothing and placed the receiver back on the hook, feeling kinship with an orphan lamb in a cage full of mountain lions.

He hurried into the bathroom to shave and shower, but of course, the water had been cold for days. He grabbed his shaving equipment and his one clean suit from a closet, dashed outside to the jeep, started up, and raced across the field to his neighbors, the Tranquilino Luceros.

He jammed on the brakes, grabbed up his shaving stuff and clothes and leapt out, heading for the front porch, just as Tranquilino stepped out to greet him.

"Hey, Tranq, what time is it? Can I use your shower? Where's Tina and the kids?"

Tranquilino followed him around, answering as best he could, with great liquid eyes asking questions from his heavy round face, his hands inside his biboveralls as if to keep his plentiful belly from tearing the threads loose.

"It is twenty minutes until three by the clock. Please use the shower. Tina and the kids have gone to the old woman Marquez to help with her granddaughter's wedding. I stay here to work in the garden when the sun is out of my eyes." He talked on about many things through the bathroom door, although Bluefeather could hear only parts of what he said.

Now he was as ready as he was ever going to be. He ran out by Tranquilino, slapping him on the shoulder. "Thanks, Tranq. Will you feed the mules for me this evening? I may be late."

He drove up in front of his house just as the long, dark blue limousine pulled into the driveway. It purred to a stop like a large metal cat with its motor still turning. There was no regular sound of the motor, only a low hum without vibrations of precision metal. There was a glare on the windshield, so the image of the driver was unclear. The machine seemed to study him with glazed eyes, making its own inanimate decision about the totality of his fate. He felt small and very alone as he stood motionless by the canvas-covered jeep, waiting.

The door on the driver's side swung open and a lady stepped out— a right keen lady. She was in a pale blue suit that matched her eyes, and the thick edges of autumn-colored hair blazed in the three o'clock sun. The orange orb had momentarily glazed his vision.

Bluefeather did not acknowledge the actuality of his jolted feelings. For just an instant, a paralyzing instant, he thought he was looking at a Miss Mary, only taller by about four inches.

Then she smiled—ah yes, she certainly did. She also spoke, although the words must have had some difficulty making their way through such a beam as that. It created considerable strain, but Bluefeather did hear her. It was Marsha. My God, it was Marsha Korbell, the deserter.

"Hello, Bluefeather Fellini."

"Marsha!"

"Mr. Korbell awaits your visit with much anticipation. Would you please get in?"

He got in. He was so stunned by her presence that he just sat immobile, speechless, as she drove away. There were things about these Korbells that called for momentary silence.

■ ■ ■

Two

Ordinarily, Bluefeather would have enjoyed the ride up through the scattered piñon and cedars decorating the foothills. The mighty Sangre de Cristos dominated the horizon above, making the world seem very big. There was glass between him and Marsha, the driver. He did not use the intercom to speak, nor did she.

As they rounded a curve, the house was revealed. It was surrounded by a ten-foot-high adobe, concrete-plastered fence partly disguised in the trees. There was a huge iron gate ahead at the entrance, but it too was painted earth colors. The sight certainly jarred Bluefeather out of his comfortable musing, for it wasn't like any house he had ever seen before.

The first impression was of a medieval castle, but the lines of old-modern southwestern architecture dispelled this impact. The curvature and soft edges of the massive structure could only be adobe. It was multistoried like the Taos Pueblo main building, but faded back in more compact layers of levels. It exuded a sense of strength, permanence, and, yes, power.

If Bluefeather had given any prior thought to it, this would be the kind of house Korbell, by his nature, would obviously occupy. One heard all the rumors of his financial manipulation. There was gossip, of course, that he was in oil, mining, manufacturing, arms shipments, and on and on.

Bluefeather couldn't remember a single interview with the man in print or on radio. However, now and then, one would see a photo of him at some exclusive international gathering with several lovely ladies surrounding his imposing presence.

Bluefeather, using his mind-voice, said, "The son of a bitch is a mystery all right, and it was one created by his own choice."

When Korbell had moved to the Southwest, the local papers, and some national ones, had simply stated—without giving reasons—that he had decided on this part of the world for his permanent home and hinted at the fact that everyone in the state would all be better for it. Personally, Bluefeather had paid little notice to the latter. It had been his minor experience that the move of big money always created that same initial reaction, even if it was later found that the wealth came to pour concrete over the hills and hide the natural horizon with all kinds of look-alike structures.

Bluefeather had been trying to quit smoking for over a year now, but he suddenly reached for his security pack in his coat pocket. He hesitantly put it back and wiped his suddenly dampened palms on the sides of his legs.

The great gate swung back in front of the limousine. Now after entering the acres of compound, Bluefeather's practiced eye saw the hidden guard boxes on each side of the gate and scattered every hundred yards around the entire estate. He had no doubt that they were being watched with careful interest.

The security commander was a huge man with a deep scar angling like a steep mountain trail carved into his face. By their subtle gestures, Bluefeather could tell that the man and Marsha were somehow close. Then he remembered seeing her with him in the Cerrillos Bar south of Santa Fe before they met.

She said, "That's Fontaine. You'll meet him someday. Now, Blue, don't go into any fits or questions. Just calm it all down and I promise you it will all come clear in the future."

Well, he might as well play along with this plot, game, or whatever it was. What, really, did he have to lose?"

They drove upon a circular graveled driveway bordered by arranged groupings of piñon, sagebrush, cacti, yucca, and other plants indigenous to the region. The limousine stopped. My God, he was about to meet the man. His brain turned into a cement mixer.

The lady opened the limousine door, waiting, still smiling.

"We're here."

Bluefeather exited, giving a weak thanks.

As they walked along toward the large antique doorway, Marsha talked casually and comfortably, but he didn't remember a single sentence she uttered. He hoped he had answered if questioned, but he didn't know for sure. The door, like the front gate, swung open before they reached it. Bluefeather truly expected a polished, British butler to greet them, but instead there stood another elegant woman of indeterminate youth, smiling.

Marsha introduced him thusly: "Elena, this is Mr. Bluefeather Fellini."

Elena shook hands in a solid way and said, "It is so nice you could come. Korbell is expecting you."

Bluefeather noticed she did not preface the name with the usual "Mister."

"This way, Mr. Fellini."

Bluefeather followed, glancing back for Marsha, but she was walking away down the long, tiled hallway without having said another word. However, the vision moving ahead of him was sufficient to hold the attention of a lobotomized lizard. Elena's long, ballerina, graceful legs floated under the flowing gown that intermittently clung to and outlined her entire body. The gown had Aztec designs of varied hues from top to bottom. Maybe Rembrandt could have given proper attention to these works of art clinging to her surfaces. Bluefeather could only think of the Great Spirit's art underneath.

She stopped at another large door, smiling as she opened it. Bluefeather was struck by the glowing whiteness of her skin and the delicate but strong chin under the slightly arced crimson lips that curled invitingly around teeth whiter even than her skin. Her hair was blue-black like the barrel of a new gun, with a large silver comb placed so that the long strands snaked around and over a shoulder, just reaching one of her slightly revealed breasts. Bluefeather had an urge to dive into the two pools of eyes that matched her hair and to swim straight to heaven, if he didn't drown first. What was wrong here? He was thinking like a beginning madman.

Then the man, Korbell, was walking across the room, smiling of course, as if he were meeting the pope or a king, but it was just plain Bluefeather Fellini.

Elena said, with the purr of a little tiger, "Korbell, this is your Mr. Fellini."

"Ah, what a pleasure to meet you in person, Mr. Fellini. Of course, I've heard about you from Marsha." He grabbed Bluefeather's hand and gave it a shake that would have torn limbs from a great oak. He turned it loose just as swiftly as Bluefeather muttered, of all things, "Howdy, Mr. Korbell. It's sure good to meetcha."

"Korbell. I prefer just Korbell."

Bluefeather would never forget the last statement even though his present retention was being shattered like a dropped clay pot.

Korbell was at best a couple of inches taller than Bluefeather, probably six three, and as lean and tan as a tennis pro with Aegean Sea eyes and a long Sherlock Holmes nose over a wide, thin-lipped mouth. His hair was, to use an ancient description, shining silver, of course—it would have to be. His age, like Elena's, could not be determined. Bluefeather guessed it could be either side of fifty. Korbell, too, had the same perfect teeth that gleamed from the ladies' mouths. Bluefeather ran his tongue over his own rather common ivories and then figured that maybe he could get a recommendation to their dentist, if nothing else. To top it all off, Korbell wore a very casual umber smoking jacket.

"You've met Elena, my adopted wife?"

Bluefeather's voice-mind clicked in again. "Horseshit and smothered onions," he thought, "an adopted wife . . . he actually said that."

Bluefeather swallowed and decided he had better just enjoy the show before he got lost in the mezzanine.

Elena vanished. Bluefeather was seated in a luxuriously soft chair as Korbell took a matching one to the right of him, angled so they could look at one another without twisting and both could comfortably gaze out a ten-foot picture window across miles of rolling hills rising through blue-hazed timber to barren, snow-covered peaks. Right magnificent.

"Well, now, Mr. Fellini, do you feel like a drink?"

"Blue. My friends mostly just call me Blue." He had to do something in self-defense. He added that he would be delighted to have a drink with him.

Another striking woman quietly appeared. In contrast to Elena, she had on a simple, tailored dress. Her brown hair was done up in a neat twist on top of her head. Bluefeather felt better when he saw that she had one tooth slightly out of line. She waited, smiling. After the introduction failed to come, Bluefeather heard her say, "Brandy?"

"Perfect," he answered, aiming to oblige where possible.

As she poured the drinks in a distant corner, Korbell looked at the boundless panorama, sighing contentedly. "What a perfect setting for our first meeting."

Bluefeather said, "Leonardo da Vinci would be honored."

Korbell chuckled slightly, adding, "Very good, Mr. Fellini. Very good, indeed."

Bluefeather thought, "The bastard has got me snake-charmed already. I'm almost ready to rise up out of a basket and start weaving to the music of his flute."

The brown-haired lady came with a large tray holding the brandy and a box of Havana cigars. Bluefeather took the brandy and placed it on a hand-carved Spanish table next to his chair. The lady hesitated just a moment, so he took a cigar along with a gold-embossed match box. She served Korbell. Bluefeather waited. Korbell lifted his snifter. Bluefeather lifted his.

"To our potentially highly rewarding association."

"Whatever that might be."

Korbell gave his underplayed chuckle again, and they drank. It was very fine stuff. Bluefeather expected Korbell to speak of some exclusive, expensive brand name, but he was fooled again. Korbell lit his Havana. So did Bluefeather, wondering when the Philharmonic would enter.

"I do so like to mix business and pleasure, Mr. Fellini. More so all the time. Much more so." With that he reached down by his chair and picked up a flat leather folder, opened it, and began to read. Bluefeather knew for sure now that the game had started. A change came over him. He was no longer overwhelmed. He knew a contest was beginning between the two of them. Overmatched? He might be, but he was pre-pared to challenge the odds. What, really, did he have to lose? He was ready. Excited.

Korbell read, muttering at first, "Now, uh huh, yes. Born 1914, Raton, New Mexico; Italian father…mine foreman, now retired; Taos Indian mother, has become a fairly successful traditional watercolorist of Indian art." Korbell continued to read, "B-student, baseball and track star in high school; assistant mill foreman before you were twenty; became gold prospector; bought property and moved to Corrales; went to war, Europe, three major campaigns…aha awarded a Silver Star at Brest…"

Bluefeather swallowed some high-priced cigar smoke and coughed out, "No, that's all wrong. It was a mistake. I didn't deserve it… I swear…"

"I like modesty in its place, Mr. Fellini, but this is not the place. I can fully read and understand a commendation. I was myself in the OSS for four years, you know?"

Then he read on briefly in silence. "I see you left the School of Mines a few months before graduating…setting third in your class at the time. Oh, well, it's not my concern why. I see you've hidden the fact that you did a stint of mercury smuggling out of Mexico recently. Not that it concerns me, but is that why you left school?"

Bluefeather had hidden the last even from himself. There would be little he could hide from this man, so why bother.

"Yes. That is why I left. I think you've already figured that. At the time the mercury movement was faster than a quarter horse track, and a hell of a lot more profitable."

"I see. The short-range profit motive overcame the long-range solidity of a degree as a mining engineer."

"I've never witnessed any solidity in the mining game."

"Game. Game did you say? You might have been ... no, let's forget this part." Korbell shuffled the papers and continued, "You did have a very successful early life considering the choices you made. You survived the Great War in good shape and were building up your investment property just outside Albuquerque. Then things started to go to hell. What happened, Mr. Fellini? What in this world happened?"

"Several markets broke, including mercury. I became jaded and careless, that's all. It won't last. I won't let it."

Korbell continued to read. "You were married briefly. Your wife, Mary O'Kelly, expired from a mining accident near Breen, Colorado. What, I pray, young man, was a woman doing mining?"

"She was very good at it. It was just a ... a freak accident. I'd rather not speak of it again."

"As you wish. Forgive my impertinence, but I have to know certain things. Oh, oh, I almost overlooked this. You killed a man in Tonopah. Self-defense. That's good."

How could this man go on so casually about the major events in his life? He decided to fire back. "Before we go any further, I want to know why you turned down the presentation on Dr. Godchuck's sage oil. It could have stopped a lot of suffering. And Marsha said you thought it was a good deal."

Korbell looked up from the papers, smiled, and said, "Maybe so, Mr. Fellini, but you see I have something that is far greater than that of the good doctor, and the time is now. You know, one may be fortunate enough to have great wealth, but it will not purchase him a single second more of his allotted time. I have things to be fulfilled and my hope is that you'll see your way clear to help." Then he returned to the reading.

"Let's see, where was I...? your father is now retired from the mines and your mother has become a successful watercolorist of Indian art. You phone her on the first Sunday of every month." Korbell was smiling so slightly that Bluefeather had to strain his 20/20 eyes to see it.

This last personal piece of information was just a little too much. Bluefeather was sure the man knew the brand of toothpaste he used. He decided to end the inquisition. "Well, it looks like you know how many times I fart each day. Let's cut the crap and get down to the deal."

"Deal?"

"Yeah, you said you needed my help. And I know you haven't invited me here for my scintillating conversation, have you?"

Korbell chuckled again, finished his brandy, and relit the Havana. Bluefeather did likewise. Waiting.

"Forgive my intrusion into your personal life, but I have a delicate proposition to make you, and one needs to know with whom and what he is dealing. I hope you understand."

Bluefeather countered with, "How about another brandy?"

Korbell raised his right hand and said softly, "Nedra."

The brown-haired serving girl entered the scene from around a latticework and they soon had their brandy. She exited.

Korbell stood up, brandy in hand, and said, "Please come with me."

Bluefeather followed him, warming the amber liquid with the palm of his hand as he walked. They wound through a hallway down a curving iron stairway beneath the house. They went through another heavy iron doorway that opened smoothly at Korbell's touch. Everything seemed to be machined perfectly around here. Everything.

Bluefeather followed him perhaps twenty steps to a like door. Korbell touched it as lightly as one might a frozen windowpane to test the cold. It swung silently open. They were in a vast wine cellar. Maybe it was average to Korbell, but it was mammoth to Bluefeather.

Korbell did not hesitate now, but strode purposefully past rows upon rows of worldly wines without even glancing at them. At last he turned and started down another aisle. Here he stopped by a tall, small-topped table that reached above their waists. He smiled around his teeth, white even in the dimly lighted cellar, and lifted his brandy to Bluefeather in a silent toast. He acted like he was in a library full of sacred tomes. Their glasses touched ever so lightly, making a ringing sound in the underground stillness.

Bluefeather followed Korbell's lead as he placed his glass on the odd-sized table. With delicacy and practiced skill, Korbell took a bottle from its resting place and very carefully placed it upright on the table between the brandy glasses and whispered, "Read."

Bluefeather bent down in the dim light, somehow knowing not to touch the old bottle. He read aloud, "Mouton Rothchild—1880." There was more fine print that he could not make out in the poor light.

Korbell whispered now as if he stood before the open casket of a dearly beloved. "That, Mr. Fellini, is one of the great wines of the world. And just as important, it pleases the palate like no other. The Rothschilds have refused to sell me another. They value each bottle in the thousands of dollars. Many thousands. It would do no good to offer more. Each year, at the end of the grape harvest, one—only one—bottle of this is opened in honor of the eldest of this noble clan. It is a priceless product to the Rothchilds, and to me. Do you understand?"

"I don't believe I do...unless...unless it is craving something one cannot buy, can't have just for money."

"Ahhh, you are partially correct, but you see I can have it...more Mouton '80 than even the Rothchilds have left in their cellars."

Bluefeather could only stare at him.

"Mr. Fellini, have you heard of Joshua Tilton?"

"The famous mining man?"

"The same, indeed." Korbell explained, "Joshua Tilton struck it very rich in mining between the two great world wars. He built large homes all over the Southwest and lavished friends with many, and varied, gifts. He was known as an eccentric—mainly, I felt, because he spent his wealth publicly and opulently on parties for renowned people from all over the world."

Bluefeather was aware that both Tilton and Korbell had become legends, even though their public approach to life appeared to be exactly opposite.

Korbell continued, "At the time Hitler invaded Poland, Tilton had become obsessed with the concept that the dictator would truly conquer the entire world. Tilton was reported to have gathered a great store of gold and silver bullion and hidden it in one of his mines. Great fortunes and many lives have been spent in a futile effort to find this treasure. If the reports were true, or if the treasure has been found, I've not been able to verify it."

He paused a moment, watching Bluefeather, his piercing eyes showing his enthrallment with the story and his curiosity at its effect on his visitor.

"Tilton's unsolved murder in a Silver City hotel during the height of the bombing of London only added to the mystery. It became a notorious incident since the head was missing from the body and has never been recovered. All the forces of the law were expended in a futile attempt to solve the case. Every lead, no matter how vague, was followed. They all petered out. Right now as we visit, someone, somewhere, is seeking the fabled fortune."

Bluefeather was aware that Tilton's bullion had become almost as famous as the lost Adam's diggings of the Superstition Mountains near Phoenix, Arizona. Elusive dreams or hard facts? The thing is, people wanted to believe in its existence, so they searched on and on.

Korbell sighed, looking at the Mouton '80 and spoke again. "I'm sure, Mr. Fellini, that your mind is racing with whirlwind thoughts of Tilton's lost bullion. Well...that is a strong rumor, but a rumor nevertheless, you see. But, a mostly unknown fact is that Tilton did hide sixty cases of Mouton '80. Sixty cases, Mr. Fellini! Do you realize what a treasure that truly is? Perhaps a million dollars worth of Mouton. Maybe more. Who knows what the careful disclosure and handling of such a find would accrue. But, you see, that is not its true value, is it? Far from it. It would be like owning half interest with the French nation in the Mona Lisa. I have the old shipping and arrival bills, proving without a doubt, that this wondrous shipment was delivered only a short time before Tilton's demise. The wine is here. Somewhere in finding distance."

Korbell was breathing like a milerunner at the tape. His eyes were staring through mountains. An obsession had possessed his being. Then Korbell recovered and got right down to real business. Real for Bluefeather at least. He informed Bluefeather that Tilton was certain to have secured the wine underground to keep an exact and constant temperature. Bluefeather was surprised by Korbell again when he admitted that the very cellar they now stood in had already been dug by Tilton and the foundations of the great house had already been poured and most of the walls laid at the time of his decapitation.

Korbell praised Tilton for his choice of this location and admitted that it was his exhaustive research on Tilton that had led him to this most perfect of all places to build his final and permanent residence.

Korbell explained that he and Tilton were of the same stand of timber; all that remained to be done was the finding and glorious consumption of their Mouton '80.

Now he led Bluefeather out of the expansive wine cellar and up to his sanctuary. It was a room almost as large as the cellar—a room hung with paintings of the old and new Taos masters: Sharps, Couses, Phillips, Berninghaus—the whole drove and more. There were the originals of world-famous Indian artists such as Woody Crumbo and R. C. Gorman's landscapes and varied styles of Andrew Dasburg, Howard Cook, and Fremont Ellis. There were long shelves of southwestern titles from such authors as Mable Dodge Luhan, Willa Cather, Oliver La Farge, and many, many others that Bluefeather recognized at a glance. It was difficult for Bluefeather to listen to more talk of lost bullion and wine when the mentors of his mother's birthplace hung about the adobe castle as casually as an old hunting dog.

Korbell forced him to return his attention to Tilton's legacy. He showed him maps of all the mines in New Mexico that Tilton had either owned, prospected, or leased, as well as the dates they had been opened, or closed, or abandoned.

Then the deal was pitched. Korbell would pick up all Bluefeather's overdue payments, thereby saving his home and land, and pay him a generous retainer for six months, renewable at Korbell's choice. If Bluefeather found the wine, he would pay one-half its immediate market value. He wanted the wine. Simple.

It did not take Bluefeather long to make up his mind. He was on the verge of losing everything that had taken so much real blood and love to accrue. It wasn't just the monetary worth of his loss. It was Old Grinder's advice that was being downgraded. Anyway, he loved the Corrales place, his mules, his neighbors. The place had to go on existing for those from the past. It hurt to think it might not be there for some future...future...? What the hell! He might as well admit it. He had goofed. His balls were in a red hot vise that was rapidly closing. Another thing that shot through his system with a surge was Marsha. He would be with her, because she definitely was part of this strange equation unfolding like the wings of a giant butterfly. Without hesitation, Bluefeather gave Korbell a powerful handshake. The act would indeed change his life completely.

Korbell held Bluefeather's hand a moment, looking through his forehead, and probably beyond, saying, "I expect the same dedication to our great cause from you that I myself have given and will continue to bestow. Do you totally understand me, Mr. Fellini?"

Mr. Fellini said, "I do." And he did.

"Fine. Fine. Now let us retire for cocktails and dinner."

Three

They sat about the great room of their first meeting. Elena, Marsha, Korbell, and Bluefeather talked about current painters, potters, and musicians of a local bent. It was easy-flowing conversation with no interrupting or domination of the talk. Nedra served the drinks and appetizers smoothly, without any wasted apologies or fuss. Bluefeather felt it was an omen that he and Marsha both asked for J. B. Scotch. The world was made of small likes and dislikes.

The hiding sun was turning the snow-peaked mountains watermelon pink. The Spaniards had long ago designated this last light of day as *sangre de Cristo*—blood of Christ. The valleys and hills had already become part night with misty blues and purples that made one think of long ago and the possibility of eternity.

The mellowness of the booze and the relief from many suffocating debts had put Bluefeather in a pleasant torpor. They all seemed to sense that. Korbell, as well, was a happy and relieved man. Marsha's eyes and rosy skin beamed like summer sunspots. She sipped her drink casually, occasionally pushing a random strand of auburn hair back from the side of her face, giving him looks that he was sure had deep meaning. Of course, those looks could only be special for him, no matter how brief. He was right. He was right. She *was* studying him, wondering how Korbell could trust him on such short acquaintance, even with all the prior information he had gathered and her own short acquaintance with him. Well, they would all soon know what his capabilities were.

As Marsha looked at Bluefeather's strong features again, she was embarrassed that she felt a quickening of breath. My God! She was feeling like a high school sophomore and praying it didn't show. She could not let him know that—not until she could explain, someday, why she had left him in Santa Fe without an answer.

Elena listened to whomever spoke with a rare raptness. As the natural outdoor light receded, her white skin again drew Bluefeather's gaze. Her large, dark eyes fastened on him like those of a master hypnotist. He wondered for an instant if they had hypnotized him—this Korbell group.

No. The mountains, now becoming one with the sky, were real. The drink he held was real. He took a small, cool swallow to verify. He pushed his own thick, black hair across his scalp. It was his own head he was inside of, for sure. Well, whatever. A few hours back, he had arrived here with one leg hanging in space above a chasm of darkness, and now both feet were planted firmly on the Indian-rugged, tile floor. Solid. Even though he felt it unnecessary, he was certain he could elevate himself to the ceiling like Dancing Bear, on command.

At the instant of this thought, the aquarium of tropical fish that he had noticed in a far corner moved toward them. It slowly circled the entire group, stopping for a fraction of a moment in front of Bluefeather. The multicolored fish swam about in little liquid rainbows, nuzzling the bottom of the aquarium among pebbles and swaying vegetation. One large, white fish looked arrogantly at Bluefeather a moment, knowing all. Then the aquarium settled down and moved on four little wheels to the great window and stopped. Bluefeather looked about—casually, he hoped—at the other faces. They had taken no notice at all; their current attention was on Korbell, who was expounding his admiration for Maria Martinez's San Ildefonso Pueblo pottery. Nedra, smiling, served as the aquarium now smoothly rose up and floated to its former place.

Bluefeather thought, "My God, how they all smile. Did rich and powerful people take smiling lessons, and ... and ignore magic aquariums as if it happened to be their due?"

Bluefeather was confident that he had maintained his composure as Korbell spoke. "Ah, yes, Mr. Fellini. I forgot to apprise you of one more item. My adopted daughter, Marsha, will be your assistant on our little venture. I trust you will find that satisfactory, as she is extremely efficient in many fields."

Bluefeather looked at her teeth lined so perfectly behind her luscious lips and said, "If you say so, sir." This was one of the closest six or seven times in his life he had ever come to dying of both shocked surprise and pained pleasure.

Marsha controlled the jumbling and jangling of her nervous system, emitted a sigh of acceptance, and nodded her head so casually it was almost imperceptible. Oddly, everyone in the room watched her minute indications of acceptance.

Dinner had been, to say the least, grand. The wine was of such a bouquet that the young guest wondered why in the holy hang-dogged hell a man ever needed to give a thought to Mouton '80. They had duck a l'orange that chewed and swallowed itself. There were many more courses, but Bluefeather blanked on what they were. There are only so many goodies a man can swallow at once without choking. He did not, however, resist when Korbell insisted that he stay the night. They all had brandies except the elegant, somehow aloof, Nedra.

Bluefeather was happy when he was shown to his room with a bed big enough for a basketball team. He was wondering about the adopted wife, the adopted daughter and, no doubt, adopted serving girl as he pulled the silken covers over his shoulders.

He thought, "By God, maybe the obsessed bastard will adopt me, too."

He was just trying to think of a single disadvantage to this as a coyote howled off toward the north, answered by one farther on, when he realized a figure stood silhouetted against the window, backlit by a rising moon. It was a female. No doubt about that at all. The scent of a subtle perfume from some faraway island wafted about and mixed with the Scotch, brandy, and wild dreams in his head.

She crawled into bed beside him. He couldn't make out her features, nor did he have a chance, for her smooth, warm arms folded over and around him. Her breasts had his chest captured and enraptured.

He croaked out, "What are you doing here?"

The unrecognizable whisper came soft as the first breeze of autumn, just as her hands found him.

She whispered, "Well, the Orientals say there are one hundred and one ways."

Bluefeather lost count at six or seven.

Later he realized he was alone. One of the three adopted ladies had permissively raped him. It was too late to care. He was too lusciously tired to stay awake and ponder.

■ ■ ■

Four

Bluefeather and Marsha were on a winding, hilly highway, heading for the place of an old friend of his in the mountains of southern New Mexico. Willy Ruger and his sister, Flo, owned a ten-room log house on 160 acres of patented mining claims smack in the middle of a national forest. Zia Creek ran right through their property. It was also a central location to search for the mines on his benefactor's maps.

Long ago, during one—or maybe his very first—meeting with his spirit guide, Dancing Bear had prophesied to his young new client that he would have a life filled with wild adventures. Dancing Bear was right. It would all speed up like an idling motor suddenly thrust into full power. The trees along the promised quixotic trail had already begun to blur from his awesome and increasing velocity.

Korbell had come through swiftly with the funds and influence to get Bluefeather's messed-up world back in order: all back payments on the property were paid and the gas, water, electricity, and phone had been reconnected. Bluefeather had hired Tranquilino to take care of the place any way he saw fit. He had even retrieved the three Patricino Barela and the two Luz Martinez wood carvings he had hocked to his insurance man. It had given him a grateful feeling of warmth to place them back in his living room alcove, where they belonged.

He was also pleased and surprised at Marsha's interest and practical suggestions when he had talked of the addition he planned for his house. She had figured out the right location for his new den. She also suggested a sliding glass door opening out onto a private patio. The enigma of the woman equaled that of the lost wine, but he held back any prying into her privacy, albeit with difficulty.

It was spring. The birds were flying about from tree to bush, trying to reach a satisfactory agreement on mating. Cattle moved about the land, chasing the tender green shoots that shoved their way up through the dead, brown remains of winter grass. The bulls were busy following the cows, sniffing, pawing, curling their upper lips, searching for the scent that signaled permission to mount the backs of mother cows whose new calves frolicked freely about with their faces white and new before the world had a chance to dirty them.

They entered the village of Meanwhile, New Mexico, population 240 people, forty cats, and thirty dogs. The highway split the town in half. There was the usual mixture of adobe and slant-roofed, frame houses. The store buildings mostly still had old frontier fronts scattered along an erratic wooden sidewalk. A few pickup trucks and cars were parked at odd angles here and there. It was Saturday, so over half of them were in front of the Dos Amigos Bar.

"Hey, Marsha, do you like burritos?"

"Yes, especially the bean and beef with red chile."

"Well good. Ol' Dominguez makes the best in the whole world."

He bent the loaded jeep to a stop. They got out and entered the Dos Amigos. Before they got inside, they could hear the jukebox playing country songs. Old Dominguez spotted Bluefeather as soon as they sat down at the whiskey-, cigarette-, and elbow-worn bar.

"Hey, Blue, where you been? Don't see you for months, maybe, huh?"

"Been dodging rocks, amigo."

"Don't see no knots on your head."

"They're all on the inside. Dominguez, this is Marsha."

"Happy to meets you, Ma'am. What'll be your pleasures?"

"Bottle of Pabst Blue Ribbon for me. What about you, Marsha?"

"That will be fine for me, too."

They ordered two burritos and ate them sitting at the bar. Of course, it took three more bottles of beer and two more burritos before they could get their strength straightened out. Marsha put away the chile, beef, and pinto beans wrapped in a homemade tortilla as if she had returned from a year in the Arctic. Bluefeather liked that.

The crowd kept gathering. Bluefeather had made the mistake of ordering a round for the house. The people of this land could smell a generous fool through a three-foot adobe wall and at least twenty miles' distance—if the wind was right. It was right, and about everybody in the whole county was showing up or sending a "rep."

Suddenly, all the old, musty cowboy prints, beer and cigarette signs, along with the comforting smell of a million spilled drinks and the sweat of miners, cowboys, and social security retirees made the Dos Amigos the only place in the whole world there had ever been or ever would be. Eight bottles of beer might have helped some. However, Marsha had sipped only two. She was laughing and visiting with every awestruck habitué who approached. She fit right in.

Bluefeather was swiftly becoming very proud and kept sneaking looks at her in the back-bar mirror. She was doing the same to him. She sat there on the bar stool in new jeans so tight he couldn't imagine how she had been able to tuck in her tan shirttail. The folded, turquoise blue scarf tied around her head looked like the crown of the most majestic queen who ever lived. Bluefeather thought all this, and then some.

He walked over to the jukebox and punched out two dollars' worth of tunes at random and asked Marsha to dance. She eased off the stool into his arms and wrapped lightly around him like a snake on a limb. Her chin fit right over his shoulder without any strain. Talk about floating; compared to Marsha all eagles and swans were amateurs. He was suddenly very proud of himself that he could control his agitation at her vanishing insult in Santa Fe. He would not bring it up verbally and would eradicate its existence from his mind. There was no other way he could handle both her and her father's deal.

By the time they finished three or four songs, two other couples had joined them on the dance floor. A whey-bellied miner was yelling every turn. The good times were rolling.

"Hey, Doming, another round for the house."

Since the place was nearly full now, Dominguez and his helper responded to the request with amazing rapidity.

Bluefeather looked at Marsha and asked, "Do you suppose Korbell will allow this party to go on our expense account?"

Marsha had a way of cocking her head to the side like a puppy and doubling the size of her big blues when asked a question. She made him feel that the fate of the galaxy depended on her giving an accurate answer. "I'm sure he wouldn't mind. He only expects results. He doesn't care at all how they come about."

"To Korbell," said Bluefeather, raising his bottle of beer. She anticipated and did the same.

"My God," she said, as if the end of the world had come and passed before she had gotten a good look at it, "I forgot my Agatha Christie book."

"You read her?"

"I love her work. Is that anti-intellectual?"

"Not at all. I've got a copy of Jack London's *Call of the Wild* in my bedroll. I've read it ten times, I suppose, starting when I was twelve or fifteen years old. Anyway, I think Christie is one hell of an underrated psychologist and a jim-dandy maker of puzzles."

Marsha was pleased and started to express it in some way when Bluefeather turned definite attention to an old man just opening the front door.

Bluefeather saw eighty-year-old Dolby enter the bar with his permanent puzzled expression on his face. He was retired from politics— not that he had ever run for office. On the contrary, he had worked in second and third position for U.S. senators, land commissioners, and mayors and as speech writer for most all of them. He had made few enemies, lived well, and had lots of fun until early middle age, when he turned to private endeavors. The wizened old man was dressed just as cleanly as he was shaven. His little fedora was cocked to the side a tad, giving him a slightly rakish look. His comfortable gray suit had grown a little too large for him. His necktie fit his collar perfectly, but the collar hardly touched the wrinkled, scrawny neck. Dolby stopped at the end of the bar and started talking right off to Dominguez, ignoring the noise and activity around him.

"I never saw so many people as there was in town yesterday. I don't understand it. Yesterday was only Friday," Dolby said.

Dominguez answered patiently, "There was a funeral. Old man Mullins was buried."

Dolby left the end of the bar and headed for the only empty stool next to Bluefeather, muttering, "I meant to go to that funeral. Musta forgot."

"Howdy, Dolby. You're looking frisky."

Dolby totally ignored Bluefeather, struggling carefully onto the bar stool, still talking to himself. "Musta forgot." The old man held a wrestling match with his knobby old hands that ended in a draw.

He said simply to Dominguez, "Whiskey."

He took the glass of straight bourbon, held it toward the light, giving it a good looking at. He turned it up as if to down it all, but only took a tiny sip. Then he turned his little dark eyes, hidden back under two bushes of gray eyebrows, and said, "The moon'll be full next week. Then we can either plant our garden or all go mad and howl with the wolves."

He waited a good thirty seconds and then said sadly, "Of course, our wolves are gone. All gone. But they'll return with the buffalo."

Bluefeather said, "I can't wait."

Marsha joined in, "Me either. I saw a pack in Canada last year...an entire pack...and there was more love between them than in all the romance novels ever written."

Bluefeather started to ask her about Canada, but Dolby was speaking again.

"I don't raise a garden anymore. Sherry does that. My part's eating it."

Everyone in Meanwhile knew Sherry—his young, Harvard-educated, East African from Nairobi, Kenya—who had come to the village several years before, had moved in with Dolby and stayed.

Dominguez asked Dolby, "How's your ex-wife getting along with her new husband?" The question was not out of place, since this was her fifth marriage. She was over sixty years old, and her new husband was under forty. Dolby was either ignoring the bartender or thinking it over. He repositioned his fedora slightly and readjusted the knot in his tie. Then he said, "A woman's love is similar to lightning—it's just as likely to strike a shithouse as a castle."

Bluefeather said to Dolby, since he had been around politics most of his life, "Who is gonna be our next governor?"

The old man raised his whiskey glass to his lips with the same fierce gesture that a thirty-year alcoholic might and then took his tiny, little sip, barely wetting his tongue. Bluefeather was fascinated with this movement, reading into it such a thing as he fools himself or others into believing he's had a big drink. It is a way to share the company of the bar—which, in effect, is Meanwhile's country club—without hangovers and little expense. Maybe, it might simply be for effect.

Dolby leaned over toward Bluefeather without turning his head. His little eyes strained sideways under the hedgerow eyebrows, however, and he said, "Beware of scared dogs and ideologues."

Bluefeather decided that was all the conversation he was going to get about the governor's race and turned his full attention to Marsha, who was politely dancing with a big hay-baler. Bluefeather could see he was pulling her closer than she liked. He started to get up and cut in when she winked and smiled, signaling that it was all right.

She did not enjoy this creature one bit, but she didn't want to create any fuss their first night in the land of hunted treasure. It would not be fair to Korbell or Bluefeather. She kept looking over the hay-baler's shoulder at Bluefeather, wondering what he thought of her. There was something tender about him, but also a force of danger contained in his easy-going and flowing body and manner. She wanted to know more about him, but Korbell had taught her above all, patience, when it was needed.

Bluefeather went to the bathroom to unload about a gallon of beer. The horizontal urinal was plugged-up looking like a dirty horse tank. A lot of it had overflowed onto the floor, but he couldn't wait for a plumber.

When he stepped out, he saw Marsha trying to sit back down at the bar and the hay-baler pulling and pawing at her. She jerked loose and threw a karate chop alongside his jawbone and the side of his neck in the same swift motion. He dropped like a sack of wet sand. Everyone, except Dominguez and Bluefeather, was yelling, clapping, and enjoying the show. The hay person scrambled up with a confused expression. Just as he took a step toward Marsha, Bluefeather side-winded his rudeness. He flopped around and down on his face. Bluefeather could tell by the way he fell that he wouldn't have to kick him. This time the fallen one eased up with great caution and stood there rubbing at his twice-jarred jaw.

Bluefeather had learned from Stan Berkowitz, the mill foreman back at Breen, Colorado, that a smiling man might be holding a knife behind his back. But the hay-baler stuck out his hand, saying with much sincerity, "Dear, dear friends?"

They shook hands. He bought them all a drink—even Dolby, who refused to acknowledge it in any manner. Then he moved over to replenish the music.

Marsha said in a low, scolding voice, "I could have handled him."

"I believe you. Believe me, I believe you."

The secret of a successful evening at a country bar was not to leave too soon or too late. They finished their beers in a casual fashion. Bluefeather ordered up a case of Jim Beam as a peace offering for his friends Willy and Flo. They both liked sipping very brown whiskey.

Bluefeather paid up, giving Marsha the eyeball signal and receiving it in return. Bluefeather laid some money on the bar and yelled, "Drinks for the whole damn house." In the midst of loud, appreciative anticipation, the two of them escaped.

They loaded the whiskey and themselves into the Jeep and backed it up. Bluefeather geared right down the highway out of town. Both were giggling like they had just graduated from first grade.

When the Jeep had been coaxed to the right side of the road, Bluefeather said, "Hey, hon', crack a bottle of Willy's whiskey, will you, please?"

She did. Taking a light sip herself, she waited for a straight stretch of road before handing the bottle to him. Bluefeather was thinking that he might never know any more about Marsha than he did right now, but even so he was going to settle in on the fact that she was one hell of a woman.

Then it smacked him and he blurted out, "God uh mighty, I musta forgot! Old Dolby was Tilton's right hand, and was for a decade, right up until the night he was beheaded."

"That's interesting to know. Very." Marsha said, reaching to take the bottle back, "Do you mind sharing with your assistant?"

"Lord uh mighty no. You can have the whole bottle if you want it."

Bluefeather pulled over at the area's only motel. Got out and checked them into separate rooms. They both thought of the waste. One room. One bed. One view. That would have to do. Both acted as if they would always sleep apart. Both were already getting used to the scent of the other, but they also had been mentored into the dedication of business first. They tumbled in the covers an equal amount of time, trying to remember Korbell's mission assignment. It didn't work. They only thought of one another. Neither would have believed the mind-images of the other.

Five

There it was. Willy Ruger's place. They were topping out over a relatively small timbered mountain. They had seen nothing for about three miles of dirt road but a few blue jays, two does, and a fawn that had crossed the road in front of them. Down in the valley they could see the log house with its barn, corrals, a bunkhouse, pump-house, chicken house, haystack, and a garden area. It looked like a small, secluded village. The meadow grass was already becoming green, and Zia Creek sparkled its eager, winding course a quarter of a mile west of the house. The sage and scattered cacti slowly mixed with the patches of timber bunched around rusty orange bluffs. On to the west, everything fused and thinned as the desert took over. To the north and east the timber thickened so that only the mightiest of cliffs bulged their way through. The mountains stair-stepped up, each higher and lighter blue than the others. If one looked closely, piles of mine tailings could be spotted from the old-time miners' attack on the earth. They had looked and dug here, over a century, for dreams seldom found, and much quicker lost. In a day or so the young couple would be doing the same.

Marsha clasped her hands together and held them to her breasts, uttering, "My God, it is beautiful. It's too much."

Bluefeather suddenly felt right and comfortable and confused at being accompanied by such a saucy, knockout assistant.

The hound dogs came to greet them first, barking furiously, but with tails wagging. There was an old World War II jeep, a pickup, and a sports car parked at random in front of the house. The last meant that Willy's niece, Sally, was home from school. Willy, Flo, and the young Sally all came out on the porch as they pulled to a stop.

Marsha and Bluefeather got out of the jeep. There was much hugging and handshaking with everybody talking at once.

Bluefeather introduced Marsha, and they all gave her welcoming hugs and handshakes.

Bluefeather asked Willy, "How're you getting along, old pardner?"

"Grandy dandy. I went to bed last night with a lot on my mind, I got up this morning and my mind had vanished. I know not where."

Flo asked, "How was the drive out?"

Bluefeather grinned and continued the silly banter. "Just like a frog going to water, steady but by jerks."

Between all the greetings, the introduction of Marsha and vice versa, the petting and saying hello to the hounds, it took them a few minutes to break free and gather up the whiskey gift. When they finally got in the house, things settled down and the sporting activities made haste. It was the time for partying. Bounteous drinks were poured. Joyful toasts were made, and everyone bubbled.

Flo wanted to know if they were hungry. She had a venison roast in the oven. They all stalled at this, settling down to drink and get the necessary small talk done before the eating started—the way things should be when old friends, long apart, get together.

Red-faced Willy's upper body was built like a jeep. Between drinks, he constantly pushed the thin gray-blond hair back on his head. He was fifty years old, but in some ways he was younger, and some ways older. His powerful shoulders and arms were bent forward as if he were reaching for a heavy rock. He had done plenty of that, for sure. When he got up to move across the room for a drink, his log-looking legs broke into a little, short-stepped run. They did the same whether in the house or on a mountain.

Flo was built somewhat like her brother, except she reared back instead of forward to compensate a bit for the two heavy weights hanging from her chest. She had a small waist, considering the fullness of the rest of her, and caused one to think about old photographs of the gay nineties girls. Her weather-lined hands and arms showed all of her forty-six outdoor years, but her face was surprisingly soft. She had always worn a hat, any hat, to block the sun from her short brown hair and constantly thinking hazel eyes.

Sally? Well, Sally was five four and filled out about as perfect as one can get in eighteen years. There was more mischief than anything else exuding from a face that moved from pretty to petulant in an instant. She wore her dark brown hair in pigtails.

"Hey, guess what, Señor Bluefeather Fellini," Sally said, "I finally made it out of high school. There's the proof right there." She pointed to the framed diploma above the couch and cast him a deliberate, flirting glance that without any guessing said, "Look at me. I'm grown up, just like you."

Bluefeather couldn't help but look at her silent suggestions. Sally could see that he saw. She warmed and glowed like a new light bulb in a cool room.

Bluefeather said, "Ain't that just keen," stepping closer to her framed diploma where it hung on the wall. "Congratulations, Sally." That gave them another excuse for a toast. Bluefeather continued, "Going to college this fall?"

Sally looked at Bluefeather, then at her mother and uncle, hesitantly saying, "Well, it all depends."

Flo said, "'Course she is. New Mexico State University over at Las Cruces."

Bluefeather knew that Flo really meant it, but he was also aware that they probably couldn't afford it. Well, that was another damned good reason to find the Mouton '80. At that thought, he asked Willy to show him around the place, since it had been quite a while since he had been here. They got another glass of whiskey each and walked out. The women were visiting like wild ducks behind them.

Willy was very excited, even though he tried to appear calm during the "showing." He was mighty proud of his overhead gas tank, the new pumps, and electric generator. He beamed like a kid on a pony when he showed Bluefeather the rebuilt smokehouse hung with dressed deer, elk, and hog meat. He reared back like a fresh-bred rooster at the solid condition of all the outer buildings, but what really made him preen was the new phone booth on the back porch.

"I like my privacy when I talk on that damn public thing. I never had nobody call me any good news on it yet. When they got that, they come in person."

The two friends sat down on a log by the woodpile, petted the hounds, and got down to serious visiting. It came out that Willy had leased his Virginia Bell Mine down at Hillsboro for three years, but the lease payments had been dropped just this month. That explained both the money to do the improvements on the place and the hesitation in Sally's voice when she spoke of continuing her education. They didn't have any source of income except what Willy hustled from leasing his mines or doing day labor on other men's claims.

The hounds were slobbering with friendliness all over Bluefeather when he noticed one was missing. "Where's Ol' Brown?"

The whiskey and the visiting temporarily lost its effect on Willy as he said, "Lion killed him. Ate him, too. Got three of our goats and a yearling heifer."

Bluefeather said, "Well, you got three dogs left—why can't you go get him?"

"Tried. That's when he killed Old Brown. You know I really ain't much of a hunter, Blue, except for minerals. Just never had the touch."

"Don't worry, ol' pardner. We'll get him while I'm here."

"If he don't bother no more... maybe we oughta just let him..."

"He will. The pickings have been too easy."

"Well, I about..." and he shook his head at the ground.

Bluefeather just couldn't wait any longer to tell Willy about Korbell. Now seemed the appropriate time. When he had finished, he waited expectantly for an enthusiastic reply from his friend and confidant.

Willy didn't say anything. He picked up a stick and started whittling on it with his pocket knife.

Bluefeather ventured, "Seeing what a pitiful financial shape I was in, I didn't see where I had anything to lose."

Willy stopped whittling, closed and pocketed his knife, picked his glass off the log, and drank what little was left in it and said, "Korbell? Well, shoot a monkey. Heard a lot of different things about Korbell. You might oughta use some extra caution with him. Sounds spooky to me."

Bluefeather felt a little bowknot tie itself inside his guts. "How do you mean, spooky?"

"Well, my pa knew Tilton some, and he dealt with Korbell some just before he died. He never could figure him out. One thing though... there's one thing for sure: papa did believe Tilton hid all that bullion somewhere down here. But wine? I never heard of no wine. Not never."

"Well, Willy, I gotta believe it. I saw the papers."

"Anybody can have papers faked."

"You're right, but then why would he put up all this time and money, sending his daughter along to watchdog me, if he didn't believe it himself?"

Willy grinned, "You got me there, Blue. Hellsfire, we'll get to lookin' for the wine startin' tomorrow. Right now I'm so thirsty I could drink mud."

"Here, have a swallow of mine. I want to know all about Sally's school plans."

"Well...she had six hundred dollars saved up to start, but that boyfriend of hers, Harvey Holt, from over at Las Cruces, done conned her out of it."

"What do you mean 'conned her'?"

"Oh, he had a sure bet on something that makes ten dollars to one in two months. Never happens, Blue. Hell, you know that. In the mining business we got 'em like Holt by the hundreds."

"Yeah. Well, what are we gonna do about it? Does she like him a lot?"

"Cain't tell. It's a lonesome country out here for a pretty young woman. He's an entrepreneur of the defecation of bulls." At Bluefeather's quick glance, Willy smiled shyly, saying, "I never thought that last line up. Heard old Dolby saying it." Then he got serious again. "But what I can tell you about Holt is, the son of a bitch laughs at ever thing you say. Makes people think they're great comedians. He'll ha, ha, ha you right out of your bank account."

Bluefeather didn't like what his best friend had told him, but he could not think of the right reason to vocalize at the moment.

Willy started his little turkey trot toward the house. Bluefeather followed, feeling great again.

They had fun like people are born to do. Flo fed them delicious venison, baked potatoes with homemade butter, green beans she had put up from last year's garden, and a peach pie almost as good as Mary's. Not quite though, for in Bluefeather's experienced opinion nothing was as good as Mary's had been. Nothing. They were full of drinks, food, and that incredibly rare feeling shared with friends who don't care what you say, and even less what you do, except to join in.

Marsha acted like she had known these people as long as Bluefeather had. They felt the same about her. She told them about spending a year on a kibbutz in Israel and quoted an old rabbi she had admired. "Rabbi Sharut said that Goliath didn't have a chance against little David, with all his mighty muscles and outsized club, because David and his people were so long experienced hunting and fighting with slingshots, they had even killed lions with them. Why, poor

Goliath was horribly overmatched. David might as well have been armed with a 30.06 rifle. Don't you see? Don't you see how history gets all turned around?"

Willy, who obviously had taken a shine to Marsha, agreed. "You're sure right about that, hon'. Look at the Billy the Kid legend. Thousands of stories and every one different, all swearing they're right. Why, the whole damn thing's a wild guess. There's things that happened during his time, and even mine, that's been told all wrong," and he launched into several examples.

Flo, sensing that he might have "whiskey tongue," interrupted cleverly, asking him to play the banjo. Willy forgot all about talking and put his mind to what really mattered, music and whiskey. Willy was adaptable.

He started out picking "Cotton-eyed Joe," "When the Saints Go Marching Home," and then went on to some real fast steppers.

Sally grabbed Bluefeather by the hand and pulled him up to dance. She saw to it that their fronts were close. So close, it both pleased and embarrassed Bluefeather. He tried to be brave and enjoy it. She could feel that he did and wiggled even closer.

All the women danced with him. Bluefeather couldn't be too flattered by this since he was the only available dancing partner. He relished it just the same. It was still cool this time of year, but everyone was sweating. Bluefeather, being outnumbered three to one, was wetter than the rest. Flo and Sally literally rubbed their precious parts all over him. The longer the whiskey and music went on, the more active the rubbing. It became more disconcerting to Bluefeather. Marsha didn't hold back anything, but she didn't push herself forward enough so that a man could make a clear judgment of her attitude. Bluefeather Fellini was disconcerted. Then Marsha pulled loose from him and did a wild, whirling Israeli dance by herself with her long auburn air flowing out like a wind-whipped flag. She got a standing ovation and bowed accordingly.

Finally, Willy put his banjo down, emptied his whiskey glass, and dogtrotted erratically toward his bedroom, saying, "Grandy dandy."

Sally tripped over the coffee table and just lay there comfortably on a bearskin rug. Bluefeather hoped she wasn't dreaming of Harvey Whats-his-name. Bluefeather and Flo gathered her up and led her to bed in the room where Flo slept.

Then Flo showed Marsha and Bluefeather to separate rooms. Flo said she didn't feel like going to bed yet. She had to clean up the kitchen first. Bluefeather knew she meant that, but he was also aware that she would probably stay up and drink and mess around the kitchen until dawn. He had seen her do just that, scores of times.

Marsha came out in a robe and volunteered to help, but Flo would not hear of it, insisting she'd had a long trip and needed rest.

There they were. Bluefeather wanted to grab Marsha and run her into his room, but he wasn't about to blow away his beloved place in Corrales just for a roll in the sheets. Not now, anyway. Maybe later he would blow up three counties for her. For now though . . . well, he would just go on aching like all frustrated youth. There was no way he could move toward her. He tried valiantly to convince himself that she had been the one who had crawled into bed with him the night he had spent at Korbell's—and lots of other things. He didn't know for sure. Anyway, he pulled himself back.

Flo said, "That's a very high-toned, regular lady, Blue. I hope you get along with her. She's what they call 'a jewel.' Understand?"

His heart did seven fast circles around his chest and he croaked out, "Yessum. I sure do. She likes you guys, too. I can tell."

"Good. Well, I just wanted you to know how much I like your new friend. I feel like she's ours, too, already."

That was all Flo said, right then. He waited. He waited some more, not moving his body purposely, although the surging blood moved parts of him. He went in and put on his robe and then slipped out into the hallway. He had decided that the only thing left in the universe that could give him the help he needed was some cool, fresh, mountain air.

He walked softly down the hallway and out on the porch. He had forgotten Flo, and almost everything, except Marsha. Flo was in the kitchen in her robe now, wiping off the cabinet. She spotted Bluefeather and motioned him to come inside. He had no choice. He tried to pull and hold the robe so she could not see his obvious problem. It did not work.

She poured him a drink, whispering, "Couldn't sleep, huh?"

He, being so suddenly sobered, took half the glass in one swallow saying, "Naw. I got a lot on my mind."

She reached down and grabbed him, saying, "I can see what you've got on your mind, Blue dear."

Without letting anything loose, she led him right out on the porch like a kid pulling a little red wagon. He went along for fear of bodily injury. Now she turned loose, as her robe fell apart too. There it was, the uppers big and inviting as bowls of ice cream, and the dark mount of Venus hairy as a black wolf pelt.

"I haven't been with a man since me and Crazy Dugan split."

"When was that?" Bluefeather foolishly gasped out.

"A year and six days and about three hours." Flo grabbed one of his hands and put it on her breast. The other she shoved between her legs. "See?" She said.

He couldn't see, but he sure as all hell could feel. She sat down on the porch and spread her strong legs wide in the ready, aim, fire position.

Bluefeather hesitated perhaps a second, thinking what Old Grinder the Gringo had once told him: "A hard-on ain't got no conscience."

Being momentarily weak-willed and out of control, he just dived right in, at the same time feeling that he was certainly young and healthy, so that left him nothing to be but kind and generous. It was quite a ride.

Flo bucked and wiggled, getting unfelt splinters in her rear. She moaned and hissed until Bluefeather got frightened and put his hand over her mouth. She clawed him in the back of the head until he felt like he had been half scalped and spurred her bare heels into his butt like a champion bronc rider.

She rasped out, "Find the pearl, honey darling. Find the pearl."

He must have found it, because he finally became conscious again. They were both unmoving now except for their struggling lungs. Bluefeather rolled off and barely clutched the edge of the porch before falling on the ground flat on his back.

A happy face soon gleamed dreamily down at him, saying, "You may not get on or off very pretty, darling, but you've sure got a pile-driving ass."

Bluefeather took a deep gulp of cool, mountain air and said, "Why, thank you, Flo."

The party was mostly over.

■ ■ ■

Six

Bluefeather and Willy went over the maps until they became blurs to their searching eyes. Willy knew the location of most of the mines, as well as their history, but there were rumors of three old tunnels that even he had never located. Somehow, Korbell had come up with faded maps to the Commonwealth, the Dutch Joe, and the Copper Star. Willy decided against taking the mules because the trails were rough, but of no great distance.

They bumped, ground, twisted, and jolted their way as far as the jeep could make it. It looked like a day's backpacking into the upper wilderness. Marsha stayed right in there, not complaining or even commenting. None of them did. The altitude and the steep climb, along with an intentionally subdued sense of possible discovery, took the chatter from their lungs.

They had lunch at about eight thousand feet. Up ahead a bit, they could see the first large stand of aspen. The grayish white bark of the trees stood out like battalions of daytime ghosts against the deep-shadowed undergrowth of the mountain. The tender, light green leaves trembled in the mountain breeze as if afflicted by a billion tiny frights a minute. To the west they could see over seventy miles across land fractured, eroded, and wind-singed into sienna, burnt orange, vermilion, and every hue of blue, violet, and velvet-purple that the eye could stand to behold. Then the land rose again to form a whole hog-backed horizon even deeper blue than the sister sky.

Bluefeather felt Marsha absorbing the ageless message of this vastness, just as he was. He was pleased without being totally aware of why. There was a combination of intensity and serenity as she looked across the immense southwestern earth as if she were somehow absorbing it into her being. Her own coloring, silhouetted against the arced sky, seemed to match and meld with the Indian-trod, snake- and lizard-crawled, coyote- and bobcat-traversed, spread-out land.

Bluefeather was developing an ancient aching, longing, for her. He could no more explain it than he could the development of penguins or cosmic dust. For now he would struggle to not even try. Besides, she was probably a spy. Even so—forgetting Korbell—he wondered if it would make any difference if she were a Mata Hari. He doubted if it would change his unformed feeling for her at all.

Willy was standing, looking up the rock-choked canyon facing them. It was a bitching climb. The old burro trail to the mine had been washed out long ago, leaving jagged boulders and wind-fallen trees covering a big part of it. They moved on up, constantly clambering over, down, and up again. They were sometimes on their hands and knees like awkward rock squirrels, but they must not stop now.

Bluefeather let Willy lead with Marsha in between them. Willy was older, slower, but a lot more knowledgeable in selecting the erratic trail. He maintained a slow but steady pace that would finally get them to their destination without killing them off. Sometimes, when the earth leveled slightly, he would break into his little trot.

No wonder Willy had lost two inches of height since he passed the forties. With the hundreds of climbs, with packing equipment up the mountains, and with carrying sample rocks down, over and over, it seemed a small miracle that he was more than four feet tall.

Not even the struggle of ascent nor the shortness of high altitude breath could keep Bluefeather from taking many glances at the rear view of a moving, twisting Marsha. There was a sensual grace about the movement of her long legs over, under, and around the hard rocks. He couldn't help it. He wanted to roll her in the shade. The extra breath he expelled at these many varied thoughts caused his lungs to work harder than otherwise.

They were past nine thousand feet now, and all wondered if they were going to run out of mountain before they found the mine. Then Willy and Bluefeather discovered pieces of green malachite copper. Marsha became grade school excited at this and acted like she was on an Easter egg hunt.

For just a few moments, she was a little girl back in her past some- where, ohing and ahing excitedly as she found the scattered pieces of the vein. Then she regained her necessary stoicism.

Suddenly, they all were side by side, an hour till sundown, staring at the mine entrance. They had found it. It had an extensive waste pile with copper disseminated all through it. Bluefeather guessed that the tunnel would be over a thousand feet deep. The mountain had shed some of its skin in a vain effort to hide the insult of the hole dug into its guts.

There was only a small opening left at the top of the tunnel. Bluefeather and Marsha wanted to go in right off, but Willy wisely said it would be better to pitch camp, gather wood, and cook supper while they still had time before dark. Willy was right, of course.

After the fire was going, Bluefeather and Marsha lay back on their bedrolls, staring at the hypnotic fire, smelling the smoke and the venison Willy cooked in the skillet.

Bluefeather was more tired than he had realized. Marsha's eyelids drooped almost shut. Then she jerked her head up and strained her wondrous, blue eyes wide. She was a stayer. She had volunteered to cook, but Willy would not allow it. Cooking outdoors was one of his prides. At home, Flo and Sally were welcome to it, but up here it was his domain. He had thrown several wads of sourdough in the combination skillet and Dutch oven to go with the venison. They ate till the wild meat and bread were all gone. Then he handed them a few dried apricots to wash down with big tins of hot coffee. They made a weak effort to visit. It did not work. They scoured the aluminum dishes by rubbing them out with clean mountain dirt, finishing them off with a precious splash of water.

They crawled into their bedrolls and were asleep before they had time to hear the night birds sing or the coyotes call.

The morning comes early on top of mountains. The sun gets first shot there. Willy had gotten up at daylight and scouted around, finding springs that were actually the headwaters of Zia Creek. He remembered now that his father had brought him up here, from a different direction when he was a kid, but the mine had been completely caved-in back then. That at least meant the mine had been opened since Tilton's time, even though the tunnel had nearly filled again. There was a remote chance of discovery this day.

Bluefeather gathered some more wood while Marsha went to the cold spring to wash. She returned to the new fire, combing at her hair. Her face had paled from the cold water, but she appeared fresh and eager for the day's adventures.

They ate the sizzling bacon and biscuits ravenously and got their gear ready to enter the mine by the time the sun had first touched the mesas on the desert floor so far below.

Now Bluefeather took the lead, crawling in the opening with his battery light. Marsha also had one. Willy carried an old, open-flame carbide light to detect poison gas if it was waiting silently, invisibly.

Willy and Marsha were right behind Bluefeather as he moved the light about the tunnel. There was a small pool of water in the overly large room in front of them. He had seen this before so many times that it pained him. The miners had found a profitable pocket of ore here and had carved out the dangerously large room in front of them. This was both greedy and foolish, because a cave-in here would not only have risked the lives of the workers, but it could also have closed the mine, necessitating digging another costly entrance. The stope went up about thirty feet above them. Bluefeather checked it as closely as possible with his light. It looked as if it would hold, although there were two piles of smashed rocks that had fallen to the tunnel floor at some time.

He led them around the edge of the pool. The lights showed the water to be so clear that the gravels, some as small as grains of sand, could be seen. The bits of oxidized malachite, azurite, and sulfide copper shined under the water like a sultan's tomb. It was just as silent. It is not known for sure why, but when people first speak in a mine tunnel, they do so softly, as they would in a library or church. Maybe being underground, at the mercy of a pierced mountain with millions of tons of rocks hanging above one's head, creates a more holy feeling than usual.

Bluefeather whispered, "Watch out for loose rock. The idiots raped another mine."

Willy excused the old-timers, whispering back, "I can understand why. They could only afford to haul high-grade from this inaccessible bitch."

Marsha spoke softer even than the others, "I feel like we just walked through time into an old, old world."

Bluefeather eagerly answered, "You got it right, lady. The rock still in place here is way over thirty million years old and was first touched by humans less that a hundred years back."

They moved carefully on. Willy and Bluefeather tapped the walls with their prospector's picks, searching for a hollow sound that might reveal a hidden side drift. The deeper they moved the better the ore looked to Bluefeather. Beyond his initial resentment, he marveled at the determination of the old-timers who had dug the tunnel for more than a thousand feet with crude hand tools, plunging for the heart of the noble mountain. The vein had a general strike northeast to southwest. It dipped to the southeast. It was in a porphyry and gneiss formation. Bluefeather knew this was good host rock for a large deposit of copper, but that was not what they were after. He almost laughed aloud when he remembered they were after wine. Wine.

They looked, too, for Tilton's metal of long ago, mined and melted and cooled into solid bars of bullion. As far as Bluefeather was concerned, the sixty cases of lost wine would do just fine. Any treasure would do, but gold. That had taken away his family—one yet unborn.

Korbell had hired him to find just the wine. Thinking of Korbell, Bluefeather inadvertently blurted out, "Don't know what we're supposed to do...what...how..."

The other two lights danced about nervously at the shock of his voice. Bluefeather felt like he had been caught pissing in the kitchen sink.

They had pecked at every foot of the tunnel on the way in. To the best of their judgment, the tunnel had not been altered. It was solid, natural rock all around. Anyway, it was frivolous to think they would find the cache on the first try. All felt a little let down, but then most everyone expects mountains to give too much too quickly. Mountains never let one know anything for sure. They only make one think so.

The three were about twenty paces from the face of the tunnel, on their way back out, when Bluefeather halted, hearing the haunting sound of an Indian flute. The others stopped, watching him, eyes wide. At first the sound came so softly that he thought it was emanating out of his head instead of into it. Then the sound swelled rapidly. Bluefeather wondered if he was the only one to hear it. His question was answered when he felt Marsha's hand grasp his upper arm for a fleeting moment.

Bluefeather turned around and shined his light back into the tunnel. Suddenly, the music stopped. There was a silence so profound that it seemed to have a singular existence, with its power being in its non-being. A small pebble fell from the ceiling to bounce on the tunnel floor, making a noise—to the only listeners—far beyond its true size. Then a larger one fell, and another. Then the face of the tunnel bulged out like a huge, stone balloon and shattered, sending large pieces of rock rolling forward. The bluish brown dust puffed forward from the rubble. A rumbling noise came from the tunnel and the bowels of the mountain like the mighty garbled voices of arguing giants. The entire face of the tunnel, the ceiling, and the hang and foot-walls started falling toward them.

Bluefeather grabbed Marsha and Willy, hurling them forward, screaming, "Run, dammit, run!"

Bluefeather held himself back with great difficulty. The tunnel filled, and its crumbling, grinding fullness moved toward them like a stone tidal wave. The air forced out by the jumbled tons of rock filling the void blasted the dust forward around and ahead of them. Bluefeather was choking, shouting at the other two, without knowing what he said. He could hear and feel the forces moving toward them like a herd of rampaging elephants on their heels. Bluefeather reached out blindly with his wildly groping hands, pushing, dragging them toward the tunnel entrance. He had lost all sense of direction and con-stantly ricocheted off the walls. Somehow he could hear Marsha and Willy coughing even in the terrible roar, above his own rasping lungs. They were slowing, for he was having to manhandle them forward, cursing, cajoling more each instant. The dust was almost unbreathable now. He felt Marsha leaning, gasping, against a wall.

He screamed right at her ear, "Hold on!" He shoved her hands into the back of his belt and felt them tighten. They moved forward. It was all darkness. The noise and shaking of the tunnel was comparable to attending a ballet during an earthquake.

They stumbled over Willy, who had fallen to his knees. Bluefeather strained up as he lifted Willy. All three struggled on. They could feel the blasts of air on their backs growing stronger, which meant the tumbling rocky guts of the mountain were gaining on them, closing in, to form a multiple, unknown grave. So-called TIME was nonexistent, because they had already experienced many light years in the thousand-odd feet of the man-made wound in the now angry mountain.

The lights had long been lost. The absolute darkness was a fear-some thing, but the as-yet solid sidewalls ahead kept them moving, stumbling erratically forward. Bluefeather could sense Willy's strength leaving his powerful old body as his lungs closed down from the dust so thick they could have been buried in midair. He could also feel Marsha's weight dragging more as the belt almost cut off his circula-tion. If it would just hold. He felt his being becoming as cloudy as the tunnel dust, certain that he was entirely without air breathing the boiling mass in and out with an effort that was ripping his lungs loose and turning his blood to cement.

All of a sudden, there was a numbness all over him—the kind that must come when a person gives in to the false warmth of a blizzard and dies in comfort. It was a teasing temptation to be seduced by the pursuing rock. All he would have to do was fall with his comrades, and in four or five seconds there would be no more agonizing effort to breathe, to find light, to live. There would be no more pain. Nothing.

Just then, he felt light. Yes, it was there. The flicker of light that pushed through the small opening at the top of the tunnel was quickly suffused with the dust, but it was definitely there, a short distance ahead of them. With the tiny beam of beckoning sun, his lungs found more air. They were all three on their hands and knees, clawing across sharp-edged rocks up toward the shiny beacon from the beckoning outer world. The tunnel narrowed ahead of them and fell, roaring, like a thousand dueling lions behind them.

With the power-granting, adrenalin-charged force that comes when all of life is based on surviving a second, or a fraction thereof, Bluefeather grabbed Marsha and hurled her like a spear ahead of Willy. It was single file for them now.

Bluefeather pushed at Willy's scrambling feet, yelling a continuous chorus of "Go. Go. Go. Go."

He could feel the mountain's masonry falling after them, making a last desperate effort to devour their flailing bodies before they reached the outer surface of its epidermis to continue life.

"Go, Marsha, Go."

Bluefeather did not remember the last few feet to the exit. He did recall rolling joyfully down the bruising rock pile, once outside, as if playing on a feather bed. He turned and watched the inside of the mountain seal the crawlway so full that several fresh azurite specimens tumbled outside, rolling down a few feet before stopping.

All three were on their hands and knees again, coughing, spitting, and coughing more. Finally, the spasms slowed and then quit. They lay back spent and limp as worn-out ropes. Bluefeather stared into the sky, trying to see beyond the blue. The sky moved back and forth and pulsated into violets and greens. It had holes and protrusions like the ground, or a cloud mass. He had just now, after thirty-odd years, learned to really see. One tiny, white cloud crossed his vision, slowly enlarging, growing by itself and then evaporating away to nothingness. He knew there was no such thing as nothing becoming nothing, so the cloud must simply have changed into another form.

The sky was the second most beautiful thing his agitated eyes had ever seen. The height of the mountain that had almost claimed them created a brisk, clean wind that refreshed their lungs and consequently their entire bodies. The first most beautiful thing on earth raised its head and turned to him speaking, "Would you care to discuss the stabilization of the world political situation, Blue?" Marsha gasped.

"Dearest Marsha," he coughed out, "it probably would be more appropriate than discussing religion. I'm afraid I've just used up my year's allotment of prayers."

It was hard for him to believe, but the Korbell clan smile radiated enchantingly from her dusty face like a second, white sun. "We wouldn't have made it without you, Blue."

"No. No, it took all three of us."

Willy let out a comforting sigh and said, "The price of metal just dropped today, but... it'll go back up in a week or two."

Then they all laughed at their silliness, which was standard, anyway, until they realized the shaking of their mirth was stirring their coughing again.

They rested a few minutes. Each one struggled to a sitting position, moving joints and limbs to test for dislocated or broken bones. There did not appear to be any, but they were a ragged, skinned, and bruised threesome.

Willy said, pragmatically, "We've got to get off this mountain before the soreness sets in."

It was a tough decision to make, but he was absolutely right. Bluefeather stood, wobbling and held out his hand to Marsha.

She said, "Thanks, but I have to know if I can do it on my own." She did.

Willy made it, too. Then they started laughing and hugging one another again. The slightly hysterical fun was soon negated by another resounding spell of coughing. After that they drank deeply from their canteens, filled them again from the birthplace of Zia Creek, gathered and packed their gear and moved out, limping down the mountain, feeling like the sole survivors of the Hundred Years War.

When they came across a rare, smooth place, Willy would break into his little shuffling dogtrot as if nothing had happened. Something had though. They all three knew it. A warning? An event? Maybe. Maybe.

Willy and Bluefeather had climbed and struggled over a lot of mountains and deserts together before today, but now Marsha had joined them. They were bound together by the unbreakable bond that can only exist between humans who have successfully survived facing the spectra together. Beauty of the voice and flesh would eventually break, but not this. The reality of the thought made the young man's tired feet bounce like a whore's butt on a steel-spring mattress. Both thoughts were good. The mountain swiftly shrunk.

Seven

Willy was right about the soreness afflicting them. They limped around like they had entertained lions in the Roman Coliseum. Flo and Sally had little sympathy. What with keeping everyone fed, clothes washed, the log house clean, chickens, mules, and hogs fed and watered, the garden weeded and watered, along with a few other chores, they were a mite busy. To be fair, Marsha pitched in and helped with the household chores. Willy's back was out. He couldn't do much but lay around in agony with his legs propped up.

Bluefeather was in the kitchen drying dishes for Sally.

"So, what kinda guy is this Harvey House I've hearing so much about?"

"They told you already, huh? But the name is Holt. H.O.L.T. They don't like him, you know? You probably wouldn't either."

"That's not the point, little darling. Do you?"

"Well, I did, or at least I thought I did, but I'm gonna break it off. Old dumb me...it took me a year to find out what an asshole he really is. I'm gonna break it off the next time he phones."

"Have you told Willy and Flo that?"

"No, I don't want them to be too self-satisfied. When he 'no-shows' for a few weeks, they'll catch on."

"Poor ol' Harvey Wallbanger."

"Mr. Harvey Shit is more like it."

"Say, don't they teach you kids anything past four letters in school?"

"I learned to talk like that listening to you and Willy long ago, Blue dear."

Marsha and Flo were pulling the new weeds out of the tomato patch when the phone rang out on the porch. Since Sally had her hands in soapy water and Willy would never make it from the couch in time, Bluefeather answered. The connection was bad, but he finally figured out that it was Willy's lawyer calling from Las Cruces. He obviously thought he was talking to Willy. Bluefeather puzzled the pieces together from the static noise of the phone and surmised that the lease had now been dropped on Willy's Hillsboro silver mines.

Bluefeather muttered to himself, "Jesus H. Christmas Christ. I'd rather be kicked in the belly by a karate champion than tell these folks that news."

He stood there by the phone trying to figure how to give the message easily. He walked out and circled the jeep about three times. Before he thought about it, he lit up a forbidden cigarette. Being so weak-willed made him feel worse. He stomped and twisted the smoke out of sight in the earth.

"Sheeeit. I might as well just go in and get it over with." He walked inside and said, "Willy, I sure hate to tell you this."

Willy was propped up on a pillow now, sensing something coming down. When Bluefeather told him about the phone call, he simply said, "See? I told you nobody ever calls you with good news on them damn things. Hell, it's happened before, Blue. You know? You know as well as I do it'll happen again. We ain't gonna die from it."

"Yeah, I know. All right. But I'm just worried about you guys."

"Don't worry your head about it. Everything will be okay. You hear? We'll figure out something."

"You're damn right we'll figure out something, old pardner. We'll pull off this Korbell deal, I tell you. We'll find that fancy wine. And not only that, we've got nearly six months of full expenses paid ahead of us. Hellsfire, we never had that much time on a deal ever before."

"You got that gathered up right, Blue."

Bluefeather knew that inside the old man was hurting, but he sure wouldn't let it show. He went back to the kitchen to help Sally, but she had already finished putting the dishes away. He intended to make some light, clever remark, but she did not give him a chance.

"I heard."

"Well now, Sally..."

She turned her perky little face to him saying, "Look, Blue, I'm used to this kind of thing happening. My God, don't look so stricken. It's not the end. There are lots of things I can do in this cockeyed world besides being a veterinarian."

"I know you can, hon'. It's just that you'd be such a good one, and your mother and Willy wanted it so much for you."

She was wiping the sink and table dry with a sponge. She squeezed it out, put it down, and stepped right up in front of him with her bold, firm little breasts barely touching him, put her hands on his shoulders, looked up and said, "Now, you listen to me, Bluefeather Fellini. I'm a big, little girl with a long way to go yet. You...you old folks just dig out your own skunks and quit worrying about me."

He hugged her up close and softly caressed her soft brown hair, knowing she was false fronting with a lot of painful courage, but the warm, little body spun his thinking machinery around. She clung to him like a spider web. He decided to go fishing and cool off.

Bluefeather gathered up his gear and sneaked out the back door, heading for Zia Creek. He forgot about all the rock bruises as he made his way through the few head of cows and on across the open grassy meadow into the trees.

Chipmunks darted from rock to rock, chattering at him. A brown squirrel shimmied up a tree and peeked around the edge, observing the intruder. A magpie flashed swift glances of black and white feathers through the limbs, squawking to all the other inhabitants of the woods.

There was no way out of it; he had to deliver for Korbell...and therefore for Willy and Company. He felt a little bit foolish, but vowed to deliver that wine to the great man's cellar, no matter what he would have to do. A lot was at stake now. He could take care of Willy and Flo's payments on the home place for a while, but it was about three months before Sally would have to prepare for college, if she was to make the first semester.

On the other hand, he did not really know if the wine existed, in spite of all the documents Korbell had shown him. At the same time, he couldn't figure what other use Korbell could possibly have for him. Was he making too much out of it? Maybe it really was just the wine. Somehow, though, he had the feeling of other invisible movements and plots.

Where did Marsha really fit in? She was beginning to obsess his thoughts. She was as much a mystery as her adopted father. Adopted? Hah. Well, no matter how much he had desired her, and that was considerably, he had been unable to bring himself to make any sort of move on her. It wasn't just bedding down with her, although that thought made the roots of his teeth ache and his blood turn to whitewater rapids, but there was an indefinable aura about her that held him back. True, she had been capable and solid on every count, so far, just as Korbell had said. Bluefeather still had a feeling, though, that she was there just to watch him. He had unintentionally caught her giving him surreptitious glances, like a spy. But what for? Well, if the wine story was true, Korbell certainly would not want him skipping off to France with it. Still, he had to admit Marsha had been open and warm with all of them, fitting in better than blood kin.

He had learned little about her past and had even suppressed his curiosity, just as he had the lust for her body. It was difficult, maybe impossible, for him to let the fact surface that he wanted her for all time. This sort of thing had last happened to him at Breen. He wasn't sure he was "horse" enough to have something that precious destroyed again. He had always just moved right in and found out quickly. His unnatural reticence was puzzling.

Bluefeather unconsciously entered a private circle of trees and oak brush. He sat down in the thick grass, leaning back against a tree, enjoying the sun's blessings more than his thoughts.

Sally tiptoed into the opening. She had her own rod and reel. Very carefully she dropped the hook until it caught in Bluefeather's shirt. Then she easily, slowly reeled it in. He muttered something, but didn't awaken completely. Grinning, she sat down in front of him after removing the hook from his shirt and felt warm and melting as she stared at his—to her—perfect features. She could have shared this private time with him for years. She was as sure of that as all young women are at least once.

He awakened slowly, surprised that he had dozed off. There in front of him sat Sally with her legs crossed under her. If he remembered correctly, she had been wearing Levis just a short time back. Now she had on a soft, cotton dress. She tucked the skirt into her crotch, which caused the hem to pull up, revealing a goodly portion of her smooth thighs.

"What are you doing out here?" he asked.

"Oh . . . a notion struck me back there in the kitchen that I wanted to go fishing with you. You're pretty when you sleep." She was grinning at him in a lopsided way. "Say, Blue, forgive me if you wish, but I'm going to get personal."

"Fire away."

"Are you getting it on with the redhead?"

"Boy! That's sure as hell personal all right. Where'd you learn to talk like that? Besides, her hair is auburn."

"Red, auburn, dark pink, what's the difference? You haven't answered my question."

"Well, it's none of your business, Sally, but, no, I'm not."

"What's the matter? You afraid you might blow your deal with Korbell?"

The night in Korbell's guest room when one of his adopted ladies had certainly adopted the wadding out of him flashed into Bluefeather's memory store again. Had it been Marsha?

When he did not answer immediately, Sally pushed forward with, "Go on, Blue. Admit you're stymied. I can tell you are wanting her. What's holding you back?"

"Okay. Okay. You're the psychologist. You tell me."

"I think you're really hung up on her, but afraid to admit it."

He had to agree that Sally might be right, but since he did not know for sure, he just plucked a stem of grass and started chewing on it.

Sally raised her legs up, holding her knees together. She constantly now spread them casually apart and back together in a nervous gesture. It was not consciously meant to tease him, but it was driving him a little mad and a little angry at both of them.

He could see all the way down her leg to her loose, flimsy panties before she closed them each time. He saw more than he thought he should, and looked away embarrassed. He was beginning to perspire and breathe heavier. His eyes returned to her. Then he raised his eyes to hers and the feeling that flowed back and forth between them was as old and new as birth.

She slowly spread her legs. Oddly, there was nothing lewd in her movement—just an eternal sensuality, an offering, a true gift.

He moved to her, and they lay in the grass, kissing, feeling, as the young of all earthly beings have always done, and always will. Ordained.

She rolled over on her back and turned her head to one side. Bluefeather did not remember her partial disrobing, but she had, because he was kissing her tight little breasts and feeling her dampness without any wearing apparel infringing.

He held back as long as he could. Then he moved. It wasn't all the way and it wasn't violent; more like the waves of a small lake lapping at the near shore. He felt her tiny convulsions under him and knew he must separate their bodies glued with the sweat of heavy courting. She knew instantly he was pulling away from her. She also knew that heavy petting was the most they would ever have together of physical love, but she couldn't help but feel thrilled that he was in pain doing so. Honor. Damn that honor. Too late.

Then she took his face in both her hands and looked him squarely in the eyes. "That was beautiful, Blue."

"Yes it was."

"I've got a confession to make."

He waited.

"I've watched you craving Marsha until it made me hotter than frying grease ... besides, I've been wanting you for two or three years."

"Quit talking like that. My Lord, Sally, you'll get kicked out of college before you even get started."

"I don't care. I'm only talking to you, my friend, my amigo, my amico, my lost amour."

"That would have been the first?"

"Yep, numero uno."

"Oh, my God." His brain convulsed as he realized she was still a virgin and he had almost taken her offer from pure weakness of desire. Trying to be a decent fellow often creates a terrible time of turmoil. He hurt worse than he had after the mine had assaulted them. Then he asked her, "Why me?"

"Why not you? I need to know about these things someday, and you, my old and beloved friend, seemed to be suffering."

"I wouldn't argue with that, even if I knew how—which I don't."

"Good, now that's settled. Go on and enjoy your fishing."

"Oh no, little girl, not after what you put me through. You're going with me, but I insist you fish the other side of the creek." At her puzzled stare, he said, "It's the only safe way. You can't get pregnant at that distance."

"You bastard," she said, hitting him in loving mockery on the shoulder.

They fished until almost dark before they caught enough for a meal. Their timing was off. It had been for several hours.

■ ■ ■

Eight

Bluefeather was fishing alone this time. His luck was better. He was having a pretty good joust with the trout. He had banked six ten-to-fourteen-inch rainbows and one ten-inch brown. There was a five-foot hole of water just before a curve in the creek, where he had fished a hundred times. It was circled by brush. He eased up, ducking low, and dropped the hooks loaded with fireball salmon eggs. The idea was not to be seen and to walk so lightly that the ground didn't vibrate and notify the fish of an alien presence.

Instantly, he felt the first tentative tug and he took it. He jerked the fish out shiny wet, flopping on the bank behind him. Bluefeather knew before the hooked fish broke the water that it was the biggest catch of the day. A sixteen-inch brown was as big a fish as the Zia Creek could support.

He was especially elated because the wary browns were difficult to catch and highly prized in this part of the state. Besides, the size of the day's catch was enough for a good meal at the Ruger household today.

He removed the hook from the slick-spotted brown's throat and cleaned and gutted his entire catch, feeling a keen sense of accomplishment at having the privilege of supplying Flo's table with a fresh feast.

As he placed the trout in his creel, he heard a flute wafting a lovely melody across the creek. He knew at once: it was Dancing Bear sitting way up in the pine tree nearest the Zia, his head and arms moving in rhythm with the music. He played on as if Bluefeather didn't exist.

"Hey, Dancing Bear. Hey, it's me."

Dancing Bear went right on playing, ignoring his client's voice. Instantly, he was on a lower limb with his back still turned toward Bluefeather.

"You old bastard, that ain't any way to treat your humble subject."

Just that quickly, before Bluefeather finished the sentence, Dancing Bear sat right across from him on a cluster of boulders, smoking a peace pipe, making signs to the four winds and chanting noises that sounded like he had a croaking bullfrog for accompaniment. Maybe he did.

"Dear brudder," he said, "a very good morning at you."

"It isn't morning, Bear. Can't you tell it's late afternoon?"

"Cannot tell that thing. Time all the same over here."

"Where've you been? We damn near got killed in that copper tunnel."

"Chure. Chure. I play the music for you in the hole of the mountain."

"How...how the hell was I to know what you meant? People play music to sing and dance and make love by."

"You got to learn some of these days, for sure. Me, Mr. Dancing Bear, I only point the way. You got to go do the right thing by your own self. That's the way it is. I have no say on that."

Bluefeather gritted his teeth, knotted his jaws, and said, "I've told you please, please, don't use that confusing dialect. I can't understand it. You savvy?"

Dancing Bear's mouth smiled into a half moon. He was silent, motionless. Bluefeather threw his fishing pole on the ground and started to cross the creek. Bear raised a palm toward him as Bluefeather stopped, saying, "Just what kind of spirit guide are you anyway, speaking in riddles and mysteries to a poor mortal, leaving me alone to figure out all these complicated problems? You're the spirit guide after all. Well, let's have some simple, helpful guidance for a change. How about it, ol' pard? Huh? Huh?"

"I've got many business to do. I been here on the fourth level about a hunnert years. Gotta get more busy. Authority is expecting me to move up."

"Move up? What do you mean?"

"I think about seven more to go before Authority give me thousand year vacation. Some peoples make two, three levels at one jump. Me...Bear...I been here on this same level about a hunnert years."

"You said that already."

"Don't talk about Authority with voice like lion in steel trap."

"I didn't mean anything by it...it's just a manner of speaking. Hey, I'm sorry, Bear."

"Now that's a good thing to hear, dear brudder."

"Okay, all right. I've got a bunch of problems and you haven't been around when I needed you, that's all."

"I been aroun' some. You maybe so busy worryin' you not see me."

"Well, I can't go around looking up at tree limbs and ceilings for you all the time, or I'd trip over something and break my cockeyed neck. Now, you know all that, don't you?"

"Maybe so that's true what you say. Maybe it don't make any difference where I'm at the way you always lookin' at that red girl. You gonna fall and break something you love more'n your neck, you not careful. Huh? Huh?" He imitated Bluefeather and let out a single continuous roar of mirth.

Bluefeather's chemicals were jumping around in his body to the point that his blood felt like it was simmering. It caused his mind-voice to click in. "That Indian guide is laughing at me so hard inside, he's having to hold his ribs to keep them from busting out of his body." He could hear the laughter spewing out now like steam from a starting-up train. Not even a spirit guide could control such comicality. Bluefeather was embarrassed and checked himself to see if anything was hanging out of his trousers. He felt around to the rear. Everything seemed covered. This waggish wimp was laughing at him just for the fun of it. Making sport of him for no reason.

"You gonna fall and break...your..."

Bluefeather interrupted the happily teasing voice and whatever raffish thoughts were in Dancing Bear's head with, "Listen here, Bear. If I could sail around in the air like you do, I'd fly over there and stomp enough shit out of you to fertilize Texas...just for the fun of it, of course."

"Be mighty big job. Why not fertilize Rhode Island? Won't take near as long."

"Look. I don't need any more funnin' around with you. No more smart-ass cracks. I need some serious advice and help. You hear, Bear? Get serious. Now, come on...please...perty please."

"That red girl...she bother you all over, huh?"

"Well, except for her being an all-around good hand, I don't know much about her."

"Hah. Now you get close at truth. Maybe so you are afraid to know more."

"I'm not afraid of anything. Well, not much anyway."

"Hah, again. You know red girl pretty like rainbow over blue lake. Pretty like little fawn playin' on long green grass of meadow. Pretty like feathered arrow flyin' through air. Pretty like..."

"Awww, oh, buzzard droppings on a dead stick, cut out that whimsical crap. If you don't cooperate, I'm coming after you when I die."

"You are not ready to crash through and come over here with me, yet."

"Well, when I am, your heart may belong to Authority, but your ass is gonna belong to me. You hear, ol' friend?"

"I hear hot wind blowin' over garbage dump."

"What do you know about garbage dumps, anyway?"

"I see 'em all over the world where I go to help. I see about a hunnert thousand...and the whole world soon gonna be one big dump. How am I gonna help people clean up their lives if they're livin' in dirty dirt?"

"Well, I'll be a puking dog. If I haven't inherited an ecologist for a guiding spirit. Hey. Hey, Dancing Bear, do you belong to one of those fix-everything-up clubs?"

"No, we make clubs out of a sharp rock with stick tied on it with rawhide. Good for fighting, huntin' and..." Dancing Bear's hands were pantomiming the construction of a tomahawk.

Bluefeather realized that he must change the direction of the conversation. He couldn't force Dancing Bear into simple, clear statements. He didn't know how. "Well, Mr. Bear, what should I know about the red lady? You tell me."

"She let you know when she ready. Squaws always do that."

Bluefeather started to tell him Marsha was not a squaw and then decided that would be a waste.

"Marsha is so pleasant about everything—enjoys every little thing so much—and she's dedicated to our search. There is no way to tell what she is thinking."

"I say to you, dear brudder, you will know this thing when red lady slide on mountain."

"That's it? That's all the help I'm gonna get?"

"I tell plenty. Use the beans in your head."

"Bear, you...you're talking under water. All I'm getting is bubbles."

"That is right. See the idee?" he said with a pleased giggle.

Bluefeather truly appreciated Dancing Bear's use of his mentor, Grinder's, words, but he still couldn't catch the message he knew was there somewhere. It always was. Always.

"Then just tell me this. Is Korbell lying to me about Tilton's wine?"

"Korbell man, he talks circles in circles. Someday circle get so small it make a dot."

"Look here, I'm not asking for instant miracles. I've finally caught on that I'm gonna have to do most of this on my own. That's the way it's supposed to be. But why in hell can't you just give me a hint where the wine is? What would be wrong with that?"

"Wine. She somewhere north."

"North? That could be in Alaska. Let's narrow that down a bit. How far north from right here?" Bluefeather picked up a stick and made an X on the ground.

"Done told you. We got no hours, no minutes, where I am. Don't got no miles either."

"Ohhh Lord. Bear, you're giving me hemorrhoids."

"Sit in hot water, maybe three times a day, rub your behind with buffalo grease, don't lift anything heavy and..."

"God, oh please, God. Authority. Number One. Please, I beg you to put words in this Indian's mouth that a common earth man can under-stand. He's changed from an entertainment director into an M.D."

"It comes clear, when you are ready, dear brudder."

"Look, Bear, I do remember clearly that you said many answers would come at the place under trees where the water burns. Well, when is that coming about, anyway? Just a hint maybe."

Dancing Bear smiled softly now, his black eyes somehow wishful, but all he said was, "You wish I play flute for you?" The wooden flute appeared in his hands as he looked at Bluefeather expectantly.

"Not right now. Thanks, just the same."

The flute vanished.

"I don't suppose I've got anything to lose by asking you about Tilton's gold and silver bullion, and maybe who killed him, huh?"

"Me, Dancing Bear, don't know all these things you ask. I think that bullion is looked after by a brain with few thoughts."

"Well, thanks a lot, Bear. Thank you ver-r-r-y much. That's a big help." Bluefeather continued even more caustically, "Three-fourths of the world is without thoughts worthy of mention." Bluefeather realized that sarcasm was getting him nowhere. Dancing Bear was having a show of combined temperament and fun this day. So he decided to try other approaches. "Say, Bear, do you need a favor? Is there anything I can do down here to help you move on up?"

"Kind thought you have there, kiddo, but to tell you a truth, I sorta like it where I am. This dog-eater, gut-cleaning Indian likes to stay busy all the time. Same thing when I where you at. Indian no more lazy than white, black, brown, yellow people. I got no prejudice. That's why I get plenty work all the time."

Bluefeather mumbled and moaned low and to himself, "Now he's converted into a cockeyed sociologist. A damned do-gooder, a full-fledged integrator."

"Better you pray for yourself, Blue. I got more business than I can handle right here where I at."

"How're you gonna know when your time comes to move on?"

"Same like you, dear brudder, with red lady. All the same. See the idee? You got to be nice to a mule or they kick the beans out of your head and the crap out of your belly, but they haul big load for you just the same when you patient and kind. Understan', dear brudder?"

"Yeah, about as well as I understand the law of gravity. If I don't watch out, a ton of rocks will fall on my head, right?"

"See there. Like I told you. You gettin' many smarts." With that he jumped up chanting and started doing an eagle dance on the flat front of a boulder.

Bluefeather yelled, "Hey Bear, come on now and stop that dancing. There's a lot more I need to know."

Dancing Bear stopped, saying, "How 'bout Russian dance?"

Before Bluefeather could answer, Dancing Bear was squatting down, bouncing around and kicking one leg out after the other, shouting like a drunken cossack. Then he appeared across the canyon, carrying on the wild dance atop a bluff. He danced right out into the pure mountain air right over Bluefeather's head, whose mind-voice explained, "He's zooming out of sight again, like a fiery-ass rocket."

Bluefeather picked up his fishing pole, his day's catch, and headed toward the house for the fish fry. It didn't seem like there was much left this particular day. Bluefeather was convinced he heard a distant voice echoing from the heavens over and over, "See the idee?"

Was Grinder talking to him through Dancing Bear? He didn't know, but somewhere in the mad conversation there were some clues of truth for him. That he knew. He smiled. No matter how disconcerting Dancing Bear could be, he always felt better for having visited him. Much better. If he had thought further, he would have realized that was one hell of a gift by itself.

◼ ◼ ◼

Nine

They were all mostly healed up now from their copper tunnel experience except for Willy's back. He was making heroic efforts to disguise the fact.

Bluefeather had gone over Korbell's maps with Willy, pinning down the best approach to the Commonwealth and Dutch Joe lode tunnels. The mines were about a mile apart and had been driven into the opposite sides of the mountain. Bluefeather decided he would explore them both in one day if the old roads were passable for a four-wheel drive vehicle.

"Willy, in a couple more weeks you'll be ready to jump over the Dos Amigos Bar from a flatfooted start."

"Two weeks, hell. I could waltz all the way to Billings, Montana, right now." He jumped up from the sofa and started his little half-running shuffle across the living room. Just before he reached the door, his back locked and he fell face down. Bluefeather had to help him up and assist him back to the couch. That took care of any protests Willy might have made about being left at home.

Flo was working in the garden and Marsha was helping Sally hang out the wash to dry.

"Marsha," Bluefeather said as casually as possible, "I'm going up and check out a couple of tunnels. Should be back by dark. Willy knows the location. If I'm not back by tomorrow noon you might come and see if I'm broke down."

Marsha said, "Oh good. We'll be finished here in just a minute. It won't take but a jiffy for me to get ready."

Bluefeather patiently tried to explain that these were safe open tunnels, and she might as well stay here and help around headquarters, where she was needed. She started to answer, but Bluefeather turned and walked toward the house to get his prospector's pick and lights. He had eaten a big breakfast and figured he could get by without any lunch. He was walking around in front of the house to his jeep when Marsha stepped right up in front of him, blocking his way.

"What do you think you're doing, anyway?" she confronted him.

"I told you. There's no use in two people going on a one-man job."

"You don't know. You may need help. Besides, I want to go."

"Look here. It's not that. I don't want you to...well, it's..."

"You made the deal knowing I was to be your assistant, Blue."

"That's right. So assistants do what they're told. That's what assisting means."

Her wondrous pearly skin was glowing so that the color almost matched that of her hair, and her eyes were speaking with sparks, "I'm going with you."

"Now look, if you're worried I might find something and hide it, then the deal is off."

She stared at him a moment before her face relaxed into her human-killing smile. "You're right. We've got to trust one another all the way. I'm sorry."

"It's okay. Hell, you're just as dedicated as I am when taking on a job. I like that."

"I like your liking it. Good hunting, Blue."

"You know now, don't you, Marsha, we have to find it for other reasons than Korbell?"

"Yes, I know. We must for Korbell and now, of course, for Willy's family, too. That is what you mean, isn't it?"

"Yes...yes." He moved slightly toward her, intending to give her a small hug and a kiss for a temporary good-bye, but she had read his intentions and so smoothly moved away toward the house that he couldn't be offended.

Bluefeather felt that he knew less and less about the "red" woman all the time, but for sure, she was as determined as a mountain goat in rutting season to succeed on their mission. She also had enough temper to start a forest fire even though she had clearly dampened it. So far, they had survived their first disagreement without rancor.

He drove until he could see the waste dump of the Commonwealth, but the rough, rutted road was blocked here from a landslide. He decided to walk on around the mountain to the Dutch Joe and save the nearer tunnel for last. After dealing with Marsha, the craggy terrain would be easy.

The tunnel still had fairly good timbers holding up the portal. He walked in with no trouble. The miners had been after gold here. In places the little gray-white quartz vein narrowed down to a thread and in other places widened to a foot. It was a good solid tunnel so far. He tapped one wall and the floor all the way in. He tested it all the way back out. The tunnel was solid. No secret rooms here.

He walked backward on the way out, however, watching and remembering like a mouse does a rattlesnake. Nothing happened and nothing of value was there. The walls were just like "the Authority" had made them.

He left this wasted dream and headed across the mountain to check out the Commonwealth. Nearing the highest point, he would have to climb a granite formation turned rotten. The surface was pulverized into billions of little pebbles. This slowed and tired him considerably because he was constantly slipping back, having to hold his balance with his hands.

He finally made the summit and started downhill over a barren patch of granite. The gravel felt like he was walking on marbles. He moved sideways to slow his descent, but even so, he fell down on one hand many times, bruising and cutting it.

There are selected sequences in life that it doesn't pay to think at all. Marsha had come into his mind again. He could see the entire woman and imagined he was feeling over her body, smelling her feminine scent. At the very moment she was opening her flesh and spirit to him, he slipped, falling onto his back, sliding downward uncontrollably.

He was going full speed, digging at the earth with his boot heels and clawing desperately at the pebbled earth with the palm of one hand. He instinctively held onto his battery light, desperately trying to protect it. It seemed silly for sure. Here he was plummeting straight for hell and was struggling to save a twenty-dollar light. His small pick was safe as long as his belt held together. As he gained velocity the gravel ripped at him even more. Then he saw the sheer drop-off about forty yards ahead. He grabbed with his free hand at a boulder that had fallen from higher up. The futile attempt didn't even slow him down. He was a goner.

Then there was flute music all around and through him. He was instantly out of, and back behind, his physical body, watching it from behind as it plunged forward to its doom. His out-of-body spirit screamed ahead for his physical body to grab a scrawny cedar tree near the edge of the drop-off.

The music stopped and he was back inside himself again. He grabbed at the tiny cedar and held. It bent, but didn't uproot or break. Bluefeather felt his arm and shoulder stretch out to the limit. His feet dangled over the precipice. He pulled himself up, straining mightily, still keeping one finger in the handle of the light. Then he sat up against a tree. He never knew how long he remained there absorbing the wonder of it all. Life. It was still his. It took all his reserves of courage—which he could have stuck in his ear with room for more—to crawl along the edge of the cliff. Inch by terrified inch, he moved until he came to a gentle slope leading right to the mine. He didn't dare walk down. He scooted on his ravaged feet and buttocks.

The Dutch Joe was caved a little here and there, but he made his wasted tests with no fear at all. The inside of the mountains had become safer than the outside. He reminded himself with his mind-voice, "You play by the mountain's rules or it will destroy you. Even then, it will occasionally remind you who is master by ripping some of your skin and jolting your liver loose."

He eased down the old trail to his jeep, just beginning to feel the pain of the mountain's recent warning blows.

It was dark when he arrived back home. The three hounds came out to meet him without barking this time. He bent stiffly down to hug them as they gave his face a good washing.

Willy walked out to greet him as he stepped upon the porch. "How'd it go?"

"Fine, but fast. Real fast," he said as he walked in the open door past his friend.

"My God, Blue. What happened to your back?"

"I got the itch so bad I had to scratch it with a mountain." Then he thought to himself, "Well, at least I'm still able to keep up the traditional silly chatter with Willy," just as his legs collapsed under him.

All three women surrounded him, commiserating something pitiful. Marsha undid the single button left intact on his shirt and pulled the torn cloth from his body. She took charge, leading him to the bathroom, telling him to undress completely. He stripped.

She checked him out from floor to crown and pushed him into the shower while she rummaged in the medicine cabinet. Then she dried him off, patting the towel softly over all his body—all over.

Then she put medicine on all the abrasions and followed that with an ointment as calmly as a registered nurse.

She yelled for Sally to get his bathrobe from the bunkhouse. Sally did, looking shyly away from his nudity, handing the robe to Marsha with her head turned.

Bluefeather thought this odd, considering she had already felt his nakedness.

Flo had been holding dinner for his arrival. She served it in a hurry now. As Willy poured him a big drink of bourbon, Bluefeather told them about the uncontrollable fall and how lucky he was to grab the lone tree. He left out the other incidents—the life-saving ones that came with the music of a flute.

After eating, he had one more shot of bourbon and headed for his room, saying, "I'll see you folks in the morning, raring to go."

"Grandy dandy," Willy said.

The soreness was coming on now, but he didn't mind. The privilege of being able to feel pain, or anything else, was what mattered. He lay on his belly, getting drowsy from the meal, the bourbon, and the day's climbing, with a deep thankfulness for the bountiful blessings he had received over the last ten hours.

He was into the first drift of sleep when he sensed a presence on the bed beside him. A hand was tenderly rubbing the back of his neck. Somehow, he knew that this time it was Marsha. He turned over in the bed and reached for her, but she was up and to the door.

He could see her silhouette there as she stopped and turned back to him, saying softly, "You need sleep most of all now. You can tell me about the rest of it when—sometime when we're alone."

She was gone.

He rolled back over on his stomach, absorbed in a rare contentment. He slept. Deeply.

■　■　■

Ten

Willy's sore back and Bluefeather's entire body healed. They hit the mountains again. Marsha went along. They studied the maps even more carefully, blocking out where they had been and where they intended to go. They climbed and climbed, dug and dug, searching carefully every tunnel and drift. When they found a cave-in they either hand-dug it out or shored it up with timbers laboriously cut and braced.

They found a lot of minerals too. The deposits and veins were mostly of marginal value at current prices. Someday, if the people of the world survived, scarcity would make their unearthing of immense value. Under any situation, they were fine homes for bats, bears, lions, and bobcats.

The mountains toughened the three in muscle and determination. They were a team now in top physical condition. Flo and Sally did not accompany them on these excursions. They stayed home and took care of the necessities. All five became very close from a hard-shared endeavor.

Bluefeather had not smoked in a month. Daily, he wondered about Dancing Bear's confusing prophecy that he would know when Marsha was ready to commit to him by sliding on a mountain. Very confusing. They had done a lot of that every day, and there had been no evidence of a mutual fulfillment to come. She remained her uncomplaining, hard-working, cheerful, dedicated self. Yet there was a gray area she reserved, letting no one in—an enigma for sure, but a deep, tormenting mystery for Bluefeather. He tried not to let it interfere with their work, and almost succeeded.

Bluefeather often wandered off from campsite, trying to conjure up Dancing Bear. But he failed to appear. The flutes were silent.

Finally, the moment arrived when they checked out the last mine on Korbell's maps. It was late day in midsummer when the three confederates exited the last tunnel. There was still no trace of the rare Mouton '80.

They had a two-mile walk downhill to the jeep. They strode without speaking, feeling a sense of failure, even though Bluefeather knew the search was not over—not at all. He would just have to wait for the appropriate moment to bring it up again.

It was dark before they arrived at the campsite. Bluefeather had expected they would drive home, but Willy was already getting his equipment ready to cook. He and Marsha gathered wood. After the meal, they leaned back on their bedrolls, drinking coffee and staring at the fire.

The sensation of loss was tempered slightly by the knowledge that they had given their best. Bluefeather had no idea what the others truly felt. However, this was not good enough for him. But this stage of defeat had to be accepted by all three. It was the way of men and women who fooled with mountains.

A night bird called, and was answered. A coyote howled his ancient statement down below. Bluefeather stood up, listening hard as he had always done. He could not verbalize what the coyote told the sky, but he thrilled as if he did. One thing he knew, the coyote had a message as yet to be interpreted by humans.

When he sat back down, Marsha said, "You are fascinated by the coyote, aren't you?"

"Yeah. They are the greatest of survivors." He felt this as an inadequate response, but couldn't gather another at the moment.

The campfire flickered across her face, highlighting one part and then another. Her blue eyes were dark now like the depths of an ocean. The shimmering flame made her hair appear to ripple and flow like molten bronze. God, she was beautiful. At just that moment she represented to Bluefeather all the mountains he had climbed, all the dreams he had or would ever have, all the light and life the sun granted. Somehow, he realized this tiny swift vision was related to a fresh-forming cloud and was part of what the coyote sang.

Willy broke his inconstant reverie with, "You know, for twenty years I didn't do anything but look at a mule's rear; then I found a silver mine that paid for a while. Not much, you understand, but enough to start me looking all over again when it petered out."

Bluefeather knew what he was trying to get at, so he said, "We've got to think of other possibilities. Right now I don't know what, but we have to."

Marsha contributed, "The wine is somewhere...we just have to look harder, think harder."

Willy looked at her with deep admiration. "Ain't nothing impossible. Look at what old Bill Mundy up at Chama did."

They waited.

"He ran down a healthy deer on foot, and killed it. Don't too many people believe it, but I was there. You see, we was out of ammunition and hungry. People do strange things when it seems important enough to 'em. Jimmy Bason over at Hillsboro killed five coons with one shot. You see this coon, this old mama coon, had been tearing up his garden and stealing chicken eggs as well. Jimmy's hounds treed her on a fence post early one morning. He ran out with a .30–30 and took a shot at the coon. He damn near fainted when five coons fell off the fence dead. Four half-grown youngsters had been lined up on the fence straight behind her. So a feller is liable to pull off anything if he keeps on climbing. Ain't that so?"

Bluefeather could tell by the way Marsha slung her head that the "one-shot" story had made her uneasy as she said, "Sad. That is really sad. The mother coon was just trying to care for her babies. Now, that is really sad."

Willy replied before Bluefeather had to. "You're sure right about that, Marsha, but Jimmy was protectin' the food for his young'uns, too."

Bluefeather tried to change the subject. "You know, right now we haven't got a new direction—but somehow..."

Willy broke in with another of his off-base comments. "Everbody in the world is a treasure hunter, of some kind or other, but most don't seem to know what they're lookin' for...much less where. We're breakin' our butts lookin' for wine when we can get it at Dos Amigos for two or three dollars a bottle. Good stuff, too. Smart, ain't we?"

Marsha chuckled warmly at this. Bluefeather grinned wide enough to do justice to the Korbell family tradition and said in the Willy-Bluefeather "silly" tradition, "Hellsfire, in spite of rat turds in the gravy we have no choice but to go on looking."

Everyone unrolled their beds and crawled in, hoping for a revelatory dream.

■ ■ ■

Eleven

Willy had nothing much to look forward to now, except hiring out as a guide during hunting season. The marauding lion had already diminished his livestock by a third and his pack of hunting hounds by a fourth. For the last three days he had disappeared in his old jeep. Flo explained that he had a girlfriend over at Silver City, and she was sure he would be back soon. Bluefeather sure hoped so, because he had already reserved rooms in the only hotel at Meanwhile for the weekend.

The annual Founder's Day celebration was coming up. It was a big day for the town. Gold had been discovered there a hundred years back, and the citizens were combining the two celebrations. People would come from all over the Southwest, and a few would drift in from other parts of the country. It had been declared an annual, official state celebration.

Bluefeather was looking forward to it for a lot of reasons. First, he wanted to have a few drinks and relax. He also thought Flo and Sally deserved a chance to have some fun and maybe meet a couple of men. It was hard to extremes on women way out here. They all needed to clear the confused air and make decisions about what the next moves were going to be.

Bluefeather had called Charlie Waters in Santa Fe to invite him down to the festivities. Charlie was an old friend from Bluefeather's futile mercury smuggling days and a bloodhound of a research man. When it came to running down records in courthouses, there was no better. Bluefeather didn't explain fully on the phone that he wanted Charlie to study all the building plans Tilton had ever had on his numerous homes and buildings. Bluefeather reasoned that the sixty cases of wine would have to be hidden under, or in, one of these structures, since the mine tunnels had turned up a blank. It was a chance they had to take so they could keep on legitimately earning the wages and expenses of Korbell's six-month commitment.

They penned up all the livestock at night while Willy was gone. He had insisted on this for weeks now. There was only a month left for Sally to register for college. Bluefeather's money draw from Korbell would keep them fed and the payments on the Ruger's home place paid until the minimum ran out. Then they would be in a mess if they didn't deliver the find. All except Marsha, of course, and yet, he felt she would also feel a great loss because of their shared closeness. However, she didn't have to worry about overdue bills, foreclosures, and food. That was a difference of some dimensions.

It was the time for searching. Bluefeather slipped out into the woods, hoping Dancing Bear would choose to be found. It was one of those summer days when the air was sparkling and undulating like rivers in the sky. The blue jays flew about like tiny solidified pieces of firmament. The squirrels and chipmunks barked all around, holding a constantly moving convention. Insects buzzed and chirped, completing the symphony.

In a wild game trail, he saw the familiar arrowhead track of a lone coyote, and on the bank of the Zia Creek, he came upon the prints of the old killer lion. He could tell it was the one all right, and the reason he had chosen domestic instead of wild stock to kill was revealed. The size of the tracks indicated that he was a tom and that he was old. It took full maturity to develop a foot that big. His right forepaw print twisted out to the side more shallowly than the others. Bluefeather was sure he had been crippled by a bullet. If it had been a steel trap it would have shown part of his foot missing. He could no longer fill the demands of his stomach on elusive, wild meat. The initial burst of speed it took to accomplish this had mostly been taken away by his injury.

A few feet from where the lion had crossed the creek, Bluefeather saw the prints of a raccoon. They were unmistakable in their likeness to the hand prints of a human baby and were similar to a bear cub's, only more delicate. Many creatures hunted and hid here. So did Bluefeather Fellini.

He listened for the music of the flute. It did not come. He tried to appear casual as his eyes searched the trees and boulders for Dancing Bear. He did not appear. He walked along the creek until he found a place he could cross by stepping on large rocks. He climbed up the opposite bank into a clearing, his mind straining a call out to his spirit guide. He was not connecting, so he sat down on a fallen log, lit a smoke, feeling guilty, but enjoying it for a moment—until in anger at his weakness he stubbed it out of sight in the forest floor.

He was in half-vision, making love to Marsha, when he heard the voice. It was unmistakably French. Since he knew only rudimentary phrases in the lovely language, he could not understand the entirety of the rapid-fire speech.

He stood up, staring around with a lot of curiosity. Soon he realized the voice was coming from above him. There, about thirty feet up on a pine limb, sat a lady in a long, exquisite dress with the waist pinched in like that of a gay nineties girl, but it was a fashion far older than that. Even from this low angle he could see her breasts pushed up and partly out. Her blond hair was piled and twisted on her head, causing Bluefeather to envision a royal ball.

She smiled pleasingly and chattered down at him under a thin, delicate nose. Her hazel eyes appeared to slant up and around her face like those of Korbell's adopted wife, Elena.

"Forgive me, but I can't understand your French."

"Oh, I'm so sorry," she said in a clear English.

"So am I. It's a lovely language."

"Thank you, sir."

"I'm Bluefeather Fellini."

"I know. I've heard so much about you."

"Oh. I don't mean to be rude, but just who are you?"

"Why, I'm Nicole Valuer, ex-mistress of Emperor Napoleon."

"*The* Napoleon?"

"Of course. Bonaparte himself."

"Could I ... I mean ... well, what are you doing here—up there?"

"Ah, that bitch Josephine had me poisoned."

"Well, I'm sure sorry to hear ..."

"No, no. Don't feel sorry for me. It was better than the guillotine."

"What I meant was ..."

"Please don't fret yourself. I'm well placed here. You see, I'm Dancing Bear's assistant. In fact, I'm his substitute today. I hope I can be of some help to you, sir."

"Blue. Just call me Blue. Why didn't he come? Bear must know I need help. A lot of help. All of us around here need help desperately."

"Ah yes, he sends his profound regrets, but he is overbooked right now. He is in London to advise one of his subjects in danger of the gallows. Falsely accused of murder, I might add."

"Well, skunk shit and cherry blossoms."

"What's that you say?"

"Oh, nothing. Just a Willy Ruger slip. How many subjects does he have? Really have?"

"Now don't quote me, but at last count he was tending fifty-six souls."

"Fifty-six! No wonder he can't keep me properly posted."

"Oh that's not so many for one so skillful. Often he has many more than that, especially in times of major wars or great natural disasters. Occasionally, he has fewer. It varies according to the number who cross over."

"How long have you been, uh, where Bear is?"

She started counting on her fingers. "Let's see. About..."

"Never mind. I know when Napoleon hooked up with Josephine." Bluefeather had ascertained that Nicole wasn't heavily versed in mathematics. He still wanted a little more assurance of her position before he got into personal problems. "Why have you been on Bear's level so long?"

"That's a good question. You see, Blue, I've tried so hard, but...well, I just haven't been able to completely shed some of the...uh...earthly talents I was gifted with while in your world. These special talents were my true calling there, and old habits die hard—even over here."

"Would it be impertinent to ask what your specialties are?"

"Not at all. I've always been asked that."

"Well then?" He waited.

"Now just be patient. You'll see very soon."

"Well, okay. Have you got any messages for me from Bear?"

"Surely. That's why I'm here. Well, one of the reasons anyway. Dancing Bear said you should get close—very close—to a Mr. Dolby."

Bluefeather exclaimed, "The old man in Meanwhile who worked with the mining mogul Tilton. That Dolby?"

"Monsieur Bear never gives me many details—mostly just messages to pass on."

"Well, I hope to Authority that's not all."

"No. No. Let me see. There was something else. Oh yes, he said the subterranean would give you many clues."

"The subterranean? Poodle poots and perfumed pee-pee. Don't tell me I'm gonna have to go plumb to hell to get any clear information."

"Oh, I don't think so. Monsieur Bear said you weren't ready for that trip yet."

"Well, thank goodness for that...but is that all?"

"Almost. Say, would you mind my coming down there? I'm afraid you're getting a crick in your neck."

Bluefeather's mind-voice cracked in: "The lady is right. My neck is beginning to swell." She was right there in front of him before he ended the thought.

"Soon is now," she said softly and welded her spirit to his tight as a rocket seam.

They were now about eight feet in the air. Bluefeather looked down over her shoulder and saw that they were now about twenty feet up and gaining altitude. There wasn't a thing left to do but hang on. They floated on up, twisting in the pure, fresh mountain air until he had difficulty discerning which end was up. All the physical and spiritual action combined with the summer sun on his back made him forget the upcoming and all past winters. It was summer forever up here. Then he forgot everything.

They were descending now. There had been a period up there of blankness. What had they done? He'd probably never know, but something had occurred, because he was short of breath. Maybe that was from fear or...Oh well, like Agatha Christie and Shakespeare said, "Old sins cast long shadows."

Then they were safely on the ground again. He kissed her some to be sure she knew how much he had appreciated the ascension.

Suddenly, he realized she had vanished. Bluefeather lay in the grass with the rest of the insects. He felt right at home.

Twelve

The day before the "Big Do" in town, Willy came straggling home. He had a red-eyed, bowlegged hangover. He also appeared weak in the joints, and one could have smelled him through three feet of adobe wall.

Bluefeather said, "Welcome home, Uncle Willy. Can I get you a drink? Might as well keep going. Tomorrow's the big day in Meanwhile."

Flo wanted to know if she could feed him. He looked as if he needed nourishment.

"Been playin' so hard I forgot to eat. Broke myself of a bad and expensive habit. Ain't that grandy dandy?" He really meant he was too sick to eat, but would never admit it. He had a large, blue knot on his forehead. He rubbed at it tenderly and explained only to a degree, "If I could throw punches as accurately as I receive them, I'd be the boxing champion of the world."

Flo did not question or argue. That stage was long past. She just poured him a bourbon, saying, "Here, brother. This will take the curve out of your spine."

"Thanks, sis. I owe you my life." With that he did a crazy little jig, slipping on a Navajo rug and tripping across a footstool. He somehow shuffled around and made the near-fall part of the dance step. Bluefeather wondered what it was with these old men like Willy and Dancing Bear—always performing these one-man dances. Maybe they just wanted to be sure of the continued ability to move or maybe they continued celebrating life itself.

Willy threw his worn, old gray hat on the couch and plunked down by it. He still held his glass without having spilled a drop. In a couple of minutes there was nothing to spill.

"Ain't somebody gonna help me out? I'm havin' more fun than I can handle by myself. This goddamn fun is killin' me, in fact."

Bluefeather felt a vast and knowledgeable sympathy and agreed to help out. Marsha, always alert, got them each a drink and then all three women disappeared. Flo went off to finish hemming her new celebration dress. Marsha and Sally retired to wash and curl their hair.

Bluefeather lifted his glass in a toast. "Here's to the gods. May they forgive us our pleasurable sins."

"And for those we ain't committed yet."

They drank. Willy felt a mite better. He ran one shovel-hardened hand through his thinning, gray-blond hair and pointed his sunken eyes straight at Bluefeather.

"Have you come up with any new ideas, Blue?"

"Yep. A couple of wild ones as a matter of fact. Say, how long has that girl—what's her name—been with Dolby?"

"Sherry?"

"Yeah, that's her. Sherry."

"Oh, I'd say 'round eight or nine years—thereabouts. She's one of them real educated gals."

"Educated? How do you mean?"

"School educated. She's one of them anthropologists. Whatever the hell that's supposed to be. Got a Ph.D. in it."

"Well, I'll be damned if that isn't a weird one."

"Yeah, she looks after old Dolby like he knew the date of the second coming. Totally dedicated to him."

"Willy, I've got to ask you some questions about Dolby, and I sure hope you know the answers. Tell me all you know about Sherry. Do you think the old man confides in her?"

"Well, I tell you this much. He got beat up and threatened about something, so he got a permit to carry a gun. Then a few months after Sherry showed up, some young buck did an ass-grabbing job on Sherry, and old Dolby shot his ear off. Don't nobody fool around with her any more."

"That's understandable. Tell me, did your dad believe Dolby made off with Tilton's bullion that everyone has wondered about all these years?"

"He sure did. Yeah, he believed it for sure. If he knew the details though, he never mentioned them to me. I believe, for sure, I would have remembered it if he had. My dad thought Tilton was a genius."

"How's that?"

"Well, making money out of mines for one thing. 'Course ever-body knows that. But there was other things. Tilton studied—or was involved somehow with science or history or something. Shit, I don't know, Blue."

"You're absolutely sure you never heard about that rare wine from anyone? Anyone at all?"

"Nope. Never. Folks around here have got plenty of interest in gold and silver, but only the winos and the church give a hoot about wine."

Bluefeather said then, "One more thing: what else do you know about Sherry besides her profession?"

"Well, not a whole lot, for sure. Talk is she was an orphan from Nairobi, Kenya. Accordin' to rumor, she's three-quarters Kenyan and a quarter French. Makes sense 'cause her adopted parents were French scientists working at Los Alamos."

"Thanks, Willy. We'll get it all tied together here before long." Bluefeather hesitated a moment, leaning toward Willy, saying with such dedication that Willy forgot to breathe for a moment. "Listen here, ol' pardner, we're gonna find that wine. You hear? I guarantee it. Somebody's gotta know something we need to know. Sixty-five cases takes up a lot of room and somebody, somewhere, remembers. Nothing is gonna stop us—no guns, no lies, no cleverness, is gonna stop us. Nothing."

Willy nodded his head in full agreement, adding, "Well, shoot a monkey."

Flo made a worried effort to get some food into Willy's dissipated body. He took about four tentative bites of the venison stew, piddled around with the peach cobbler, and took off for bed without saying a word. Willy was in search of lost sleep.

Bluefeather sat at the table sipping his last drink while the ladies cleaned up after the meal. They all seemed to be talking at once and enjoying it. He didn't even attempt to hear anything specific as he drank and thought. As soon as Flo and Sally said their good-nights, Marsha poured herself a light drink and sat down at the kitchen table with Bluefeather. He was glad, having just enough of a buzz on that he didn't relish drinking alone.

She said, "I know you don't like to drink alone, so I'm going to have exactly two with you."

"Exactly? I don't know what that word means."

"Two. That's all. So you might as well make yours strong enough to compensate. Personally, I want to feel good tomorrow."

"You will. I'm gonna see to that." He hesitated. She waited, sensing that he wanted to talk other than about the weather. "Marsha, are you certain, without any doubt whatsoever, that the wine actually exists?"

"Yes. As certain as a human being can be about anything. Korbell is far too obsessed with it to be wasting his emotions. He doesn't waste things. He makes use of them or... discards them swiftly."

"That makes me feel better. If it exists then, we're gonna find it. Nothing on this earth can stop us. You know that don't you?"

"I know. I'm ready to work it as long as we shall breathe if that's what you and Korbell wish, and that seems to be an obvious truth."

Bluefeather whammed a fist into a palm, smiled in unison with Marsha and said, "Good. Good." He felt comfortable and full partners with her.

Then he told her about his talk with the hungover Willy. About Dolby and Tilton. She agreed that was the only lead they had going for them right now and that they should pursue it with full energy and dedication. Bluefeather knew she wasn't faking it just to make him feel good. She had already proven in many surprising ways that she was a sticker. He did make his drinks heavy and hers light as she had stipulated. He sure didn't want her to leave.

When she had emptied her second glass, he blurted out, "You know don't you, Marsha, that I care for you very much?"

She cocked her head over in her puppy dog fashion and laid her big, blue lookers on him, saying softly as a baby's kiss, "Yes. Yes, I know you do. And... I feel the same about you."

"Then what in the whirling world is holding us back?"

"Nothing. We're just not ready yet."

"Jesus H. Christmas Christ, I'm as ready as a lit firecracker."

"I speak of the both of us, darling." She got up, walked around the table, and kissed him on the cheek. Placing her fiery hair over his shoulder, she gave him a quick hug. The feel and scent of her essence thoroughly slammed extra blood into his temples and half closed his access to air.

Then she walked out of the kitchen, adding, "Would you please pen up the dogs? Willy forgot."

"Oh yeah. Sure. I'll take care of the dogs." He stumbled out into the night confusedly from having been kissed on the cheek by the woman he was rapidly becoming goofy over. The cheek. What a raging romance this had turned into. It was hard for him to accept how cowardly he had been in his approach. This woman made him feel like it was his first day at school and he was emperor of the universe at the same time.

He called the dogs with a smile in his voice, though. They came running, wagging their tails. Bluefeather wagged his all the way to the pen.

Willy felt so sick the next morning he declined the trip to town. They tried to get him an eye-opener, but he refused all offers of help, explaining that he couldn't leave the place alone when the killer lion might strike again.

Thirteen

On Founder's Day the population of Meanwhile usually doubled, but tied to the gold strike celebration, it more than quadrupled. People came in every kind of vehicle, pickup trucks and cars, most pulling campers and trailers. The streets were lined with commercial stands of all kinds, selling and trading every sort of knickknack from homemade quilts to Indian jewelry. Other booths offered an assortment of foods—hamburgers, hot dogs, barbecued beef, chile, pancakes and eggs, and country gravy with sourdough biscuits.

Visitors came from all over the Southwest and other parts of the United States—business people, government employees from Alamogordo, Los Alamos, Albuquerque, and Santa Fe. There were artists, Indians, miners, cowboys, and kids. Kids were running everywhere—yelling, dodging about among the grown-ups, the boys teasing the willing girls. Old acquaintances were renewed and new ones made. The teenagers moved about, trying to act older but glancing quickly and constantly about, measuring the opposite sex with a forced casualness.

The small-town parade was supposed to start at ten. Just as parades everywhere seem to be tardy, this one got moving at eleven A.M. There was an old stagecoach pulled by four bay horses. Old-timers in fancy dress of the period rode in it. A real, bearded prospector led a mule with a pack on its back. Working cowboys, mixed with western-dressed dudes, rode finely made quarter horses. A team pulled a wagon with a country band playing in it. Various dances were done by a group of Santo Domingo Pueblo Indians. Their colorful costumes made wildly colored flashes as they turned. Children with their pets followed the proverbial convertible hauling the day's queen and her attendants—all in long formal dresses. The audience quit shopping, visiting, and drinking until the parade had passed, then resumed their choice of activity.

After the parade one could see long lines of people waiting at the many food dispensaries. They knew eating now was not only a pleasure but a necessity, for soon the music, dancing, and drinking would swiftly gather momentum.

Bluefeather's group had watched the parade amid the scores of handshakes and hellos to friends. They had a twenty-minute wait to get the huge and juicy barbecue sandwiches. It took about the same amount of time to eat them and enter Dominguez's Dos Amigos Bar.

Bluefeather had been searching through the outdoor crowd for Dolby or Charlie Waters. He had seen neither out there. Now he spotted Charlie standing at the crowded bar. Charlie grinned at them from a well-chiseled face under thick crew-cut brown hair. His lips pushed his cheeks up from the pressure of his smile so that the brown eyes seemed as merry as those of a professional Santa Claus. He and Bluefeather could have worn one another's clothes without alteration of any kind.

Bluefeather introduced him to the three women and Charlie ordered them drinks all around. They had to wait a spell for that too, but Marsha spotted a table being vacated and grabbed it while she could. They all sat down at last with their first drink of the celebration.

So many local people were stopping by the table to visit with Flo and Sally that Bluefeather had a chance to talk to Charlie between introductions. The noise level was so high that he wasn't afraid of being overheard. If he had been able to pursue his hobby of blind-listening, the variety of pure thinking and feeling in this little town would have pleased him very much.

A table of loggers was discussing their jobs.

"My salary is so very damned small compared to what I do."

His friend settled the fate of a glass of beer, belched, and replied, "The return on my expenditure of energy don't match my paycheck either."

A retired banker talked with a teacher of sociology. The banker said, "We do not need more voters. Half of the ones we have are functionally illiterate. We need fewer voters. Should make 'em all take tests to qualify like they do teachers and college entrants."

"Aw, hogwash, you'd wind up with a monarchy with that method."

"So what? I would make the politicians take a much harder test than the voters before they could even think of running for office."

Then a water well driller told a table of drinking buddies, "His mouth didn't fit his stupid face, so I rearranged it so that it did. He did look more natural when he got out of the hospital."

Then another voice added, "He dealt the cards slick as a fresh-laid egg. Sure enough, I got three deuces to his three aces. That's why you folks should buy me a drink. Soon as I start drawing aces, I'll start buying the treats."

An old rancher walked from the men's room, through the crowd, back to a table. He walked so stiffly he could have been a bunch of weathered boards nailed randomly together. After his wife died, he had sold his ranch and moved into town. He never would have done it, but he had finally got to the point that he was physically unable to mount a horse. In his youth, he had been six feet two, but the constant jamming of his bones by horses, one way or another, had left him at about five eleven.

His face was aimed toward the chair, his upper body a few degrees to the left and his lower body angled off to the right. One stiff elbow stuck out from his side, permanently positioned awry. His nose had been knocked sideways by the slinging head of a bronc. Instead of being flattened, the bridge was mashed thin and curved like the inner portion of a hay hook. His hips and tailbone were smashed and tilted under him from fifty years or more in the saddle. Only by watching his eyes could one tell his real direction—the rest of him moved at different angles. He finally got seated across from the university professor of history of the American West, to continue their conversation that the professor was instigating with much acuity.

The young professor, perhaps in his early forties, had authored a couple of books and several journal articles expounding to his readers his version of a world-famous time just past. He had a large balding head and the required beard, shoulders of a football tackle, hands of pianist and blue, curious eyes as active as baby brother's.

The battered cowboy sitting there in front of him was the perpetuation of the living past through his father and grandfather, all the way back to Juan de Oñate and his horses. The two men were fated. The horseman was the end, and the professor was, he must be, the honest continuation. That was what he had studied, lived, loved, and dedicated his life to. They were both privileged to have met at this exact moment in infinity. The professor must observe, teach, write, and enshrine these truths with as much energy and commitment as the old horseman and his ancestors had lived them.

The professor spoke first. "Now, according to my research on . . ."

The old rancher, who had lived both the old and the beginning of the new West, raised a long, battered hand. "Whoa, there. I've been listening to you all day. Now you listen to me for a spell. The only true record of the cowboy comes from the skin of the human ass glued to the leather of a saddle for twenty or thirty miles a day for a long, long time. Horses have killed and crippled far more cowboys than all the lightning, snakebites, booze, and bullets combined."

"How's that?" the professor urged him on.

"Well, first there's the gettin' tangled up in a rope tied to a thousand-pound bronc and getting jerked almost in half, or a bad dally around the horn after catching a big old steer and gettin' a thumb or some other finger jerked off. Then, of course, a lot of 'em were forced to ride their horse under a tree, where a posse or lawman tied one end of a rope to a limb and the other to their neck and then spooked the horse out from under them."

"But . . . but . . ."

"Just a damn minute, son. It's my turn, my turn before it's too late."

"I'm sorry . . . go on."

"Well, a lot of cowboys went to whatever reward they had coming, from getting knocked off, or thrown off, and hangin' a foot in a stirrup. Them horses sure enough resent a cowboy in that position. They'll run until they've batted his brains out against rocks, trees, or posts. Sometimes they'll run through barbed wire and cut both of 'em to death. If all that don't get the job done, they're more than likely to kick the cowboy to jelly. When they fall by accident—ranch horses don't fall on purpose—they can mash a feller's guts flat as a stomped centipede or break him so's he'll never walk in the same direction at the same time ever again. Just like me. This I know, you see?"

"Well, yes, but there are other things I have found in my research, such as . . ."

"I ain't got time to listen to things that I don't know and you're not real sure about. The way I see it, perty soon now, pickup trucks will kill more cowboys than all the guns, crazy horses, and other accidents combined."

The professor was both agitated and excited. He was taking mental notes right now, but he would sneak off and write them down later. He was too experienced to make obvious notes that might halt the natural flow of the old cowboy's wisdom. This conversation was also his work and life. He must not waste it.

"'Course, you know, young man, that horses come in all sizes, colors, and dispositions. There are those beautiful paints, golden palominos, kingly blacks, noble bays, browns and chestnuts and sorrels so perty they'll melt a dude's heart just to gaze upon 'em. Those very creatures will do all I've told before and more, like run you under a limb trying to break your neck, slam you into a tree trying to crush your leg beyond repair. Sometimes by accident—sometimes on purpose. Young broncs, or spoiled horses, especially, like to buck you off onto piles of sharp-edged rocks, into mud holes and cactus. That's a specialty a lot of horses enjoy. There's been plenty of cowboys flat-ass bucked to death. Sometimes it took only a few minutes or months or years to die, but their innards never healed right, savvy?"

"History is as important as the future. I'm not going to back down on that, no matter how many of your truths you tell me," he slyly urged the rancher on.

"I'm not sure you fellers should be mixing the fun myth with the hard reality. You're gonna get everybody as confused as politicians."

"Exactly what do you mean by that?"

"If you can't figure it out for yourself, after what I just told you, then I ain't got the time to waste trying to explain it any better."

The professor was revising something in his head somewhere. He opened his mouth to speak, but the old ex-cowboy-rancher decided to finish his little say and then shut up about it.

"Now don't get me wrong, professor. I've loved some horses just like a man naturally loves some women, but I just wanted you to know a simple, broken-up truth before you go on writing down all this research again. Horses was it. There wouldn't have been no West without 'em, I don't reckon, not even in all those make-believe picture shows and books. They are a hell of a lot of fun, but I'm not sure they've got much to do with how it really is, or was, or what you been talkin' about. Hellsfire, for one thing, real dedicated, working cowboys was too poor to buy bullets to practice shooting. Mostly it was mind-sick, town dudes dressed up like cowboys, twisted-brain meanies and roundup quitters that learned to shoot. Now listen careful, these were the people who went around robbing banks, stagecoaches, trains, and mostly shooting people in the back. Real working cowboys and their horses were way too tired to even think about racing all over the West committing these murderous fairy tales."

The old rancher was quiet a moment, looking way back. The young professor was quiet with him, honestly trying to feel where this real, old cowboy had been.

Then the rancher ordered them each another drink, grinned through seven scattered teeth the horses had spared him and said, raising his glass of brown whiskey, "You can count on one thing, though: cowboys do a lot of laughing when they get together, because they all know they've somehow survived being killed by horses. It was mostly those lovable horses that did 'em in, son. That's just the way it was."

"I've appreciated this enlightening conversation, but I'd like to ..."

"We're done talkin'. Let's have some fun."

"I was just going to say that you surely told me ... something all right."

"Yeah, I surely did."

Great and varied noises of this tiny portion of the West talked, laughed, danced, flirted, and plotted, cascading around them like the incessant roaring of a waterfall.

Bluefeather did hear through the pulsating energy of sounds someone say, "Hey, ain't this the keenest day that ever was? I had a good breakfast, ain't in jail, and I'm already half-drunk and it's still six hours before closing time."

Then he thought he heard a sort of prayer. "Oh, great mystery in the sky, I am too insignificant for you to answer my personal prayers, but I beseech you to give approbation and save us all from these greedy, screaming, Bible-waving puppeteers."

Another voice finished, "A great big happy amen to that."

After considerable small talk, Bluefeather finally told Charlie what he wanted—plans to every house and building that Tilton had ever had anything to do with. It was Charlie's nature to enjoy any job he liked enough to take. He was fairly wiggling in anticipation of getting after this one. Bluefeather handed him an envelope containing enough cash to get the job done, if it was possible.

Charlie swallowed his drink and said, "I think I'll start at Silver City, where the killing took place. I might as well head over the mountains right now. I can get checked in tonight and begin when the courthouse opens in the morning. I got a camper on my pickup so it won't matter what time I get in." He said the words to Bluefeather while staring at Sally.

Bluefeather had seen Sally taking several quick, interested glances at Charlie, so he told his friend, "Charlie, you might as well stay here tonight. We might think of something else important to hunt. Anyway, we're having too much fun here at Meanwhile's unofficial country club."

As nearly always, Charlie was agreeable. "Well, since you put it so high classed, I believe I will. The only way I could get in a real country club would be to buy it."

"Okay, that's settled."

Charlie raised his six feet up and headed for the jukebox. He wasn't going to waste any time starting the fun. He went about any job he did the same way. He was soon back, moving agilely through the crowd, and stuck his hand silently out to Sally. They were in each other's arms, around tables and out onto the dance floor, smooth as flying squirrels.

Bluefeather felt real good about that. He touched Marsha on the shoulder and said, "Our luck's beginning a run."

She raised her glass in a quick toast of agreement.

Harvey Dixon from Albuquerque, who owned two Mexican restaurants, sent them a round of drinks, then came over to say hello, asking Flo if she would care to dance. She did.

Bluefeather was glad again. Harvey Dixon was a go-getter about the age of Willy but without the wear and tear of climbing hundreds of mountains and swinging an ore pick uncountable thousands of times at hard rock.

Bluefeather was exulting. The three women he escorted were all so attractive. He was one proud ex-mining man. He looked at Marsha, grinning like he had just invented chocolate pudding, and said, "It's our turn now."

She gave him back that old magic Korbell adopted family smile and said, "Agreed." But, being the brilliant lady she was, she suggested they wait until one of the other couples sat back down, so they wouldn't lose their table.

"You're right there. This place is filling up like a church at a rich man's funeral."

"I like it here," she said. "I don't know when I've had more fun. Yes, I really like it here. You know, I feel right at home. I was raised near a little town about this size in the High Sierras, not too far northeast of Fresno, California."

Bluefeather was both amazed and honored that she had finally volunteered something about her life before she had been adopted by Korbell. That explained her knowledge of the outdoors and more. He felt so flattered that he made a circle with his hand to Carmelita, Dominguez's sister, denoting another round of drinks. She nodded an acknowledgment. Things were working.

As Harvey and Flo sat down, he led Marsha to dance. They did several. The music stopped as the machine automatically changed records. He unglued himself from Marsha with regrets, saying, "Boy, I hate to leave now, but I gotta go look for Dolby."

"I know."

She did, too. The fun was fine, but they had a chore, a big chore, that hadn't been taken care of.

Fourteen

Bluefeather walked all over the two-block-long main street. There was an old-time fiddler's band making music from long ago. The seniors were sashaying back and forth, feeling and loving the nostalgia of other times. Their times. Farther down the street a country rock band was blasting out for the younger blood, and they were shaking their bodies, swinging their arms, and really getting after it. The conglomeration of different ages, colors, and styles, mixed with the natural attitude of abandonment, was contagious.

It was extremely difficult for Bluefeather to concentrate on his mission. He walked the side streets and alleys looking for Dolby's collector's Bentley. It wasn't there. Maybe he didn't intend to show up at all. If not, it put Bluefeather in a poor position. He knew it would be far better if he ran into him accidentally. His move had to be ultrasmooth to get any information out of the crazy old man. Hundreds of others had tried before him, even using force, and had failed.

He walked on, looking.

Back in the Dos Amigos, a little middle-aged, sparkle-eyed man named Mac Brown introduced himself and asked Marsha to dance, saying, "It's okay, darlin', for you to dance with me. I'm Mac Brown. Blue won't mind at all. I've prospected, and got drunk and been in jail many times with oh' Blue."

She said, smiling with dangerous whiteness, "That's the best line for qualification I've heard in a month."

He was surprisingly agile and, though several inches shorter than she was, also surprisingly strong. He whirled her out and away and back again with a hand that held hers tight as set concrete.

Other dancers respected Mac, she observed, because they left them a larger space to dance in than the other couples. Then Mac, still holding her hand, dropped coins in the jukebox and punched up a lot of slow music. They needed less space now.

Marsha noticed that several local couples danced by them and scratched Mac in the middle of his back. He paid no mind at all, as if it was either his due or he had no feeling in that portion of his anatomy. Most of them smiled and said something to one another as they circled away.

Finally, she could take the curiosity no longer and asked him, "Why do those people keep scratching you on the back?"

"Oh, that. Well, that's a joke. A joke on me. They're just friends lettin' me know they remember."

"Would you care to share the joke with me, or is it none of my business?"

"Ah, you'd just be bored."

"I truly doubt that, and I am really curious. Anyway, you'll find that a friend of Bluefeather's is a friend and confidant of mine as well."

"Now that you put it that way, well . . . alrighty, I'll give it a try. You see, I used to be a workin' cowboy. Then I got me a little ranch of my own and married up with Norma Mae. She was a good wife and perty as six new kittens. She didn't much like me going off runnin' coyotes with hounds and lookin' for gold mines."

Marsha said, "Something must have been neglected among all those activities."

Mac beamed and fast two-stepped at her statement. "Now you're gettin' it, gal. I was neglectin' the ranch and Norma Mae, too. 'Course, I didn't realize it at the time."

"I guess that would be pretty good grounds for argument, Mac?"

"Yeah, but the truth is, it was more fightin' than arguing. She had a tendency to pick up things and hit me with 'em, and if she couldn't get close enough, she'd throw 'em. Things was always nervous and chipped 'round our outfit."

"Are you still married? Where is she?"

"Don't rightly know. You see, I'd been gone 'bout three months, up in the Gila region, and got drunk over at the S-Bar-X Saloon in Hillsboro on the way home. She was mad. I'm telling you, she was real mad." Mac danced on about ten whirls, receiving another unacknowledged scratch on his back, saying nothing.

Marsha said, "Well, go on. You can't quit on me right in the middle of the story." And she was serious. She just had to know how it ended.

"Yeah. Well, we got to cussin' at one another and the next thing I know she's comin' at me with a butcher knife. I jumped around her, trying to get to the door, when she stuck that damned knife in my back hard as she could. I'd reach..." he was demonstrating right on the dance floor, "with one arm over my shoulder, but I couldn't quite get a hand on it. Then I'd reach back and under, but I couldn't get hold of it that way, either. I was just standing there helpless with a knife in my back. She musta been studying that unreachable spot for years. All the time I was stumbling about screaming and trying to reach that knife, she was packin' her clothes. I musta looked like one of them magicians that's tryin' to get out of a straitjacket. Only I couldn't help myself. I started to beg her to pull the knife out, but instantly thought better of it."

"She just might have done it, Mac. What did you have to lose at that point?"

Mac stepped back from Marsha again, saying—swelling with indignation, "Lose? What did I have to lose? My head, I reckon. I'm sure she would have pulled it out and cut my dumb head off."

Marsha wanted to laugh at his description but choked it back admirably, not wishing to hurt Mac's feelings.

His little eyes enlarged along with his nostrils as he said, "By the time I got that damned butcher knife out, she had driven off in our pickup, taking what little money and prospecting gold I had, and vanished. Just disappeared like a coyote in thick brush. Never showed up nowhere again. Never. Musta gone foreign, I figure. Way off somewhere foreign."

"How did you get the knife out, Mac?"

"Oh, that."

Mac stopped dancing, walked over to the wall, turned his back to it, and rubbed hard right and left. Right and left. Unbeknownst to him, his local friends had witnessed and recognized the show he was putting on for Marsha. He received an ovation of appreciation.

She had enjoyed his story and the dance. She gave his sore back a light scratching and one-hand massage. Then she told the old man, whom she had enjoyed so much and now strangely felt close to, as if he were an older version of Bluefeather, "Your back will never itch again."

He danced with her again, so slowly they came to a stop, as he said, "Danged if you ain't cured me, darlin'. Cain't feel a thang back there but staring eyes."

Then Mac held her close and she was both radiant and safe as her mind turned him into Bluefeather for a few moments. The jukebox was playing a popular song, "Tears on My Pillow." Somehow the misty mood of the music mellowed her body and her heart so that she constantly glanced over Mac's shoulder at the door for Bluefeather's return. Then she asked in a voice soft as a dropping feather, warm as a wool coat, "How long have you known Bluefeather?"

"Ohhh...let me think. Something like ten or twelve years. You get to know a man real quick when you work the desert or the high mountains with him."

"Yes. Yes, you certainly do..."

Mac was silent a moment, but being a man of deep, mostly hidden, feelings, he knew Marsha was sincerely casting a fishnet.

"I'll tell you true, and for barn rat sure, that man's as loyal to his friends as a loving mother is to her firstborn."

She was surprised how his words thrilled her and made her feel safe. There was no danger from Korbell or any of his adoptees. For that one moment, there had never been any wars in the history of the world; hateful jealousy and grinding greed were nonexistent. Just for that little moment, there was just Marsha and Bluefeather.

Then the music changed, but she didn't hear it. She stopped and leaned down, kissing Mac on the cheek, saying, "Thanks, friend of my friend. Thank you until there is no more."

Mac led her politely to the table, thanked her for the dances, and wondered what she meant by the "until there is no more" stuff. He went to the men's room to cogitate. Marsha smiled after his healed back.

Bluefeather re-entered Dominguez's place and rejoined his group. He gave Marsha a tiny head signal out toward the dance floor. He wanted to let her know what had happened even though he had been unsuccessful. Other things were moving along as wished.

Charlie and Sally were holding hands, laughing, and giggling at every statement they made, no matter how silly. Harvey Dixon had one arm partially draped over Flo's back. They were both talking and enjoying themselves almost as much as Charlie and Sally. This was, at least for the moment, good enough for Bluefeather. He worried all the time about Flo and Sally's dedication to taking care of Willy, because he had done the same for them when Flo had been widowed. Just the same, it sure restricted their chances at a love life, living in such an isolated place.

Three couples that Bluefeather was slightly acquainted with sat at an adjoining table. Among them were Pearl and Bill Dozier. Pearl was an old friend of Flo's and yelled meaningless things at her now and then. She never stopped talking, whether she had listeners or not. She mouthed on about her garden, her dog, her kids; then she would repeat the same subjects. Her husband was a retired air force colonel, but he wasn't giving any commands here. He drank mostly in silence, giving a nod when one of the others tried to wedge in a sentence.

Suddenly, there was a crash. Bluefeather's instincts directed him to duck and whirl, leaping back ready to defend himself. The colonel had crash-dived to the barroom floor. There was a doctor from Las Cruces sitting at the bar. He gave Bill mouth-to-mouth resuscitation while Bluefeather pumped rhythmically on his breastbone, trying to revive him. Dominguez yelled for someone to get the emergency squad that was always present at these celebrations. They came and slipped an oxygen mask over the colonel's face. It was too late. His heart had evidently worn out from listening to Pearl's endless repetition of superficialities. She had actually talked him to death. It was slow murder and she would get away with it amid much sympathy and honor.

Some people led Pearl out of the room. She was screaming, over and over through her tears, "How could he do this to me?"

The whispered voice of tragedy witnessed washed about the bar for a brief time; then everyone gradually returned to drinking and dancing.

Flo said, "Well, old Bill flew through five major campaigns without a scratch, and it only took Pearl three years to talk him to death. Gotta give her credit—she's still maintaining her average. That's about how long it took her to cash in her two previous husbands."

The empty table was taken up by three husky young men with two-day beards and soiled baseball caps. They were accompanied by a pretty, if unwashed, eighteen-year-old girl in very tight Levis.

Carmelita was trying to clear their table so she could serve them. The largest, with a growing belly pushing his pale gray-checked shirt out over his belt, rubbed Carmelita's rear, saying with a shared grin of sleaze, "Lookee what we got here. A regular quarter horse mare. What time you goin' out to pasture tonight, Sugar Doll?"

Carmelita moved away, taking the dirty glasses without comment. His two companions made remarks just as dumb. When she returned with their beers, they chorused even more stupid utterances. If there was anything that could unlock Bluefeather's controlled anger it was some idiot making rude, suggestive remarks to waitresses. He had always felt they had a tough enough time serving people, standing up and running around, hour after hour, on their tired feet, without having to defend their private parts from some smart-ass, numb-headed, macho fool.

Every time they finished a beer, one of them would snap his fingers at Carmelita and yell, "Hey, you," like she was his personal slave.

Bluefeather figured they would probably leave a fifteen-cent tip. It was difficult indeed for him to keep his breathing down. He could feel the scar across his nose searing and the hairs itching on the back of his neck. His face was becoming flushed. He tried to cool himself by hoping some cowboys would take up Carmelita's case even though he craved to bash the Neanderthal skulls. Then, too, he and Marsha had fought with a similar dunce the last time they had been in here. He didn't want any trouble as long as there was a chance Dolby might show. At that thought he heard flute music. Indian flute music.

There in the middle of the dancing couples stood his spirit guide. At his stare, the flute disappeared and Dancing Bear indulged himself with an Irish jig even though it didn't fit the music.

Bluefeather excused himself as soon as Dancing Bear jigged to an outside circle. Bluefeather walked by and whispered for him to follow.

"We gotta talk."

They walked past the restroom and out the back door. There was no one out there to interrupt them but one drunk cowboy who was leaning up against the building by the palm of his hands, trying to keep from vomiting on his expensive Paul Bond boots.

Bluefeather held onto a cedar post holding up a drooping, barbed wire fence with one hand and relieved his kidneys.

Dancing Bear sat on top of an old gasoline barrel. "You know, dear brudder, old man Phillips, he tell me this. When he was young man he have to put his thang under the wire to keep from peeing in his face. Now when he get very old he have to drop his thang over the wire to keep from peein' in his boots." With that Dancing Bear started laughing and stood up on the barrel, holding up one leg in the stance of a Masai hunter.

"I haven't got time for your worn-out jokes, Bear. You've been playing around in London and Authority knows where else, while I've been in desperate need of help."

"That's for sure. But I send substitute with many messages. She give it to you? Huh? Huh?"

"She gave...well, let's put it this way. I couldn't figure out what she meant."

"Don't tell me this thing. Sometimes you smart boy. Sometimes you don't do so good."

"Good? By the almighty Authority, you tell me how."

Dancing Bear said, "Now don't get your bowels in uproarious condition. Things movin' along pretty good. I tell you this truth."

"I gotta admit some of the crazy things you tell me have come to pass. But they've only created more confusion. Korbell's not going to wait on me, or anyone else, forever."

"Korbell wait like horny buck for doe to tell when time she's right. Like that 'red' girl do it to you, huh? Ain't that about right, for sure."

Bluefeather felt like running back into the bar and drinking all the whiskey in Dominguez's place, but he was too confused to find the door. Instead, he said weakly, "I haven't figured out all I know about this world right here, much less the one you inhabit."

"No matter. I been 'round a hunnert years, maybe more, and I haven't learned but a..."

"Please, Bear. Please. I beg you like a little baby brother to help me right now. Just give me something solid to hang onto. Anything. All you've been doing is handing me pieces of broken limbs and shattered bottles."

"Sure as sun smile on morning dew, sure as mother's milk, sure as moon make ocean tides, sure as buffalo return, sure as the snow turn to rivers in the spring, sure as..."

Bluefeather's ears went numb. His head felt like the wheel of a windmill in a tornado. He felt for certain he had sunk into the earth up to his waist.

"Shut up!" he yelled. "Just shut up that poetic flea shit and tell me. Just plain tell me what to do. Oh, what did I ever do to deserve you?"

"You just lucky, I guess. All the time you white men hurry, hurry, hurry like rabbits making million baby rabbits. Then the coyotes, the bobcats, the mountain lions, they all come and eat 'em to pieces. Poor dumb rabbits. They got to jump on one another, hurry, hurry, before they all gone. Then..."

Bluefeather stumbled toward the bar.

"Wait one step, dear brudder." Bluefeather stopped without turning around and Dancing Bear said to his slightly humped up back, "That pretty Mexican waitress, Carmelita..."

"Carmelita?"

"Yes, her. She show you the way to where the moon don't have no chance to glow. That girl don't know she gonna do this for you, but, dear brudder, you watch what happen like one thousand eagles. Huh? Huh?"

Dancing Bear then leapt from the gasoline barrel to the top of an old shed and started yelling at the universe, doing an expert rainbow dance. Then he shouted at his subject, "You like Scottish fling?" He flung himself from the shed out into the crisp, mountain air. He did such an expertly executed dance that it would have made a real Scotsman rupture his bagpipe in awe.

Bluefeather walked past the drunk. He was now sitting down with his head back against the building and his still-clean boots shoved out in front.

"You need any help, old buddy?" Bluefeather asked him.

"Naw, I'll be ready to get after it again in just a minute."

Bluefeather entered the throbbing bar. It was the time of insanity. It would do nothing but improve until two o'clock in the morning.

Flo said, "We were just about to send the militia to look for you."

"They wouldn't have me."

Charlie said, "Hey, Blue, we were thinking about going somewhere to get something to eat. Dominguez is outa burritos already."

"You folks go ahead without me. I gotta wait here for somebody."

Marsha volunteered, "Tell you what, folks, Sally and I will go get something and bring it back here. Any idea what you would like?"

Harvey Dixon said, "Anything that's not talking."

Everyone left it up to them. Food was simply fuel now. Naturally, the table with the three scummy baseball caps and the soiled, but pretty, girl had to yell after two women as fine looking as Marsha and Sally. That was excusable for the moment. Those two women would have drawn a reaction from a mummy.

Harvey said, "You know what, Blue? I think I'm falling in love." He grabbed Flo around the shoulder and pulled her to him.

She liked it, but said, "Aw, shoot, he's just had enough drinks to start smelling roses in a catbox."

Bluefeather said, for no reason he could think of, "Watch out for him, Flo. An uncle of mine was going broke and he decided he'd slowly teach his dog not to eat. Soon as he got him trained, he died."

There they were just as one-track-minded and silly as all the other drunks in the world. Right now they were all thinking of the food to come.

Bluefeather decided he should ask Flo to dance. They did.

"You kinda got the itch for Harvey, haven't you gal?"

"We'll know about that by morning, Blue."

"Well, there's not a drove of people around that I'd recommend to a friend, but Harvey's about as right as you're likely to run across these days."

"He's a lot of fun anyway, but I wish Willy was here to share with us."

"Now you listen to me, Flo. Willy's just hungover and worried about a lot of things. Listen to your buddy Blue. Everything's gonna be honey and grapes before you know it."

"Okay, boss. If you say so."

"Guaran-goddamned-teed. I got it on high authority. We'll just stay hooked to the wagon even if the axle breaks."

Marsha and Sally returned with the food—green chile burritos and barbecued beef sandwiches. This would take care of them for the rest of the evening.

Bluefeather ordered another round of drinks from Carmelita. She served them from the side of the table so the sweat-stained idiots couldn't grab at her. Bluefeather must remember to watch her as Dancing Bear had insisted so adamantly. He did. Sure enough, she stopped at the bar to speak to someone. It was Dolby and his Kenyan lady, Sherry.

Bluefeather uttered, "Slapping thunder. It's Dolby."

He felt Marsha's hand on his arm, silently speaking to him. It was suggesting he take it calmly. It was a difficult chore for him to do, but his nerves quit jumping. The bar table inhabitants chattered on with reasonably intelligent conversation that could only come from comfortable company appreciating each other.

Then it happened, of course. One of the three cretins was trying to pull Sherry away from old Dolby onto the dance floor. He made the mistake of saying, "Come on, honey, your old daddy won't mind."

Sherry was trying to tug her arm free, looking helpless and angry at the same time. Dolby was slowly becoming aware of the intrusion. Bluefeather saw his hand start under his coat for the pistol.

There was no time now for thinking things over, being cool and all that. Everything Korbell was paying wages for, and he and his friends had been struggling for, was about to be blown away by one worthless half-wit. The strong lock that Bluefeather kept on his anger broke apart into powdered metal.

Bluefeather decided this had to be done instantly. He reared up and ran at the abuser of women, shoving a thumb and forefinger in each of his eyes. Then he kneed him forcefully in the groin. The baseball cap's lungs were partly paralyzed as he bent over, agonizing out a howl that denoted pain.

Bluefeather grabbed him by the top of his head and with both hands pushed down hard, bringing up his right knee to meet the descending face with much force. They met. A number of things on the victim's face squashed and the blood splattered about like water from a busted garden hose. He dropped. Thunk.

Charlie had another "baseball cap" down and was pounding the dog piss out of him. The third one had poor Harvey on the floor doing the same to him. Bluefeather charged through the milling, yelling crowd to give his friend Harvey some relief. Marsha beat him to it. She had one knee in the assailant's back and was opening both of her arms wide and then whamming both palms against his ears. The third time she did this he fell off Harvey onto the floor, screaming, "I'm deaf. I'm deaf."

Bluefeather jerked him up and whammed him across the nose so hard he could feel the bones splinter. Now the whey-bellied "cap" was without proper hearing or smelling abilities. Charlie was trying to kick him blind to make his deserved punishment complete, but a throng of peacemakers were pulling him backward toward the bar, handing him refreshments to cool him off. The crowd's action was correct, for a change. Any more punishment would go unfelt and waste good party-ing time.

The defeated ones' little girl companion was about to faint, so Bluefeather handed her the only drink that hadn't been spilled.

"Here Miss, try this."

She took it in shaking hands and said, "Thank you. I just met them today and I've been embarrassed ever since."

The Dos Amigos went through the after-fight bedlam of the law arriving, and the losers trying to fake breaking loose from restraining arms to fight some more. The officers talked to Dominguez, Carmelita, Sherry, and a few others, then hauled the three caps away. One of them screamed back vengeance.

The place slowly returned to more peaceful drinking and dancing. The usual accompanying yells quieted for a while. Their table was sent many complimentary drinks from other patrons. Some of them added that Bluefeather's bunch had saved them the trouble. The night was about normal for a hundred-year celebration: one dead colonel, three whipped smart-asses, several new romances in progress, and old and new drunks dancing again.

Old Dolby was calmly sipping his drink, without having had to fire his pistol. Sherry was talking seriously into his ear. He would nod almost imperceptibly to her. Then a stool emptied next to Sherry and she put her purse on it, motioning Bluefeather to join them. Here it was. The main move. Indeed, for once—this once, when it counted the most—Dancing Bear had clearly guided him to the desperately needed connection. The success of the meeting would be entirely up to Bluefeather. By defending Sherry without hesitation, he had just earned the sudden trust of both Dolby and his lady.

Sherry moved over at his approach so that he would be sitting between them. He glanced back at Marsha as he sat down, shaking hands, and their eyes locked in space with understanding. These moments would be it, one way or the other. They both knew it. Dolby was the only entrant left in their shell game. Unbeknownst to Bluefeather, he had just become the finalist in Dolby and Sherry's desperate search for a partner.

"Thank you, Mr. Fellini," Dolby said.

Bluefeather started to tell him to drop the mister, but Korbell had worn him out on that subject. "My pleasure, I assure you. They had been insulting Carmelita, too."

"We both thank you, Mr. Fellini," Sherry said.

"Please call me Blue," he felt free to suggest to her.

"Of course. At any rate we are deeply appreciative."

"Hey, it's just part of the celebration. Perfectly normal happening."

Dolby didn't look him directly in the eyes, but stared far away at some distant cloud bank or mesa. His mind seemed to be only partially here.

Oddly, Sherry Rousset had that same expression of a knowledge that only the two of them could share. There was a vast loneliness emanating from these people as if they sat at a bar in some other world and time.

Bluefeather was struck again by the huge, black, shining, African eyes whose outer edges arched up around Sherry's head as if she had the peripheral vision of a chameleon. Her light, milk chocolate skin pulled over the cheekbones as tightly as little drums, but her full-lipped mouth had a hidden sadness about it.

Dolby's face, under the slight shade of his little fedora, showed lines that could have been etched by a linoleum cutter. He stared at the glass of whiskey in his bent, bony hands as if the ultimate answer of existence was being revealed in the amber lights flickering there. They were a couple out of context with this milling, sweating, laughing, celebrating little world around them.

Bluefeather thought of the larger world, of other cities in other nations. In his mind-pictures the couple was unique, no matter where he placed them.

"Do you visit?" Dolby asked in a whisper, turning his little eyes toward Bluefeather without moving his head.

It threw Bluefeather off, but he answered, "Yes. What do you have in mind?"

"The millenniums are less than seconds."

Bluefeather just simply did not know how to reply.

Sherry placed her hand gently on his forearm and spoke lowly, "Would you come to our house—alone?"

"Now?"

"If it would be at all convenient for you."

Dolby emptied the few drops of whiskey left in his glass and said, "The vassals and vessels are empty. It is the time of conceptions."

Sherry interjected, with only a trace of urging in her voice, but Bluefeather felt it quivering in her being, "If you could come now, please. He . . . he is ready at last."

Bluefeather nodded yes, went to his table saying, "Have fun, kids. I have to leave you for a while."

Marsha reached out and took his hand, squeezing it with a soft strength that made him feel warm, calm, sure, and just plain good.

■ ■ ■

Fifteen

Sherry drove the perfectly tuned Bentley along the well-graded, graveled dirt road. Dolby sat in front with her. Both silently stared straight ahead. Bluefeather sat in the back, looking out at the sagebrush and yuccas. The foothills became larger, and the cedar and piñons began to thicken. In openings around curves he could see the mountains climbing in green, then blue, layers, furred with spruce and pines.

They came to a huge fence and a guard post. There were two men in their seventies with rifles slung across their shoulders. They were in dark, loose uniforms. Without the belt and holsters for revolvers, their dress could have been taken for monks' robes. The age of the two, who pushed the buttons to swing open the huge electric gates, surprised Bluefeather. Behind them was a big guard house with a tower and dark port holes all around. There was no way of knowing how many guns there were here.

Bluefeather's recently jubilant mind was now somehow tilted out of kilter at the old men and their raiment. There, across a lush, heavily grassed valley, was the house nestled against the last big foothill at the base of the heavily timbered mountains. It was a huge, brown brick against the bluffs. Because of its low profile and the long, hexagonal sloping roofs, the compound of buildings blended into the background as if it had been carved there by a giant sculptor.

There was another artfully designed fence and guard gate nearer the house. It was perhaps twelve feet tall. Bluefeather was certain it was electrified. The fence had been painted in army camouflage colors and was hard to follow as it wove erratically through clusters of natural trees and vegetation. The guard house was even larger here. There were several old men and two elderly women dressed in the same unique warrior-monk uniforms.

One leaned over and spoke into Dolby's ear so softly that the words were indistinguishable. The car pulled across the cattle guard into the grounds area, where there were no lawns, just gravel and stone pathways winding through natural vegetation. A massive wood and iron-laced door opened and let them into a rock-fenced area that closely surrounded the entire house.

Sherry turned sharply to the right, into a huge garage that housed several jeeps, pickups, a new Buick Roadmaster, and another Bentley. A couple of old men were slowly moving about, checking and cleaning the vehicles.

"My God," Bluefeather's mind-voice elevated, "Dolby's got a combination old folk's home and senior citizen army here. Why? Why and more whys?"

As they got out and entered the house from a doorway connected to the garage, Bluefeather saw a hallway perhaps twenty feet wide and eighty feet long, just like the one at Korbell's. It was even floored in a similarly colored design of Mexican tile. The paintings—some of which he instantly recognized as Taos masters—hung on the walls. There was one great difference: instead of being escorted in by Korbell's beautiful, adopted wife, Elena, two great danes and a mastiff were lined up, staring at them motionlessly from the end of the hallway.

Sherry gave a hand signal and they fell from formation and came to meet them. Bluefeather was certain they would smell his fear and take three parts of him for play. They all gave him a slight touch of the muzzle.

Then Sherry said, "Hello guys. This is Mr. Fellini."

They wagged their tails now, fully smelling Bluefeather's legs and allowing him to touch their massive heads. They actually roughhoused a little with Sherry, but not enough to give up their dignity. Bluefeather was surprised that he wasn't surprised at them totally ignoring Dolby's existence except to circle him without looking or smelling.

They walked through an archway into a large living room full of old prints and dark walnut furniture. Great urns and brass objects were placed about. Bluefeather didn't have a chance to study the room's contents, but he got a feeling of ancient things residing here even though the main compound itself couldn't be over twenty-five or thirty years of age—at least it was new for the land of the vanished Anasazis and Mimbres Indian tribes.

Sherry smoothly led the way into the combination kitchen and sitting room area. Bluefeather sat in a modern, rounded chair. Dolby took his own matching one, as if from long habit. The dogs scattered about in a semicircle on Navajo rugs, lying heads up, watching, listening. For what? The young man did not know.

There were richly colored draperies hanging beside the huge picture window facing mountains to the north—just like Korbell's. All sorts of green living plants flourished in pots of many sizes around the room. In this room the paintings were much more modern than those in the hallway, done in broad and brightly colored strokes. They varied from barely recognizable figures—ghostly, religious, devilish, both delicate and deformed—to wild, almost unrecognizable, landscapes. Two long sets of bookshelves balanced the sitting room. One held leather-bound tomes that appeared scholarly, the other books of a more recent vintage. He couldn't read the titles from where he sat, but he had an almost irresistible urge to go and search for old, familiar names with which he had spent so many wondrous and adventurous hours. He kept control somehow, and yet he had this feeling of déjà vu, as if he were back in Korbell's mansion being set up again.

He looked out past a great landscape, over the small lake in the valley and felt another charge of electricity tingle all his skin. There were at least thirty gorgeous mules—some grazing, others turned head to rear, swatting flies from one another. A couple of younger ones raced about in a mock running fight. There were bays, browns, and blacks along with one gray. They were so solidly fleshed, so sleek of hair, that he could tell they were exercised and fed to perfection. Well, that was one thing for sure he and Dolby had in common—the mules, man's most useful partner of the entire animal kingdom. There was so much he bubbled to ask and discuss that he had to grit his teeth to refrain. He was here for greater—if mostly unknown—purposes than discussing common likes and dislikes.

Sherry brought liver pâté and cheese wedges with little crackers and placed them on the coffee table between the two men.

"Now, what would you like to drink?"

Usually, the drinks would have been served first, but this turn-around seemed proper to Bluefeather here—now. He asked for Scotch and water. Dolby was served his usual glass of sipping whiskey. Sherry poured herself a rich, red burgundy wine.

They were all seated. Sherry raised her glass in a silent toast. Dolby raised his along with them, staring at the glass only. He seemed to see things in the lights and tiny bubbles that no one else could envision. Dolby took a tiny sip, moving his lips soundlessly. It was as if they should know his thoughts without the interference of words. Now the old man seemed to be staring across vast landscapes, looking for the fountain of truth.

Sherry sat a moment, slowly whirling her wine after the first sip. Her thick, black, minutely wavy hair picked up reflections of blue and brown as did her large, slanted eyes with the whites gleaming around them in contrast to her coloring. She was indeed striking. Her eyes penetrated the space beyond the strongly sculptured face and looked into Bluefeather's head. He felt as if she saw all the way through so that she could have computed the hairs on the back of his neck, if she so desired.

"You are searching for something, Mr. Fellini. Something very special?"

"Well—yes. Aren't we all hunting something we don't have?"

"Surely. But the rare few seek the difficult—the impossible. Impossible to most of us, I should say."

Bluefeather fished forward. "I've done a bit of gambling in my time—with cards, of course, but far beyond that."

"We're aware of that. That's why—among other reasons—we asked you to join us here."

Dolby mumbled, "The world cannot control all that is in it any more than it can the human mind."

Sherry glanced at him with obvious fondness and appeared to understand what he meant. Bluefeather admitted to himself that he sure as hell didn't. Lord, he was mixed up, what with the riddles of Dancing Bear and the unexplained, almost invisible games of Korbell and now the incoherence of the seemingly senile, imponderable utterances of Dolby.

It was the time of decision. Sherry Rousset made it.

"Blue—I recall you wish to be called Blue—as Dolby said earlier, 'It is the time to move on.' We might as well start now. Right now. We have decided to put our trust in you with multiple, and what will at first be shocking, revelations. We're not going to ask for guarantees, either verbal or written, that you will keep faith. Faith is only as good as a person's heart and honor. We, as of now, accept yours. Let me add, however, that even if you keep it, and we believe you will, it could still lead to disastrous and momentous events. If you do not keep it," she paused a beat, "well, it will mean certain doom for many who do not deserve such a fate."

Bluefeather could not resist, not for a second, the promise of such unknown escapades. It was imbedded as deep in his blood as coyotes howling. Bluefeather Fellini was a natural-born yearner. He committed.

"Whatever it is, I will give you my best."

Sherry's face now softened a mite with a slight smile. "We, as you shall see, have waited a long, a very long time. Our waiting must come to its agonizing end now. Now," she repeated louder, looking at Dolby.

A metamorphosis took over the old man. He straightened. His pallid skin gained color. His eyes moved thoughts to their surface from hidden recesses. He finished his drink in a single swallow and stood up, suddenly animated, exuding the forces of life. For just a moment he looked into Bluefeather's dark eyes with his recessed blue ones. The old man's dry stare was as merciless as the gaze of a tiger hunting to feed her young. He must never forget this look, thought Bluefeather. Never!

Sherry rose now, saying, "Come then. We shall begin."

Dolby led the way, momentarily in charge. He pushed lightly on a shelved wall of Mimbres pottery. It moved back, opening into an empty concrete passage. He pushed on another wall—again not unlike Korbell. It swung back, then closed precisely as they moved on down curving concrete stairways.

Bluefeather had felt, or believed he felt, a slight quivering. He even believed for a moment he could hear, but he wasn't certain, giant motors running somewhere. The curving stairway slope was long and gentle, and old Dolby negotiated it with confidence.

They circled many times, going deeper and deeper under the compound until they came to another wall of the same material. There were soft lights from indentations in the wall showing the way to it.

Dolby swung the wall open with another light push, and they were in a room possibly forty by eighty feet. At one end there were wheel handles of a large steel vault. Heavily reinforced file cabinets lined part of the room. There were tables filled with microscopes and all sorts of chemistry tubes and glasses. Several shelves were loaded with metal boxes of bones. Bluefeather could not, at a glance, tell what was skeletonized.

Sherry moved forward and slid a panel back over a narrow, heavily glassed window. She motioned Bluefeather to have a look. Down below was a large power plant humming the sound he had felt and heard. A couple of old men—as old as Dolby—sat on stools conversing, watching the machinery.

Sherry said, "We call our workers the Olders. You'll understand why later. This is our own private electrical plant fueled by our own thermal-powered wells. No one knows about this outside the compound. You'll see why this has been a requisite as we move you forward into the greater aspects of our installations and situations."

There was a film projector at one end and a pathway through the other items in the room to a large screen. There were six softly made chairs facing the screen.

Dolby pointed from one end of the great room to the other. "We could show you many astounding things here, but Sherry shall take you to see the real thing."

Sherry opened a gun rack—more like a small armory—which included automatic weapons, handguns, and hand grenades, even two flamethrowers and several rifles with grenade launcher attachments. She handed him an M-16 and a belt of cartridges. She placed a huge pair of binoculars around each of their necks.

She said, in a soldierly manner now, "We probably won't need the weapons today on so short a trip, but..." She picked up a battery light as big as a loaf of bread, saying, "We have lights installed for miles, but just in case." She shook the handlight, testing it. She pushed a file case on smooth rollers away from a wall and spun a combination lock behind it. Then, with a push the same as Dolby had used, a huge concrete and steel door three feet thick swung open with precision movement—soundlessly.

Dolby said, "Not past station C-One for now, Sherry. Understand?"

"Yes," was all she said, and they entered.

In the next few hours Bluefeather had a slight understanding of what Dancing Bear had meant about the subterranean and there being no time in his dimension. What he saw down below was so real, so very real, and so unreal, so believable and unbelievable, so unearthly, and yet, more earthbound than he could have dreamed with the mind of Edgar Allan Poe.

Upon their return, they ran the film of the subterranean. Bluefeather remembered again that Dancing Bear had used the word more than once. He was in a state of exhilarated shock. The film had been such an addition, revealing wonders past—far on past—those he had just seen with his naked eyes.

Dolby finally slept as the last hour of the unimaginable reality of the documentary film unreeled. Sherry shut off the projector and, with that, Dolby awoke and sat up, staring again at Bluefeather. Waiting.

Bluefeather asked, "Why me?"

Dolby stated, matter-of-factly, "I'm not going to be here much longer—that's pretty obvious—and I need the assurance that Sherry, and the project I've given my life to, are safe from the greedy clutches of...an old adversary."

Bluefeather took a deep breath and said, "I'm honored, Mr. Dolby, to be part of your world—your world inside a world." And he was.

Sixteen

Back in the sitting room, Sherry Rousset served strong, aromatic Turkish coffee. They needed the caffeine jolt to hold on for the dawn assembling itself outside, painting away the night with sun rays brushing the northern peaks pink on their eastern tips and violet in the valleys. The outer world, the one that suddenly seemed commonplace, had made a complete circle during their short trip to the interior.

The coffee tasted good, but Bluefeather did not really need it to keep awake. He could literally feel the nerves of his entire body vibrating like a driven jackhammer.

"Well, folks, it will take me a while to organize everything—since we can't hire any strangers. You'll have to trust my people just as you have me. My experience in the mines and World War II, the trips back and forth across the Mexican border, may be useful to us now."

Dolby spoke as alertly as an Olympian finalist, "Of course, Mr. Fellini. We are totally committed now. All of us. You make the necessary preparations. We shall comply and help you with all our physical, financial, and mental resources."

Sherry looked at Dolby with a strange reverence in her eyes, exhaling a deep sigh of relief, saying, "At last, dearest one, at last."

The first smile Bluefeather—or anyone else—had seen, crept across Dolby's face with the words, "Yes. Yes. The fulfillment. The finality is near."

She answered considerately, "Only the finish of one magnificent step. It is really endless."

Dolby answered, "You are correct, precious one. It is in fact, perpetuity. No recorded beginning...and no end."

Bluefeather said to himself with his mind-voice, "As for me, old dumb-butt Bluefeather, I'm growing speechless, mute as a mummy."

Seventeen

Sherry drove Bluefeather back into town as the sun was beginning to warm the east side of the scattered homes of Meanwhile. People were already up and stirring about. Some were shaking the night before from their sleepy, still half-drunk eyes, while others were starting to cook breakfast over open fires and in the trailers and campers.

"Don't get impatient now, Blue. We'll contact you a few days ahead of the expedition," Sherry said.

"I'll be getting ready, nonetheless, as fast as possible. Say two weeks. By the way, thanks for..."

"Forget it. We're on. All the way."

Sally and Charlie were just getting out of his pickup camper, which was parked by the hotel. Bluefeather didn't waste any time. He handed Sally the key to his room so she could clean up and told Charlie to wait. He went over and pounded on Marsha's door until he woke her. He told her to pack her things—they had business to attend to. He asked Charlie where Flo and Harvey were. Charlie pointed to Flo's motel room.

"Good. Now you guys all stay here and finish your playing today. Then, Charlie, you get after those maps. Harvey can take the girls home tomorrow. Say, get plenty of olive greens, climbing boots, bedrolls, the whole bit, just like we were going into the wilderness for months. Don't need any food or weapons though. We've got plenty of both." At Charlie's quizzical look, he explained, "Look, ol' pardner, we're goin' after a big score. The biggest ever. You're just gonna have to trust me. Call in every day at Rugers'. I gotta know where you are all the time."

"Well hell, couldn't you just give me a hint at what's up, Blue?"

"Not now. Anyway, you probably wouldn't believe it," Bluefeather said, shaking his head. "I want all of Tilton's floor plans. Then I'll explain. Marsha and I have to get on out and talk to Willy. And then I've got to get hold of Pack."

Bluefeather and Marsha were about a mile from Willy's when he finished telling her where he had been and everything he had seen at Dolby's. She sat silently around several curves. A doe and fawn bounced across the road and vanished into the timber.

"My God, Blue. What you have told me will alter human history. Earthly history, as well, I suppose. I'm completely dumbfounded."

"We'll probably get the bullion, too," he said.

"What does it matter now, after what you've just told me?"

"It matters even more to me. It's, well, shit, Marsha, it's just part of what we set out to do. It's our job. Our duty."

"No. No, it's not. We started out to find the Mouton 1880. That's all."

"Yeah, maybe. You gotta remember Korbell did make a strong point about the bullion. I know that wasn't part of the deal with him, but it has become our deal. Ours."

"Well..." and she shook her head, dismayed to a degree.

They drove to the front of Willy's house. Old Brown was on the porch but did not come to meet them as he usually did. He looked awful. One of his ears was shredded, and he had several scattered cuts.

Bluefeather yelled for Willy and got no answer. They entered the house. Willy sat there on the couch with a glass of whiskey in his hand and a bottle on the floor within reach. They had left Willy at home a wreck and he hadn't improved in their absence. He looked like he had been kicked by a mule and crapped on by an elephant.

"What in hell happened to you, Willy?"

Willy stared at his drink like old Dolby and finally choked out, "The lion. The lion killed Toby and Jumper and made off with a calf."

It was another brain-shaker. They had come here to tell Willy about their monumental challenge and now this. Right here, in the woods with his dogs, was Willy's world. They would just have to forget the other fantastic, subterranean one right now and take care of his.

"When did all this happen?"

"Jist 'fore dawn. The racket of the fightin' woke me up. I got the gun, but it was already too late. I done buried the dogs. Jist finished 'while ago. Forgot, goddamn it. I jist forgot to pen 'em up."

Bluefeather checked the .30–30. It was loaded. He got a holding leash for Old Brown.

"Marsha, if you want to go with me, we have to move out now." She nodded "yes." He handed her the 357 Magnum. "The lion will be full of calf meat and bushed up somewhere. We gotta get after him while his belly is full. It'll slow him down."

Willy stood up, weaving, silent tears washing over his blunt, drawn face. "I'm ready."

"No, you're not, ol' pardner. You're gonna stay here. It won't take long."

They left him standing there, making feeble protests. Bluefeather knew damn well Willy had suffered all the killing he could take in his condition. Besides, Willy had an admiration and deep feeling for the very creature that was destroying his livestock.

Bluefeather ran the cotton rope through the iron ring on Old Brown's collar and held the two ends in his hand. This way he could control the dog until he was ready to turn him loose by simply dropping one end of the rope. Release would be instantaneous, and one second might decide success or failure with the obviously survivalist cat.

In spite of the pain from his mauling, Old Brown was pulling hard ahead of Bluefeather on the rope, excited and anxious. He was a hunting dog and that's what he was doing with all he had. He led them to the spot of the previous night's battle. The grass was torn up in spots and bits of bloody hair were scattered about. They followed, with little trouble, the signs of the calf being dragged to the creek. There the lion had turned north, looking for a place to cross with his kill.

Bluefeather said, "The old dickens still has plenty of power left. That calf had to weigh around two hundred pounds—but he's lost most of his speed."

Marsha was amazed at the crippled lion's strength. She said, "You have to admire him, no matter what."

"Yeah. Just like us. He's making a living, the only way he knows how," Bluefeather contributed with a slight grin.

They found where the lion had. crossed. The wet blood left a visible trail. Then, on a rise in a small circle of short brush, they found where he had fed. He had picked a spot so he could escape in any direction if interrupted.

Bluefeather whispered, "The cache won't be too far from here."

It was, however, over a half a mile uphill before they found the calf's remains. The cat had dropped it in a vacant badger hole and half covered it with dirt and sticks.

Bluefeather scooped the covering off and they saw that the cat had eaten a good third of the meat. Some of the bones were stripped relatively clean. The oldster had been desperately hungry. Without any interference, he could have loafed around and fattened up for several days.

The man, the woman, and the dog followed the lion's tracks, observing that the right hind foot twisted to the side from the old injury. This slowed him.

Old Brown strained harder against the rope as the scent became stronger. Bluefeather admired both the dog and lion very much at that moment. Both were doing the best they could under difficult conditions.

Suddenly, Bluefeather saw that they were a lot higher up in flat rocks and boulders than he had noticed. Then Old Brown became confused about the scent on the rocks. Because of the bad leg, Bluefeather surmised that the old lion had made an erratic climb, looking for a safe lair in which to sleep and digest his huge breakfast. Old Brown moved back and forth, once giving Bluefeather a glance like, "Hey you, a little help is in order."

Now they were stalled because of the rocky terrain directly in front of them. Bluefeather motioned to Marsha and softly told her to circle out to the left to look for a patch of soft earth so they could pick up the tracks again. He would do the same with Old Brown, to the right. He also warned her to be very careful. The lion would not be charmed at having a rare meal disturbed.

She nodded and holstered the 357. As Bluefeather and Old Brown scrambled through the rocks and brush he had a sudden regret of having let Marsha go off alone.

Then Old Brown lunged against the rope so hard he almost jerked Bluefeather off the rocky slope. The dog bellowed. Bluefeather turned one end of the rope loose and Old Brown was gone. Bluefeather wadded up the rope, jammed it in his belt, crawling, climbing, and running when he could, after the hound's cries. The dog was out of sight now as the slope got steeper and the rocks bigger. Bluefeather could tell by the intensity of the baying that Old Brown was on a hot trail. The lion was moving on up, just ahead of them. The sounds were as clear and full of information as a telegrapher's message.

Bluefeather forgot everything in existence but this hunt. He was tearing through brush and clawing recklessly over the rocks without thought of injury. At this moment, he lusted to be there when Old Brown treed the lion, more than anything in the world. It had always been so with man.

Then he saw a flash of Old Brown through some cedars and looked on up where the heavily limping lion was leaping off a rock and moving higher into the massive boulders. It was becoming very steep here. Bluefeather was slipping and falling now and then, grabbing at the jagged stones with his free hand. By training and nature, he protected the rifle beyond himself.

Now the sound came, terrible, clear, and beautiful. Old Brown had treed the lion. Bluefeather stopped and looked up, but could not see either one of the animals. One thing was obvious: there was no tree there. The lion's run had been stopped by a bluff, and there he was, making his stand. Bluefeather could tell by Old Brown's sounds that he was frantically trying to get at the cat. If he did, he was dead.

Bluefeather caught a glimpse of Marsha higher up on the other side of the confrontation. It was all coming together like the instruments ending a Wagner symphony.

His mind blurred but his body's adrenalin pushed him on. On up, up. Now he was on a little promontory. He saw them. Old Brown was leaping back and forth, trying to get a foothold up the ledge where the enemy was backed against a bluff. The lion moved to the edge and made a swipe at Old Brown, just missing.

Bluefeather yelled. The lion backed up again. Bluefeather still had to climb down a few yards before climbing back up. He was crawling on his stomach, slipping, digging his feet at pebbled rocks, using elbows and clutching for any kind of hold with his free hand. At last he struggled to an angle where he could get a shot. He raised the rifle as he levered a shell into the chamber.

Then he saw a blur on the rocks above the lion. It was Marsha. She slipped, letting out a cry. The 357 dropped down by the lion. She hung by her fingers a few yards above him. Old Brown was filling the mountains with his voice of the kill. All eternity collided in an instant. Marsha's fingers were losing their grip. If she fell, it would be right on top of the lion. Mountain lions seldom attack humans. In all known history, only a few instances exist where they have. In most cases they had been wounded or cornered, just as in this tragic moment.

Now Marsha was holding on with one hand, clawing desperately with the other. Old Brown had, by chance, found a foothold and was moving awkwardly almost to the edge of the shelf. Bluefeather was near enough to see the saliva in the mouth of the overheated lion.

Bluefeather took all this in at one glance as the big cat turned to face him, his fangs revealed under his stretched-back lips.

Bluefeather centered the gun sight between the yellow-brown eyes. For one unmeasureable piece of time, he stared into the soul of the universe. He pulled the trigger and said, "Forgive me, brother." Death was instantaneous.

Marsha dropped on top of the lion's limp body, thereby saving broken bones. Old Brown scratched over the ledge and chewed at the lion in victory. Bluefeather crawled on over and held Marsha to him without words. Only the growling of the dog interrupted the silence. No birds sang, as yet. All lizards and other earthlings were frozen, still listening.

Then Bluefeather grasped that it was over and lay down on the shelf, panting heavily. He held Marsha to him. He could feel their hearts pounding the blood of life through their slowly relaxing bodies.

He caressed her hair against her neck and held her cheek, damp with soundless tears, against his. Then she moved her head and her mouth sought his. They kissed in a mist of tenderness and warmth-giving that enveloped them as a golden protective shroud. She removed her clothes without haste and spread them on the rocks by the lion and laid her naked body upon them. He removed his own clothes and eased between her thighs. There was no waiting, no tricks, no games, as their bodies joined with the delicious commitment of love. Yes, love. There on the rocky side of the mountain, by the body of the valiant lion and the exhausted hound, they gave all they had to each other.

Bluefeather slept. When he awakened one of his arms was under her head, her face turned to him, and her enormous blue eyes studied him. She smiled so slightly it almost wasn't there. With the tips of one skinned finger, she touched his lips. Then she stretched back, her breasts catching the late sun. He touched a nipple and it stood up stiff. He touched the other and then closed his hand on its firm smoothness.

This time there was the ineluctable pleasure of their separate parts. At the last moment, she let out a cry of pleasure that echoed across the hills into the sky, part of all and of him.

They came to a creek. He took the bloody lion hide from his shoulder. He could not let all of this majestic creature go to the vultures. Willy must have it to admire just as he had when it lived. Marsha, Bluefeather, and Old Brown knelt together and drank the cold liquid gift of mountain snows.

■ ■ ■

Eighteen

Since Bluefeather was afraid to talk on the phone to Korbell about his current knowledge and pressing needs, he was pleased and surprised when the man agreed to come to Willy's place.

He came sweeping in with three large helicopters. The multiple roar made the cattle run, the mules circle, heads high, and birds fly from tree to tree in clattering panic.

All the present Ruger household and the heroic Mr. Brown hound joined Korbell and his retinue where they landed in the meadow.

Before the country bunch could offer any amenities, a large portable table was assembled and set with fine linens and exquisite silver. There was also a bounty of food—including Bluefeather's favorite, wild quail. There were at least six people working on the lunch setup. About a half dozen armed, security personnel stood about, professionally studying the landscape for they knew not what.

Bluefeather recognized Fontaine, Marsha's adopted brother, the one he had first seen at Korbell's guard tower—the one who had a deep scar completely cutting his face in half at a forty-five-degree angle. The seven footer was obviously in charge of this tiny army. He reminded Bluefeather of the arrogant SS officers they had captured at Brest, France. Bluefeather felt Fontaine was just as dangerous.

Korbell was dressed all in white, including tie and shoes, which emphasized the sleekness of his silver hair. His thin, butcher-knife face was accentuated by a perfect golden tan. The adopted wife, Elena, wore a formal black dress that matched her hair and eyes, giving them tremendous punch. His adopted assistant Nedra was also dressed formally in a burnt orange, exquisitely fashioned cocktail dress with Aztec designs.

At first, Bluefeather was puzzled by the formality of dress and dining. But somehow he knew this was part of Korbell's smooth intimidation. However, he reasoned, the man with skillful utility would again expertly, in fact, exquisitely, mix business and pleasure—just as Korbell had told him when they first met.

Amid plentiful small talk, everyone was introduced with enough smiles to hypnotize Satan.

Nedra poured Chateau Lafitte '53 and they feasted as they visited. It was pleasant, indeed, here in the meadow with a soft breeze teasing the warm air, stirring the vegetation that reflected emerald green in the noonday sun. The purple shadows under the trees and the blue-violet haze of the mountain canyons served up a background worthy of the table's bounty that all so eagerly consumed.

Marsha slipped Old Brown several bites under the table. Nedra had arranged the place settings so that Bluefeather was next to Korbell, who naturally sat as head of the table.

Korbell raised his glass of fine wine and said, "May we dine with pleasure, work with total dedication, and win with relish." All raised their glasses at Korbell's movement and drank to his thoughts. He sounded so sincere, Bluefeather felt guilty when his mind-voice broke in with an unsolicited warning. "If that man asked me for a loan, I'm dead certain he'd insist on a cashier's check."

Now Korbell turned his head slightly toward Bluefeather and said, "I assume you have a lead on the Mouton Rothschild, Mr. Fellini."

"No, not yet. Something far greater."

"Indeed. Well, now, knowing the depth of my feeling for the rare wine, I can only consider that you have made a discovery at least equal to the conquering of gravity."

Bluefeather strained to catch some sarcasm in his voice but could not. The man sounded as sincere as the ringing of church bells. Bluefeather was having some difficulty following up on his end of the conversation. He knew that Dancing Bear was somewhere near, having a little fun at Bluefeather's expense, because they were all now sitting at a table that was approximately forty feet in the air. No one appeared to give this fact the attention Bluefeather felt it deserved. The entire group dined and chatted as if they were on solid ground. Bluefeather moved his feet up and down in the pure, thin mountain air. There was no question he was aloft in spite of the others absolutely ignoring the spatial situation that was so obvious to him.

"If you don't mind, we'll have a private talk after lunch," Bluefeather said to Korbell.

"Of course, Mr. Fellini."

What Bluefeather really desperately desired was a conversation with his guiding spirit. He strained mightily, trying to project his mind-voice to the dancing trickster. For once it worked!

There he was, down in the meadow, dancing with one of Willy's mules. He believed it was a waltz. 'Round and 'round they went. The jenny mule followed gracefully, flawlessly. The music was being presented by the Zia Creek. It suddenly changed into a fancy-stepping fox-trot. The mule was leading Dancing Bear.

Now he looked up at Bluefeather, grinning like a chicken-stealing fox and said, "Oh, dear brudder Bluefeather Fellini, it is very good to see you again. How you likin' this dance I do here in grass with my friend the mule? Huh?"

"Two well-matched asses, I'd say," so spoke Bluefeather, not knowing where the words came from. At this Dancing Bear and the mule stepped swiftly, perfectly, together, finishing exactly when the music did. They both turned to him and kneeled, bowing three times in faultless unison. Bluefeather shook his head three times. It changed nothing. The sun punched a hole between two clouds and spotlighted the pines, piñons, and cedar trees that clapped and waved their branches wildly in appreciation.

Bluefeather had to take three quick swallows of Chateau Lafitte '53 to keep from choking.

Dancing Bear, obviously thinking that Bluefeather was triple toasting his performance, said gleefully, "Thank you. Thank you. I appreciate you like my dance so much. I do another good 'un for you. I do tree dance for sure."

Dancing Bear tried doing a Texas two-step with a sixty-foot ponderosa pine but soon said, "Too tall, dat tree."

Dancing Bear was directing the nearest rock bluff—where Bluefeather had killed the lion—in some kind of symphony. Slim slags of stone slipped loose from the bluff's efforts to match its music with the lightning action of Dancing Bear's arms. The pines remained motionless, and their cousins the piñons only applauded lightly out of courtesy. Bluefeather knew, suddenly, that Dancing Bear had blasted his brains with these apparitions for a purpose, but he wasn't going to show his gratitude until after the hoped-for revelation.

In an instant, he was on a limb of a dead pine next to an exultant Indian spirit guide. He was grinning as if he had just sold a shovelful of fresh horseshit for the price of platinum.

"Dat's enough dancing for dis day."

"That's enough dancing for a full year, and don't you start using that cockeyed Indian dialect on me, again. That's for the tourists. You hear?"

Dancing Bear ignored his subject's insolence and said, "Now, dear brudder Blue, I ready to give you plenty good guidance."

"It's about time you showed some responsibility to me. I've got an extremely dangerous and daring venture to perform. There's never been one like it in the history of the world."

"Whooo-eee," said Dancing Bear, "that's a big one, all right. The world she been goin' on pretty long time."

"I'm telling you, Bear, this is so important you may have to ask the Authority for advice on how to give advice."

Dancing Bear jumped upright on the limb and sailed over on top of a big orange bluff. He sat there with his chin in his hand, like Rodin's sculpture, thinking hard. Then he zipped right back on the limb.

"I talk with Authority. He tell me that I done had about a hunnert years to learn, so I gotta do advice for you by my own self."

"Well, as deadly and provident as the final adventure is, I may just have to go over your head, old friend."

Bluefeather looked down at the dining table; there sat his other self right where he had left it, taking another drink of the fancy wine. He could tell from way up here on the pine limb that he had overindulged in that wonderful stuff.

"Listen, Bear, you've got to stay with us all the time when we do the subterranean. We can't pull this off without your help. The last discovery we reveal down there will have to be kept in total secrecy until the hour we move underground. It would scare and muddle our associates' minds out of reason. I'm not telling anyone but you and Marsha. Anyway, there's plenty of wonders to work on until we're ready for the finals."

"How long, dear brudder, before you do this great thing?"

"I think we can have everything ready in about ten days to two weeks."

"That's gonna crowd your friend Dancing Bear. I got to go to Canada and help my trapper buddy. His wife leave him and run off with police that mount. Then I got to go to Andes for to see my Inca friend. He got himself a big dose of screaming clap, and he give it to five of his six wives."

"He's got six wives?"

"No. No. He don't got any. None wives. These are his amigos' wives. That's the reason he need help so very much. Savvy?"

Bluefeather nodded that he understood, but the wild Indian dancer was still avoiding a full commitment.

"You notice today, dear brudder Blue, how I use both Spanish and English? Authority make me learn nineteen languages. Only one I don't know is Ethiopian. I go there tomorrow for conference on how to make money. Some folks still eatin' buzzards for beef and drinkin' muddy water for milk. That not good for Dancin' Bear, Bluefeather Fellini, or wide, wide world."

Bluefeather was beginning to wonder how he could possibly compete with all the problems Dancing Bear had to solve when his ragged thoughts were interrupted by, "Problems. Problems. When white men discover this country, Indians were runnin' it. No taxes. No debt. Women did most of the work. Indian men hunt and fish all the time. White man dumb enough to think he could improve a system like that?"

Bluefeather burst out laughing and so did Dancing Bear. In fact, Bluefeather almost fell out of the tree, forgetting for a moment he was a temporary spirit. He grabbed Dancing Bear just in time, reminding him who he was. At that he just rolled over and over in the air, spinning like a floating top, both hands on his belly, trying to stop his Indian sense of mirth. Laughter has no accent.

Dancing Bear finally controlled himself, soberly asking Bluefeather if he would like a special dance before he left for Canada. "Maybe Lithuanian? Huh? Huh?"

The young adventurer told him "no" in several different tongues that he had just invented. He repeated one last time his need for help and advice.

"Hokay. Okay. You got help. Sure as I tell you truth. Sure as moon make blue-colored nights. Sure as long-lasting rain make long-lasting grass. Sure as cactus spine make hole in skin. Sure as winter make frozen water. Sure as pretty red woman make you jump and...and..."

Bluefeather had to stop him right there or otherwise he would leap from the limb, hoping to get a clean but fatal break in his neck. He yelled desperately, "Enough. Enough of hearing about you watering rare orchids with skunk piss. Just give me one pure word of advice. Just one."

"Go!" said Dancing Bear and danced off across the sky on his moc-casined toes like a mad choreographer of ballet.

Bluefeather discovered his numbed self walking along Zia Creek with Korbell. Four of Korbell's security people followed discreetly with their automatic weapons held ready for action toward he knew not what. Bluefeather was playing poker with a professional devil, but at least he was a charming one.

He said, "Mr. Korbell, if it would be possible for you to accept my word about the significance of this discovery without my spelling it out, I would be forever grateful."

Korbell took two Havanas out of his leather case and handed one to Bluefeather. Even though he had finally conquered the vile smoking habit, he could not turn down Korbell or resist lighting up with him.

"I shall respect your wish, and I must say, I respect you for undertaking what must be a great risk and challenge."

"Thank you, sir. Yes, it is all I say it is and much, much more."

Korbell replied to Bluefeather, "There are a lot more 'never beens' than 'has beens,' let me tell you."

Bluefeather took about three more steps before he got the man's meaning. The words made Bluefeather realize that Korbell had as many levels as the Grand Canyon, and one would only forget this at great peril.

"Is my daughter contributing her share to your efforts?"

"Marsha is first cabin all the way. Thanks for providing her presence."

"Ah. That is good to hear, Mr. Fellini. Yes. Uh..." He stopped walking, and his companions did likewise. He turned, looking straight into Bluefeather's eyes, saying softly as a snake slithering over silk, "You know of course that love—love is giving up something?"

Before Bluefeather could answer, Korbell looked at his heavy gold watch and said they must depart, turned quickly on feet as deftly as a tennis champion, and strode back toward the choppers.

Bluefeather followed. The good-byes were swift, without waste or hesitation. The thank-yous were accepted and waved off. They were gone, falling into formation up in Dancing Bear's realm, clacking out of sight over the horizon as if they had crashed through the wall into eternity.

Bluefeather's bunch was all alone again. It was suddenly, sweetly quiet. They walked back to the house before they conversed again. Marsha held his arm all the way across the pasture—not possessively, but affectionately. The gesture felt good to Bluefeather and, even better, comfortable.

■ ■ ■

Nineteen

Tina and Tranquilino had certainly kept Bluefeather's place up in style. The mules were solid and healthy from a balance of grain, grass, and exercise. Bluefeather and Marsha petted and conversed with Miss Mary and Nancy, bringing them up to date as they would long-lost relatives. The mules listened and moved their ears. The trees, grass, bushes, and even the vegetable garden were watered and fertilized and growing happily.

Marsha picked Big Boy tomatoes, cucumbers, squash, green beans, and lettuce from the garden. She made a huge fresh salad with wine vinegar and olive oil dressing. Bluefeather made up a big pot of his grandmother Fellini's special sauce to pour over the pasta. It took a lot of careful time, but in the end the Marsha Korbell and Bluefeather Fellini repast would have pleased even the rulers of the Vatican.

"I'm bragging, of course, but this salad is heavenly."

"I'm bragging, of course, but this sauce was inspired in heaven."

They both laughed and acted fun-silly for a while.

"I think you must be missing your family right now, aren't you?"

"Grandmother Fellini's sauce caused it. And this Italian wine we're having has created a certain nostalgia."

She had been reading his mind a lot lately. She was at it again, saying, "You must take me to meet them soon."

They were both quiet for a moment. Then he said, "Yes, soon."

"I'll surely be happy when we've finished with it," she said. "The trip—the job, I mean. I love to work in a garden. Well, I mean I would like working in a garden of my own."

He just pulled her up close and let her know he understood and knew what she meant. It was a nice feeling all the way around for both of them. So they just left the table and climbed into bed as if they only had ten minutes to make love before the world would come to an end.

For a few moments afterward, Bluefeather did not much care if the globe was finished. There was nothing to look forward to better than this. After they had showered and changed into fresh clothes, another form of adrenalin started to flow. They dropped by Tranquilino and Tina's for a visit and to bring their caretakers' pay up to date.

Tranquilino refused to accept it, but Tina was more practical—there were three children to get through school. She let Bluefeather slip the money into her apron pocket. She put it in a cigar box full of knickknacks. The Luceros would have an extra feast or two out of this, and Tranquilino would never know how it happened. Their children were in Socorro with the grandparents for their last visit before school started.

Marsha and Tina got along as if they had been friends since childhood. While they visited, Tranquilino and Bluefeather slipped out to the barn. He could tell Tranquilino wanted to talk in private.

"Hey, amigo Blue, you got one good girl there, so don't you let her jump the pasture fence, huh? What you think, huh?"

"I think you're right as rainwater, Tranq, but she's the kind of woman that can't be fenced in unless she builds her own corral. Savvy?"

"Ahhh, *si, si* for sure, I do. Just help her build it, okay? Tina and me, we sure like to have one more good neighbor."

They chatted on about rain, crops, who was in trouble, who was making money, who was getting married, having affairs, and getting divorced.

Then Bluefeather got the 357 Magnum pistol and the Remington 30.06 rifle and took Marsha out to the shooting range south of town. He asked her if she had any experience shooting.

She replied, "A little."

He put her on a hundred-and-fifty-yard target. It was small—very small. She shot a tiny pattern, six shots all touching or in the black center of the paper target. After seeing this, Bluefeather prudently decided not to risk showing her his own abilities. She knew he had fired thousands of rounds in the war, anyway. They moved on to the pistol range. Bluefeather was only average at best with the small arms. He decided to shoot first and get his embarrassment, if any, over with. He put in the ear plugs and drilled the small target seventy-five feet away dead center.

Knowing this was pure luck, he handed her the 357 pistol before she found out, and said, "Your turn."

Marsha held the weapon out in front in both hands. She blasted away the second he had hooked the ear plugs over her thick auburn hair that glistened in the mile-high sun like burning wire.

She shot a three-inch pattern with the remaining four bullets. Then she looked at him with her head tilted over in her puppy dog way and smiled with her eyes, saying, "Will that do, Master Fellini?"

"That's all right for now," he said, proud as a first-time daddy. "You'll do until something better comes along. It's none of my business, I guess, but where did you learn to shoot like that?"

She answered, "Korbell. That's one of the qualifications one must fulfill to be adopted by him."

Since he had varied emotions about eventually being adopted himself by Korbell, he didn't pursue it. They went home and got "spiffed up" for an evening out.

They drove down Rio Grande Boulevard, turning left on Central to the Sunset Club. The club had a large dance floor and a fine, popular band that was playing "Amapola" as they entered. There was a huge dining area that offered space enough for privacy to visit while enjoying a meal, the music, and other action in the background. Politicians, promoters, ranchers, and local business people were the main customers. The steaks and all the Mexican food was superb.

They chose a table in a far corner and were on their second glass of house wine when Bluefeather finally overcame his childhood training not to ask questions and quizzed her about how she had been adopted by Korbell.

"Well, my parents were killed in an airplane crash when I was fifteen, and I went to live with my aunt and uncle in Los Angeles. At seventeen, I won a scholarship to USC in communications. My sophomore year in college, I was at the top of my class when I was interviewed by one of Korbell's people. The next thing I knew I was meeting Korbell and Nedra in a suite at the Beverly Hills Hotel. I was shocked that he would propose adopting me right then and there, with the understanding that after graduation I could take a position in one of his companies—or directly with him. It's very difficult to explain, Blue, how he can influence people. It sounds self-serving, I know, but his whole empire has been based from the beginning on acquiring the best talent in the world. When he decides, there is no hesitation. Just like he did with you. Remember?"

"I don't think anyone can criticize his approach to that. The record is there for all to observe," he answered.

"It wasn't that easy. My aunt and uncle wanted to adopt me as well."

"So do I. Right this minute."

"All right, now. You wanted to know about Korbell, so no more unsolicited remarks, okay?"

"Yeah. Okay."

Marsha continued to explain. "Finally, after checking out his company, the quality and attitude of his main people, my uncle—who is a banker—and my aunt—who is a horsewoman—reluctantly agreed. So, I chose to work for the main man himself as a combination publicist and troubleshooter. And that's the story of my little life."

Bluefeather knew that was a small portion, but he decided not to ask any more questions. What in hell did he care anyway, as long as she felt about him as he did for her? Besides, if they survived the trip into the earth together, there could never be anything else to question. Never.

He said, half-jokingly, "Maybe he'll adopt me if I deliver what he wants."

"Oh, no. That would never do." At Bluefeather's questioning stare, she continued, "You see, my darling, we'd be brother and sister then, and I don't believe in incest."

"In that case, I'll never be a son of Korbell's."

"In that case," she returned, "I have something to give you. I've been waiting for the right moment." She reached into the soft leather handbag hanging on the back of her chair and removed a flat package wrapped tightly in colorful paper. She handed it to Bluefeather with a nervous smile.

His heart was pounding from the suddenly surging blood of anticipation. Marsha did not pass out gifts, of any kind, lightly. He struggled to remove the paper without letting her see his shaking hands. It was a book. A large book. There on the front was a photo of himself, his head held high, looking off toward Taos Mountain. The angle was dramatic and so was the effect on Bluefeather. The photograph showed him wrapped in a blanket, Taos Pueblo style.

Bluefeather was really taken aback. "My God, I was just a little kid," he said, looking at the lettering on the dust jacket of the book that said, "Bluefeather," and at the bottom, "Photos and Text by Lorrie Friedman."

He looked through the book, being instantly teleported back to that time of beginnings, of his mentor Grinder, and his love for Lorrie and the lands and spirits surrounding his half-home, the Taos Pueblo. It was shocking to know that Lorrie had taken so many shots he had been unaware of. There were those up Twining Canyon he remembered, but there were many on Taos Plaza and at the pueblo with his grandparents, Stump Jumper, and others of his clan that he had been unaware of until now. His stomach was tingling delicately from nerves throbbing from old, warm memories and ancient nostalgia. On the back of the dust jacket was a photo of Lorrie. She was as beautiful as he remembered her. He read underneath that she now lived in Connecticut with her husband and twin daughters. The tears dewed his large, black eyes as he cast them with scattered emotions at a waiting Marsha.

"Thank you. I don't know how to..." He swallowed twice and sniffed, then went on, "Where on earth did this come from?"

"From the publisher, in New York, in 1946, the year you returned from the war. It's selfish of me, but I hoped you were unaware of its existence—that it would be a surprise that pleased you."

"I wonder how I missed it. Of course, I missed most everything in forty-six, except drinking, laughing, and raising hell. Hey, forgive my numbness. I do thank you for it with all my heart. I had no pictures of Old Grinder except in my mind, and those tend to get fuzzier as the years pass. Come to think of it, that's the only kind I have of Lorrie. She was always promising me copies, but never gave them."

"Well, she has now. There you are and there she is on the back of the book. It's obvious from the photos she took that she loved you very much."

"I suppose I did her, too, at the time. Yes, yes, I surely did love her as much as I knew how. It all seems so very long ago."

"What happened, Blue?" Then she quickly reversed. "No. Forget I asked that. It's none of my business."

"No. Really. It's all right. Her mother wanted to bind us together by buying me, that's all. It wasn't Lorrie's fault. None of it was. The blame must be with me and her mother, Candi. That was one powerful and beautiful woman. Now that I think of it, your adopted mother, Elena, reminds me of her." He stroked the book. "I shall treasure it always...not just because of the photos of me..."

"Oh, I know."

He thumbed quickly, embarrassedly, through the book again, stopping only to look at Grinder and himself standing with the burro Tony in his Taos home pasture. He could visualize Lorrie behind her camera, moving, squatting, seeking the perfect light and angle. He could hear her lilting laughter and see her warm eyes looking into his, enjoying a mutual reaction of joy. Then he closed the book saying, "That was a very special thing for a very special lady to do. Where did you find it? A rare bookstore?"

"No. I stole it out of Korbell's collection."

"Thanks again to a lovely lady, who is not only special but very daring and brave as well."

Bluefeather felt grand all of a sudden. The nostalgia of the past was gone, replaced by the splendor of his lady now and the grandiose escapades they were about to share. They lifted their wine glasses in a silent, but understood, toast.

"Say, Marsha, I've been wanting to ask you a crazy question."

"It would be rather childish for us to hold anything back now, wouldn't it?"

"Yeah. Sure...well, is Korbell magic?"

She laughed out through her perfect teeth, "A lot of people seem to think he is when they're dealing with him, but he is not a Merlin, if that's what you mean."

"Never mind. You answered my stupid question. One more. Did you come to bed with me the first night I spent at Korbell's castle?"

"Good heavens, whatever made you dream up something like that? Not that it wouldn't have been a good idea."

"Oh. I don't know. Maybe I had more drinks than I realized."

After a thoughtful moment, they turned the subject back to Dolby. He told her about seeing the room of gold.

"Where is it hidden?"

"Under the house, in a huge concrete vault. The door must be four feet thick. Sherry said they had spent the silver bullion, and about a tenth of the gold, on fixtures underneath in the..."

"My God, Blue, do you realize there was over forty million in gold when it was only twenty dollars an ounce?"

"Yeah. I tried to figure up what it would be worth today and make a projection twenty years into the future. It was too much."

Marsha's wide, blue eyes became more so. She said, "I'm just now beginning to realize what we're really in for. Wars between entire nations have been fought for less than that."

"Yeah, that's true, but beyond the uncountable riches and altering the concepts of world society with the knowledge we're going to attempt to verify—we, you, me, Pack, all of us, will be changed forever, as well."

Bluefeather worried a moment. He wondered if Pack, much less all the others who would accompany them, could accept the reality of a world so different from their own. Even seeing it on film had rattled his own senses like multiple lightning bolts striking his body all at once. He had time now to adjust his mind to the vast differences of this new world and its creatures. His friends would not.

Marsha said, "Yes. Well, while we still have time, let us order dinner."

They had enchiladas. The red chile sauce was perfectly balanced in flavor and heat. They had another bottle of wine, but part of the taste was lost because no matter how they tried now, thoughts of the phenomenal experience shortly to come kept intruding.

Then it hit him. He had to get Pack out of the mental hospital at Las Vegas, New Mexico.

He explained to Marsha, "He's the most sane crazy person one is ever likely to meet. I knew him in the war and we partied some afterward. He ran guns to Latin America in every revolution he believed in, and if he didn't believe in it, he supplied guns to the defenders. Pack is one of those men who go on long-lost weekends that sometimes turn into years when they are unable to find work that has a chance to save the world."

"What's he in for now?"

"Oh, he has many ways of going on 'vacation.' That's what he calls going to a mental institution. He usually throws something, or someone, through a plateglass window to get the attention of the straight-jacket crew. This last time he showed more class. He was discovered sitting on the curb in front of La Fonda de Santa Fe, nude except for one item."

Marsha looked at him now with the tilted head and a quizzical gleam in her blue, magic eyes. She pushed a thick strand of hair from her face. Seeing her like this made it hard for him to carry on about Pack.

"Well? What was the item?" she prompted.

"He had a red, wool sock on his dinger. That's all."

"That should do it," she said, laughing.

Bluefeather didn't think Pack's last "entry fee" was that funny, but he was caught up in her glee and made as much happy noise as she did.

Surprisingly, she picked up her glass of burgundy and said, "To Pack. How do we acquire his services?"

"I can't. But your father—Korbell—can get him out."

"I'll call him then."

"He'll never talk to you, Marsha, about using his influence like this on the phone."

"Yes, he will. I know how to talk to him in code."

The last would have certainly surprised Bluefeather a few months ago, but now he accepted it as the norm. "Go ahead then, if you don't mind."

She stood up, saying softly, "When do you want Pack out?"

"Oh, tomorrow would be just fine," he said casually, half joking. Then he thought to himself, "We've been accomplishing the impossible by joining up with Sherry Rousset and Dolby, so why not ask for more miracles?"

Marsha walked away to the pay phone in the entryway. There wasn't a man or woman in the place who didn't stop eating, drinking, or talking to watch her smooth, thoroughbred walk. Class.

He poured a little more of the dark red in his glass and thought about how good it would be to see Pack again, although his old friend's impatience for action would be a strain.

Marsha returned with all the patrons' heads following her in the opposite direction as if they were watching a slow-motion tennis game. She sat down matter-of-factly, unaware of the halt in conversational ideas, maybe permanent changes in the flow of people's lives, that she had innocently created by merely passing by.

"Done," she said. "Two P.M. tomorrow at the main office in Las Vegas. Say, it's off the subject, but I'd like to know: How did Dolby come by Tilton's silver and gold? That is, if you feel free to share it with me."

"I suppose it's okay. Sherry said it was too late now to worry anyway. We four have to trust one another whether we like it or not. There's no choice now. The story goes: contrary to what all of us have heard, Tilton was not taking care of his partner, Dolby. In fact, he had cut him completely out of his will. Sherry swears that Dolby has no idea why, to this day. The fact that he had spent twenty-five totally loyal years of his life in the service of Tilton's wishes and wealth made Dolby's actions at least justifiable to himself. The reasons for Tilton still being listed as missing are all clear in Dolby's mind. He knew there was no record of Tilton's fingerprints. So he just cut off his head and took it with him when he left that Silver City hotel by the fire escape.

"My God, Blue, what earthly reason could he give for committing such a barbaric act?"

"Not barbaric at all...in his way of thinking. It was simply the right thing to do. No fingerprints, and along with the missing head, dental records would be useless. He took clothing, jewelry, and everything but the nude torso. There was no one around to say the remains were Tilton's. After that Dolby..."

She cut him off there with, "I believe you've answered all the questions I care to know, darling. I'd as soon leave it there. Could we go home now?"

The last question caused Bluefeather to almost dislocate his elbow waving at the waiter for the tab, and by nature he was most often a shy man.

Twenty

Bluefeather drove alone through Las Vegas, New Mexico, hunting the street that led to *La Casa del Locos*, as the local Latinos called the mental institution, with some fondness.

The mighty Sangre de Cristo Range sheared the sky west toward Santa Fe and north to Taos. The massive architectural clouds piled up, creating spots of shadows so deep that the terrain mostly vanished under the cloak. But there were portions of the landscape and the town where the sun splashed shoutingly down, revealing intense patches of green and yellow like falling gold dust.

Scores of the old frontier buildings still stood, some with repairs just beginning, others being historically maintained to give a frontier aura unsurpassed in America. Just north of town was the famous old Montezuma Castle. Its earlier occupants had ranged from Jesse James to Theodore Roosevelt.

Las Vegas caused Bluefeather to feel as if he had one-half of himself in the Old West of Billy the Kid, Wyatt Earp, Doc Holliday, and many more of their ilk who had once inflicted the town with their persons. Then too, the old issues of the *Las Vegas Optic* revealed such prominent names of the past as Flyspeck Sam, Cockeyed Frank, and the Dodge City Gang, who once ruled the town under the tutelage of one Hoodoo Brown.

Bluefeather slowed down and looked at a one-story building facing the old town plaza, where General Stephen Watts Kearney had taken possession of the territory of New Mexico for the United States. He enjoyed looking at the century-old Plaza Hotel—now restored to its former glory.

Ruts of the Santa Fe Trail could still be found outside town, yet here he was, Bluefeather Fellini, driving to pick up Sergeant Pack, a modern-day warrior, from the institution and go on a trek of dimensions far, far beyond the local history of Las Vegas, New Mexico. Yet, it seemed to the young man that this was the perfect place to launch an expedition of such wondrous—though deadly—potential.

He had wanted Marsha to share the day with him, but she had politely and wisely refused, saying she felt he and Pack should have some time alone. She also felt it would probably be good politics if she returned home for a short stay while he and Pack prepared for their inestimable travels into what might be the infinite. The subterranean journey could possibly be "forever" for the entities already there as well as for those en route.

Part Two

THE CAVERN OF WONDROUS MARVELS
AND THE SECRET RIVER OF RICHES

Twenty-One

It was the time to take great and spectacular risks. As Bluefeather drove Pack into the edge of old Santa Fe, Pack broke a twenty-minute silence with, "What happened, Blue? Those people at 'The Institute of Incapacities' were going to offer me a manager's position if you hadn't shown up."

"Korbell called. That's all."

"Not the Korbell who owns the world?"

"That's the one, old pardner. He doesn't own it all yet. Our friend Dolby is way ahead of him."

"That's some going. How'n hell did you wind up involved with both of them? My God, that's like having dinner with Churchill and Napoleon."

"One introduction was on purpose and the other was planned luck."

Bluefeather had answered most of Pack's questions and explained all the details by the time they were seated in Maria's Mexican Kitchen on Cerrillos Road, having a drink before partaking of Maria's famous enchiladas.

Bluefeather ordered a margarita from Gilbert Lopez, Maria's husband. Gilbert handled the bar orders and did most of the visiting while Maria cooked the meals and oversaw the kitchen. Bluefeather enjoyed looking at the Alfred Morang murals on the walls. The oil paints were so thick and bright it reminded him of some childhood dream.

Pack said, "Gimme a liter of the cheapest red wine you've got." At Gilbert's puzzled look, Pack went on seriously, "Ain't any need to be poor, when you can be rich for two dollars."

This would have been beyond most bartenders, but not Gilbert. He laughed and joined right in. "Makes sense to me. For four dollars you'll probably not only be rich but be a free guest of the city—the part with the crossed iron windows," he said, chuckling.

Bluefeather raised his margarita to Pack's glass of wine. These would probably be the last drinks they would have for a long time. Neither one had ever drunk alcohol during the battle of work or the work of battle. They knew they could die quicker that way.

"Here's to the world and all that's in it, Pack, and the old days and old ways we survived together."

"Yeah, Blue, yeah." Pack thought a minute and then grinned. "Hey world, there's no way out, so let's just plunge right on in."

Bluefeather was amazed again at Pack's almost common appearance. He was about six two or three but didn't strike one as being of that height, because sitting, standing, running, or walking, he always slumped a little, as if it was just too much bother to straighten up all the way. His small blue eyes were faded and always seemed a little extra damp, as if he could cry or laugh himself to tears instantly. He never quite did either one that Bluefeather was aware of.

There was a perpetual, almost imperceptible, smile on his face. In the intensity of battle and death, Bluefeather had never seen him without it. It was as if he was constantly on the verge of caring deeply about something, but never quite making it.

Bluefeather had always been amazed by the physical power of the thin body that showed no musculature at all. Pack looked soft, easy, even weak. At the thought of this, Bluefeather laughed, and then choked it hurriedly back, for this man before him could be so mean he cast a shadow over the sun, and so gentle he could turn dog turds into tulips. No one could pin down what his thoughts, conversation, or actions might be about anything but battle. There, he was as dependable as a grandmother's love.

Bluefeather suddenly felt comfortable and confident having him along on the great venture. They started naming off acquaintances that would fit well in the expedition. People whom they could trust with their lives and, even more difficult, keep what they saw inside their heads. Hard choices. They had talked an hour and the only person Bluefeather had come up with was his neighbor, Tranquilino; and then he decided he could not bring this upon his friend. Tranquilino had too many children and other dependents.

"What do you think about Felix Hadley?" Blue asked.

"He's a talker."

"Oh, well, then old Gene Smedler? He's a hell of a fist fighter."

"Aw, he don't like dogs."

Bluefeather finally named three miners and one cowboy he had known. He gave the names and last known addresses to Pack—who had made a few bar napkin notes himself.

Bluefeather handed him a sheaf of folded hundreds and said, "Use this to gather 'em up. If you can find them."

They agreed to rendezvous at Willy's in ten days or less. With the business talk out of the way, for the moment, they talked of other random things, such as Marsha. Bluefeather had told Marsha about Pack and how their friendship was cemented with blood as the binder.

Bluefeather had gone to the pay phone and had tried to call her several times. Now he wanted Marsha to meet Pack, but he couldn't get past a strange voice on the phone, explaining that Marsha was unavailable but would he please leave his name and number. Anger and disappointment moved through him at the same time, but he subdued them and continued drinking and visiting with Pack.

After Maria's delicious enchiladas, Pack discussed the three wives he'd had since the war. "How lucky we all were—no offspring had to suffer through the split-ups," he said by way of a minor explanation. "You see, Blue, I never knew how to pick out a new suit either. I was proud when people asked me how much it cost. I'm so dumb I always thought it showed my good taste." Pack sat silently a moment, staring at the almost empty liter, then continued speaking so quietly from his soft, unlined face through his thin lips that Bluefeather had to lean forward in a strain to hear: "The battles with the wives were never really worthy wars." And that would end the discussion of Pack's marital difficulties from now on.

Bluefeather was having more and more trouble with his annoyance and puzzlement at not being able to get a phone call through to Marsha. To his surprise, he had a momentary cold feeling of being deserted, but of course it couldn't be—she had risked her life in the dangerous, old tunnels with him. She had backed him to the limit in the barroom fight. She had loved him with all he could have ever hoped for, physically and mentally. And most important of all, they had had much fun and laughed at many ridiculous things together. No, it was just a temporary mistake. She simply had not expected him to call so soon. Or maybe Korbell had her tending to one of the chores he had adopted her to do. This thought didn't help him at all. Korbell had chores around the world. For a fleeting moment, a little pain of loss stabbed him under the breastbone and spread into his stomach.

Then the thoughts of the subterranean expedition came again. The solid wealth and opiate power of the stacked bars of gold in Dolby's vault grew even heavier and larger before his mind-vision. In spite of his past dispersions of the metal and his vows to defeat its sorcery of seduction, he could not help but feel exhilarated.

He suddenly felt as much an imposter as all the pretend Indians beginning to infiltrate the Southwest. He had made a vow, unthinkable to break, at Miss Mary's tomb, that he would never let gold even start to possess him again. He blinked his eyes, and his mind-vision, hard. The craving for the yellow metal vanished and the one for Marsha returned. It surprised him how the two longings had been so closely allied in the spectacle of his mind-picture.

He came back to his outer self, hearing Pack talking on. He was saying, "... By working him over with the hammer handle I had saved him from the wrath of his returning peers." Bluefeather let that one slip on past, but when Pack added, "Somebody hung the sun up for a stoplight and then turned it green, so, it's time for everybody to get going!" Bluefeather decided that Pack's rare conversation was as erratic and puzzling as Dancing Bear's. He decided it was also time for a nightcap. He ordered a double brandy and explained to Gilbert, so he wouldn't have to worry, that it was a nightcap, for sure.

Pack said, "Hey Gilbert, I desperately need a cyanide and root beer." For an instant, even Gilbert was thrown off, but there was enough of a grin on Pack's face to actually be visible in the dim restaurant candlelight. "But I'll take a brandy with ol' Blue, instead." While Gilbert poured the brandies, Pack continued, "Now don't let's ever forget..."

"Forget what, Pack?" asked Bluefeather.

"Oh... that all the world's clever schemers and plotters have great advantage over the few dreamers and lovers of beauty."

"Understood, sergeant. If the 'accumulators' abuse our trust, we shall send them to the far beyond."

"With pleasure—and with skill."

Maria came out of the kitchen with her tired, lovely face expressing gratitude for their business before she said it. Gilbert took the money, dawdling over it, making change slowly, as he finally said, "You guys don't wait so long to come back."

"Thanks, Gilbert, and thank you Maria, for the usual great meal."

"Likewise and double," said Pack.

As they stepped out the door, Bluefeather spoke to the night: "A single coyote's howl circles the earth forever like cobalt rays and touches everything." So for that very reason he tilted his head back slightly and howled at the Santa Fe half moon.

Pack clapped his soft, long-fingered hands silently together twice and did a tiny, lazy two-step that would have made Dancing Bear close his eyes in shame and groan in misery.

Since Pack had lost his apartment soon after he placed the red sock over his privates, Bluefeather got them a double room at La Posada. They slept.

When Bluefeather stumbled up the next morning, Pack was sitting up in bed trying to drink a glass of water. His hangover drooped all the way off the bed onto the carpet. He did, however, speak with considerable valor. "What we need is people of every color, type, and mixed blood for our little venture. Thoroughbreds don't much like this kind of continous rough goin'."

Bluefeather said, through a bale of cotton in his mouth, "Agreed. Go get 'em."

They shaved, showered, and had breakfast—huevos rancheros with really hot chile and tortillas—in the dining room.

"This is the only medicine that'll cure a hangover…and you can enjoy it at the same time," Bluefeather said. Pack agreed with whole-hearted appetite as he attacked the food with a purpose. "This stuff here will cure fleas, sinus problems, and evil thoughts."

They ate the rest of the fiery meal in silence, planning and preparing for, as Pack had said, "The great, big, audacious quest."

Twenty-Two

Bluefeather had been back at Willy's place two days when Charlie Waters showed up. After the hellos and an ardent kiss from Sally, he told Bluefeather he had all the maps there had ever been on Tilton's properties. The two men excused themselves and went to the bunkhouse to look them over. The whole Ruger family had asked Bluefeather about Marsha, and now Charlie was doing the same thing.

"She's got some chores to do for Korbell. She'll be here in a day or so."

He couldn't get his mind on studying the maps, even though he had something important, not quite revealed yet, on his brain relating to them. Instead, he decided to risk confiding somewhat in Charlie— not enough to scare him, but enough to grasp what his attitude was about what Dancing Bear had first named "the subterranean journey." It was enough to make Charlie's face radiate questions.

"Okay, Charlie, you're in. Sally can't go. She has to stay here with Flo and help her look after the place. Okay?"

"I understand that, and I'm damned relieved. I'd be worrying about her every minute."

Bluefeather didn't tell him how true the statement would be.

They went back to the house and he used Willy's porch phone. This time he said, "Look, Miss Whoever-you-are, I'm at Willy's place. Got it? Willy Ruger's place. Have her call me here today. You hear? Today."

"I'll convey your message, sir."

He was relieved he hadn't brought Nancy and Miss Mary. He walked out to the corral to talk to the other mules, feeling selfish, because they would all have to go. He went back to the phone and called again and again, first for adoptees Marsha, Nedra, Elena, and finally for Korbell, the adopter himself. He couldn't reach anyone but the message person.

He had to struggle with himself to stay out of his jeep. He wanted to race and ram right through Korbell's mighty iron gateway, blasting anybody who tried to stop him. Instead, he took off walking swiftly through the meadow, across Zia Creek and climbed up on the first rock ledge he reached. He leaned back, breathing more from anger and anxiety than exertion. He rubbed at the thin scar across his nose and pondered the questions. What the hell kind of mess was he in? What had happened to her? Why had she deserted him after all they had shared together?

Bluefeather was in a quandary—one he had asked for. He now had to work for Dolby for a chance to fulfill Korbell's search for the wine. It was an extremely tight place to be in. He was just now learning how deadly the competition was between the two men, and now more pressure was added by Marsha's vanishing act. Such strained loyalties.

He still felt his obligation to find the wine for Korbell, if at all possible. After all, the wine deal had saved his home in Corrales, his jeep, and his phone. Ah hell, Korbell had just plain saved him in every way, financially. He had even given him his only adopted daughter as an assistant and she had become his lover. No. She was more, much more, than that. She was his love. He knew. He knew because of the dull, seemingly incurable ache he had in his center.

Had they planned it this way all the time? Bluefeather wondered if she had deceived him and had told Korbell what he had asked her not to divulge. For a moment, he hated Korbell so hard he considered ways of putting him to sleep in a marble orchard.

Were they already plotting to move on Dolby and Sherry's domain— one that Korbell, with all his shrewdness, power, and will could not have even dreamed existed? Not unless, of course, Marsha had broken her vow of silence. This was unforgivable to Bluefeather's Italian genes. Deceit must not matter now, though. No matter how his heart hurt. He had made an agreement with Dolby far beyond all other deals. That one he had to keep regardless of anyone or anything else in the entire world.

His thoughts turned to the spirit world and he began looking around for Dancing Bear. He listened to the softly whistling wind for the sound of his guiding spirit's flute. Dancing Bear didn't come. He strained to see any angle, light, or shadow of Marsha's face, but all was just a blur. He could not conjure up Dancing Bear, and he could not visualize Marsha. The two who were closest to him were out of his imagining reach.

He leaned back against the rock, staring into the sky at an eagle circling, making unseen tracks in the air like the ectoplasm of souls. He watched until the powerful bird glided out of sight behind the first mountain, the circles appearing smaller as the distance increased.

He walked back without speaking to the mules or the dogs and entered the house. Flo and Sally were fixing supper and Charlie was drinking coffee and listening to Willy. Bluefeather got a cup and sat down on the sunken couch next to Willy, who started trying to cheer him up.

"Heritage? It's here, right here, Charlie. My old daddy said, 'We're all remnants of history. You just can't see it anymore.' Now I'm finally beginning to see it. It's just like my old daddy said, but it don't do me much good, yet. Now in just a few days we may be making history, but how in hell are we gonna know? What seems like history one minute may be a little, dying dust devil the next."

Bluefeather appreciated Willy trying to help out. "Willy, I think you're on the right track," he said. Bluefeather felt better, and remained so through most of the fine country supper. But he just couldn't make his part of the conversation move. So he got up saying, "'Night, everybody. If I get a phone call, wake me up no matter what time it is."

He heard Charlie come in from walking Sally in the woods about midnight. Then he went into a tossing, dreaming, but never-remembered sleep.

The silent sun woke him up with the first beam that changed the color of the top half of New Mexico. He was out of the bunkhouse and into the kitchen in a few steps. He had just made a pot of coffee when Sally came in, rubbing her face and pushing the hair back. They would have a chance to visit alone for a brief spell.

"Blue, I want to thank you for trusting Charlie enough to include him on our... your venture. He's a good person. I'm sure he'll prove to be an asset."

Bluefeather said, "I hope you understand why you and your mother can't go with us. And I know you wouldn't want to leave Flo here by herself. She just couldn't take care of everything here on the place without your help."

"Sure, I'm fine about it, don't worry. And mom is, too. Anyway, she's getting along real good with Harvey Dix, so she hadn't even thought about going with you all. He'll be out to see her regularly. Of course, she wants me to get a veterinary degree so badly she'd do most anything to help. God bless her."

"We've all got plans to get your education taken care of, Sally, but Charlie may have other ideas."

Sally's face turned a little red, and she took a quick swallow of coffee to hide it.

"Say Blue, forgive me for getting so personal, but I can't help it. Is anything wrong between you and Marsha?"

"Not that I know of. Why do you ask?"

"Well, you've been itchy ever since you got back and, well, I know she's really plumb nuts in love with you."

"How do you know anyway? Did she tell you that?"

"A woman can tell about another woman that way."

Bluefeather could not bring himself to share his anxieties about Marsha and Korbell possibly double crossing him, nor could he force himself to express his sense of loss. He had to force it down and away. There were things more important even than the love between a man and a woman. Even more than that of this man, Bluefeather, and that woman, Marsha, no matter what the depth of their dedication and instinctual feeling toward one another. What awaited at the end of the trek was more, far more, important than anything he could ever have imagined. Even with such heavyweights as Korbell, Sherry, and Dolby, along with Pack, Marsha, Charlie, and the Rugers—who were bright, tough, and finalists—any way he looked at it, he, Bluefeather Fellini, had somehow become the catalyst and the glue. He was it. Without his total commitment the whole venture would crash and crumble into a disaster of formidable, maybe everlasting, consequences. Bluefeather had so many thoughts he could hardly keep them in his mouth.

Flo came in, followed soon by Charlie and Willy. Flo fixed a breakfast so huge it seemed wasteful for people who lived on the edge at least half the time, but it was the last they would have as a family alone for a long time.

Wordlessly, quietly pleased with her labors, Flo set the table with milk gravy, sourdough biscuits, fresh-gathered eggs, hand-cured bacon, homemade butter, and jams. She refilled each coffee cup before it was empty. It was her personal gesture, and though everyone made polite complaints about getting fat, being foundered and never having to eat again, Flo relished the rapid disappearance of the last breakfast. It was her unspoken contribution to the eminent subterranean journey.

■ ■ ■

Twenty-Three

The men and women of adventure arrived one and two at a time by pickup truck mainly—a couple in cars. Pack had not wanted the route to the Rugers' to look like a military movement. He was a quarter of a mile up the road, checking the potpourri of mercenaries in. He came back and reported to Bluefeather as he would a company commander. Bluefeather was amused at their reversed roles, since he never figured he was anything but a "get-by" soldier.

They were all in camouflage clothing. They arrived with a minimum of equipment—a small bedroll, packs, and a few personal supplies. No surplus. The encampment hid their personal vehicles in, and behind, the barn. Those left out in the open were covered with camouflage nets. The trucks would arrive the following morning. The ex-sergeant of infantry had delivered expertly as expected.

Bluefeather had never considered anything else from Pack but a premium performance. He made his last possible phone call to Marsha from the Rugers' place. His mind must now be on the men, women, and equipment. Bluefeather explained to Pack that he would rather not be introduced to the group until they were at Dolby's, where the chain of command would be explained explicitly. Pack understood.

No one slept much that night. Bluefeather stayed at the house with his friends. Pack was with the "chosen ones" beside a campfire near the forest. There were sounds of quiet laughter, a song or two, and then the silence of the individual dreams and thoughts intermingled with the talk of night birds and coyotes.

Just after daybreak the two trucks arrived. One canvas-covered truck would haul only people, and the other would carry Bluefeather and Willy's mules. The elderly drivers from Dolby's headquarters caused a slight side casting of eyes from the younger, uninitiated troops, but there were no comments. They had all been regimented in various battles and high-risk endeavors before.

Bluefeather waited, watching carefully, until all was loaded. All the other friends and family close to Flo and Sally had told them good-bye.

Then Bluefeather went to Flo and Sally and hugged them. "Flo, you and Sally being here taking care of things is going to be as important to us as anything anyone could do. Maybe more so. I'll look after your loved ones the best I know how," Bluefeather assured them.

"I know that, Blue. Don't worry about us, darlin'. I know bein' conceived or born or simply climbin' a tree is all part of the risk of this life."

He could feel her heart beating hard against their two chests, as he said, "See you 'round the corner, Flo. Love you."

"Love you too."

He hugged Sally and said, "Take care of your mama, you hear? Love you both."

He turned and walked to the waiting truck loaded with men and women ready to gamble their lives. He crawled in the front with the driver. Unlike the war, when he could not make himself cry, his eyes were blurred as he glanced back from the large rearview mirror on the truck and saw Flo and Sally waving good-bye until they were out of sight. The trucks ground away until the forest and bluffs absorbed all their sounds.

Twenty-Four

Pack was training his troops in hand signals. Willy and Dolby's old mule keepers were readying the animals and the packs. Bluefeather was in the great room below and beyond the house in conference with Dolby and Sherry.

Sherry pointed a stick at a map, saying, "Okay. Now, Blue, here we have way stations for going and coming pack trains to pass. Each station has protective shelter with water and food for several days." She indicated the stations in blue. "The three main points, or posts, are in red. Here is a scale map for you and one for Sergeant Pack. They are absolutely water- and fireproof."

Dolby sat up as straight as a broom handle. He crooked his eyes sideways under eyebrows that were thick and long enough to have been fertilized and irrigated. He said, "And the Lady Marsha? She is to arrive today?"

"Today or tomorrow," Blue answered, hiding his concern.

"And if she doesn't?"

"I think it will mean that she has been forcefully detained or that she has joined against us."

Dolby said, "Correct. I'm pleased that you have an open mind."

"In case Marsha has divulged any information to Korbell...I suppose..."

Dolby interrupted and finished the sentence. "It will present an attainable difficulty—a contingency we have prepared for."

"On the other hand, Mr. Dolby, when Marsha arrives, as I believe she will, we should be secure. You have sufficient armed resources aboveground to protect your interests below, and besides, Korbell surely wouldn't risk jeopardizing the life of his only daughter."

"All settled then, Mr. Blue. Let's just hope she shows."

"Yes," said Sherry. "I predict she will."

Bluefeather could feel the large, slanted, African eyes boring into him, studying him for he knew not what. He wondered how this woman, Sherry, could be so certain Marsha would show up. There were less than thirty-six hours left until they moved underground. He felt like a traitor to himself, but he believed that Korbell and the huge, scar-faced Fontaine and his force would be waiting for them when they returned from below. If, of course . . . well, he must not think like that.

From where he stood, Bluefeather could see, through a crack in a doorway, several smocked, old men working in the large laboratory that had been empty of people when he had been down here before.

Sherry observed Bluefeather looking and explained. "That is where we process the minerals—some from the star material—break them down with chemicals and separate the different structures with heat. There is another huge, blind vault under the northwest corner floor. It is almost full of the precious and invaluable products. That is just one more critical reason we have to move now."

Dolby joined in, "We are starving our souls with an abundance of riches, Mr. Blue. You do totally understand the criticality of the urgency to proceed so that a final decision can be made?"

"Mr. Dolby, I don't know what to add to the knowledge you have just shared with me, but I've already committed my life to you and your truly majestic dream."

"So you have, my boy. So you have," Dolby said. "Well now, Sherry, will you proceed ahead of us to see that a proper last supper is served? Also see that Mr. Pack is invited. I need a few more moments of discussion with our commander."

Bluefeather wondered at this phraseology relating to the military. Why not "our boss" or "our leader" or "our control?" Why "our commander?"

Sherry was gone by the time he closed this thought and turned to face Dolby—a now standing old, old man. His look was far away again, just as it had been before they became associates. Dolby spoke in a monotone as he slowly opened the door to the vault.

He said, "You could live in a tomb the entirety of your life, Mr. Blue, covered with the strongest sunblock lotion. You could be buried on a moonless night and the sun would still make grass grow over your grave. You could be sealed a thousand feet inside an arctic glacier and only a few million years afterward the sun would finally melt it and you would wash into the open to be touched by its life-giving beams. Whole civilizations exist in a grain of sand washed by the great blazing orb."

The massive door on the vault moved slowly, ever so slowly, open. The monologue continued. "You must remember that the force of the sun has been everywhere in one aeon or another. Everywhere—with no exceptions where things breathe, until... until, well, until now."

The door was open and again Bluefeather stared at the little Fort Knox of mined, extracted, melted, rectangularly formed cords of gold. Their dull yellow edges did indeed reflect the artificial lights as if they were suns. He stared at scores of millions and millions of dollars' worth of reflected, yellow suns, hand-formed in the laboratory.

"You must remember," Dolby continued, "no matter the difficulty, that the treasure you gaze upon is nothing, absolutely nothing, compared to the other rewards of your task."

Bluefeather could not answer all of this. He did not understand it anyway. Oh, he understood how his heart served notice of his mind's greed at the sight, how it was difficult to keep Dolby from seeing his chest rise as his lungs expanded, searching for more air.

Then he did manage to speak: "I have already conquered that urge, Mr. Dolby. Long ago."

He knew it was a lie. Dolby knew it was a lie. He was still in battle against the yellow-yearning, and at this moment the golden swords of color were piercing his resolve, his word, his faith and his promises to Miss Mary near Harmony Creek long years before.

The aged servants served the meal in movements so smooth they were hardly visible or noticeable. The talk was of the business ahead and below, but it now had an almost celebratory tone.

Dolby, the only one drinking anything alcoholic, sipped at a glass of ruby red wine as delicately as he did his bourbon, saying, "Of course, Mr. Blue, if your research fulfills our promise, our dreams, then the fun, and then the worldwide entertainment, I might add, will begin."

"I admit the difficulty of keeping our minds locked in the present," Bluefeather agreed.

Sherry said, "I always favor beginnings as much as finishing. I suppose it is simply the anticipation."

Pack listened to her so carefully one would have thought she had written the Bible. Bluefeather was startled at the obvious and instant fascination Pack had shown with Sherry. He had hardly glanced at any-one else, and it was very doubtful if he tasted the tender veal and steamed vegetables at all. He had as much as admitted to Bluefeather that his other marriages had been more or less an attempt to fill up a space of boredom. But now, right here, Pack the warrior had finally fallen. Bluefeather felt that "stricken" would be the proper word to describe Pack's emotions.

"My God," he thought, "we are involved in one of the few great escapades left for humankind and my sergeant has a stabbing case of quixotic love."

It caused his temples to throb in tune with the motors and other vibrations of the Dolby compound. As they had dinner, huge dynamos and engines pumped electric power and water far below the surface. Old men and a few old women were dining. Others tended the machinery of power, and some, with their failing eyes, were at guard posts, protectively studying the surrounding terrain, their hands near warning buttons and automatic weapons.

The gracious, patient mules ate high-grade hay and oats, awaiting their return to the strange winding up and down trails below. They could be counted on as solidly as a cathedral cross made of mahogany. The dogs circled and listened in their enclosures. Phones and radios were constantly checked and spoken over, maintaining constant contact between the nether and outer worlds. Yes, a decrepit but proficient and powerful force did actually create a tiny, but steady, oscillation of the floors and walls of the building and the surrounding earth. Bluefeather could feel it in his feet as it moved up his body, right on out his fingertips.

The meal was done.

Dolby said, "If all you see is black and white and gray, then those are your colors." His eyes now looked backward into his head.

The three of them were on their way to fulfill his awesome visions. Not one of them existed for any other reason now—if at all.

■ ■ ■

Twenty-Five

The mules were packed. Batteries and big handlights were issued to all. Two flamethrowers, the automatic rifles, the handguns, and a razor-sharp machete for each had been issued. After several conferences with Sherry, which Pack had conveniently arranged, it was decided that hand grenades would be taken, but not issued, as yet.

Now the troops, so to speak, were lined up in a casual manner like guerilla soldiers. Sherry and Bluefeather stood a few yards out in front of the line as Pack faced down it and spoke.

"Men, women, these are your leaders," Pack said. "In case of the need for action of any kind, to protect our endeavors, I report to Commander Fellini. You report to me. Miss Sherry's position is one of total adviser to Commander Fellini. Understood?"

"Yes sir!" they all shouted.

Pack moved down the erratic line. "This is Moosha. He's from Africa. I fought with him in a small revolution there." The ebony African stood rigid and implacable. His powerful body radiated an energy of force.

Pack continued, "This is Hector Garcia of Las Cruces, New Mexico. He worked with your commander, Mr. Fellini, in a minor smuggling operation."

Hector grinned at the words, his short wirelike body anxious to move out.

"This is George Tack Won," Pack said. "He is a professional ambusher of political plunder from Indonesia. We're friends. This is Jimmy D. Ratchett, a former pro football player who went wrong in the sports booking business. Now he's in the cooking business. He'll be our chef. If you don't like the food, don't you dare tell him."

They all looked at the two hundred and fifty pounder and had a little laugh.

There were six more of Pack's friends: Kowalski, Kubeck, O'Malley, Davis, Dunning, and Osaka.

"All friends of mine." Pack smiled as he said it.

Bluefeather whispered to Sherry without turning his head, "It seems like the crazy bastard has the United Nations as an ally, but rest assured, that is an illusion. He has simply chosen the best, that's all."

She smiled with her wondrous, raven-colored eyes only.

Then Pack introduced the last three swiftly: "Jody, Estrella, and Charlene. These ladies are professional entertainers from Las Vegas, Nevada. Early in their careers they worked the streets enough to become proficient in the use of knives and guns. Besides their expertise in protection, they will be available for entertainment appointments at proper times, and through me."

Bluefeather spoke softly to Sherry again, "Our warrior, army organizer, and special employee is now a blasted pimp."

He was surprised when Sherry said, "Great foresight. Napoleon was aware and made use of these needs."

For just this one moment, he felt more Italian than he ever had in his life. Here was "his" family standing around him, ready to die if he asked them to. He felt a surge of power that the Florentine Medicis must have sensed as they developed their papal and art connections in the Florentine Renaissance. He felt as tall as Giotto's tower in the heart of Florence. He was Romulus, the mythical and efficient ruler of ancient Rome. He was as dauntless as Garibaldi, who had twice come back from exile to free his country in the nineteenth century. He was a poet of the scope of Dante and a painter and sculptor equal to Michelangelo. He could still the explosions of Mount Vesuvius. He could out-sail Columbus and sing along with the great Caruso. Then, just as suddenly, he was plain Bluefeather. His history was here among these men and women of all bloods and soils.

Pack brought him all the way back to the eminent instant, saying, "Now our commander has a few words to say. Hear him well."

Bluefeather said, "Men, women, associates, we are embarking on an adventure that could change the thinking of the world's inhabitants. A remote chance, I admit, but possible. We are the chosen. You have already made a blood oath to Pack. Let me say, now, that it is too late to pull out. We're all in it to a finality of either riches and glory for all, or we die in the effort. Are there any questions?"

There was a wild shout of excitement from the entire group.

"Well," Bluefeather continued, "then we'll now..."

The increasing "clack clack" of a helicopter stopped his words and thoughts. It came in high above the bluffs to the north. Instinctively, Pack's section spread out and aimed guns, awaiting orders.

Bluefeather shouted, "Hold fire."

Pack repeated it.

Sherry turned and hand signaled the guard towers to do the same. A figure plummeted from the machine's side and then the little parachute jerked the large one open. It drifted toward them and would have made a precise landing, but a gust of wind caused a slight stagger, just enough to roll the figure. The face under a cream-colored felt hat, of a Riviera style, tied down with a cord, rose to look up into the barrels of many guns. The figure scrambled to its feet while others gathered up the parachute. The blue, seven-seas eyes stared straight at Bluefeather.

The fashion model face uttered serious words. "Reporting for any duty, sir." Then it broke into various grins ranging from exultant to pitiful. It was Marsha, the only adopted daughter of Korbell the Mighty, and once, a short time back, the lover of confused Commander Bluefeather Fellini. She had her own private .45 automatic side arm, a sheathed dagger, a pack that contained a deflated bedroll, personal necessities, and a World War II carbine with extra ammunition.

The entire section now numbered eighteen eager and capable bodies. They moved to the mule entrance, where Willy would join Dolby's associates on the twelve-animal pack train.

Marsha walked expressionless now, behind Bluefeather. Sherry's face had an "I told you so" smile. Bluefeather's mouth was dry. He swallowed over and over what seemed like chips of sandpaper, but he would truly expire before he would let anyone know of both his torment and relief.

The great gate—disguised as a cedar-covered rock wall—swung open. The entire section, the mules and the youngest of Dolby's animal tenders (who was probably sixty-five) entered the gateway to the earthen deep. The electricity sealed the gate behind them so solidly and faultlessly that the avaricious eyes of a tax collector or the hungry ones of a young eagle would never have known it existed. They had disappeared from the sustaining world of the sun.

■ ■ ■

Twenty-Six

The cave entrance was cemented for about a hundred yards. Soft electric lights protruded from sunken sockets. The mules' hooves made echoes bounce from the walls. Everyone felt more natural when the concrete ended and they entered rooms that widened and narrowed for about a quarter of a mile. In places, they needed a couple of handlights to guide them.

Just as they were getting excited about what might confront them around each turn of the human-constructed trail, they hit a large irregular opening with diffused sunlight shining through cracks in the earth above.

Sherry reached into another indentation and pushed a button. A large beam of light emanated about the cave room and revealed a clean, emerald pond perhaps forty yards across. The intake of breath was audible from all. It was a huge liquid jewel. Back from it was a way station with camping facilities, corrals for the mules, electric plugs for additional light, water faucets and stainless metal sinks, hidden chemical toilets, and wooden tables and chairs to seat at least twenty-five people.

It was a pleasant shock to all when Sherry's message was passed on from Bluefeather to Pack that all could go for a swim in the pool and enjoy a stopover of many hours. The packs were unloaded, the animals cared for. Hector Garcia stripped off all his clothes and dived into the precious pool. Soon everyone followed. The naked, variously hued skins of the men and women of The Section flashed under and around the lighted liquid like porpoises shouting and splashing water on one another with the abandonment of children.

They had not broken even a mild sweat, as yet, and here they were in paradise. What was all this talk of life-risking situations, anyway?

Sherry slung a small leather pouch over her shoulder and led Bluefeather, Marsha, and Pack on a private excursion. Hector Garcia, now Bluefeather's corporal, would be in charge during their absence. Willy stayed behind with the old man, Gordon, and his mule packers, taking care of the animals.

After an undetermined, but certainly not great, distance they turned off to the right into a side cave. There Sherry switched on another series of lights. Before she had a chance to point them out, Bluefeather's half-Indian eyes had seen the petroglyphs chipped into the cavern walls. There were pictures of deer, mountain goats, dancers, hunters, medicine men and women, and other designs he did not recognize.

"These images were made by the lost Mimbres tribe. As you probably know, their pueblos were scattered over wide ranges of southwestern New Mexico and southeastern Arizona. Hundreds of pueblo locations still exist and not one piece of viable evidence is available as to what might have caused their disappearance many hundreds of years ago. There are, of course, the usual drought-famine-war-evacuation theories, but until now, the late fifties, none have been validated."

Sherry noticed her companions' special curiosity at one carving of a rabbit—a circle with twenty-three points seemed to be dropping off a hind foot—so she tried to explain it in layman's language. "To the Mimbres, the rabbit is the man in the moon. In other words, it is a space creature. In approximately eleven hundred AD, a royal Chinese astrologer recorded that he observed a star exploding that formed the crab nebula, millions of light years from our earth. The constellation, as you know it, is called Taurus. The Chinese said that the supernova was visible for twenty-three days. That circle falling from the rabbit's foot has twenty-three rays. Count them."

They did and there were certainly twenty-three.

Sherry continued, "I've found a book with the same drawing that dates to about eleven hundred AD. What I'm saying is, the Mimbres Indians saw, and recorded, the forming of the supernova. So we must not sell the observational abilities and intelligence of any creature short. Ever. Especially those we shall soon be meeting."

They studied all the carved drawings, entranced. Sherry continued, "I know how intriguing they are, but I'm impatient to show you . . . well, come on. Follow me."

They did, and after a while they came to a rocked-in wall of sandstone rocks fitted together with perfection, except where one side had collapsed or been knocked out. The debris had long ago been stacked neatly to the side by Dolby's people. They all tiptoed unnecessarily through the opening. Then it became so dark they all had to use their handlights.

Sherry stopped. She asked them all to turn off their lights when they reached her side and to link hands. She moved ahead, leading them along the left wall. In the dark, measurable distance vanishes, and any measurement of time is distorted beyond human comprehension. Their muffled footsteps and breathing were hardly heard.

Then Sherry stopped. "Wait just a moment, please. Ah, here. Now ease forward beside me. There. No, up a step. Here, let me place you. Now." She flipped a switch.

The light shocked the pupils of their eyes and revealed a large, auditorium-sized room filled with people—dried, mummified, Indian people. They sat around in seven separate circles as if having a hunting or root gathering powwow. Bluefeather momentarily expected heads to turn toward them, but then realized that the entrance was cut off with layers of heavy glass. The window was several sheets wide, and in front were chairs with sealed binoculars embedded at different eye levels and angles. There was one sliding partition for cameras.

"The last of the Mimbres tribes," Sherry said. Then she opened a large cabinet door and pulled out, for each, a small oxygen bottle attached to a breathing mask. She helped them put them on. She said, "Come," as she opened the heavily glassed door with a large key that she pulled from her leather pouch. "No one is allowed in except on special occasions, and then only with masks. Our breath, you know? It corrodes ancient things." Then she led them through three airtight doors, assuring that no human breath or outer air could follow them into the room of historical wonders.

Bluefeather was honored beyond expression. Walking carefully, fearfully behind Sherry, they entered the first circle of the dead, looking themselves like space beings. The air had been so dry there that the animal skin breeches still hung on the bodies, and placed by each one was painted pottery, shell, turquoise, and bone jewelry. Hide drums were still intact. Bows, arrows, tomahawks, spears were laid out alongside others.

At first Bluefeather almost fainted from the fear that he might be desecrating this ancient spot of his possible ancient kin. But soon the enthrallment of discovery eased his concern. He shone his light around the circle into the dried, hollowed eyes, and the lights and shadows made the Mimbres heads seem to see at one moment, move their head slightly at another, and eternally grin through the dried lips stretched back, revealing ground-down, short, and often missing teeth.

Sherry seemed to be tuned to their minds as she said, "They're all viejas—the old ones. After years of study I now believe that these were the ones who were too old to migrate and were brought here near the pool, which had to be a sacred place, for them to die in dignity. I'm certain, for now, in my mind at least, that all the others migrated south. I'll get to that evidence later."

Their voices were muffled by the masks, but the more they conversed, the better their hearing adjusted.

Marsha asked, "Is it possible that the Mayans contributed to their disappearance?"

Sherry answered the best she could. "Yes. It is entirely possible that the Mayans deceived and destroyed them, but considering the evidence in this room, I'd rather think they were enticed south and assimilated into the cultures of other tribes."

There were great clay jars called *ollas* scattered about, corn grinders, and water jars—some with clay handles, others with rawhide. The quality of preservation was the most dramatic any of them had ever seen.

Bluefeather looked into the jars, saying, "Well, Sherry, the corn seed in these ollas is very small and drought stricken. They probably had to move somewhere. Huh?"

"We only know one thing for sure...they vanished forever from their home area."

Bluefeather felt a hand touch and hold his arm. It was Marsha. He stepped away so that her arm dropped back to her side. He felt guilty at his continued reticence at Marsha's possible deceit. She was here, but he still couldn't help his feelings. However, the wonders of the Mimbres remained.

They visited each circle and Bluefeather made silent chants and prayers in each. It was impossible not to visualize crackling ceremonial fires, dances, sings. Timeless time.

Sherry pointed up with her handlight, enhancing the beams of the floodlight, at the walls for over a hundred yards where there were richly colored paintings mixed in with the line carvings. All the Mimbres pots and jars were in black and white, making the colored ones stand out. This pointed to the presence of other tribes. Some of the designs were definitely Mayan.

One painting was, as Sherry explained, of a Mayan pot, and on the floor just below the painting sat its model. There was sequence writing and an alphabet in use as well here. On one pot was a figure of a howler monkey that could only come from knowledge of the jungles far to the south. This vision, in part, explained to Bluefeather why, as far north as his own Taos Pueblo, the shamans still sought and used parrot feathers in their ceremonies. There were no indigenous parrots in the land of the Mimbres or the Taos. They had come in the form of trade from the jungles far to the south.

Then they spent several hours studying primitive, but somehow explicit, cave wall carvings of what Sherry believed was, at least in goodly portion, the last history of the Mimbres. It was obvious, too—because of the Mayan symbols intermingled with the Mimbres'—that they had made the long perilous journey back and forth from the Mexican jungles to the New Mexico high desert, trading in apparent friendship. There was one outstanding painting in reds, umbers, and blacks of the Mimbres sharing a deer kill with a figure from a different tribe. Sherry believed he could only be a Mayan. The richness of the colors gathered from oxidized iron and copper and many natural plants was dazzling. Even though here and there a chip had fallen, the record was brilliantly intact and just as important to the ancient Mimbres and Mayans as the Dead Sea Scrolls were to the Jews. When they had sealed the dry, ceremonial cave of darkness with rocks, no doubt the ancient laborers felt they had left their old ones, plus their painted records and all their belongings for use in another world, safe for their gods.

Bluefeather felt that Sherry and Dolby had done a priceless job in protecting the valuable find. Now, as Sherry pointed out the positions of the old women next to their men, it was apparent that the women had outlived the men, even back then. Some of the male figures were accompanied by one to three elderly females.

When everyone's awe finally subsided to simple elation, they dared ask Sherry questions.

Marsha led it off: "How did they die sitting up like this? They look as if they'd just walked in and squatted down for a ceremony."

"It took us three years in the lab to test the relaxant of peyote and the poison of the loco weed that killed them. The combination was probably painless and they died with visions before their eyes and in their minds, but the cause of their lifelike attitudes has escaped us. I sometimes feel that was done spiritually, though I have no idea how, as yet. Someday I intend to discover the answer."

Pack could hardly speak for his perpetual examination of Sherry's classic African beauty, but he forced out, "Maybe they just went to sleep along with their visions. What do you think, Miss...Miss..."

"Please call me Sherry from now on, Pack."

"Yeah. Yeah. Sure. What do you think, Sherry?"

"It sounds as reasonable as anything I've come up with."

Pack grinned, pleased at this faint praise.

Bluefeather knew now that Sherry could already have become world famous and the winner of many anthropological awards and generous grants for her voluminous notes and theories about this discovery. He could not imagine the courage, the patience, it had taken to go on studying all these long years while subduing the terrible desire to share her massive historical find with her colleagues. A hell of a woman here. Pack might be foolish, but he was correct in his admiration of Sherry. Deserved. All of it.

Bluefeather did not ask her a question, but his statement was directed to her. "I'm beginning to feel at home down here. Right now I don't know the living from the dead."

Hours had passed in seconds here. Finally, with reluctance, Sherry led them out of the sanitariums. They all turned, still staring back, seeing their own private, different visions. Bluefeather heard a chant old as wind and an accompanying flute playing somewhere inside the gathering of the ancients.

Sherry turned off the floodlight, and in that moment before the first handlight was thumbed on, all of the figures inside the sanctified room and those by the triple glass shared a second of eternity.

Twenty-Seven

They left the peace of Way Station One, the emerald pool, and the haunting rock hall of mummies and headed along the trail down, ever down. Sometimes the path was wide and safe through tunnels; at other times it narrowed and even the mules hugged near the wall as they moved. Now, Bluefeather's concern increased at how his command could handle what they would soon witness. He wondered if even he could take the massive change in thinking, feeling, the acceptance that would be required. They were all, every one, proven in battles of some kind or other, but what they were about to see would be mind-altering if they were not stronger, by far, than they had ever been before or would ever have to be again. Well, for now there were acceptable wonders to enjoy. Later?

Stalactites hung from the roofs of the large rooms, formed there over hundreds of thousands of years from moisture dripping through the massive deposit of limestone. The stalagmites growing up from the cavern's floors were just as impressive. When the two joined together they formed columns. They were of every shape and color according to the mineral content of a particular portion of the host limestone.

Bluefeather marveled, as they all did. Occasionally, Sherry would switch on one of the recessed buttons and floodlight a particular majestic formation for them. There were mineral curtains ten stories high, flowing down in places as if once a mighty wind had penetrated even the billions of tons of stone and frozen them forever in a graceful flow. In places pagodas towered above the group so high in rippled patterns like melted matter that the entire pack train appeared minute. Specks. Sometimes there would be dry spaces, but mostly, now, one could hear the infinite drip of water eternally changing the underworld to ever more beautiful and uncountable designs.

They came upon a dripping spring of fresh water that ran into a side cave. Since there was a way station nearby where they could pen the mules, Sherry led The Section into the dark dampness. Their handlights revealed creatures slick, hairless, and blind from living in the total blackness so long. There were sightless salamanders and crayfish smelling out a rare blind beetle that survived on fungi.

In several pools there were white fish about three inches long. Sherry had to shine the light close to point out the tiny suggestion of eyes still remaining since their evolution. There were translucent cave worms and a pure white beetlelike creature with long, ever-moving tentacles of delicate feeling, hunting its prey with the same deadly efficiency as a jungle leopard but with different senses. There were little white frogs, not much bigger than a thumbnail. It was difficult to discern that some of their backs were clutched by young ones no larger than a match head. It was a cave of the blind and the white.

Sherry asked everyone to switch off their lights and then imagine the miracle of how these creatures had adapted to the total darkness. The silence, except for their shallow breathing and the "drip, drip, drip," only emphasized the wonder of things moving, killing, eating, defecating, and mating in an inky world all their own.

Sherry said, "Even now the whole of the cave and the pools are crawling with life." She waited a couple of beats and then switched on her light and revealed three pearly fish swimming slowly about. One darted forward and swallowed a tiny transparent shrimp. They were all humbled at Sherry's demonstration.

By the end of the next day, they had reached Way Station Six. The Section, and even the mules, were tired enough to crave a rest, but Sherry took Pack, Marsha, and Bluefeather into another cave.

The creatures here were three, maybe four, times larger. It was disturbing, and Pack had to know, "What could possibly cause this change in size in such a short distance?"

"Well, we're in farther than it seems. But this growth is unique in the recorded world of caves. The mineral content of the limestone, and consequently the water, is very high, and the deposits get richer the deeper we go. Maybe—maybe, I repeat—that could be part of the answer."

One white beetle, its tentacles wiggling out ahead—ceaselessly moving, searching for prey or predator—seemed to be transfiguring into a different creature than those above.

Everyone crouched down to study it when Marsha grabbed Bluefeather's arm again, leaning forward excitedly. "Look. Look. It's transparent. My God, you can see the heart beating, actually pumping blood through its veins."

It was a difficult to believe their eyes, but nonetheless, there it was right before them: a critter that defied all traditional thinking. Bluefeather did not move his arm until Marsha removed her hand.

When they got back to the way station, Ratchett had started preparing powdered eggs, fruit, and biscuits. It was a good meal and he was pleased to please.

They all rested now except Sherry and Bluefeather, who walked down the trail aways to a dry shelf and sat with one handlight for illumination.

"Blue, it would be prudent if you advised Pack to alert The Section from here on. There are a couple of points of extreme danger between the next two way stations. Sometimes they are totally without mishap, and on other occasions, permanent harm has been done." She explained about the wind and the flying beasts. "The wind we call simply 'The Unholy' and we have no control over the flying beasts except our preparedness."

Bluefeather hesitated, then blurted out, "Unfortunately, Pack has fallen so in love with you, he's not his usual deadly, efficient self."

"Yes, I noticed. However, when you alert him to the upcoming hazards, I'm sure another form of adrenalin will take over his mind and body."

Bluefeather couldn't think of an apt reply to such a perceptive statement.

They went back to the camp and crawled into their bedrolls. Sherry left on one partially hidden light that shone so softly it could not disturb sleep. Bluefeather's eyes soon adjusted to it and, just before pulling his head all the way into the bedroll, he saw the face peeking out of the cloth cocoon next to him less than a yard away. It was Marsha staring at him with eyes deep and dark blue as the deep Atlantic, but even in this cavern far below the earth, the slight artificial light created rings like the ripples on a pool in her orbs. She did not blink, nor did Bluefeather, until they closed their eyes for the night. Both could see things under their clamped lids. Things they hurt and craved for but couldn't bring themselves to reveal openly.

They arose at Sherry's waking call. For now, only she could guess at the hours to move and the hours to sleep. A different rest cycle existed here. A definite one would have to be settled on later, deeper.

Gordon rode out ahead of the mules, following the leaders, Bluefeather, Marsha, and Hector Garcia.

Pack walked in the middle of the hoofed and booted train to better control both ends. Moosha brought up the rear with the rest of The Section scattered from front to back. The mules' tie-ropes had been undone and every animal had a personal trooper leading it. It was the best formation Pack could figure out for the movement of the operation, having never faced such threats before. It was difficult for any of them, except Sherry, to believe there was any danger.

She had temporarily switched on enough lights to reveal the enormous circling rhythms of the caves. There were circles in circles in archways—blue-whites, creams, orange, brown flowstone like shiny marble rivers. Some had grown so large they cut off certain cave entrances.

Pack realized this surfeit of dazzling beauty could be, and was becoming, dangerously hypnotic. One could look on and on until the eyes were dead and never see the end of original shaped formations and unlimited subtleties of color. He walked up and down the line from Bluefeather to Moosha, keeping everyone alert, and a good thing too.

Sherry was tuned to the noise first, since she had heard it so many times in the past. But before she could comment, Bluefeather noticed the low growl like a tiger on the other side of a hill. It slowly grew louder until all could hear and begin to feel a slight suction pulling their clothing.

The mules' ears and nostrils were working and their hooves clicked against the floor quicker and more erratically. They pulled now and then nervously at their halter ropes and their eyes rolled around, showing more of the white.

The roar came now in almost solid sound at times with a deep bass underlying tone, pierced occasionally by stabbing needle sounds that screamed in a high tenor through the deepening roar. The mules, flicking their large ears with twitching pain, were skittish and wanted to break and run from the unknown forces pulling at them.

The lead mule tender, Gordon, had dismounted now and was holding the animal's reins up close to the bits and walking on the left side, which was on the down side of the wind. It was more dangerous for the humans on this side, for the mules could bolt and shove them off into the numerous stone crevasses filled with up-jutting spear points of stalactites. However, to control the animals from the windward side would be futile. No one can hold a mule if it decides to break free. The presence of comforting, warm flesh pushing against them was absolutely requisite here.

Now they were nearing the great tunnels to each side that wound throughout to some lost and hidden openings far apart, forming an enormous tilted chimney with mighty powers of suction. It was, in fact, the world's largest, longest flue.

Gordon fell and his mule whirled, slipping, stepping over him, somehow without trodding on him. His shirt had ripped as he had fallen, and it was sucked downwind into blackness so swiftly it could have been shot from a cannon. The dark brown animal was loose, stumbling, trying to flee ahead, almost falling off into the dark emptiness with nothing but flesh smashing and spearing stone at the bottom.

Marsha tried to lift Gordon, but the wind pulled her over and away from him. She started to slide toward the crevice. She dug in with her fingertips, seeking an indentation to halt her slide to doom.

Bluefeather reached with one hand and grasped Marsha's wrist. He gripped Gordon's belt and dragged both of them to a pagoda column, which split the wind. He yelled for them to stay put. Then he forced his way into the opening again, leaning into the moaning blast and taking short steps sideways. As each person and each mule came to him, he grabbed and shoved them along the path until they were in the area of the columns.

The wind screamed around these uneven stone posts with a sound of horrendous agony, but the people and the mules could now keep their feet, even while sliding and taking halted steps in the air at times. Eternity is eternity. One can live only a single eternity technically, but all members of Bluefeather's section had lived them before, and again this day. This hour. This moment.

Pack had held the middle of the train on course by pure human will and that strange resource of strength that came to his lax muscles in time of action.

At last, Moosha was ushered on past as Bluefeather struggled in the invisible fury to Marsha and the shirtless old man, Gordon, looking as weak as a straw blown from the top of a weathered haystack.

Then there was the time of the blur, like a full-blown barroom brawl. They came out of the haze safely. Now they struggled forward with eagerness, for each few yards they could feel the force of the The Unholy subside as well as its nerve-ripping devilish voice.

The path widened and slopes became gentler again. The flailing fingers of The Unholy reached out for them futilely now and it seemed to be crying with sad regret.

All were safe but O'Malley's mule. It had gone over, trying to claw at the steepening roll of stones with all four hooves. Helpless. Gone.

As everyone checked their person, the remaining mules, the packs, and each other, an air of survived togetherness caused them to shake hands and strongly embrace in relief.

Sherry consoled them with, "Anyway, when it doesn't kill, it serves to cleanse the dull, musty air from the entire cavern. Although frightfully dangerous, it is a necessary safety vent." She explained further to all how weather conditions on the surface of each opening in the outer world evidently made the force of the air either a springlike breeze or a hurricane-force wind. She said, "Someday we'll probably understand the unpredictable winds completely, but for now, we must move on."

They did, stepping alive and lively, on to the comfort of Way Station Seven. Suddenly, the full realization that they were safe became apparent and no one wanted to do more than drink a lot of water and rest. In the morning the soreness and stiffness would reveal at each step that The Unholy had actually tried to blow their flesh free from their bones and their minds out of their skulls. They felt lucky. They were.

Twenty-Eight

They were awakened from exhausted slumber by anxious shouting and the "clop clop" of hooves of an upward-bound mule train, or what was left of it.

The leader, Verner, wore the same bluish black soft cloth uniform as all the other Olders. He would talk only to Sherry. He told her that they had been attacked by the screechers at the worst possible place along the ledge above Needle Canyon.

They had broken about even in the battle. Verner himself had finally fired enough lead from his .45 automatic tommy gun to down one screecher into the canyon and had wounded two others. They had lost a loaded mule, a handler, and had three more packers wounded.

Pack, always in the forefront to tend the injured, along with Hector Garcia, who had been a combat medic with the 36th Infantry Division in Italy, immediately examined the wounds and treated them with efficient care. They were painful injuries, but the two Olders would survive. One had his left shoulder muscle ripped through as if a madman had swung a razor-sharp hay hook through it. The other was luckier. He was raked from his waist all the way up the back. Two ribs were revealed slightly, but no crucial tendons or muscles had been severed— painful, but survivable. Way Station Seven was as busy as any combat command post for a while. Even in the excitement of the unexpected arrival of the damaged mule train, the muscles of The Section felt as if they had been mashed by a ten-ton vice. The power of The Unholy would be felt for days, but now others had to be cared for. They, too, might soon have to face the screechers.

Three of the mules with flesh rakes were doctored by Willy and Gordon, the latter so infirm that he was mostly in the way. It was decided to take the walking wounded on back down with them, where there was an infirmary. Finally, everything was attended; man and beast and the battered mule train would proceed on up with the precious concentrations of ore. The upward-bound would, of course, wait until The Unholy was in a period of relative quiet, no matter how long it took.

Sherry called a meeting of the leaders into the phone and radio room of the way station compound. Sherry, Bluefeather, Pack, Hector, Moosha, and old Verner met over coffee uselessly prepared the night before and now reheated.

"First, I'd like to relay Commander Fellini's compliments on your individual bravery and self-control at The Unholy," Sherry said. "It was a particularly hard blow, but usually our losses are much greater when we've been trapped this way."

"Luck," said Pack. "Pure luck."

"Nevertheless, my congratulations, as well," Sherry said, shooting a swift glance at Pack.

Bluefeather had noticed that in contrast to Pack's constant gaze upon the entire physical being of Sherry, she never looked directly at him.

Sherry continued, "Before I proceed fully, I must explain once again that my opinions, although backed up with several degrees and considerable experience, are expressed in layman's terms. I shall always use layman's terms with you. Only inferred guesses are possible. It's the best any of us can do when we're working in the frame of scores of millions of years."

"The screechers, as you might have gathered by now, appear to be half bird and half mammal. They do fly, but they also leap along the earth in great bounds. I do not know if they have moved up from the floor of this cavern—an area of the most fertile grounds and waters imaginable, as you will eventually see—or whether their genes are driving them upward in a belated return to the outer world. I don't know if they're progressing up or down. They may have migrated down aeons ago and slowly have metamorphosed into this new form. We do know this: their attacks on the trains are so erratic that they're totally unpredictable with a single exception. After one of them has been wounded, they apparently carry a grudge for a while, and they do like the meat of mules." She went on to explain, "The screechers, in some amazing way, although as blind as the salamanders we have just studied, find their way back to the River of Radiance for hunting. They have been seen flying back with fish weighing a hundred or more pounds."

Pack asked, "Shall I break out the flamethrower?"

"I leave it up to you, but if they do attack, it always seems to come by surprise. I imagine lighter weapons would be more practical."

This made sense to Pack, and anyway he would have taken her word about the creation of all thought without question.

Bluefeather said, "I believe a full meal will help us think."

Hector said, "When did we eat last? Maybe we could have a couple of screechers for dinner, huh?"

Sherry smiled. "We tried it once. They tasted like I imagine buzzards would. Not too appetizing."

Moosha said, "Sergeant Pack and I once ate buzzard."

"Not by choice, Moosha. That wasn't the only strange thing we ate on that little venture on ... ah, hell, forget that one." He bounded up from the bench. Suddenly, his usual little, misty gray eyes jammed with excited lights and his naturally slumped and lazy-appearing body had turned into long muscles of spring steel. Battle might be done. It was catching.

In a while they were on the trail with the wounded, guns fully loaded, sharp, holstered machetes flopping against thighs and hearts singing with their blood suddenly surging with the chemicals of warriors.

Pack said to himself, "By God, this is going to be thrilling." All his warring and warning nerves vibrated in anticipation. Hector and Moosha's adrenalin had reacted the same as Pack's.

Sherry thought, "These crazy people don't realize we have far greater things to accomplish than killing screechers, but I'm glad they're ready. Ready? Hell, they're eager."

Marsha thought, "Oh, dear God, protect everyone, protect Blue— and even myself, if you will. I've got to try to explain things to him before something happens to us."

Bluefeather's mind-voice cut in. "We've gotta get on past this area of danger if we have to kill every screecher and its kin in the entire cavern. We've got honored promises to fulfill and—and I'd like to somehow be alone with Marsha. We've got to have an understanding, a truth, about Korbell and—us."

The rest of The Section was charged up like sparks from broken high lines. The threat of possible imminent death gives life an intensity of fear and buoyancy like nothing else.

Since there was no hiding from the enemy, they were free to talk if they so desired.

Willy, looking over the multitudes of caverns that Sherry kept switch-lighting ahead of them and darkening behind, said, "This here makes Carlsbad Caverns and Mammoth Caves look like prairie dog holes."

Charlie Waters thought of Sally, "I'm here, and I'm glad you're there." Then he said aloud to the others, "This would make one hell of an orchestra pit."

"Or a hay barn."

"Or a bomb shelter."

"A way station for the gods."

"A great place for the world to end."

"Or begin."

And then Sherry motioned for Bluefeather to stop The Section. There was a covered box of switches. She opened it and pulled several. Ahead and far down into the Canyon of Needles it was lit up. The canyon gleamed here and there, looking like pearly, ice cream–filled bowls many yards wide. Between them were the sharp formations that gave the canyon its name. Hundreds of pointed stalactites stabbed upward, threatening anyone or anything that fell into the enticement of the milky surface of the seductive, deadly translucence.

Bluefeather adjusted his binoculars as Sherry had. All shifted about, seeking a position to focus in closer on the canyon.

They saw three of the great screechers feeding on the remains of the mule carcass. It was obvious now that they had been named properly from the shrill sounds they uttered. Their beaks must have been over a yard long and they hopped about like giant African vultures with their wings constantly spreading and folding. When they stretched their wings all the way out, three long, fishhooked, lionlike claws dropped down from each tip. There was a straighter, sharper one on the edge of each elbowlike appendage. Similar claws came out of large pads on their feet, giving them a powerful grasp and a base from which to launch their awkward but effective ground leap. Their color was white with patterned ripples of pink through it. Each had a large knob on its head that was its main sonar reflector. Even with the help of field glasses, the blind indentations of their receding eye sockets were so small they were barely visible.

The birds had the amazing ability to pick at the remaining scraps of flesh on the mule's bones with both the beak and the deft, clawed hands at the tips of their eight-foot wings. Even more astounding to all viewers was the fact that the extensive wings smoothly folded inward so that the outer hands could deliver the flesh to the beak with ease. The screechers were equipped with five appurtenances or, in their case, five extremely useful weapons.

The mule had fallen and was pierced by several needles, but the screechers had pulled and torn at the carcass until it was completely askew. They flung the bones in random directions with a jerk of their huge heads. They alternately hopped above the needles to touch the side of their heads several times to their own dead—in a ritual of grief or beyond—then returned each time to rip viciously at the mule's carcass in both hunger and apparent anger.

Sherry said to Pack, Marsha, and Bluefeather, "It does seem as if they have the beginning of recognizable anger and grief, doesn't it?"

Before anyone could give more than a thought to her combined statement and question, one of the screechers acted out her prophecy. The creature flapped its wings up and down, holding itself in place like a hovering hawk. A needle pierced the buttocks up through the area of the privates of a fallen mule tender. The screecher dropped down, clamping its beak on the human body and jerked it up and free from the rock spear. The shrieks the screecher made were so loud, shrill, and piercing that The Section wanted to go deaf. In fact, Jody, Charlene, and Osaka did clamp their hands hard over their ears. Others started to do the same and then forgot it as they observed, stunned at the screecher screaming in what sounded like horrendous delight as it flew high above the canyon floor with its victim.

Its two companions circled underneath, their sounds just as loud, and even more excited. The massive one purposely dropped the body, while another, with its sonar in perfect pitch, soared and grabbed the limp, bloody carcass and flapped upward like the other. Then it, too, dropped the lifeless form, continuing the game. They tossed the body in the air like children playing with a ball. Their cries were pitched to the volume of a thousand mad people in a tin building, echoing back and forth in the caverns so that it sounded as though a screecher was sequestered in every recess of the seemingly limitless limestone. The now nude cadaver was shredded and red. Finally, they dropped it onto a needle that pierced what was left of the chest and neck. It hung there halfway down the point with strings of flesh like a rag doll ripped into strips by a mad dog.

The mules, skittish and frightened as holed rabbits at the touch of a badger's claws, were somehow controlled, but The Section was in a rage, as the screechers had been, at the defilement of one of their own. They charged forward, closing in to fire, but when they were close enough for vengeance, the screechers had disappeared. They all swung about with their weapons ready. Bluefeather and Pack, having once before gone mad at Brest, France, performing heroic acts because of a sudden mutilation of one of their own, reacted like the rest of The Section, but now there was no visible enemy to kill.

Now it was silent. They stood. They waited.

Pack spaced his armed people about, facing both ways where one great cavern was above them and one below. On beyond the Canyon of Needles, he and Bluefeather stood in the middle, surveying the dark silence of the far-reaching space. They each grasped the nozzle of a flamethrower.

The silence became the enemy. They thought it was truly insulting. Then from above came the screech. It was so far away it sounded like the cry of a red-tailed hawk in a high wind. Another cry came, and yet another, from above. Then they were screeching from below. Now their great, blind bodies moved forward from both sides. Their sonar control overcame their blindness with extremely sensitive sound echoes. The extraordinary large and receptive scent openings on each side of their beaks made them even more frightening. There were no eyes to blind with a spray of bullets or flame. None of these tactics would work here. Only solid death would do.

Nearer, louder came the painful sounds. Crescendoing.

Bluefeather shouted, "Hold your position until they're in a clear beam of light. Their shrieks are one of their main weapons. You hear? You understand?" He raised his voice now to be heard above the enemy. "Ignore their little, baby screams. Aim where the throat joins the breast."

The screaming stopped with shocking suddenness, but Bluefeather could hear the mighty wings whoosh as they displaced air. He said softly, "It's a trick. Here they come."

Pack had trouble holding his fire. His washy blue eyes were filling his sight with flashes of crimson. "There!" he cried.

Bluefeather yelled at the same instant. "There the bastards are!"

The attacking birds' sonar might have been slightly disoriented by the spread-out explosion of bullets and their huge scent glands thrown awry by the smell of gunpowder, but their heat indicators worked perfectly. The screechers were surprisingly aware of the searching blazes and veered away without even nearing the burning flare. Pack and Bluefeather resecured the flamethrowers on their backs and picked up their semiautomatic rifles.

The screechers arced again swiftly into the light from the front and the back. The spread-out troops stayed kneeling while they fired, leaving space above for Pack and Bluefeather to blast away. The ones with the mules needed both hands to control the animals. They were the most vulnerable. But for now the screechers' heads smelled and felt the sound-shattering explosion of the shells and headed into the barrage. The terrible noise of the mighty birds and the loud echoing clatter of the weapons created a maelstrom of frenzied action and sound.

Bluefeather saw one screecher circle high and come down in a straight angle at him. He pulled off three shots straight into the circular indentation of the thorax just above the huge breastbone. The creature twisted and flopped, crashing into a pagoda-style pole, fluttering in a wad, missing Moosha by inches. It tumbled on over the ledge and down into the needles, sticking there like Christ on the cross.

Another had been wounded about fifty yards away and had fallen, but now came leaping at them twenty or thirty feet at a time.

Bluefeather slapped another clip in the M-II and fired, trying for the vulnerable spot. He could see bullets tearing into the creature, crippling it, but on it came. Then it made a huge leap, a strangling cry, and rolled over in a desperate attempt to control its forward direction. Now its flopping was accompanied by gurgles instead of screams. It managed to thrash its way within about ten feet of the troops when the blood poured out of the blueish veins as big as water pipes that were clearly visible on the surface of its thin-skinned body. The bird's blood coursed down the satin-smooth rocks, making little rivers and richly colored designs. A beautiful death.

Pack and the group on the other side of the ledge had maintained such heavy and accurate fire under his orders that four screechers were blasted down into the needles: two pierced dead, two crawling and flopping about, crippled.

Then a different call came. It was one of retreat. It sounded as if the screechers consoled one another for their losses.

Bluefeather knew now that the screechers were valiant—caring deeply for one another—but not foolish. They were like the Comanches—if out-gunned, retreat for another day's battle.

He started back to the mules as Pack and Hector commenced caring for the injured men. He was within forty steps and was thrilled to see that they had held the caravan of frightened mules and the two wounded Olders all together and safe, when he heard the noise below. A screecher, too full of holes to fly, was nevertheless determinedly limping up the more gradual slope here toward the group.

Bluefeather pulled the trigger on the M-II. It was empty. He jerked out his sidearm and fired, feeling the weapon kick in his hands as he could see the heavy magnum shells jolt and slow the screecher, but it strained on up, slipping back a tiny bit at the very edge of the canyon.

The mules were squealing and bolting now as the creature clawed to the edge, struggling to make its final attack. Bluefeather jerked out his machete and leaped at the creature, cutting at the knob, slicing it in half. Then as one clawed hand of a wing tip reached for Marsha, Bluefeather smashed the blade down, splitting the wing. He swung now with a force that was actually beyond his normal strength. The wing dropped, but the one claw held the edge while the other reached out weaving back and forth, searching for flesh.

Bluefeather ducked under the flailing to his knees and chopped down with a prodigious swing, almost severing the clawed foot that clung to the edge. The screecher tumbled down now, bouncing, flouncing, making feeble grabs at the slick wall with its remaining usable appurtenances, then fell into darkness. One last feeble sound came up, then was sucked back into its body in final silence.

It was over.

The mules were scattered up and down the trail; all but one was safe. Pack had three men wounded from wing claws. O'Malley, who had lost the mule, had a rip in his left chest muscle. The top of Moosha's head had been raked to the skull. He would have a permanent part now. Kowalski's side was sliced open to his entrails. He was in serious condition.

Bluefeather gathered together all mules and people while Pack and Hector patched up the wounded, giving antibiotics and even sewing up some. They gave Kowalski morphine.

Then Bluefeather found a cave with a narrow entrance that widened inside to form a room big enough to accommodate all. Fortunately, there was a clear pool of water here. Pack set up two guards at the entrance. Willy, Gordon, and Charlie unpacked the mules and rigged a rope into a cavalry-type picket line. They watered and fed them oats. There would be no hay here.

Hector was making the injured comfortable by blowing up their air mattresses and covering them with blankets and coats borrowed from others for extra warmth. Everyone checked their own personal equipment and weapons. Sherry had told them that nobody would know for sure when the screechers would attack.

Ratchett had a portable gas stove going. He heated water to cleanse the wounded and to prepare a meal.

Bluefeather said, "Our compliments again, troop. You held solid and kept up the fire, otherwise the screechers would be playing catch in midair with us."

This got a few nervous but needed laughs. In spite of Kowalski's serious wounds, some began joking their over-stretched nerves into submission. Willy let out a belch so loud it made the roar of a lion seem timid.

Bluefeather said, "Shhh. Shhh, Willy, you're going to give away our position."

Willy replied, "When I'm hungry and scared my stomach talks to me like a used car salesman. Don't be concerned, though, because everything is goin' to be grandy dandy from now on."

They all broke up in relief laughter. Even Kowalski grinned in his morphine daze.

Marsha came and sat beside Bluefeather on his bedroll, saying softly, hoping that no one could hear but him, "You dirty bastard. You've saved my life twice in the last two days. It's unfair to make me owe you so much."

Then she went back and got a wash pan from Willy, dipped it in the cold pond, and returned to her bedroll. She splashed her face and dampened her red hair, then dried it with a towel. She took a lipstick and tiny mirror out of her bag and put some color on her lips. She began brushing her red hair. Even in the dim light of three Coleman lamps, the bronze and gold streaks shined.

Bluefeather was trying to get his equipment in order and clean his rifle, but he had seen almost every feminine move Marsha had so deliberately made. She knew it. She suddenly turned her head and gave him a world-class, Korbell adoptee's smile. If there had been any candles around, their flames would have seemed dim compared to its radiance.

In spite of his numb, dull-pained aching of believed deceit, he much desired to motion her outside and go frolicking—if necessary, among the bloody needles—but thought maybe they had better wait. The possessive screechers might resent fornication amid their deceased. He was mostly certain that Sherry would resent them risking antagonizing their worthy opponent so soon.

■ ■ ■

Twenty-Nine

Before moving out the next morning, or noon, or night, Bluefeather asked Sherry if he should give another warning to the group, even though they had held up well through The Unholy and the screechers. She agreed he should.

"Listen up for a moment. You must, do you hear me clearly? You must, this very moment, start adjusting yourselves for many shocks—yet to come—of what you are going to see and experience. Remember, remember well, that you will soon think of it as normal—it is normal for here. We are the abnormal here."

They all looked at one another to give reassurances, comfort, and to get it.

The march on down into a lower level of the cavern was fearful for a mile or so as they all watched with nerves and senses tingling, waiting for the screechers, but they did not return.

As their nerves relaxed, the wounds, bruises, strained ligaments and muscles made them appear remnants of soldiers retreating from Napoleon's defeat in the Russian motherland. Bluefeather took the lead now, setting a survivable pace. Pack and Hector moved back and forth, talking, joking, consoling those who moved between. Moosha guarded the rear drag.

As they limped out of the cave trail into a great room, they gazed upon a vista that could only have been envisioned by a happy Dante. It welcomed and soothed their tired eyes.

They saw a human-constructed palace of many rooms against a mighty wall. Powerful recessed lights illuminated most of the outstanding features. There were fences of metallic material with dagger-length barbs all about and other mysterious material they did not recognize. There were old people moving about. Some had been waiting for The Section's arrival after receiving the phone message from Dolby's outer world.

The vast limestone room spread up and out farther in some places than the large electric lamps could beam, revealing a world such as no earthly other. There was every conceivable color and variations thereof in the endlessly shaped stone. Stalactites and stalagmites with bases sometimes bigger around than the combined circumference of a hundred redwoods stood taller than a thirty-story building. There were some hanging like huge icicles twirled until the points dropped in the suggestion of giant spirals, gold-hued soda straws and strands of gypsum crystals like clusters of long glass needles. There were drapery formations sizable enough to decorate ten glass buildings.

There were hanging crystals of calcite, chandeliers of aragonite, a wetly gleaming paradise of forms and colors so dazzling that the whole of the room could only be, and was, called God's Castle, and in fact, between two five-hundred-foot draperies was a soft orange-colored throne formation that only a god would be worthy of sitting upon.

Beyond, and down through a large opening, was another room that dwarfed this one. Bluefeather had seen this Cavern of Marvels on film at Dolby's home, and he had told Marsha and Pack about it. There was an eerie, soft-glowing light of violets and greens emanating from there. It was not from electricity. This light was…well, every mind-voice there was wondering, questioning: "How? How could there be a natural light this deep into the inner world?" And indeed, as if to mystify their mind-voices even more, now and then there would be a soft, red flare through the colored space like lightning reflecting from a far-distant sky. They could hear no thunder. It was soundless.

Later they would understand, but for now Sherry suggested Bluefeather halt the column short of an enormous arched gate and guard tower made of some strange metallic-looking material.

Sherry walked forward to greet several Olders in their gray-rose coveralls. It was the uniform of all the old ones. She talked animatedly, looking back at Bluefeather, gesturing with her arm. The Olders stood holding their weapon barrels cradled across one arm at first, but now carried them casually as one might carry an umbrella on a clear spring day.

Bluefeather could see them nod slowly, now and then looking at The Section.

Then Sherry returned, "Since I have been, and will be for some time, your official guide, please follow me. First, however, I would suggest that you greet the Olders at the entrance with civility and politeness but not in a personal manner. Commander Bluefeather will give you a full briefing later."

After the recent adventures on the down trail and the awe-inspired look at the castle room, it was easily possible for The Section to accept the size and surprising modernization of the castle compound. Once inside the strange metal walls, they saw pools of water surrounded by plants analogous to reeds, branching out into sticklike limbs that forked in straight, angular designs. In some cases they had been trimmed so that the total effect was as circular and varied as the caretaker-designer pleased.

Bluefeather marveled at the soft, violet-green lighting effect that seemed to emanate directly from the obviously living plants. He had been sure, until now, that plants could not live without photosynthesis from the sun, but these weirdly glowing objects certainly contained some kind of life.

There were tiny quartzlike pieces of tektite embedded everywhere in the host rock. The quartz reflected the electric lights, as well as the lights from the strange plants, into little specks, giving an overall effect of one huge partially revealed jewel.

There were walkways throughout the frontal compound from one pool design to another with stone benches of creamy marble flows that had been laboriously secured from some secret place in the immense, rock auditorium.

Some Olders of both sexes and all types of skin tones ranging through black, brown, yellow, pink, and white were here, lounging around these delightfully decorated spots, watching their visitors with controlled concentration.

Sherry introduced Willy to Adam and Toliver, the mule keepers. Adam was a veterinarian and separated the wounded mules into padded stalls for treatment. Willy nearly choked when they showed him how to feed the strange, hollow stalks that they had seen glowing in the front grounds to the mules. The animals ate it with relish. Willy was assured by the Olders that all nutrients were plentiful in the plants. They called them the "trees of light."

There were stalls for about fifty mules in all. Even now a team of packers was ready to move out toward the top with the ore sacks full just as another would return with many varied supplies from above.

Kowalski, O'Malley, and Hector were taken to the infirmary for immediate treatment. The latter two were stitched, medicated, and released, but Kowalski remained in serious condition.

There was a large entryway into God's Castle not unlike a hotel lobby. In fact, the entire structure curved around the natural limestone walls. The foyer was made of different rhythms, colors, and textures of rock quarried from some unseen place in the natural auditorium. They were fitted together perfectly like outer world marble, only many times softer and more beautiful. In fact, they would soon find that all the outer halls and entry rooms were constructed of this multitextured material. Obviously, the limestone was available everywhere to finish making the necessary cement.

Some of the natural crystal chandeliers hung about the lobby with lights strategically placed to create a soft glow below and illuminate a sparkling treasure above. There was furniture of heavy oak and cedar from the outer world. It was stained to blend with the pearly gray lustrous sections of cave marble that dominated the other colors. There were large maps in one corner like one might find at the entrance to a national park. They were framed with the cured hollow bushes, trees, vegetation, or whatever they were called that decorated the outside front. It was the same vegetation the mules found so delicious.

Bluefeather was shocked to see four young people. He guessed they were in their mid-twenties. They stood up in a formal row to greet them. The Youngers, two men and two women, smiled by force of will. All bowed. They did not speak until Sherry said, "These are your room engineers. They will help everyone to their habitats and will be on call at all times should you need anything."

Then, as formally as their stance, they said in sequence, "At your service, sir. At your service, ma'am."

Sherry went on to explain that she and Bluefeather would go ahead first, as they had to confer. It was suggested to the others that they be shown to their rooms. There were bathrooms in each suite and some snacks. They were to wait until their commander gave them further orders.

Sherry was placed in the first room by the stairs. There were elevators, but Sherry explained that they were used by the Olders, who were on the first floor of the palace for obvious reasons.

Sherry was accompanied into her room by a yellow-skinned young woman with eyes almost as large and certainly as slanted as Sherry's.

A young man with a face as white and fresh as new paint accompanied Bluefeather, saying, "Here sir. I'm experienced. Just sit and rest while I place your things."

All the room furniture here was made from different-sized trees of light. Some had lost the soft luster and others had only a trace of glow left. The furniture was uniquely comfortable and relaxing.

Bluefeather sat back in a lounge chair for a moment and looked around the room. There were original paintings on the wall, but all abstract. Not a single landscape or certainty to suggest anything from above was there. He got up and patted the huge bed and found it was soft. Across the room was a solid blue wall. As he gazed at it, he realized there were many shades of the outer world sky color so subtly blended together that it teased the mind and the eye to try and discern the difference. In doing so he dozed off for a moment.

He was awakened by the unnamed young man saying in a voice without accent, "It's all done, sir. Now let me show you the rest of your home."

"Home?" Bluefeather thought.

There was a large cave-marble bath and shower with real gold fixtures. He had heard about these luxuries but never dreamed he would spend a night with the metal that had haunted his entire life. It was used all around him as plain hardware. There just did not seem to be any way he could escape gold, unless, of course, he was trying to find its natural formation in the desert. Then it became as elusive as waterbugs.

There was a large combination kitchen, containing a refrigerator and an electric cooking unit, and a dining room with eight chairs and a table. Naturally, air conditioning was not needed, but there was a vent to give circulation. All but the living room and bedroom had been dug from solid limestone, then cemented in with more oddly decorated stones. There were false windows with casements made from some of the larger half logs of the hollow trees of light. And amazingly, stone draperies had been fit together so perfectly that Bluefeather almost tried to part them before he realized they could only be separated by a jackhammer, and then after doing that, all he would have been able to see was more stone. In any case it was a room unique in all the world and felt soft, restful, and secure for the moment.

The young man bowed again, saying, "Instructions are by the phone. When you call, either I, or one of my relief, will be available to you at all times."

Bluefeather showered under the gold spigot, shaved and changed into the soft uniform of God's Castle. However, there was one difference.

His was far more rose-colored than pearl gray. He was sure the others of The Section would find theirs the same. They did.

The phone chimed softly. It was Sherry. "Are you ready for the tour and the conference?"

"Ready."

She showed him the large dining halls and the kitchens, where huge freezers hung full of wild fowl, lamb, beef, and frozen vegetables imported from all over the outer world.

The tour moved on to a special room where the trees of light grew. They ranged from some so small and tender that they were sliced as part of a dinner salad to others, just a bit larger, which were bundled for mule fodder. The largest ones were cut to make all sorts of furniture, frames, ladders, and design decorations. Bluefeather decided that this tree was a true wonder material. It was food for man and beast, building and art material and, no doubt, when they finally arrived at Way Station Nine where it grew, they would see many other uses for it.

Sherry showed him the entertainment hall with a bar, a bandstand, comfortable chairs, and tables of such smooth and creamy stone that it made Bluefeather think of Chinese silk and milk frozen so hard it could never melt. Many lampshades were made of spider web calcite, thin and spiny as strings of cotton candy. Turtle-shaped crystal formations and blue diamond clusters of glasslike rocks formed little jeweled worlds set casually about on tables, serving no use but the greatest of all—beauty. The dance floor was of such amber smoothness that at first Bluefeather walked with short, cautious steps, but soon he found it was smooth without being slick. He did a dance in honor of his spirit guide—a combination waltz, two-step, Cherokee stomp, and Taos alley wobble.

Sherry clapped vigorously and joined him for several careless whirls, saying, "More later."

She led him to the conference room, where the decor was a miniature replica of the entertainment room, except one wall was painted so red it seemed to be bleeding. In its very center, all alone, was a blown-up photograph of Dolby when he was a youthful futurist of fifty, but already the eyebrows were beginning to look like cacti and the eyes seemed to tear holes in the photographic paper on which they were processed.

Sherry said, "I have other rooms to show you as we progress, but for now, I want to explain a few things that were needless to spell out before we reached our present post."

"First, the Olders—they're here because of misdeeds such as murder, fraud and the like. Dolby recruited people desperate to escape life in prison. He lured them in here with luxuries and promises of a life secure from the force of the law. It worked. Once he had them under his spell of wealth and wits, they stayed too long. For many years the great front gates of the 'Outer' have trapped them. There's no escape."

"None have ever returned aboveground?"

"None, Blue. Not a single one has ever seen the sun again after entering the caverns."

"These are tough, mean people; surely they've rebelled at some time or other at this...this velvet prison?"

"Some did, but he had his old loyal troops you saw above, and they crushed all rebellions until an acceptance set in as you see here now. They are reasonably content, finally, and age has mellowed them. This is home now. Here. They perform their duties slower, but surer, and take more pride than the Youngers. On average, over a year's span, they out-produce the young people by about thirty percent."

"What about the Youngers? Has Dolby just now recruited them?"

"No. They arrived as babies, and some of the women were unknowingly pregnant."

"You mean to tell me, Sherry, that these young men and women have known no other world but this one right here?"

"Yes. That's correct, Blue. Oh, they've overheard talk of an outer world and they see the pack trains come and go, but they've been brainwashed to believe the upper world is full of evil wars and poison air."

"Well?"

"Oh, of course, we know that could be made a truth, but there is the other side of the mountain still left. There are many things of beauty to try and save. People of dignity and bravery are still scattered about everywhere, Blue. You know that as well as anyone."

"Oh, I know you say a truth, Sherry, but Lord, what a tragedy that these young people have never seen the sun coming up over the Sangre de Cristos or listened to the talk of Twining Creek."

"Well, that's what you were chosen to do—help prove that we have the wealth Dolby believes is here, the wealth to absolutely control this magic world, to show it to the scientists, anthropologists, and the thinkers of the earth in freedom, along with the vast knowledge of all life that I know is here. I'm sure you'll soon see this for yourself."

Bluefeather realized now that Sherry was just as mind-controlled as the others in some ways. Sure, she was the one who would save and present it all, if it was within her personal power. He did not doubt a digit that she would give her life to this incredible endeavor one way or another. Then the question crossed his mind: How was a smitten Pack going to approach such a dedicated and flint-willed woman?

"This seems pedantic compared to all the rest, but why haven't the young bred here? I haven't seen any children."

"Oh, they have," she said and laughed with her great eyes and teeth that shined like the light of white suns against the background of her ebony skin. "They surely have, but Dolby felt that birth control, without exception, must be maintained for the work to get done in time."

"In time?"

"His time. He's old. He wants to see the mammoth task to the end." She became defensive now. "Who among us can possibly blame him? It was his discovery, his risks, his money, his mind that brought it to a point where it might, just might, be saved from a grabbing, greedy, stupid world. The knowledge here in these connected caverns opens up old, old worlds and presents the possibilities of new ones far, far into the future. What more can one ask? What more, indeed."

Her usually controlled voice had risen as her eyes had squinted and her lips pulled back like a forest animal ready to defend or attack.

"Look," Bluefeather said. "Look here, I'm with you to the end as I've said before. I just want to know as much as possible so I can contribute the most. I believe, girl. Do you hear ol' Bluefeather? I believe."

"I know you do. I'm too damn defensive, but that's how I've survived all the years of holding back my own growing awareness of what lavish physical and mental rewards await us—await everyone here. God, how I've longed, even craved, to share my notebooks with my colleagues around the world."

"I do understand the agony of that. I had to hide something once...long ago. Something I'd—we had—earned."

"You've got to call The Section together, I know, and explain the Olders to them. After they've eaten. I think it best if we time their first sleep. We have found, over the years, that the best average rhythm is ten hours of sleep and twenty awake. And, oh yes, I might as well say it just to you. Only the two of us can share what I'm about to say. Agreed?"

"Agreed."

"If the research of our present expedition doesn't come up to Dolby's expectations, we'll be here forever—just like the rest. He has the early tunnels wired with huge explosive charges. There would be no way out. He can press one button and the return route to the outer world and the light and power and water coming down from it, is gone. 'Boom!' 'Poof!' That quickly. That final." She snapped the fingers on one and then the other hand in time with her words.

Bluefeather felt a shower of icy sleet in his stomach at this terrible and lonely fact Sherry had stated. Then the fires of his ancestral Indian-Italian blood—and as Old Grinder had intoned "his separate Bluefeather blood"—scoured the cold away and he felt suddenly ready to face, with all his experience and energy, anything. Anything.

"Then we'll just have to win it all, won't we, dear Sherry?" And he gave her a smile—a Korbell smile that was the equal of her African one. Hell, he might never be adopted by the Korbell powers in this ultimate game, but now, at last, he could smile as grandly as they.

Thirty

With Bluefeather's help, Sherry had started to get The Section on the twenty-hour-ten-hour rhythm. They lounged about, enjoying the lighted view out in front of God's Castle and the seemingly unending delights of the courtyard. They were fed gourmet food and drinks and spent an hour and a half of their ten-hour sleep rhythm segment in the artificial sun, sauna, and exercise room. The wounds and stiffness receded and the vigor of youth and anticipated adventure surged through the entire section.

They had adjusted to the polite reserve of the Olders and the gracious service of the Youngers. Curiosity about many unanswered questions naturally nagged at them, but even that subsided as their bodies rebounded with vitality.

During the next twenty-hour awake period, they were to have what Sherry called a "princely pause." They were to dine and dance just this once as long as they cared to maintain the fun, for after their recovery and careful preparation, they would all depart for Way Station Nine and the River of Radiance in the Cavern of Marvels.

But this day, before the first and final celebration prior to that, Sherry took her command personnel of Bluefeather, Marsha, Pack, Hector, and Moosha on a tour of outer space inside inner space.

"It is the time to witness wonders," Sherry said, leading the other five around a sharp curve in the cliffs.

The compound wall curved with the building even after it ended. Then they exited another gate and guard tower and followed a trail for perhaps a mile. They were armed for protection against migrating screechers outside the fortified and weaponized metal fence. Sherry and Bluefeather had high-powered prospector's magnifying glasses. They all carried the short-handled prospector's picks in their belts.

Sherry pointed out the increasing numbers of tiny quartzite flecks and showed them a few heavy dark mineralized chunks of the material that the guard fence was made of—pieces created from the impact explosion.

She explained, "They're much larger than they look from down here. The quartz and its flakes were formed from the remaining heat of the meteorite. We call it a star. For some reason the Olders like to think of it as a fallen star. Maybe it's the memory of other sights and sounds. Maybe it is their genes recollecting; nevertheless, all these are stars."

Now they came to rows of loose chunks of metal forming a sort of fence. A couple of Olders stood guard at a tunnel entrance. They nodded to Sherry as she led her command inside. A portion of the cave wall was rusty, irregular, and dark for at least half a mile from its portal. Sherry nodded and spoke to the Olders softly as they passed. "We will return when we've finished our inspection, Grady."

"Yes, ma'am," was all he said. The other tall, bent guard—with a face as gray as old milk, eyes withdrawn and near-blank—nodded a bony head on a turkey-like neck and sat wearily back down on a tree of light chair.

The tunnel floor was level and well lighted, although Sherry carried a powerful handlight. There were no timbers or reinforcement of any kind here. They walked on solid, shiny, crystallized metal. Now and then she stopped and picked at a loose piece of metal from the tunnel wall and handed it to Bluefeather, the near-geologist, and held her light so he could examine it with his glass.

"I've never seen meteorite rock crystallized like this. The luster is mostly metabolic with fractions of quartzite. This kind of crystallization is unheard of in such a small specimen. I see the hexagonal, isometric, tetrahedrons, on and on."

Sherry held the light steady but lifted her head to explain to the others, "Our labs show heavy concentrations of palladium, iridium, platinum and lesser amounts of nickel and iron. Ordinarily, iron would dominate even a small meteorite—but one of this size..." She waved a hand at the solid concentrated metal all around forming the whole tunnel.

They walked on and then suddenly curved out to the left. To the right, facing them, was a much darker, different looking matter.

"Here is the heart of the star. Diamond bits shatter upon it. It was an implosion in the center and explosion on the surface. The core is so dense, we can't mine it except by acid. Look," she said as she pointed down one curving tunnel and then the other. One side of the wall was the dull silvery metal, the same as the tunnel they had seen all the way from the portal to here. The other side of the wall revealed a core dark, even forbidding, in its feeling of heaviness, as if it had closed together forcefully during its long journey from the heavens, preparing to protect itself from the eventual collision. It had actually done so, and consequently survived the impact mostly intact, carving a canyon five miles long before it finally entered the mountain range, with its center still imploding until its long journey had finally stopped right here.

The five section members followed Sherry around the mass, sensing a fearful power within it. Then they heard grinding sounds ahead. Four Youngers were working—two drilling and two carefully sorting what had been blasted earlier.

Bluefeather said, "Of course, they are only working the surface metal free from the concentrated core."

They all nodded in acknowledgment and then Sherry continued her necessary illuminations. She showed them how they used wax to hold sulfuric acid that slowly ate through the core metal. There were fifty of these wax troughs set up against the core about three feet apart, forming squares of the same dimension.

Sherry explained that once the square was cut with acid to a depth of four or five inches, the metal could be peeled with prize bars in relatively even layers. So far, it was the only way they had found to extract it.

Sherry said, "We tested a piece of it aboveground with a 105 armor-piercing shell and it bounced off like a dropped needle. Now, allow me to suggest to you that if—and I emphasize *if*—if this kind of implosion had occurred on a huge scale in outer space, it would have left nothing visible to the strongest telescope but a black hole. Though there are several million tons in this meteorite—I mean, star—it's only a miniature replica of what's supposedly occurring at all times in the universe. Now, please understand that only a few people of science have even suggested this theory to date, but here is living, priceless proof before your eyes. It will take the scientific community ten years to get over the shock of this discovery and a thousand years to break it down into its understandable parts."

She went on to explain to The Section's speechless members that there were three heretofore unknown metallic elements that they had already found and no known earthly mineral was even near their hardness.

Bluefeather took Sherry's light and shone it on the core, studying it carefully with his naked eye and then with his glass.

He said, amazed and dumbfounded, "It's made up of hexagonals from the most minute to those wide as a hand. All are hexagons except for some binding substance of many different lusters and apparent multiple gravity."

Beyond his present bewilderment, being a man of minerals his entire life, his mind whizzed, trying to compute even an estimate of the enormous and rare values of wealth contained here. It would stagger a half dozen of the richest and most powerful nations on earth. He must stop these wild thoughts this instant and get his mind back on gold, where it now appeared to greedily belong.

Sherry helped with, "On a more practical side, folks, can you imagine what chemists, metallurgists, designers, engineers, manufacturers of high technology, scientific minds of every kind would give to walk into the center of an imploded, currently unexplainable star?"

"Not to mention plain, wealthy tourists," said Marsha.

"And mercenaries," added Hector.

"And soldiers of good fortune—any fortune," said Pack.

"And me," said Moosha.

"And me, too," Bluefeather agreed.

That was the best they could do with frivolity. The far-distant universe surrounded them. They walked along the tunnel quietly, afraid of God, afraid of sound. Afraid.

Bluefeather said, "Parts of this are what the galaxy is made of—our world, even us. Yes, us—before evolution, before..." he couldn't express what he felt any further. It was just too much for a mere human to explain in just one attempt.

Then he had to try again. There might never be another chance. He turned and stared into the blank face of the massive, blackish monolith saying, "Look, look into its void of solidity and see the beginning and the end of yourself."

All looked. All were silent.

Then, a few steps on, outside the star, the artificial lights revealed colors and wondrous formations enough to remove the ponderous, unbearable weight from their beings and they stepped briskly along now, all chattering at once, except Sherry. She smiled inwardly, contentedly.

"The first wonder of the world. The greatest wonder of the world, but what world?" Bluefeather said, as Marsha put her hand on Bluefeather's pointing, waving arm. He covered her hand with his and gave her a smiling look as they walked on. Everyone was talking great sense and nonsense, with no one able to truly hear the messages.

They went to the lab, where the old men showed them how the star metal stopped heavy radiation totally, and on to the infirmary, where they met an old nurse who was as pretty-faced as a twenty-year-old. She was the first Bluefeather had seen among them. She slowly, with pleasure, moved a little piece of the star metal, far heavier than gold, back and forth in the air above Kowalski's terrible screecher wound. She smiled proudly down at his scar with its flesh almost healed. The old doctor stood back, seeming bored as he watched his nurse and these children of the surface earth exulting over a simple process he had been performing for over two decades.

Sherry said, "It won't make a new liver or a new heart, but it does radiate something that heals cut flesh in a miraculous manner."

They could all see the results.

Kowalski sat up, stepped from the bed, and said, "I heard we're gonna have a princess party."

Sherry corrected, good-humoredly now, "A princely pause."

"Goody. That, too. When do we start?"

"Whenever you're ready."

They all left to prepare for the get together. Sherry had accurately planned it all, for as each entered the door of the luxurious "homes," the weight of the universe and its metals dissolved and misted away. She had performed proudly with The Section's commanders. Relief untold relaxed her whole being. There were still sixteen hours left of the awake time. Perhaps that would be enough to get in a "kingly" princely pause.

Thirty-One

It was the time for relieving cavernous concerns. Bluefeather had washed himself clean as decency. He impulsively phoned Pack's room.

"Hello. This is ol' bother. How're you feelin'? You ready to party?"

"I feel great. I had a good breakfast and I'm not in jail yet."

Bluefeather had heard these words before from his old sergeant, but always welcomed them.

"Meet you in the entertainment room."

"You'll have to hurry to beat me there."

The musicians at God's Castle consisted of four Olders—three men and a woman—and two Youngers—the Asian girl with the classic eyes who tended Sherry and a Jewish lad who played the violin. There was a piano, a clarinet, two violins, a bass fiddle, and a drummer. Bluefeather did not exactly identify the specifics of the orchestra. He was just happy to listen. All were.

The bar was open. A sleek, dark, young Apache of fine temperament named Alonzo Martinez was bartender. Pack and Bluefeather ordered Scotch and water. Everyone gathered in small groups, excitedly enjoying the soft music of Strauss waltzes in the background. The softness of the lighting, combined with the jeweled spots of natural chandeliers and strategically placed lamps and other cave-grown decorations, created an ambience that both soothed and excited the emotions. They were all compadres who had survived The Unholy and the screechers' attack successfully together. That was enough to bond them for the rest of their lives. They had shared great danger together, surviving together. Thereby, they now enjoyed the only true and total love.

After two or three cocktails, Sherry told them to seek out their tables, for dinner would soon be served. Bluefeather, Marsha, Pack, Sherry, Willy, and Charlie were seated next to one another at a table.

They were served by two polite old gentlemen who ignored any attempts at light joking, although Bluefeather thought he sensed a longing for new friendships in them. Nevertheless, they served with quiet dignity and efficiency, as all their compatriots seemed to perform their varied tasks.

What a feast it was—pheasant and quail, ham and roast beef topped off with a tree of light salad with tender green onions and spinach leaves. A large tray of assorted cheeses, fruit, and fresh bread was placed on each table. The suggestion of candles was provided by sixteen-inch sections of fully glowing trees of light.

They drank. They talked. They ate. Soon they would proceed to the glorious horrors of Way Station Nine. Now they enjoyed.

Pack was the first to dance. He stood in front of Sherry, trying to straighten up his slumping frame in the rose pearl uniform that somehow fit him like a worn-out bedsheet. He held out his soft, killing hands. She took them, rising without looking at him directly. The music changed now. It was original. None present had ever heard it before. It had a slow but underlying beat of something about to explode. They simply moved with its airy flow and created their own personal, original steps.

Bluefeather could not help watching Sherry and Pack's first tentative steps until she leaned to him and placed her head upon his shoulder. Pack started moving with a slow but irresistible smoothness and strength just as he did in battle. He was a warrior of the dance floor as well as the foxholes. With all of Sherry's brilliance of studied knowledge and experiences, beyond most in this world, she was caught up in Pack's strange spell. They danced seven sets together until the dampness created between their fronts forced a break.

Bluefeather observed that his friend had increased the size of his tiny perpetual smile enough to last a week. Everyone had danced, except Bluefeather. As Hector brought Marsha back to the table, Bluefeather went to her. She looked up at him before she arose. The Korbell smile did not appear. There was a rigidity about her, even though she followed him with expertise.

Then he said, "I've missed this—this holding you."

"You haven't shown it."

"Yeah. Well, you're right, and I'm sorry, but..."

She moved with him now and they both forgot, for this moment, here in the ballroom far under the earth, what separated their souls. They were warm, comfortable, with bodies that felt tiny spasms of ecstasy tingling under the surface, longing with a delicious ache for full expression.

As Bluefeather guided her back to her chair, they both had to control their breathing.

Pack was expressing one of his often puzzling statements: "The more ants in the colony, the deeper they have to dig and the greater the size of their beds. Nothing ever vanishes. Nothing. It all goes somewhere."

For the first time, Sherry had her great African-French eyes riveted on Pack. At that moment Bluefeather thought it possible that Pack's far-out statements were as unfathomable as Dolby's. Neither one spoke in riddles to compare with Dancing Bear, but both uttered sensible, occasionally brilliant thoughts out of context—assuming that the listener understood what came before and after. But it had meaning for Sherry. It related to a decision Dolby would soon be making, using the final efforts of The Section as his arbitrator on the future human habitation of this Cavern of Marvels.

Jody, Charlene, and Estrella danced with poise, but in between, they quietly slipped away with the surplus men of The Section, doing their duties in their chosen profession with eager and appreciative partners. They eased tensions and contributed amiably to the contentment of the troops.

Now the Olders served liters of wine made from fermented trees of light extract. All marveled at its delicate balance and body.

Bluefeather said, "Here's to this magic plant. Its uses are endless—wine, food, furniture, candles, mule fodder, and no telling what else. The world hunger problem can be permanently solved with this honorable growth."

Glasses of its bounty were raised with shouts and toasts of agreement. Pack leaned over and whispered to Bluefeather, grinning for the first time in his life like an alligator full of ducks, "We're gonna start a new baby boom."

Bluefeather did not or could not answer directly, but he did raise his glass and click it against Pack's, whispering, "A full bowl must be emptied."

Pack's smile went back to its barely visible permanence. His little bluish eyes snapped and gleamed in partial, but strained, understanding of Bluefeather's words.

"Good fortunes for him," thought his longtime friend Bluefeather.

Charlie decided he would sing along with the orchestra, but "Rock of Ages" was somehow out of synch, and he gave it up with a finishing coyote yell. Others from the dance floor and the tables echoed back shouts that resembled those throated by territorial lions, babies with the colic, winners of horse races, howler monkeys, and losers of virginity.

It was the time for listening. Bluefeather could not help this habit he had had since childhood. He looked at the decor of a distant wall, but did not see. The Section, in its time of joy, was sharing silly things, which Pack knew as a good omen of solidarity for a fighting force.

Bluefeather's ears increased their sensitivity as his eyes dimmed.

"Hey, you don't have to worry about Korbell. He's trying to figure out the secret of thought."

"Figure it out, hell, he ain't even discovered it yet."

"Old One Lion was the best animal instructor I ever knew. He was so cheap, though. He trained his dogs not to eat and then they died." He recognized Willy's favorite story, even though he didn't wish it.

"I really didn't want any conversation from the arrogant bastard. When I kicked him in the nuts, it knocked all the dignity out of him."

"This dude says, 'Hey honey, how much for all night?' And I told him, 'Oh, maybe a thousand.' And he says, laughing, 'For a thousand, I could buy me one to keep.' Then I says, 'That might be so, honey, but then you would have to feed her every day.' Then he laughs and says to me, 'Okay. Okay. How about a hundred for an hour and you feed yourself?' And I says, 'It's a done deal, dandy.'"

"Hey, foolish one, there have been many other important things in the world besides Bolsheviks, booze, and books."

"Yeah, I know, but that's all the little cells in my head could understand."

"Hey, Willy, when you gonna dance with me?"

"When Tack Won turns loose of your thigh, Charlene."

"Oh, he's just warming his hands."

"Well, come on then, 'fore he burns it off..."

Bluefeather started seeing again as soon as he recognized his friend Willy's silly talk. He tilted the liter of homemade wine into Marsha's glass and then his. They toasted wordlessly, minds still foolishly shadowboxing.

A sound flowed from the bandstand now that none of The Section had ever heard before. All but one musician were playing flutes carved from the slender growths of the trees of light. The other one used two thin sticks of this same material to beat rectangular drums in strange rhythms.

Bluefeather, having been raised half the time around Taos Indian drums, felt the odd beat and the disturbing, chaotic rhythms from the flutes and the "whack, crack, click, click, boom, toc, toc, toc" from the long drums as part of the rhythm of the caves and its creatures. The slowly rising vibrations entered his blood and joined that of the liquid blended from the same plant that was the players' instruments.

Now they all began to dance. Slowly at first. Then imperceptibly the intensity of the music increased and so did their movements.

Bluefeather whirled Marsha as swiftly as possible, holding her body against his, and then they broke apart. He danced in a complete circle around the edges of the hall, waving his arms above his head. She did the same, whirling on the far side from him. They held a very special eye contact as he yelled at her in tongues from so far back in eroded history that they were naturally unrecognizable but truly felt by all, especially Marsha.

Perspiration soaked all their uniforms to charcoal color. Everyone slowed now as Bluefeather and Marsha continued their steps to the ever-wilder music. Their eyes locked on each other's bodies following the wild cave refrains. The rest of The Section, whether dancing in pairs or singly, slowed to watch.

Willy yelled, trying to echo those louder expressions of Bluefeather. Charlie, Pack, and Sherry smiled with gratified personal knowledge. The others were infected with the musk that impregnated the air between the two dancing lovers. Had there ever been such a galvanic dual dance? Now they wove, shook, whirled, moving across the room, coming together with the sweat of flesh and fun. A rousing shout full of many meanings rent the room. At that second they quit all movement and clung together like long-separated souls of sameness. The orchestra suddenly stopped. It was time for the ten-hour sleep period. Everyone knew it. Everyone left.

"My God, I've missed you," Bluefeather said.

Marsha responded, "I've hurt for you so I thought I'd perish."

"Don't ever leave me again. Never. Never. Never."

"Now. Now. Now?"

"Yes. Yes. Yes."

"Oh. Oh."

In the residual flush of the dance of splendor and the night of the princely pause they made love—Bluefeather Fellini and Marsha Korbell.

■ ■ ■

Thirty-Two

Bluefeather had breakfast ready for her at the beginning of the awake time. They had danced and loved away any possible hangover. It was known only to Sherry that the last wine was of very low alcohol content, but so delicious one felt inebriated and exhilarated anyway.

Bluefeather had scrambled some fresh eggs with chopped ham and green chile. There was toast, jelly, orange juice, and lots of hot coffee.

They ate and gossiped about the wondrous night.

All over God's Castle, section members were awakening from the sleep period. They all knew they had two more such times free to heal, rest, relax, and adjust to the new sleeping-working schedule—to do whatever they needed most before training began for the final segment of their venture.

Bluefeather and Marsha made love again with no words intelligible except to longtime lovers. They lay in the bed, staring up at the ceiling, shoulders touching until their breathing subsided. All their flesh and bones felt so relaxed that they were sure they could never be coaxed to move again.

Slowly, Bluefeather's mind-voice ticked at him: "This is wonderful lust of love, but what about her unexplained absence before the formidable undertaking? What excuse could there be for her neglectful silence—not even a phone call—when they had already shared laughter, love and survived disasters of life and death? What? What?"

Bluefeather showered, put on his clean uniform, and opened the door out on the balcony as silently as possible. He looked across the barely lighted front gardens. The trees of light glowed little residues of illumination in spots. The distant environs of the cavern melted the soft light into a darkness far beyond any he had ever seen on the surface. He heard the distant, traveling calls of sonar location between screechers. The almost loving sounds moved on through the suet blackness toward the glow above the River of Radiance. The birds were going hunting.

The slowly diminishing talk between the massive creatures of both earth and air left him suddenly forlorn. It was all so very old. Such timeless mysteries of the aeons had transpired here that he felt for a moment he had never been conceived or gifted with thought. Infinitesimal. He listened for the far, far sound of distant planets for an explanation, but he couldn't hear them audibly.

He physically shook his body. He stretched the strength of the muscles in his arms and an unrestricted feeling of power and optimism suddenly permeated his being. As if on signal, the clocks of cavern time switched on the abundant electric lights and the inspiring distant sight of God's throne gave credence to his living self. Regardless of the dangers or restrictions, he decided to visit and touch the throne during this twenty-hour period. His mind was afire with the sudden shining scheme.

Then he felt Marsha's arm in his and her head leaning possessively into his shoulder. For just an instant, the awesome lighting spectacle causing the swift alteration of his feeling and her touch was everything. One.

Then the primitive parts of his humanness transcended the eternal, and he pulled loose, stepping back from her, saying, "You sold me out to Korbell, didn't you? You broke a sacred vow and revealed our mission to the bastard. You told him our secrets, didn't you? Even after he himself had agreed that my knowledge of the bullion was all I needed to tell him for now. You told him about it all, didn't you?"

With eyes like round turquoise, she tried to interject. "Blue, oh, Blue, for God's sake. Listen to me. It's all going to..."

"Don't lie to me, Marsha. I know. I can tell. You've done it. Don't the lives of your lover and friends, the knowledge of the ages mean more to you than...than...?"

Before he could say Korbell, she turned with sudden resentment, saying, "You have a right to be upset, I guess, but I don't have to explain or excuse Korbell to you or anyone else."

"The hell you don't. He no longer amounts to a fart. All his real estate, money, power and political briberies are nothing. Nothing. They don't even amount to a whisper in the center of a hurricane, not a single splinter in the Amazon Forest compared to the offerings of this great cavern. Don't you understand the difference? Can't you see...see what's important? What's lasting? What's falsely temporary? Well, can't you?"

"Don't sell me short like that, you unreasonable bastard. I've given you all I have to give and more."

"Well then, answer me, just answer me, Marsha. Now. You can't blame me for insisting...before we leave for the river. You owe it to me, just as everyone in The Section owes loyalty to one another. It's our survival—and the survival of all this." He swept his arm in an arc, pointing at what he felt was the obvious.

"All right. Yes. I did lead you on, reporting to him how highly I felt about you and your abilities. I did tell Korbell what you told me. He cajoled me. He intimidated me with kindness, the loyalty to family, and all that crap. Then he threatened me with every known torture. His daughter? Can you believe it? His only adopted daughter? Do you care about that? Do you care about me? Or do you just care about yourself, Bluefeather Fellini?"

"Did that son of a bitch abuse you? Tell me? Huh? Huh?"

"No. They drugged me and I suppose pulled it out of me."

"You don't know, for Christ's sake? You don't know for sure exactly what you told them?"

"I think I know. Of course I know, because they didn't bother me anymore. Just the opposite. I was coddled, pampered, and had full cooperation and offers of anything I wished. So I asked for the helicopter to fly me to you."

"Bullshit, Marsha. You're here to spy for him. He'd never let you come back, knowing you'd let it slip out one way or the other. You were leading me on and setting me up all that time with the Godchucks in Cerrillos and Santa Fe, weren't you?"

"I've told you the truth, you bull-headed jerk. That's the best I can do."

"Well, that's pretty damned good. Do you think I believe for one second that you're on our side? What kind of fool do you take me for, anyway?"

"A big one. The biggest one I've ever known," she screamed, "except for myself. I'm not only a fool, but a blind one at that, to have ever believed in you."

"You believing in me? Now doesn't that frost the governor's balls. Hah."

"You go to hell, Bluefeather Fellini, and stay there until you grow horns out your rear." She charged the door and slammed it heavy as a dropped anvil.

He turned, looking outward again and ground his teeth, breathing like an exhausted marathon runner and gasped out, "Dumb. Dumb. Dumb." But he wasn't sure whom or what he was describing.

Then he made up his mind, at least all of it that would allow him access. He would somehow believe in her until proof solid as the star core was revealed. He must. He wanted to take back the harsh tone of his last words to her, but those words could never be returned to his tongue. He would have to show her some way how much he cared, so that his anger would be ignored and eventually forgotten.

Marsha was in her room furiously combing at her hair. Then she slowed the motion and wished she had somehow muted the anger in her voice. In truth, he really had the right to at least question her loyalty. She had expected him to feel it—not have to hear it. She took a shower, soaping more than needed.

Thirty-Three

Over Sherry's protestations, Bluefeather finally got permission to go to the throne alone. She insisted he take hand grenades as well as his semiautomatic, a machete, and a handgun. The exhilaration of the trip caused his worried war with Marsha to subside for now.

The endlessly changing beauty of multiple-colored formations and crystallizations would have caused the best of the Great Spirit's helpers to skip a week of work in rapture. There was a ridge of rock animals—suggestions of lions, elephants, and horses—all walking through deep cake frosting in a combination of perpetual motion and never-ending stillness.

He saw the room full of great rock horns, in shapes that suggested all those ancient musical instruments that signaled battles, crownings, and celebrations from great occasions of the past. He could hear their trumpeting across hills and through the streets and archways of history.

Dazzling jewels gleamed under his hand-carried light that only angels would be allowed to wear. Then he came to the hill of pearls. There were thousands, from small as a pinhead to the circumference of a grapefruit. For thousands of centuries, the ceiling above had dripped the calcite just right to form perfectly smooth, opaque ovals of indescribable colors—hints of soft tan, a touch of violet under his handlight. Some had a tiny suggestion of white blended into gray-blue green. They all had been formed around a seed blown down here, or a speck of foreign rock, or even a tiny particle of an insect's bone. They lay in slight indentations, like stone birds' nests, and had been formed by the dripping over unmeasurable time.

Bluefeather, without conscious thought, picked one up and put it in his pocket for Marsha. Even this minute removal of the minuscule pearl caused him to feel like he had committed a sacrilege against the insides of Mother Earth. Fifty yards on past the field of pearls, he found the hill of sea urchins. Their rounded forms bristled with short, sharp stalactites of a yellowish orange similar in color to the coat of a golden palomino stallion.

Then he came to a natural flow bridge like those in some national parks in Utah and Arizona. He had cautiously crossed and was now settled on conquering the hypnotic variety of views and getting on to the great throne itself.

His hunter's blood caused him to hear the unmistakable "whoosh whoosh" of the screecher's huge wings. He froze his movement, then slowly turned toward the sound so there would be no noticeable sudden action to be picked up by the land-air creatures' sensitivity. There were three of them between him and the searching lights of God's Castle. Two of them carried a fish of perhaps a hundred pounds in their claws. The third one had either dined at the

River of Radiance or intended to share with its companions, for it carried nothing.

Bluefeather held his breath in fearful obedience as they air-lumbered past. He turned his head with them, eyes locked on the follower. They were just past when the last one circled away as the leaders moved on up and out of sight. It came circling slowly above Bluefeather with the knobby antenna atop its head moving, searching for him. The edges of the bridge seemed to be slightly distorting the returning echoes, but the screecher knew something alien was there. It made a low dip, then swerved back up to a half circle. A paralyzing sound emitted from its throat that seemed to send waves of unseen wire, piercing the air, flesh, stone, everything.

Bluefeather knew the searcher had honed in very close on his hidden spot. It was just him and the screecher now. The outer world, the galaxies of stars, the universe, and the Cavern of Marvels did not exist. Only the two of them and infinity were real. There was nothing else. His heart made noises that a deaf-mute could have heard—so it felt and sounded to him.

Now the screecher, with wings spread and sloped to stop his flight, landed on a prominence, tilting its sightless head from one side to the other with the beak bigger and sharper than a factory bellows. It listened, seeing with the echoes the exact forms all around, smelling Bluefeather's exact shape as well. Silence. More silence. A forever silence. Then the head slanted with the receptor knob directed straight ahead. Bluefeather knew that the silence of Pharaoh's tomb was being split apart by echoing emissions sent back to the screecher that were beyond his own hearing but clear as cathedral bells to the bird-animal.

Bluefeather waited for that immeasurable, instinctive movement between the hunter and its prey that decides which attacks first, which lives. He jerked the pin from a grenade, counting off as the bird crouched to launch its leaping charge. He hurled it in an arc at the bird as it arose. It was just hitting the cave floor to spring forward again when the grenade dropped, exploding under its breast, knocking it over and crippling one wing. The screecher struggled upright, nevertheless, with the weight of the dragging wing slowing it and clawed closer and closer to Bluefeather.

He jerked his finger on the trigger of the rifle as swiftly and smoothly as all his years of training and nature had taught him. The bullets pierced the sunken area just above the protruding, foot-thick breastbone in the spot where the neck joined it. It slowed. It stopped. Then came on anyway.

He desperately, but with precision, jammed another clip in the rifle and concentrated on the antenna knob. He missed the first shot because of the screecher's movement, but now he could feel out through space right with the bullet as it thudded into and through flesh.

The screecher was only a couple of short, jumping jerks away from him now, but he had thrown its radar system off and it leapt on past him, one huge claw raking at the top of the rock formation under which Bluefeather threw himself. Then it turned, wobbling out of balance, pecking with its beak in space toward him. It reached for him with one claw, using the other foot and the unharmed wing, with its own retractable swords, to make a final launch and devour him like a bug.

Bluefeather grabbed for another ammunition clip, rolling down a slope just as the screecher leaped, dropping on the exact spot Bluefeather had just vacated. He lost the clip in his tumbling fall but leaped up, pulling out the razor-sharp machete. The screecher slipped sideways, awkwardly, incapacitated from its many wounds, down toward him. Bluefeather leaped as far as his legs could possibly take him to avoid being mashed into a smear by the two-ton brute.

He was struck by only a glancing blow from the screecher's good wing. Even so, the contact knocked him a good six feet sideways, but his surging body chemicals of conflict enabled him to recover and charge on top of the fluttering beast's back. He started slashing and stabbing with vicious abandon and even after it was still and dead, he stood on its back and stabbed, over and over, with the bloody machete, until the realization of certain survival caused him to stop and fall down on the soft, helpless wing of the screecher until he could breathe and think clearly again. Close.

He reached out, his chest still heaving, and patted the velvet-soft wing, gasping out, "I'm so very sorry. Please forgive me, my dear, blind brother."

As he walked through the glazed underworld toward the throne, the high from battling with the screecher subsided. His mind-voice spoke to him. "Is this entity you just killed a beginning thinker like mankind once was? Is it being driven by a genetic force away from the watered field of stones to seek the outer world? Of course, it couldn't survive there a day. Someone would kill it, just as you have, whether it be self-defense or not. It is not even settled whether it becomes an animal of the ground or a fowl of the air. It will take scores upon scores of thousands of years yet before that is decided. Ponder on it some, Bluefeather. You are supposed to be the creature of thought and reason, so start living up to your abilities, your gifts, your privileges, you foolish man."

Ponder he did, but then the elegance of the surroundings overwhelmed thought with feelings of reverence. So he knelt his blood splattered body on a smooth parapet and said aloud, "Ah, Great Spirit, I'm doing the best I know how toward fulfilling my commitments to those two villainous forces of efficient greed, Dolby and Korbell. I ask you, oh Great One—and smart one, too—what are the limits of my obligations to these causes? Illuminate my thinking brain. Enlighten my soul, oh Great Tutor. Kick my dumb ass into righteous and proper obedience. I am lost on the subject of those two satanic bastards. Help me find the invisible path of nobility. Then make me run up and down that son of a... son of a saint, until my ability to cogitate is no longer impaired and my butt is so tired it's bouncing off my boot heels. You got it down correctly, oh Splendid One? Be sure of it now. Please."

He felt better as he walked between the two immense calcite curtains filled with enough oxidized iron to give them an orangish luster the same as the remarkable throne. He was there.

He slowly raised his head, absorbing the beauty by degrees so he would be sure of containing it. Up. Up. Up. His eyes moved right on up to the seat of the throne of God's Castle. What was that way up there?

He turned and carefully walked backward so he would have a better angle of vision. He turned and tilted his head and eyes upward again. "What is that speck defiling the seat of the great one? Is it a fly turd?" he questioned. "Is it the droppings of a sickly mouse? Huh? What is that tiny pile up there that stinks like all the sewers of Bombay, all the garbage of New York City, and the combined flatulence from all the beans ever raised and eaten in the whole states of New Mexico, Oklahoma, and Texas? What is it, I repeat?"

"Dear brudder, it is Dancing Bear, your friend and spirit guide." Dancing Bear kicked his soft, leather moccasins back and forth where they hung over the throne so small and fragile-looking. Bluefeather had to take a look with his binoculars to be certain he was there.

"What are you doing on that throne, you smarmy pretender? How could you be so presumptuous as to think you're the Authority? Come down from there for your chastisement. Remember my last begging words to you? Huh? I asked with all humility for your constant help in this..." he waved an arm all around, "this world of caves and monstrous events, and now, you show up, playing at being the Authority. The next thing I know you will be setting at His desk, feet up, smoking His cigars."

"He don't smoke."

"Well you'll be reading His mail then."

"He don't get no mail. He get important news on the TP."

"No. No. No. Tell me you lie, tell me my ears are deceiving me. Authority just can't get his communication from all the people of the universe on the TV."

"No. No. No. Like you say, dear brudder, No, no, no again. He gets messages from TP—T like in tap dance and P like in pardner. That means telepathic. Now you savvy?"

"Telepathic, huh? Well that makes more sense to me."

"That's what I'm here for, dear brudder."

"What's that again?"

Dancing Bear stood up and leaped out on the curtain, sliding down its rippling curves on the seat of his leather breeches, yelling, "Wheee, Wahhaaa, hey yehhh and whoa now." He pushed upright on his feet and did a Balinese dance, waving and undulating his arms and hands, jerking his head from side to side like his neck was out of socket, bending his knees and pointing his feet sideways. Then he bounded up on top of a column about six feet from Bluefeather, crouching there on one foot, saying proudly, "I learn that one in Bali."

"I could tell. I could tell."

"Now, dear brudder, now what can your kind helper and friend forever do for you?"

"Well, friend forever, I got lots of chores that could use plenty of help. Let me count the ways, as the poet person said. First of all I have a broken heart. I busted up with Marsha—well...we had a terrible fight—I guess we broke up. I'm pretty sure Korbell has washed her brain plumb out of her head. I got Dolby setting up there on top the outer world trying to decide whether to open this entire damn Cavern of Marvels up to the scientists and tourists and thereby get richer than all the world's banks combined and nearly as famous as Alexander the Great and Shakespeare. Again, he might decide to blast the whole thing shut for that 'forever' you just mentioned, leaving us down here so long the word 'forever' is meaningless. On top of all that, I've got many friends to worry about and the screechers and the goddamned fallen, collapsed star and a palace full of olden coots to boot. Now, Mr. Bear, let me tell you that I've spoken of only the beginning. The River of Radiance has got more wonders yet to behold and conquer than seven thousand erupting volcanoes, on a world bigger than the sky, composed of twenty-four-carat gold, redwood trees, strawberry plants, and poison ivy..."

"Wheee whooo-eee. You got perty near close to 'bout half my problems. We got to have a talk."

"Wait just a damn minute. That isn't even half of it."

"Well then, we got to have a bi-i-i-g talk."

"Yeah, I suppose so. I don't have any idea what Korbell has planned for us."

Dancing Bear perched on the other foot now, squinted his eyes and tried his best to look worried, saying, "Now, that is a big worry right there, dear brudder Blue. My most profound sympathies are offered."

"Bear, old buddy, spirit guide and forever friend, it is not sympathy I gotta have, it is wisdom I crave. Wisdom of the ages. Wisdom of the Great Spirit, wisdom from the Great Dancing Bear."

"You beginning to sound just like me, so maybe some good judgment has possessed you. I say to you sometimes this truth, dear brudder, the cement is still wet. Nothing is set for sure yet. Maybe you know many answers when someone else makes their decisions. Huh? Huh? Maybe..."

"Oh, dear Authority, please enlighten your servile associate before I'm doomed. He talks into vapors and thinks with his head in a bucket of worms. Help this poor, lost spirit."

Bluefeather sat down on the bottom of the cave a while, staring between his feet. "You know what, Bear? I'm not getting anything from you but conversation. I've prayed to the Creator and begged his associate, who is a lower class one for sure, but part of the 'Big Deal' just the same. All I can show for my efforts is a brain slowly spinning into numbness and a heart cold as early morning icicles. Your congeniality is appreciated, but your lack of solid counsel is disheartening. I shall by all that's holy or unholy do whatever it takes by my own damned self." Bluefeather stood. He picked up his rifle and started walking, winding up and down and around toward the distant comforts of his companions, saying back over his shoulder, "Good-bye ol' dancing pardner. It has been interesting knowing you."

Dancing Bear leapt from one stalagmite and pagoda pillar to another, playing his flute, doing war, peace, rain, and fertility stomps. He turned somersaults in midair and invented songs and poems in nineteen languages, but Bluefeather Fellini moved on up toward his problematic destiny without glancing even once at the great performer.

Thirty-Four

Sherry led Bluefeather through the cave. Each had a handlight, although they didn't need them as yet. This cave was dry. No moisture followed the cracks of the surface earth to this lower level.

Then they came to another stone door. Bluefeather wondered what it was with these accumulators—the gatherers of the world's treasures—that impelled them to hide their acquisitions behind iron and steel doors of such magnitude. They all seemed to guard their protective doors with heavily armed little armies as well—only existing in prisons of riches belonging to others. He decided that fear and vanity made up their greed. What else?

He was so accustomed to Sherry, Dolby and Korbell opening these fortresslike entrances that he didn't even watch as she did it. Instead, he noticed how small her waist was and how voluptuous the wide perfect curve of her hips as they slanted back into her strong graceful legs moving like perfected machines of flesh under the soft cotton cloth coveralls. No wonder Pack was shell-shocked over this woman of such classic beauty, courage, and such dedicated intelligence.

He must stop thinking these compliments to hear, and observe, the message of their sojourn. The cave suddenly forked so that now there were three openings. They took the left one. It was a gloomy passage and there was a smell that Bluefeather recognized instantly. It was very subtle at first. Then Sherry shone the light along a wall of hand-dug niches, each about fourteen inches high and seven feet long. In every one there was a body. Most had a burial raiment of a canvas-type sheet. The hands were folded in skeletal exactness over the chest of bones, and the skulls peered upward at the limestone a few inches above them, in perpetuity.

"These are the honorable dead. Those who died of natural causes, accidents, or attacks from beasts of the cavern. Sherry stated this as matter-of-factly as a tour guide, and she swiftly cast her light down the other wall, revealing the same sort of open tombs, saying, "Just the last few years, Dolby has allowed burial at the River of Radiance—which is a form of cremation, as you will soon see."

He had seen so much of death and dying in his young life that Bluefeather only felt a loneliness here. The bones were present, still in their burial cloth, but the spirits had departed. He could feel no vibration or residue of ectoplasm.

The next—the central cave—was different. It was a shrine for any anthropologist on earth. "This is mine," she said proudly. There were bones scattered about a room that had been chosen because it widened suddenly and was extensive enough to hold the huge remains of creatures unlike any he could imagine. Sherry had completed the reconstruction of one that was only about four feet high, but with its tail it must have been thirty feet long. The head was big as an elephant's and longer than a crocodile's. There were only three ample neck vertebrae. Bluefeather reasoned that if there had been more, it could never have held up the weight of the elongated head. The teeth were alligator-like, except much longer, and the tusks were about the size of an ancient Siberian tiger's.

Noticing his interest, Sherry explained, "This is one of the few carnivorous animals we find at the river."

Bluefeather was a fairly brave man, but the thought of contesting one of these malevolent-looking beasts made the perspiration form on his upper lip, his heart rattle, and his rectum pinch down like a python's throat.

She continued, "I have, of course, recorded proper technical names for all the creatures we've been fortunate enough to identify. This one is named, in layman's terms, the chomper."

"Apropos as Jack the Ripper."

"Thank you, Blue. Oh, come here."

He followed the path through the deliberately scattered cluster of bones from many species to the outer edges of the extensive room. There was a creature with tiny, almost transparent, bones. In fact, Bluefeather was not sure whether they were bones or hard ligaments, so he asked Sherry about it.

"You've missed your true calling, Blue. These structures are in fact a combination of bone and ligament-like material. In the living animal they are translucent and only become partially opaque after death.

This one specimen has taken over a year of my life to get its form laid out properly."

"My Lord, it must be as big as a mastodon."

"Far bigger, and almost as rare."

"Would it be an imposition to ask?"

"Its technical name? No, of course not. We call it the Khyber. If you think of the Khyber Pass and its great battles and intrigue over the centuries, you will possibly understand the why of the name."

For now he did not. Later he would.

"Blue, I could happily—and in fact, do hope to—spend the rest of my life right here, but now we must move on to the third cave." There was hesitation in her voice, but she led him forward almost too energetically.

Then her steps slowed, and she beamed their way totally with the handlight. Bluefeather instantly switched his on. Now he felt the spiritual turmoil of earthbound spirits. They were there in the room of killing—of murder. The bodies had been tossed about in piles. These skeletons lay across one another as if they had been dropped at random from a rooftop. The skin was dried and preserved here and there on some of the human chassis.

Sherry just held her light in one place, although there was a slight quiver to the beam. Bluefeather wandered around with his spot, seeing the bullet holes in some skulls. Others had been bashed in from some heavy object; a few heads were completely severed. He could hear screams and cries for release from somewhere far away, but he couldn't reach there. Torment. Torment of the trapped.

He turned his eyes toward her. She was already staring at him. She read the questions projected from him and knew she must give some kind of an answer. She sensed he would not settle for less than a true one.

"These are the rebellious—those who attempted to return to the outer world. Some were rule-breakers who would have jeopardized all of Dolby's sacrifices and dreams of contribution to the world of heretofore unknown knowledge, unheard-of wealth and a surplus of mysteries and revelations from far away space."

She talked on in a monotone that Bluefeather refused to acknowledge. It was a speech she had prepared for a very long time. One she had memorized for whomsoever was chosen to lead the last expedition before the final decision was made on the disposition of the Cavern of

Marvels. She was performing the duty she had trained and prepared for so long. But it didn't work with Bluefeather Fellini.

He placed his light on the floor between piles of the dead, stepping carefully nearer the woman. Her face was powerfully lighted from below so that the whites of her eyes and the forms of her living bones under the light chocolate skin waited for his reaction. She knew she would have to face him someday, but she dreaded it all the same. It was, however, going to be now. Here.

"Sherry, oh, Sherry, how do I speak to you of such things? Can you really believe that these bones lie to us any more than those left after the Fall of Rome, the Holocaust, or the Crusades? What are the odds, my darling woman, of Dolby sparing us any more than these—" he waved his arm around, "these wasted ones here in this room of rock?"

He waited. She stared on at him, immobile of body, but her full lips were moving slightly, trying to give voice to tangled thoughts.

Bluefeather, seeing her hurting from her terrible turmoil, went on, "I know that a trainload of reasons could be made for this—this taking of lives. It can be, and has been, said all through recorded history that it means nothing to take the life of a thousand to give greater glory to a million or to kill a million to benefit a billion, but when has it ever really happened? Is it any more likely to happen here than at Buchenwald or Devil's Island? Is it?"

"I don't know about those things you speak of. I can't see the final results defined. But...here...here I know only a portion of the good that could come to all the world, and it is enormous in its ramifications of knowledge leading to more knowledge, of the whole of the world realizing how truly miraculous it is that life is marching on and on, evolving toward individuals—entire societies—that can think, reason, invent, compose, laugh, love, and..."

"Please. Please don't think me rude for interrupting, but I, too, have already seen all those possibilities you speak of, and we have yet to enter the really bravura part of the expedition. I will not cause you to despair again. I will move on with all the energy I've got, letting my actions come from the beliefs that are presented to me."

"I know you will, Blue. You've already proven that." Suddenly, she stepped to him—pressing her head into his chest a moment—then raised her face to his, saying in a voice that was partly from ancestors so far back in time that the generations were unfathomable, "I don't know either, but we must not let these thoughts out of this room. Ever."

Bluefeather touched her tenderly on the cheek with the flats of his fingers, saying, "You can trust everyone in this room to keep the secret with silent tongues, except the two of us, and we don't have any other choice."

"I couldn't have said that much better myself." She smiled.

"I'm sure you could say it much, much, better. However, I'll settle for breaking even on this deal. How about you?"

"Even?" She thought a moment. "Yes, even would be fine," she said. "Even means everyone comes out equal, right?"

"That's about it, but I think the deceiving odds of it happening are about the same as Dolby turning into a missionary and Korbell into an archangel."

They marched along jauntily now, arms linked, heading together toward the palace that Dolby built.

Sherry said, "I feel so goddamned saintly I could lead a church choir."

"I feel somewhat divine my own dumb self," Bluefeather replied.

They chuckled together like two misbegotten cherubs.

Thirty-Five

The Section shaped up for the final phase of the Dolby expedition. They trained by alternately walking and running two hours each awake period; then they did calisthenics, cleaned weapons, ate gourmet food, and mostly enjoyed one another's company.

Pack had taken a shortcut to heaven. He had his dream of Sherry looking at and speaking to him. His section comrades were shaping up, eager and ready. Even Ratchett was extra happy. He had been allowed to study in the gourmet kitchen and help the Olders prepare the meals. The aged and the youthful had their own separate but patterned training methods and areas. They were still helpful, courteous, and pleasant at all times, but there was no fraternization between the "inners" and the "outers," with one exception—Shia, the young Asiatic lady, who respected Sherry close to worship and somehow escaped censure for her attendance thereby. In fact, Shia had been accepted as Sherry's assistant by all. The unheard-of order could only have come down from and been approved by Dolby.

Bluefeather only got glimpses of Steinberg, the palace commander. He could be seen standing taller than any down here. He was thin, but appeared in fine physical shape for his age—or any age for that matter. He led the Olders in their exercises with weapons and gave orders to the leader of the Youngers, as well. He wore a beard of iron gray and a mustache that was still as naturally dark as it had been forty years past.

Curiosity did nothing to diminish Bluefeather's astonishment that Steinberg was Dolby's only remaining friend below. They seemed so different at a distance. One thing was for sure: his being down here in charge, and the only one ever allowed above, proved beyond any question that he was an extremely loyal and tough entity.

The Section had adjusted now to the twenty-ten awake and asleep pattern so that it seemed as natural as any schedule they had ever followed above.

Bluefeather checked with the stables. He was amazed over and over at how the cattle, chickens, ducks, and geese all seemed to thrive on the mulch feed made from the trees of light. The mules were shiny and alert.

"Hey, Willy, you got your mules ready to take us fishing?"

Willy said, "These mules are over-trained, over-fed, and underbred."

"Those last words are all that fit you, my dear ol' pardner."

Charlie stopped brushing one long ear and joined in. "Don't listen to the old renegade, Blue. He's been visiting Jody on one shift, then Estrella the next, then Charlene—all in turn."

"That's all I been capable of—just visitin'."

Bluefeather said, grinning, "Well, ol' pardner, I better not hear that the other men are missing their turns because of your greediness. Bad for morale, you know?"

"I'm safe, Blue. Haven't you noticed—all your section boys go around smiling like they just discovered ice cream and cake?"

"I thought it was better than dessert the first time, myself," Charlie added.

"My gosh, is that all you guys think about?" Bluefeather asked, smiling.

"Naw, I think about goin' fishing once in a while," said Willy. "Hey Blue, they tell me the underground river holds some whoppers."

"Yeah. They're whoopers all right. They never quit bitin'," Bluefeather assured him.

Bluefeather joined in a few more fun and silly remarks before going to make his last call before dinner.

He knocked on Marsha's door and the voice came from just the other side. "Who is it?"

"Blue."

She slowly, wordlessly opened the door. After a moment she pulled it back for him to enter. He walked around the spacious room, then sat down.

"I don't know what's right to say, but I gotta say something," he uttered.

"I think we've already talked enough . . . too much, in fact," she said.

"Yeah, well, I agree."

She had just washed and dried her hair. Now she sat down in front of the dresser mirror with her back to him. She had on a robe and nightgown of peach-colored satin. She could see his face reflected in the mirror. He could see both her face and the back of her auburn hair as she combed it. Her special feminine movements made him warm with desire and a craving to erase all the harsh words and thoughts forever.

He had that feeling of déjà vu that comes from half remembering an almost identical actuality. He knew he had sat like this in torment, wanting her, sometime before, but couldn't peg it exactly. He could smell her from somewhere long ago. It was her true body perfume that teased his memory through his olfactory senses. There was not any use torturing himself further.

"Might as well get to it, Marsha. We go on down into the caverns day after tomorrow. It's the 'Big Do,' you know? A lot of people have died down there attempting to solve and solidify a hold on that world. You have no idea how many," he said softly. "I told you what I saw on the film, but the rest of it—the real thing—is something else altogether, and..."

"Well, if you're concerned about my dedication to this project..."

"Yes, I am concerned about everyone's dedication. One misstep, just one person sloughing off, and the consequences and the loss are too much to contemplate. Do take my word on this."

She put the comb down and walked over to him. Her body lines showed smoothly under the slippery fabric. She stood in front of him with one hand on a hip. Her waist, even with his line of vision, and the faint scent of her perfume so near made it very difficult for him to hear what she was saying. Lesser men had been doomed by these simple gestures. Armies and political careers and kingdoms had fallen to this essence that spoke without words.

"I will obey all commands with the best of my ability and be alert for any danger from any place at all times."

He lifted his body and, reluctantly, his eyes as well, saying, "No one can ask more." He started out of the room, stopped, turned, and spoke again. "To try and pull off the imagined impossible is to leave oneself wide open to both great and minuscule forces."

She replied, almost flatly, "It seems the impossible is our motto. We're already experienced at that, aren't we?"

"Yes. Yes, we are, sort of, but it's only a beginning, as we'll all soon see." He was talking at an angle away from her now, fighting to keep from whirling and lunging back to her body.

He went out the door, aching like an abscessed tooth from the pearly floor to the top of his dark-maned head. He said to himself, with his mind-voice, "Bluefeather Fellini, you are one dumb sucker, but you courageously, and at great sacrifice, listened, heard and absorbed every word the woman said, but...but it's not relieving that half-raised staff just under your belt buckle now, is it?"

"Shut up, shit head," he replied rudely to himself.

Thirty-Six

Mules and human packs were loaded; weapons were cleaned, oiled, prepared. Bluefeather stood behind Pack and Sherry; Marsha and Shia were immediately behind him.

Pack voiced the roll call. "Estrella."

"Here."

"Jody."

"Here."

"Charlene." And on down the list: "Garcia, H.; Waters, C.; Ruger, W.; Moosha, Z.; Tack Won, G.; Ratchett, J.; Dunning, R.; Kowalski, B.; Kubeck, A.; O'Malley, B.; Davis, C.; Fielder, M.; Osaka, M." All answered with a resounding "Here."

Pack said, "Your Commander Fellini will address you."

Bluefeather said, "This next moment we move out on one of the greatest adventures in the history of humankind. Let's go get the job done and celebrate a thousand years. Are you ready?"

There were cheers of such exuberance that Pack immediately strung out the train and started it moving. It would be downhill all the way and only a five-hour trip.

At about the halfway point, a string of screechers moved down parallel with them toward the widening otherworldly light emanating from the river. The entire section stopped, immobile, except for their eyes, which followed the leaping and soaring of the massive creatures. The last one leapt in the air and circled, pointing its knobby antenna toward them. The mules' small hooves shifted around nervously, their ears worked constantly as their eyes rolled. The Section's hands tightened on their weapons, perspiring. A call from a screecher just reaching the River of Radiance was heard, and the beasts sailed on down to seek food in more abundance. Easier breathing returned.

As the panorama of the deep widened, a profound feeling of discovery, of stimulation, of privilege overtook them all. The natural light spreading here thousands of feet underground was so old it transcended the seemingly impossible by such a margin that they rapidly prepared to accept almost any vision. It was a good thing. Rounding a curve in the trail, they could see occasional geysers of fire across miles of steamy water and eerie patches of many-hued greens and blues. The steam clouds were moving violet above, radiating slowly over vibrating rainbows. The musty smell of ancient, heretofore unknown life-forms, permeated everything now. The Section would soon adjust to this, too, but for now, every step, every breath, every nerve, every glance, was the very old becoming the very new.

Then the trail widened and Sherry said, "We'll take a short break here. It's only a couple hundred yards on to the elevators."

With the vision and awareness of the ethereal light came primitive sounds of living, loving, and death rattles, creating an everlasting symphony of the inexplicable. Bluefeather had heard, and felt, a similar music only on the sides of Taos Mountain.

Hector Garcia said, as if speaking to the keeper of the pearly gates, "*En divina Luz.*"

Someone translated. "The divine light."

Marsha's eyes were as wide as they could be by nature, trying to pull it all in at once. She uttered in awe, "As Charles Darwin said of the Amazon Jungle, 'it is a vast, untidy, hot house.'"

Someone else muttered in a voice suggesting the sacred, "It's a festival of fire."

Even Willy Ruger only whispered, "Grandy dandy."

Bluefeather said to Sherry so that only she could hear, "I think you had better explain a few things to The Section."

She understood. Sherry was the only one present who had been here before—many times, in fact. But even now on this new pilgrimage, in an attempt at a final penetration of the "Hills of Hell," her own body juices were playing intermezzos of trills.

"May I have your attention, please." Hypnotized eyes slowly turned away from the sight of all sights. She paused a moment, then said, "First, as I've told you before, my suggestions are only theories spoken with my best professional judgment. There seems little doubt that the light scattered all about the river and its environs is that of minute organisms and heavily condensed luminescent bacteria. The occasional increase in illumination comes from the trees of light impregnated with these bacteria. Some of the surface algae as well as the bush-trees also have unexplained qualities of luminosity that flare in nearby locations for several hours after an eruption of fire. It has never been identified like this before, but many scientists suspect there will be such discoveries on the great reefs of the ocean someday.

"The earth we now stand in was supposedly formed about five billion years ago by gases. It is guessed that the first upright animals came from the great rift of Africa some three and a half million years ago. What you are about to witness here is probably just as old, or new—a million or so years, one way or the other."

Sherry stopped a moment, looking across the vast inner panorama of seething elements, searching for a simple way to explain it. "Well...you know that Rome fell in AD 476. The gap between that seemingly ancient time and this minute is so inconsequential here that the greatest of all scientists would be unable to discern any change in the evolution of the creatures we are about to visit."

"As for trying now to explain this, this..." she waved her hand across the River of Radiance, "...we'll just have to experience the best we can as we move into the river regions. Let me add one thing more. We gaze upon the living primeval."

The acceptance of Sherry's explanation of the entities of the caverns and lights was surprisingly immediate, but Bluefeather knew from the film he had watched that the wonders and danger they had experienced successfully could be destroyed instantly by what was upcoming.

He added to Sherry's talk, "In any museum of natural history you can see models and reconstructed bones of creatures from a time in the past fully as exotic and natural to their wetlands environment as these we have been seeing and those we are about to encounter. Soon, you will realize they are a properly evolved part of their surrounding elements. All I ask is this: Prepare your minds for openness. I already know your courage. So there is nothing else to ask. Thank you. Let's go see it all."

They moved on now to the elevators. There were two heavy iron ones here under a latticework of steel that went down, surrounding and protecting them. The stone barracks and its compound below were enclosed in a protective arc of steel all the way to the river. Three-foot long, ice-pick-sharp spikes protruded from every cross section, forming formidable and sometimes deathly barriers to any charging or flying invader. The entire system was wired to electrify as well, though now it was seldom used. The primitives had learned the lessons of sharp steel and electric pain, and had somehow spread the message. With all of that, the human inhabitants could easily see out between the spaces of the lattice.

It took three trips for Willy and Charlie to deliver the packed mules but only one trip for the rest of The Section. There were perhaps twenty Olders as caretakers of the last outpost and eight or ten Youngers. All had waited and been trained most of their lives for this final assault on the river's treasures so fervently protected by fire and other sweet and devilish things.

They were there. It was millions and millions of years since their ancestors had crawled out of some ancient surface water probably similar to that just below. Now they had arrived to fulfill, or fail at, a destiny begun so infinitely small and so immeasurably long ago.

It had been a hell of a trip for humankind—about three and a half million years, in fact—and now it would reach its apex in only a few more days.

Bluefeather could hardly wait to see the end of it. But first the mules must be put up, fed, watered, and brushed. Each of The Section was assigned small, spare rooms with running water and a chemical toilet. Dolby might be a defiler of humans, but he insisted no unnecessary pollutants touch the river or its air. Here, where the wires from far above ended, they cooked with electricity. Here, too, the last contact with any sort of so-called civilized world ended. Outside this iron cobwebbed fortress was the other mystery, filled with nuances of the incomprehensible.

Sherry, shadowed by Shia, retired for a short time to write in her notebooks. All the others were unpacked. After while, Ratchett called them to the outdoor dining room. They fed on fresh fish, some kind of meat they had never tasted before and other dishes of vegetables and fruits that were frozen or dried. There was little talk during the first meal here, just low mumbling and stares out through the lattice.

The weather, or temperature, was constant here; even the flares of fire seemed regularly timed. Bluefeather figured the temperature at about seventy degrees here at the outpost. He asked Sherry, and she verified that he was close. The temperature fluctuated only a degree or two, which was caused occasionally by The Unholy taking a cleansing breath for the entire living organism of the cavern. Even so, he figured that quite a drop from the fifty-eight degrees at the Mimbres burial chamber in the Cave of the Dead.

As the last one finished eating, Sherry said to Bluefeather, "Well, let's get the obligatory tour in motion, commander."

She was suddenly all professional anthropologist, getting things that were mundane to her out of the way so the paper and bone chase could continue.

The entire compound was covered by the iron latticework right to the river's edge. Here and there, in proper places, were sliding doors of the same material. It was like an extra-long circus tent except that it was made of latticed iron. She showed them the boat ramp, where they toured the shallow steel craft—the special one that was encircled in cork all around its middle, which they would use for their last voyage. They would learn later its purpose. The inside was covered solid with asbestos underneath a rubber matting securing it all in place. There were two gun turrets with double levels fore and aft. The upper level was armed with 20-mm cannon, the lower, more open level, with a 50-caliber machine gun. Two heavy engines powered the craft. They would use only one at a time, saving the spare for an emergency.

The boat crew was the young of both sexes. They stood by at attention as Sherry explained, "This ship we call *The Columbus* has been tested on all depths of the river. It works. However, it has never been into the area of the Hills of Hell, where we are going, for the simple reason that we can only afford to risk it one time. Our gunners are well trained and we have survived short excursions and attacks from the screechers and the chompers. The ship and crew are as ready as we can make them for the final thrust."

All looked and listened carefully with wonderment. Bluefeather marveled at the labor that had gone into constructing the boat: the heavy pieces of iron hauled down from so far above at such great risk, the engineering, the welding, the motors that had to have been brought below in parts, then reassembled. The petrol that filled the tied-down barrels could only have been hauled in ten-gallon cans at the most. All had arrived and been prepared by force of Dolby's will over his laboring militia and the burdened backs of mules.

They followed Sherry on through three gates. Finally, the armed Youngers slid a half gate, and the river was open before them. Sherry motioned everyone back but Bluefeather.

The Youngers kept automatic weapons ready. But nothing attacked. It was peaceful—this moment.

Bluefeather could hear an inexplicable music, again reminding him that the only other place he had heard such an uncanny sound had been on the side of Taos Mountain. The fact that the mountain was above and far north of these depths puzzled him greatly. Nevertheless, he could swear their source had to be the same.

Sherry motioned the whispering section to silence and produced from her shoulder pack a metallic instrument that could be squeezed so that it was soon making the sound of a dozen castanets. She played it—there was no other word—like little metal drums in a broken but constant rhythm. "Clackety, clack, clack. Clackety, clackety clackety, clack."

Then, after each session, she would pause and stare out across the river. All watched curiously, with little electric signals from their brains teasing countless nerve endings about their bodies.

Bluefeather saw the movement on the water's surface even before Sherry did. Gray-white creatures were sliding into the river at the nearest peninsula. It was too far for him to discern what form they might be, but they entered the water with a singular purpose, he was certain. Then they disappeared under the river's surface.

Sherry continued the clacking sounds with what seemed to Bluefeather a little more urgency now. Her hand must be tiring. After a time that no one could measure, Bluefeather saw the head. Then Sherry saw it. Then the young guards, and at last the entire Section, saw one head rise above the water and duck back under instantly. Then another and another performed the same movement with as-yet-indiscernible faces turned toward Sherry's clacking. In unison, all disappeared under the dark blue river for perhaps a full minute. It seemed like hours to The Section, of course.

Bluefeather could sense the tension and radiating nerves in the fine figure of Sherry. He could smell the electricity emanating from the pores of those behind him.

Then. Then a dream of reality, in such perfect harmony they could only be of one mind, rose above the water. These creatures walked on it with arms that had flaps connected from the insides, partway down their bodies. Their arms flailed so fast the flaps appeared like motorized sails, speeding them along the top of the water at least as fast as the most expert of water-skiers.

The Section braced, as the triloids, in perfect synchrony, turned toward the open gate of the iron tent. Then they came to a halt on the surface and sank down to their shoulders, waists, and mid-legs at the edge of the river, according to the depth of the water. The greatest of all Bolshoi ballet corps could not have executed the maneuver with more perfection. Their arms hung just to the knees. Their skin flaps were not noticeable now. Their legs were both short and thin so that tendons could be seen underneath the gray-white hairless skin. There was no use for hair here where the sun never shone.

They had tiny waists from which hung brief clothing made from the softened skins of some other cave creatures. Stone knives, with handles made from trees of light wood, hung from the belts that held up the leather breeches. The knife handles were secured on the stone blades with strips of rawhide and sinew. They had crossed leather suspenders over their chests and shoulders down to the breech cloths. Behind—on each back in a leather, open-ended holster—were short spears made exactly like the knives except the stone points were a little wider and the handles longer.

The triloids' heads were shaped like a short-billed bird's head, about the size of small human heads. Their mouths stretched back from the front perhaps three inches on each side. Their eye sockets were inverted vertically in their heads with extra-long eyelids to cover them. The vertical sockets were thin, and a slit perhaps an eighth to a quarter of an inch is all that was revealed of the eyes. The shape of the orbs projected a feeling of hidden meanings and immense cunning to The Section. The triloids' chests were large and protruding like proud roosters. The females had two large breasts located almost the same as a human's, but each had two nipples.

So, Bluefeather thought, they were placental. Then suddenly, he observed that they had reason and thought as well as the mass migration movement and techniques of most birds, fish, and grouped land animals in the outer realm.

One female stepped forward to the clacking of Sherry's castanets, clicking her teeth together in return signals. The action proved the existence of a form of thinking and reasoning, because they could converse with a creature from out of their ecosystem. The upper lips lifted and their bottom lips lowered as the teeth clicked sounds of a message in return to Sherry.

Bluefeather thought by now his quotient of surprises was exhausted, but the teeth were all in a solid piece, looking like porcelain bone. The upper and lower teeth could make contact with amazing speed and power to crush all but the largest bones. There was in actuality one single, curved tooth above and one below. However, due to the protruding shape of the mouth, they could also rip with them.

The ears were wide, rounded, and as high up on their heads as coyotes'. They were flexible and cupped both in front and back, receiving signals from all angles, pouring them into the head.

"Her name is Dolla. The leader of this group," Sherry said softly.

The two females were so natural with one another they could have been having an over-the-fence, backyard conversation. The final proof of intelligence was revealed to Bluefeather when Dolla and Sherry smiled at each other. Each raised a knee and touched them together. The ceremonial movement was the same as a kiss and a hug. The triloids had the magic gift of friendship.

As Dolla raised her knee, Bluefeather noticed her feet. They were very flexible, about five inches wide, and had toes that were partly short claws. Then his eyes went to her hands. They were like her feet, but with longer, retractable claws similar to those of earthly felines. Both male and female had the same. Their jaws, feet, and hands were all weapons, so the unarmed knee was a perfect part of the anatomy for a gesture of friendship. These triloids, although not quite as heavy as the humans before them, were armed in five very different ways. The observers had seen that they could swim under water like fish and walk—or rather, run—on it, too.

Dolla and Sherry spoke in their special way again. Then the triloids all turned, following Dolla. They raced upright along the shallow water, up on the banks to some rocks bluffs. They climbed them as agilely as squirrels do trees. Powerful, ringed muscles in the bottoms of their feet and hands gripped the bluff as if they were part of it. When each reached a certain height they "showed off" in space, one after the other, their arms spread wide so that the flaps formed a perfect sail-wing. The updraft from hot spots in the river and on the land allowed them to circle, gliding sometimes higher, sometimes lower, on across and beyond the river to become lost in the ever-moving mists. They couldn't exactly fly, but how they could sail.

Sherry turned to The Section, saying, "It took me five years, but we are friends. They've gone home to prepare for our visit later."

Bluefeather knew now why Sherry had included the "tri" in their species name; they were creatures of the water, earth, and air. Incredibly appealing and adaptive beings high on the ladder of subterranean evolution.

■ ■ ■

Thirty-Seven

Sherry had directed them straight to the conference room and immediately began to explain: "As you have seen, life has been developing here on the River of Radiance for millions of years. Some of the creatures are still blind from the far back time of total darkness. After the moving earth plates below us opened tiny cracks to its molten core, luminescent light particles formed. Because of that, some—like the triloids—have slowly developed eyesight, weak to be sure, but a much-needed addition to the sonar mind-sight so highly developed in all the creatures here. Our friends, the triloids, have both. Consequently, they have a physical, as well as an intellectual, advantage over all else in this cavern of impossibilities. Of course, the closer to blindness the denizens are, the greater their olfactory abilities. I do believe they can actually smell the outline and movement of any living thing as clearly as we see it with our eyes."

Sherry patiently answered many questions from the group, emphasizing that it would take thousands of minds greater than hers at least a century to even partially explain the beginning and development of the life system here.

She said, "These creatures of the cavern river are not museum pieces of some long-lost time. This is their time and place, right here, right now."

Pack did not seem to be bothered so much by the marvels as he was by Sherry's suddenly relentless, professional attitude. Bluefeather could tell Pack took it personally, while he knew himself that it was a focused drive to furnish Dolby his long-pursued dream before it was too late.

She almost brusquely dismissed all but Bluefeather, leading him to a special room high up on the bluff overlooking the river and the smaller caves within the overly monstrous cavern.

The room was long, fairly narrow, with windows that easily slid open. Two large telescopes stared out over the innerscape. There was a comfortable, raised swivel chair in front of each. But what caught Bluefeather's vision first upon entering the room was a five-foot-tall iron rod secured in the floor. The last foot of it appeared to be made of solid gold, and on it perched a gold-plated human skull staring blindly out of its hollow, yellow eye sockets between the telescopes. There was an incongruous wig of scraggly hair sitting atop the smoothness of the gold plating. It was askew and ridiculous looking.

"That's Tilton's head with his own scalp on top. Dolby wants him to look forever, helplessly, out on the richest world ever known," Sherry explained.

"His vengeance would appear to have been artfully completed," said Bluefeather, staring at the partial remains of another accumulator who had, with his evil, instigated considerable early twentieth-century history here in the Southwest. Dolby kept that same acidulous emotion moving around the bone of Tilton's severed head even today. By the Great Spirit, Dolby had not only decapitated Tilton, he had also scalped him as a Comanche might have and had tanned it, for at least some per-manency. The seemingly unlimited lengths to which Dolby would go to avenge or control were more extreme than even one with Bluefeather's experience in mental and bodily violence could fully acknowledge.

"I hope Dolby likes me—I mean, really likes me—especially when it comes to that 'forever' business."

"He does, Blue, just as he does me. As long as we perform and deliver. Delivery, that's what Dolby expects, not excuses. Delivery," she said, as if to herself.

She adjusted a rod connecting the two telescopes so they could look in synch, seeing the same things. First, she slowly moved the tele-scope upriver through alternately spurting and subsiding geysers of steaming water, on past spear points and needles of burning rock pierc-ing the floor of the cave, building and forming tiny islands as they lit up the caverns in an ever-moving glow.

There were other balls of light, oscillating, dipping, dancing, with no patterns to their movements whatsoever. They were like many UFOs seen in the above land, coming at one with amazing speed, then twist-ing, turning diagonally or vertically with immense velocity. They were there most of the time, flashing in and out of steam, mist clouds, and caverns, circling—sometimes feverishly—'round and 'round the mighty stalactites and stalagmites. They teased the eye as well as the brain circuits and tantalized the natural timing of all else here. Bluefeather figured they were gas balls squeezed up from plates of earth grinding below. They were an energy of life somehow, as were the fire and metal and other living things that began breathing here in many different manners over the ages. It was a circus of lights celebrated where once the darkness had been supreme and the consequent blindness had created creatures that could only look inward in order to look outward.

Sherry moved the powerful glass past the fiery fissures to the now dead blackish Hills of Hell. There would have been no surprise to either of the two if they had seen devils dancing in delight around suffering sinners.

"There you see, Blue, do you see the dark Hills of Hell?"

"Yes, I see them. Looks like they've been dead for aeons. Speaking of hell, well, how in the hell do we get there and why?"

"In the boat, of course. There's no other way. Once we brought pieces of a helicopter down here. Took us a year to haul and assemble it. We set up strong radios and relay stations. The two chosen ones flew on over the dark hills and perhaps ten miles beyond before the cave narrowed into blackness and the river vanished over a void."

"We recorded the radio reports on the return trip. They landed on three of the terrible hills—giant fumaroles is what they are, built from cooling minerals of the deep. Anyway, the copilot's voice is recorded as saying that the hills appeared to be burned and condensed down to the most precious of metals. At that announcement, Dolby ordered their return. From their last spoken words, just instants after takeoff, we can only surmise that a Khyber grabbed the chopper and they crashed. You can hear it on the tape. I'll play it for you later. We expect to find the remains of the chopper on the big hill."

Now Bluefeather knew why all had happened before—all the labor and lives sacrificed. It was still the power of riches they were pursuing for Dolby's obsession with greed and conquest. He was suddenly stunned that such a wondrously creative mind and soul as Sherry's could not see it. Her work, her world of knowledge scribbled in the notes, her own foolish dream of believing Dolby, would open and share all this information. Clues to the origin and future of the universe, life, and even reason itself would be abandoned to fulfill an evil old man. Bluefeather believed this. He ached because of it with all the pain of the billions of dead creatures over the millions of years of their own hurt to get to here. Right here. Now. This instant. He felt all their hurts at once, and he momentarily blacked out from the unbearable thoughts.

When he gained awareness again, he subjugated all these feelings to the "nowness" of the telescope. He would speak and act later. He must not spoil these minutes, these hours, that Sherry had shared with no one else but Dolby. They saw creatures like miniature dinosaurs that Sherry had named Dinahs. She explained that they laid eggs in concealed places on the edge of small backwater pools, hidden in and around fallen bush-trees. Down here, the Dinahs were food for many—especially the triloids—just as rabbits and squirrels were for the earth animals above.

They witnessed a struggle for the carcass of a horned creature that would have in the outer world appeared to be a cross between a hairless buffalo and a mountain goat. A chomper and a dragonlike animal with six legs, its feet armed with claws like Arabic daggers, rolled and ripped at one another, blood spewing and flowing, until they were solidly covered and slick with it. Both died.

Before Sherry could move the glass, screechers swooshed down and settled their blind selves in the blood and flesh to feast their huge, bellowlike craws full. Even through the constant cacophony of multiple sounds, Bluefeather and Sherry could isolate the shrill and now sometimes choking cries of the massive hopping flyers.

"My God, I keep forgetting what ravenous things they are."

The glass moved on, revealing all kinds of snakelike, alligatorjawed, slithering, lighted, electric eels. The quantity of living, moving things was enormous per square acre. They flourished with a bounty of riches from the fiery center of gravity itself, mixed with the water to make a richness of nutrients and life unparalleled in earthly experience.

Sherry said, as if to a student, "This is no sci-fi comic book. This is as real as a tyrannosaurus once was or a kangaroo is today."

"Square on, Miss Sherry."

Bluefeather had forgotten Dolby's wickedness now. He had forgotten the flesh and soul of Marsha that he constantly craved. He had even forgotten Sherry. They had become, one or a trillion, of the same grand destiny peeled bare before them to its feral fauna.

He said, "The Great Spirit invented little bacteria and told them to make what they wished."

"Yes. Yes, and here before us are the mighty works they've created."

"We stare at the most lavish cauldron of existent life on earth, without question."

"Yes. Yes. Yes." She answered him as if she were having an orgasm for the whole world.

Then out from the interior of wonderment, the incessant ringing of the last phone finally reached them. It could, of course, only come here, way down here, from Dolby.

Reluctantly, Sherry removed her eyes that had seen so much in the glass, stood up, and took a very deep breath that raised and protruded her breasts—pushing them tight against the front of the pinkish gray uniform—turned and zombie-stepped to the instrument linking them to the above land.

Bluefeather was trying to turn loose, to free his being, of the underworld they had just been living in. It seemed like many minutes before he realized that Sherry was talking to him. He could not coordinate his thoughts or her words. She understood. She had been in his condition many times these past years.

Sherry hauled off and slapped the robin piss out of him. At first he was blank again, but then his head cleared in opposite reaction to the blow.

"Blue. Listen, Blue. There's a large man with a scar," she made a motion at an angle across her entire face, "hanging around the bar at Meanwhile asking questions about Dolby. The Olders have seen him 'glassing' headquarters. Do you think you might know who he could be?"

"I think so. It sounds like Fontaine."

"Fontaine. Who is he?"

"Fontaine is Korbell's man. His only adopted son, in fact."

"Oh. Then we might have another problem, huh?"

"If Korbell wishes, we've got an oversized problem."

"Dolby's troops will handle anything that comes up. I'm sure of it." She put her hands flat on his chest, looking up into his eyes. "Isn't that right, Blue?"

He knew it was a goddamned lie, but he couldn't help himself. "Dolby can swallow Korbell like Hitler did Poland."

She placed her head against his chest between her hands. He caressed her hair a moment, trying to make the terrible responsibilities she bore a little lighter. Then, inexplicably, she said, "I'm so hungry I could lick the shadow of a cactus tree till it's as shiny as new money."

■ ■ ■

Thirty-Eight

When The Section came out of the third sleep period, they found Sherry in a regimental mode of action. She lined up everyone in the entire compound—the Olders, the Youngers, The Section—and read off the names of those who would go for the underwater walk. Bluefeather headed up the list but was dismayed that Pack was not included in such a dangerous assignment. He eased around and asked Sherry about this privately.

"Look, Sherry, we're going to feel terribly confined in the river cage. I'd like to leave Marsha out of it. I'm afraid worrying about her will weaken my concentration. She can help Pack and the rest get things ready for the Hills of Hell excursion. Okay? Please."

"That's one of the reasons Pack can't go. I should have thought of it myself." Agreeing with his concern, she announced to the group, "Sergeant Pack will remain here in charge. We cannot risk both commanders until the final voyage."

There was no time wasted. They had rehearsed for three days. Now they went under. The iron submarine was nothing but a latticed miniature of the huge protective tent above and around them. It had wheels under the entire oval, mounted below hydraulic systems to fluctuate with any change in the bottom of the river. There were even more iron spear points, thinner and sharper, welded to its outside so that it appeared at a glance to be a large porcupine. There was cork all around a rod underneath to make it lighter in the water. Another rod was welded around the entire inside, standing out about a foot from the shell. It was grooved to make holding it easier. Only hands pushing and pulling here would control its direction going down into the unknown waters. A large steel cable tied to the device would unwind with their descent. It was connected to a powerful electric motor at the tent compound. When the striking of the cable in a coded rhythm occurred, the engine would be reversed and draw the object and its people back to shore. Every few feet on the push rod there hung heavily stitched canvas bags ready to receive the nodules of rich minerals from the floor of the river. There were extra oxygen tanks latched securely inside as well as several dozen spears for the three spear guns in holsterlike rigs. The oxygen-fed suits were of the finest heat-resistant material science could devise. There was a water bottle on each of their backs with an attached tube inside, next to their mouths. They only had to turn their heads slightly to suck the water to prevent dehydration from the heat. The circular glass windows they looked out of were ground glass as precious and strong as that of an expensive telescope. There were large battery lights that could be controlled by a switchboard in front of Bluefeather's position.

Bluefeather's section of the crew that Sherry had selected gave him some comfort because they were all top troopers: Hector Garcia, Moosha, Kowalski, George Tack Won, Davis, and Osaka.

They entered the river, pushing ahead and downward. The attached steel umbilical cord was slowly unwinding, allowing their penetration toward the river bottom. There were enough concentrations of luminescent microbes to provide sufficient light to move on. The trees of light, which of course had absorbed and concentrated the infinitesimal particles of light, waved very slowly in rhythm with the barely moving water.

The eerie, otherworldly luminosity revealed an abundance of life beyond ordinary comprehension. They soon adjusted to pushing over the wavy terrain in bumps and jerks softened by the water pressure around them. The brilliant colors were at the very least equal to those of the Great Barrier Reef's creatures. They saw striped fish of every shape that looked like swimming rainbows and fish that were so small they were only visible because they swam in such vast numbers. There were mollusklike crustaceans on the floor and white crabs with a single, perfectly round, black dot in the center of their backs that at first looked like a bullet hole. There were floating things similar to jellyfish, but so transparent they were almost invisible until they moved. A six-foot-long, green and yellow fish with a head like a rhino's and blue teeth—sharp as broken glass and uneven as tornado-ripped timber—dined on the jellied ones constantly.

A ten-foot-long fat fish floated beside them like a large, pink balloon. The odd fish easily coordinated its speed with that of the slowly moving explorers. It had several eyes, forming a perfect hexagon. The change in the density of the luminescence made the eyes appear to be lighted from inside the strange floater. It had a webbed mouth without teeth. Bluefeather surmised that it must filter tiny water creatures very efficiently into its system to be so rotund. He wondered how the pink, tender-looking bulk kept from being eaten by the flat-nosed sharks that were now becoming more numerous, circling the cage with a curious confidence.

Then one shark made a presumptuous lunge at the fat fish. The pink skin suddenly opened hundreds of tiny portholes and shot out a yellow cloud of acidic juices that made the sharks roll over in the mud of the bottom in agony.

Bluefeather and his comrades were all relieved that the gang of flat-noses had dispersed. One of them could easily have shoved its huge frontal object under the craft and caused great destruction. Everyone kept touching his razor-sharp machete. Bluefeather, Moosha, and Hector felt the spear guns now and then for comfort, as a baby does its mother's breasts.

The kaleidoscope of swimmers and clingers to the river bottom was so great that the initial astonishment and awe was already becoming the norm. They watched with great care as Bluefeather began picking up a few of the slowly increasing number of nodules and scraping off the rust-like crust to study the heavy metals underneath. Some were mainly of manganese; then he would find a cluster that had malleable metal that could only be an undetermined mixture of silver, platinum and gold.

Increasingly, Bluefeather was realizing what caused Dolby to create such a climate of murderous dedication. Already he had seen rich minerals that could easily be hand-mined, of such quantity that one could purchase any mid-sized city in the world. He only saved a few of these first samples, handing them to his cohorts and signaling which bags to put them in. He wanted to keep the load as balanced as possible.

Now the loss of the thought of time possessed all of them again. Space as an actuality vanished as well. Time as measured by a mechanical instrument was even more changed here than it was by the infinite sounds and sights of the mighty Cavern of Marvels directly above them. In a few yards it seemed that a decade had sneaked by them. In a hundred yards they had breathed and moved through a millennium of time fractures. Sherry had warned them of this hypnotic danger.

Bluefeather signaled them to stop and needlessly inspected the condition of all equipment, and every user, just to break the rhythm of their internal systems and to get the adrenalin of discovery flowing again.

There were areas in the river where no luminescent materials were concentrated, and it seemed as if they had entered the darkness at the center of the great meteorite itself. They automatically pushed harder against the handbar, shoving their feet more strongly against the primal wetness of the floor. The darkness turned to total black, making them feel as if they moved in solid mud. Bluefeather saved the switchboard lights for a dire emergency only. They broke free of this area and the light slowly brightened. There appeared a nicely rounded hill in front of them. As one body now, they all pushed to the side to skirt around it.

Then, Bluefeather, as usual, spotted the vision first. His breath was pulled back into his lungs so hard at the sight he almost became giddy from the increase in oxygen in his lungs, and consequently, the blood that rushed to his brain.

A herd of four-legged green fish-horses with purple and orange manes was moving in single file across the hill. The movement caused the stiff manes to wave in the water as if blown by a high desert wind. They had tails that dragged behind them like true wild mustangs of the early Spanish West. Short, incomplete, pointed stripes marked their sides.

All the humans had stopped, mesmerized by the real but miragelike vision they were witnessing. The fish-horses even seemed to have fetlocks until one realized they were connected all the way up their legs to their bellies, translucent as glass beer mugs. It was a soggy dreamscape of bewitchment. The crew was paralyzed with entranced delight.

The spell was silently shattered then, as a one-ton, twelve-foot-long, saber-toothed monster moved past, jaws chomping in anticipation like massive maws. The three eyes that stuck up above the head like periscopes centered on the remuda of fish-horses. Its white and unevenly black-and-red-patterned sides undulated forward so powerfully that its bulk and power caused the water to move strongly in the cage. Its silence seemed louder than a runaway train. But before the ogre could create successful carnage, the lead fish-horse sent an unseen signal, and the startled adventurers saw the entire herd of horses flow swiftly, efficiently, into one stolid form. The manes and the tails were poisonous barbs, and what had in effect appeared to be short stripes on their sides were daggerlike pins that now protruded in a solid mass of protection as they all together formed the shape of a single giant watery porcupine.

The three-eyed saber-tooth hit the mass and separated it some from the force. As it pulled back from the piercing pain, the fish-horses fell back into a single unit again. The swimming beast bit at the hilt below them, trying to rip the entire earth apart from its agony. It shook about in the water, forming foam and unseen ripples, whirling like a dog chasing its tail in an attempt to clamp the monstrous jaws on itself. Failing this, it rolled over and over wildly in the water and then circled a bit before charging straight at the iron-cloistered group. The impact lifted the cage despite the full weight of eight people trying to hold it down. The iron spears shoved into its face and mouth and sent clouds of blood black as motor oil spurting into the water in jets. It came again in such a random, wanton rage that the cage threatened to completely tilt over, but this time the barbs were too much, along with stings from the horses. It turned and erratically vanished into a large, dark hole.

When the cage had tilted, unseen by all, a flat-mouthed shark had swum into the cage and now had Kowalski around the knees and was shaking him like a goose-down pillow. One leg dangled loose from a tendon and the other was ground and cut until it was ready to drop from the upper portion. Davis fired a spear just above the tiny eye of the shark. Its thrashing had knocked several men to their knees, where they held to the iron strips, struggling to get at their weapons.

The human blood now mingled with that of the departed saber-toothed beast. Bluefeather swung down with the machete before he realized that that sort of action was only partially effective against the resistance of the water. He stabbed and stabbed into the head and side of the shark as Sherry managed to fire another spear that pinned the shark to the river bottom.

Even when he could hardly see, Bluefeather stabbed on at the lifeless brute. Kowalski, with his lower legs severed and the oxygen gone from his shattered diving suit, floated up to the top of the cage, then slowly sank as the air left the insides of his upper body.

One at a time, Bluefeather checked his crew in the murkiness. Then he saw Davis floating about a foot from the bottom. His glass viewer on his diving suit had been smashed by the shark's tail. He had drowned, and no one had even seen it in the bloody and sudden melee.

This unperceived death struck Bluefeather hard. He felt helplessly deceived, as he had by the two unscathed soldiers he had tried to awaken from their concussion death way back in the Normandy hedgerows. There was no time for guilt here as back there. He wondered, just the same, how much longer he could negate and subdue the awful feelings of losing those he had become so close to—like members of his family now. That's the way wars, no matter how small, had to be fought, if they were to be won. The grief must be saved for later, or all of them would be doomed. He must not become immune to it like Pack.

Bluefeather choked back the tears and banished the numbness in his stomach by pure necessity. He had to make a quick decision. The dead were past his present help. Everyone had signed on this expedition aware that they might die at any moment from unknown forces. It had happened.

After turning on all the battery lights and studying the near waters for any danger and finding none, Bluefeather signaled the men to lift one side of the cage. It took such effort that they all marveled at the strength of the saber-toothed beast. Bluefeather shoved Davis and the remains of Kowalski into the wet forever world. He had a struggle pulling the spears loose from the riverbed, but he finally did and was able to shove the dead shark out. They pushed the cage away from the two bodies that were so very slowly turning, turning in their vast grave.

Now they were numbed against the beauty of the light and darkness blending into the mysteries of uncountable and unfathomable creatures formed here so long ago by chance of time or by the design of gods. Who could say for sure? Who, indeed?

They did not see the fish-horses instantly separate and walk in mid-water, forming the same single file as they headed away, above the river's floor. Their legs, now used as fins, headed to some private destination this group would never know about. Ever.

An eyeless worm, a yard around and fifty feet long, came at them but turned away at the last instant, its sonar sensing and reading the sharp steel. It flashed through Bluefeather's mind that for every animal on the surface of the earth, there were a hundred similar forms in the water worlds.

A mighty electric eel struck at them three times, causing jolts to their bodies and minds but no permanent damage, as their heavily treated diving suits gave protection from most of the electric shock.

They had never before seen sparks such as were created each time the slick, overgrown, linear creature stabbed itself with the steel. The deviant and enigmatic attacks were like underwater arc welders, until the eel burned and electrocuted itself only to be devoured by a hundred rapacious fish before it could settle to the bottom.

In spite of the rapid series of jolts and disasters, they couldn't help watching in growing awe the actions of the wheel fish. Their forms were perfect circles, perhaps eighteen inches across and very thin in width. There were red and black stripes radiating from their very center, where a golf ball–sized eye looked out from each side. They floated in a seemingly uneven group. Some spun like wheels until all the spoke-like stripes ran together and the fish practically became an invisible blur. Others turned slowly, if at all. But their own personal mass sonar message was there just the same. As a shark moved near them, they all, in one motion, flipped up horizontally, with only their inch-and-a-half edge visible. This threw the shark's sonar signals, sight and smell into such confused disarray that it circled a couple of times and moved on, seeking simpler pleasures.

The wheel fish moved as erratically again as they had on first sight. Then a mighty demon fish, with rhinoceros-type horns of odd lengths over all the front of its armored body, moved toward them. It had one eye in the moving tube atop its head and another eye circling and searching below. The tube—the size of a stovepipe—was extremely flexible and could turn the eye in any direction, but now they both were aimed, weaving toward the group of wheel fish. A jaw that had nine rows of teeth sharper than machete blades, and almost as long, opened up as wide as the arms on a lounge chair.

The group thought many of the wheel fish were doomed. Then, with amazing speed, they all whirled into vertical positions. Little fins suddenly opened in a circle inside the circle. Teeth like large, sharp diamonds suddenly appeared around their thin edges. Spinning in bunches, they surrounded the massive, horned fish like saw blades, as they did indeed prove to be. One group spun, slicing right through the head of the fish, the armor, hide and bone like a lumber-mill saw. One followed another until the victim was almost cut in half lengthwise. Then the other groups whirled in from the sides and the diamond-like teeth sliced the meat into ever-smaller pieces. They were river butchers to perfection. Each retracted the teeth now, and the tentacles with little suction cups pulled the smaller shreds of meat into their bodies, swelling the parts around the eye until it was almost invisible. The pieces that were dropped created another free feast for thousands of flashing, diving, smaller fish and other forms of frenzied feeders. The sated wheel fish formed a single line behind an obviously designated leader and circled their way to a ten-foot-high bluff and slowly disappeared into its cracks and crevices. They had precisely served their evolved purpose for now, feeding themselves and thousands more.

This last underwater show had exhausted everybody. They didn't care now, as they moved on, bent over, testing the nodules that were becoming so thick on the river floor that all walking was difficult. Bluefeather had mined, prospected, and studied enough to know that all minerals were formed by magma and gases penetrating fissures in contact with water. Here, so far below the surface and so much nearer the magma, combined with a huge water source flowing interminably, the creating forces had been magnified many, many times. He could barely raise one huge nodule. Even with the lifting effect of the water he had to put it back down.

Then he took a hatchet from his belt and struck at it and became so excited at the yellow revealed that he risked the sharpness of his machete by scraping and cutting at it. The object contained a high percentage of gold. The battery lights did not distort the color. There were others that were more silver and platinum. With all his vows, and the violent deaths of his comrades just behind them, he felt the old familiar surge of his body juices exciting, compelling, transforming his whole being at the thrill of the find. The kill of the hunt after a long chase. Did it never change? Could it? God. No matter.

Now Bluefeather struggled, controlling his emotions and actions, as he proceeded professionally, guiding the crew along the edges of the thousands of visible tons of nodules and dropping a sample into the canvas bags every fifteen or twenty steps.

Other uncountable, great fishes and entities of phantom shapes inspected them. A few with teeth made to tear, rip, and chew tested the steel barbs and resentfully backed away. The bottom-boat moved on, in and out of darkness, as if it sensed that they were close to completing a mission of the inconceivable. They turned on the weakening battery lights in the black holes and switched them off as the glowing microbes gave form and sight to all again.

They passed area after area of fumaroles, where the hot water spewed out and up through the pipes of blackish metal and stone, some the size of a water hose, others as big around as a sewer pipe. At one time or another, they had helped form the huge mineral deposits of the river basin. Shrimp and other crustaceans large as rabbits fed frantically on the sulfides, white crayfish and slow-moving isopods formed a great food source, and there was no telling what else was being emitted from water heated by the very core of the earth. Some fish, adapted to the three-hundred-degree temperature next to the fumaroles, feasted on the shrimp. There were other sulfide-addicted critters who had developed the ability to turn most of the poisons into food and life. Some of the wormlike creatures glowed red with blood formed from the hot sustenance of the fumaroles.

The sweat poured down out of the explorers' bodies and made a squishing feeling around their feet. They conservatively sipped at their limited supply of water.

One geyser fifty feet away shot up with such force it jarred the cage sideways and blinded everything with bubbles. The suddenness of the shock caused George Tack Won to slightly dirty his rubber breeches. Bluefeather and his old buddy Hector just dripped a little more moisture down to their feet. Heavy perspiring caused by the scattered areas of hot water had afforded a considerable reduction in their weight over the last hour. Even the Youngers, who had been trained for this job much longer than Bluefeather's associates, sweated profusely.

Finally, the ore bags were loaded and the crew's energy was depleted. The reserve oxygen tanks were now only a quarter full. It was the time for retreating.

Bluefeather pulled his machete, opened a sliding hatch and whacked the coded signal hard against the cable, and waited. He held his uniformed hand lightly against it, but no signal returned down the cable. They all looked at one another through glass and water. Fear.

Bluefeather repeated the signal against the cable, and again he touched it with his hand. Cold, cold fear. Waiting. Waiting. At last, he felt the tiny tapping that had raced down the steel cord from their life source at the river's edge. It was a living, pumping heart to his hand.

He turned and gave a raised clenched fist of affirmation to his surviving crew and they all gave it back, resisting the urge to celebrate their apparent survival with the natural human gestures of shaking hands, hugging, or slapping one another on the back. There were smiles inside the glass apertures of different sizes and shapes, but all with the same meaning—life.

Bluefeather's mind-voice spoke. "Funny how the green pines and sunlight of the outer world, that once were taken for granted, will now appear as wondrous and new as the depths of the Cavern of Marvels did a few weeks back."

The Great Spirits, or pure luck, had saved one last vision-gift to partially make up for the loss of their buddies, Davis and Kowalski. Now they looked over an area like a farm of fumaroles, which had formed castles of crystals. They ranged from the size of a cube of sugar to as tall as church steeples. They were mostly hexagonal, but Bluefeather's trained eye saw many other geometrical arrangements such as tetrahedrons and twin systems of crystallizing. He could not help but play the battery lights across such artistry from the deep, showing clear calcite and quartz crystals; others were probably of green and blue tourmaline and beryl; some were rose- and amber-hued.

The totality of their glittering perfection was beyond the capability of mere eyes to behold properly. One had to breathe and become mentally suffused with them. The entire formation could easily be viewed as a small fantasy city with tilted bridges, streets, and buildings—the tallest being a cubist cathedral.

Long leaflike crystals of silver and gold grew next to huge clusters of iron pyrite—no doubt associated with many other minerals of great value. All the jewels in all the royal vaults of the world would have looked small and dull compared to this watery display of beauty in its most glorious form.

Then the fish-birds came and enhanced this gifted vision even more. There appeared over the fantasy city with wings moving them like great eagles flying into a wind storm. Now the movements of the fish-birds captured the group's view with their tantalizing flying swim. They were about half as large as the screechers, but more streamlined. Flat tendrils hung from the wide-stretching wing-fins, giving the appearance of feathers.

They dived as if from above the Rio Grande Gorge into a group of yellow stripers. They had tongues with barbed points that flashed out and pierced the victims like Comanche spears and jerked them into their open, beaklike mouths. Then they folded the barbs to release the catch into their throats. They swallowed them whole.

As six or seven of the flyers dived, swept up, circled, and stopped, like courting scissor-tails, the river turned into a baseball-sized area of fluid motion, creating newly formed bubbles in circles of tinted brightness oscillating in such splendor that The Section was paralyzed.

That was enough, and more, for a final vision of the deep, but they couldn't help watching the rippling psychedelic lights sending flashes of rainbow colors back and forth through the fish-birds' bodies. The chemicals created an incandescence that rushed down to their swishing wing tips, sending a wake of bubbles of every color in existence that slowly diminished behind them, forming a protective diversionary barrier from any possible enemies. It was as if they had been born from the mating of two fumaroles of magma and had retained all the colored flames in their beings.

Then the fish-birds, all in one swoop, water-flew back over the city of crystals, disappearing just as the bubbles blinked to blackness in the void.

Everyone felt enormously blessed, as if they had been truly, tenderly touched by the hand of the Great Spirit. Eyes stared through glass a while in reverent thanks for the river's gifts. They turned their bodies in unison, up-slope. The supreme show had been a special gift that helped ease some of the terrible pain and awareness of their recent tragedies. Bluefeather wept silently, unseen, now, giving thanks that he had left Marsha behind, waiting safely for his return.

The cable slowly rewound, pulling the cage upward. They adjusted to its tilting, sluggish movements, holding onto the iron rail with only one hand, walking freely, but carefully. Very carefully.

Bluefeather jested to himself, "Just another dull day at the office, dear. And how was your day?" But of course, only he could hear his silly satire. He laughed uproariously just the same.

Thirty-Nine

They rehydrated. Sherry was so thrilled at their river-crawling success that Bluefeather felt she had forgotten the human cost. He wondered if that part of the Dolbys and Korbells of the world wore off on everyone they touched? If so, the world as he dreamed of it finally being could never exist. Where in the hell had honesty and honor gotten lost? Somewhere. Where? He knew if the day came when a majority of the people had given up their proper portion of truth and dignity for the fragility of greedy gain and vanity, the forests would fall, the air would become rancid, and the entire earth would turn to ice and sand, dying of starvation and thirst just as all its inhabitants had before.

He finished his report on the inferred mineral values of the small portion of the river they had covered. He put the assay reports, just returned by mule-back courier from God's Castle, beside them. He clipped them together and started out the door to deliver his findings to Sherry.

He took two steps past Marsha's doorway, turned back, and knocked. She opened the door, eyes wide and solemn, waiting wordlessly to hear his verbal approach.

Bluefeather circled the small room a couple of times. He could smell her fragrance with every breath. He tried not to stare at this woman he was in such conflict over, but he could not help himself there. The turquoise robe emphasized the curvature of the body he had enjoyed so much and made her matching eyes seem even bigger and more absorbing. Even her hair showed tints of fire among the autumn auburn he had never seen before. Not to hold her was painful. Not to talk with her of nonsense and laughing matters was numbing, but a sharp knife of doubt had sliced them into separateness.

"Marsha, I'm really pissed."

She stared silently. He waited for a question. It didn't come.

After an uncomfortable awkwardness, he said, "I keep getting this feeling that you not only gave all our venture's secrets to Korbell, but that maybe it's also making it possible for Dolby to use us, our lives, our souls for nothing but a moment of great power before he dies of old age."

"We've been through this before, Mr. Fellini," she said formally, "and it got us exactly nowhere."

"That's because you keep on lying about what you told Korbell."

"I don't like being called a liar. I think my actions make a travesty out of that statement."

"See. See. I told you. You keep avoiding, circling the real issue. You are leaving us vulnerable to these two greedy bastards of evil. They're probably gonna join up and bury us all here just as soon as we prove up the immensity of the wealth."

"They respect, but despise, each another. That should be very obvious. Even worse, they carry vast hidden jealousies. No, they won't join forces. No way that could happen. Anyway, don't blame me for all of that."

"You see these papers?" He waved the reports out toward her. "Entire nations would go to war over this information. And you stand there and deny that Dolby and Korbell aren't planning to do us in as soon as we make our run at the Hills of Hell? Huh? Well?"

"I'm certainly no clairvoyant. And I haven't denied anything but their partnership. You've been in too many wars. You're losing any semblance of the reasoning you once had. You are letting your imagination run rampant."

"Bullshit, Marsha. My imagination hasn't got anything to do with this. I have seen proof of evils you can't even believe. And this evidence has opened my eyes and mind so that I really know what's possible."

They both breathed heavily now a moment. As their anger subsided the breathing returned to normal.

"Ah, shitfire," he said, with more regret than ire in his voice. He walked out the door, not looking back, but saying, "I hate these doubts I feel, but dumb-ass me, I love you anyway."

The truth he had failed to admit to himself was suddenly clear. It didn't make any difference about her domination by Korbell. Who would not be intimidated under the conditions? He was arguing to try to find an excuse to cut her out of the final deadly trip. If he survived, he wanted her here waiting for him. It was no use, though. If he cut her out now, she would never speak to him again.

He took the papers to the headquarters room, where Sherry was on the phone. She said, "Don't worry, here's Blue now with the reports. I think you'll be enormously pleased. No, no, I'll call you back in an hour or so. I still think you have plenty of protection. What could he do? He can't bring in army tanks and that's what it would take. Okay. Okay. I'll be back in touch as soon as I read the reports. Okay?" She hung up, saying to Bluefeather, "Dolby's getting concerned at Fontaine's presence. He's thinking about having him hidden."

"Hidden?"

"Forever."

"There's that Dolby word again. It suggests an awfully long time. A longer time than I like to think of. That's one word that doesn't make sense. We all keep using it. Forever! Forever! I wish the dictionary would drop that word."

Sherry's tilted eyes widened even more at this unexpected tirade about a single suggestive word. Nevertheless, she smiled with immense relief in her voice, saying, "At last. At last," as she took the papers.

He sat down, then quickly got up and stared out at the river world as she read. No matter what one's emotion, the fact of the sacred cavity's visual and audible existence eased his concern for the upper world. He was becoming—by the day, maybe by the second—pulled into this other world here, far, far below. All his youth he had heard the legends and myths of the underworld from many different Indian nations and pueblos. Here he was in it. A wonderment indeed. For just a moment he was startled that he already felt more at home here than he did above. How could it be? This ancient system down here had already killed some of his best friends and his favorite mules. Making the expedition at all had cost him the love of his woman—and they hadn't even started on the deadliest part of the trip yet. Then he knew. This underworld would kill them, just as they might have to kill some of it. But it was honest survival—survival of the fittest; survival of the honest; survival of...

He was humming out loud, smiling to himself, when Sherry interrupted his reverie with, "It's mind-shattering, Blue. My God, there's enough riches in the river to buy New Mexico and Colorado."

"Yeah, with Arizona and West Texas thrown in. My dear woman, please be aware that therein lies the joker."

She ignored this, saying, "Dolby is going to be out-of-his-mind thrilled. His dreams, his visions can actually come true now. We could have the power to open these wonders up to the world and protect and share all this for science, for medicine, for knowledge. Just think of it, Blue. The possibilities here in the Cavern of Marvels—this cavern of impossibilities—will leapfrog understanding of the earth, the galaxy, the universe, even ourselves, by millions of years. My mind is exploding with excitement. Have you thought about it?"

"Oh, I've sure been thinking about it, all right. That's for sure. I've certainly been thinking overtime, Sherry."

At that moment, his heart had overcome his desire for the greatest of all adventures. He would have given it all up to be back at Corrales fixing his grandmother Fellini's sauce for a pasta and wine dinner with Marsha. Then he eradicated these warming thoughts. He had to.

Sherry's scientific mind was racing on beyond his temporal thoughts. She said, "The schools and pools of positive facts here will prove and disprove theorems by a thousandfold."

She had suffered the silence of her knowledge, so carefully recorded in her many notebooks, so long that Bluefeather could not bring himself to interfere with her very natural enthusiasm.

He started to tell her that none of this gracious and glorious gift to the outer world was planned by the powerful ones above. There would only be, in the final face-off, just another use of power for more power, until there was no force left with which to destroy. They, the little group of them, could save it—give her dreams a chance—if they were aware and stayed open with the truth. If, of course, they survived the next and final journey of the expedition. The Section had already taken the risks and paid the price—some of it terrible, some of it glorious. Only they—as a solid, dedicated unit of love and reverence for earth, for flesh, for guilelessness—could save it. It would be their choice. It always was. Choice.

He talked on with her in the most hopeful terms he could dredge up, and being a natural-born optimist himself, he was soon, even if temporarily, laughing and planning great and momentous occurrences right alongside her.

"Well, Blue, none of it would have happened if Dolby hadn't had the wisdom to choose you as the leader."

"I'm flattered, but I've always hoped it was you who really convinced him."

"Well...I think maybe I had a tiny bit of influence. Maybe," she said.

"Tomorrow we go visit the triloids?"

"Yes."

"Is it really necessary, Sherry? I would feel better if we launched our excursion to the Hills of Hell now. Too much anticipation, like that of making love, can take the edge off The Section. Waiting too long can create a mental dullness in the best of soldiers—and a big increase in causalities."

"I understand what you're saying, but believe me when I tell you, all of us will enjoy it, and the visit is a critical part of our venture. Critical."

"Good enough for me then."

"Fine. We'll depart after the next sleep period."

He started to leave and then stopped. "Uh, say, Sherry, I know...I know you'll think this a strange request, but...see these nodules here?" He had selected the richest of the lot and had set aside about four hundred pounds of them. "I'd like for you to have one of your men load these in the leather panniers on a couple of mules and have them camp above the elevators until we're on our way back to God's Castle. Okay?"

She looked at him strangely, but then figured that it was somehow part of his geological work and said, "You've got it. It's done."

"Thank you. Dream well."

"How can I miss? Dear Blue, you've given me whole worlds of dreams and reality."

Forty

Bluefeather was admitted into Pack's room and instantly saw that eternal wisp of a smile was completely gone from his pale face for the first time he could remember. He had come here positively exploding with something he had to tell someone, and his old friend Pack had been chosen. But Pack was already mumbling things that he strained to hear.

"I don't know about that Sherry woman. Ever since we got down here she has been as cold as four-day-old oatmeal. Looks right through me like a dose of salts."

"Hey, old pard', she does the same to me—to everyone—unless she's giving specific instructions. In her mind she is carrying the future of our planet on her already weary back."

Pack sat back down and continued his ceaseless cleaning of the weapons of war. "I s'pose you're right, but ..."

"Listen, soon as we get back from the Hills of Hell and return to God's Castle, you're going to see a regular Sherry. That woman is gonna pour her happiness all over you like icing on a wedding cake. She just prepares for battle just like you do, huh? That's why you like her. She's a female version of Sergeant Pack."

The little delicate smile was back now. "Aw, shit. She's ten times smarter'n me."

"You think for a whistle that I like what's happened to me and Marsha? Hell, I wanted to leave her with Flo and Sally. But if I had she wouldn't have been waiting for me there or anywhere else. Patience, Pack. That's the way for you. When we complete Sherry's dreams, she'll turn them all back to you. I swear it."

The little hint of a smile returned to Pack's thin lips. His slumped shoulders lifted some. He said, "Okay. That sounds reasonable to me, Fellini."

Bluefeather had done his duty to Sherry and Pack; now he had to rid himself of a heavy inner load of constant concern that wouldn't be a worry at all for his friend.

"Pack, listen to me. Listen close and careful."

Pack stopped wiping the surplus oil from the rifle and carefully rearranged the six grenades in a hexagonal shape on his bed, listening hard.

"I finally figured out why we keep on doing these crazy, dangerous things," Bluefeather continued. "All addiction is plain memory, whether it be the first high from booze, sex, or your first shot fired in war. You can never forget that adrenalin rush when you pan your first color of gold. The swift surge of thrills is imprinted for a lifetime, many lifetimes. The instant dreams of luxury in all things, opulence, and glory become possible. The dream and the memories continue. At the time the memory genes remind you of past thrills and highs, they are conveniently skipping the struggles, the sacrifices, and only fill your blood with past resplendency and pleasures—especially those dreams attached to the idolized yellow metal. Goddamn it, Pack, that's it. I know where the fever and loss of control comes from. It has taken me my whole ignorant life to figure out such a simple thing. Now ain't that something, ol' pardner?"

"Yessir, Blue, that is one hell of a something."

Bluefeather Fellini was so happy that he pounded his friend on the back so hard that Pack's throat momentarily jarred shut.

"It's sleep time now, sergeant." He started for the door, then said, "Oh yeah, I almost forgot. I've arranged to provide enough of the river minerals to take care of us, just in case—close to four hundred pounds of about eighty-five percent gold. Not bad, huh? Just thought you might like to know that, after my speech and . . . before you go to sleep." He left, stepping with bounces.

Pack stared at the closed door, picked up his rifle, and aimed it at the heart of anything.

Forty-One

The boat crew of the Youngers was ready and, surprisingly, anxious. Guns were cleaned, polished, loaded in the turrets, and all The Section was armed, just as they would be on the final charge down the River of Radiance. The trip across to visit the triloids would be a rehearsal. Barrels of gasoline were latched in place. Ammunition and extra grenades were in a gun box. It was welded onto the bottom of the boat and had secure latches that could be easily opened with the knowledge that had been imparted to all. The two flamethrowers were also secured, ready to be unhooked. They would not be needed on this day, so they remained in place. Sherry stood upon an ammunition box.

"Attention, please. Attention. We're going to visit a pueblo of our neighbors, the triloids. We've been invited to their territory. I know how tempting it is to compare certain traits of theirs with ours. Chimpanzees, dogs and wolves have some actions similar to humans', but they are not us. Neither are the triloids. They are their own entities and we must respectfully treat them so." She motioned to the motor man. "Crank it up."

He started one of the large engines, leaving the other in reserve. The boat quivered a little like a race horse in the starting gate. Everyone took swivel seats and dropped the simple safety belts over their laps. They could, if need be, be instantly removed. A group of Olders waved them away from the dock. They had visited the triloids with Sherry before.

The boat trip had the thrill of a first hayride or the first unpacking of goodies for a family picnic. Since the river moved as slowly as cooling molasses, the ride across was a smooth joy. Everyone opened up and chatted about the majesty of the great multi-lighted cavern and the dark blue river. They made curious gossip about the triliods. All was festive.

They saw the head and arcing back of what could only be called a monster. It circled the boat fifty or so yards out. Its head and corrugated-appearing neck arched out of the water to stare at them. Then it went under except for the undulations of its spine, creating strong waves that began to rock the boat as it continued circling.

The gunners in the two turrets kept it in their sights most of the time. Their first flash of fear had now turned into intense interest.

Sherry soothed them by explaining, "We call it Nessie after the legend of the Loch Ness monster."

She had no sooner said this than the huge creature turned away in a spray, heading with amazing speed down the river until all that was left was the wake.

Two-thirds of the way across, Bluefeather saw some triloids waiting on shore, pointing at the boat and communicating with one another in obvious pleasurable anticipation. Several sailed above with spears, looking all around protectively.

Sherry said, pointing, "They are on the watch for screechers."

Then they were there.

After Sherry clacked her odd castanet in greeting to Dolla and was jaw clacked in return, the crewmen leapt down and secured the boat to a tree-bush. They would have to stay with the boat. Sherry was taking no chances of any kind this near the end of the long, long struggle and wait.

The triloids stood in a row. Sherry directed The Section to do the same. She and Dolla raised their left knee, then their right, to touch in greeting. The other triloids and The Section understood the official greeting gesture, and all did likewise.

This over, Sherry and Dolla walked along an ancient trail, wide as a road, like two neighbors heading for a shopping trip together. They were preceded by spear warriors, while sailing warriors protected them from above. The Section automatically fell in a column of fours with Bluefeather, Garcia, Moosha, and Marsha leading. Pack and another chosen three brought up the rear guard.

There were ponds formed by the river inlets and trees of light grew in patches around them along with bush-trees. Here and there, where the path led them by the edge of dampness, algae had crawled out and taken hold in uneven patches on the limestone, providing a grazing source for the plentiful Dinahs that darted now and then from one source of cover to another. At times the trees and the luminous concentration of the microbes thinned so that a space of near darkness formed in the thick, damp fog. This was no problem, for they simply followed the glowing handles of the triloids' knives and spear shafts. It was not unlike the great candle-bearing processions of the Old Mexico Indians.

Pack said, "I feel like I'm in a dust storm somewhere near Texas." The easy, sometimes senseless banter of soldiers marching to a rest period before battle rippled back and forth through The Section.

As they walked in the middle of the darkest air hole, a UFO or gas bubble, as Bluefeather guessed it, whizzed silently toward them. It stopped right above them, illuminating every nearby stalactite or stalagmite, revealing the creases in the rock pagodas and outer cavern walls and dimming the other distant light sources to nothing.

There was a slight increase in the teeth clacks of the triloids, who had been born to this phenomena and had accepted it, countless generations back, as commonplace. The Section, however, stopped, transfixed, shading their eyes, yet attempting to see into the great ball of light. Then it zoomed sideways at such speed their sight could not follow. When their vision did catch up with the gleam, it was whirling and dancing a mile away.

They moved on now in a slight trance. Bluefeather was feeling and hearing the cadences of the caverns: the animals; the fish that also crawled on land; the screechers; the Dinahs; the pursuers; the captured; the spewing of thousands of steaming geysers, some with spouts as small as a pencil, others as big around as ice-skating rinks; shafts of molten rock spurting up from fissures and breaking into droplets as they returned to water and earth, building little islands one place, causing holes to sink at another. He was hearing the sounds of a virgin jungle.

Bluefeather fully realized now that the world inside and out made constant music. Everywhere. Great composers simply heard it cleaner, more clearly and rearranged what was there for all the rest. Always.

The clacking sounds increased in intensity. They were there. A two-hundred-yard-high face of limestone cliff fronted them in a half arc. There were homes of holes all over its face, starting about seventy feet up. They had been partially porched in and had unlighted river reeds tied together with dried sinew as a combination door and window. Some had rock ledge perches. Others were constructed from the river reeds, similar to a huge eagle's nest. Guards watched from properly spaced perches. The rest of the triloids, perhaps a hundred or more, waited. When Dolla clacked a signal, they moved forward en masse.

Some females were suckling from one to four babies, who hung on their mothers with claws that surprisingly seemed to give no pain. There were young ones who followed right next to both the fathers and mothers with much shorter, but imitative, steps. Then there were those The Section would call teenagers, walking to the rear.

Now they lined up in a half circle and all but the babies raised first the right leg and then the left knee out prominently in greeting. The Section was a little late in its movements but fulfilled the ceremonial gesture anyway. The triloids seemed satisfied.

Now each of those from the outer world was led to be seated in a partial circle and the triloids finished filling it in. In the middle were cooking pits with river reeds as fuel. There were spits made from thin rocks, and on them some of the triloids turned huge fish and many Dinahs. There were multiple metate-like bowls at which some sat slicing the cut saplings of trees of light, then grinding them with another, smaller hand-rock into a flour—a process not unlike that used by the ancient Anasazi grinders of corn. The powder was mixed with water, crabmeat, and other delicacies that not even Sherry recognized.

Sherry walked over to The Section accompanied by Dolla and her teen daughter, Reesha. Then they were joined by Dolla's mate, the father, whom Sherry had named Odad.

Sherry went on with her explanation. "Today we have been invited to Reesha's wedding. Soon the members from another pueblito will arrive with the groom."

The feast was about ready. The triloids' guests were all nearby, hidden, awaiting the signal to be asked to present their son to be wed.

Bluefeather was personally thrilled to know there were fourteen pueblitos scattered up and down the river. The triloids lived peacefully in their own territories, similar to the pueblo nations of the Rio Grande. Certainly half of him felt at home here by blood and instinct, and the rest by genial invitation.

He looked at the Dolby Youngers so eagerly absorbing the visit. It was as new to them as it was to him. Steinberg had trained his militia well. They obeyed orders instantly and efficiently. A sudden pang grabbed Bluefeather's throat when he realized he would never get to know their minds, or souls, or dreams. Dolby had already arranged that. His eyes moved to The Section. Only Pack was aware of their loves, desires, families, and childhoods. There had been no time for him to know them outside battle. Maybe later. Maybe.

His sight jumped to Marsha and he moved down next to her, squeezing her hand. She squeezed back so lightly he almost missed the pressure.

Then his mind-voice plugged in: "Why, we could live here with the triloids, Marsha and I. We sure could. Let the rest of them go on and risk their lives, while Sherry fulfills old Dolby's ambitions. Marsha and I could survive here on our own skills—and those learned from the triloids. We could live and love and laugh and mate, like we're supposed to." The mind-voice fell silent and he came back to the reality of the near-unreal.

It was the time of the wedding. Dolla clacked her teeth a certain way. Four triloids, two old males and two even older females, moved into the circle with drums of rawhide stretched around stems from the magical trees. Their drumsticks glowed from the microbes, and the ends were leather-wrapped in such a way as to create perfect percussion.

They sat in a square and suddenly, at an unseen signal, simultaneously pounded a powerful rhythm on the drums. Out from the crevasses of the bluffs, and up from behind indentations in the earth, out of ponds of reeds, the guest triloids suddenly arose, watching as the young male left their company and moved out toward the opening circle where Reesha now stood alone, waiting. The host triloids widened the circle smoothly to allow all the visitors to enter it, creating one twice as large.

The young groom, whom Sherry called Metza, moved to the very front of Reesha. They lifted and touched knees one at a time, stepped back a yard, then advanced and repeated the greeting thrice. The drums suddenly stopped. Metza clacked his teeth at Reesha. Then again. Again. Now she answered. His sounds of conversation became louder, faster. So did hers, lagging just behind his.

Then he started a sort of shuffling dance, circling her, moving first one hand and then the other out toward her midsection, each time getting an inch closer to touching her. He circled more and more, faster. Now his hands touched her, and touched her, and touched her, all over. Her clacking became shallow and fast as her breasts were moving in and out. Suddenly, she dropped to her hands and knees as the drums began pounding, pounding blood rhythms. He circled now on his hands and knees. It seemed impossible, but the drums increased in volume. The others, both human and triloid, stared—mesmerized.

Metza circled swiftly now and then mounted her from behind like a dog, a stallion, or a bull, and he pumped away with the rhythm of the drums. To the shock of the above-grounders, the two young triloids were making their first love. They rolled on the ground, holding each other close, their flaps pulled and wrapped in such a way that they appeared to be a huge, round baseball.

They rolled in circles that became more erratic with each pounding sequence of the drums. Then the gray-white ball almost stopped—whirled jerkily, swiftly, three or four times—and then the two fell apart as the drums reached a crescendo at such speed that it was one beat.

They unfolded and lay side by side, their breaths heaving mightily. They were wed. No one paid them any more attention. They could wander around the compound within safe limits doing anything they wished, totally ignored. Later, when the visit was over, Metza would lead Reesha, following his tribe, to the new cave home he had built for her on down the river in his territory.

The drums played softly now, accompanied by some others beating a rhythm with the sticks cut from the endlessly useful trees of light. They drank slightly fermented juice from a tube of the same. The fermented plant gave them a mild sensation of mellowness no matter how little or how much they drank. Everyone lined up and sliced their own meat onto plates of woven reeds. From the metate dishes they dined on food of many varied textures and shapes. It was a feast of difference—a wedding feast, a friendship feast—but a feast nevertheless.

At first, Bluefeather had been taken aback by the fact that the triloids cooked their food, but, of course, with their obvious reasoning powers and fire rising and falling over all the basin, they could hardly have escaped discovering its delights.

Suddenly, such practical thoughts became unimportant as he had a desperate urge to grab Marsha and dance in wild circles and take her to the mating mat with him as Metza and Reesha had done. He controlled this powerful drive by forcing his thinking in the direction of Taos Mountain and all the secret canyons he knew surrounding it with deer, bear, bobcats, and squirrels. Its own song came to him for a moment, above that of the cave, and soothed him, quieting his lust and making him feel foolish for having thoughts of actions that might have appeared impolite to his hosts. He wondered what all the rest were feeling. Partly the same as him, he was sure.

They were all rescued from their varied musings by Sherry and Dolla, who took them on a tour. The triloids had their own fish farms with gates to hold and control them in the pools around inlets from the main river. Then they were shown the waterfall that came out of a cavern upon the bluff and formed a deep fresh waterhole. They had dammed it up with rock work.

There were a bunch of young triloids waiting on a ledge high above the water for a signal from Dolla. She clacked her teeth and raised an arm, swinging it down hard by her side. The entire section, except for Sherry, gasped as three young triloids raced, leaping off the high ledge, rolling up into round balls, plunging down at the speed of gravity's pull. Then their ball-like roundness rolled over and over in the air. When it looked like they would strike the surface of the pool with such force that they were in peril of being splattered into bits across the landscape, they unwound. The folds under their spread arms caught the air, and they sailed off in circles without ever having touched the water.

One by one they circled back up like well-guided kites to the proper altitude, rolled into balls again, and plunged into the pool, resurfacing swiftly and water-walking right out on the bank. They stood in line and raised their knees in unison to their guests, who started to clap but then realized that Sherry was imitating Dolla, raising her knees in swift applause and slapping a hand on each. Everyone followed this example, trying to be proper.

The teens smiled with what could have been taken as a snarl if The Section had not already seen Dolla do the same at their first meeting. Then Dolla tilted her head back, looking way up on the precipice, and gave her signal again. This time a dozen of the young raced and leaped off the edge, spreading their wind flaps. They sailed along the same air drafts as the others had, in a flying ballet—in and out, up and down, in a gorgeous harmony of slow bird movement. They circled lower and lower above the pond. One by one they formed a ball and dove into the pond. Each stayed under water until all had joined them. Then the ripples subsided so that the surface of the pond was almost smooth. "Boom!" All twelve of them came out of the water at once. Flapping their way on the surface of the pond in curving single file, they moved faster in a bubbling, frothing race around the pond, doing figure eights and double figure eights, leapfrogging one another with foaming speed.

Charlie Waters said, "If I could dance like that I'd own Broadway."

Hector Garcia intoned, "Such a *baile* would fill Bernalillo County with tourists from around the world. No?"

Willy said, "I wouldn't travel this far to see it, but I'd pay a lot for a ticket if the show was put on close to home."

The ex-football player-chef, Jimmy D. Ratchett, said, "The Superdome would fall down from the applause."

Bluefeather could tell by these and other remarks that the watery dance was a stunning success and much-needed relief for the troops. It was a show such as no one above, and not many here below, had ever seen.

Shortly, Bluefeather would find out that Sherry had made a bargain for the triloids to follow them into the Hills of Hell, giving whatever support they could. So they also were putting out extra effort to entertain and to enjoy, for the tomorrow of all their tomorrows was near.

The dozen young leapt up out of the edge of the pool in perfect synchrony, coming down softly on the cavern floor with their flaps folding just as they touched stone, rolling, all together, right over in front of Dolla, Sherry, and The Section, unwinding and standing up at the same time, lifting their knees to form a perfect chorus line.

This time The Section lost control. The recognition of such a performance could not be held back. They clapped and yelled, "Bravo! Bravo! Bravo!" raising fisted hands in the air and making bent-over side motions with arms of excited approval.

Bluefeather thought of the purity and rareness of this welcome given and performed for strange creatures from another world above them, who had intruded on their domain. Incomprehensible beauty. Pureness.

They had shared with them an intimate wedding, a feast, a performance of life-risking action, and had volunteered to follow them to hell. Totality.

It was time to return to the boat. There was nothing left to receive from the triloids without great embarrassment. Fortunately, for the hosts, the triloids didn't have that last word in their clacking, clattering vocabulary, as yet. They had never done anything to warrant its invention.

Forty-Two

Bluefeather lay back on the couch and tried to put things in order before going to bed. They would leave for the hills right after the sleep time, which was going on now for most of The Section, as well as the Olders and Youngers, but his sleep did not come. Then it struck him—it was the Mouton '80. That's how Korbell had trapped him. Step by step the man had taken control of his life so smoothly Bluefeather had almost failed to notice.

The Mouton '80 had done the trick, all right. It sounded so reasonable for a man of such wealth and power, who could buy almost anything, to crave what he couldn't find or have. Nothing unusual there. He was willing to pay good money for skilled services. He had even assigned his adopted daughter, Marsha, to assist Bluefeather in order to make the deal seem true. Korbell had shrewdly figured that Bluefeather's friends, the Rugers, would eventually lead him to the contact with Dolby. They had.

Then Korbell had relied on Dolby and Sherry to recognize a good hired hand. Being both a soldier and a near-geologist, Bluefeather would fit all their plans. Marsha, his love, had been there all the time, giving to him—or giving for Korbell? That was the mainline question not answered with any definity yet. Korbell had probably known all along that Dolby had beheaded Tilton and taken the gold bullion. It was the accursed yellow metal that Korbell had wanted all the time.

It was difficult to cogitate upon, but Marsha had to have told her father of the filmed images here below, and—as a nation covets a strategic seaport or energy source, a farm or timber belt—his natural powers of acquisition and greed had taken over.

Marsha? Marsha? Marsha? Had she been the manipulator all the time? It could be nothing else. The wine search had been forgotten too easily by the both of them. The original deal had been subordinated.

However, if this was one-hundred-percent true, why did he worry so with a nagging presentiment that something terrible was going to happen to Marsha on this next trip? Why did his fleeting dreams almost reveal the cause of his feeling of dread for her? Why? Why? Why? Again and again.

Now he was working for both Dolby and Korbell—two respectful enemies—and innocent people were dying. Well, in spite of Korbell or Dolby or Marsha, he was going to fulfill his obligations to Sherry and the surviving Section now or he would burn and sink in the River of Radiance—that river of riches, river of revelations. He would pursue the Tilton maps that Charlie Waters had acquired for him. He would search every inch of every building and he would find the wine and fulfill his word. Then, and only then, would he decide whether to kill the two greedy bastards or not.

If The Section pulled off the last phase of the expedition successfully, one or the other, or both, of the world-class accumulators could control the largest, most precious and rare mineral deposits in the world. The winner would be able to swing money and stock markets at his will. He could, at the movement of a finger or the uttering on one word, "yes" or "no," make kings from paupers and vice versa. Then, of course, other accumulators would start plotting and planning, and in a decade, a century, whatever, take it away from him. By so doing, the avaricious cycle of the powerful, the rich, the imprisoned, the tortured, the beheaded and disemboweled would start all over again. Endlessly.

From the other viewpoint, Sherry's, the galaxies could be studied right here in the cave of "the star." The whole of the creation of old worlds, giving clues to the new, was here to be studied and the knowledge applied to those above and beyond. In the blackness of the center of the fallen meteorite, great curative powers, plus every metal of the earth—and several as yet unidentified—had been concentrated in the great kettle of fire and water intersecting here.

The plants called the trees of light were a miracle of creation and bounteous giving just by themselves. The wonders of the life-forms here would have to be totally respected and protected or they would soon deteriorate and suffocate, as those on the surface were rapidly doing. There was the possibility of vast knowledge for the youth of the entire world here. Wonderment. That's what they could commonly share—that necessity of all young things without which they become half blind and half dead and so inwardly directed that they create only half lives for themselves. Wonderment. Yes, wonderment was abundant here. Awaiting—making it the greatest of all gifts or the greatest of all sins—its destruction.

However it went, Bluefeather was going into the Hills of Hell and would return to face Korbell with the whereabouts of the wine. He laughed, alone and aloud, at himself. His mind had leapt from the priceless rocks of heaven and earth to twenty cases of wine—and he was guilty of equalizing them. The grand questions became practical and singular after all. Still, one had to have both.

With this thought he decided it was time for a half-vision. It did not come easily or clearly; it was more like the mists of the Cavern of Marvels.

Dancing Bear sashayed toward him, but he knew this only by the movement of his head and hands, for his lower body was in fog. He was doing some of his favorite dances—a nameless Greek step, segueing into a Scottish fling, a Cherokee stomp, a Taos round, and a Russian tippy-toe. Although the moccasins were lost in the low mist, Bluefeather could not miss the motions he had seen a hundred times.

Bluefeather whispered, "Iceland. Do Icelandic for me."

Dancing Bear only smiled and Hawaiian hip shook and New Orleans tap danced himself into Marsha, who smiled until all he could see were her teeth. Then she receded into Miss Mary, who first waved at him in greeting and then beckoned him to come with her into the filminess. Miss Mary. Oh God. Then he was thankful that guitarists Ramon Hernandez and Antonio Mendoza played a duet just for him. Could it be? Yes it was. *La Golondrina.* Then they did an old Italian classic in such harmony as to be one.

He now caught swift glimpses in the clouds and there he saw the Friedmans of a Taos summer—both mother and daughter—and Old Grinder yelled at him from the fog above the fading music, "Get the idee? Get the idee?"

His two mules were clearer than all else. They were contentedly eating oats there at home in Corrales, looking up now and then, watching for his return.

He came out of his half-vision just as he was saying, "I'll see you in a while, little darlings."

They switched their tails and moved their ears back and forth, hearing something from somewhere. He slept.

■ ■ ■

Forty-Three

It was the time to attack beyond the beyond—even farther, if needed. At the departure, Sherry had said, simply, "This is no sci-fi film we're going to attend; it's real. Real as homemade fudge."

All listened, all heard, all understood. At first it was easy. The boat purred along the smooth waters with no threats from the water or air. Sherry instructed the motorman to slow down and pull over next to a nearly sheer bluff that joined the river where it became narrower for a quarter mile or so. He stopped the boat. She pointed out watermarks etched into the stone of different ages with different lines and colors. There were ice ages, great droughts, years of heavy snows and rains, tales told as in the rings of redwood trees. Here was the history of the upper and lower earth for aeons—a geological map.

Sherry had long ago photographed and catalogued this Morse code from the far and near past. These water messages on rocks could tell why and when great herds of animals and pueblos of Indians had migrated. There would be fossils and sediments of large lakes and seabeds above to match these linear messages down here—a bulletin board from the long ago.

Sherry had done some work on its ancient signs, but she would need help from the world's scientific minds even to get a start on the massive information stored everywhere one gazed, stepped, or breathed.

They moved on through the narrows and into a wide area where there were many side shallows. Sherry pointed out the triloids moving on the ground, parallel with them. At times they climbed the endless formations with their muscled palms and foot soles, leaping free and sailing in circles, always staying protectively even with the progress of the boat.

It seemed that every mile or so the number of steam geysers and the amount of magma increased, as did the light, noise, and heat. The triloids were having to move forward with more and more effort, even though they were still a good distance from the spewing, erratic, half ring of fiery geysers that protected the entrance to the dead—the reportedly gold-rich Hills of Hell.

Bluefeather's eyes were first on the danger. He spotted seven or eight wide water wakes moving toward them. Even so, he had almost been too late. The heavy chomper came leaping and diving over the edge of the boat and grabbed the two-inch pipe railing, biting it in half as Pack let loose a burst of M-II lead right into its nostrils. Several chompers were now attacking all sides of the low-slung ship, rocking it down to the cork rim, encircling its entire outer shell.

Bluefeather yelled for the people in front of him to hit the deck. He let loose a blast into the open throat of the huge-jawed chomper that had chewed a piece of the boat edge loose as a rat might the cardboard around a box of cheese. The gun mounts were useless now. There was too much chaos, and personnel movement, to fire such high-caliber weapons this close in.

Pack emptied another clip into the short neck where it joined the great chest. He had found the weak spot—the same as on the screechers. The beast fell slowly backward, claws hanging till the last on the ship rim. Blood spewed in the air from its dying bellows like a lawn spray.

Bluefeather had just slapped another clip in his rifle when Jimmy D. Ratchett let loose a burst with his .45 tommy gun, shooting enough off the top of its head to reveal its brain. Moosha sunk his razored machete into the opening, plunging it back and forth until the chomper slid away to end its day.

Bluefeather whirled to look for Marsha. She, Sherry, and Willy had all emptied clips into one of the attackers without seeming to slow him down. It had snapped the railing like a toothpick and bit a bolted-down swivel chair into junk. It turned on Bluefeather as it opened its jaws again.

Marsha took a terrible gamble on all their lives. She made an instinctive, lightning decision as she jerked the pin from a grenade, screaming, "Hit the deck!" All that were standing did. As the animal opened those terrible jaws of teeth—bigger, sharper by far than those of the largest of the Australian whites—Marsha hurled the grenade down its throat with all her strength. The creature instinctively, and with great good fortune, swallowed. A couple more steps and the beast would have crushed or bitten some of them in half.

The grenade lifted a hump in the brute's heavy frame and blew holes in its sides. Streams of blood gushed out the wounds, along with its guts. The overly heavy head dropped, and it clawed weakly with its front legs a few times. Then a death sigh of "war lost" was emitted. It was still.

The gun turrets were firing now at those that had failed to make it to the boat's rim. The 50-caliber machine guns and 20-mm cannon turned them into rolling tails and heads that splashed water and blood. Their yellow-white, perforated bellies turned upward and thrashed wildly about, over and over, until the boat pulled away, leaving a thousand, smaller, sharp-toothed fish and other swimmers dining well. It took most of The Section to lift the dead chomper and roll it over the edge of the boat.

Only Moosha and Willy were injured. A couple small pieces of the grenade shrapnel had exited the chomper, striking Moosha along the ribs, breaking the skin but not penetrating the bone. Willy had received a metal sliver in his bicep. Pack and a couple of the Youngers gave immediate first aid. They did a good clean job of it.

The temperature of the air and water was getting hotter. Now little bits of mist, almost steam, lifted here and there, even from areas of the river where there were no geysers or bottom fumaroles. They were now in a vast humidifier.

Bluefeather checked with everyone to be sure of no more injuries. When he came to Marsha, he said quietly, "Thanks. Thanks—from all of us. That was magnificent."

"I didn't even think. I just did it," she said fearfully.

"There was no time for anything but action, little darling," he said without forethought, but he was actually still possessed with the premonition of something terrible happening to her. He couldn't let his concern show to the others, not a particle. None. Especially Marsha. The slightest nervousness revealed could lead to disaster for all.

Sherry kneeled on the ammo magazine, watching all around. Shia stood, rifle ready, as close as possible to Sherry at all times. Unlike the rest, Sherry was all she cared about.

Then everyone went on full alert. Bluefeather and Pack took over, posting guards in proper positions. Bluefeather assigned the young female first aides the job of filling and refilling canteens so that no one would dehydrate in the huge cooker. The sweat poured from them so that they looked like fully clothed users of country club steam baths or denizens of a Navajo sweat lodge. The canteens were emptied and refilled twice in a brief period.

They now traveled in torrid unpleasantness. The rubber-covered asbestos and the titanium steel hull held together and kept them from seriously burning, though. The ship worked.

The Youngers in the gun turrets raised the steel flaps and took more drinking water than anyone else. The great plumes of smoke from the gas and magma fire geysers both darkened and lightened places in the cavern up ahead, but they could still see relatively well, at least for a while.

The Section forced its collective nervous system to prepare for the upcoming passage through the Ring of Fire. Adrenalin charged everyone up again. It was a good thing, for soon Sherry heard the loud and worried "clack-clack" from their friends, the triloids, penetrate the fogs to her ears, warning of the screechers.

Sherry shouted to all, "Screechers. One o'clock high."

Five of the massive, air-ground creatures were following above, along river updrafts, which were strong enough to keep their hollow bones floating with only an occasional flap of the wings for guidance. They floated easily, conserving most of their energy and strength. Their ear-numbing shrieks shafted the air and the heads of the boaters like millions of minute needles. The occupants' hearts pounded from this assault of sound the same as they would have from exploding bombs.

To the amazement and relief of all on the boat, a score or so of the sailing triloids attacked their number one enemy first. The triloids angled in from all sides on the leading bird. Hurling spears into its bulk, then arcing out and back to jerk the weapons free, they circled until they were in range again. Some of the projectiles sank a foot deep into the screechers' bodies.

One especially daring triloid landed right on the lead screecher's back and stabbed up and down into its flesh, but another screecher swept down, grabbing and crushing the brave triloid and dropped its form into the river. Other triloids were hooked on the scimitar claws at the ends of the screechers' wings and were ripped apart like swords slicing jellyfish, falling in their own spray of red to feed the millions of odd-sized jaws waiting below. They were losing members, perhaps seven or eight already. They zoomed in and out, around and up under the mammoth screechers.

The boaters were shouting encouragement. They suffered every wound of the triloids and exulted with each piercing of a spear into the enemy.

The screechers were so busy trying to fight the constant stabbing circles of the little gray-white enemy—attacking with the ferocity of killer bees—that they had broken formation and no longer considered them mere pests to be slashed from the air like biting flies. The birds were angered, pained, and losing life fluids—although not enough to cripple one as yet. Nevertheless, as accurate and exact as their sonar, scent glands, and mind-vision were, there were just too many moving objects coming at them from too many angles. It became impossible for them to keep the formidable weapons of wing and feet claws and the slicing, crushing beaks in proper killing mode. Their attack on the humans had been disorganized.

Now one of them lost control of a wing and circled off toward the shore. All the triloids, sensing an actual kill, followed it like vengeful wasps. The message of memory had been passed among them. Here on this boat were the true intruders. The attack of the triloids, while injurious and unexpected, was nevertheless part of the nature of their domain. The uncounted creatures of the water and air were part of the allness in this vast habitat, but those on the boat were foreign splinters.

The triloids were victorious. All the screechers but one were now being dined on and assimilated into the food chain by the thousands of smaller water creatures.

The last one splashed so near the ship, the shocked waves of water almost capsized the boat, throwing everyone crashing into each other and battering everyone against chains and the sides of the boat.

Kubeck, struck by Ratchett's heavily tossed body, was knocked overboard to the feeders and only had time to raise one arm and yell for help twice before he disappeared. His hurtling body had saved Ratchett's life.

A part of the screecher's wing had struck the engine mount so hard that it had bent the frame of the boat.

The survivors crawled up out of the sloshing deck water. They could feel the ship shaking as the engine pushed its unevenness against the water's constant bulk. It was barely moving.

Bluefeather ordered them to activate the other engine. With both propellers now shoving, the craft moved somewhat faster, although constantly shuddering, trying to alter its course. The boatmen were struggling mightily to keep it moving in the general direction of the Ring of Fire. They succeeded.

Pack said, "Hey, you guys, get it back together like we were when we left port. There ain't been any shrapnel here. Just flying bird guts."

Those unhurt or only lightly wounded did a celebratory dance of victory and then a more somber one of respect for the vanquished. The latter action was cut short when Dolla made a Sergeant Pack-type speech of her own, with different sounds but the same meaning. They would have to reorganize, winding their way in the air above the intermittent and erratically blazing fire line; otherwise, they would rapidly bake to a nice brown on the hot banks of the river.

The seriously wounded were stabbed in the heart and rolled into the water. This was a rule of battle the triloids had followed for epochs. All who were capable fought on. All unable died quickly. This kept the forces intact to win. No sympathy. No regrets. They survived their constant wars healthy, intact, or they would never have survived at all. Venerable. Dolla ordered the able-bodied to the walls and pillars of stalactites and stalagmites, where they hung like large, pale bats.

Sherry was looking ahead at varied geysers with daring exuding from her eyes and stance. She, above them all, had waited to enter this deadly approach so long that the dangers seemed secondhand now. To the others, the geysers, the smoke, the rising and falling mists, the constant roar of the most powerful forces of earth—fire and water—were fearful and enticing at once. Nevertheless, as the mists became heavier, hotter, and the magma flares ever brighter and louder, their fears tilted to the greatest opiate of all—the enveloping intoxication of possible instant life, or death. The ancient hairline of the ultimate thrill was upon them.

Bluefeather signaled the directions with arm movements to the waiting motormen. No verbal instructions were possible. The burning gases and the boiling spouts of water coming up from the molten center of the earth were as loud as an exploding volcano. They moved into the fiery, watery abyss. No return tickets at this point.

Several dropped from the heat as if struck by an invisible, invincible force applied by the gods. The standing leapt about, keeping the faces of the fallen out of the bottom water, where they would have drowned. Marsha swayed upright beside Bluefeather, then moved on to help the fallen. The center of hell surrounded them below, above, and on all sides—churning, burning, roaring with the voice of all the forces of life, death and doom, of birth and rebirth.

They had been in the vortex of Hades for timeless time. A coven of craven witches brewed mixtures of devils all around them. The Section's ability to regulate reason was gone, though they were sane. Their senses of direction had been scattered, but they moved on. They remained ready to live or die as the call came. Bluefeather held their direction together and now his voice could be heard. It seemed remote, planets away, but was recognized as the voice of their commander in the sound receivers of their brains. Louder, clearer.

"Now left. Now right. More. Now straight ahead. Hold it there. Straight on, troops. Forward!"

They were in a lake of placid water before they knew it. The great fumaroles that had formed the dead Hills of Hell had dammed the river enough to create a lake. It drained out a narrow opening on one side, a mile or so beyond the island that in itself formed a holding dam. None of the natural inhabitants of this deep place cared a damn about gold. All they wanted to do was eat, any way they could, and reproduce their own kind.

The remaining Section members came out of the necessary daze slowly. Their breathing returned. Bluefeather ordered the motors at half power to ease the jolting of the bent ship. Eyes began to clear and little smiles broke through the grime-coated faces.

Sherry crawled up by Bluefeather on the shattered gun turret. She looked across the smooth surface of the lake and at quiet dark hills, hugging him silently from the side. The motion conveyed her thanks and the depth of her feelings with no need for words.

They had made it. Unbelievable. True.

Forty-Four

It was so peaceful puttering across the lake that for a while a lethargy settled on them. Even such experienced warriors as Pack and Bluefeather moved about the boat as if they had been dining on opium for a decade. The cuts, bruises, and fears were all numbed for a spell. The din of the peerless line of fire and water in conflict with itself receded behind them, so they ignored its existence. The subsiding of their lifesaving adrenalin and electrified thinking of battle, followed by the confusion of the fiery fissures, left them in a peculiar and pensive mood. Tranquil. The only surprise came when they casually swept their eyes across the new, yet ancient, landscape and discovered that the triloids had beaten them there. They waited with obvious patience—guards strategically posted on various low rises. The triloids' appearance ahead of them was almost instantly accepted as normal.

They tied the boat to an upswung rock and slowly disembarked. Bluefeather, Pack, and Sherry eased back into a cautious command mode, checking all equipment, including the saws, axes, and the large canvas ore bags made to fit on a special backpack. All weapons were loaded, clips filled, grenades secured. The flamethrowers were unloaded from the craft but not back-slung as yet. Long drinks of water were taken and canteens refilled.

Then Bluefeather positioned different members of The Section on the moonscape shore so that a watch could be kept and still leave someone to visit. Besides, the triloids occupied higher ground and would front any danger if it existed. Nothing threatened them for now. Nothing at all.

They sat on the rocks and had a lunch of hard energy candy that had melted together into a slab but was now broken into servings by good-humored Chef Ratchett. Sherry was becoming extremely anxious to finish the final journey but knew they would need the nourishment and subsequent renewed strength to climb and work the hard metallic hills.

Bluefeather took two pieces of the candy and eased over and sat next to Marsha, handing her a chunk. She took it, smiling her great smile through the grime of the day. Bluefeather's heart turned to newborn magma. The successful trip together, through the torrid line of fizzing fissures, and the survival of the battles had erased all sins against one another—no matter what they had believed or imagined. Vanished. Gone. Never to matter again.

He touched the back of her now blackish hair as if it were new silk and said as simply and sincerely as sunshine, "I sure do love you a whole bunch."

Her Korbell smile would have lighted a Yankee Stadium night game with enough left over for New Year's fireworks.

"I love you too. About this much." She started with the palms of her hands about three inches apart and then spread them slowly until her arms were spread as wide as possible. Then she flung them around him. They held one another closely, warmly, and hard.

Bluefeather saw Sherry stand and order a Younger to sack up all the lunch waste and put it back on the boat. He knew it was time for her final lap.

Pack and Ratchett put on the flamethrowers. Everyone took positions as Pack designated. Nothing was in sight or sound to hinder them, but back at God's Castle they had trained and prepared for any eventuality. Sticking closely to the prior plans had gotten them to this last destination.

They climbed up the hills toward the triloids, who moved much faster and had taken up positions far ahead of them around the sides of the large hills. They were glued there comfortably with their powerful suction muscles.

At the beginning of the slope of the largest hill, Bluefeather made his first cut with the axe. He chopped through the dark, burned crust that crunched under their feet with the sound of cinders. His axe cut into the mostly malleable metal, revealing spots and streaks of yellow and silver dominating the harder and widely varied colors of other rare metals. The long, long time of intense heat had boiled and melted the weaker metals—such as iron—away, leaving only this surface crust to cover the massive volume of unfathomable richness underneath.

Bluefeather ordered George Tack Won to slice a linear chunk out with the diamond-surfaced chain saw. Won pulled the cord and the gas motor started on the second yank.

The metal was very heavy. The Youngers, with their packs, were sent back and forth from the cuts, carrying the precious metals to the boat. Pack watched the triloid guards for any danger signals as Bluefeather worked. Bluefeather and Willy measured the distance between cuts with a long, steel tape. Bluefeather recorded them all in a wax-wrapped notebook.

Clock hours passed and even the relative coolness became hot as they marched on from one totally barren hill to the other, cutting, measuring, carrying the heavy samples again and again to the boat. The richness varied. They had now sampled out about a square mile of metal with obvious depths in places above the river, ranging from a few feet to three hundred.

Bluefeather, Willy, and the carriers were exhausted. Now Bluefeather paused and really looked at the landscape here for the first time. Not a blade of grass, not a sprout of a weed or a cactus or a seedling of any kind—not even algae from the lake's edge—showed life here. Where once hellish fires had flamed and cooked, there was only a crust of burned iron and underneath enough wealth to control the flesh of most of the world and the forests, bushes, and grasses that covered it. He was too tired to analyze any of the results of their current labor, even for a moment. But Willy did.

Willy said, sitting down and leaning back against a small dead fumarole, "You know, this stuff looks like it's over half malleable metal to me. So, if all we did was mine this an inch deep, there would be enough reserves to buy Germany, Japan, Roosha and all the Hawaiian Islands. Don't you reckon, Blue?"

"I hear you, old pardner, and as soon as we can stand up, I'm going to call it finished."

"Good. I'd give half this Island of Gold for six bottles of cold beer."

"When did you switch from whiskey?"

"Oh, about the middle of that goddamned firestorm. I figured a change would do me good."

"Makes a world full of sense to me."

The two old buddies were just on the verge of silly-happy when the unmistakable warning of the triloids' clatter came clicking out across the dead, black hills. Everyone who was sitting leaped up. Those standing crouched. All were looking and listening for the cause of the triloids' warning.

It was so huge and nearly colorless that everyone but the triloids missed it. The object of their notification was so much bigger than any creature the humans had ever imagined, it was at first indefinable.

Bluefeather's superior eyesight saw it looming up over the hills into the sky of the cave. It was translucent and only shadows of light gave it any form at all. In fact, most portions of the as-yet-formless body were transparent. Then he saw the red, throbbing thing inside it. His eyes tracked the thin lines of red fluid pumping throughout the body. That pump was its heart and the liquid its blood. It had no eyes, but it had all the other senses of the cavern's blind ones. It had, in fact, begun to take on a nameless shape something like forty transparent elephants metamorphosed into one. It had two mighty bluish white trunks at least fifty feet long with a mouth at each end that widely opened and closed, over and over. It had glassy, but tactile, arms, similar to a giant octopus, along each side. In between these were tentacles that swiftly rolled up into balls, then flung themselves open, reaching out twice the distance beyond the mouths of the trunks. Its main body was almost like a huge, transparent, rectangle of a box, but with rounded corners.

Willy whispered in awe, "That thing's big enough to use the moon for a volleyball."

Charlie Waters gasped, "We are in dung of great depth."

No one seemed to hear them. All eyes went to the boat, where the remaining cannon and 50-calibers were, but there was no way to reach them now. The Khyber beast had that area easily covered with writhing, searching protuberances.

Simultaneously, it seemed everyone heard and felt the triloids change their warning sounds. A look, far back downhill, revealed another Khyber crawling onto land with its hundred legs moving in impossible cohesion. There was total pause of everyone and everything. No triloid, no human, no Khyber moved. It lasted less than a gasp of air but seemed like the length of a three-day blizzard.

The first movement came from the triloids. En masse they leapt into the air and attacked, circling high above, then plummeting down to within a few yards of the Khyber. They stretched out their underarm folds to brake just on the surface of the now moving, bluish white mountain of molecules. Their spears, knives, and four-inch claws appeared useless. However, as with their charges at the screechers, they had slowed the Khyber's attack by diverting its attention.

Bluefeather and Pack scattered their troops and attacked. They had no other choice. Without the boat they were—every one of them—doomed.

Now all recognized the beating, red heart and poured round after round of bullets into the transparent body until the lead looked like flakes of pepper in mashed potatoes, but none of the slugs could penetrate deep enough to reach its heart.

A tentacle reached into the air and plucked a triloid like an apple from a tree. With an amazingly swift, accurate movement, the Khyber tossed it into the nearest octopus mouth. The discernible triloid was sucked down the long trunk into another tunnel to the clearly visible stomach and, before their stunned eyes, was swiftly digested into juice.

Moosha and Hector remembered Marsha's action with the grenade. Each pulled a pin, holding the hand trigger closed as they charged the octopus's mouths. For just a moment it looked as if they had a chance to wound the Khyber, but the tentacles snaked out and encircled them so swiftly that they were jerked loose from the grenades. Both grenades fell, exploding in midair, doing little more damage than the hundreds of bullets the Khyber had now absorbed.

Moosha dropped down one trunk-tube and Hector down the other, right into the stomach. Both were melted by the acids and mixed invisibly with those of the vanished triloid.

Bluefeather and Pack started firing rifle grenades. The Khyber was jarred and torn enough to make it hesitate. Fielder and two of the Youngers made a run for the ship's guns. They were almost there when the Khyber shifted in what seemed like slow motion because of its massive bulk. Its tentacles swished out like living bullwhip sinews and captured them, curling the bodies back and into the tube for the same visible fate.

Almost as shocking to Bluefeather as the liquid deaths was the fact that Sherry suddenly knelt down, opened her notebook, and started writing. Shia knelt in front of her, offering her body first as Sherry wrote: "The Khybers are soft-bodied fauna organisms without shell, teeth, or bone. It appears that they are halfway evolved in the development from soft tissue to bone. Considering their size, this is an amazing discovery."

Bluefeather had a flashing thought: "My God, in the face of imminent death Sherry is momentarily ignoring everything to record a few lines for a posterity that is in extreme doubt."

Sherry secured the notebook and stood up to join Shia and the rest in the desperate situation. By now, seven of The Section had been savaged in less than a minute. Three more triloids were hurled inward. The stomach juices had become so thickened with the plenitude of other bodies that the victims now kicked about like small children playing in a wading pool before they dissolved into shapelessness.

About half the triloids were making dives on the other advancing Khyber, delaying it temporarily. Some of the grenades from the launcher had shattered and slowed the tentacles.

Now Osaka's last grenade was attached to the rifle launcher. He advanced. The crippled tentacles searched for him and came within inches. When he saw the Khyber move the other undamaged mouth, spreading wide to suck him in, he fired and fell. The grenade entered the opening with much force. The grasping mouth dipped to suck him up. Osaka was lifted several feet from the ground as the grenade exploded. The grenade burst the transparent flesh open just behind the trunk-mouth, and blood flowed down like bayou rain. Osaka was dropped—jolted, but intact—on the iron crust.

Pack dashed forward with the flamethrower now and burned the tentacles from around the mouth. The scent of seared blood filled all the survivors' nostrils. Even though the Khyber had workable arms left, it stopped a moment. Somehow its mind-voice was telling it for the first time ever that it was no longer invincible.

Jimmy D. Ratchett had gambled with the grenade instead of the flamethrower and lost. He joined the multiple liquid bodies in the stomach of the Khyber. O'Malley had hurled grenades and charged, firing his rifle to the last empty clip, and had been crushed into a little flat roll by a flailing, impaired tentacle.

Bluefeather saw that in spite of the triloids' valiant agitation of the companion Khyber, it kept on advancing, narrowing the terrible vise.

A female Younger was the first and only one to crack. She did so in style, charging, screaming at the beast, slicing with her razored machete in one hand and firing her handgun with the other. Surprisingly, she didn't have a wasted death. The Khyber was so awkward with the injured tentacles that it fumbled attempting to tuck her into its remaining usable mouth. She emptied the handgun into the more sensitive parts of the interior and cut and sliced with the machete all the way to the stomach acids.

Major damage was done to the nerves of the beast. Pack sensed this and struggled forward again with the flamethrower cooking the ends of the tentacles and burning most of them from the Khyber's remaining mouth. It was weakened but still held them at bay with its crippled but wildly flailing tentacles.

The triloids had occasionally fought the Khybers back from their personal territories throughout the millennia. Now they sensed the weakness and the chance. One raced up to the very top of the dominant Hills of Hell and leaped upon a thermal, circling as high as it would carry him. Then at a selected point, it dropped, wrapping itself into a ball. It plunged for the Khyber as fast as gravity could propel it, penetrating deep into the creature, jarring itself dead only three or four yards from the Khyber's heart. Another followed and another. All missed the heart and were lodged there, looking like tiny balls of cotton from where the humans watched.

Then a triloid raced up the side of the highest hill. Its suction muscles worked in perfect rhythm to let it gain speed. It got a much greater leap than the others had. The thermal gave a boost as well and lifted it up, up, up on its outstretched flaps until it was very high. It circled, aiming its tiny body at the colossus. Then it rolled up and the living cannonball plummeted down, down, faster and faster, entering the same wound pioneered and dearly paid for by its predecessors at a slightly different angle. The sacrificial triloid ripped through the already weakened flesh and struck all the way to the heart of the beast, bursting it apart. Its oozing redness spread rapidly in the cavity around it.

Sherry, Bluefeather, Marsha, Charlie Waters, Willy, and Osaka raced toward the ship. Pack held back a moment. His flamethrower was still burning nerves in the few floundering tentacles.

Bluefeather grasped Marsha's waist and hoisted her up. They all made it on board, falling over the railing in heaps. Willy started the motors. Bluefeather headed for the remaining 20 mm and fired four direct line shells into what was left of the quivering heart of the Khyber. Pack fell on board so tired he could barely keep his head out of the water.

The ship moved away, desperately trying to escape the last throes of the mammoth creature. Sherry leaped upon the ammo box. She took the castanet from her bag, clapping it together over and over on its fulcrum with astounding sound. The remaining triloids heard and retreated from the other, enormously energized Khyber. The fatally wounded behemoth's hundred legs all crumbled under its weight. With feeble movements of its distressed extremities, the Khyber slowly sank sideways until the gravity of its main body gained speed and slumped in a mass of huge waste, slipping on its own slickness into the lake. It created another wave, but the boat was too far away to be in danger.

To the survivors' surprise, their part of the lake became so peaceful-looking it was almost holy. At the dying Khyber, though, the water frothed with creatures that had risen from the depths to tackle the biggest bait of all. The other Khyber stopped there, helplessly seeing its mate being eaten by creatures so small a hundred would not make a taste. Even so, their tiny working jaws had turned the lake a darker color of blue by far—a reddish blue. The living Khyber's transparent body emitted little sounds of despair, like a rabbit's last muffled squeal as a bobcat breaks its neck. Then in a sliding, lumbering movement, it turned back to seek out the dark void of the far unknown part of the cavern—its home—where no human had ever gazed.

They were the conquerors—those who had made it to the ship. They had prevailed where others, and other things, had perished. After such an awesome adventure no one was wise enough to judge what the reaction would be of those remaining alive.

Sherry said, "It just occurred to me: we never did see the remains of the helicopter. Do you suppose the Khybers swallowed it?"

"Wouldn't surprise me none," Willy said. "I believe those critters could swallow a whole penitentiary, barbwire and all, without even belching."

Bluefeather gave instructions: "Willy, turn her left, right over there. I picked us out an opening through the fire when we were making our highest measurement on Khyber Island."

Willy said, "Done."

Marsha said to Bluefeather, "I guess this sounds frivolous right now, but god, I would love a meal, a bath, and about twelve hours' sleep."

"Well, there's plenty of hot water for the bath. Have at it," Bluefeather said with a grin, motioning to the rings of fire.

"This particular hot water isn't exactly what I had in mind. And come to think of it, forget the sleep part, too. I might miss something."

Charlie agreed. "You got that right." He took a deep swallow of water from the canteen, emptying it.

They went on with the necessary, silly survival talk as Bluefeather directed Willy and the boat to relative safety. Then they all became very, very quiet, not even hearing or feeling the motors turn the propellers that shoved the boat jerkily, steadily toward the compound—much heavier with gold, much lighter with loving flesh than it had started out. All the molecules of their beings longed for peace now. It was the time of repose.

Forty-Five

They were drinking water and cooling down now after safely negotiating the melting heat line. Willy kept the motor at low rev to prevent the bent boat from shaking them any more than necessary. On the banks and in the air, the triloids followed, parallel. They had lost fifteen percent of their numbers but were staying with the remaining Section all the way.

Pack had taken over the one unbroken 50-caliber turret. Bluefeather counted the survivors over and over. No matter how he tried to stretch it, there were only eleven of them left. He inspected Marsha with loving eyes and counted her a hundred times. The premonition was wrong, it seemed. He gave silent thanks to all the Authorities that had ever been.

He named them off once more: Marsha, Sherry, Shia, Pack, Willy, Osaka, Charlie, three Youngers, and himself. That added up to eleven. No more. All must be kept on the alert or none would return to report the astounding results of the costly victory.

He recognized the narrows coming up. Nothing had bothered them on the in-going trip until they had been well past this point. Everyone relaxed several degrees now. The triloids were out of vision, blocked by the solid walls arcing here into a stone tent as big as ten circus coverings above their heads.

The river widened again. Even at this slow progress they were only a couple of hours from the lower base camp. They passed the easily identifiable spot where the water-etched lines of ancient history had given Sherry so much priceless information for her notebooks.

Then Bluefeather saw them coming from the port side. Giant, undulating white worms with pointed, hardened noses.

He yelled, "Pack, three o'clock," and automatically reached for a grenade. There were none. All had been used against the Khyber.

Pack turned the 50 into the Nessie. It churned wildly as some of the en-masse attackers were shot into shreds. There was an early effect this time, but those that came on struck the ship with such force that their snouts penetrated the hull and rocked the boat. Where the metal had previously only been impacted, now holes were punched all the way in. Fortunately, the worms were not physically equipped to make it over the edge of the boat unless it listed much lower.

All but Pack thought, "Would there forever be one last war—on and on until nothing is left? Nothing?" Pack, the war-lover, loved on. But his lust for battle was unknowingly tempered some now by his love for Sherry.

Osaka sliced his machete down on the heads of worms that got through the steel and asbestos, then kicked their remains back into the river.

The Section had damaged the worms enough to stop them. They had lost no more of The Section, but now the *Columbus* was taking water so fast that all hands were using buckets instead of guns. They didn't have to worry about the worms anymore. A group of chompers had started feeding and fighting with the pieces of worms that wiggled and stabbed on with their saber-snouts even after the large-jawed beasts bit them in half.

The triloids came in formation now, water-walking with all their speed, but they could see the worms' battle with the humans was finished. The two kinds of water beasts fought one another in a frenzy of killing and feeding that overwhelmed any possible interest in human or triloid presence. The triloids stood on the water, their bent-over figures kept afloat by the whirling of their arms and the winglike flaps.

Dolla clacked at Sherry, but she could not stop the bucket brigade to look for her castanet. They were in very real danger of sinking.

Bluefeather had to risk The Section, the ship, and its treasure now. He shouted for Willy to give both motors all the power they could produce even if it shook the ship apart. Slow sinking would have the same final result, anyway.

As the motors revved, Sherry painfully clacked a message to Dolla with her own teeth. At first Dolla was so surprised she missed it, but not for long. She led the rest of her tribe swiftly ahead.

The *Columbus* was vibrating so hard that the occupants were not only sure it would split into shreds, they also felt their brains were being bruised against their skulls.

The water was sloshing almost up to their knees now, but they kept on bailing in strength-draining desperation. The triloids joined the struggle now as Sherry had asked. They were pushing behind and pulling in front of the crippled boat in a last effort to get it into its shallow dock.

The Olders and the Youngers at the compound had been waiting in shifts with telescopes aimed down the river. They had witnessed the attack of the giant worms and the subsequent nearly fatal damage to the ship. They acted now.

The cable had been unhooked from the submersible unit and made ready to attach to the injured *Columbus*. Several of the Youngers, standing chest deep in front of the deck, hooked the cable to the ship. The powerful motors now assisted the two boat motors, and the craft was pulled three-quarters into dry dock. Only a moment ago The Section had been bailing water with arms so stiff, pained, and exhausted that each lift of the container had been like chopping wood with bones cracked and split from compound breaks.

Now they steadied themselves, getting some control of their breathing, and watched the water drain out the holes made by the charging worms. Everything critical to the success of the expedition was now retrievable. The iron-webbed gate was closed over the entrance and they were finally safe.

Sherry retrieved her castanet and went to speak with Dolla and her tribe through the webbing. After all these years, she had never learned how to signal "thank you." Even if she had, the triloids would probably have failed to comprehend such a gesture. Friendship and loyalty were total with them, so the meaning of the signal would not have been understood. In lieu of this, she gave as close an approximation to saying "the trip was fun, and we'll have to do it again sometime." Sherry gave a huge, forced smile with only her face. Her heart did smile, but she was too weak to be sure it was projected to her friends.

Dolla returned a smile even bigger—because the size of her mouth stretched around her face and away from her large solid teeth. It was magnificent, this gesture, this smile. All the other triloids imitated her.

Then with the invisible signal of birds and fish and triloids, they all turned in unison and breezed their way across the river toward home—a home tens of hundreds of thousands of years old.

Sherry stood, instinctively putting the castanet away, and allowed a few tiny tears of love and gratitude to escape from the corners of her eyes. Shia watched her every move and imitated her tears just as the triloids had Dolla's smile. Then they wiped their eyes and joined in the effort to unload weapons and mineral samples of much richness.

It was not the time for celebration until the garden of treasures was secure in its proper place. Then she would call all the survivors together—The Section, the Olders, and the Youngers—and properly compliment them on their sacrifices and successes. That done, she would phone their victory to Dolby. Afterward, they could rest and heal before The Section's victorious return to the surface with riches and knowledge enough for many worlds.

Bluefeather pitched right in with all the rest helping to carry the heavy mineral samples. It was all soon displayed in the conference room. He was already planning many things, but he felt good that he had had the foresight to ask Sherry to have two mule-loads of the river nodules waiting above. One thing for sure—the gold in the nodules was solid and real. He would die to see that his surviving friends got to share the comfort of a little financial security. He did not, in any form, trust Dolby or Korbell to pay them what they deserved for their bloody striving. He made silent prayers for them to be fair for once if for no other reasons than to save more complications leading to more casualties.

He prayed hard for those persons with so much greed that they became bloodhounds of gold. He knew that he, too, was infected with the yellow virus, but by admitting his illness he had been able to keep it mostly controlled. The trouble with praying for accumulators like Dolby and Korbell was that they were unthinking and blind to any defect within themselves. It was always others, they believed, who were flawed and should be used up, then destroyed. Bluefeather knew what he was facing to get his friends through this and safely out of the widely spread fences of folly the two powers would try to herd them into. He was ready to wrap it up, and he did not have to doubt the dedication of his surviving companions. These people were fulcrums of friendship.

He brightened at the certain feeling that he and Marsha could live long lives, enjoying Corrales while they made their minds up about what they really wanted to do. Of course, he still had to find the Mouton '80, but he was sure that the diagrams of Tilton's building plans would reveal the undiscovered hiding place without too many problems.

At this he quit praying, giving many complimentary thoughts instead, and went to clean, oil, and reload his weapons—again.

Forty-Six

Sherry called every citizen of the compound to the meeting. Bluefeather had expected her to be full of smiles and commendations for the survivors of the killing trek. Instead, there was a solemnness about her as she said right off, "I know you deserve a rest and a celebration. You know it, too. However, I've decided we'll gather our wills together and move on up to God's Castle so we'll have the proper luxurious amenities for the victory pageant." She forced a quick smile and then ordered all the samples loaded onto mules.

Everyone was armed with full packs. The Youngers would go with The Section. Bluefeather requested that Willy, the mules, and the two mule keepers, Adam and Tolliver, go ahead and wait above with the gold nodules. The Olders would follow at their own pace. All the rest would force-march ahead to fittingly prepare for the ceremony.

There were none who did not sense something out of kilter. Sherry's attitude and orders seemed unnatural, considering the situation and the exhaustion of the returnees. No less afflicted were those who had waited at the compound without sleep during a seemingly endless spell of wrenching anxiety. Their fate hung with those on the front lines. Now they were all to be marched away without even a few grams of rest from their last murderous journey. A slight dose of relaxant was essential for those whose mightily strained muscles were already stiffening. Nevertheless, they obeyed without complaint and made ready to ascend to the next level on the elevators.

The line moved with Bluefeather leading it. Behind him were Marsha and Charlie. Sherry moved back and forth from Bluefeather to the Youngers, in constant motion. Willy and the two mule packers trailed behind the Youngers with the heavily loaded mule train. Willy resented this extra weight on the mules but had tried to see that it was balanced equally among all. Pack guarded the rear. Osaka walked to the side as the flank guard. The Olders moved at the only pace they had—slow.

In spite of the near-exhaustion suffered in many forms, they kept a wary lookout for the screechers. The unpredictable power of these ground-air creatures was deeply imprinted in the genes of all.

Now that Sherry was sure that her gold samples, her notebooks, and her associates were all moving forward in the best possible shape, she walked up beside Bluefeather and whispered, "The phone line was dead to Dolby's." That's all. Then she continued her edgy walking up and down the line.

The entire progression was slowing. Muscles could no longer be sped up by the force of will alone. Willy's chest felt like two boulders were pressing on each side. He said nothing but felt much. Bluefeather was able to maintain the pace without too much exertion because everyone else was lagging. It was the same with Pack in the rear. It felt as if there was extra heavy leather on their boots and as if the seams of their trousers were surely sewed together with lead thread. The packs with the blankets, shovels, the battery lights, and the personal items had all fallen in love with gravity and pulled downward. Slow clock hours. Slower cave hours. Slower mind hours.

The lead mule heard it first. He stopped and raised his head, all muscles tensed as his ears worked back and forth, distilling the sound. It was gunfire.

Then everyone heard it. There could be no mistake. It was not Steinberg directing target practice. It was the sound of a small war. There were no mortars, of course, their being useless because of the terrain. There was no noise of artillery, but Bluefeather and Pack recognized the exploding sounds of intermittent grenades and handheld rocket launcher projectiles. They had heard them often, long ago in France and Germany. There was also the "crack, crack, crack" of semi-automatic rifle fire and the heavier, faster rattle of a 45 Thompson. It didn't matter. An M-II rifle bullet could kill one just as dead as any 150-mm artillery shell or hydrogen bomb. Death played no favorites. A rock, a spear point, a bullet, and a bomb were all the same to death. The means was meaningless. The results certain.

Bluefeather knew someone had to take total charge instantly. It should have been Pack, he supposed, but somehow he felt the responsibility of it all was rightfully on him now. He halted the column and told them to take protective cover even though the battle was obviously farther on at God's Castle.

He moved forward at a trot now to reconnoiter alone. He climbed a large gypsum slope, seeking a high point. Static muscles were forgotten, but not war. Damn. He had really had his share. No use regretting, no use worrying. There was another one to face now. Even so, damn. He fell belly-down, knowing that when he raised his head he would gaze upon its craven face again. It was harder to do this time than ever before. No matter. It was there in front of him.

He rose up reluctantly. He could make out bodies inside the star-metal walls—many bodies—but the sounds and most of the movements were beyond. This surprised him. The castle occupants had obviously attacked "out" from the protection of the strong, solid fence. He focused his binoculars on the castle courtyard. Around the bulwarks of the fortress fence the bodies were clustered heavier.

He saw where the three girls—Jody, Estrella, and Charlene—lay dead, almost side by side. No doubt they had been hit by the same burst of bullets, having never been taught to disperse. He tried to take a guess at the number killed and the number still fighting. Numbers—love was like numbers, full of addition and subtraction. There was never a meaningful evenness in either. Being even or getting even was neither winning nor losing; winding up even is impossible in love or war or life.

The gun turrets had been knocked out by fire through the portholes. He could see the movements of the castle brigade around the massive dropping and rising fingers and abutments of the lighted cavern along with other endless, smoother, varied formations. The brigade circled, fell, climbed, leapt, fought, and died.

There was old Steinberg, his tall grayness limping heavily but giving orders and firing, in charge of his battered troops with a wounded flair. The elegance of a true command filled the viewing glass.

Now Bluefeather's ears adjusted to the sounds and realized that nearly every bullet was ricocheting—most of them many times—so that one shot sounded like a dozen coming from all angles. Gradually, as he watched, the entire picture came to him. The ricochets, the grenades, and the shoulder-held bazooka shells had all been helpless against the strength of the star-metal fortifications. When fired over the top or the powerful fence into the rock abutments and ceilings, they had been able to decimate Steinberg's forces. The castle and all its research facilities, its hidden and protected knowledge of the Cavern of Marvels, the Star Cave, the Cave of Bones and so much more, would have been lost to attrition if Steinberg and his forces had stayed in place.

Steinberg had no choice but to attack. Bluefeather could see where the scattered bodies of a squad had moved outside the half circle of the fortress wall to draw fire so Steinberg's remaining force could attack through the great archway of the main gate. It had worked—at great cost, of course, as evidenced by the scattered bodies strung out in a zigzagged line. The squad had offered its flesh so the main group could reach outer cover and return the fire on a more flexible front.

Bluefeather had no doubt that everyone in and out of the courtyard, the Olders and the Youngers, had been committed to the engagement of forces. All those who were not lifeless were now fighting in the rocky formations. He focused the glass closer on Steinberg and saw him take another ricochet in his left side. He reeled back and straightened, still able to fire and shout encouragement.

From this angle, Bluefeather could see a little movement of the enemy as well. Then he recognized the figure, the movement, of Fontaine, even though he couldn't glass close enough to see the scar that angled across his entire face. It was not necessary. The man's powerful athletic mobility was unmistakable. He raced with three men to the cover of a large pagoda, motioning two others to different forms of protection. One from each group fell from the firing. One was still. The other crawled on toward cover. Movement.

It was impossible for Bluefeather to figure the number of combined fighters left to either Steinberg or Fontaine. But the latter's presence confirmed that Korbell had attacked Dolby's domain. There was probably no one left alive above to answer Sherry when she phoned. Of course, that was the worry she had denied all the previous weeks, hoping within prayerful hope that her suspicions were unfounded, right up until the first mule heard the shooting. At least now the uncertainty was over.

The map of the entire battle was there before Bluefeather to read. The story was as clear as if he had been in the middle of it all. Clearer. Much clearer. His picture-mind rolled the war past at high speed, in color, with full sound effects. The only things this part of his brain failed to show him of the immediate past was the pain and the shocked screams before the bodily systems were nonexistent.

He would have liked to believe that Steinberg could have held out and won without them, but the bodies kept falling on his side. Steinberg's ranks were thinning faster than Fontaine's. He had been surprise-attacked, and the first gunpowder war between humans here below had taken a terrible, early toll. He now fought with a mixture of the Olders and a few surviving Youngers.

No, The Section couldn't wait. Fontaine might take the castle and he would not care about the damage. If he got holed up there with its large armory and food supplies, Bluefeather's small force could never dislodge him. The last thought was all the analysis he would give for or against joining the bloody fracas.

Bluefeather leapt and slid his way down from the gypsum hill and ran back to his waiting friends and loved ones.

"Willy," Bluefeather shouted in a whisper, "you and the keepers stay behind us with the mules. Be as quiet as possible. Surprise is our greatest weapon." Now he had become like Sherry. So many had died for the cargo in the mule packs that they must save it, along with themselves.

All moved at double time now, and as silently as possible, following Bluefeather to the rise he had just left. Every one of the command staff was ordered to glass the situation as Bluefeather explained it.

"Sherry, the Youngers will never stay organized except under your command. Take them in the back gate, through the compound, and out the front gate to support Steinberg. The rest of us will circle right and come in on the flank. I saw Fontaine. They are Korbell's men. Move out. Now."

Marsha said quietly, "Oh, my God. Oh dear God." Nobody heard her. She moved up beside Bluefeather and no matter how he climbed, slid, twisted, rolled, or turned, she stayed right with him like a shadow of flesh.

Sherry, Shia, and the Youngers did not have nearly as much trouble. Their way down undulated in smooth surfaces with only an occasional pointed stalagmite to circle. There was no direct gunfire as they moved through the red-spattered compound. It was difficult for a few of the Youngers to follow her because they saw the bodies of their parents and all recognized friends, even in the eternal blue fog of beginning battle. But on they moved behind Dolby's right arm, Sherry following her to their death, if need be.

Bluefeather's section obeyed his every move, every signal, as a single mind—almost as well as the triloids. They moved forward, crouching when he crouched, stopping and listening when he did, racing or slowing as he did. They moved unseen to scattered positions selected by Bluefeather and made ready to fire. He sent word down the line for all to select targets of opportunity for one mass firing. Then they would be on their own until a new victory was won. Yes, another. They waited for his signal. He held back, for they could all see Sherry and her Youngers advancing from one pillar to another in uneven fashion. Some fell forward against the stone floor of the cavern as Fontaine's men increased the firing on the fresh, young, moving meat.

At last the fourteen or fifteen survivors of God's Castle had joined the wildly erratic line of Steinberg's remaining force. Sherry's group moved up on the left flank and Bluefeather's was ready on the right. It would be a three-pronged attack.

Bluefeather dropped his raised arm, shouting, "Fire! Kill the invaders! Fire! Fire!"

They did—circling, ducking, dodging into the new three-pronged battle of erupting frenzy. Bluefeather caught a glance of a dark blue uniform moving low toward Steinberg's position. He mind-sighted and fired. The figure doubled up, arching its back, then kicked with both feet, falling flat and dead.

Bluefeather had lost track of his Section except for Pack and Osaka, who were on each side of him. They were firing, crawling, rising, looking and firing again, just as he was, and all around the ricochets became frenzied like the drums of a rock band, like the whine of breaking guitar strings, like a wail of insane thoughts flashing through a brain and bouncing off one part of the skull to another. The invisible diagrams that the ricochets drew between cavern walls and ancient pagodas would have destroyed all known geometrical concepts and caused the makers of spider webs to fight in frustration.

Now three of Fontaine's men dashed successfully across an opening to a large pagoda. Bluefeather and someone else fired, but too late. The three were at a protected angle to easily exterminate several of Steinberg's fighters. They did. Bluefeather watched them fall. Because of the ceaseless singing, zinging hive of bullets bouncing from stone to stone until they were expended or embedded in soft spots of limestone, no one knew from whence their death came.

Bluefeather saw Osaka charge through an undulation of rocks very near them. Osaka pulled the pin from a grenade and rose to throw it, absorbing several rounds in his chest. He fell on the dropped grenade, already dead. The grenade didn't give a damn. It exploded anyway, scattering pieces of Osaka about the surrounding terrain. One piece of bone struck Bluefeather on the cheek; another stuck to the top of his left shoulder. He brushed its warmness away, pulled the pin from his own grenade, and played billiards. He hurled it at a stalactite just past the one Fontaine's little group was fortressed behind. It was a good bank shot and certainly counted more than most. The grenade bounced left and back behind and exploded with extreme beauty. It blew one gutted enemy out to the side. Another was slapped up against the stone like a doll made of cheesecloth. Half of his upper head and one hand was missing. Since there was not enough left to identify of the third one, Bluefeather let his picture-mind work in slow motion as portions of the body drift-floated apart like a dropped, overripe watermelon. Now, as all three fighting organisms closed on the enemy, it became only the ageless, twenty-yard circle for each combatant to call home. There was no more world than that for now. Anywhere.

Bluefeather rolled over some rocks and fell on top of a dark blue uniform. The blue clothes covered a living body. It tried to shove the barrel of a rifle in his belly, but Bluefeather grabbed it, twisted, jerked it loose, and threw it aside. In continuous movement, he gouged so hard with his thumbs at the man's eyes that one burst like a grape and the other popped, dangling across his cheek. Then he battered the blind head until the back skull bones were chips inside the mushy head. He bashed all the memory out of him. He gathered his rifle and moved on, firing at everything that moved and some things that didn't.

Bluefeather had forgotten his oldest and best friend, Sergeant Pack. He had forgotten his love, Marsha. That was what moments of war do to people's minds. Now his thoughts and feelings turned just as suddenly the other way. Where were they? They had to be alive, those two; no matter what, they must survive beyond all. The cavern and its treasures of gold and knowledge were instantly worthless to him. Only those two were in his immediate thoughts. That's all the time that mattered, whether measured by earthly or unearthly standards. Oh, Great Spirit—oh, Dancing Bear, my spirit guide, take me to them so I can love and protect those two. Before his prayers were finished he had fallen behind a rock formation where Pack fired and jerked back down to reload on one edge and Marsha crouched on the other, just finishing reloading.

He sat down right by her. The bullets sang less now because there were far fewer fingers left to pull the triggers. There was even one of those sudden battle lulls that happen without explanation. It was the oddest war ever fought. More than half of the front lines were old men and women. Reversed.

Bluefeather and Marsha looked directly into each other's eyes and saw there something of such a craving for perpetuating life that wordlessly they fell together, removing and separating enough clothing so that their love, through their flesh, joined in the ancient movements creating future. The continuum. It was violent in its fleshly moist tenderness. It was a desperate seeking of all the senses of one another. A joining of renewal. Their bodies lustfully, but lovingly, drove hard together, increasing in intensity as Pack gave covering fire next to them. They were coming to the indescribably delicious finish of abandonment together.

Then Bluefeather lay atop his love, both spent to perspiring limpness. The instant after the grand finale, she had sighed two words, "Oh, Blue."

He moved his lips over to kiss her eyes. The first one was wet, full of tears. He moved his damp lips over to kiss the other lid, but the eye was open. He raised his head to look into both her wondrous blue irises that had thrilled him so much so many times. Only one was visible. It stared up blankly. The other socket was empty except for a pool of blood with a tiny stream running out the corner. A couple of drops, the size of a lemon seed, dripped from his mouth to the delicate crease above her chin and splashed into little red patterns on her pale dead face. A ricochet had struck her straight on, entering the socket and then the inner skull. She had never felt it. Marsha had died from a bullet sent here by Korbell, her own father.

Bluefeather stared, paralyzed, stricken. The old scar across his nose burned with a cutting pain he had never felt before. Then he rolled from her, took the three grenades from her belt, and screamed at Pack. "They killed Marsha. The bastards killed her."

Pack recognized now the madman Bluefeather had once seen in him years before at Brest, France. Pack grabbed for him too late and followed after his friend's madness, just as Bluefeather had once followed him. They both fired at every edge of rock visible and were separated from each other by these same rocks. Bluefeather screamed oaths, both silently and aloud. Every survivor on Steinberg's side heard and understood. Bluefeather hurled the grenades in a magical manner. Each one floated or drove just right to encircle, reach behind, and shatter the enemy.

The madness had given him the force of not caring. There was absolutely no fear. It was subdued beyond belief by the raging of his temporary derangement. He hurled all the grenades with deadly and efficient effect, emptied all his ammunition clips, pulled his machete and could find nothing to slice or stab.

He saw Fontaine and another man vanish into the edge of the dim light at full retreat. His reason slowly returned. There was no firing, no sound now that he could hear above his own heavy breathing.

He stumbled around a pillar and fell over Pack's prone figure. He reached out a hand, crawling to the body, feeling for, and finding, an erratic pulse. He pulled himself to a sitting position and took Pack's head in his lap. The bullets had got him in the lungs. He knew. He could hear the inner rattle of Pack's diminishing breath.

He rubbed the side of Pack's ashen face and rocked back and forth like an abandoned child with Pack's head cradled in his lap. His old friend opened his eyes slightly. There was the tiny little grin on his thin, white lips he had seen so many times in battles and barrooms.

The lips moved slightly and Bluefeather bent his head to hear, "Did we win, Blue, ol' pardner?"

"Yeah, we beat 'em good, sergeant. We beat 'em real good."

Pack was so still, Bluefeather thought he was gone. Then he strained but heard the last whisper Pack would ever make. "Take care of Sherry, Blue. I loved her, you know?"

"I will, Pack. Don't you worry about..."

Pack's head rolled over. Bluefeather got up on his hands and knees, straightened Pack out, placed his hands over his chest, and touched his eyelids closed. He stood up, saluted him, and turned away. One cannot weep in battle, for one cannot see to shoot with accuracy.

Bluefeather walked and walked among the dead, looking for Marsha, circling back on himself. He found the still body of Dunning nearby. There was no use moving around now. He sat down on a stone rise and yelled, "It's me. I am here. Here by the orange-stained pagoda. It is me. Bluefeather Fellini." He waited and yelled again. "They're all gone. The Korbells are all gone. It's me, I say, Bluefeather Fellini, from Raton, and Taos and Corrales, New Mexico, by way of the rest of the world and a great portion of the landscapes of heaven and hell. Now, if there are any friends or enemies left, you know who I am."

He heard the movement behind him. Even now he expected a bullet in his spine, but no powder exploded. He heard a voice say, "Blue? Blue, is it you? It's me. Charlie, I'm...I'm here, Blue, alive."

"I'm Blue. Here. Right here."

Charlie came and sat by his side. His head and arms dropped forward. Then Sherry and Shia moved in front of them silently. Sherry's eyes, which were big enough to see many worlds, stared—frozen in position in her head. She knelt in front of the two and put her head down against a leg of each and hugged them with both arms. Shia knelt behind her, her Oriental face pale as ivory. She reached out hesitantly with one hand and lightly, automatically patted Sherry between the shoulders.

Bluefeather pushed their hair silently out of their faces and tenderly rubbed their cheeks and temples for a long while before he realized that Charlie felt no more.

Then he gently rose up and said softly, "Stay here, Sherry. Don't move until I return."

He walked away in full control now. He passed over many bodies, some several times, until he found Marsha. She must have a tomb safe from the screechers, for they would, by nature, clean the cavern, and by desire, dine on the remains of the now vanquished enemy. He accepted this as inevitable for all but Marsha, his Marsha.

Then he searched about until he spotted a crevice. He gathered her up and eased her tenderly down into it without looking at her face. He pulled over two sloughed sections of limestone and dropped them to seal the crevice. He removed his pack and took the perfectly cylindrical rock-pearl and placed it on top of the tiny tomb. He had saved it, intending to have a silver necklace made for her after they returned to their adobe home at Corrales.

He took a pocketknife from his trousers and, with a strenuous effort, crudely carved: "Marsha—who died with love."

He didn't date it, for dates were meaningless in the context of caverns and caring. As he walked away his mind-voice spoke soothingly to him, "It is part of the overallness that we finally bury the ones we love or they us."

Then he heard a mule bray, and another in the same direction. He spotted the orange-stained pagoda and said to the waiting Sherry, "Did you hear them? The mules called from way over there."

She had heard. So they moved toward the sound that did not come again, shouting unintelligible things so that the mules and Willy and Adam and Tolliver could hear their approach. The trio had forgotten the war, but Willy hadn't. He had a rifle fully loaded, dead centered on them as they rounded the stalactite carelessly, for they had forgotten fear in their silent grief.

Willy stood up, grinning with monumental relief saying, "Well I'll be damned. My two best friends are here…and a new one. Say, ain't that keen?"

They all embraced and then admired the pack train, whole and healthy, even if Adam and Tolliver had died from the strain—one of heart attack and the other from a stroke.

Willy laughed. "Hard to believe, but the old farts never knew that every single one of the thousands of bullets missed 'em. Now ain't that a puzzle to ponder?"

Forty-Seven

The remains of The Section moved with the mule train safely past the deep, climbing cave of screechers. Bluefeather knew why. He had heard their signal cries moving through the multiple caverns; the screechers were finding their way to the feasts of war. If any of the Olders or the Youngers left behind were alive, they would have very little cleaning up to do.

At each way station, Sherry turned the electric lights off behind them, explaining that it was too much of a strain on the power plant above. Luck moved with them on through The Unholy and past Needle Canyon.

They were safely beyond the place of violent winds when they felt a tug—a suction—pull at them. It was like the cavern had given a great sigh of relief at their leaving and let them move on. They had, many weeks before, given up clock time, but now they had lost the sense of distance. Everything was different with battery lights reflecting in such a small area. The dark swallowed the end of the frail light beam and ate it shorter and shorter as their batteries weakened.

Bluefeather thought again, "Strange how the sunlight and green trees that once seemed so common will now appear as wondrous and new as the depths of the cavern had only a few weeks before." He experienced déjà vu. He believed that maybe this same thought had come to him before while deep under the River of Radiance.

They turned off their handlights now as another set of strong reflection bulbs revealed the endlessly changing formations again.

Just as Sherry moved toward the switch box, the lights were extinguished. The totality of the sudden darkness was a shock to all. Even the mules pulled against their tie-ropes nervously. Sherry turned on her handlight again—as did the others. She moved to the switch box and pulled it up and down several times. No one said it, but everyone knew, without words, that the darkness was permanent. It was a desolate darkness. The power plant had either been shut off from a breakdown, or someone had simply pulled a plug or the wires had been cut. Well, at least now the button that Dolby had hidden to push and blast-seal the caverns was useless.

The small Section and the eight mules stepped up their weary pace. If they did not reach the area of the Mimbres before they were without lights, trouble was an insufficient word for the problems they would have to solve. One step off the regular trail and one could wander in the darkness through a thousand miles of both connecting and dead-end caverns. But of course, no one could beat such odds. There were crevasses so deep that a dropped rock could not be heard hitting bottom and uncountable formations sharp and penetrating as daggers. Once they were past the Mimbres Cavern of the Dead there was a chance they could follow the wall on the man-carved trail and make it to the first stone gate. At that thought came another. Would it be open or sealed? Would there be anyone to open it for them? The phone line was dead. If they made it that far, the tunnel could still be their tomb of permanent darkness. There was no going back.

The adrenalin of fear increased in their bodies as the beams faded from Willy and Sherry's handlights. Bluefeather's light was only a rusty little shaft that he led them with. Bluefeather held the lead rope of the front mule. Sherry clasped Bluefeather's belt. Shia kept a hand on top of Sherry's shoulder, constantly grasping and releasing. Behind them all, Willy stumbled along with the last mule's tail in hand.

It was a slow movement, and even in the cooling temperatures the sweat drenched their bodies and began to weaken them beyond the carrying capacity of the dredged-up adrenalin. All had enough sense left to ration the water in their canteens.

When they came to a drip pool, Bluefeather said, "Willy, walk carefully up here to my light." He did. "Now kneel around the pool and get it located with your hands. Okay. I'm turning off the light while you drink and fill our canteens."

The blackness made the amazing guidance systems of many of the blind creatures below seem pure magic. With their fingers in the pool, they had awkward moments tending to such simple chores as Bluefeather had ordered.

"Are you all filled up now?"

"Yes," they chorused.

"Okay. Wash yourselves down." They did so. The cool water and the little rest refreshed them a lot.

Willy felt his way along the mules until he took up the last tail again. Everyone moved clumsily into position, saving the tiny, precious light for one last move forward. All made prayers now to reach the ruins before the batteries died just as dead as the Mimbres mummies.

They edged forward, the mules bunching up and bumping all along the line, then loosening until all the guide ropes, as well as the arms of the survivors, were stretched full length. They were bunching and unbunching over and over again, moving now around a sharp curve. The beam only strained out feebly about six feet in front of Bluefeather, into space, dark and huge.

The shots came as a surprise in a way, even though Bluefeather had figured Fontaine and his comrades had already made it past the Mimbres. It was the miss that was to be honored. The ricocheting whines and wails created a great anger in him at first. He had seen the flash of fire from the muzzles, though, and as he pulled back a step around the curve, he felt both elation and depression. Were Fontaine's lights used up as well as theirs? Or had they simply heard them and attempted a blind ambush in the raven-dark air?

The four were very still, but the delicate shuffling of a mule's hooves made sounds. Bluefeather listened above that, though. The enemy was not moving. His mind-voice gave him lectures that were not easy to hear. "You and Willy are miners. How could you not be prepared with long-lasting carbide lamps?" His other inner-voice answered, "Because we were assured there were several backup generators at the main plant as well as God's Castle. You don't want any more fights no matter how small, do you?" He answered himself quickly. "No, oh, no. I never did." Then the inner-voice said, "I'm truly sorry you fools, but wars have always existed in the past. Top professional gamblers would give big odds it will remain so in the future." At this Bluefeather closed off the voice. It was not helping anyway.

He took from his belt the grenades that he had salvaged from the fallen at the battle of God's Castle. If he demolished those who were still trying to maim and kill them, maybe they would have lights to lead them on. It was a chance. Even though a very thin one, it was enough to give him a sudden charge. There was no longer going to be any need to remain silent.

He spoke as if starting a dinner conversation. "You know what, dear friends? Sergeant Pack, the war-lover, once said, 'Life would be miserable, and hardly worth living, without my hand grenades.'"

Bluefeather stepped forward, pulled a pin, hurled a live one, and sent the second on its way before the first exploded, laughing so hard he shook and choked right through the explosions.

"Stay put," he whispered, holding the dim light out to his side as far as he could reach to give a misplaced target. He crawled forward on his knees and one elbow, holding a cocked handgun as ready as the awkward movement would allow. He need not have bothered. Fontaine stared up—his entire body ripped with shrapnel. The other man had slid or crawled in a trail of red several yards down a slope.

Bluefeather searched Fontaine for any kind of light. He found none. He scrambled down the slope and could find nothing on the partially disemboweled body there either.

He tried to shout at the others, but his voice was barely above a whisper. He walked back to join them. Now they followed him, locked together again. Just as they reached Fontaine, the battery spent its last tiny charge and all was darkness.

No one spoke for a moment, and then Sherry's usually strong, solid voice, quivering and haunted, sounded, "Blue? Blue, what do we do now?"

"Everyone ease back against the wall, sit down, and rest a few moments. Then we'll try and decide."

Sherry said, "You're right. If we're going to perish, we might as well get our breath back first." Now it was Sherry who became protective of Shia. Her love for Dolby had been decimated by his terrible deceit. And Pack was gone. She pulled Shia to her with a strong hug that spoke silent words in the darkness. She would have been pleased if she could have seen Shia's face upturned, smiling in near worship.

Willy said, "I crawled out of saloons and into my living room all through my youth. Might as well complete my old age in a familiar position. Don't you folks worry none, I can feel this path all the way to the surface. You think I'm gonna waste all this experience and wisdom? No sirree, I ain't."

In spite of the black shroud surrounding them, they had a small chuckle at Willy's attempt to give hope. They sat down and leaned back. Bluefeather held the lead rope of the mules. It was his job, and the connection to the noble animals gave him comfort.

Bluefeather was straining his entire being trying to come up with an answer for his friends, beyond the remote one—and injurious one—of Willy's crawling them home on solid rock.

The only answer there had ever been to darkness was light. Any childish idiot knew that. He couldn't conjure the tiniest flicker that could be visualized beyond the interior of his skull. Interminable.

Then there was Dancing Bear, searching and removing a small box of matches and a cigarette lighter from the pockets of the recent corpses. Bluefeather felt like a fool. That would have been enough erratic light to have moved them on a bit.

Bluefeather spoke to Dancing Bear in their own private, unheard dimension. "Well, Bear, it's sure nice to see you. How have you been? How's the spirit business these days? Where have you been? Would you care for a drink of canteen water? Do you happen to have a flashlight on you? If not, do you think it would be forward of me to ask for the loan of the matches and the lighter? How's your assistant Nicole? How's the Authority?"

"Whoa, whoa, dearest brudder. You sound just like me sometimes."

"I thought I'd beat you to it for once so we could get down to some serious conversation about getting us out of here."

"Dear brudder, Nicole is fine, just fine."

"Now that we've got all that settled, Bear, could we cut the clatter just this once, while there's still a once left, and solve the final, and almost certainly fatal, problem?"

"Dearest of all brudders, I have to combine the real and the magic to get you out of here. I just don't have the resources to do it any other way."

"What do you mean by that? I can see you...so I follow you and the rest follow me right on to safety. What's so difficult about that?"

"Well, for one thing, it ain't in the rules, dear brudder Blue."

"Now listen, Bear. I know you remember that old cliché about rules being made to be broken."

"Chure, chure, a hunnert times ago. I hear 'em."

"Now, cut out the Indian dialect right now. No more, you hear?"

"Okay, okay. Your people know you can't see in the dark like a screecher?"

"Of course."

"Well, my people won't let me carry magic that far. It's the rules. The 'from now on' rules. You gotta help yourselves some. Besides, I can't afford to be breaking no rules right now. I'm up for a promotion to the next."

"Next what?"

"Aw, you know—the next dimension. It's a big leap. I'll have a lot more assistants and won't have to travel so that I'm worn down like a ghost all the time."

"Well?"

"I go before the Authority and the board in just six—maybe nine—days. Gotta work by the book now. I been here about a hunnert..."

"All right. All right. What do you suggest?"

"Well, we can't let people who are not ready for it see true miracles performed. You—that's okay, but these people are too risky. They might jeopardize my promotion. Anybody—fakes, cheats, liars, and greedy frauds—could make them believe anything after witnessing a true miracle. We can't have that. It's too easy. Folks gotta have faith in their own strength."

"Lay out the rules. Please."

Dancing Bear was dancing slowly around in a one-yard spot. "This is the dance of the thinkers," he explained, taking the band from his skull, pointing at his heavily furrowed forehead, saying, "See the hard-thinking lines in the front of my head?"

Then he went on dancing the thinking dance. Suddenly, he stopped as accurately as a powwow dancer does on the last beat of the drums. "I got 'er. I got 'er. Here, you take the lighter and the matches. Here's what I been thinkin' this very second, dear brudder. I'm gonna go with my spirit body half in one dimension and half in another. Very dangerous thing, but the sparks from the friction will give you a light to follow. You gotta figure how to do a white man's lie to your friends. Okay?" Then Dancing Bear started dancing harder and wilder than ever before. It was the buffalo dance he performed. Soon there appeared a buffalo head over the top of his skull, its skin flapping down his back.

Bluefeather rose up and announced to his friends, "It's possible that these matches," he shook the two small boxes, "and this lighter..." he flared it quickly with his thumb, "can light our way. Because a tiny flare of light every now and then could fatally confuse you, Sherry, I'm gonna insist you hold onto my belt and follow my pull with your eyes closed. Shia, hold onto Sherry and don't let go, no matter what. Willy, you do the same with the mule's tail."

All they had to do was grab hold and they were as ready as they would ever be. Bluefeather had told a truth, but he didn't want his cohorts to have any time to mull it over.

Dancing Bear danced away from them, then poised like a marathon runner. Bluefeather held the lighter in the air and snapped its flint into a brief light.

Dancing Bear ducked down so that the horns exactly split the different dimensions of time and matter and charged the line of separation at full speed. As he hit the dividing line, he slowed, but struggled valiantly, the friction creating sparks, just as he had said.

The Section followed and, true to the half lie, Bluefeather snapped on the light every so often. It was an unusual sight Bluefeather followed. Half of Dancing Bear was invisible as he worked in parallel dimensions. The single horn left in the sparkling sight, the one leg and one arm and half a body, were a sight Bluefeather could have remembered in the depths of amnesia. Dancing Bear also sawed his head up and down against the invisible line and it showered light like a Fourth of July sparkler.

Sometimes Dancing Bear would run too far ahead, and would yell out in pain, trying to reach the finish line. Bluefeather reminded him that he was the one who had had the idea in the first place and that he must control those urges to run off and stick his searing head in pools of cool water.

The lighter fluid was about used up. Bluefeather could tell this because he now had to thumb the wheel several times to get a flame, but they had made remarkable progress by the time the lighter failed. He started in on the first box of matches. Of course, this slowed them down some, as he found he couldn't strike the little fire sticks while moving without wasting some.

Now Bluefeather was down to the last box of matches and Dancing Bear's smoking buffalo skull sent so much heat into his altered self that he was weaving off line a bit. Sometimes three quarters of him was visible—other moments only one-quarter. The followers and the mules were totally dependent on Dancing Bear's continuing charge forward as he courageously moved his head up and down against the line of different planes of being. Just the same, it had all been timed like a Shakespearean play.

As Bluefeather struck the last match, there was a loud ripping sound as Dancing Bear strained forward far beyond even his blessed and multiple talents. He fell, weaving wildly and exhausted, and "crashed through" out of sight into the invisible side of his heroic advance.

At that instant they all saw the gorgeous flow of light coming through the open stone doors. They had—Sherry, Shia, and Willy with eyes closed—and Bluefeather with his eyes only on the buffalo skull— moved right past the Mimbres area without being aware of it.

The smell of singed buffalo hair vanished from the fresh air that followed the light. The great Dancing Bear vanished with it. Bluefeather thanked him anyway, even though, just as he had insisted, it had taken valiant efforts by all. Dancing Bear could go before the Authority and the promotion board with a clear and hopefully clean conscience.

It was the mule entrance that had been blown up by Fontaine's men, they discovered. The four who now constituted The Section were trying to breathe the sunlight along with the outer air. In spite of the recent struggles, Bluefeather found that not keeping them alert for a possible last battle was one of the great failures of his life. No matter how he warned them that some of the enemy might still be here, they, for the first time, ignored his pleas. At the very last, his ability to com- mand had failed. Or had it? Everyone seemed to know, along with the weary pack mules, that all was safe now. However it came about, Bluefeather's weary brain could not understand, but he joined them in their quietly joyous entry into the new old world.

They were locked in a circle of nineteen guns pointing straight at them from different positions on the rocky foothills and around the corrals—but they instantly became friendly guns. Ten men and nine women slowly rose, lowering their guns, and came forward smiling, walking the circle smaller. They moved faster, now, on their old legs, laughing and closing in to embrace Bluefeather's little bunch.

Then the Olders' story unwrapped a layer at a time.

Korbell's soldiers had caught them by surprise just before daylight, knocking the outer compounds useless by bazooka and machine-gun fire from the outside, reaching the gates by crashing heavy reinforced trucks through. They had landed other troops by helicopter in the pas- tures. The battle had been swift, ferocious, and over in a short time.

They, the nineteen, had long ago been trained as "last resort reserves" and had retired by secluded, prearranged passage to the rocks above. Korbell had made the same mistake as Hitler had in Russia and Normandy. He had split his forces, consequently losing the battle of

God's Castle and not fully securing the upper compound either. The casualties here had been continuous and heavy on both sides. Korbell's forces had managed to blow the tunnel doors and breach Dolby's lower rooms in order to raid the vault. But the nineteen gunners on the hills had made transporting the gold bars to the helicopters costly indeed.

At last, both sides had called a truce to dispose of the dead. They had been hauled away. Korbell himself had overseen the hauling of the dead and wounded around the other side of a near mountain to an old ghost town with many deep mine shafts. There they had been dropped in and rocks pushed on top of them. There was no other way.

Korbell had disposed of all the dead and living evidence except the nineteen Olders. He knew they would not talk to or contact the social world. They couldn't. Their long-brainwashed minds would see to that. The last phone call out by Fontaine had indicated that Steinberg had counterattacked and driven them back, and then the phone had gone dead. Korbell could not know this, but he had to surmise that the underground battle was a loss, or in such jeopardy that there was no way he could control it. So he pragmatically settled for the large acquisition of bullion to soothe his losses.

Sherry led the entourage around the buildings to the front gardens, dreading the description of Dolby's death, when a couple of Olders appeared around a hedge, leading Dolby by both arms. He walked in little, short, shuffling steps. Sherry was so joyous at his appearance that she momentarily forgot what he had done to them all and leapt forward, hugging him, kissing his old face and thanking all the gods and their minions in the heavens.

Everyone stood waiting, seeing what Sherry in her enthusiasm and relief had missed. The world that Dolby had often retreated into over the past thirty years was now his permanent abode. His eyes stared inward only. His ears heard only the sounds from whatever his eyes saw inside. He did not recognize Sherry or anyone else in any way. He lived elsewhere. He was dead out here where the sun shined.

When Sherry finally shuddered and saw his true condition, she was suddenly back in control of her remaining and just-beginning destiny.

While Willy and some of the Olders helped unpack the mules, secure their golden burden, and water, feed, and brush them down, Sherry, Shia, and Bluefeather moved down to the lower rooms with a dread tempered by the almost impossible gift of their being alive.

The vault had been blown open. Dolby had obviously not given in to the threats of torture or provided Korbell the combination. For some reason Korbell had left an even dozen gold bars. A gesture. Saying what? Who would ever know for sure what Korbell had in mind? Possibly, it was some kind of weird statement to his only daughter and son if they survived. They hadn't.

Sherry did not puzzle on this as Bluefeather was doing. She leapt in the vault, counting her notebooks of the deep from the last seven years. They had been ignored there right beside the gold—overlooked because of the tens of millions upon millions of dollars' worth of the rectangular yellow. The treasure of all outer-worldly and inner-worldly treasures had been treated as a trifle—no more than a bookkeeper's ancient labors. Worthless.

Sherry had forgotten the note bag still slung over her shoulder. She removed the new notebooks and placed them tenderly atop the still neatly stacked older ones. She stepped out of the vault, pushing its injured door shut, and turned to Bluefeather. Her great, dark eyes wetted with a smile of relief beyond her speaking, beyond moist imaginations, but not beyond his. He held her a moment, caressing the beautiful, valorous head so full of inestimable knowledge.

They repaired the damages done by bullets, picked up all the shell casings, and disposed of them. Shia worked harder than anyone when she wasn't marveling at the hand-built and God-built surroundings. They were as new and wondrous to her as the Cavern of Marvels had first been to the mesmerized Section. It would take her a while, but she would adjust to the upper, just as they had to the lower.

Willy stayed on and got all the mules in good shape and patched up the damage to the outbuildings. The power plant was easily restored to service. They had been correct about Fontaine overlooking or ignoring it. Cooks, repairmen, chemists, and guards from the Olders soon separated into their own units of service.

Sherry and Bluefeather took Dolby to El Paso, Texas, and put him in a private and highly recommended home so he would be well cared for and could finish whatever time there was left for him to fill up his small, useless space here in the world of humans. For a while each time Bluefeather had even a glancing thought of Marsha, or Pack, or Hector, or...he wanted to cut the old man open and toss starved rats into the cavity, but these feelings soon dissipated.

Dolby was a voracious murderer, a dreamer of both greedy and noble visions and a complex mixture of acid and roses. He was all of us, only more so. He just turned the wheel one way while others twisted it another. But in the end, he had cared deeply for, and respected, Sherry. He had long ago given her full power-of-attorney over all his holdings, his many bank accounts, stocks, and land, but now his will also showed her as the sole beneficiary.

Bluefeather had to attend a final meeting with Korbell. Korbell knew it and waited with the patience that huge wealth affords. He looked forward to it as much as Bluefeather—almost. But first, Bluefeather, with the help of a couple of Olders, melted down the nodules into small bars, and at Sherry's insistence, all but three of the widely separated samples from the Hills of Hell. She wanted those for further study, as she put it. All told there was enough to pay off Willy's place, send Sally to college—as Bluefeather had sworn would happen—and give Flo and Harvey a good start in any business they desired. His friends, the Rugers, were now provided for. They had earned much more but were overly grateful for—and for a short time even guilty over—what they received. Zia Creek could flow on without interference from bankers or builders at least through their lifetimes. Bluefeather also was left with enough to make him, as country folks say, "fairly well-to-do."

Now that the compound was running smoothly again, Bluefeather and Sherry sat on the terrace in front of the thirty-foot window, absorbing the sunshine and the green, growing grass, trees, and bushes. They gazed with delicious delight and appreciation.

Their conversation dodged all around what must be done about the "below" world. They advanced a thought here and there, both pulling them back, afraid, searching for some answer they could settle or believe right between them. It was all up to them now. Just the two of them. Shia and Willy would remain totally loyal and silent unless told otherwise. The decision would be momentous, with chances for terrible destruction or boundless gain. The indecision became destructive stress.

They must decide now.

They agreed that a few of the Olders, and possibly some Youngers, had enough food stored and live chickens, cows, pigs, and the bounteous giving of the trees of light to survive quite well. They had known nothing else, anyway.

"Look, Sherry, the system below has survived uncountable aeons without us. It can surely advance without us now—it even might be destroyed with us. Don't you think?"

"I would never let anything permanently injure the lower cave system. We never have."

"I know, but you and Dolby were the sole controllers. There's no way it can be maintained. Look how close Korbell came to taking it. Think about how many died trying to win it and how many died to save it. The percentage rate is astronomical."

"Of course both sides had different goals, Blue, I . . . I well . . ."

"Listen, Sherry, let's admit what's going on around us with the destruction of the forests and poisoning of the rivers. The wolf and grizzly are being pushed back into what few old forests are left and are losing the race of extinction. There is an endless, growing chain of babies—hungry babies, beautiful babies, lovable babies, irresistible babies—crawling across the entire globe, spreading, taking up all available space and finite resources. Babies being conceived, birthed, bathed, fed, fed, fed—cartons, diapers, bottles, cans, cups, glasses, plastics, clothes, toys. For all the surplus babies scrubbed and fattened in one spot, even more will be starved to death in another."

Sherry was so motionless, Bluefeather felt she had quit breathing for a moment, and in truth she had been trying not to hear what he could not hold back. It was beyond his control now, however, and the long-suppressed feelings tumbled out of him in words.

He continued. "Then those babies grow up, Sherry. Their stomachs are bigger, it takes more to fill them, and more trash to wrap the food in and more poison chemicals to make the rapidly dying land produce. Don't you see? It tilts the world and all of nature off balance. It's simply an unthinking mass suicide."

"I know, I know. I can't stand to think of it, and I don't want to hear it anymore."

"But we have to think about this surface earth, dwell on it, in fact, and then act, act, act. And even now we may be too stupidly, greedily late."

"Oh, Blue, I know. I'm having selfish thoughts of continuing Dolby's dream—my dream—of sharing it all—the sights, the smells, the notebooks."

There were over eighty thousand privately owned acres of hills, mountains, canyons, and forests like earth auditoriums all over the

Cavern of Marvels. It was surrounded by national forests, most of it inhospitable even to hunters. Sherry could certainly protect any outside discovery of a crack or hidden cave during her lifetime that might lead the accumulators and desecrators down below.

Bluefeather asked her if these things were not true. Sherry agreed they were. It was her deeded land to protect now. Only she, Bluefeather, Shia, and Willy would know during their allotted breathing time.

They both sat in the warm, kissing, ancient sun that would forever be new to them now. Sherry tried to move her mind back to the decision she and Bluefeather had to make, but it kept glancing at, and stumbling over, the glory of the soul that would come from revealing to the world all she alone held inside her head, heart, and in the leather-bound pages of her notebooks. Pains came and were fought away at the images of Dolla, the triloids, their river, Dolby, the Star Cave, God's Castle, and the smell and feel of Pack. At this instant Bluefeather was missing his friends Charlie, Pack, all the others, even the Youngers, who—except for Shia, alone—had never had a chance to know the difference.

Bluefeather's vision was convoluted with pictures of Marsha's eyes, her hair, her walk, her laugh, her, she, Marsha, Marsha. He saw the never-to-bes they would never have, tempered by the always-ones they had shared. He forced the mind-pictures in fast-sliced images on to the great room of pearls, the iridescent horse-fish, the diving and dancing triloid young, and more.

Sherry and Bluefeather were back in the same shared space. They would have to weep and mourn or perish, but for now their mission was untidy, unfinished. Weeping must wait again.

Then he spoke softly aloud. "You know what? Blood and gold and beauty are made from the same chemicals."

Sherry came up out of her reverie of disassembled truths, saying, "What? What did you say, Blue? I'm sorry."

"Oh, nothing really. I was just kinda talking to myself, I guess."

Sherry said, "Would you like a glass of wine?"

"I sure as hell would."

It was served in a full decanter, purple and radiant in the sun that had created the mother grapes of its beginnings. They made a silent toast and sipped, delaying with some pleasure the inevitable agony of final decisions.

Then Bluefeather's mind-voice clicked in from somewhere far away in his head and spoke with authority: "Beware, beware, ye pioneers, for vultures will follow and become fat on your discoveries." After a moment the voice continued. "Korbell. His heart is as cold and stiff as a Siberian thermometer. Never forget it."

Sherry spoke aloud now, her voice was as surprising, and suddenly painful, as a paper cut. She said, "I can't. I can't just bury it all, Blue. That's what we'll have to do, isn't it? We'll have to bury it so no one can find it? Well, I can't do it...I just can't. Because then...then all the years of study...knowledge in my little books will be gone, lost. I...I..."

"I know. Well, I know part of what you are feeling. Just a small part, but..."

Her great eyes were so wide and deeply disturbed, searching, that Bluefeather could no longer look into them. Instead, he stared at the blue, misty mesas, all the way to the western horizon.

Then he finally said, "As of right now, the Cavern of Marvels and all its multitude of inhabitants are very much as they were before humans discovered the use of fire. They'll most likely continue to evolve aeons after mankind has destroyed this world...and long after the little human empires of wealth and pitiful power have crumbled and vanished. Forgotten. The greatest cities—the mightiest nations—will change boundaries over and over and will probably collapse into piles of matter. This, too, will finally be flattened by the ever-changing heat and cold, wind, and rain, and disappear as if these things had never been."

Sherry knew, but was trying to hide from herself, the point that Bluefeather was so desperately struggling to impress upon her. She said, "Blue, I think I know what you are driving at. And I know you are trying to make this easier on both of us. But I...I just can't let it go...yet. It's like losing my...well, my soul. I just can't explain my feelings. I suppose it's even a certain kind of greed...not money greed, but greed all the same."

Bluefeather hesitated a full minute. She waited, frightened, knowing he would not give up.

"Well, I sure as hell understand about greed. That cockeyed, yellow metal has haunted my dreams uncounted days and nights, but I fought it, and I think I've won. You're going to have to do the same about the cavern. Oh, God, Sherry, please forgive me...the last thing I mean to do is preach or lecture to anyone in this world, much less you. It's just that I'm filled up with all these worries about that wondrous world. I can't help myself."

"But we'll lose everything we've found. It will all be gone. It will all be lost forever. I can't stand the thoughts of it."

"But, darling Sherry, there is a remote chance that all this below could surpass and survive and maybe, in some far-distant time, one or more of its creatures might crawl from a fissure in the earth and out into the sun. You know—just as others came out of the ocean to the land and air and eventually climbed trees. That might be the only chance left." He stopped and looked straight at her before saying, "We do have to bury it. We have no choice, do we?" Then he was quiet.

The desperate effort to convince Sherry to give up the almost limitless knowledge of her life's work pained and drained him. Her eyes looked on through his, out the back of his head. Then she stared straight ahead, motionless, as if in a trance for five or six minutes. Eternity.

Finally, with a start, she blurted out in complete contradiction, "Of course, dear Blue, of course. Let us do our duty and drink to it. What have I been talking about? Who do I think I'm fooling? Not you. Not me."

They had survived hellish wars and pressure together. They had both lost their loves and lovers. Their minds had swiftly become meshed by necessity and now were even more together by respect and love.

"Blue, can you do it so no one outside this compound will ever know?"

"I can do it, but Korbell knows."

They both thought simultaneously that Tilton's gold had been moved to Dolby's vault and now it, along with its evil spirits, had gone on to a new vault with a new master—or slave. They must act. They made a last futile search for Dolby's explosive button. It was not to be found. Maybe it had never been there. The threat was as good as the truth with such an overpowering man.

"Then let's get after it and worry about him after the fact," Bluefeather said as he stood up to phone Willy to come help with the planning. Willy was overjoyed with the decision. It was decided just like that.

Bluefeather had always been naturally good at dynamite blasting. Willy was also an experienced expert. Even so, it took days of drilling to angle and space the holes and measure the powder exactly right. They had to blast the concrete tunnels into rubble so that the next explosions would cover it all. It had to be perfect.

At last it was as ready as it would ever be. One more time they had to be perfect. Just once. It was important to everything that had ever been or ever would be. All the electric lines had been connected to the explosives.

The little group—Bluefeather, Sherry, Shia, Willy, and all the Olders—stood about, staring at the box with the plunger raised. All eyes were centered on the plunger.

Bluefeather said, "Sherry, it's your honor."

She looked at him, and then moved without hesitation, knelt, and pushed it down. The earth jarred under their feet. The foothill dropped some of its surface in a landslide of the perfection they had sought. The entrance to the underworld was covered and hidden as if Mother Nature had created the rockslide. Maybe she had, actually. It looked as natural as all the other slides over the entire range. The continuum would be left to the vagaries of chance and the progression of evolution in the cavern far, far below.

They stood silently for several minutes. Then the four went back to the house and sat on the terrace. They stared in appreciation of all the precious greenery of the meadows and mountains, absorbing kisses from the sun playing sweet symphonies of shadows for their grateful eyes.

Bluefeather raised his glass of fine wine and toasted. "As I've said before, here's to the gods, goddamn 'em and bless 'em, too."

Sherry said, "And to their daughters, sons, and heirs."

Willy clicked his merry glass against theirs and offered, "Grandy dandy. And here's to dancing, to singing, to love, to growth, for folks cain't have no real fun without 'em all."

They cheered in agreement, laughed, and drank their wine with joy. Then, as Willy had suggested, Sherry caught a hand of both Bluefeather and Willy, tugging them up. The three of them danced on the surface of the secured Caverns of Marvels. Shia watched, clapping in rhythm. They danced in small circles, hands on each other's shoulders, smiling, then giggling, then laughing, so that birds and squirrels moved and chattered about in the trees at the happy disturbance.

Forty-Eight

Willy had returned home several days earlier, and now Sherry walked Bluefeather down to his jeep. Neither spoke. There was too much to verbalize.

He opened the door and turned back to her. "I've got a very necessary chore to attend to."

"I know."

"I'll be back to see you—when I finish."

"I'll be looking forward to hearing from you."

They held one another a long moment, feeling their everlasting bond.

"I love you."

"I love you, too."

He climbed into the jeep and drove on out through the new guard gate. She stood looking after him a long time.

He went by the Rugers' and picked up the Tilton property maps that Charlie Waters had gathered for him with such unquestioned dedication. He talked to Sally about how brave Charlie had been and finally managed to get her thinking about school again. He drove on over to Albuquerque and shopped a while and saw a lawyer before going home to Corrales.

The Tranquilino Lucero family was so happy to see him that they wanted to throw an immediate fiesta. He explained that he had some studying to do and an appointment to keep—then they would celebrate.

He handed Tranquilino two envelopes, one sealed, one open, saying, "Now I gotta have your word and your handshake that you'll accept these envelopes with no hesitation, no apologies, and no regrets."

Tranquilino stared at him, at his wife and children, then smiled widely and warmly said, "Okay. Okay, amigo. Okay. My word and my hand."

They shook hands. It was done.

As Bluefeather left to go see the mules, Nancy and Miss Mary, he could hear the happy cries of the excited family behind him. Tranquilino burst out on the porch to yell at him but remembered his vows and re-entered the house.

In the open envelope was the title to a new Ford pickup truck to be picked up by Tranquilino. He had no idea the truck bed was heaped up past the rim with delicacies of all kinds, educational toys and many books for the whole family, a silver concho belt for the lady of the house, and an inflatable boat for Tranquilino to fish in up at Fenton Lake in his beloved Jemez Mountains. More. Yes, more, for Bluefeather had signed the deed to his house and acreage over to the Luceros with one restriction—that he could pitch camp there at any time in the next three years and would have a place for his two mules the same. He felt very good about this. It would give the Luceros enough paid-for land to make a living from without having to give in to the greed of overdevelopment.

Bluefeather was amazed that the mules remembered him. They were sleek, shiny, and solid muscled. Tranquilino had obviously fed them well and exercised them properly. Of course, he had only been gone—how long? Nine weeks. Twelve? Fifteen? He couldn't remember, for it seemed, even now as he talked to and petted his long-eared partners, that he had trekked for a thousand generations at least.

"I don't want to leave you, my exquisite ones. Oh no. It breaks my tired heart, but I must fulfill my present destiny. Do you understand, sleek ones?"

They moved their ears, hearing and comprehending every inflection of his voice as before. They watched him with dark, moist eyes made of the essence of stars and loyalty—the latter prized above all by the half Taos Indian and half Raton, New Mexico, Italian—now meshed, as Old Grinder had demanded, into just simply Bluefeather. Now he could weep, here with his familiars. He sobbed and shook so that his ribs were near breaking and his lungs bursting. He wept for Marsha, for Pack, for all who had perished, and even for the dream itself. He finally wept for its success and failure and even a little for himself. The weeping was over at last. The silent grieving would be slower to withdraw, but it would—mostly.

He acquired a suite of rooms at the Hilton in downtown Albuquerque and stayed there four days and nights—all alone. He used room service only, so as to study Tilton's maps undisturbed. He would stay put as long as it took. That is the way he was. But at midnight of the fourth day he was satisfied. With his picture-mind, he saw Tilton's golden skull staring across the River of Radiance and said aloud, "Thank you, Mr. Tilton. All small favors are deeply appreciated."

He picked up the phone and called Korbell. With a little explanation as to who he was, Bluefeather was put through to him.

"Ahhh, Mr. Fellini, no less, the midnight caller. I've been expecting your call. The timing is perfect. I often stay up until two or three in the morning, studying and enjoying the silence and . . . my collection."

Bluefeather didn't ask him what collection, since he owned some part of the world somewhere, and a bit of everything in it, along with about fifty million dollars' worth of Tilton's metal.

"When shall we meet? I have information that might lead us toward closing our original deal."

"Ah, yes. The Mouton '80."

Bluefeather was enjoying Korbell's cautious cleverness on the phone, as if he didn't have every means to discover a phone tap.

"Yes, the eighty-eight."

Bluefeather wondered if the man had gotten his double entendre about the Mouton 1880 and the deadly German eighty-eight shells they had both once been so very close to.

"Afternoon after next. Three o'clock. I have some old friends from various parts of the planet arriving for a small soiree. Informal, of course."

Bluefeather held the phone a moment, looking at it after the other end was dead. He could see the "Korbell smile that spoke" all the way to where he sat.

◼ ◼ ◼

Forty-Nine

It was the time for rounding up loose ends and tying them together. The guards shook Bluefeather down at the gate to Korbell's retreat. They seemed surprised he was clean. Nedra smiled and complemented him on his health, his sport jacket, and his general attitude all the way to meet Korbell. The man with the silver hair and the silver voice left a little covey of worldly citizens, greeted Bluefeather with enthusiasm, and introduced him to men and women from London, Bombay, Tokyo, Paris, Houston, and Bogota. There were others he met and to whom he said the "Happy to...honored to...pleased to meet you" party gargle.

Korbell spoke their languages flawlessly, with naturalness, with each guest, except for the oil men from Houston. He slightly overdid that particular foreign accent. Bluefeather covered for him there, since he had the southwestern, geological drawl down to its beefsteak, pork chops, and red-eye gravy. He liked it.

Even with the Scotch in his hand and the huge patio with the small pool in his vision—things were a little blurred. Bluefeather wasn't here to focus his mind-camera on these people so practiced, planned, and perfectly casual in all ways. The dress, the conversations hinting at power and wealth were barely, but strongly, suggested among those who really had it. The worshipped power was presented, along with an attitude of responsible respectability, as smoothly as an Old Vic play. Only here, their stage and the masks were real. The rest was the play itself. All the actors wore masks of opaque illusions. Magic was made by little tricks of cleverness. Sincerity was acquired by the purchase price—lovely appearances in expensive disguise.

Bluefeather even gave Korbell a complimentary thought. Korbell recognized all this, but he was not aware that Bluefeather had seen him glance over his adopted wife Elena's shoulder at him. Korbell had long ago won all the other games, including the games played here. Bluefeather was the only prey left.

Bluefeather walked along the hors d'oeuvres table filled with every imaginable delicacy. He picked at the food, setting his drink down carefully, untouched. He never drank alcohol when he worked. Right now he was very busy indeed. He moved a china plate in deliberate misdirection—an eye-fooling trick he had learned in his card playing days from Nancy of Tonopah—and stuck a carving knife in the back of his belt under his jacket. He moved on around the table and with the same smooth motion placed a bread knife in the inside wallet pocket of his jacket for extra insurance. Then he took a few nibbles of shrimp and waited. He was trying to make himself invisible until Korbell could separate himself from his guests.

When the mariachi band started up and all eyes and ears were drawn in their direction for a moment, Korbell moved to Bluefeather, saying, "Come with me, Mr. Fellini. We have things to discuss in private, do we not?"

"Indeed we do, Mr. Korbell." He didn't emphasize the "mister" but got it slipped in anyway.

They moved easily through three rooms to a hallway. Korbell opened a door, switched on a light and led Bluefeather down two turns of circular concrete stairs underground. Then he touched a stone door. It swung open, moving as smoothly as a snake on Italian marble, revealing a vast wine cellar. Even Bluefeather's awareness of Korbell's hobby had not prepared him for this.

Korbell marched him grandly around, pointing out and describing different bottles of rare vintages. He often picked up a special bottle to read the impressive label.

Bluefeather's perception of the bottles and of Korbell fused. He could no longer waste any faked interest on what they both knew was a formality—a hollow one at that. Then, at the very back northwest corner, Korbell reached under and between two bottles on the second shelf and pushed a hidden latch. The shelves swung outward, revealing a solid-looking wall. Then Korbell easily pushed the great stone door open. The massive two-foot-thick block had been cut so mathematically, so flawlessly, that Einstein would have published a paper on its precision.

Bluefeather noticed that Korbell left this door open. There was a huge, hidden room unmasked before them. It was full of treasures on shelves and in glass cases—treasures from around the world. Bluefeather saw Ming vases, Egyptian mummies in solid gold uniforms, a nugget that must have weighed five hundred pounds from a Brazilian placer mine, and a diamond the size of a prizefighter's fist. Surrounding it were piles and clusters of smaller blue, white, and yellow diamonds of all sizes and cuts. There were old, old Mayan and Aztec masks—objects of a unique, and sometimes tragic, beauty. There was a Rembrandt painting of a golden-lit lady, dazzling to behold. Renoirs of dancing light and moving shadows. An El Greco figure, twisted, long, lean, elongated, so it seemed to stretch up past the picture frame to the ceiling.

Korbell proudly, profusely, eloquently described the value, the place of origin, and even his acquisition of the mostly stolen goods.

It was not lost on Bluefeather that the accumulator seemed to enjoy incriminating himself to Bluefeather. On and on it went—the riches cut, carved and painted so long ago by great artists and craftsmen who were now all worm-eaten dust.

Korbell's chest was rising and falling in exhalation. Now at last they came to the corner shelves, where a waist-high narrow table fronted them. The shelves were all replete with the same vintage wine bottles. To the side was a very old-fashioned but elegant wash basin with solid gold handles and pipes and a glass case full of wine glasses above it.

Korbell stopped between the case and the table, reached in and took out two glasses. He placed one in front of each of them. He moved around a moment, then, leaning over, pushed a plush chair, sending it rolling away toward a couch. All the furniture was on rollers to move easily over the smooth tiled floor of a neutral color with a tiny unobtrusive pattern.

"I come here, Mr. Fellini, and sip my wine. You see, I enjoy sitting here and gazing at many of the greatest treasures and artifacts in the world. I take great pleasure in knowing they are all mine and I am the only one in this world left alive, except you, who knows about this room's existence. Selfish to the extreme, huh, Mr. Fellini?"

"I would agree with your last judgment totally."

Bluefeather knew now what was coming. Korbell never intended him to leave the cellar alive. He couldn't allow it, now. Not after his admissions.

"Don't you find it a revelatory irony that Tilton invented this room, and these marvelous doors, just for me? For me, Mr. Fellini. None of us, not one, ever knows in the end whom we have really been working for during our lifetime."

Bluefeather had finally seen that exact same truth on Charlie's maps two nights before at a minute to midnight, but Korbell—with all his knowledge—was not aware of this.

"I agree with you in totality, and if and when you ever find out, it's probably too late to change it," Bluefeather said, studying Korbell, sensing the slight bulge cleverly hidden under his armpit. He didn't believe that that was how Korbell meant to kill him, though. The gun was only protection against his guest. Korbell would surely have a more subtle method.

Now, as Korbell reached to the shelf for the wine bottle, his face was a vibrant pink, his eyes turned to shiny pearls, and his smile was one of near orgasm. He set the bottle on the table ceremoniously and wiped it carefully, lovingly, with a white silk handkerchief. Then he turned the wine label toward Bluefeather, staring at him in what could only appear as a form of gloating glee.

Bluefeather calmly read aloud, "Mouton 1880."

"Forty cases of it, courtesy of Mr. Tilton. Of course there are a few bottles I've sipped while perusing my...my little cache."

Bluefeather had known that the wine could be no other place than here. One of Tilton's architectural drawings revealed the front cellar and the one where they now stood. He must not let Korbell know this yet, for he intended to kill him some way soon.

"You sly rascal, you," Bluefeather grinned. "You've had the wine here ever since you bought the place. Tilton had already hidden it here before he finished the upper house. Pretty slick." Bluefeather reached over playfully and tapped Korbell on the shoulder, but let his hand swiftly feel the gun. It was there all right. He had to watch every tiny move now. "You were after the bullion all along, right? Huh?" Bluefeather laughed.

"Of course, Mr. Fellini, and I must say you delivered. Delivery— that's the word. That's all that matters. Here, let us celebrate our victory with this rare liquid treasure." He expertly removed the old cork, smelled it as his eyeballs rolled up in mock thanks to God, and then, as delicately as a mother kisses her new baby, poured them each a glass.

Bluefeather watched for any movement of misdirection, of deceit, as Korbell tilted the bottle with both hands. He could discern none, but a warning coldness tingled on the back of his neck and the once-split nose itched more with joy than anger now. They raised the glasses and stared straight across them at one another.

"To the best of everything, Mr. Fellini, and to the bonus you shall receive momentarily."

"To your dedication, Mr. Korbell, and to a bonus you so abundantly deserve."

They both laughed and then tasted the rare liquid extravagance.

"Ahhh," admired Korbell, savoring a second swallow. "Ahhh."

Bluefeather was taking no chances of Korbell palming poison or flicking it from under his fingernails. One or the other had to be the method of his murder, he figured.

He must get the carving knife out before Korbell could reach his revolver. He was counting on his more youthful, swifter physical movements to beat his opponent.

Bluefeather held the glass at half-toast position as he swung one arm in a gesture that included the tennis court-sized room and said so softly that Korbell would be compelled to strain his hearing, "You killed your only daughter and forced me to kill your only son for the bullion when you already had this room of treasures—and a thousand times more. Why sir? Why, I ask?"

"It wasn't supposed to happen. I underestimated the loyalty and courage of Dolby's people."

"You underestimated your daughter as well."

"Yes, I admit that. We tried every form of bribery and even threats to get the information from her. She was tough. Very tough. Of course, she was tough. I had trained her that way myself."

"Of course."

"Yes. It took a very large and dangerous dose of truth serum to get it out of her."

"Well, here's to your diligence, Mr. Korbell." Bluefeather raised his glass, continuing the toast, "and my many wishes that you enjoy every drop of wine on that shelf and gaze upon nothing but beautiful treasures such as these the rest of your life."

Korbell had just caught onto the satire in Bluefeather's voice, because the pink in his face dissipated into gray and the smile turned down at its edges.

Bluefeather grabbed and swung the half-full bottle of Mouton '80 with extra swift force and speed just as Korbell opened his fingers ever so slightly, preparing to grab his gun. Korbell had miscalculated and given away his position at last. The bottle struck him full on the chin. He fell with a comforting thud, his head bouncing a little on the tastefully tiled floor, adding to his present blankness without permanent injury.

Bluefeather grabbed a bottle with a loose label from the shelf. He quickly finished peeling it off, took a pen from his pocket, and wrote on the inside of the label, "Enjoy. Eternally yours, Mr. Fellini."

He set the bottle of Mouton '80 next to the note, moved to the stone door, and closed it carefully behind him. Now he had use for the carving knife. He forced the point into the almost invisible crack of the door and drove it as a wedge into the space. He pushed with all his might. It now fit exactly. Then he broke the blade off even with the door and wall. It would never move again. The perfection had been prized away by the knife blade. Now it was a perfect prison. He pushed the wine shelf against it. The door could not be seen at all now and the recessed latch was invisible. Perpetuity.

Korbell's luxurious entombment had been necessary so that they, the triloids, and all their companions, were permanently free of human intervention. The world would not be aware of that action, but now Korbell was hidden underground as well. The public would never know what happened to him, either, but would spend uncounted hours and million of dollars searching and guessing.

Bluefeather smiled a smile of such brilliance it would have dulled those of the Korbell tribe all the way back to cave frogs.

He walked up and out into the sunlight, visiting, just as casually corrupt as the rest of Korbell's associates. He was enjoying his third Scotch—he was through working, so he could indulge himself a bit. He heard Elena asking several people nearby, and finally him, if they had seen Korbell.

Bluefeather said, "No. I have been enjoying your guests so much, I didn't notice his absence."

"Oh, well, he's always just disappearing like this. Sometimes he's actually gone for days. One never knows if he'll return or not."

"I'm sure that's true," Bluefeather agreed, as he wound around the gardens beyond the patio with the New Mexico mountains swallowing the rays of the warm, early fall sun placidly. Content.

A lady in delicate costume came toward him on a curving path. He recognized Nicole, once mistress to Napoleon, poisoned by Josephine.

She smiled and spoke. "Please, Monsieur, have pleasant thoughts about me. Am I not worthy?"

"Oh...yes...you certainly are. What are you doing here, Nicole?"

"Oh, Dancing Bear sent me to substitute again."

"Well, I'll be honest with you, Nicole. I expected Bear here in person to celebrate our victory."

"I'm sure you did, Monsieur Bluefeather, but he asked me to give you this message exact. He said you would understand."

"Of course," he said, mimicking his fallen foe's precise speech. She quoted Dancing Bear "exact": "Tell Blue that I got the promotion from Authority, but he sends me to the Bahamas to heal. Buffalo who runs a mile uphill with his skull on fire needs a vacation."

"I can certainly understand that—and sympathize."

Nicole reached out, took his hand, and they floated over the compound's walls, out over the forest, up onto a little white cloud not much bigger than a king-sized bed. Down below a sheepherder stopped to listen. He would always swear he had heard voices from the sky saying, "Lower. Lower."

"Higher. Higher."

He would spend the rest of his life searching for the meaning.

◼ Part Three ◼

THE TIME OF DECISION
The Great Quandary and Embarkation

Fifty

It was the time to die. Bluefeather could feel all the natural crippling ailments of old age coming on strong. He would beat them at their timeless game. He had lived an extremely active and exciting life. It was not his nature to go bedridden, mind-fogged into the other realm. No, sir. He would go bouncing at his best. He felt especially blessed that he—along with coyotes, Eskimos, turtles, and cicadas—knew this.

It might take a few days. Just the same, he felt it was upon him. He had been here long and the thinning legs beneath his body were increasingly uncertain. He must get away from the town. It reached out and surrounded him. He could feel its grasp tightening. He could hear his mind-voice saying, "Come, old Bluefeather, and sit on the porches of my dusty streets in the shade of my trees. Stay and loaf and dream in the sun and warm your worn old legs by the log fires of my houses. Stay and die slowly here, looking at the far distant hills of your youth, in the easy time."

"No!"

First, before dying, he had chores to tend. He sat at the rough, handmade table in his three-room house and wrote his will on a yellow pad. The hands that held the pen looked like twisted oak limbs. He would leave the residence to his amigo, Artesimo Gomez, a prospector like himself. They had drunk the same blood and seen the same lion.

Bluefeather explained in the note about the high-grade silver ore piled in the corner of his bedroom. He had made this heap of rock his retirement. He could hand-crush the ore and retort it down to silver ingots with a few chemicals and a blow torch as he had need for it. There was enough in the pile to take care of Artesimo for several years—if he was frugal.

Bluefeather thought of leaving his twenty-acre mining claim in the Black Range above the tiny village of Kingston to his godson, Brian Rousset, who had been adopted as an infant by Sherry. Then he changed his mind and decided not even to mention the claim, letting it revert to the forest service, which had owned it first. He had never patented it, but had simply turned in his yearly assessment.

Near Hillsboro, big copper companies had recently spent scores of millions of dollars core-drilling and building mills, but due to price fluctuations, they had left with nothing but the sad experience. The bonanza-hungry, the greedy, the simple fools, along with the stock promoters, had come and gone all the years Bluefeather had been plugging away here. A few had hit nice pockets of ore on occasion but had raped and ruined most of the tunnels.

He stared at the paper a moment before signing it. His dark eyes glistened out from a face that appeared to be chiseled from the hardest granite in the mountains, but the tiny smile was tender.

Bluefeather fixed himself a large breakfast of sourdough biscuits, sowbelly, and sorghum syrup. He ate ravenously and felt elated, younger, much younger. His old legs seemed suddenly solid beneath him. He marveled at how making the ultimate decision of freedom had restored his body and his spirit as well. A small miracle, maybe.

After the Cavern of Marvels expedition and completion, he had drifted south in the Sierra Madres of Old Mexico and then back to the Big Bend country of Texas, without anything but survival deposits. At the border town of Terlingua, he had made a small mercury strike. Then he had worked his way to Globe, Arizona, and panned a nice pocket of placer below a mountain of low-grade ore.

He spent several years wandering with his mules from Prescott, Arizona, down to the Superstition Mountains near Phoenix. Then he moved on over into southern New Mexico. He headquartered at Hillsboro, to be what he felt was an easy half-day's drive from Sherry— near enough to feel her presence but not to bother her. It seemed just the right distance. Any nearer than this and the old haunting of the Cavern of Marvels might have a chance to obsess them again. Anyway, he loved the wonderful diversity of such a small place. Besides, he had finally found the silver deposit—of the exact richness—that he desired.

Hillsboro was inhabited by a few retirees from larger towns and old prospectors, cowboys, and artists of various kinds. Bluefeather had decided that this village would be his last hometown.

All his "early life" friends, including most of his family members— at least the ones he knew personally—had long ago "crashed through" to other dimensions. Besides Sherry, Brian, Shia, and a few Hillsboro friends who were left from his younger days, he also had Tranquilino's son, Little Tranq, in Corrales. The last few years their visits had become fewer and fewer, but their thoughts of one another were projected many times a day across the mountains.

He had often gone to visit Sherry at what they still called Dolby's Ranch, spending a week or more at times. Even though it was an easy drive from Hillsboro to Sherry's place, they had both quit driving for themselves now. Nevertheless, they could have if they had wished to concentrate that much. They didn't. Brian was always glad to drive either direction whenever Sherry or Bluefeather wanted to visit. They cared deeply and enjoyed each other's company more than that of anyone else on earth.

Shia had long ago adapted to the upper world, making a fine and trusted companion for Sherry. She insisted on running the household and doing a lot of the cooking herself, which suited Sherry just fine.

Sherry's son, Brian, was now mature and capable of handling the ranch headquarters. Besides being general manager, he was also the gamekeeper. There was an abundance of elk, deer, bear, and mountain lion, along with saddle horses, pack mules, and donkeys.

Sherry had long ago set up the huge acreage in a trust as a summer camp for the Girl Scouts of America. Before the trust was signed, all trails and campsites, lakes and streams had been designated. One Mimbres ruin—with her help—had been excavated by the University of New Mexico and a small museum of its artifacts and history built near the site. The trust restricted any exploration for minerals or excavations of any kind. It was an unspoiled paradise of the wild for the young Girl Scouts of America.

Bluefeather's life was quiet and uncluttered now. He did have a favorite radio station that was devoted exclusively to classical music. He enjoyed this a lot, but he seldom used his television, read a newspaper, or talked on the telephone. All these things were mostly a waste to him, for his active mind was a private and very real television set, turning on, at will, a wild animal show, a mountain storm, Saturday night dances, or a mineral strike—and without having to touch a single button. He often thought of his young times, which were now the old times, and knew that these present happenings would soon be the old times, too.

He reread his beloved Jack London. He also read Cervantes, because miners constantly tilted at *unseen* windmills; Balzac, because he once rode a donkey across rough and barren land, for many terrible days of pain to his soft body, to buy a copper mine; and Twain, because he had loved miners and mules and had written about such courage and foolishness as this. The latter trait was sufficient for all-time respect from Bluefeather. Movement. Eternal.

He had, for many years, kept up a correspondence with his kin, but it had slowly dribbled away to nothing as his relations had died or forgotten. He knew they had been hurt at his "apartness" in the early years. He had told himself over and over, as he had wandered in his youth, that Italians had always been heavily family bound and that the Pueblo Indians had their clans hundreds, perhaps thousands, of years old, but he had been gone so long in other worlds that he could not bring himself to gather up his blood ancestry. He couldn't explain this to himself, much less his kin. Bluefeather's parts were all synchronized in *his* world, but they bent the wrong way to fit the dominant one that made up the rest of human existence. He would never forget Old Grinder deeming that he was just an American called "Blue."

Fifty-One

Bluefeather had learned long ago, through the experience of the desert and mountains, that mules are kinder, smarter, more enduring and more affectionate than horses and most other four-legged creatures of the world.

He yelled, "Haaa. Hooo," in greeting to the two brown mules. "Haaa, Nancy. Hooo, Mary." They walked up to him, with their delicate and evenly paced steps, as he poured the oats in a metal trough and stepped back to watch them dine. It always made him feel warm to see working animals enjoying their feed.

He mumbled a few unintelligible things to them and then said, "Ah, yes, my beautiful creatures with wings on top of your heads, eat heartily, for soon we make the final journey together."

They moved their long ears back and forth, acknowledging his familiar voice. Chewing, Mary raised her head and looked at Bluefeather with her wise and tender eyes.

Now he returned to the house and got the three, fist-sized pieces of rose quartz with the wire gold laced throughout like yellow metal worms. One was the rock his father-in-law, Ludwig Schmidt of Breen, Colorado, had first shown him that had started the search for the mine that destroyed their Miss Mary. The second specimen he and Miss Mary had dug from the vein of Ludwig's dream. The third was one he had saved in remembrance of the glory days at Harmony Creek.

He put them into a small canvas bag and walked toward the single business street of Hillsboro. He took his handwritten will along to get the two necessary witness signatures that would make it legal.

First he stopped by the post office and asked for his mail. He was relaxed and joyful at the same time. Sonya Rutledge, who had been here fifty years, looked in his box. She knew, and Bluefeather knew, there was little chance for mail. He thanked her and stood a moment. He wanted to tell her good-bye but didn't know how.

He said, "Looks like an early fall, Mrs. Rutledge."

She smiled and said it sure did.

"Mrs. Rutledge, would it be too much trouble to ask you to witness my will?"

"Of course not. I'd be happy to help you any way I can, Blue." She signed it after only a swift glance.

He thanked her, bid her a good day, and walked on down to Roy's Hillsboro Texaco station. The gas pumps were gone now. It was just a repair garage. Before the pumps had quit paying, he and his friend, Artesimo, would stop here for gas when they drove to Truth or Consequences, the county seat, to fish in Elephant Butte Lake and drink and dance on Saturday nights. All hoped for the gas pumps to return. It was a symbol of survival for this small town and thousands more like it across America.

Bluefeather was pleased to see his two rancher friends, Jimmy Bason and Sterling Roberts, here getting their pickups greased and the oil changed. They were teasing one another about a horse trade.

Sterling said, "Jimmy, you knew that old gray horse you traded me was stone deaf. He don't know 'whoa' from 'go.'"

Bason laughed and said, "Don't be blaming me. I tried to tell you that horse couldn't hear too good. You checked him out and thought you were stealing him."

Sterling said, "Well, he looks better than he performs."

"Hey, so do you."

Bluefeather had to pass through Bason's F-Cross Ranch to get to his mine. The rancher allowed this without question because he knew that Bluefeather left his camps so neat and clean a coyote would have trouble locating them. Bason was one of those people who would go a mile out of the way to pick up a loose scrap of paper or a soda can. He cared deeply for the land and its animals. He did not take lightly to fools defiling it even in the smallest manner.

Jimmy asked Bluefeather, "Hey, Blue, would you like a Coke before Sterling drinks them all?"

"No thanks, I'm saving room for a beer with Artesimo a little later." Again, he could think of no way to bid his friends farewell, so he just went to the restroom and then back down the street to Sue's Antique Shop to get the second signature on his will.

Sue Bason was Jimmy's ex-wife. She, like the post mistress, had always been especially nice to him, selling his rock specimens when he really needed a little cash. She greeted him when he walked in, although she was busy with a customer.

"What have you been up to these days, Blue?"

"Oh, the same old stuff. Managing to stay out of too much trouble."

"I'll be with you in a minute, Blue."

Sue was a fine watercolorist, and Bluefeather moved about the shop, looking at her paintings while she finished with her business.

When she had completed the sale and they were alone, Bluefeather asked her if she would witness his document. She did. He thanked Sue and presented her the gold-bearing rock.

She exclaimed, "Oh, Blue, this is truly a beauty. This is real gold, isn't it? How much should we ask for it?"

"No, no, Sue. This one is for you. This one is not for sale. It belongs only to you. It's a memento from my youth."

"I don't know what to say—except, of course, thank you. It's so lovely and..." Her eyes, as dark blue as Bluefeather's were black, beamed with pleasure and puzzlement, because the old prospector had already walked out and was angling across the street toward the S-Bar-X Saloon. Sue Bason stared after him and then back at her rock, sewn together by the gods with thick threads of gold.

Bluefeather walked on the flat ground with broad back and powerful arms moving jerkily sideways to keep his balance. Since he had spent most of his life straining over and through mountains of rocks, his slightly bowed legs were unsure on level ground, like an old sailor's.

Bluefeather knew it was almost noon and his friend Artesimo would be halfway through his first beer of the day. Coke Jandro, owner and sometimes dispenser of drinks, was behind the bar. It smelled of spilled whiskey, tobacco, and ancient dreams. There was a traveling salesman and a local retiree from Santa Fe sitting at the long bar.

Bluefeather, unlike Artesimo, had quit most of his drinking ten, maybe fifteen years ago. Well, at the annual Apple Festival on Labor Day weekend he had kicked over the wagon, and sometimes on the Fourth of July and Christmas he'd have a few toddies, but, of course, that didn't count as regular drinking. Today, though, he ordered a Mexican beer—Corona. He raised the bottle in a toast: "Here's to Hillsboro, New Mexico, the greatest one-bar, one-church town in the world."

Jandro said, "You're only half right, Blue. The S-Bar-X is Hillsboro's country club and family entertainment center."

Artesimo, or Arty, as his friends called him, said, "Hey, Amigo, whatcha do, find the mother lode?"

Bluefeather took a pull at the Corona, wiped his mouth, placed the canvas bag on the bar, and stretched the drawstrings open. He said, "See for yourself, feller."

Coke Jandro, the bartender, and Arty Gomez, the prospector, were impressed. They were also instantly curious as to the location of such a find. Finally, Bluefeather broke through their mesmerized state and presented them each with a precious rock. The actual feel and sight of the snaking gold intertwined in the quartz pulled them back from the sudden dream world. Reality.

Coke stuttered his thanks. Arty caressed the rock and slapped Bluefeather on the back. The gesture said it all.

He must leave the young friend—the dispenser of relief to the walkers and dreamers of mountains. He must leave his old friend, with whom he had shared the secrets of the earth for so many decades. There was no stopping now. The last great call had possessed him. He must heed. He must.

The bartender set the drinks out, saying, "On the house, for sure," and went back to turning in his hands the rose-colored rock containing twisted treasure.

Arty took his prospector's glass out and studied the magnified beauty of his gift.

Now was the right moment. Bluefeather walked to the jukebox and put all his change in it. He punched a mixture of country tunes and popular love songs. He walked out the back door and wound around the old buildings toward his home. The sound of the music faded with each step. The images of his friends blurred. He felt the irresistible pull of the final act.

He walked determinedly to his home. A van was parked there in front. It was Sherry's son, Brian, sitting on his front porch. This was a discord. As much as he loved his godson, he was messing up Bluefeather's life before his imminent death. Brian walked toward him, smiling. They gave each other an embrace.

"Sorry it took me so long, Blue, but I had to wrap up a bunch of things for mother."

Then it dawned on Bluefeather that Brian had called a couple of days ago, saying he would be over to pick him up to drive him for a visit with Sherry.

Bluefeather recovered quickly, saying, "We're always causing you problems, son."

"No problem. Mother had everything in good shape as usual. Just wants to see you. Hey, you're looking ten years younger, Blue. What have you been doing, taking extra-strength vitamins?"

"It's all the dirty, sinful living I've been doing."

They both had a little chuckle.

Bluefeather put his toiletries in a small leather bag, took a change of clothing from the closet, and said, "Hey, young'un, we're wasting time standing around here."

Bluefeather always enjoyed the drive to Sherry's. It had both mountains and desert. The van purred smoothly around the curves. Brian was a careful driver and didn't talk so much that he interrupted Bluefeather's musings at "that" mountain, "that" canyon, "that" heavy stand of junipers, all of which he had been on or in.

They rode relaxed, comfortable, and caring. Brian was enjoying it as much as the old man. He had always looked up to Bluefeather as a best friend, an uncle, and a father. Bluefeather had taken Brian on his first prospecting and fishing trips, his first country dance, and had taught him what all the wild animals and plants mean to each other and humankind. He had done more, much more, for him, including kicking his butt a couple of times when he had gotten out of line with his mother.

Shia, with the slanted eyes of mysterious loyalty, served Sherry and Bluefeather out on their favorite terrace. They sipped comfortably, looking across the valley to the long rows of Girl Scout cabins half hidden by trees. When Shia served the meal, Brian left the two of them alone to eat and visit. He went to help his permanent crew winterize the scouts' compound. The last of the girls had left for home and school only a couple of weeks ago. Shia, too, politely vanished back into the house.

It was a delicious meal of pasta and a special Italian wine. Bluefeather rejoiced that he had given Shia his grandmother Fellini's recipe for the greatest of all pasta sauces. They had benefited often from this little bit of sharing.

Bluefeather tasted the wine, saying, "Shia hasn't aged a month in the last twenty years. She's caught that look of perpetual youth from you, Sherry."

"Ah, you old flatterer. Don't you know I've caught on to you after all we've shared through the years? But...don't misunderstand, I still love to hear it. And I'm sure Shia will tremble in delight when I quote your words to her."

"It's true. It's true or I'd never say it." He changed the subject. "What is the standing situation on Shia and Bob Miller? Are they still engaged?"

"Yes. They're actually going to finalize the marriage next month."

"My gosh, what's the rush? They've only been engaged nine years."

The Bob Miller in Shia's life was the principal of Meanwhile's high school. He was a widower with a seven-year-old daughter and ten-year-old son who were in effect, if not by blood, treated like Sherry's grandchildren. Sherry adored them and used every excuse, and considerable cunning, to get Shia to bring them to stay with them every feasible chance. She even spoke of them as her grandchildren. Bluefeather was happy to feel her happiness at the upcoming marriage.

Her black eyes beamed as she said, "Brian is getting pretty 'thick' himself, with a nurse from El Paso. He spends at least two weekends a month down there and they've worn the phone lines to shreds."

"Do you like her?"

"I adore her. She's pretty, practical, and, even better, she genuinely loves Brian and she seems to like Shia and me, as well."

They talked on quietly, relaxing in their pleasure of family gossip. For they were all family, cast together from many winds. The night came and chilled them. Inside the great house Shia had prepared a crackling piñon fire in the fireplace to greet them. Soon they were both nodding off and went to bed.

The next morning, Bluefeather hugged Shia and then held Sherry to his breast for a full minute. Each could feel the other's heart beating. They never said good-bye to one another but the old man could not help glancing back one last time to see the two figures, Sherry and Shia standing arm in arm, staring after him as Brian drove him away and over the mountains to Hillsboro for the last time. He was a happy old man tinged with a touch of soon-discarded sadness.

As they got out of the van, Brian said, "Come here, Blue, if you please." Bluefeather followed the young man around the vehicle. He opened the back doors and there in a box were four shiny, silvery, metallic cylinders about eighteen inches long and ten inches in diameter.

At Bluefeather's puzzled look, Brian said, "Don't ask me what they are. I'm just following mother's orders. There's a sealed envelope in the box." He picked it up and carried it in the house for Bluefeather. They both stared down at the objects on the floor. Then they locked eyes for just an instant, embraced again, and embarrassedly, Brian said, "I've got a lot to do, Blue. I'm going on down to El Paso and see my girlfriend, since I'm nearly there anyway. Sorry we can't have a visit. Maybe in a little while you can come back over and stay longer with us. Huh?"

Bluefeather also felt perplexed at being so impolite that he didn't insist on Brian staying for coffee, at least.

Brian yelled out the open window of the van, "Be seeing you soon, Blue. Take care now."

"Yes . . . yeah, soon, son."

How could he tell him that he had never been worth a damn at good-byes anyway? Even as he picked up the sealed letter and moved to his cluttered desk for an opener, he felt as if his only son were driving away for good and he hadn't even protested. This thought vanished as he both expectantly and fearfully opened the letter. He put on his over-the-counter reading glasses and sat down to read:

Dear Blue,

We have long shared a great glory. It is all contained in the notebooks in these time capsules. You, of course, know about the little notebooks that are more than my blood. I'm told that these capsules will last millions of years. Dear, dear, Blue, please forgive me for leaving the awesome responsibility of their destiny in your adroit hands and heart. I weakened at last. I simply cannot make the final decision regarding their disposition.

I've finally been at peace and happy these last few years except for what's contained in the notebooks and what it took to fill them. Soon, now, I'll have Shia and Bob's children as my own grandchildren. It is unfair, the way you've always taken care of me, to leave the burden of this knowledge to your judgment alone. I'm doing it anyway. Whatever you decide will never be questioned by me. I love you and will do so forever.

Sherry

He sat staring at the single last page, last words from Sherry Rousset. Then he looked at the containers so shiny, so permanent, containing the most powerful thing in earthy existence—knowledge. Knowledge of riches, of stars, of the beginning of life, and maybe the means to stop it from being destroyed or the catalyst to launch its doom. What a pitiful thing that humans were such that this wonder had to be questioned and concealed at all. It had only been a few decades since there had been nine billion passenger pigeons in America. Now there were none. Not one. It caused Bluefeather to ponder seriously where the possible effects of this additional awareness would lead.

Bluefeather said aloud, "Aw, shitfire, why did all these smarts have to come along and mess up a person's life? He had felt, a few hours earlier, the peace of final decision, and now he had been handed a judgment to make that only the Great Spirit should be asked to even contemplate. There was no use dwelling on what might have been. He was into what *is*. He and Sherry had certainly done that when they had closed the only known entrance to the Cavern of Marvels with Mr. Nobel's invention. He simply had to decide what in holy hell to do with the most precious of all treasures. His decision alone. Simple? Sure it was.

Fifty-Two

It had been just a year ago that his compadre, Artesimo Gomez, had driven him to Albuquerque. He hadn't been there for twenty-five years and had been filled with both fear and exultation.

Bluefeather had a special purpose for the trip. He wanted to go to a used bookstore and look for volumes he'd missed by Colette, Joyce Cary, and Alberto Moravio. They were among his favorites now.

Artesimo had been born there in the suburb of Corrales, not far from where Bluefeather had once lived and loved. This had given them a special association. The trip was simply a fine excuse to please his friend and look up Little Tranq.

They stopped at the Owl Bar in the village of San Antonio for one of their famous green chile hamburgers. Each had a bottle of Corona to wash it down properly. They moved on northward on Interstate 40, feeling pretty damn good. Then Bluefeather became disoriented right on the freeway. Everything looked so different to him. Houses and franchises had proliferated in such abundance that the landscape of the old man's memory was shattered. He slid lower and lower in the seat, trying to block out the fearful view. Arty tried to talk him into some form of acceptance, but it didn't work.

When they got to Little Tranq's rambling adobe home in Corrales, Bluefeather finally overcame some of his fear of the city. The Rio Grande was only a football field away, and the trees of the *bosque* hid everything to the east except the majestic crown of the Sandia Mountains.

He had longed to see his old home next door, but now he had a hard time looking at it. It was the same but different as well. The house and barns were smaller than he remembered but the trees and bushes much larger. As soon as his mind-vision showed him a glowing Marsha working in the garden, he turned away and never looked again.

They stayed the night. They talked of old times in old familiar spots. A great meal of chile, tortillas, and homemade wine in his honor caused Bluefeather to relax. It gave him much pleasure. He was astounded each time at how much Little Tranq and his wife reminded him of Tranquilino and his wife, Tina.

The next morning, he could hardly wait to go to Old Town to start their shopping. Arty noticed Bluefeather shoving his feet almost through the floor of the car and grabbing at the dash with sweating palms as the traffic increased.

He walked stiffly around the Old Town Plaza, sticking so close to Arty that they were constantly tripping and bumping into one another. Bluefeather didn't find his books there, but he was told where he might.

Arty patiently made the drive and, after successfully making his purchases, Bluefeather immediately insisted that they drive around the massive Sandia Mountains. As always, the mountains were his refuge. He could think of nothing else that would ease the terror that was stabbing at his body. The enormity of the apprehension that numbed his mind and soul was indescribable.

Arty drove east on Interstate 40, ever closer to the mountains, and he talked of it to his friend. "Ah, amigo, how fortunate these city dwellers are to have the forests and the coolness so near the city. Ah, yes, it is still untouched higher up."

Bluefeather Fellini was having none of this consolation talk. He saw the tract houses pushing at both sides of the freeway like the pincer movement of a mighty army. "My God," he said, "what has happened to the world since I was here? Only twenty-five years ago there were still large patches of space all around and now it seems that all the people of the world have huddled together and covered all the virgin hills with concrete." He forced words out like the irresistible desire to mask the pain of a throbbing boil. "Turn off, Arty. Turn off here. Drive to the mountain."

Arty said, "I thought you wanted to go all the way around them."

"No, I've changed my mind. Please turn off at the first exit. I want to look at it here...here on its western slopes. I prospected here when I was a young man. I slept here on her sides for many nights with the deer and the bear."

Artesimo pulled off at the Tramway exit. In a little while he had wound through an area of beautifully designed homes in the foothills of the Sandias.

"Stop. Stop right here," Bluefeather shouted, his voice loud and quivering.

Gomez pulled over near the end of a cul-de-sac. They could see between the houses and up a canyon for perhaps a quarter of a mile that was still free of development.

"See, way up there? See? That's the way it was. The way it all was, Arty. It was like that all the way up to the tall timber and all the way over the east side to the prairies. See?"

Arty looked and could no longer hide his own feelings for the benefit of his friend. He sighed and settled back in his seat, letting go of the steering wheel and allowing his gaze to wander with Bluefeather's across the hundreds of houses, streets, and the automobiles parked by them and constantly moving to and from them. Then they talked the real truth as real friends must.

Bluefeather said, with a voice that came from thousands of years back, "They are building the city on the only mountain they have. Don't they know that the mountains make all our precious rivers? Don't they care?"

Arty Gomez agreed. "Sad to say the destructive developers are way out ahead of the dutiful defenders of the soil, old amigo."

"*Si*, my amigo, the promoters are leading the preservationists by many lengths...and...and the finish line is near. They are shitting in the bears' front yard."

The two old friends sat a while, silently looking at the brave mountain and its afflictions.

Suddenly, Bluefeather laughed. "Ha, we sit here and preach to one another alone like we are full of wisdom. You know what I think we're full of? Huh? Huh? We should be at Elephant Butte Lake fishing, but first, before we start for home, let's swing by the Indian Cultural Center and see if by chance some of my relatives from the Taos Pueblo might be there exhibiting some work. You never can tell."

Gomez was delighted at the sudden, courageous change in his friend's attitude and drove down from the foothills of the mountain toward the center of the city, toward the Pueblo Indian Cultural Center. They enjoyed the exhibits, but there was nothing there done by Bluefeather's family.

They didn't look back at the mountain then and they didn't look at it as they drove south toward the state's largest lake for some bass fishing and then on home to the wonderfully small, lost little paradise of Hillsboro, New Mexico.

■　■　■

Fifty-Three

Bluefeather moved out in front of the mules almost straining beyond his reach. The voice of the town became weaker with each step. With each step he was nearer his true home—the hills. Up there somewhere was a secluded spot where he could die as he pleased without interference from the town. No one could force him to tell stories that belonged only to him...tales that he alone could understand.

Old Bluefeather had lived as he wanted. Surely then he could die as he wanted. He had expected a lot from this world and had done much to return its favors. And all he asked now was a hidden spot of hard earth on which to lay his head and depart. What was the use of being buried in a fenced-in plot, causing trouble and pain? He would offer his body to the coyotes. They could make a meal of him and have strength for several hunts. Yes, he would give himself gladly to those singers of the night who had been his partners for these many decades. Partners they were, for they too had scratched their breath and sustenance from these lonely hills. He knew that they were the true contact between man and the animal world.

He felt no pain. His heart still pumped his blood with some strength, and though his legs were stiff and very old, they kept him upright. Still, it was his time, and like a gut-shot wolf he hunted his home. There it was out ahead...dry, washed, worn, cruel. It was his. That was the difference.

He stopped after a while. The mules stopped. They grazed about in the thin patches of grass as Bluefeather looked back. He had made better time than he thought. It was about noon and the paved road splitting the historic village looked narrow and fragile. He could see the trucks. He could hear the trucks. The endless drone that spoke of things he could be no part of. Maybe by nightfall he would be free of their sounds.

He was on the bottom slope of Mount Dubois, named after a noted roper, Frank Dubois, who was also secretary of agriculture for the state of

New Mexico. It was five miles northwest of Hillsboro near Percha Creek on Jimmy Bason's F-Cross Ranch. The mountain stood almost alone, like a huge female breast. It was scattered with cedar, juniper, and blue grama grass. A good place to camp. He had done so many times before. Just behind it the mountains would become steeper, rougher, and there in the pack was a problem he was trying to forget—Sherry's time capsules. In spite of his efforts against it, his mind wandered back down Dubois mountain to the history of Hillsboro—a minor part of it his own.

For well over a century, Hillsboro had been a running, yelling, stump-jumping town. After the first strike of silver and then gold, it had roared like a fresh-trapped cougar. From the Bridal Chamber Tunnel alone the miners had taken two and a half million in silver in just one year.

Bluefeather recalled making many pleasurable trips the twenty miles south from Hillsboro to Lake Valley. He would stop just past the Berrenda Four A Ranch sign and move carefully along the east slope of the foothills west of the road until he found the proper spot. He could see the Bridal Chamber mine portal and the railroad bed where miners had actually driven the train inside the tunnel and dug the ore directly into the cars. From his favorite spot he had been able to see the little town and the school and to the right the graveyard on the hill. He could see almost to Skeleton Canyon, where the Apaches had lured a bunch of drunken miners, ambushed, and slaughtered them. He would often imagine himself as a youth working in the Bridal Chamber Mine, where the silver ore was so rich it often had to be sawed. He worked, he danced, he fought, and he loved here just as he had actually done in real life. Silver. It had taken silver to pull him away from the haunting of gold. And the Bridal Chamber was the richest silver mine in the world for a long time. The ghosts of the mine and Lake Valley helped and succored him.

Certainly, many infamous people had lived at Hillsboro. Albert Fall, who had been secretary of the interior in 1921, was one example. He had been mostly responsible for the teapot dome scandal that rocked the nation. And then there was Toppy Johnson's slaughterhouse headquartered on what is now the F-Cross Ranch—so aptly named because of the number of competing rustlers that were butchered there along with the cattle. There was Sadie Orchard, a madam, a dead-shot gun woman, and owner of a stagecoach line. Sheba Hurst, one of the men who had inspired Mark Twain's *Roughing It*, had come to the area.

He was buried a few miles west at the tiny town of Kingston. Later, a Colonel Bradley, who called Hillsboro home, owned horses that won the Kentucky Derby four times. Oh, there had been scores here who made names all across the West and the nation. It was amazing to him still that so many big things had emanated from such a tiny town. Even now, sometimes on a Saturday night, the miners, cowboys, artists, and a few adventurous tourists blew a little wild at the welcoming S-Bar-X Saloon and burrito joint.

But all history was done for Bluefeather Fellini. He'd made a little history himself here, but its sight and sound slowly faded away like a soft breeze in a deep canyon. His vision was far over the mountain ahead.

The packs on the mules should have been light, but the metal containers had changed that. Soon he would free them of their burdens and turn them loose. They, too, could roam free and unmolested. But he would need them for a while yet.

"Haaa, Mary. Hooo, Nancy. Let's move out." The burros raised their heads and followed, their sharp, black hoofs pitching tiny balls of dust at each step.

It had been a damned good and exciting life. That was for sure an understatement. He had enjoyed its various pleasures. The drinks, the tender women, the feasting, the dice tables—they had been his, and more. But it had always been the call of the hills and the search for the days of little wind that had meant the most. It had been but a blink with fog-filled eyes.

Those sunken, black eyes pierced out beyond the sharp, eroded cheekbones to the land ahead. The great red and white mesas' edges cropped up in the distance here and there. On beyond, the high ridges of mountains called like ancient beasts.

He watched the buzzards circle off to the right. Would they find him before the coyotes? He hoped not. It was a chance he would take.

What had started this search of his so long ago? What had kept him at it without fail? Was it the gold? He mumbled to himself. Was it just the gold? He couldn't answer that. He had tried a thousand times to answer that and probably had, but he simply could not remember the result of his questioning. It didn't matter now. He had been young when he started. How old? Just a kid from the mines at Trinidad. It didn't matter. He had been strong then, and he had been strong for years after. He felt strong right now, purposefully so.

Before his first strike he had had other moments. That was for sure. He had dug and panned nine hundred dollars worth of gold one summer so far past. When a hundred dollars was three-months' living. What had the woman said? "We can start a business of our own. You can settle down. You can sleep in a feather bed each and every night. You can possess my body and my heart." Something like that.

How pretty she had made it sound. What was her name? Nancy? Mary? Both? Of course. That's why every burro or mule he'd owned, no matter the sex, had been either Mary or Nancy. His mind was much sharper than this. Why was he forgetting all these things? Did his slow gain in altitude make him grow denser? What did it matter?

He tired now. What used to be foothills suddenly seemed like mighty mountains to his old legs. He hadn't looked back for a long time. He would not look back until the night was upon him. It came swiftly and all at once. He knew that the sky had been filled earlier with gold lights, but he could not make himself look. He could see a good open camping spot above.

Now he shouted words to encourage the mules and himself. "Haaa, Mary. Hooo, Nancy. You listen now with much care because I'm gonna tell you a great truth."

The mules stepped on faster, ears working back and forth as they certainly heard their long-time partner.

"Your great, great grandfather many times over was the burro who carried the Mother of Christ on his back while she carried the Son of God in her belly. Step with pride. Haaa. Hooo." They all three raced the night uphill with inspired strides, painfully bellowing lungs, and hard-drumming hearts.

He gathered some wood and built a fire. They were still some distance from the high timber of the mountains. He was warm from the blaze now. He fried the bacon and took the hard sourdough bread into himself with little taste. It was merely to sustain him until he reached his goal.

He felt, and heard, the whish of the night owl's wings at about the time his old friend gave voice. The coyote sang to Bluefeather. He told in his lonely wail of the Marys and the Nancys, of other warm firesides. He talked to Bluefeather of the things he missed; but even more he spoke to him of the things he had found, those things that only the coyote and

Bluefeather could understand. Then again, Bluefeather allowed himself to think of the four metal containers in the panniers filled with Sherry's words of observation, study, and soul. He stared and stared. They were right there—imprisoned. Only he could turn them loose to spread across the globe . . . like what? He didn't dare ask the Great Spirit for help yet. He didn't even call on his representative, Dancing Bear. He, the American called Bluefeather, must make the terrible—or hallowed—decision alone. It was hanging around his neck like log chains.

Now Bluefeather looked and listened downward again. There it still was, the lonesome drone of the mighty trucks. He was not nearly far enough into the hills. It would take another day at least. Maybe two. He could see the tiny, flickering lights from the village below. They looked like a small cluster of earthbound stars.

He had long ago learned that war was hard work, but he had never thought simple dying could be so difficult. Everybody did it. No exceptions.

Bluefeather slept little that night. He lay in his blanket and stared and felt the earth throb beneath him. This earth was his. It was his mother, his father, his brother. It was his love. He craved to have it devour him. But he must live the night out and move on beyond those lights and noises below. He must decide the undecidable for Sherry, somehow.

It was the longest night of his life. But occasionally the coyote kept him company, crying into the darkness from one valley, then the next, raising his head atop the hills and voicing his great concern for those who sleep alone on the high desert mountains.

Fifty-Four

For the first time in years, Bluefeather's ancient and fading eyes saw the deer before the mules heard it. It was a Coues deer. They are much smaller—a miniature version of the whitetail that also roams the mountains west of Hillsboro. The little deer, not much larger than an average-size dog, poised on an up-slope, looking back at them. Somehow the deer knew the man and his mules would not harm him. He held the elegant pose, as if frozen in a painting, until the trio moved from his sight around a cut bank.

A couple of blue jays flickered across an opening and landed. They stared down from a scrubby pine at the travelers, chattering as if in a heavy discussion with the entire forest about the whys and whats of the menagerie of three moving slowly but ever higher.

Now the acuteness of Bluefeather's observation lapsed back in dream-walking. His old muscles were relieved for a time from their natural aches by the anesthesia of his mind-pictures of the past.

He saw his parents and the entire family, cousins, uncles, aunts—the Italian family—on a running, playing, laughing, eating, drinking picnic near Raton and Dawson. Then he was fly fishing in Taos Pueblo Creek, halfway between the mighty adobe structures and the sacred mountain. The dancing, sparkling water was talking to him, telling where he could catch the fighting, native, brown trout. He was filling the banks with them and wishing this was a real night dream, for catching big trout was a sign of upcoming fine fortune if you saw it in your sleep.

Now he was with the gringo, Grinder, in a Taos lounge. This time there was no fight. They drank beer so cold one could only stay warm by leaping up and dancing, dancing on into warmth, keeping ahead of the coldness of the beer. Then he was eating a huge plate of the finest chile *rellenos* ever made. The smoke from the fireplace only enhanced the taste of the food and the entertainment value of the beer in his blood. A treasure of a time they were having. And then there were Nancy and Mary, and bloody battles, and hot deserts, and cold mountains he walked over and sometimes right through.

When he sensed the slight tensing of the mules at the narrowness of the real trail they were on, the kaleidoscope faded away and he saw and heard the flashing black and white flight of the magpie, and its piercing cry brought him back to his true task of climbing safely upward toward his final adventure.

He felt the ache of bones and the worn muscles tied to them again. He had no choice, it seemed, but to go back to Miss Mary with the hair that had fire in it. At the first perception of her swimming naked in Harmony Creek, he vanished it. The time was not ready for these sorts of visions. Later, it would be fine to look back—after he had made his decision about the metal capsules. As he had packed the mules back in Hillsboro for his departure, he had thought of giving the capsules to the archaeology department at University of New Mexico or maybe to his old school, New Mexico Tech, at Socorro. He thought maybe he should place them in the archives at UTEP, the University of Texas at El Paso, to be opened in ten, fifty, a hundred, or a thousand years. His experiences in the Cavern of Marvels had made known that this much clock time was nothing—not even a single breath. Would humankind have changed enough in that time to deserve and use the priceless information properly? How could he believe it? What should he do? Had ever a man been handed such a terrifying trust? Why did it have to be him? Well, it was him. So? So, he had to resolve the dastardly dilemma somehow in order to "crash through" in peace and possible joy. Bluefeather dropped the forbidding thoughts and decided his old legs needed a rest.

He and the mules came upon the spring. How could he have forgotten the location of such an invaluable source of water here in the high desert mountains? It was only an hour past noon, but he pitched camp, such as it was: simply his blankets, oats for the mules, and a little food for himself.

He averted his eyes from the alluring containers for now. Hellsfire, why was he in such a rush to his final passing on? He and his two partners might as well enjoy the early autumn sun and go on tomorrow refreshed and rested. There was an inviting shelf of grass against a rock bluff facing south.

He watered the mules and buckled the *morrals* full of oats over their muzzles. Later, he would let them graze in a little grassy meadow below. He splashed his face. The friendly sun equalized the chill from the spring's cold water. He had a little to eat and for the first time in years got out his old pipe and tobacco.

As he leaned back against the warm rocks and gazed across the seemingly endless, isolated landscape, he lit the pipe and laughed, talking to anything that might be listening. "I wonder if this tobacco is gonna kill me before I go to meet the Great Spirit." He was surprised at what an instant dizziness the dried plant gave his body after a couple more puffs. He knocked the tobacco out of the pipe and mashed the fire away. That had been his first smoke, except for medicine-making ceremonies, in many years, and it would be his last here on this particular earth.

Bluefeather felt good the way he was so easily and rapidly shedding earthly habits and accoutrements. Things that had seemed so bad— seemed so critically necessary—were truly mostly meaningless after all. He was so relaxed that he dozed with his eyes half closed.

It amazed the old man how, right here, so near the end, his memory-diary was suddenly so vivid again. The gallery that held the portrait of his beloved Miss Mary was always open whenever he wished and followed him about as open as an angel's arms and as intimate as his shadow. He dozed, and she came smiling to him in his dreams, as well. In spite of his reluctant vows. He welcomed her with permanent pleasure.

Fifty-Five

The old man was bent like the hook on a chain hoist as he slumbered astride the mule. The path was narrow and the Nancy mule followed behind, taking careful, even delicate, steps. The drop-off to the left was steep.

Bluefeather Fellini did not purposely start recalling the great World War. The first year after his return, he had cringed at every sudden noise, a few times dropping to the floor or street for cover, getting back up embarrassed and glancing around to see who watched him. He had also spent many nights trying to burrow through the mattress away from the eighty-eight shells of his dreams and the machine guns of his imagination. Just the same, they were as real to him as the taste of his tongue. But soon he gradually put it away, and it only returned a few times during each of his many surviving years.

He felt the mule Mary stop and his senses shifted from the hedgerows of France to the mountains west of Hillsboro as suddenly as his aged brain would allow. In spite of Nancy's care, a part of trail rock cracked at the weight of Blue and Mary. It simply dropped out from under Nancy. Instead of attempting to reach for the earth with her two hooves on the falling side, she had miraculously whirled with one foot solid and pushed herself so she was facing down the slope with her forefeet out in front and her hind legs tucked so far under her belly that her hindquarters were dragging. Without this instant reaction she would probably have tumbled over and over, crippling herself permanently, destroying and scattering the contents of the pack as well. Mary did not bolt but held the trail and turned her head toward the noise just as Bluefeather had. Nancy went on down the slope, dangerously gaining speed until it curved out into a much gentler grade. She still had to run a piece to hold her footing, charging between twin pines. The space was too narrow for her to pass through with the pack on her back. She was jammed there with a very sudden stop.

Bluefeather was looking at her, and then at the slope, trying to find a safe place to crawl down to dislodge her. Then he decided he had better ride down, as it might take the combined strength of both him and Mary to free her. He could see the tops of the canisters gleaming in the sun.

Finally, up ahead, he found a nice round ridge sloping toward Nancy at an angle that was safe to ride. As they moved toward her, Bluefeather saw that she struggled mightily to get on through the trap. No go. She stopped without any movement except her ears. Then, just as they were about to reach her, Nancy solved her own problem. She easily, as if it was the most natural of actions, simply backed out and waited calmly, ready to follow them back up to the trail before they reached her.

Bluefeather looked up into the sky as straight as his tired body would allow and said, "Thank you, oh Great One, for the company of your most majestic invention—the mule."

Soon they were back on the trail, moving on upward to Bluefeather's final destination. Damn it. He had, just yesterday, occasion ally started thinking way, way back to the Normandy hedgerows. As unpleasant as it was, he would rather think about the near destruction of the whole world all day long than think a single second on the rocky demise of his beloved Miss Mary of Breen, Colorado.

Now it was taking the images of Miss Mary to draw him away from conjectures about the time tubes. He would think of one of his other loves, the mines, the veins in them, and the float rock that often led to their hard-to-get booty.

Three thousand years or so ago, the first humans like him had started mining copper on Cyprus, with the help of what were to become metallurgists. They had mixed different metals to make arms to hunt wild animals for food and to protect their families from pillaging and death from competitors. Finally, printer's type had been made from miner's metals to record the whole movement of the human race—which might not have survived at all without metal swords, spear points, and machinery in a land of huge beasts and great natural disasters. The human race had held on precariously. Its ultimate existence, survival, and history itself came from minerals. Nor could anyone lay the blame on the diggers for the recent defiling of the earth. Greed had become boss of the mine workers and the whole earth. Greed. Bluefeather was proud to have been a considerate miner. Whether one liked it or not, without the ore diggers, the jaguar would be president of Mexico, Central, and South America; the lion would reign as the ruler of all Africa; the wolf would hold, along with a wildly trumpeting elephant, sovereignty over most of Asia; and the grizzly bear would rule unopposed as the monarch of North America.

Fifty-Six

The shock of the near loss of mule Nancy from the trail caving in under her had tired old Bluefeather Fellini early this day. For the second time since they had left Hillsboro—seeking the right place to die—he quit in mid-afternoon and pitched camp. His eyes were hurting in their sockets, trying to stare past Sherry's containers.

He found a reasonably level spot against a bluff facing southwest. He would have the sun here, as well as a breeze. He leaned back. It was the time of half-vision. But today it did not work; he went on past the vision stage into a warm, comfortable sleep with just ordinary dreams.

He was back in Raton, playing hide and seek with two of his friends at the age of six, both joyous and frightened because the next day he was to start school. Of course, his fears would turn out in real life to be unfounded, because his mother had already taught him to read, and that had put him way up on the other students.

As he dreamed of his childhood, he was being carefully observed from a bluff. Across the meadow, scattered with timber of spruce and large ponderosa pines, a mountain lion lay watching him through a thin bush. There was no malice. She was just being cautious because her den and three cubs were only a short distance around the edge of the bluff. They were at the age of concern for her—big enough to feel adventurous and at the same time small and inexperienced, making them vulnerable to eagles, bears, and man.

She licked at one paw, sore from leaping onto a pile of boulders the day before at a three-year-old deer. The deer had felt her presence while she was in midair and had leapt aside so that she only scraped its sides lightly with this sore paw. Having missed, she had whirled in midair to maintain pursuit, jamming the paw into a rock, catapulting down the rough slope after the needed prey. She caught the deer from behind, hurling it over a ten-foot drop. Twisting back violently again, she had dropped down on the young buck's back just as it regained its feet, hooking her claws deep where the shoulders joined the neck, sinking fangs where the skull joined the first vertebra. It was over in a roll.

She feasted and brought her cubs to dine. Then she dragged the carcass up higher and nearer their den, covering it with brush. An hour later, she suckled her cubs and listened to the meat digest in her stomach. The end of her tail switched now and then as she licked her bruises. She had decided the man and his mules presented no danger. She stared now out of curiosity—safe, full, and secure about her cubs.

Right around the corner, in a hollow of a great ponderosa pine, a spotted owl had listened to the mules' hooves and had taken a peek, staring from the darkness at the camp. Watching. Just watching.

Farther up on the cliff, forming a half circle of animals around Bluefeather, a red-tailed hawk watched the camp's inhabitants only casually. Its eyes, strong as a telescope, searched for other things. Its head moved as slightly as its feathers that occasionally lifted in the southwestern breeze.

A lizard watched from a four-inch space under a rocky ledge ten feet from Bluefeather's sleeping body. Yesterday the hawk had dived at it here, missing the lizard by a fraction of an inch as it leapt to safety. The hawk was not dismayed. It simply waited for another chance.

In a smaller, new-growth pine, a tufted-eared gray squirrel peeked from around the trunk of the tree, observing the camp, the hawk, and the presence of the lion. Suddenly, it chattered in defiance, the sound breaking across the silent foothills and ledges as a shattering intrusion. The hawk moved its head an unseen bit. The spotted owl lifted a leg and then dropped it. The lion twitched the end of her tail three times in succession. The lizard jerked its eternally tense body around half an inch, and the mules grazed on, flicking one ear each toward the noise.

One part of Bluefeather's mind was hiding a fact from the other. He was delaying the once-relished trip of finality because of the quandary, the duty, of what to do with the containers of precious notebooks.

He woke up refreshed, stood up stiffly, stretched his tightened old muscles, took a drink from the canteen and, before cooking his supper, spoke to the mules.

"Haaa, little darlings, isn't it wonderful to be in the wilderness again? Huh? Huh? Just the three of us all alone?"

They were all three rested and decided to climb another mile before making camp for the night. He felt the nearness of a long-favorite stopping place.

Now the old man looked up ahead expectantly. Yes, that was the rock formation he had anticipated. He wanted to camp here near the rock ruins of an ancient Mimbres hunting campsite because it had a large, bubbling spring. He was sure the waterhole had been active and used way back then, in the time of the Indian tribe's existence. This spot also gave them an almost three-hundred-and-sixty-degree observation point.

He staked the mules so they could reach the water but not disturb the ruin. The outline of the single rock camp house was clear. It had been about half underground and half above to give the maximum protection from both the temperature and any enemy. The upper half had caved in, filling the lower part centuries before. Even so, he could always find pieces of pottery and a few flint objects as the rain and wind revealed them. It would be at least an hour before the sun temporarily yielded its power over to the night.

"Look here, Miss Mary, sweet Nancy. Look here, where they camped and hunted maybe a thousand years before us. There were no motor sounds to make the deer and elk retreat to the most hidden spots. Now, even the bear, mountain lions, and coyotes quiver and spend more time watching for intruders than they do hunting for themselves. They didn't have precious pardners like you ladies to help with the burdens of carrying their necessities. No—just their own backs and shoulders. Listen, and you can hear their music, their singing. Hear? Hear? Ahhh haaa. I can feel them as well. Yes, they are here with us, and I can tell they wish us well, for we have no desire to defile their domain."

Old man Bluefeather spotted about an inch of pottery sticking out of the mountain soil. He bent down casually to pick it up. It broke the shallow dirt for about five inches around. He lifted it from the earth, surprised by its size. He carefully hand brushed it and, to his pleasure, saw that the drawing on it was part of a howler monkey. There was no doubt. He had only seen this once before, so long ago, back there in the Mimbres cave of the dead, with Sherry, Marsha, and Pack.

He sat down on the edge of the ruins and stared at the shard. He slipped into half-vision, seeing many things. Hearing and feeling The

Unholy again and the battle of the screechers, and now The Section walked sore, wounded, but with great relief, toward their first look at God's Castle and all the Olders and Youngers.

Fifty-Seven

It was almost noon the next day before the stiffness left his legs. He could no longer roam these hills of home. It only proved how right he was to make this final decision. Just a little more now and he would be finished—his long, fast run would be over. He walked, nevertheless, leading the mules.

He heard the rattle of a diamondback. He had known it was there. He felt the lead mule pull on the rope and turned to look as they tossed their long ears forward and shied sideways. It lay coiled, black tongue flicking, quivering in tenseness. The rattles were a blur on its tail as it shook its warning.

"No need for that," Bluefeather muttered. "I'll give you back your land. I will walk far around you. It is yours. Take it."

The stoop in his shoulders was great as he climbed on up through the thickening timber far above the desert floor. It was now a great effort to put one foot in front of the other, but on up he moved. He saw the deer and the bobcat tracks in the soft sand of the washes, and he saw the fresh droppings of his old friend, the coyote, matted with rabbit hair.

He turned and looked again, taking his ragged, old hat from his grayed and tangled hair. One more look back. One. It was gone. The village was finally gone from sight. He strained his ears. No sound except the distant calling of a magpie came to him. He was beyond it. But still he felt unsafe. So they moved on up, the three of them.

They topped the high, long mesa and struggled up into the thicker timbers. Bluefeather could feel the blood beating hard in his ears now. His breath rasped through his broken, worn teeth.

Then he found the game trail into the oak brush. It was very steep. The timber thickened. He knew from the "rat-a-tat" of the woodpecker that he was high up. He saw, in the trail, a lion's round track as big as his hand. Yes, he was near his destination, for the lion feared the very thing that was in Bluefeather's heart. He, too, had moved to the outermost reaches. It was just a matter of finding the spot—the right place to return to his earth. But first he would take a last look at his mine. It was near, and there he must make the final decree about the capsules. The mules had recognized the terrain and stepped lively now.

As Bluefeather topped out on the trail, he saw two does and a fawn raise their muzzles from the spring below the High Line Tunnel. They looked at him an entranced moment. Then, in unison, they bounced downhill, vanishing into their world. Bluefeather was pleased that the wild things were sharing the spring he had so laboriously kept clean these many years. Anyway, it had been theirs first.

He unpacked the mules with care before he turned them to the spring. They were very thirsty, but before they drank, they took the time to roll in the dust near the log cabin, shook themselves, and moved with deliberate calm to the water and drank patiently, politely. Under similar, exhausted conditions, horses would run to the water and possibly founder or bloat themselves.

The old miner could not resist reading the map of wild animal tracks in the mud around the spring. There were the deer, of course, the rounded paw of a bobcat, the arrowhead-shaped prints of the coyote, the pronged turkey sign, but now there was something new at this altitude—the rooting marks of the wild hogs, the javelina. This shocked Bluefeather. He knew that, for a reason yet unknown, the javelina had been ranging into higher terrain the last few years. According to authorities on the subject, they had remained in the desert areas of northern Mexico, extreme southwest New Mexico, and southeast Arizona for many millions of years. Now, suddenly, they were working for a living at a heavily timbered eight thousand seven hundred feet. Unheard of and puzzling. For just a brief moment, Bluefeather knew why they were changing and learning to survive at this height of harsh winters. Then the little seed of knowledge was gone. Haunting. If the time was ever right they would return to lower levels.

No matter, he had to tidy up the mine site. It must be done with an attitude of servility to the place the mountain had so generously loaned him. He went first to his powder box, which he had dug into the earth with the door facing across a wide draw, away from the site, for safety. The dynamite, explosive caps, coiled fuse, and hand plungers were all safe and dry. There weren't many real mining individuals left who cared about the land. Now most were violators of the earth's fragile crust. Big, mostly foreign mining companies were strip-mining gold all over the Nevada desert now, ripping the fragile soil away from its creatures and poisoning it with leaching cyanide. Soon, he supposed, the corporations' destructive greed would drive them to tear up beautiful Arizona, as well. No matter what, a mechanized world must have copper, lead, zinc, tin, iron, and such, but destroying an entire desert for gold to glorify human bodies with jewelry was a sacrilege, in his eyes. There was already enough unused, hidden gold in vaults to accomplish this ten thousand times over.

Then he carried water from the spring and washed and dried the tin dishes, the hand-hewn tables, bunk beds, and cabinets. He braced, nailed, and tied up the poles and lumber of the little corral and mule shed, tack room, and small hay barn. He checked the mining tools in the work shed and arranged them in corners on metal hangers. He fed Mary and Nancy each a half gallon of oats and a block of alfalfa hay.

He gathered up his hard hat with the carbide lamp attached, poured in a little fresh water, let it settle among the carbide for a bit, then flicked the lighter into the gas jet. The flame lit just right. He put the hat on and walked under the portal timbers into the tunnel.

This mine was a mere pinprick on the whole of the mountain, but a lot of Bluefeather's years, flesh, and soul had been depleted here. It was a good tunnel and required no timbers once past the slough of the mountain's skin.

He walked on through the silence that heard only his own movements. He stood a moment to appreciate it, as he stared at the seven-foot tunnel face with the tiny vein of quartz weaving through it like a little frozen creek. He tilted his head closer to the vein and strained his eyes to try to see a particle or a thin string of silver. He was not sure, but he thought he saw one.

He straightened up, reached out slowly, and touched the spot, saying softly, "Forgive me, old mountain."

Then he turned and walked away from the face of ore for the last time, not looking back. Now it was too late to finish his chores here.

He had no desire for food. He must get to bed, for he had powerful things to do in the morning. Otherworldly duties to attend. Then... then on up above to the inexplicable spot of finality.

He stood in the front of the cabin and said, joyfully, "Good morning stately trees. Everlasting blessings on you, precious grass. Dear rocks, may comfort and compassion befall you for aeons. A thousand wishes, sweet mountains that all your trees, bushes, and grasses will have wet summers and mild winters. Oh, and the best of mornings to you, Mr. and Mrs. Beetle Bug."

It was the last morning here. The mules were tied to trees. Bluefeather Fellini was almost ready to make his final prayers and Indian medicine. It was a problem of choice: from his Italian blood came a strong Catholic belief; from his maternal side came the Indian conviction; and from inside himself came a third that was simply his. He would do his best to uphold all three. He was an advocate unto himself.

He still had no hunger, but suddenly the nose scar, which was visibly long lost in the roughness of his aged skin, started to itch and burn. The time capsules! For an immeasurable vacuum of a moment, he almost turned back down to the technical world with the idea of calling the media, the geologists, the anthropologists, and the archaeologists all together—dumping out, at once, the entire contents of the metal containers. The implications and the temptations were equally enormous. The notion passed.

He spread out his medicine pouch on the ground and knelt by it. He decided to get his personal part of this religious business over with first.

"Oh, dear Lord and Jesus, I sure do thank you for giving me the special privilege of choosing my own time to leave. I realize what a problem this must have been to you since so many folks are probably pestering you to death for the same favor. Anyway, gracious tidings, and thank you very much."

Mary and Nancy watched with curious eyes and tilted ears, sensing something different in their partner's voice and overall demeanor. Mules are like that.

Bluefeather climbed up the tailings pile to the tunnel entrance and nailed a cross he had made on the portal timber. Then he crossed himself and said several Hail Marys and got down to the plan.

"Ah, sweet, thoughtful Saint Anthony of Padua. I know you take care of many problems and give your loving protection to many creatures, but I also know you specialize in burros—or donkeys, if you prefer. Please bless the donkey half of Mary and Nancy that is your special domain. Thank you very much."

Mary and Nancy must have felt the call, because they actually switched their tails and stared at Bluefeather even more attentively.

He crossed himself again and put his fingers and palms together just under his chin in supplication. "Now, my friend, dear Saint James the Greater, I know beyond any possible doubt that you will bless the horse half of my beloved Mary and Nancy. They have been my faithful, hard-working, tender, loving companions for over twenty years. I am forever grateful and beholden to you and thank you very much."

Bluefeather's voice had been rising both in volume and intensity. Just as he finished his thanks, Mary raised her head, opened her mouth, and brayed. Nancy did likewise. The loud gasping two-part symphony made Bluefeather know that the blessings he asked for had been presented and properly received. Who could doubt the happy, accepting song of the mules?

He didn't spend quite as much effort on himself, saying to San Raphael the archangel and patron of travelers, "Dear Sir, I ask that you send me whatever direction you wish, and if there are rocks to climb or rivers to swim, please point them out and I shall meet the challenge, knowing you are a benevolent saint who would have much compassion for travelers in the alien dimensions of unfamiliar worlds. May this interloper do justice to your kindness. My deep appreciation for hearing me."

The mules must have known that their part of this particular ceremony was completed, for they dozed contentedly in the midmorning sun.

"Dear St. Francis of Assisi, patron of all animals, birds, peace, reconciler of the family, and patron of all needs and all virtues, please join this humble servant in his next, and last, adventure. Thank you very much."

And then to himself, Bluefeather said, as he whacked one heavy hand into the palm of the other, "That ought to do it!"

His own private creed and the Catholic creed had been reverently disposed of. Now he must conscientiously fulfill his duties to his Indian heritage. Then he would be free to seek the ultimate solution. To act.

He took the dry cedar twigs and leaves from his medicine pouch, crumpled them in a prospecting pan, and set it on fire. He smothered the flames so they would smoke heavily. He danced about with the smoke from the pan. He chanted softly as he wafted the smoke with an eagle feather over the mules, the outbuildings, the log house, the spring, and the tunnel of the mine. He danced back on his worn old legs to the spread-out pouch, took corn meal and tossed it to the four winds, straight at the earth and then directly upward into the sky. Now all the elements had been fed. He pulled the Earth Spirit from the ground and turned it into a swiftly flying peyote medicine bird. Already it was ripping the sky apart as it neared the domain of the Great Spirit, whose spectra controlled all the earths and all the skies. The message had been delivered.

Now Bluefeather placed the coyote fetish inside a circle of cornmeal with one little opening. He scattered the dried seeds in the circle and he did other things as well. Then he stood and yelled "Yiiiiii" up into the sky, and his voice boomed as strong as a young Milano opera singer's.

"Oh, Great Spirit, I know that a human's life is made of seconds, and any one of those can be the last breath. I know this thing, Exalted One. How many times have I breathed past the burning fuse? How many times has the mountain held its insides above my humble head without falling on me? Huh? Of course, you know these things, my Ennobled Guide. Yes, for sure. I have been through many, many dangers, and yet, here I am, me, Bluefeather Fellini, mostly in one piece. Thank you again for allowing me to pick my own time and ground. What a lucky man you have made me." Bluefeather was breathing heavily now, but he felt he had played as nearly a cinch with the various gods as a mining man would ever get.

Then the burst of illumination struck. His prayers must have worked. No more uncharacteristic indecision now. He took the time capsules one at a time and set them fifty steps inside the mine, side by silent side. His breath came in gasps, but he paid no mind. He stepped back perhaps forty yards from the mine portal, carefully surveying it, calling on all his engineering skills in his mind's survey. Then he easily hand-drilled holes in the dirt crust and under rocks of all sizes above the tunnel, on up the side of the natural mountain aways. He armed the dynamite with caps and fuses, his lungs hurting and his hands shaking dangerously from the exertions that would have tested his strength fifty years earlier.

He ignored the pounding in his chest and the pain of old, used-up muscles and ligaments trying to tear. He lit the fuses and slid down. The mules would not mind. They had heard thousands of sticks of dynamite.

The mountain shook all the way under his feet. The dust boiled above and around the portal while Bluefeather waited anxiously for the southwest wind and gravity to reveal its new form. Perfect. It looked exactly like a small natural landslide. He was sure he heard the mountain sigh in relief.

He exclaimed aloud, as he whacked his fist into his palm again, "I'm getting to be a better hider of treasures than I am a finder."

It was no longer up to him. He had done the only thing he knew. He had entombed these priceless objects just as he had other beloved objects in younger years. He had blown the final placement and use of Sherry's little books into the discretionary hands of the High Authority. He was no longer responsible. The odds were heavily against anyone trying to open up the little one-man mine so high in the mountains. If it was ordained, someday, someway, someone, would dig here and make the greatest discovery of all history to that date. If not—then that was the way it would and should be.

"Good-bye, friends. Thank you very much."

He folded up his medicine pouch and stuck it inside his overalls. His recent heavenly exertions made him decide to ride Mary to his sacred spot of ground, wherever it was. He got an old McClelland saddle out of the tack shed and, along with a bridle, fit it on the mule. He took the halter from Nancy's head, because she would follow. He led Mary over to the edge of the tailing pile, shuffled his feet up, and swung stiffly, but surely, astride her back. Without looking back, he reined her away from the mine site into the wilderness. He loosened the reins and gave Mary her head. She would find his singular spot.

Mary curved her way carefully upward. Far up. Bluefeather was piercingly aware of all their surroundings. He saw where a lion had covered its deer kill with brush. He would not worry about the lions getting the mules. They had instant reflexes and could kick to the side with devastating force, whereas a horse could only kick forward and backward. Man would take care of them, for they didn't exist without humans to assure the breeding of a donkey and a horse or vice versa. They were mutually dependent in many ways, but the mule's very existence was at the pleasure of humankind. They had paid back in full, millions of times over through the millennia.

Bluefeather thanked the mules for all the years they had carried the powder, hay, tools, grub, and on and on. No matter what the weather or difficulty, they had delivered.

He continued. "Did you know, my precious ones, that George Washington, who is called the father of our country, loved and respected you mules? Huh? Well, it's a fact. When he died he owned over sixty head and willed them to a few special friends and his slaves. See? See how special you girls are?"

The mules responded with increased speed yet sureness of step, one under him, the other right behind. He had a feeling of sublime peace, then exultation. He tilted his stony, weather-etched face back and yelled at the universe.

"Hiiiii yiiiiii, I'm Bluefeather Fellini, the last free man!"

They moved on toward his final departure with elation and relief. He talked to mule Mary now. Her long ears worked back and forth eagerly, recognizing that Bluefeather's voice was meant for her.

"You see, precious one, the other Mary would have made you very proud."

Every now and then the mule rolled her great limpid eyes to the side as if she were trying to see back in time along with him.

It was the time of musing. Bluefeather felt he had been blessed abundantly. He had been born into two cultures that he had loved and that had loved him in return. A fine childhood had been his for sure. The early Taos days with his pueblo family, Grinder, Lorrie, and more could only be thought of as a period of divine gifts. The Breen, Tonopah, and Corrales eras were laudatory remembrances. Even so, one never knew when an alliance of evil would germinate and alter the surface of the earth with scars, defilement, and human horror. Look at pitiful little Adolph Hitler, failed artist and architect, whose growing thirst for vengeance on society, and the power to extract it, could only get him up to the rank of corporal during the First World War. Yet, he had finally gathered around him Heinrich Himmler, a mad mystic, as head of the Third Reich's dreaded police; Joseph Goebbels, a failed writer, to be his head of propaganda and publicity; Hermann Goring, a dope fiend, to lead the economy and later to attempt to bomb the world into servitude or death.

Bluefeather felt good now about having fought this maniacal quartet the best he could. There had never been any war like it, and there never would be again until the very last one—and maybe not even then. Over fifty million people had died and hundreds of millions had been permanently wounded in flesh and soul. Bluefeather knew now, in hindsight, that only one more year of hesitation by the United States in joining the massive retaliation with food, guns, and flesh would have absolutely doomed the entire world to slavery. As it was, Hitler had been only about six months away from having atomic energy when he committed suicide in his bunker. The Germans had already invented the jet airplane and had been manufacturing them at the time of their doom. Very soon they would have ruled the skies. He already had rapidly improving missiles to launch against the rest of humanity. Close. Very close for this world that Bluefeather now walked and rode over. The billions of people under forty-nine years of age would not have been here at all. They would never have existed, for their copulation, conception, and birth would have been forever altered. Other entities would have existed, but none of those that were here now. None. America alone had committed ten million troops. Only one out of eight had fought on the front lines. America alone had had over eight hundred thousand casualties. Eighty percent of those had been in the infantry. The other twenty percent had been scattered among all the other services. It had cost them three trillion one hundred billion dollars, an uncountable sum in today's currency. And unthinkable, if not impossible, for the future, because too much of the earth's finite resources had already been turned to smoke and dead dust. The Allies had stayed firm and, with a massive will and sacrifice, had given all the world the chance to be free. Amazingly, only a third or so of the world's leaders had chosen the route of democracy that so terribly much had been sacrificed for. The so-called little wars—some more, some less— had never stopped. Even now, as Bluefeather moved upward to seek his well-earned peace, people were butchering each other somewhere in some manner. In Asia, Africa, Central and South America, the Middle East, Mexico, Yugoslavia, all over, groups of various-sized, foggy obsessions were tearing one another into bleeding shreds to make chattels out of the survivors. Little Hitlers still arose in ceaseless succession around the lovely, blue globe.

Well, he and his comrades of the Caverns of Marvels had fought a short, decimating battle to save the sanctity of all the natural earth and the beings below. They had won at great cost, with a casualty rate that had been almost one hundred percent. But they had not died in vain, as those in other wars before and after them had. Not yet, anyway. They had allowed the savage and delicate beauty, so many aeons in developing, to progress in nature. Bluefeather felt content now with their costly decision down there. He had to admit that he had probably learned just one thing of importance in his entire fruitful, fortunate, and celebratory life: the greatest mistake of human existence was the still-growing belief that wealth, fame, and the power that comes with them are the same as intelligence. This massive, human, judgmental error was rampant.

Then, suddenly, all these memories were behind him—history. He felt jubilant as his mind-voice pointed out the multitudes of rapturous events he had been so privileged to enjoy in the deserts and over the mountains of Hillsboro and most of the West.

A warmth, like first love and misted sweets, enveloped him. It was the time of times. He must go into his last half-vision now.

He rode eagerly into it. Sure enough, as so often before, the sacred Taos Mountain filled the distant background. He heard the music before he saw the players. Ramon Hernandez came on in a black, silver-fringed costume of both New and Old Mexico. His wide mouth grinned around his face and his dark eyes were full of music and fun. He was followed by his long-ago friend, Antonio Mendoza, whose whole body expressed an attitude of joy as they played a resounding medley of Spanish music and, slowly moving, danced delicately ahead of many followers who were just coming out of the aged mists into view. There was his mother, Morning Star, and father, Valerio, his grandparents and his Chicago cousin, Hog's Head, along with Stump Jumper—all doing little dance steps, smiling, occasionally waving at him with casual friendship. There were his Raton relatives shouting bravos at him. And behind them were mama Anna and papa Tony Marchiondo, proudly pointing to Billy and Johnny and the rest of their sons and daughters, who were dancing along, happily escorting them in the great eternal procession of timeless life. Then his mentor, Grinder the Gringo, chewing and spitting tobacco, shaking his happy head up and down as if approving Bluefeather's life and loves, danced on in the procession. Oh, there were too many. Too many to carefully observe coming in and out of the mists. Lorrie Friedman followed Grinder, sinuously moving her arms at times and at others raising an imaginary camera, taking imaginary pictures of everyone in pantomime. She passed on by, turning, dancing backward, waving at him in a movement of greeting, not good-bye. Dr. Godchuck and his Aunt Tulip dippy-doed and smiled as he twirled his bull-prick cane in his smooth hands like a cheerleader—and they both moved just as lively.

Oh, how the music whirled and did its own dance of sounds across the sagebrush and foothills of the most special of mountains. There. There was Nancy of Tonopah, and she was doing a cancan, kicking her lovely legs in rhythm to all the sound of the world of cantinas. Then, then Miss Mary and old Ludwig shuffled gleefully out of the mists, both acknowledging Bluefeather's image with gazes and grins so beautiful that birds started singing along with his old friend's music. Miss Mary blew him a half dozen kisses that turned to white roses and landed between his legs and the leather of the saddle in a perfect bouquet. There was Daniel Wind doing an Osage shuffle, still wearing the steel army helmet that never seemed to fit. Marsha just beamed out of the lowering mists, her hair fiery as the magma of the Cavern of Marvels and her teeth showing strong and bright as the sun on arctic snow. She waved—with her fingers snapping, joyously whirling—to a shuffling Willy Ruger and a tap-dancing Flo. Then Marsha turned her wide, loving eyes toward Bluefeather. At each turn, she tilted her head in its puppy dog way. Oh, how they danced and laughed. Oh, how they smiled and waved. Oh! Then there was Pack, with his silent little smile, motioning for Bluefeather to advance. Hector Garcia followed a few steps behind, obviously inventing new dance steps but becoming more buoyant each yard. They had all casually, almost delicately waved for him to follow. The entire Section danced on by, along with other figures, not quite clear. Ghosts. The ectoplasm of memories, maybe.

Now came ancient relatives dancing from way back in his heritage—strong, purposeful, but radiating warmth and approval as they smiled at him. Turning swiftly in exuberance and stomping his moccasined feet in festive steps came Dancing Bear the spirit guide. Who was that with him? Who was that great dancer of endlessly skilled steps following him? Why, it was Bluefeather Fellini, as a young man of Taos, of Corrales, of many places, and then he turned into old Bluefeather of Hillsboro. The two friends from different dimensions were doing a special dance just for themselves now. It was the laughing dance. They twisted, stepping in time to the undulating stomach-aching, eye-watering mirth. They danced faster and faster around each other, giving one another swift, knowing glances of sidesplitting merriment. They roared. They howled with glee and fun. Then the laughing dance was suddenly done.

Bluefeather was absent, gone, from the procession and was back here in the Hillsboro mountains. Ramon, the entertainer of loving kindness, played on for all who listened, all who followed him, weaving their way through the desert, through the village of Taos and to the pueblo, on up the sides of the magic mountain.

The music and the snaking figures slowly vanished over a rise into the timber. Silence.

Then the sound of the mules' carefully stepping hooves returned. Dancing Bear's early prophesy of Bluefeather's great adventures had come true and had been fulfilled. Old Grinder's recognition of his being "a yearner" had also been correct and verified—all but this last one. He was anxious to get on with it—the dying—for no doubt it would be the greatest adventure yet. Bluefeather had experienced huge helpings of love, war, and gold with an almost equal amount of hell and rapture.

They couldn't go much higher on the Black Range. Sure enough, he found the proper place—a flat area on solid rock.

He dismounted and looked over to the west across the Gila Wilderness, created by President Theodore Roosevelt as the first of its kind in America. Bluefeather felt especially privileged to look upon such rare, grand, protected areas once more before it was all gone. It was perfectly suffused with shades of purples and deep blues.

He then cast a last glance back across the Aldo Leopold Wilderness Area, named after a great conservationist who believed, long before it was fashionable, that the world was a single, living organism, and who had written and preached this endlessly until he died. A lot who heard and read him knew he was a prophet ahead of the time of no return, but all who truly listened would never see the earth the same again. They would come to respect the delicate miracle of a breathing world. And there was the massive 330,000-acre Ladder Ranch, now owned by a world-famous communications couple.

All this area was the ground where the great warriors Geronimo and Chief Victoria and the black buffalo soldiers had roamed. It was all emerald green to him now. He could see as far and wide as his old eyes could search. Without thinking, he felt the insects, the birds, the wild animals, the grasses, the bushes, the trees, the rocks of thousands of square miles of earth. He heard them as well, and there were no vulgar interruptions of grinding steel mechanisms to wound the natural sounds. There was no town. No road.

"It is the rare time of perfection," he thought. "The blessed time."

He unsaddled Mary and took the bridle off. Both mules stared at him, puzzled. He raised his arms and told them to go. Then, seeming to understand, they turned and moved hesitantly away, down through the brush and timber. He hung the saddle from a tree limb with the rein of the bridle.

He slowly, carefully stretched his body out on the flat part of the rock—his back down, his face straight up. He started to fold his arms across his chest but stretched them out by his sides instead. He took his final look at the local sky. The golden element he had sought—then tried to deny—throughout his struggling life was minutely disseminated in an unlimited sky. There would be no more climbing over sandpaper rocks, no digging in the impervious earth, no scalded feet and bleeding, blistered hands. A simple upward glance had provided it all for free. Free.

He closed his eyes and became motionless, as the gold dust drained from the sky and turned into darkness.

The pinks and violets of dawn spread across the morning sky, and later a great shaft of reddish sunlight broke between an opening in the timber and shone on the still, still figure prone there on the rock. The soft, awakening sounds of the daytime creatures were mixed with those of the retiring night hunters. The sun caressed all the eastern slopes of the peaceful Black Range now.

Then the sudden, shattering noise of two fighter jets in training caused the top of the earth to vibrate with a terrible sound—the scream of a thousand doomed and tortured souls—the rending and ripping of miles of metal. As they passed on, vanishing over the mountain horizon beyond the speed of sound, the "chop, chop" of a Forest Service helicopter whirled and whacked its way through the air of the nearest canyon.

A tired coyote registered one more howl of defiance. An eagle screamed at nothing. The blue jays became raucous, and down below them the magpies chattered at one another with high-pitched screeches. A three-hundred-pound black mother bear stood up on her hind legs and roared loudly. Her two cubs squealed like pigs and climbed the nearest pine tree. Several squirrels chattered like little machine guns. Hearing all this from a quarter-mile distance, Mary and Nancy widened their nostrils and snorted and brayed with all the power of their lungs, adding to the crescendo.

Bluefeather was now sitting on the edge of the rock, staring straight out into a blankness. With both hands, he pushed himself up and stumbled stiffly over to untie the saddle and bridle from the limb. Taking the bridle in one hand, he walked downhill into the timber, his steel-toed miner's boots feeling surprisingly lighter with each step, as if they barely touched the ground.

Then he yelled angrily to the forest, "It's too damn noisy to die!" He followed the tracks of the two mules. All the nearby creatures of the wilderness could hear him calling, "Haaa, Mary. Hooo, Nancy. Haaa, Mary."

■ ■ ■